Rave reviews for Jac

"A well-defined and i_____
distant future.... Every_____
colorful, from the techn_____ to the human (and humanoid) characters. Author Bedford's world-building feels very complete and believable, with excellent descriptions bringing it all to life." —*RT Book Reviews*

"Bedford mixes romance and intrigue in this promising debut, which opens the Psi-Tech space opera series.... Readers who crave high adventure and tense plots will enjoy this voyage into the future." —*Publishers Weekly*

"A nostalgic space opera.... Bedford's prose is brisk and carries the reader quite sufficiently along." —Tor.com

"I'm very, very excited to see where this series goes next. The foundation that Bedford has laid has so much potential and promise. This is an author I will watch."
  —Bookworm Blues

"Space opera isn't dead; instead, delightfully, it has grown up.... A fine example of a novel which has its roots in the subgenre but grows beyond it."
  —Jaine Fenn, author of *Principles of Angels*

"The first of a new space opera series that delivers the goods and holds lots of promise of things to come."
  —SF Signal at kirkus.com

DAW Books proudly presents
the novels of Jacey Bedford:

The Psi-Tech Novels

EMPIRE OF DUST
CROSSWAYS

CROSSWAYS

✦ ✦ ✦

A PSI-TECH NOVEL

JACEY BEDFORD

DAW BOOKS, INC.
DONALD A. WOLLHEIM, FOUNDER
375 Hudson Street, New York, NY 10014

ELIZABETH R. WOLLHEIM
SHEILA E. GILBERT
PUBLISHERS
www.dawbooks.com

Acknowledgments

My thanks to all the team at DAW, to Josh Starr, and especially to my lovely editor, Sheila Gilbert, for her valuable input and for commissioning the fabulously talented Stephan Martiniere to do the cover. His artwork gave me a severe kick up the imagination. Thanks also to my agent Amy Boggs, and all at Donald Maass Literary Agency, for enthusiasm, expertise, and guidance.

I'm a great believer in peer-to-peer writers' critique groups. *Crossways* went through the mill at both the annual Milford SF Writers' Conference and at several quarterly meetings of the Northwrite SF writers' group. The Milford writers and the Northwrite writers overlap considerably so some lucky folks got to critique the same bit more than once. Special thanks go to: Northwriters: Tina Anghelatos, John Moran (and his wife, Sara), Terry Jackman, Ian Creasey, Sue Thomason, Liz Sourbutt, Gus Smith, and Tony Ballantyne for their forbearance, especially when I was obsessing over Chapter One endlessly.

In addition I'd like to thank Milford attendees in 2013 and 2014: Guy T. Martland, Mike Lewis, Sue Oke, Phil Suggars, James Maxwell, Al Robertson, David Allan, Jim Anderson, Nick Moulton, Pauline Dungate, Vaughan Stanger, Jaine Fenn (and her husband, Dave Weddell), Bob Neilson, Matt Colborne, Heather Lindsley, Mark Bilsborough, Deirdre Saoirse Moen, Cherith Baldry, Tiffani Angus, and the ever helpful Liz Williams. Thanks, too, to Kari Sperring, N. M. Browne, and Karen Traviss for encouragement and words of sound writerly advice. All of these guys have books and short stories published. Do yourself a favor and seek them out. In addition I have to thank my singing partner in Artisan, Hilary Spencer, for her proofreading skills.

An extra-special thank-you and much love to my husband, Brian, offspring, Ghillan and Joe, and Mum, Joan Lockyer, just for being there and tolerating my obsessive, post-midnight keyboard pounding and other writerly foibles.

And lastly, thanks to you for buying, reading, talking about, reviewing, and recommending not just my books, but all books. Without you there would be no books. You rock! Keep up the good work.

Jacey Bedford
Yorkshire, April 2015
www.jaceybedford.co.uk

Chapter One

WANTED

IT WAS ALL IN THE PLANNING.

Forcing people to go against their nature was almost impossible. The trick was to ascertain their true nature and allow them to indulge it—at the right time and in the right place. That was the art of the true puppet master. One of the problems with being so far from the action, however, was that once you set things in motion, you had to wait. And that was the hardest part.

Gabrius Crowder glared at the deepening purple sky outside his window, high up in the Trust's administrative headquarters. Arkhad City glowed bright in the distance, artificial light overtaking the natural as Chenon's fifty-hour day slid into its long dusk. Down in the compound below, tiny figures scurried between warehouses and the immense packing station next to the shuttle port, some on foot, others with float carts. Unobscured by trees or buildings, a kilometer of manicured, pink vegetation rolled to the perimeter, where a glistening curtain of pure power, beautiful but deadly, kept out unwanted visitors.

Crowder turned and gazed at the holographic galaxy hovering in the middle of his ops room. Tiny pinpoints of white light marked the Trust's colonies while the jump gate hubs blinked rhythmically in green. The platinum-producing planets glowed blue. Not enough of them. Never enough. The jump gate network devoured platinum as fast as the megacorporations could refine it. Platinum, or lack of it, was the curse of the interstellar age.

He reached into the display and touched Olyanda, platinum rich and almost in the bag for the Trust.

Almost.

Soon.

The puppets were in the theater, the show had begun.

He put his hand to the dressing covering his ear. Itching was a good sign, wasn't it? He pressed gently with his palm, releasing a small dose of topical anesthetic until the fierce itch faded to a mild annoyance.

If his plague had done its job, they'd all be dead by now: Benjamin, Carlinni, the psi-techs and settlers ... even Ari van Blaiden. He squashed the flutter of guilt. He was a compassionate man, fond of cats and small children, but he couldn't afford to let sentiment get in the way of platinum.

Getting rid of van Blaiden along with the rest would be a bonus. A dangerous enemy, an even more dangerous business partner, co-conspirator, frenemy—whatever. Crowder's relationship with van Blaiden had been complicated.

He strode through to his office and dropped his ungainly bulk into the float chair which dipped and swayed before stabilizing beneath him. The backrest molded to his lumbar region and cradled his spine.

He'd always thought of himself as a good man, a moral man. Had that changed? No. A general who sent troops to die in a war was not a murderer. Sometimes you had to do the expedient thing for the greater good. He was fighting a war on behalf of the Trust. An undeclared war, maybe, but a war all the same, not only against Alphacorp, the Trust's closest rival, but also against the other megacorporations, singly and together. The Trust was on top of the heap, but they couldn't afford to get complacent.

His holo-screen showed a direct call waiting. It was Bibby, one of his insiders in Alphacorp. A man with expensive tastes in chemical relaxation.

"Bibby, what have you got for me?"

The first page of a report flashed up in front of him. He spotted the words Olyanda and van Blaiden before Bibby snatched it away again.

"This is big news, Mr. Crowder. It's worth five thou."

"Your grandmother isn't worth five thou."

"Six thou. Every time you hesitate the price goes up. It's an eyes-only data package for . . ." He flicked his gaze upward to indicate it was for the very highest authority. "I could sell it to any one of the megacorps for double."

"Not unless you want to spend the rest of your life — your much shortened life — on a penal colony."

What had happened? Van Blaiden's name linked with Olyanda on a report intended for Alphacorp's CEO was a potential disaster. Crowder's considerable belly churned. "Has she seen it yet?"

"I'm good, but I'm not that good. This is a copy."

"Six thou, all right."

"Seven."

"Seven." He'd get back at the little shit later. For now, the report was what mattered.

Bibby smiled and nodded. Crowder docked his handpad with the reader on his desk and his slush fund was instantly seven thousand credits lighter.

The report appeared on his screen. Bibby's image shrank to a pinpoint and vanished.

Crowder read, the hairs on the back of his neck standing to attention. He could almost feel his blood pressure rising.

It was a fiasco — a fucking fiasco. Olyanda was lost. There were survivors. Any survivors were bad news. Benjamin and Carlinni — that was a disaster.

He'd paid a million and a half for that plague. What in all-hell had gone wrong?

He read on, sweating over what would happen first. Would the news break like a tsunami across the space-logs, or should he expect silence and a visit in the middle of the night?

He was going to have to scramble to minimize the damage.

At least Ari van Blaiden was dead, that was one blessing; a dangerous connection dissolved. He frowned. The report revealed that Alphacorp had been watching van Blaiden. How much did they suspect? How much did they know for sure?

He checked the report's author, but the name Kitty Keely didn't mean anything to him. It was probably an alias anyway. No one was really called Kitty Keely.

Despite the climate control in his office, a bead of sweat trickled down Crowder's face from forehead to jowls. If Alphacorp had proof of his involvement they'd use it not just against him, but against the Trust. That was a given.

He swallowed hard to dislodge the lump in his throat.

Hold steady, don't panic. It's a setback, it's not the end of the road.

Some setback!

The Trust had lost a prime platinum resource to the mobsters on Crossways. That was bad enough, but the psi-techs, once his own employees, now knew that he'd tried to wipe them out along with the settlers.

It was only a matter of time before someone came after him.

Crowder rubbed his hand over his ear, resisting the temptation to poke his finger through the dressing. They were still growing him a replacement, and the new eardrum graft was delicate. Benjamin could easily have killed him, probably would if they met again. That must never happen.

He took a deep breath. First things first. Slap Benjamin and the psi-techs on the Monitors' most-wanted list. He knew one Monitor in particular who had a personal grudge against Benjamin. It was time to feed Alexandrov the relevant information. He attached an unsigned message to a transfer of funds. *Benjamin heading for Chenon. Apprehend.* That would be enough.

Now for the second thing: so far the space-logs had been silent. Of course, it had only been a few days. There was still time. If Bibby's report was correct, most of the survivors had been evacuated to Crossways already and might be sending trouble his way at any time. The S-LOG network was slow between systems. Transmission of data packets through the jump gates was bound by the laws of physics. The tel-net was faster: short messages passed from Telepath to Telepath across space and then fed into local networks. Once a message hit the planetary net it could go viral in minutes, handpad to handpad. Crowder couldn't do anything about the tel-net, but he might be able to silence Crossways' direct chatter by pinching it off at the jump gates.

"Stefan," he yelled for his secretary. "Put in a call to Legal." He hoped the tech guys could block a route as quickly as Crossways' hackers could open one. Crossways housed any number of resourceful criminal gangs.

With van Blaiden dead, Crowder could probably shift blame and retain plausible deniability for himself and the Trust. He had a breathing space, but he needed to make full use of it.

In his head he was already concocting a press release. A headline, something like: *Olyanda Plague Survivors Break Quarantine*, followed by a scare article. *Threat level red. All planets should deny landing rights to colonists from Olyanda or vessels from Crossways, where plague carriers have taken refuge.*

That should do it.

Quarantine notices and warrants wouldn't be enough, though. He needed to deal with Benjamin and Carlinni immediately and with extreme prejudice.

Good thing he knew the right someone on Crossways.

◆ ◆ ◆

Ben Benjamin eased the *Solar Wind* into realspace with only a faint shimmer in the flight deck air. His version of reality resumed, though the dizziness took a few moments to subside, as usual. The transition was as smooth as it could be, which meant his connection with the ship was functioning damn near perfectly.

And . . . relax . . .

It was a good day. Ben counted the ways.

One: Ari van Blaiden was dead. Two: Ben's psi-tech crew had survived the Olyanda mission and they were all individually rich, or would be as soon as the platinum mines on Olyanda started to produce, which admittedly might take some time yet. Three: they had allies on Crossways, home to some of the most talented criminals in the known universe. Four: the spaceship he'd stolen turned out to have teeth. And, best of all, five: Cara Carlinni, love of his life, had not tried to kill him today.

Not yet, anyway.

He took stock. Five of them on the flight deck, pilot, co-pilot, comms, systems, and tactical. One by one the other four nodded back to him.

"Ship status?" he asked.

Cara relayed his question telepathically and cut him in on the reassuring responses from the crew in medical and engineering as well as from those off-duty in their cabins.

"Time?" He turned to Wenna at the systems monitoring station. Unflappable, dependable Wenna, his second during the Olyanda mission.

"Subjective time in the Folds: three minutes fifteen seconds." She swiped her left hand across her hard-screen, favoring it above the biosynthetic right, despite having been right-handed when both her arms were her own flesh and bone. "Objective elapsed time in realspace: two hours forty-three minutes."

Ben worked it out roughly in his head. Seventy seconds had passed in realspace for every one in foldspace—a much higher ratio than when transiting via jump gates.

"Log it."

Solar Wind was one of those rare vessels with her own jump drive, which made transiting foldspace simultaneously less restrictive and more dangerous. They were still trying to figure out her parameters. The time differential could be fluid. You couldn't predict, you just had to go with it, though the longer you stayed in the Folds the less likely you were to get out again.

Ben subscribed to the theory, unpopular in Academy circles, that once you entered foldspace you ceased to be real in any accepted sense of the word.

He glanced across to where Cara sat at the comms station.

"How are you?" he asked her softly.

"Holding up." Her short fair hair couldn't hide the thundercloud bruise radiating across her cheekbone, and she held herself stiffly. He guessed her rib was still sore despite the fancy bone regeneration equipment in *Solar Wind*'s sick bay.

He flexed his shoulder, knowing that only the drugs from his buddysuit dulled the pain of his healing burn. Neither of them had come through their trials on Olyanda without injury, but they were both still alive and upright, and that was what counted.

Cara's scars were more than physical, however. Broken bones and blistered skin healed faster than the deep mindfuck Ari van Blaiden had administered.

But that was over now. He, Cara, and the rest of his crew were still flying.

He turned to the newest member, still unproven, in the copilot's chair. She was supposed to be, like him, a psi-tech Navigator, but he'd felt her doubt herself during the fold-space transit. "Kitty?"

"Sorry, sir, I froze." Kitty Keely combed her fair, shoulder-length hair off her face with her left hand and scrubbed at the back of her neck with hooked fingers to massage out the stiffness.

She looked drained. Flying the Folds was tricky at best, deadly at worst.

"It happens," Ben said, remembering his first time flying a jumpship. "We'll try it again another time. And I already told you, no need to sir me. We're not in the service now—unless you want to go back to Alphacorp. I can still arrange that if you do."

"Uh, no thanks, si . . . er . . . Boss. I've had enough of big business." She shuddered.

And enough of the likes of Ari van Blaiden, Ben guessed. Cara had never told him the worst of van Blaiden's excesses, but he'd seen enough. Young Ensign Keely had been sucked into van Blaiden's plans just as Cara had been. She was in an impossible situation. He was almost obliged to offer refuge.

That Cara had eventually come out of it sane was almost a miracle in itself.

He glanced sideways at Cara again. Well, at least she seemed sane.

Cara noticed and gave him a half smile, her gray-blue eyes crinkling at the corners.

Sane enough.

He dragged his mind away from Cara's smile back to the job at hand.

"You have the coordinates, Kitty?"

"I do."

"Okay, take us to Chenon."

She nodded. "Estimated flight time eighteen hours."

You trust the rookie with your shiny new toy? Cara asked mind-to-mind as Kitty linked to the ship's systems.

Ronan did a psych evaluation and gave her a clean bill of health. Whatever's wrong with Alphacorp, it isn't their flight

*training program. She's a sound Navigator and a good pilot—
in realspace anyway—Ari van Blaiden was wasting her talents
having her run errands just because he liked her ass.**

**She's lucky she never needed to get on the wrong side of
him.**

Like you did. It was as close as he ever came to asking.
Yeah.
*About that . . . *
When I'm good and ready.
Whatever you say.

She gave him another half-smile.

"So . . . Chenon," Cara said aloud. "Security's pretty tight
as I recall. How do you propose we get at Crowder?"

"Quickly, before news of what happened on Olyanda
breaks. I'm gambling that he'll still be holding his breath
hoping everyone is dead as planned."

"And if he isn't?" Cara frowned.

"Well, I guess we'll have to improvise."

Crowder was their best chance of locating the diverted
ark, carrying thirty thousand missing settlers frozen in cryo.
Ben had vowed to find them.

"Ship ahead. Closing fast," Kitty said.

"Identification?"

"It's not broadcasting any."

"Assessment." Ben turned to tactical where Vijay Gupta,
grizzled veteran of many military campaigns prior to joining the Trust as a security specialist, was quietly checking
out *Solar Wind*'s armaments.

"No weapons lock at present, but she's running hot, torpedoes primed and ready. Do you want me to—"

"Stand by until we see her intent."

"Got it, Boss."

"Cara?"

"Trying to contact them now. Unidentified vessel, you
are on a direct intercept course, please state your identity
and purpose." No response. "Unidentified vessel, you are
on—"

"*Solar Wind*, this is the Monitor Ship *Lomax*. You are
impounded by law. Please stand down and prepare to be
boarded."

✦   ✦   ✦

Ben tried to control the adrenaline spike. The Monitors should be the good guys, independent law-keepers, but too often they were just the instrument of the megacorps. They relied on levies from the colonies to fill gaps where their fleet was thinly spread, which often put planetary interests over interstellar law. He'd been in the Monitors himself in what seemed like another life. He'd joined up to make a difference and found the law was not the way to go about it.

How in seven hells did they know we were coming? Cara asked. *Maybe the mercs back on Olyanda have a long-range Telepath we don't know about.*

How doesn't matter, Ben said. *They know, which means Crowder knows.*

Gupta's hands twitched toward weapons control.

"Stand down, Gupta." Ben held up a hand. "Once we fire on a Monitor ship we're beyond the point of no return. Cara, patch me in." He opened the vox channel on the collar of his buddysuit. Play the innocent for starters. "MS *Lomax*, what are your grounds? We're civilian vessel *Solar Wind* out of Xerxos heading for Chenon. Our course is filed with—"

"*Solar Wind*, we know exactly who you are and what you are. There's a code red quarantine notice out for you, and in addition we have warrants for the arrest of Reska Benjamin, Cara Carlinni, and your crew. Three hundred persons in all."

"Do we look big enough to carry a crew of three hundred?"

"Transmit us a full crew list, *Solar Wind*, and stand by to be taken to the nearest quarantine station."

"I want to see your warrant."

"Transmitting now."

"Got it," Cara said.

An official-looking document flashed up on the screen, long and detailed, with mug shots. A quarantine notice followed it, saying that *Solar Wind* was transporting plague carriers from Olyanda.

Ben switched off his vox while he skimmed the warrant. "Murder, terrorism, armed insurrection, hijacking, grand theft, and kidnapping." He raised one eyebrow. "Crowder must be getting desperate. Maybe I'll admit to grand theft." He patted the control pad. "Or does the acquisition of the

Solar Wind come under hijacking? Personally I regard her as spoils of war."

"This is serious!" Cara snapped at him.

"And I'm taking it seriously, believe me, but let's find out exactly what we're up against. Patch me into *Lomax*, please."

She did.

He touched the vox again. "MS *Lomax*, the plague on Olyanda was a malicious false report."

"You know I can't take that for an answer."

"Okay, then, another question: who am I supposed to have kidnapped?"

"Forty thousand Ecolibrian settlers. You don't know that, Benjamin?" It was a different voice on the comm now.

It wasn't the words that bothered him. He muted his vox again. "Shit!" He looked at Cara and shook his head. "I know that voice." He hit transmit again without waiting for a response from her. "Sergei, when did they bring you back from the Rim? They must be getting desperate."

"That's Prime Alexandrov to you, Benjamin. Why am I not surprised to see you on the wrong side of the law? It was only a matter of time."

"You seem to forget which one of us was taking bribes back in the day."

"Unproven. And I don't forget anything, including three months in rehab. You, however, broke every rule in the book."

"I bent them a little, but only when they didn't make sense."

Cara didn't interrupt with anything that might be overheard, but she quickly stood and moved to stand behind Ben, her hand on his good shoulder.

It's a commercial warrant, she said on a tight telepathic band.

Alphacorp or the Trust?

There was a slight pause. *Trust,* she said.

At least it's not both. The day that Alphacorp and the Trust start talking to each other we're screwed.

"Their missile ports have opened," Gupta said, reaching for the weapons controls.

Ben muted his vox again and shook his head. "Much as I'd like to fry Alexandrov, stand down. There are a hundred

Monitors on that ship who are just doing their job. Kitty, bring the jump drive online. Quick as you can."

Ben squeezed Cara's fingers and then he let her go to focus on the ship. "Everyone sit down and strap in."

Cara slid back into her seat and broadcast telepathically to the crew to alert them to prepare for the jump to fold-space without giving away their intent to the *Lomax*. Though they had cabins for thirty they were running a skeleton crew on this trip.

"*Lomax*, stand down your weapons, we will comply," Ben broadcast.

We will? Cara asked.

Course not. He closed down his vox.

The *Lomax* fired an energy pulse. It went wide.

"Is that the best they can do?" Kitty asked.

"That was just a warning shot," Ben replied. "The next one won't go wide. Is the jump drive online yet?"

"Thirty seconds," Kitty said.

"We might not have thirty seconds."

Hold fire, Lomax. We're complying. Cara sent out a verbal and a mental broadcast that hit every Telepath in the Monitor ship. Even if Alexandrov had a personal grudge against Ben, his crew should make sure he stuck to protocol.

Or not.

"Hard shell torpedo launched," Gupta said. "Twenty-five seconds to impact."

"Twenty seconds," Kitty said without prompting.

Lomax, you're not playing by the book, Ben broadcast via Cara's telepathic link. *Who's your Second?*

Second Officer Jessop, here, Ben.

Jess? Is that you? That prime of yours is going to get you killed. Pull away now.

Too late. Sorry, Ben.

No, I'm sorry. Hold on to your hat, Jess. Bumpy ride coming up. Stay out of our wake. Give my best to your kid when you see her again.

Ben engaged the jump drive and felt the yawning pull of the Folds.

❖ ❖ ❖

Cara is used to transiting foldspace through gates. Does a jumpship access different regions of the Folds? The disorientation is worse and the visions more vivid on *Solar Wind*. She feels as if she's being turned inside out. First the ship is perfectly still and she's sucked into her own personal vortex, then the whole thing reverses and she's still while the ship whirls. She closes her eyes, realizes they are already closed, and forces them open. The flight deck looks normal except for the crew, all in various stages of trauma. Gupta has spun his chair around away from the weapons control, but the chair itself has turned two-seventy degrees, and now his hand is clawing for the board. Luckily he can't reach it. Ben has both of his hands clamped on the arms of his chair and he's pushing himself back, away from something only he can see.

"Five seconds to impact," the onboard computer announces calmly.

No. Surely they've left the torpedo behind them in realspace. They are deep inside the Folds now, safely away from the MS *Lomax*.

"Four."

Bloody hell, what's the matter with the system? Does it think they are still in realspace or . . . Cara freezes. It's theoretically possible that when the jump drive fired, it sucked in anything in close proximity. Oh fuck! They've pulled the torpedo into foldspace with them.

"Three."

She manages to turn toward Ben.

"Two."

He wrenches his head around to meet her eyes, nods and mouths, "It will be all right." His voice catches up with her ears a split second later.

"One."

The nose of a hard shell torpedo punches through the bulkhead silently and in slow motion, but there's no rending of metal and ceramics, no explosive decompression sucking the air out of the flight deck, no flash of light or searing heat. Instead the torpedo pierces the flight deck and shoots out of the far bulkhead like a ghost, leaving not a trace.

Ben grins, white teeth contrasting against warm brown skin, a mixture of relief and smug I-told-you-so.

"To Crossways," he says, his voice still half a second behind, like a badly synchronized vid.

Where they should have been heading all along, Cara

thinks. Ben's anxious to find the missing ark ship, but it has been lost for months already. The settlers are either dead or they'll wait a few more days. They need a little recovery time after the events on Olyanda. Hell, her rib is only half-healed and Ben's shoulder must be hurting more than he lets on. She glances across at him again, but he's focused on finding the right exit point from foldspace. Please let him do it before the ghost of Ari van Blaiden finds her again.

She wonders what will happen to her and Ben now that Ari is dead. Can they reclaim their relationship? Maybe too much has happened.

Ben's making light of it, but sooner or later it will come to a head.

✦ ✦ ✦

Cara shook off the last remnants of her foldspace visions.

Her screen bleeped.

"I've got a visual on Crossways," Kitty said.

"Relay it ship-wide." Ben hit the internal comms. "Take a good look, people, it's going to be home for a while."

Cara stared at the screen as the scale resolved itself in her brain. The vast man-made habitat hung in space, orbiting a yellow dwarf star, Amarelo, at a distance of two AU. It looked as if it had been slung together by a lunatic with a giant construction kit. Its central spindle supported a series of fat doughnuts perched on top of each other like a child's toy, probably the original station. From that had sprouted a huge outer assemblage of concentric rings which looked as though they had been made and remade several times over, expanding organically with encrustations and additions which owed little to long-term planning and much to immediate necessity. Massive cylindrical structures jutted from the outer rings, presenting weaponry always at the ready.

White floods on the external docking cradles glinted off the solar collection tiles that covered almost every exposed surface. On opposing sides of the main station, two additional wheels, each big enough to be an independent station in its own right, pivoted on projecting arms.

"I knew it was big, but . . . that's big," Cara said.

She knew Crossways' history, its grab for independence, but she'd never quite appreciated its size before. Seeing huge liners dwarfed by its bulk brought it home.

"The outer ring is ten klicks in diameter, with eight levels," Ben said. "And that's before the additions. You've got to admire a good engineering project. The station supports close to a million people, and she's armed to the teeth: pulse-cannon, torpedoes, lasers, and enough fighters and fighter drones to make even the Monitors wary of approaching without permission."

The Olyanda survivors were here, somewhere, saved from the immediate double-threat of plague and hostile incursion. Mother Ramona and her lover, Norton Garrick, the station's head crimelord, had given assurances that they'd be safe, but how could any station, even one of this size, absorb ten thousand displaced persons?

"See that section there"—Ben pointed—"the one that looks as though someone's taken a giant bite out of it . . ."

"It looks like old damage," Cara said.

"It's from Crossways' war for independence," Ben said.

"But that's a century ago," Kitty butted in. "Couldn't they have fixed it by now?"

"It doesn't look like they want to." Cara kept her eyes on the screen. "Sometimes keeping the damage visible is a good reminder not to let it happen again." She didn't even realize she'd said that out loud until Ben glanced over with a sharp, suspicious look before turning back to answer Kitty.

"Crossways survived and prospered while the megacorp that tried to subdue it withered," he said. "That's a point of pride for the locals, some of whom are descendants of the original revolutionaries."

"Not all criminals, then?" Kitty asked.

"There are a lot of legal businesses, some legitimately occupied in supporting the illegal ones. In fact, unauthorized crime is dealt with just as quickly here as anywhere, perhaps even more harshly."

"There's such a thing as authorized crime?"

Ben shrugged. "Most of the organizations on Crossways have learned not to shit on their own doorstep. It operates in much the same way as any station, except with a wider range of services on offer, no questions asked."

Cara had experienced Crossways only once before, and it had not been under the best of circumstances. She wondered whether she would ever be able to settle here.

Chapter Two

A NEW HOME

BEN TURNED TO CARA. "FOR BETTER OR WORSE, Crossways is home, at least for a while," he said. "You once told me you didn't want to live the rest of your life on a space station."

"I didn't. I don't. But we can't go back to either Chenon or Earth, can we?" She shrugged. "Your home? My home? They're all closed to us. We don't work for the Trust anymore."

"I think Crowder trying to kill us makes a pretty good case for constructive dismissal," Ben said. "Besides, we're wanted criminals now."

She sighed. "Well, we do seem to have stolen a spaceship. I guess that means we've descended to the criminal classes."

"Ascended, I'd say," Ben said. He was relieved when she grinned back at him.

The *Solar Wind* could give them a hell of an edge. He intended to keep her, since she wasn't ever going back to her original owner. They'd left van Blaiden's ashes scattered on Olyanda, and good riddance. A nastier individual would be hard to find.

Having a fancy boat like this just might make a difference in the future. Whatever it took to keep the wolves away from the sheep. These days there were more and more wolves, and the sheep were spread out thinly among the stars without a shepherd.

Ben felt the familiar buzz of Cara's implant handshaking with his own.

Mother Ramona, she said. *Calling from Crossways.*

Okay, ready. Ben was used to Cara's touch inside his head. It never seemed intrusive or abrupt. His own Psi-1 rating was in Navigation. He could barely throw a thought from here to the wall by himself, so he needed a strong Telepath like Cara to run comms for him.

There was a slight internal lurch as the focus shifted and Mother Ramona herself arrived in Ben's mind, front and center, routed through Cara on *Solar Wind* and Ully on Crossways Station. Mother Ramona, a marble-skinned, genetically engineered exotic whose criminal activities included smuggling, identity manipulation, espionage, counterespionage, and network hacking, had stuck to every deal they'd made. Without her they'd never have extricated the settlers from Olyanda.

Benjamin, you took your time, Mother Ramona said. *Your settlers are driving us crazy. If Garrick hadn't signed a contract to keep them safe I think he'd have spaced them by now.*

Sorry about that. Had some business to attend to. Turns out it wasn't as simple as I'd hoped. There's a warrant out for our arrest.

I know. Even Crossways has received it, though I have no idea why. She laughed. Even mentally her laugh was more like a cackle. It was the one thing that made her seem older than she was, or perhaps it gave away her true age, which otherwise she hid very well.

Good thing you have no extradition treaty with any of the megacorporations. Ben didn't try to hide his own amusement at the thought.

If we did, half of Crossways' upstanding citizens would be in the chokey. Mother Ramona's mental voice went from humor to worry. *They've pretty much thrown the book at you, though.*

We know. Had a bit of a brush with an old friend. He frowned. *Not exactly a friend, to be honest. Long story.*

I look forward to hearing it sometime.

Me too, Cara echoed.

He shot Cara a look and she pulled back out of the conversation.

Mother Ramona continued, *While you've been tying up loose ends we've been trying to accommodate ten thousand pains in the ass who've never even seen a space station before. We've had to corral them in the stadium. It's not pretty in there. Your psi-techs have set up camp in the upper bleachers while the settlers are down on the pitch. Victor Lorient is . . . well let's just call him high maintenance. Even his wife won't talk to him anymore.*

There was a reason for that which went beyond the current settler situation, but it wasn't up to Ben to divulge it. Lorient, the settlers' ultra psi-phobic leader, had been more than just a pain in the ass throughout their time on Olyanda.

I get it, Ben said. *We'd better find the settlers a new planet soon, or else.*

The audio comm buzzed into life and Crossways Control announced, "*Solar Wind*, you're cleared for docking. Proceed to Port 22, Green Sector."

Ben saw Cara touch her vox. "Thank you, Crossways," she said. "On final approach."

Be with you, soon, Ben told Mother Ramona. *Your flight controllers have cleared us for docking.*

Port 22 is Garrick's private dock, Mother Ramona said. *I've vouched for you personally, so mind your manners.*

Will do, Ben said. *Can you do us one more favor?*

How much is it going to cost me?

Nothing. It will cost us in the long run, Ben said. *Can you find us a space we can take over? I don't care how spartan it is. Even an empty warehouse will do. I'd like somewhere I can get my psi-techs away from the settlers.*

I'll see what I can do. I guess there's not much love lost.

The settlers are a bunch of Ecolibrian fundies, Ben said. *They're never going to like implant-enhanced psi-techs, no matter how many times we save their asses.*

Mother Ramona gave the mental equivalent of a suppressed laugh.

I'll see what I can find.

Ben turned his attention to docking an unfamiliar ship in one of Crossways' internal docks. There was little room for error.

"Harnesses," Ben broadcast ship-wide. "Safety lock-down for manual docking."

All battened down here, Ronan Wolfe, their medic, responded privately to Ben. *How is your shoulder?*

Sore but holding.

And Cara?

Making light, but I've seen her try to ease her ribs when she thinks no one is watching.

Ben lined up *Solar Wind* with Port 22's blue access lights. The station filled the viewscreen, her pulse-cannon obvious from this distance, barrels sticking out like bristles on the side of a porker.

Port 22 grew from a small dark rectangle on the bulbous end of one of Crossways' huge projecting caissons to a gaping maw that swallowed them whole. The screen view switched to a functional glideway with a run of central guide lights.

Ben cut the power, feeling a slight bump as the grav buffers caught and the ship regained weight. *Solar Wind* settled gently into her landing gear and the clamps engaged. The air lock began to cycle.

Home—for now, at least.

❖ ❖ ❖

As the rest of the crew left the flight deck, Cara sat back in *Solar Wind*'s comms chair.

"Are you sure you don't mind?" Ben asked.

"Of course I don't mind. I've been waiting for you to suggest it."

She swiveled around to face him.

"It won't tire you too much?"

"Stop trying to give me an out. You need to talk to your Nan. Yes, it's a long way, yes it will be tiring, but it's what I'm trained for. Now do you want to do this or not?"

He nodded. He'd hoped to be able to bring his family off Chenon, but Alexandrov had foiled that plan along with his attempt to get at Crowder.

"Okay."

Cara breathed deeply and closed her eyes, sitting perfectly poised. Bruise or no bruise, she looked beautiful, even in a severe black buddysuit that disguised the curves he knew were there.

Ready? she asked.

He followed Cara's mental link as her thoughts ranged out toward Chenon and Nan. Ben could feel her concentrate on seeking out his fierce and formidable grandmother, matriarch of the Benjamin family, or what was left of it: Ben's older brother, Rion, and Rion's two boys, Kai and Ricky.

Cara! He felt the moment of contact as Nan recognized Cara's mental touch. *Is Reska all right?*

Nan was the only one who ever used Ben's given name. He'd been Ben Benjamin since his first day in the Monitor Cadets, just as Jessop had become Jess.

Ben's fine, Cara said. *Here, see for yourself.*

She pulled back, leaving Ben and Nan to talk to each other through her link.

Reska. It's been too long—

Sorry, there was a reason for that, Nan. Things went south very fast on Olyanda and I didn't want to put you in danger by giving you information others might want, but you need to know now.

Tell me the worst of it.

Nan never wasted time on irrelevant explanations.

We found platinum on Olyanda and Crowder betrayed us to get it all for the Trust.

And did he?

Get it? No. I sold it to Crossways, but it was touch and go for a while. He tried to wipe out the colony with a plague.

But you're all still there.

Still alive, but not on Olyanda.

What do you need us to do?

Get the first shuttle off-planet to a neutral station. I'll meet you there.

There was a significant pause before she answered. *Not going to happen. Ricky would love a trip off-world, but you think I could possibly get Rion off this farm?*

Ben fought down rising frustration. His older brother might as well have been welded to the land.

I'm worried Crowder will try to use you as a bargaining chip.

You think we're in danger?

*I'd be happier if you all found a bolt-hole and kept your heads down in case someone comes calling. Can you find an

*excuse to bring Kai home? He's a sitting target in Arkhad.
The university's too close to the city.*

**Kai's on a field trip to one of the moon arcologies. He's
safer than any of us.**

**That's good. Warn him, but don't trust the house's regu-
lar comms links. Your line might be bugged already.**

Understood.

Ben saw Cara begin to sway sideways. The call had taken
long enough.

**That's it for now, Nan. We'll be in touch again as soon as
we can. Love you.**

Love you, too, boy. Take care, both of you.

We will.

He felt Cara close off the conversation and her eyes
opened.

"Thanks," he said. "You followed all that?"

"I did. Will Nan be able to persuade Rion to leave the
farm?"

Ben thought of his brother. Stubbornness was his
strength and his failing.

"Probably not, but at least they're warned now."

❖ ❖ ❖

Kitty Keely pushed down panic. Had she overstepped her authority? Would she get a medal or a reprimand? Hell, she was
so out of her depth her feet might never touch the bottom
again. It had all started when Akiko Yamada, Alphacorp's director, had called her into her office in Sandnmore, Alphacorp's headquarters in the Saharan Rainforest, and
personally instructed her to spy on Ari van Blaiden. She
wanted to know all his dirty little secrets.

"You're van Blaiden's type. You're ideally placed in his
department. Get close to the man."

"How? I mean . . ."

Ms. Yamada had looked at her over her entirely unnecessary retro-fashion spectacles and said, "Use your initiative, Ms. Keely."

She'd swallowed. "You want me to sleep with him?"

"No, Ms. Keely, sleep is the last thing I had in mind. I
want you to fuck him bowlegged if that's what it takes. I
don't care how you do it, but win his confidence. My Telepath, Rufus, will contact you for a weekly report."

"But you can't order me to—"

"Your reluctance is noted. Perhaps I can sweeten this for you a little. You mother has recently been diagnosed with Ren-Parry Syndrome."

Kitty swallowed and nodded numbly. It was curable, but the treatment was expensive and not available in Shield City. She'd applied for a loan—Damn, was that how Ms. Yamada knew? Weren't those things confidential?

"Forty thousand credits," Ms. Yamada said. "That's the full cost of a course of treatment. Such a pity to lose a loved one for lack of a mere forty thousand credits."

Forty thousand didn't seem mere to Kitty. "I've applied for a loan."

"Which will be refused."

"What?"

"But I will personally make sure your mother receives the best of care at Alphacorp's clinic in Switzerland. Keep the reports coming and your mother's course of treatment will continue."

"What if I can't get him interested?"

"That would be a pity. I understand that unless the course is one hundred percent completed the treatment isn't effective at all."

Kitty had left Ms. Yamada's office in shock. She'd taken the York flight from Sandnomore with her mind spinning in circles. She was the right size and shape and the right coloring to fall into the category of Mr. van Blaiden's type, and she was certainly in the right place—his office was just down the hall from where she'd been posted, fresh from flight school—but she was no spy. What did Ms. Yamada suspect him of? She so didn't want to get involved in anything clandestine. She'd been hoping for a proper posting in the far reaches of space. Getting involved with politics was going to screw her career.

When she'd realized she was making her lip sore by biting it, she'd activated the sound baffle around her seat and picked up the comm only to find a message from her mother. The image wavered, but the sound was clear.

"Kitty, sweetheart, I don't know what to say." Mom was smiling like Kitty remembered her doing when she was younger and healthier. "That nice Doctor Pinder came in person and explained everything. I'm booked on a flight to Switzerland first thing in the morning. She said not to worry, once the treatment is complete I should regain the sight in my left eye and the feeling in my feet and there won't be any further deterioration. And I have you to thank for it, my girl. You and Alphacorp." Her face clouded, just a little. "Can we really afford it? I mean, I know you're drawing full pay now, but . . ."

She responded. "Don't worry, Mom. It's all taken care of." She really had no choice. "Just get well soon. I love you." She hit send.

Ari van Blaiden, get ready, 'cause here I come. Damn and blast it!

Getting close to Ari hadn't been as easy as that, of course. He'd seemed supremely disinterested until she'd mentioned the fact that she'd taken the advanced class in jumpship flying. Then all of a sudden he'd started sending her flowers, which quickly led to the bowlegged fucking thing, except it had been her on the receiving end. That man could go. Despite the fear of being found out, it had been fun at first, when he'd been in the wooing stage. After that—well—she'd rather forget what happened later.

Ari had never suspected, though.

She'd continued to report until the day he'd tried to use Carlinni to take down Benjamin and it had all gone horribly wrong. She'd reported van Blaiden's death and then asked the Telepath, "What happens to my mother? The treatment isn't complete. Tell Ms. Yamada I did my best."

Rufus had simply shut off the conversation and hadn't been in touch since.

So when Kitty had spotted the opportunity to attach herself to Benjamin's psi-techs she'd gone for it. Once again she had information worth something, and hopefully it would pay for her mother's continuing treatment. All she needed to do was to get a message to Ms. Yamada to restart those regular links.

Of course, she needed to make sure she stayed on Benjamin's good side. She wasn't going to be able to get to him the same way she had van Blaiden, but he did need another jumpship pilot. That could be a way in. She needed to try harder next time.

❖ ❖ ❖

Mother Ramona has found you a warehouse space.
Mother Ramona's personal Telepath, Ully, came through as

Ben followed Cara down the tube to *Solar Wind*'s main deck. *She's arranged for a real estate agent to meet you at the dock and take you straight there. Her name's Bettina Mirakova.*

Ben gathered his skeleton crew at the top of *Solar Wind*'s extended ramp. He noted they'd all removed the Trust's insignia from their buddysuits. This wasn't the place to show affiliation to any of the megacorps, especially since that affiliation had been irreparably broken.

"Crossways isn't like most space stations," Ben said. "Despite what you may have heard, there are rules. Stay together. Don't get into trouble. Gupta and Jon Moon are on duty here to look after things, so the ship will be available if you need a bolt-hole. Cara and I are going to check out a potential home space. I'll let you know if we find somewhere we can all hang our hats. After that we all have decisions to make about where to go from here. If you have to get in touch with your families, limit what you tell them. Remember there's a warrant with your name on it. Don't give your family the responsibility of keeping your secrets if the Trust knocks on their door."

"What about me?" Kitty Keely asked.

"What about you?" Kitty was trim and fair, maybe a couple of centimeters shorter than Cara. It was easy to see how the two women fell into the broad category of Ari van Blaiden's *type*, yet Kitty didn't interest him at all. She was pretty enough in a superficial way, but his attraction to Cara wasn't all about beauty.

"You didn't promise me anything more than Crossways, and I appreciate I didn't do so well with *Solar Wind*'s foldspace jump, but I'd really like to stick around. Do I lose myself here or am I joining the team?"

"Good question. Until a few days ago you were on the side trying to kill us."

"You know I wouldn't have signed up for that if I'd known what I was getting into."

Ben glanced sideways at Cara.

She's telling her own truth as far as I can judge, but what do I know? I believed Ari, too. At first, anyway. Cara was the first to admit that her Empathy skills were intermittent at best.

Ben dipped his head fractionally in acknowledgment.

"We'll decide how permanent it is later when we know our next move, Kitty. Stick with Gupta for now. He'll find you something to do."

She gave him a tight little smile and turned back toward the ship as everyone dispersed, leaving Ben and Cara with Wenna and Ronan Wolfe, the dashing young doctor who had worked with Ben on several missions before Olyanda and was, along with Wenna, one of the survivors of the ill-fated Hera-3 debacle.

"Aren't you two going exploring?" Ben asked.

Ronan shrugged apologetically. "As your doctor I feel obliged to make sure you two follow my instructions to take it easy. Besides, Jon has drawn guard duty, so I find myself temporarily without a partner."

"And since I never had a partner in the first place, you're stuck with me, too," Wenna said. "I'm too old for singles bars. Besides, I'll set off every scanner alarm I pass through until I register this with Station Security." She touched her right arm, prosthetic from the bicep down, with her good left hand, a self-conscious gesture that Ben still winced to see. She'd survived Hera-3, but not without injury.

She was right about the scanners. Crossways was particular about security. With a population laced through with criminals, opportunists, misfits, mercenaries, and free-thinkers, it had to be.

It was good to have the *de facto* president of Crossways on their side, though. The extra layer of protection was useful. Garrick owed them for the platinum deal, which would make him several million credits richer as soon as Olyanda started to produce, though that was still six months away.

Only the Trust had lost out. And Ari van Blaiden, of course.

They passed through the vast hangar lined with three ship-servicing gantries, two in use, one idle. The whole place was gray medonite, clean and workmanlike, but with touches of individuality: Mother Ramona's simple "R" logo and Norton Garrick's colors, dark green with a red flash. One of the ships in dock was Garrick's private yacht, cigar-shaped with a crystal observation deck topside, the other a guppy-shaped runabout, unmarked, that looked as though it had met with some trouble. Ben supposed trouble was an everyday thing for someone in Mother Ramona's line of business—the softer side of crime, but equally dangerous in its own way.

Smart private guards, dressed in Garrick's livery, escorted them all to the door. Exiting past the security station, they emerged onto a utilitarian concourse divided by a sunken track for the auto-cabs that looked more like a fairground ride than a transport system but sped efficiently around Crossways' complex spiderweb of interconnecting routes.

A tub-cab, garishly hand-painted yellow, red, and blue, pulled up. Serafin West stepped out, trim for seventy, but with a face wrinkled like a walnut. He had a satchel of small engineering bots slung over one shoulder, which he was able to connect to, mentally, via his implant. He called them his boys.

"Hey, guys." He grinned at them. "Glad of an excuse to get out of the stadium for a while. It's good to see my fellow criminals looking so well. I hear you ran into trouble."

Ben shrugged. "Had to change our plans about Chenon. Crowder outmaneuvered us. We'll get settled here first and try again."

A second cab pulled up, equally bright. Gen Marling, nearly four months pregnant and just starting to show, leaned into the protective embrace of a tall settler with a brush of dark hair. Ex-settler, since Max Constant had thrown in his lot with the psi-techs, even going so far as to have an implant fitted, though he'd barely learned how to use it yet. His civilian suit set him apart. Maybe that's why Gen had elected to leave her buddysuit behind. She wore leggings topped by a lightweight tunic in blue with a spray of peacock colors emblazoned across the front that flattered her small bump and set off the golden undertones in her skin.

"Will you two get a room?" Wenna said.

"Got one," Max said. "The stadium's not the place for us to hang out. I may have been forgiven my romantic indiscretion . . ." He squeezed Gen's waist. "But having an implant fitted is one step too far for my former settler colleagues."

"So we figured we'd come house-hunting with you," Gen said. "I want to make sure we get somewhere decent." She patted her belly. "We don't know how long we'll be here and I don't want to bring up baby in a dump."

"How come you know where we're going?" Ben said. "I only asked Serafin to come and do a structural survey of the place."

"Ah, my fault," Serafin said. "I may have mentioned it to a few people as I was getting the boys together." He patted his satchel.

"All right." Ben sighed a mock sigh. "Come on."

◆　◆　◆

"Coffee, Mr. Jussaro?" Crowder pushed a lidded cup toward the squat, genetically engineered individual with a serious case of monobrow and unsettling nictitating third eyelids. His dark purple-black skin, slightly scaly, was designed to be impervious to the cancer-causing radiation that swamped planets in the Hollands System.

Jussaro blinked his inner eye membrane sideways, like a reptile, and reached for the cup, hesitating just short of grasping the handle, as if he wasn't quite sure whether the offer would be snatched away. He glanced toward the clear panel on the interview room door to see if anyone was observing.

Crowder opened his hand to indicate the coffee was his, free and clear.

Jussaro nodded and drew the cup between his palms, holding it under his nose and breathing in the fragrant steam before sipping slowly. "Nice. Thanks."

"You're welcome. No need to be uncivilized. I believe you've been Mr. van Blaiden's guest on Sentier-4."

"You might say that."

"He wanted to know the whereabouts of Cara Carlinni, I expect."

Jussaro put the coffee on the table and sat back, eyes suspicious. "I've not seen van Blaiden for weeks . . . months . . ." He jerked his shoulders. More of a nervous twitch than a shrug. "Maybe longer. It's difficult to tell." He held up his left hand, showing a ridged scar on the back where his handpad had been ripped off. They'd cut him off from the world, removed his ID, isolated and dehumanized him.

"Please." Crowder pushed the coffee back toward the little man. "So . . . Carlinni."

Jussaro frowned and shook his head.

"I don't need you to tell me where she is," Crowder said. "I already know."

Jussaro didn't react, rising in Crowder's estimation.

"You might also be interested to know that Mr. van Blaiden met with an unfortunate accident."

"Fatal, I hope."

"As it turns out, yes."

"I see. Good." Still the poker face.

"Did you know he used to work for me before he defected to Alphacorp? He was a great disappointment in so many ways. Mr. van Blaiden was not a friend to this department."

"That might mean more to me if I knew which department we were in," Jussaro said.

"Forgive me. You're safe with the Trust, now, Colony Division, Chenon."

"Safe. Ha!" Jussaro's face twisted. His laugh was like a bark and contained no humor whatsoever. "The Trust, Alphacorp, Ramsay-Shorre, Arquavisa; you're all as bad as each other. Megacorporations are the curse of our time. You think a stranglehold on jump gate travel and ownership of the psi-techs gives you trading rights throughout the colonies."

"Ownership?"

"Well, what would you call it? They toe the line or they get decommissioned." He touched his own forehead. "Sure, they can move from one owner to another for a transfer fee, but they can't go independent unless they can buy out their own contracts—and how many of them ever have the resources to do that?"

"We care for them, provide for them. They want for nothing."

"You make sure you bill them for every damn implant checkup, their apartments, their uniforms, every last piece of equipment. That's how you tie them to you. It's economic slavery, only it's soft enough that most of them don't complain."

"Still continuing the rant that got your implant decommissioned in the first place, Mr. Jussaro."

"Damn right."

"No matter." Crowder waved one hand to dismiss the past. "Doctor Zuma has finished conducting her tests. You have a very strong natural psi talent. One that has survived the termination of your implant. I've checked your records. Two periods of Neural Readjustment after being found guilty of encouraging psi-techs to go rogue."

"If you call leaving their employers going rogue."

"Do you know how much it costs to find kids with psi potential, fit neural implants into their skulls, and train them? We have contracts for a reason."

"Yes, to keep them on a tight leash."

"So you went rogue yourself. Formed a breakaway group of psi-techs. Sanctuary."

"I didn't form it, but, yes, all that's a matter of record. I helped kids to get free of the megacorps and I paid for it. You nixed my implant." He fingered his forehead again where a faint scar still glistened. "There's nothing else you can do to me except kill me, and there are times I think that would be a mercy."

"There is something we can do." Crowder tried to make his smile reach his eyes. "Not me personally, you understand, but Doctor Zuma tells me that you're a suitable subject. She can refit you with a new implant."

Jussaro's face traveled through the whole spectrum from derision to hope via the realization that his principles were about to be sorely tested. After a moment of indecision, his eyes shone wet and his mouth formed an oh shape, but no sound escaped.

Got him, Crowder thought.

"What would you do to have your Psi-1 status restored, Mr. Jussaro? What would you do?"

Chapter Three

DAMAGE

CARA STARED IN FASCINATION AT THE SUN-
ken roadway. It was alive with automated tubs whizzing
past, each cab competing for the annual bad taste prize, all
of them dipping into tube-like tunnels and emerging equally
suddenly into stations and pull-ins.

The real estate agent, Bettina Mirakova, hopped out of
her tub to meet them. Cara had never taken too much notice of fashion—it was too hard to keep up when you spent
chunks of time away, and every world had its own local
styles—but she desperately hoped this look was not currently in vogue on Crossways. Mirakova almost outdid the
tubs. She wore a spotless white lace top, a formal purple
vest, and a plaid kilt in shades of purple and green with
matching purple knee-length boots, flat heeled. Her dark
hair was pulled back into a severe knot, emphasizing the
planes of her face and her tightly sculpted curves.

"I was only expecting two." Mirakova eyed the seven of
them. Her tub would take no more than four. "I'll take Mr.
Benjamin and Miss Carlinni and here's the address." She
paused to scribble on the back of a business card and
handed it to Ronan. "You five grab another tub and catch
up with us."

"There's room for a little one." Serafin waited until Ben

and Cara had settled themselves in the tub with Mirakova and then muscled in. Mirakova shot him a dark look, then quickly replaced it with a bright smile. Their tub, the interior blissfully gray, whirled away into the traffic, leaving the other four on the concourse.

Cara settled back into the seat, still feeling drained from the long-range talk with Nan. The whole tub experience was damned uncomfortable and a little dizzying, but efficient. Mirakova was all sales pitch. She talked too much and too quickly, obviously anxious to make the deal. That was real estate agents the galaxy over. They'd swear black was white if it secured a sale.

"Of course, it needs some work," Mirakova said, "but I gather you've just come into some funds."

"Not yet," Ben said. "But soon."

Needs some work . . . Cara aimed a thought at Ben and Serafin. *That probably translates to near derelict and barely holds an atmosphere.*

"We have excellent builders on Crossways," Mirakova babbled on, unaware of their shared thoughts. She was probably on commission from the builders, too.

The tub popped up out of a tube and slowed to a halt in a private pull-in. Mirakova had been talking for the whole journey. Cara had zoned out.

"Not sure that we'll be needing builders." Ben offered Mirakova his hand as she exited the tub. "Not even sure how long we'll need the place for. Things are still fluid."

Cara hopped out unaided, followed by Serafin.

The street, if street it could be called, was empty. It was just more gray medonite with a low ceiling and broad featureless walkways on either side of the transport pull-in. Cara could hear the whir of traffic along the main thoroughfare, but this branch remained deserted. There was no sign of the second tub.

Are you guys on your way? she asked Ronan.

Took us a while to get a cab, he replied. *Does it look okay?*

Only just arrived. The whole area looks a bit run down. No one around. You'd expect a station this densely populated not to have any deserted bits, but we seem to have found one.

Cara stared around the warehouse district and sup-

pressed a shudder. Most of the units were vacant or shuttered. The overall impression was of locked doors and
boarded windows. The ceiling, just a couple of meters above
Cara's head, was low enough to be oppressive.

"I thought this would be perfect for you," Mirakova said.
"It doesn't look like much, yet, but this whole segment is
about to be redesignated as a mixed residential and commercial zone. Pretty soon it will be awash with cafes, shops,
and apartments, but right now the space is up for grabs. I
believe you have a lot of people to accommodate."

"Not sure how many yet," Ben said.

Mirakova swiped her handpad across the doorplate. A
quiet beep accepted the connection. The wide loading door
grumbled back to reveal a cavernous interior full of crates
stacked in blocks and bays.

"I thought this was supposed to be available right away."
Cara started counting the stacks and lost track where the
shadows swallowed them up.

"The previous tenant is clearing them later today.
They're mostly empty." Mirakova skimmed her handpad
over a control panel by the door and punched in a series of
numbers on the keypad. Lights in the ceiling immediately
above their heads sprang into wakefulness, obscuring the
rest of the warehouse in shadowy gloom.

Serafin reached into his bag and loosed a handful of
mind-controlled mini-bots to scurry like demented spiders
across the floor, up walls and along ceiling beams. Mirakova
stared at them and Cara sensed extreme agitation, but
maybe the woman was just not used to being around Psi-
Mechs. Cara admitted that the little spider bots were un-
comfortably insect-like. Serafin tossed another handful to
the floor and they scuttled away, probing, calibrating, calcu-
lating, and sending information back to him on the structural integrity of the warehouse. This was an old station,
never designed to be in service for centuries. Many parts
had been renewed and strengthened, but sections could be
prone to materials fatigue.

"This way, quickly. Quickly." Mirakova led them deeper
into the warehouse and away from the bots at a brisk pace.

"Why the rush?" Serafin muttered, turning to check on
the bots as Mirakova strode on.

We're here, where are you? Ronan asked.

Inside. Cara glanced toward the door. *Can't see your tub. You sure you're in the right place?*

Warehouse district. Looks quiet. Some workmen in the unit across the way. No open doors apart from theirs.

Nope, definitely the wrong place.

My sweetie says he thinks he knows where you are, Gen butted in. *Be right there.*

"Miss Carlinni, this way, please," Mirakova called.

Cara turned to follow, feeling uneasy.

Somewhere outside a tub clanged to a halt. "Sorry we're late," Wenna called from the doorway. "I think you gave us the wrong address, Miss Mirakova."

"We'd never have found you," Gen said, "but it looks like Max is shaping up to be a Finder."

"I just said it felt as though they were around the next corner." Max looked bewildered. He obviously didn't know what a big deal it was to show signs of a specialty this early after having an implant fitted.

"That's the way it works, sweetie." Gen grabbed his hand and pulled him toward her, bumping her little round belly into him and giving him a swift kiss on the cheek.

Mirakova glared at them as if kissing in public was against the law. Cara caught a wave of anxiety from her. Why should she be anxious? Did she have another appointment? Was she afraid of losing a good commission if she failed to sell them the warehouse? After all, the more of them there were, the less likely it was that there would be an instant and unanimous decision on the first viewing.

Ronan strolled in behind Wenna. Ah, good, his Empathy rating was stronger than Cara's. Perhaps he could help pin down her feelings.

As they moved further into the warehouse the sensor-lights lit their path and darkened behind them. Serafin's bots kept pace, but Mirakova strode ahead.

Ronan, there's something not right with Mirakova. Can you sense it?

Cara opened up a comms channel and brought them all into it, even Max, who still felt very green. She showed them what she felt: a sense of unease, maybe anticipation, emanating from Mirakova.

Serafin sent his bots scuttling ahead.

There's someone else in here. Ronan was staring into

the shadows. *Four of them,* he said. *Concealed behind crates.*

Trap! Cara blasted out a warning.

✦ ✦ ✦

A shadow moved behind the crates. *Take cover!* Cara shoved Max and Gen toward a gap between two stacks. She reached out for Mother Ramona's personal Telepath and snapped out a mayday call.

Mirakova spun around and produced a pistol from beneath her kilt. Ben and Ronan each ran for a different gap. Separated from the others and caught out in the open when the first zap of a bolt gun rang out, Serafin fell, arms flung wide. He jerked once and lay still.

Another shot clipped the corner of the packing case above Cara's head. *I called Mother Ramona. I sure hope these aren't her guys.*

I trust her, Ben said.

You trusted Crowder.

She shouldn't have said that. It was a low blow. Cara's tiredness vanished under the adrenaline spike. She opened a mental link and drew them all into a gestalt, feeling Max's surprise as his world opened up to five other minds. Hell of a time for his first experience of hive-mind.

A hail of bullets peppered the crates close to Ronan. *Shit, that was close!* he said.

Status, Ben said.

Fine, Gen and Max said together.

Ronan?

Okay.

Serafin was an aching absence.

Where's Wenna? Ben asked.

Here, Boss. Bastard shot my arm.

Which one?

The one that doesn't bleed, but it's hit the servo. Bloody useless unless I take it off and beat someone to death with it.

Cara released the lobstered helm from her buddysuit collar pocket. It unfolded and covered her ears and brow. She flicked an ultrathin face mask into place. She felt Ronan turn his concentration on Serafin, pouring willpower toward him to try to hold body and soul together.

One of Serafin's bots scuttled along the ceiling. They'd be

dead if he was. She felt relief prickle her scalp. The bot dropped suddenly and there was a yell from behind a crate. Those little devils were tiny, but they were equipped with drills and cutters big enough to go through a man's skull or into his eyeball.

She ignored the wave of panic from the bot's victim and reached out with her mind to seek the other attackers. Her Empathy could at least tell her how many and where they were. *Three more plus Mirakova,* she broadcast. *One of them is psi.* A weak Psi-4 Telepath at best. Cara could do something about that one. *I can put him out if you all let me draw some whammy.*

Go for it, Ben said.

She felt Max begin to question what they wanted of him, but she figured he'd get it soon enough as she took over their combined power, channeled and aimed it at the man's implant. She wouldn't have been able to do this before experiencing what it was like to be at the mercy of Donida McLellan's ruthless mind manipulation, but now she used it without a qualm.

See how easily the abused becomes the abuser.

She kept that thought to herself, or hoped she had.

As she bored into the mind of the assassin she learned that he was supposed to let someone know as soon as she and Ben were dead. This was a trap made for two and the assassins had been dismayed to find themselves five against seven.

Five against six with Serafin down, and all of them weaponless. Damn, they were stupid for obeying Crossways' rule of not carrying sidearms in the street. She guessed Ben had his parrimer blade, but that was no good against a bolt gun and projectile weapons.

She pressed on the Telepath's mind and choked off his ability to get a message out, then heard him gurgle, just off to her right, as she slammed him into unconsciousness. There was the sharp sound of a weapon clattering to the floor.

Ben, he's close to you, she said. *To your left.*

Got it.

Cara relinquished the borrowed power, taking a few seconds extra to make sure Max hadn't been completely freaked out.

I'm okay, Max said.

Good. Keep down and keep Gen down. You're the only two not wearing buddysuits. We don't want to lose anyone else.

She was aware that Ben was on the move. A moment later there was another grunt as a second attacker fell.

Two weapons, now, Ben said. *All I have to do is pinpoint the bastards.* He fired off several rounds on a spray burst to cover Ronan, who was working his way over to Serafin. *Catch.* Ben slid the second gun skittering in Ronan's direction with an urgent shove. *Max, can you get a fix on Mirakova?*

There. Max wriggled close to where Cara crouched behind a stack of packing crates and pointed.

Take this. Cara detached the cuff-light from her left wrist. *Point the light, and then get down.*

Max closed his eyes and directed the beam. It stabbed through the gloom and straight at Mirakova's eyes. Two of Serafin's bots dropped from the ceiling into her hair. She flailed at them, unable to quell the usual human reaction to bugs, and staggered forward.

Ben moved and fired as she stepped into range. Mirakova gave a ragged shriek and dropped.

Ronan, covering Serafin's body with his own, fired randomly in the direction of the other two attackers to keep them down. Cara ducked back behind her crate.

Five combatants were now two. With Mirakova down the odds suddenly became much more favorable, but a fair fight was too much to hope for. There was a dull clunk and the sound of something rolling.

Grenade!

It didn't take Ben's warning to have Cara twisting away from the opening and pushing Gen and Max down even further, covering as much of them as she could with her body, hoping that the armor built into her buddysuit was enough to deflect the worst of the blast. But instead of a bang there was a hiss.

Gas! she warned.

She pulled out her breathing tube and pushed her face-mask seal tight to her skin. It covered her eyes and nose, but not her mouth. She clamped her lips together. These guys were out to kill so this wasn't going to be a simple knockout gas. Gen and Max didn't have buddysuits. She had to get them out.

Cover us. She rolled to her knees and shoved Max hard. *Get out now. Don't speak, don't breathe. Quick.*

Gen was already on her feet crouched low over her belly. The three of them scuttled between obstacles while bolts splintered crates around them. She heard Ben and Ronan returning fire, but she couldn't stop to see what was going on. Max stumbled and Gen grabbed him by the arm. Cara heard his breath rasp. Oh shit. Hopefully the concentration of gas was less this far from the grenade or Max was a dead man. He coughed and doubled over. Cara grabbed his other arm and she and Gen hauled him bodily back toward the main doorway.

Guards wearing Garrick's colors boiled out of two tubs as they reached the street.

"Gas!" she yelled, and they pulled out breathers.

Max dropped in a heap at her feet and Gen doubled over coughing. She must have caught some of the gas, too.

"Medic!" Cara yelled, trying not to lick any residue from her lips.

A woman wearing a full protective suit stepped forward, scanned them with a sensor and slapped a blast pack to the side of Gen's neck then to Max's. "Clothes," she snapped at all three of them.

Cara knew the routine. There could be enough gas trapped in the folds and creases of her buddysuit to kill. Especially in the confines of a space station. She peeled off the suit and dropped it into a hazmat bag, shivering in her singlet and briefs.

Ben, help's coming.

A loud bang and flash from inside the warehouse ended the sound of bolt guns. Ben and Wenna ran from the warehouse and started stripping off their gas-coated suits. A medic jumped in to help Wenna when it became obvious that she only had the use of one hand. Garrick's guards emerged a few moments later, prodding along two of the would-be assassins at gunpoint.

A gurney team, with Ronan in attendance, brought out Serafin, already hooked up to a drip. Not dead, then. Cara felt dizzy with relief.

Garrick's medic waved Ronan back. "He's in good hands, Doc. Let us take care of you for a change." They whisked Serafin off in a tub with Gen and Max.

Wrapped in foil blankets, Cara, Ben, Wenna, and Ronan piled into another tub and let themselves be given the antidote.

"Taking you straight to Dockside Medical," an orderly said as he squeezed into the tub with them and punched the locator pad. "It's closest, and also the best."

The tub whirled them toward the traffic lanes.

"What was all that about?" Wenna asked, clutching the blanket about her with her good left hand. "Van Blaiden's dead. I thought we were in the clear."

"But Alphacorp isn't dead," Cara said.

"And neither is the Trust," Ben said. "That could have been either of them. And if it was both of them working together, gods preserve us."

✦ ✦ ✦

Cara suffered the indignity of thorough decontamination, every crack and crevice being cleaned and swabbed. Once out of the final head-to-toe dunk in something slightly more pleasant smelling than the previous three solutions, she gratefully accepted a robe and followed a young woman to a separate unit for an extensive checkup. It might have been any medical facility in any part of the known universe. They all smelled the same and looked the same, every corridor in the ubiquitous hospital green, only marginally better than plain gray medonite.

The orderly left her with a polite instruction to wait and pointed her toward a sitting area dominated by a holographic mural depicting a beach scene on some planet with a red sun, yellow sky, and black sand.

Ben and Ronan were already waiting, freshly scrubbed and gowned in white.

"Efficient here, aren't they?" Cara said as Ronan moved along the bench to make a space for her next to Ben.

"Very." Ronan wriggled in his seat and screwed up his face. "I'm usually not on the receiving end of this kind of treatment."

Ben turned to Cara. "All right?" he asked her.

"I think so. I feel all right, anyway. Is all this really necessary?" She nodded to the exam room.

"Let them do your bloodwork again," Ronan said. "Make sure the gas is out of your system."

"Cara . . ." Ben looked uncomfortable. "The Telepath you took out . . . he never woke up again."

"I killed him? How is that even possible?" She turned to find both Ben and Ronan, the two men she trusted most in all the universe, looking at her as if she was a stranger. "No."

Their silence said yes.

"Perhaps he had a bad heart."

Ronan shook his head.

When she didn't speak for a few moments Ben asked again. "All right?"

Was she? She'd killed a man with her mind for fuck's sake! It wasn't supposed to be possible. No one had ever warned . . .

She took a deep breath.

A man who'd been trying to kill her and her friends.

She nodded. "I'll have to be."

Counseling? Ronan asked on a tight band that bypassed Ben.

She jerked her head once in a brief nod.

The double doors opened and Wenna entered in a float chair, saving Cara from continuing the conversation, though it didn't stop her gut from churning.

"Wenna?" Ben's voice held a hint of alarm.

"It's okay, Boss. Not sure why they don't trust me to walk. It's my arm that's busted, not my legs." She waited for the float chair to settle and stood up, her right sleeve hanging loose.

"Miss Phipps." A nurse in an antiseptic-looking ice-blue coverall came out of the treatment room and called Wenna in first.

"No Gen or Max yet?" Cara asked, trying to sound normal.

Ben shook his head.

"Want me to find out how they're doing?" Without waiting for an answer she reached out to Gen. *You all right?*

Yeah, but Max is making such a fuss. They want to keep me in overnight for observation, just to make sure the baby's not been harmed. I feel fine, now, but I think we'd better stay.

Good plan. Be safe.

Cara passed on the information.

The beach mural changed to a mountain scene. This time

it looked vaguely familiar. *Matterhorn*, Cara thought. She focused on it and tried to calm her thoughts. Every now and then *I killed him with my mind* surfaced, but she fought it down. The thought was abhorrent, but beneath it there was the strangest tickle of a thought: she'd never have to be afraid of another Telepath like McLellan again.

As the Matterhorn cycled to a forest scene, the double doors opened and Mother Ramona wafted in on a cloud of expensive perfume, looking very different from the last time they'd seen her, kitted out in combats and body armor. Cara never washed up that well. She spent too much time in a buddysuit and boots to feel comfortable in high heels, but Mother Ramona's sure had an effect. Even Ronan— comfortably gay—seemed to appreciate the clingy black dress, which showed off her girlish figure.

How old was she? Older than she looked, Cara thought. Her refined features and her smooth skin, delicately marbled in shades of blue and gray, showed no wrinkles, not even laugh lines. Her hair, a vibrant cerulean blue, had white highlights and was cut fashionably spiky. Maybe the clue lay in her crone-like cackle.

Cara ran her hand through her own cropped mop wondering if she should make more of an attempt to look feminine and then realized what she was doing and self-consciously sat on her hand.

Most exotics were genetically engineered to enable them to survive on a less than hospitable planet. Cara's friend Jussaro, from her time on Mirrimar-14, had purple-black skin, heavy brow ridges, and even nictitating eyelids, all to combat the high radiation in the Hollands System. Marta Mansoro, the supply officer on the Olyanda team, had scaly skin and gills that enabled her to function on the water planet of Aqua Neriffe. But Cara couldn't begin to guess where Mother Ramona came from or what her physiology might be adapted for, other than looking gorgeous.

"Dreadful business. You kids look shattered. You need sleep." Mother Ramona pulled up Wenna's empty float chair and sat down opposite.

Ben started to protest, but Mother Ramona cut him off.

"Garrick sends his apologies, he has business to attend to, as do I, but you can go and rest up at my place. It's a bit less ostentatious than Garrick's Mansion House, but don't worry, it's perfectly safe. I don't spend much time there now. I'll send Syke with you, our captain of security."

"My team . . ." Ben began.

"Already recalled to the *Solar Wind*, and the dock's been secured."

"That's where we should go."

"If you prefer. Syke will provide protection. Here, wear Garrick's colors. It would be a very foolish person who interfered with one of his visitors. We should have issued you all with a band on arrival." She handed each one of them a green armband with Norton Garrick's distinctive red flash. "In case you're wondering, Mirakova was a fake. The real Mirakova will take you to the real warehouse tomorrow."

"We should get off Crossways as soon as possible," Ben said. "We still have thirty thousand lost settlers to find."

"And three hundred psi-techs who possibly all have different ideas of what they want to do with the rest of their lives," Cara said. "Their lives have been turned upside down, too. You—we—can't ignore them."

"And you'll soon have a fortune in platinum stocks to manage," Mother Ramona added. "You cut your psi-techs in for a percentage, but money has to be earned and then it has to be managed. You're in business, Benjamin, whether you want to be or not."

"Hardly," Ben said.

Mother Ramona cackled. "Better get used to it. You're not rich yet, though I've arranged a line of credit against your expectations. In the meantime you have a debt and a stolen state-of-the-art jumpship to support. What are you going to do, sit back and sip cocktails all day? That's not your style. The Trust isn't paying your bills now. You need to make your money work for you, otherwise one day you'll turn around and it will all be gone. There are crooks on Crossways, you know."

She winked at them.

Cara watched the beach scene cycle back into view. How would it be to have nothing to think about except the next few hours in the sun, the drink by your elbow, and the book in your lap? It was a long time since she'd relaxed with a novel.

I killed him with my mind. Shut up . . .

But . . .

Shut up!

It was only thirteen days since the showdown with Ari. Even without the new revelation, she needed recovery time. Ronan's regeneration treatments had helped, but her ribs were still sore and her bruises still livid.

She'd been hurt too much, and not just physically.

Never again.

She could kill with her mind.

She wore that thought like armor.

Never again.

"Thirty thousand settlers."

Ben's words cut into her thoughts. He was right, of course. Thirty thousand missing settlers trumped everything.

"I'm looking for a lead on your settlers," Mother Ramona said. "My sources are tracking jump gate records. Give me a few days before you go shooting off. It's been months already, a little more time won't hurt."

Cara could feel Ben's impatience, but he nodded agreement. The missing settlers could be anywhere: dumped on an inhospitable planet, left in cryo, running on automatics on an outbound trajectory to nowhere, fired into the heart of a star, or lost in the swirling black of foldspace. Ben had promised Victor Lorient that if they could be found he would find them. And he would, or die trying. That was Ben. Nothing if not true to his word.

How could she love him and resent him for it at the same time? Life would never be easy with Ben. He'd never do the expedient thing, only the right one.

She sighed inwardly. The settlers were innocent victims of Crowder's attempt to grab Olyanda's platinum for the Trust. Maybe the search was futile, but if the ark ship was still out there to be found, she'd give the search her best shot. She owed Ben that much at least. After that, she'd see.

Chapter Four

THE FREE COMPANY

DRESSED IN ONLY A SKIMPY SINGLET AND shorts, Kitty Keely jogged the whole length of Port 22 for the fifth time, pivoted, and jogged back, ignoring the burn in her thigh muscles and the grab in her chest from the dry space station air. She was still questioning her sanity in joining Benjamin's crew.

What if she'd done the wrong thing?

Ms. Yamada was not, by all accounts, a forgiving person. She didn't even have a way of reporting securely until Ms. Yamada's Telepath, Rufus, contacted her, and as yet he hadn't. She was a respectable Psi-3, but she couldn't transmit across the galaxy.

She needed to get a message to Alphacorp. They didn't even know she was here. Did anyone even care that she was missing? Ms. Yamada no doubt had bigger concerns than one missing pilot.

What had happened to her mom's treatment? It was barely halfway done when she'd left Earth for Olyanda with Ari. Her mom had been cheerful throughout and had nothing but praise for the staff at the Swiss clinic. How cruel if Ms. Yamada withdrew treatment through no fault of Kitty's.

What if Kitty had outlived her usefulness? Had Ms. Yamada cut her adrift? If so, there were worse places to end

She seemed relieved. "Come on, then," she said.

Was that an invitation?

Only to sleep. She picked up his thought and responded. Gah! He must be tired if he'd let his shield down.

He followed Cara to the cabin they'd been sharing during the journey—well, not exactly sharing, as she'd managed to take her sleep breaks when he was on duty. This was the first time they'd hit the bed together since . . . when? Since before van Blaiden.

She was bound to be twitchy. More than twitchy. He'd tried to talk to her about it, but she wasn't ready to open up. He'd waited for some signal from her, let her make the first move, but though she'd touched him in public—a hand on his shoulder, a casual brushing together of elbows, the light slide of her fingers across his, briefly igniting fire in his belly—she'd been much more circumspect in private. It would take as long as it took, he understood that. They were working their way through everything that had happened, but she was still fragile—even more fragile after today—but he didn't know how he could help her to get over it, if indeed it was his help she needed.

"I still feel like an intruder in here," Cara said, dropping down to sit on the wide berth. "Ari obviously had this built for himself. He never liked sleeping alone."

"It's a bit excessive." Cara's former lover was always excessive. Ben was glad she'd never shared this particular cabin with van Blaiden. "Just say the word and we can tear it apart and rebuild it. Or we can let Ronan and Jon have the space and move to another cabin, or separate ones if you prefer."

"Is that what you'd prefer?"

"You know it's not."

"You're going after Crowder again." It wasn't a question.

"As soon as we've settled things here. He's the obvious starting point."

"He tried to kill us all." Cara shuddered.

"That's why he's the obvious starting point."

"You think you can dodge the Monitors and get in and out of Chenon without anyone noticing? Even if you can, Crowder must be eyeball deep in his own security by now. He knows you. He'll be expecting you."

"I'm working on it."

"You're not planning anything . . . terminal . . . are you?"

Ben opened the door to the fresher and activated the shower.

"Ben? Answer me."

He ignored Cara's question and jerked his head toward the shower. "Want to share?" He released the touch-and-close fastenings that held the top half of his buddysuit to the bottom, unclipped the shoulder catch and shrugged out of it, feeling the suit's sensors peel back from his skin.

"Do you want me to?" she asked.

He turned to look at her, saw her face suddenly serious, and stopped undressing.

"I appreciate all you've done for me, Ben, but . . ."

Snakes began to turn somersaults in his gut. "But thank you and good-bye. Is that it?"

"I tried to kill you on Olyanda. Twice. I almost got you killed. Your shoulder—"

"Almost as good as new." He flexed it, hiding the stab of pain from half-healed muscle. He'd looked at it once, using a mirror, soon after the dressing came off: a livid stripe, pink meat against brown skin. After that he'd avoided looking at it again. "Ronan says it won't even need a graft. It'll barely scar."

"That doesn't make it right."

"Cara . . ." Oh, gods, where to start? He sat next to her, carefully not touching. "I thought we'd worked all this out. I thought we were good. Olyanda was tough, but we survived. Together. What am I missing?"

"Ari van Blaiden."

"He messed with your mind. It wasn't you."

"They couldn't make me believe all the things I believed if I hadn't had some lingering feelings for him."

"What about us, Mrs. Benjamin?" He felt something slipping away that he'd let himself start to rely on.

"Don't call me that. We lived a lie for a few months. It doesn't make it real."

He'd wanted it to be real. "What do you want me to call you?"

She didn't answer.

"Cara . . ."

"That'll do. Cara Carlinni. I need to find out who I am before I become someone else."

"Are you saying you're leaving?"

She shook her head. "Only if you want rid of me."

"I don't."

"Even though I tried to kill you and had sex with Ari? And, for fuck's sake, I killed someone with my mind!" There, she'd said it at last. "And I don't even feel sorry."

"You can't go through what van Blaiden and McLellan did to you without it changing you."

"For better or for worse?"

"Not better, not worse, just different. I love you, Cara. I've never made any secret of that."

"I know that, too." She smiled a small, sad smile. "I think you're nuts, though."

"So sue me." He reached out and covered her left hand with his right. She froze for a moment and then turned her hand to grasp his.

"Can we just take it slowly for now?" she said.

"As slow as you like," he said. The snakes began to settle. Maybe there was hope.

◆ ◆ ◆

Cara and Ben lay in the generous bed, not touching. Aware of Ben at her back, his warmth prickling her skin, she thought she'd never sleep, but as soon as her eyes closed, she felt the blackness sucking her down into its warmth.

With only a hazy impression of fast-fading dreams, she awoke to an empty cabin.

Cautiously she opened her eyes, stretched and sniffed. Fresh bread and coffee, real coffee by the smell, not just caff or regular CFB, coffee-flavored beverage. On the table at the foot of the bed stood an insulated carafe and a copious breakfast cup, plus a basket of hot rolls and a selection of pots and jugs: cream, milk, fruit preserves, and honey. It looked like Mother Ramona had sent a care package.

Ben's used cup stood still half-full, with cream congealed on the cooling surface. That man had no taste. He preferred caff to the real stuff. It probably came from being raised in the colonies.

She showered and dressed quickly before Ben returned, then grabbed the coffee and rolls with real strawberry jam. Did Mother Ramona and Norton Garrick live like this all the time? Luxury goods were rare on a space station. Their lifestyle said a lot for their affluence, and the platinum deal was going to add to that considerably.

She was halfway through her second cup when the door opened to reveal Ben with a carton of caff from the galley in one hand.

"Good morning," he said. "Good news on Serafin. He's out of surgery and resting comfortably, though still on a respirator. Suzi's with him."

"Are you going over?"

"They've said no visitors yet. If you're ready, Mother Ramona has arranged for us to see the real warehouse this morning."

She was grateful he didn't try and take the conversation back to where they'd left it last night. She could manage this level of normal.

"Coming." She gulped down the last of her coffee, grabbed another roll from the basket and closed the neck catch on her buddysuit.

Gen met them in the corridor. "Not so fast. We need to talk."

Max stepped out of his cabin, dressed in a brand-new buddysuit.

"New gear. Nice." Cara pretended to brush lint off his shoulder.

"I went for basic black. Do I look the part?" Max twirled.

"Combat ready," she said. "Do you know how to use that thing?"

"Light here. Hood here. Facemask here. Breathing tube, emergency drugs, noise canceling earpieces, full spectrum eyepiece, cuddly toy, bottle opener, pack of cards, and . . ." He patted his pocket. "Somewhere I think I have a tool that takes stones out of a horse's hooves."

Gen turned and gave him a light smack on the arm. "You promised not to be flippant."

"Oww! I only said I'd try. This is all a bit new. Gimme a break."

"The suit'll give you a break if we run into trouble."

"She's right," Ben said. "Don't forget it has armor, too, and it's specially strengthened on the outer edges of the forearms if anyone comes at you with a knife."

Max's eyes widened. "Is that likely?"

"You can ask that after yesterday?" Cara said. "You're going to need some combat training."

"I'm pretty good at duck and run."

"Good, then all you need to learn is when to do that and when to hit back."

"In the meantime, we have business." Wenna joined them.

Cara was relieved to see she was back to normal, with the prosthetic arm completely indistinguishable from her biological one.

"Who's we?" Ben asked. "This corridor is getting a touch crowded."

Wenna stepped back and turned. "You'll see."

She led the way to the *Solar Wind*'s mess, the biggest communal space on the ship. Cara tagged along. She'd only been part of this crew for one mission, and that all gone to hell, partly because of her.

At the door Wenna paused and by a gesture waved Cara in with Ben. "Promise you'll listen," was all she said.

Gen and Max crowded in behind them. There were probably fifty or sixty psi-techs crammed into a space designed for half that number, many of whom had been roughing it in the stadium billet: Ronan and Jon; Gupta; Marta Mansoro, gills covered by the high neck of her buddysuit; Cas Ritson, their other Psi-1 Telepath; Mel Hoffner from medical; Archie Tatum, Serafin's Psi-Mech second; Lewis Bronsen, a Finder; Yan Gwenn, pilot and ship's systems engineer; and even Kitty Keely. The hubbub of voices died away.

Ben inclined his head and looked at the crowd. "Wenna says I have to listen. I'm listening."

"We wanted to let you know we've decided to stick together," Gen said. "With you, that is. No one here intends to desert."

"It's not about deserting," Ben said. "It's about family and commitments and about independent people deciding where they want to be. I'm not Commander Benjamin anymore. No one has to do what I say."

"Well, since Crowder slapped a warrant on all of us, where can we go?" Gen asked. "First listed as dead, now listed as, at best, Typhoid Marys, at worst, criminals on several counts. We're probably the most wanted semi-corpses in the galaxy."

"There are plenty of colonies where one of Mother

Ramona's new identities wouldn't be questioned," Ben said. "Anyone with a partner and children or parents and siblings at home might want to gather their family and start again. Their platinum share will give them the resources to do it."

"And they might prefer to bring that family here and stay with a group of people they trust and a boss who looks out for them," Gen said.

"There's no longer anything for me to be boss of."

"There's the Free Company."

"What's that?"

"Us. The Olyanda survivors—most of us—or two hundred and eleven of us to be precise." Gen waved expansively. "The Free Company doesn't belong to you, it belongs to all of us. We've all agreed to invest half our platinum money, and we've elected you as boss. Max is our accountant, Wenna our company secretary."

"And what do you expect the Free Company to do?"

"Anything. It doesn't even have to be legal." Gen frowned. "That is, if it breaks a few stupid laws, we don't care, as long as it's moral. While the platinum holds out it doesn't even have to make money."

Cara had been watching Ben. He'd been trying not to react, but she recognized his small tells. Body inclined slightly forward, mouth set in a line as if he was deliberately trying not to smile. Oh yes, he was up for it.

"I can't do anything until we've found the missing settlers," Ben pushed out the suggestion and waited to see whether it would float.

"Then that's our first job," Gen said. "Come on, Boss, you know you don't really want to cut us all loose."

"On one condition," he said. "That you can un-elect me any time."

"It's a deal," Gen said.

Cara saw a smile begin to twitch at the corners of Ben's mouth. That's settled, then, she thought.

◆   ◆   ◆

Kitty waited until the general hubbub had died down. Everyone was excited by the prospect of the Free Company and it took a while for them to disperse back to their temporary accommodation. Three of Yan Gwenn's ship engineers stayed behind to familiarize themselves with *Solar*

Wind's systems and to check for any nonstandard mods they still had to find.

Gupta had called all his security team to a meeting on the dockside, twenty-three of them, hardly an army, but Gupta was taking the attack at the warehouse more than seriously and was going over options and revising procedures.

Which meant he had more than Kitty Keely on his mind.

She tagged along behind the last few stragglers heading back for the stadium.

Better them than me, she thought to herself. By being no trouble and keeping a low profile she'd kept her berth on *Solar Wind*, which meant she could watch whatever move Benjamin's renegade psi-techs made next. Of course, it hardly mattered to her if they did something to hurt the Trust. In fact if they did, it could only benefit Alphacorp.

There was no getting close to Ben Benjamin. She'd flashed her most dazzling smile at him a couple of times, but he hadn't even noticed. He was never less than polite and professional, but it was pretty obvious that he only had eyes for Cara, even though she wasn't totally sure it went both ways. Cara had been messed up by van Blaiden. It took a while to get over that.

There was no one else worth pairing up with. Ronan Wolfe was utterly gorgeous but settled in a relationship with Jon Moon. Wenna would be the obvious one to chase, but Kitty had watched her closely for days and still didn't know where her preferences lay, if, indeed, she had any. Wenna never showed any interest in either males or females. If Kitty made advances and was wrong, she'd mess things up. She certainly wasn't going to settle for Gupta or Yan Gwenn, or someone further down the food chain. They were definitely not the first people to know what was going on.

Maybe it was better not to form relationships with any of the psi-techs, though it wouldn't do any harm to get on the right side of the cute guard, Wes. He'd already helped her to get one message out to "Mother," though she hadn't had an answer yet.

Time to go and see if he was on duty today.

She slowed down to let the others get ahead as they neared the entrance to Port 22. There was one guard on the gate, and she could see Wes inside the gatehouse.

He stepped out just as she got there.

"Hey, Kitty." He really did have a nice smile; she had little difficulty returning it.

"Wes."

"Going somewhere? I get off duty on the hour."

She checked station time on her handpad. Fifteen minutes. "I could wait. I was just going to explore."

"Let me take you on a guided tour. I thought you lot weren't supposed to go anywhere on your own."

"I won't be on my own." She winked at him.

"I suppose not."

Five minutes later Captain Syke arrived with six fresh guards and Wes' shift ended.

"Sorry you had to wait." Wes lifted off his helmet and scrubbed at his scalp one-handed. "Damn thing just makes you want to have a good scratch once it comes off."

"Good to be off duty, huh?"

"Sure is."

"I'm not spoiling any plans, am I?"

"Not a bit of it. I was going to Ag One, but I can go later. There's a community farm there. I volunteer."

"On a farm?"

"Community farm. They keep domestic animals, chickens, goats, sheep, pigs, a horse, a couple of ponies, and cows in milk. It's for the kids. Crossways kids only ever get to see animals like that on vids. It does them good to see what they feel like and smell like, even though most of their protein comes from a vat. There's nothing bigger than a cat allowed outside of the farming area, and that's only to keep the rat population down."

"And you volunteer?"

"Sure. I show the kids how to milk the cow and I lead them around on the ponies. Not just me, of course. There's a rota."

"Well, you are a surprise, Mr. Orton. I'd love to see your farm sometime."

He held out his hand and Kitty took it.

Chapter Five

QUARANTINE

"HOW ARE YOU FEELING, MR. JUSSARO?" CROW-
der leaned over the recovery bed. "Dr. Zuma tells me
the implantation was a complete success. Ready to join the
living again?"

Jussaro blinked, then smiled.

"Before we activate your implant fully, there are conditions, but you knew there would be, didn't you?"

"I guessed as much." The smile faded, replaced by wariness.

"You'll be leaving as soon as you've recovered. I want
you to go and find your friend, Carlinni. That's no great
hardship, is it? We'll even give you passage and a cover
story."

"I won't kill for you." Jussaro's mouth was set into a hard
line, but there was worry behind his eyes.

"Of course not. I wouldn't ask you to."

"Information, then, is it?" Jussaro looked relieved.

That was the trick. Make them think the worst and then
when you asked for something smaller it didn't seem so bad.

"Information." Crowder nodded. "I'm not a mind reader,
but I'm guessing right about now you're wondering what's
to stop you from skipping out on your obligations. Am I
right?"

Jussaro didn't answer.

"Of course you are. So you need to know about the modification to your implant."

This was almost too easy. Jussaro's reactions were too predictable. He began to wonder whether the man was as naïve as he seemed. Maybe he was feeding Crowder the reactions he thought were expected of him. It didn't matter. Crowder had him sewn up.

"Modification?"

Was that a hint of fear in Jussaro's question? He hoped so.

"There's a switching device in your implant; effectively a kill switch."

Jussaro shrugged, not giving anything away in his expression now. "What does it do, blow the top of my head off?"

"Nothing so crude. It induces an electrical cascade in your brain, a stroke. You might survive it, barely, in some kind of vegetative state perhaps, but your implant won't."

Crowder let the information sink in. "We can trigger it from anywhere. You can run, but you can't escape. And just in case you're wondering, there's a dead-man switch. If I don't hear from you every seven days your implant is toast. And, of course, if I die . . ."

Jussaro's eyes widened.

"Carlinni and Benjamin have several good reasons to want me dead. You have a very good reason to want me alive. I'll expect to hear from you on a regular basis, or rather, my Telepath, Mr. Leyburn will. I won't be opening up myself to the possibility of attack. I know what Cara Carlinni did to Mrs. McLellan. Your friend is a dangerous woman."

"Is she? Tell me more."

❖ ❖ ❖

Ben had an appointment with Norton Garrick and Mother Ramona before going to the warehouse.

"Coming?" he asked Cara. "Or would you rather meet me there?"

"I'll come."

He felt absurdly pleased.

They took a tub hubward, accompanied by two silent guards in full-face helms, hurtling into the fast lane to make the six-kilometer journey in just under ten minutes. The Mansion House was right in the middle of Crossways, in a district known as Center-Spindle. It faced out across Hub Park, a green space surrounded by the homes of the wealthy. The artificial azure sky, far above their heads, seemed convincingly real. Built on Palladian lines, the Mansion House's main living area was above street level and accessed by an impressive outer staircase leading to a columned portico. It almost looked like real stone, a clever artifice. On the ground floor, below stairs, Norton Garrick had his personal offices, distinct from Crossways' administrative headquarters, which were a block back from the hub.

Garrick's slight figure and pale skin stretched tight across the planes of his face spoke of deprivation in his youth, but his clothes and the single small diamond in his earlobe showed the restrained good taste of someone who no longer needed to flaunt excessive wealth. His brown wavy hair, cropped stylishly short and graying at the temples, could have belonged to a businessman rather than the pirate that he was, or maybe had been. Whatever Garrick's former occupation, he'd reinvented himself as an entrepreneur and politician. Crow's feet around his eyes spoke of a ready smile.

He wasn't smiling today.

"Bastards!" Garrick spat the word out and then looked up. "Not you two. Bloody Alphacorp. They just stopped a shipment of provisions at the Athabasca Terminus. The bogus quarantine notice for Olyanda has been extended to Crossways. We appear to have taken in ten thousand plague victims and are now in imminent danger of infecting all human life in the known universe. Any ship docking on Crossways won't be allowed to dock in Alphacorp or Trust ports without spending ninety days in a designated quarantine holding area. In other words, the independents can deliver their cargo here, but they're not going to be able to trade anywhere else for three months after that."

"Just Alphacorp and the Trust?" Ben asked.

Mother Ramona entered the main office from a door at the back of the room. Today she wore an elegant business suit that contrasted sharply with her marbled skin. "Arquavisa has just been panicked into joining in. The rest will follow. That means we're under an effective trade embargo. No supplies in, no goods out—from and to the megacorps-held planets anyway."

No station in space, especially one the size of Crossways, was entirely self-sufficient, despite intensive food production. It would take a while for shortages to kick in, probably nonessentials at first, but once it started to hit the staple food stocks it wouldn't be pretty.

"How long before supplies run out?" Ben asked.

"A couple of weeks before people start to notice they can't get everything they want. A couple of months before supplies get dangerously low. We could introduce rationing, but that's going to cause unrest."

"You don't need this," Ben said. "Forget the warehouse, we'll go."

"Where to?" Garrick gave him a level look.

"Fair point." Ben shrugged.

"Besides, Alphacorp has always wanted an excuse to stick it to us. You could leave tomorrow, but they wouldn't lift the embargo. We have to change our trading patterns to deal with the independents only—build up new networks."

"Where are the nearest independent planets?" Cara asked.

Mother Ramona hit a panel on the desk and a holographic galaxy materialized in the center of the room. It was very like the one Crowder had in his ops room, and for a moment Ben was back to being a young ex-copper staring at Crowder's favorite toy in amazement as colonies twinkled in front of his eyes. In the intervening years he'd helped to put more bright white dots on the map. He located them: Rostov, Occania, Kemp's World, New Canada, Eyonore ... and there was Hera-3, glowing blue to designate it as a platinum planet administered by the Trust.

Alphacorp's colonies were green, Arquavisa's yellow, Ramsay-Shorre's red, and a number of others glowed in shades in between. Dotted among them all were worlds he didn't recognize, picked out in violet.

"Those are the independents," Garrick said.

"I didn't realize there were so many." Cara stepped in past Ben to get a closer look. "That's quite a network."

"Plentiful, but not close," Garrick said. "In the past it's suited us that Crossways is off the beaten track with only one jump gate, which we control. A lot of the independents have picked their locations carefully, far enough away from a jump gate that transit is going to take anything from four to twelve weeks. Many of them are happy to trade with us, but we have a logistics problem. Did you enjoy your coffee this morning?"

"Mmm, lovely," Cara said.

"Very kind of you to send it, thank you." Ben tried not to look at Cara as he sidestepped the question smoothly.

"From here." Mother Ramona pushed her arm into the hologram and brushed her finger across a violet world in the Perseus Arm of the galaxy. "Blue Mountain, the ultimate coffee-producing planet in the Tegabo system. Settled by a breakaway bunch from Drogan's World. Their nearest gate is fifteen weeks out from the planet."

"And while coffee is not an essential . . ." Garrick said. "Well, not to me at any rate." He took a sidelong glance at Mother Ramona and gave a twitch of a smile. "Cereals would take eleven weeks' transit from Prairie, bulk protein powders five weeks from Massukos, even supposing they have the surplus to help us. If they don't, then the next nearest producer of any size is Keynes, which is nine weeks from its nearest gate."

Ben stared at the hologram. "The megacorps don't have quite the monopoly on fast transit that they think they have," he said. "But it would certainly help if we had a few more jumpships. That would solve a lot of transit problems."

"You said 'we,'" Mother Ramona said.

"Huh?"

"You said 'if *we* had a few more jumpships.' We, not you. Does that mean that you're with us?"

Ben blinked twice. "I guess it does. I can't speak for everyone. Some of the psi-techs want to leave and find somewhere quiet to settle down, but over two hundred are staying." He glanced sideways at Cara, but her face was expressionless. He wished he knew where her head was.

"The scruffy engineer woman!" Mother Ramona snapped her fingers several times, pressed her lips together and screwed up her eyes. "What was her name? Kept busting through security to rant about retrofitting jump drives."

"Kennedy," Garrick said.

"Dido Kennedy, that was it. Didn't you give her a few hundred creds and tell her to go away and work on it?"

"Seemed to be the best way to get rid of her." Garrick shrugged.

Ben jumped at the news. "Someone's working on retro-fitting jump drives?"

"Don't get excited, Benjamin," Garrick said. "It could all have been hot air."

"Worth checking out, though."

"On your own head." Garrick shrugged. "You'll find her in Red One. Woman is mad as a bag of snakes."

"And it's not a very nice neighborhood," Mother Ramona added. "Take backup."

"You think there will be assassins?"

"In Red One they could all be assassins if you look like a victim. Nothing personal, but half the folks down there are looking for a business opportunity, and that could come from anyone who looks as if they have something worth stealing. Even the underclass has an underclass."

"Noted. It's worth investigating, though. Jumpships are the way forward. I've used some of the independent gates," Ben turned down the corners of his mouth. "Some are old but robust. Others are held together with string and a prayer."

"I don't think there's one person on this station who can fly a jumpship, Benjamin," Garrick said. "Or at least, no one who's owned up to it. Just you and Miss Marling so far. Jumpships are important, but so are pilots to fly them. If we can retrofit, buy, or even steal jumpships to bring in supplies, we're still going to need pilots and Navigators who've got what it takes. Can you train them for us?"

"Damned if I know." Ben shrugged. "Gen's a Psi-3 Navigator and she can do it, but Kitty Keely just doesn't have the knack. If I knew what gave Navigators the ability to fly a jumpship free-form, rather than transiting via the gates, I'd be closer to knowing whether I could train them."

"But you'll try," Mother Ramona asked.

"If it doesn't take up too much time. We still need to find those missing settlers. Crowder is the obvious starting point. We have to get to him on Chenon somehow, since he's not at home to telepathic callers."

"Don't throw yourself away on something you can't win," Garrick said. "The settlers may be long gone."

"I made a promise."

"I know, I know." Garrick held up both hands, palms out-ward. "You always keep your promises. I have it on good authority." He exchanged a knowing look with Mother Ramona. "My fiancée is your biggest advocate."

"You want something else," Cara said.

Cara had always told Ben that her Empathy, her ability to read people's feelings, was intermittent and unreliable, but this time she seemed to have hit the spot.

Garrick nodded. "You have information that could damage the Trust and Alphacorp."

"Yes." Cara moved to stand closer. Ben could feel the warmth of her. "A download from Ari van Blaiden's handpad."

"We don't know the extent of it, yet," Ben said. "There's a lot of data and we've hardly begun to look."

"Will you share it?" Garrick asked. When neither of them answered straightaway he continued. "The megacorps can't stand that Crossways fought for its independence and won. They've always been worried that others would follow suit. Alphacorp has a spurious claim to ownership because it bought out the Larssen Corporation, which first put the station out here. We've always known that one day they might try to enforce that claim."

"The trade embargo is the first step," Mother Ramona said. "We think they might use Olyanda as an excuse. We need to find a way to fight them." She took Garrick's hand. "And we need to get all the independent planets talking to each other. Alone, they're in danger of being swallowed up every time they have something that a megacorp wants, but together they can stand strong."

"And if the megacorps lose their grip you get a whole new trading network to support Crossways," Ben said.

"Exactly," Garrick said. "Only that should be *we*, Benjamin. Are you in? You and the Free Company?"

"News travels fast."

Mother Ramona cleared her throat. "I might have had a casual conversation with your Miss Phipps."

Ben looked at Cara. She gave him a curt little nod.

"I'd say take all the time you need," Garrick said. "But I'm not sure how much time we have."

"We don't need time," Ben said. "Thanks for the offer. It's a good idea. Cara says yes. We need a base and Crossways is it. We're in."

❖ ❖ ❖

You like Garrick, don't you? Cara asked, using a tight telepathic band to keep the conversation private.

They were on their way to the warehouse, crammed into a tub with their silent guards.

Like is too strong a word. I trust Mother Ramona and she trusts Garrick. I've seen a few people come and go at the top of the Crossways heap. Garrick is something different. He thinks big and he's not just at the top because that's where the profit is.

That's what I mean, she said. *You like him.*

I like his vision and I respect him. I'd rather give someone the benefit of the doubt than live my life expecting to be let down. I find if you put your trust in people they often come up to your expectations. My grandmother taught me that. Of course there are occasionally exceptions.

Crowder.

A big exception. I confess I didn't see it coming.

Neither of us shines in the character-judgment department. Cara sounded rueful.

She put on a good front, but she wasn't over the Ari van Blaiden fiasco, yet. Maybe it would always leave a scar. Van Blaiden's pet Telepath, McLellan, had messed with her head appallingly, conditioning her to protect van Blaiden against all her natural instincts. It had almost killed them both until Cara had managed to turn the tables on McLellan, get inside her head and smash her down.

Oh! He had a sudden insight into the way Cara had put down the Telepath in the warehouse yesterday. McLellan had turned her into a killer.

Ben took her hand and squeezed it. *I trusted you. I still do.*

That's more than I deserve.

The moment begged for her to say she trusted him, too, but she didn't. An aching gap opened up between them. He let go of her hand. *It's a start, isn't it?*

✦ ✦ ✦

The warehouse was in district Blue Seven, close to where they'd been attacked the day before. The back of Ben's neck prickled. Too late. Why hadn't he had warning shivers yesterday?

"Déjà vu," Cara whispered as the little transport tub bounced into the bay.

"This time I'm ready." Ben patted his buddysuit thigh pocket. "Not getting caught like that again."

Cara patted her own pocket. "Derri?"

"Derri," he confirmed.

One of the guards cleared his throat. "I'll pretend I didn't hear that." The voice was female. Ben revised his opinion hastily.

"The no-firearms rule could hardly apply to something as low powered as a Derri," Ben said.

Even smaller than its antique counterpart, a palm-sized Derringer delivered twenty stun bolts without recharging time between shots. It was short-range, but had laser-point accuracy over a distance of twenty meters and the advantage of being able to shoot around corners, or at least bounce off any shiny surface. It wouldn't kill, not unless you pumped five or six bolts into a person on rapid-fire, but it would give you an edge in a street fight. You really had to want to kill someone to make it lethal.

The warehouse door stood open. The female guard commed ahead and received the all clear. No traps waiting for them today. They stepped into the cavernous, well-lit space, their boots echoing on the medonite floor. No packing crates this time, good. A knot of people had gathered a little way in, where Wenna, Gen, and Max stood with a young woman in a sober business suit. Archie Tatum, Serafin's young Psi-Mech second, was above them on a gantry examining structural beams.

"Hey, Boss, Cara, come and meet the real Bettina Mirakova." Wenna waved them over.

"I heard what happened yesterday. I'm so terribly sorry." Mirakova stepped forward and offered her hand. "I wouldn't want you to think we're all savages on Crossways."

"Miss Mirakova." Ben took the hand and then stood aside for Cara to shake.

Well? he asked, close range.

As far as I can tell she's who she says she is. Damn, I should have realized something was wrong with yesterday's Mirakova, but I took her agitation for anxiousness to make a deal. I was careless.

We both were, and we nearly paid the price.

"Please, call me Tina," Mirakova said.

"This is the warehouse Tina was supposed to show us

yesterday," Wenna said, "but her appointment got canceled by your secretary."

"I don't have a secretary," Ben said.

"I know that now," Tina said. "I'm sorry."

"No need to keep apologizing. It was a good setup, a team of professionals. We were taken in as well. Caught off our guard. Slow and slack-witted. It won't happen again."

"What do you think?" Tina said. "You can use this space for anything legal."

"Legal?" Cara said. "I thought this was Crossways."

"A lot of things are legal on Crossways that might not be legal elsewhere." Tina smiled. "But killing Mr. Garrick's guests is definitely not."

"I like it." Archie recalled a small flotilla of engineering bots no bigger than his thumbnail. They came zooming to his bag as he scrambled down from the gantry, scuttling down from where they'd been examining structural beams and wall skins, transmitting information directly back to his neural implant. "The boys say the outer structure is sound and the floor"—he stamped hard—"is strong enough to support whatever we want to build. There's potential to install a back door to Blue Eight and a direct link to Upper Blue One." He glanced upward. "We could have our own docking cradle."

"And a communications hub to connect to Crossways Main and the intersystems banking grid," Max said. "We'll need to invest if we're going to make the most of the platinum."

Ben sometimes forgot Max had a previous career in accounting before he signed up for the Olyanda Colony. He might need training in survival skills, but he left them all in the dust when it came to finance.

"We should send a recovery party back to Olyanda, Boss," Wenna said. "I know we're going to be filthy rich in platinum, but there's no point in wasting some of the good equipment we left behind."

It seemed they'd settled matters of the Free Company between themselves. Ben tried not to smile. The secret to running a good team was that a really good team ran itself. All it needed was someone to nod or shake their head a time or two at appropriate moments.

He nodded.

Wenna and Gen high-fived. "You won't regret it, Boss," Gen said.

Wenna hugged him, her newly fixed prosthetic arm squeezing just a little tighter than a human arm might have.

"Oww! I already do."

He turned to Cara, strangely silent through all of the discussion. "Are you in?"

Am I invited?

Of course.

She gave one brief nod. *I'm in, then.*

Relief flooded through him. He'd been worried she'd cut and run.

◆ ◆ ◆

Kitty was dozing in her bunk when she felt a mental handshake, implant to implant.

Remus, thank goodness.

Ms. Yamada wants to know what the hell you are doing, Keely.

Making the most of an opportunity.

Have you considered the opportunity you'll give Benjamin if he figures out who you are working for?

He won't. I aced the psych test. Put all my feelings about Ari van Blaiden right to the front of my mind. After what happened to Carlinni, they've given me the benefit of the doubt. No one suspects.

They'd better not.

I can make my way home if Ms. Yamada prefers.

Since you're there, let's have a report.

Kitty tried not to feel smug, since Remus would notice.

Benjamin's psi-techs and the Olyanda settlers are all on Crossways, but there's a plan to move the settlers out as soon as possible.

To where?

I don't know. I'm not sure even they know yet.

What else?

Benjamin's psi-techs, or most of them, have officially formed the Free Company and they're setting up a base here in Blue Seven district.

As mercenaries?

More like psi-techs for hire, problems solved, that kind of thing, but their first job is searching for the missing settler ark.

You don't know—

If I did, I'd tell Benjamin. Thirty thousand settlers. Kitty shuddered at the thought. *Ari van Blaiden didn't tell me anything. I wish he had. Whatever happened to them was arranged before I hooked up with him.*

What about the psi-techs who are not joining the Free Company?

Going their own way with a new identity. They'll be laying low, heading out for the independent settlements. Shouldn't be any trouble. They won't want to draw attention to themselves.

Not sure Ms. Yamada will agree with your assessment. Secure a list of those new idents in case we need to seek them out at any time.

I'll do what I can.

Yes, you will.

Remus, what about my mom?

Stand by for further instructions.

She waited until Remus returned.

Ms. Yamada says don't worry about your mother for now. She wants to be kept up to speed on everything concerning the Olyanda platinum. Mining operations, production schedules, the lot. I'll contact you every three days. Stay sharp, Keely.

Kitty felt sick.

While she'd been waiting for Remus to contact her she'd been worrying about her mom, but now she was worrying about herself again. She felt supremely inadequate at the spying game, but she was stuck with it.

Chapter Six

RESOURCES

SQUISHED IN A BOOTH BETWEEN WENNA AND Archie, with Gen and Max opposite, Cara glanced at her handpad for what felt like the hundredth time and resisted the urge to order another beer. Alcohol had a suppressant effect on her implant, so she rarely overindulged.

Sam's Bar. There was a Sam's Bar on every station from Earth to the Rim. Few of them were run by actual Sams, but that didn't matter. This Sam's Bar was around the corner from their new premises and was unpretentious, clean enough to be comfortable, and quiet at this time of day. Each booth had a privacy baffle, so they couldn't be heard, though the general noise from the bar filtered through at a low level. Wenna turned down the musak, a monotonous fluctuating tone designed to be soothing. It did nothing for Cara. She preferred the classics if she had to listen to anything, but music wasn't her thing. Syke had arrived, checked the guard and left four of his men on duty. They sat at a table by the door, trying to look inconspicuous in their livery with glasses of juice in front of them and weapons ready below table level.

How long did it take to interview would-be assassins? Cara knew why Ben had taken Ronan instead of her, but it galled her. They weren't even psi-techs, how could she hurt them?

"So are they trying to kill just you and Ben," Wenna asked, "or are we all in danger? And who's *they*?"

"I guess Ben and I were the main targets yesterday," Cara said. "But Crowder was willing to sacrifice everyone on Olyanda to secure the platinum, so no one's safe."

"So anyone who's not staying in the Free Company is going to have to watch out when they leave." Archie stirred his caff. "Not that I'm thinking of leaving, you understand. I don't have any relatives waiting for me."

"No one can leave without getting new idents," Cara said. "And a fix for their implant so they can't be traced."

"Everyone needs one of those," Wenna said. "Whether they're staying or going."

"The ones who are leaving are the first priority. The rest just as soon as we can afford it," Max said. "Do you know how much those things are? I guess it's a seller's market."

Wenna took a long pull of cinnabeer. "So with limited creds we have to resettle Lorient's Ecolibrians somewhere safe."

"While finding thirty thousand lost settlers." Cara bit her lower lip. "That's Ben's top priority."

"And establishing the Free Company here on Crossways," Gen said. "It seems obvious, but we're going to have to split our resources."

"I'm no good to anyone in the field until this arm is fixed properly," Wenna said. "It looks okay, but it's not fully functional yet. I'm happy to stay on Crossways and refit the warehouse into Free Company Central."

"And Bump's not going to get any smaller over the next few months." Gen patted her belly. "I'll take care of new idents and safe passage for those who are leaving." She turned to Max. "With me, honey?"

"Huh? Oh, yes, sure. Whatever you want."

Cara smiled. They were holding hands under the table. So sweet.

Ben and Ronan walked in through the front door, stopped to order at the bar, and then slid into the booth as everyone shuffled up to make room.

"Well?" Cara asked.

Ronan shook his head.

"They know nothing," Ben said. "Local hires. Mirakova— or the false Mirakova—did the hiring, and she's dead. The psi-tech apparently had a single contact to make when the job was completed, but as far as we can work out he was just a link in a chain."

Cara thought back to the moment she broke through the Telepath's defenses. Was there any residual memory she could find? Damn! She hadn't meant to kill him. She really hadn't. But yet, her only remorse was for the way she'd done it, and the possibility that she'd given everyone linked to her the vicarious experience. She felt especially sorry for Max, who was still a novice.

"Alphacorp or the Trust, Boss?" Wenna asked. "What's your best guess?"

"Let's assume it's either or both." Ben pinched the bridge of his nose, then shook his head as if to clear it. "Garrick's not pleased. Crossways is a megacorp-free zone and he intends to keep it that way. He's stepped up security, but there are close to a million people here. How many of them could be sleeper agents? If I were running Alphacorp or the Trust or any of the corporations, I'd have agents here."

They all sat back as the bot delivered more drinks, caff all around and a sharing plate piled high with savory chimichi rolls. It trundled away from them with quiet authority and delivered another plate of rolls to the guards.

"We can't keep using Garrick's private army," Ben said, nodding at Syke's men who had waved thanks for the rolls.

"Well, we need some security, and Gupta's only got a small team," Cara said.

"Hiring might be problematical right now," Gen said. "We could easily be hiring our own assassins."

"Wenna was talking about going back to Olyanda to pick up some of the equipment we left behind," Cara said. "But we forgot one of the biggest resources Ari left us." They all looked at her blankly. "His mercenaries."

"They were trying to kill us just a few days ago." Wenna rubbed the stump of her arm above the prosthetic.

"Of course they were. That's what they were being paid for, but they were cool and professional and tight as a drum. And now they're kicking their heels on Olyanda and wondering if they're going to be able to negotiate their way off that rock. Ari only ever employed the best. They have the advantage that they've been tied up on Olyanda for long enough that they've not been in a position to accept a new contract to kill us."

Ben nodded. "Let's see what they're made of."

Cara realized they were all looking at her. Oh, right, contact the mercs. She steeled herself. The last time she'd had any direct contact with Captain Morton Tengue she'd been his prisoner. She knew he'd lost men in the fracas that followed Ari's death. She hoped she'd judged him correctly and that he proved to be a man who didn't hold a grudge.

How would he react to a suggestion to come work for the Free Company? Only one way to find out. She'd met him face-to-face, she could find him mind-to-mind, though his telepathy rating was moderate, a Psi-4 at best.

She cleared her mind and let herself concentrate on Tengue as she'd last seen him, a buzz-cut, thick-necked soldier in a dark blue buddysuit with a white flash at the shoulder, his unit's uniform. She thought about what she knew of him: tough, professional, undemonstrative, impersonal. All good outward traits in a soldier for hire. She wondered what lay underneath that. Surely there was more to Morton Tengue. Ari had hired him, so he must have come with a good reputation. She got the impression that all the mercs had served together for a long time, so loyalty played a part in their makeup. Mercs weren't generally loyal to a commander who wasn't loyal to them, so that gave her another aspect of Tengue to fix on.

She let her mind range out. Though most Telepaths had a limited range, distances meant very little to a Psi-1—that's why they were so important to the megacorps. Instant communication was often the difference between the success of an enterprise and its abject failure. It wasn't just what you knew that counted, it was how quickly you knew it. The only limit was the length of time she could keep the communication open. The longer the distance, the shorter the call.

She felt her implant handshake with Tengue's.

Who?

Cara Carlinni. She felt him on the verge of clamping down and cutting her out. *I've got an offer for you. Can we talk?*

There was a long pause. *I'm listening.*

We're willing to set the past aside if you are. We'd like to employ you.

Who's we?

A new outfit. The Free Company. Not affiliated to any megacorps. Working out of Crossways.

Who's running it?

Ben Benjamin.

He was on the point of cutting her off again and she needed to keep his attention and finish this quickly before her energy levels drained.

Please. Talk to me.

You and Benjamin took out two of my best men.

And you led us to our execution. Have we got that out of the way? You were doing your job. We were trying to stop you. Our fight was with van Blaiden. Sadly you picked the wrong boss. I made the same mistake myself once. It's easily done. The bad guys don't always wear black hats.

Ben had said that to her once about his time in the Monitors.

You come here in person and we'll talk. Face-to-face. You and Benjamin.

Cara could feel his wariness, but he was giving them a chance.

Done.

❖ ❖ ❖

The back of Ben's neck prickled. Mother Ramona hadn't exaggerated when she said Red One was not a great neighborhood. Located in Crossways' maintenance layer, the station's underbelly, it was a space the wealthier citizens avoided. The roadways were all narrow canyons with exposed conduits for power, coolant, and waste. Crossing them either meant jumping a three-meter-wide tub-way or walking to one of the rickety looking metal gantries to clamber up and over. The third alternative was climbing down to track level and taking your chance between passing tubs.

Syke loosened his sidearm in its holster. Ben still carried a derri, as did Cara, but he didn't draw attention to it as they climbed out of the tub.

Ronan climbed out of the second tub, leaving his guards behind.

"We should come with you," Syke said.

Ben eyed the three teens lounging against the wall. There had been four when they arrived. One had gone to alert others.

"Three of us are less threatening than eight. Better stay here and make sure we've still got transport if we need to get out quickly."

"So we're your getaway drivers." Syke hrmphed. "Yell if you need us."

"We know the routine." Cara tapped her forehead. "We'll keep in touch."

"Ronan?" Ben asked.

Just teens, wary as hell, but not a threat.

Ben, Cara, and Ronan breezed past the teens as if they hadn't a care in the world. *Don't look like a victim.* The only way into the neighborhood from this direction was via a narrow walkway down a featureless tunnel, brightly lit. There were no hidden openings, so no place where an ambush might occur, but an attack from either end would be like shooting fish in a barrel.

The teens behind them didn't follow them in.

They emerged into an open space with a ceiling that felt too low.

Red One was close to the spindle, a wedge-shaped block of workshops, storage areas, and tenements. This central open space was the closest Red One came to having a commercial plaza.

"I think we hit lunchtime," Cara said.

There were maybe sixty individuals gathered in groups. Every single one of the adults was looking toward them as they emerged from the walkway.

Surprise. No malice, Ronan said.

Agreed. Cara nodded.

The smell of cooking—salty, spicy, savory—fought with the smell of hot grease, or maybe the grease was all part of the cooking. An open stall with a row of steaming cauldrons was doing good business ladling something into folding bowls the customers had clipped to their utility belts. About a third of the people, men and women, wore green coveralls that said they worked for the station's maintenance crew, low-paid manual workers, but the others were dressed in a variety of inventive styles from the occasional buddysuit to sarongs—on both men and women—or the collarless shirts and straight-legged trousers that were common on-station.

A few children, from toddlers to teens, clutched their

own bowls and stood in line with parents, though a group of five- or six-year-olds played tag through the crowd. A shout snapped out brought them all up sharp. They stared at the strangers, wide-eyed, peeled away from each other and skittered back to their parents.

Most of the diners took their food to a seating area furnished with packing case chic, crates and boxes either used as they came or reworked. It didn't look as though these folks let anything go to waste. Upcycling was an art form.

"Looking for Dido Kennedy," Ben announced over the heads of a group of diners.

There was no answer.

"Dido Kennedy," he repeated.

"Who wants her?" A plump woman with her hair shoved untidily under a leather cap stood up. She wore what might once have been a buddysuit, but the trousers were now a separate garment. The sleeves had been ripped out of the top and the remains hung open above a grubby shirt.

That's her, Ronan said.

"You're Kennedy," Ben said.

"Might be." She sniffed. "Depends who wants to know."

"Benjamin," Ben said.

"Wolfe," Ronan said. "Doctor."

"Carlinni," Cara said. "Garrick sent us."

Ben glanced around to see if anyone else was interested. They weren't. In fact, their disinterest was so studied that he guessed they were taking in the whole scene. Ronan didn't seem worried.

"Ah, shit! Just about finished this anyway." She picked up her bowl and slurped down the last of the contents. "You eaten? It's good today."

"What is it?" Cara asked.

"There's vat-meat, fifty cents; razorfin, forty-five; or *don't ask*. That's forty, but you get a hunk of bread with it and it's got real vitamin supplements."

"Don't ask?"

"Yeah, that's right, don't ask. Most of the folks around here grew up on Casey's *don't ask*. It won't kill ya. Want some?"

Cara shook her head.

Kennedy just shrugged. "Suit yourself. You won't get better value anywhere on-station, specially not once supplies start to dry up."

She raised one eyebrow to make that into a question. Word traveled fast. Ben neither confirmed nor denied it.

"Come on, this way." She led them to a narrow entrance between a closed door and a station maintenance hatch. "Mind where you put your feet, I ain't too particular about where I drop stuff down."

Ben caught his toe on something that scuttled away with a metallic tinkle.

"I said be careful. I only just fixed that little feller."

"Sorry."

"Yeah, right."

The dark passageway opened up into an Aladdin's cave. Shelves and racks overflowed with what some people might call junk. If there was a space, there was something stuffed into it, leaning against it, or hung in front of it.

"You a real medical doctor?" Kennedy asked Ronan.

"Yes, real as they come. You need a doctor?"

"Not me. Never sick." She patted her chest. "One of my kids, though." She looked around. "Shanna, come out from under that workbench."

A stick-thin child with big round eyes emerged, dark hair hanging in rats' tails over her face.

"This one?" Ronan beckoned the girl, squatted down in front of her and asked for her hand. He grasped her wrist and after a few moments said, "Nothing wrong with this one that a few square meals wouldn't cure. You don't feed your kids well around here."

"As well as we can afford. It's her brother that's the problem. Shanna, go ask your mother to send Ez. Tell her we got a real doctor who's going to take a look at him for free. That's right, isn't it, Doc?"

"Sure." Ronan glanced at Ben. *You go ahead, I'm still listening in.*

Ben stared around the room. Tool chests, none of them matching, climbed on top of each other making a bid for the ceiling, and there were three workbenches, one covered with tiny parts in neat rows, another with a tarp thrown over something lumpy, and a third, the one Shanna had been hiding beneath, littered with the detritus of what appeared to be a dozen failed experiments. In one corner was a couch with a throw over it that Ben strongly suspected was where Kennedy slept.

"Yeah, before you ask, I know where everything is, so no touching."

Ben put up both hands in a gesture of surrender. "I wouldn't dream of it."

"Did you make all this?" Cara asked, a slightly glazed expression on her face.

"Lord love ya, girlie. Course I didn't." Kennedy gestured at the shelves. "Folks bring me stuff they can't use anymore. Sometimes it's stuff they've . . . found . . . in a finding kind of way. I make it work, get a few credits for it, pass the profit back so I get the best tech to play with. I take it apart, see what makes it run, make it run better, do more. Sometimes I get lucky and sell on a new design, then we're all in the gravy for a while. I've been working on jump tech for a few years now. Figured someone would pay a lot for a system that didn't lose platinum, or a system that could recover the platinum it lost. It's got to be possible. That other universe out there, foldspace. Somewhere in that big old chunk of nothing there's a big old chunk of platinum."

"Tell us something we don't know."

"I only said that was what I was working on, y'know, in general. I figured that this time I could sell Garrick something different—jump drives small enough to retrofit. You interested?"

Ben nodded.

"I know what Garrick thinks of me. I saw it in his eyes. Fat, ugly woman, can't be too bright or why's she in Red One? 'Cept he thinks maybe, just maybe there's something to what I say, so he ties me into his debt with a couple of hundred creds for materials and sends me off to play pretty."

A small disturbance in the entrance announced the return of Shanna with a small boy, even skinnier and paler than she was. Ronan knelt on the floor and took charge of both children.

"And how's it going?" Ben chose to ignore Ronan.

"It's going good. I got this."

Kennedy pulled a cover off a block of wires, tubes, and pipes that looked like an explosion in a spaghetti factory.

"What is it?"

"That's only the big old drive that brought half of a clapped-out O'Neill cylinder through the Folds to be tacked on and used as Crossways' farm."

"That was—"

"Yeah, I know, close on fifty years ago. Don't touch!" She slapped his hand away.

"How does something that size punch something as big as an O'Neill cylinder in and out of foldspace?" Cara asked.

"Ain't the size of it, it's the power that it packs and that's all about the compression ratio in the antimat— Hey, you don't need to know that. All you need to know is that if I can reverse engineer this thing and squish it down some, you can have jump drives."

"Can you?" Ben asked. "Reverse engineer it, I mean? And if you can, how come no one else has tried?"

"I'm halfway to understanding it." She settled the cover back into place. "And the reason no one else has tried is because they didn't believe the thing survived its trip here. The story always fascinated me. Some tomfool Navigator brought an O'Neill cylinder through foldspace, then got sucked into the black when the thing cracked apart. They looked for the drive but they didn't find it, so they figured it was lost, too. I figured it was more likely buried. You wouldn't believe how much shit I had to dig through— literally. I found it in a sump under one of the barns." She patted the cover gently as if her favorite dog was sleeping beneath it. "Course, it's fifty years old, so there's a containment problem, but, hey, you wouldn't want it to be too easy, wouldya?"

Ben hastily checked the readout on his buddysuit, but background radiation levels were normal.

"Relax." Kennedy smiled. "I ain't going to put anyone in danger. My friends all live here. I got external containment. Should hold it while I work."

"So what do you need to move forward with this?" Ben asked.

"Platinum. Can't test anything without it. Four rods."

Ronan? Ben asked.

She's playing you about the platinum. Going to ask for more than she needs, but she's straight up about the jump drives. She honestly thinks that she can do it. She was right about the boy, too. Got a heart murmur. Routine surgery will cure him completely. Not likely to be something the good folks down here can afford.

Ben jerked his head toward the doorway and the people

outside. "This area doesn't strike me as the safest to keep a fortune in platinum."

"Well, I wouldn't shout about it, but, yeah, those folks out there are only ordinary folks. Just as cream rises, so does scum." She jerked her head toward the ceiling. "The real hardcases are all on the upper levels, fleecing the fancy folks. No point in robbing the piss-poor." She turned to Ronan. "How's Ez, Doc?"

"Needs a little surgery, nothing serious."

"Expensive?"

Ah, Ronan said. *She's overdoing the platinum to cover the cost of surgery.*

"Not so much. We can include it in the deal." He nodded to Ben.

"Surgery for the boy, five hundred a month, two platinum rods and you give us first refusal on whatever you come up with. Deal?"

"Deal!" Kennedy's eyes lit up. "Five hundred in advance?"

"In advance. Expect a man called Yan Gwenn," Ben said. "He'll have what you need. He's also my best engineer, a Psi-Mech specializing in ships' systems." Ben looked at Cara, who confirmed what he suspected with a tiny shake of her head. Dido Kennedy didn't have an implant.

"Yeah, whatever. Send whoever you like. Just make sure he's got my paycheck and the platinum. Shanna, go tell your mother to pack a bag for Ez. He's going with this nice doctor. Right, Doc?"

"Right." Ronan stood up and scooped the boy up as if he weighed nothing. "He'll be back in four days. Does his mother want to come too?"

"She might want to come, but she's got another three little ones to look after," Dido said. "You could take Shanna, though. Four days of feeding up wouldn't do her harm."

Ronan nodded and the little girl slipped her hand into his free one.

It's my guess her paycheck will be feeding half this sector, Ronan said. *And it looks like they all need it.*

❖ ❖ ❖

Ben couldn't put it off any longer. With departure imminent, he had to make a courtesy visit to Victor Lorient and see how the settlers were getting on in their temporary quarters. The multipurpose sports arena seated twenty thousand, so the sanitary facilities were sufficient, if basic, and Garrick had organized enough food vendors. Those who'd extended their menu beyond the usual snack foods were doing good business. It was all working on extended credit, though, until the profits from Olyanda kicked in.

The stadium looked like the refugee camp it had become. Unlike some of the planet-bound grapple arenas, the spectators' benches only filled the lower half of the sphere and, though steep, were perfectly safe when gravity was on. There were safety straps for when gravity was off for a game. The bottom of the sphere was flattened off for track events and gymnastics. Currently ten thousand settlers were crammed among rows of beds, nothing more than a blanket on the ground for most, air mattresses for the lucky. The psi-techs had made a more private space for themselves on the lower spectator benches, but they looked anything but comfortable.

"We need more sonic shower units." That was Victor Lorient's opening gambit.

"Hello, Director, how are you doing?" Ben extended his hand and from force of habit Lorient took it, though he didn't remove his glove.

The man looked tired and unkempt. His dark hair flopped over one eye and he'd lost weight. His nose dominated the landscape of his face, his features turning from chiseled to gaunt, his eyes deep set. Once handsome, now Victor's features had lost their vigor and he'd become haggard. How had he aged so much in such a short time?

Victor snatched his hand back as soon as he could. "The players' facilities are inadequate and this whole place is starting to stink of the unwashed."

Ben couldn't deny it.

"Let me show you." Lorient walked a few paces, then whirled suddenly. "Are we prisoners here?"

"You're confined for your own protection," Ben said. "Crossways can be dangerous for anyone not used to its ways, but Mother Ramona can arrange for anything you want to be brought in, or for small groups of you to go out, escorted, of course."

Lorient scowled. "We had to leave so much behind on Olyanda."

"But not one life lost."

Lorient sighed. "I'll grant you that, Commander Benjamin. You were right about van Blaiden and his thugs."

Ben wondered if he could get that in writing, or maybe chiseled into tablets of stone two meters tall. He suppressed a grin. It was the closest to thanks Lorient would ever come.

"Commander Benjamin." Rena Lorient picked her way across some of the makeshift beds and held out both hands to him.

"Mrs. Lorient, how are you doing?" He took her hands and she squeezed. Ben hadn't seen Rena since she left Olyanda with the first evacuees. He'd expected her to look tired, but she looked energized. Throwing herself into work was probably her way of dealing with the loss of her son. Ben had heard that all was not well between the Lorients since Danny's death. Losing a child, especially in such tragic circumstances, could either strengthen a marriage or tear it apart. The jury was still out on this one, but it wasn't looking good.

"I'm doing well, thank you. Keeping busy. There's so much to do here, and since I arrived early, most of it has fallen to me." She gave Victor a long look, but he didn't respond.

There was an awkward silence, so, thankful to have avoided a guided tour of inadequate showers, Ben moved on to practicalities, getting a list of everything they needed, noticing that during the whole conversation the Lorients only spoke to him and not to each other.

Chapter Seven

DEALS AND ALLIANCES

"HEY, WAIT FOR ME." WES CAUGHT UP WITH Kitty as she ran a second circuit of Port 22.

"Keep up if you can. This girl waits for no man." She smiled as he fell into step with her.

"I thought we could maybe go somewhere together—a drink or a meal." He delivered his invitation as a string of staccato words, snatching a breath with each one.

"You should run with me more often, Wes. Sounds like you're out of condition."

"I'll show you out of condition. Race you to the gate. Loser buys dinner."

"You're assuming we're going out for dinner."

"Well, yeah."

He said it to her back as she lengthened her stride and pulled away. She heard his boot soles slapping on the deck as he pounded after her. Only a last-minute spurt got her to the gate half a stride before him.

"See . . ." He gasped for breath. "Now you've got to come out with me because I owe you dinner."

"So you do." Her own breathing wasn't so labored.

"When?"

"Give me ten minutes to shower and change."

"Now?"

"Why not?" She smiled at him. "Besides, if we don't go now it will have to wait a few days. I'm shipping out to Oly-anda first thing in the morning."

His grin touched a genuine spark and she found that her response was not altogether fabricated.

Ten minutes later after Kitty had been through every-thing in her small wardrobe twice and settled on the only dress that she had, a pale green calf-length sheath with a short, practical jacket, they stepped into a tub-cab. "My place first," Wes said.

She raised one eyebrow.

"Nothing funny, but I'm not taking you out to dinner in my uniform."

Kitty looked at Wes, the planes of his face, the way he towered above her without looming or making her uncom-fortable. Maybe she wouldn't mind a little funny stuff to wipe out the memory of Ari van Blaiden.

"Okay, your place before dinner, but before your place I need to send another message to my mom." This time it really was to her mom. *Don't worry*, Remus had told her. He hadn't exactly said not to try and get in touch. Her mom could send a message back via Wes. No one at the Free Company need know about it at all. What harm could it do?

The cab dipped into Crossways' tunnel system.

"Where do you live?" Kitty asked. "I hear that Saturn is the best real estate."

Saturn was one of the two independent wheels, about as far from the core of the station as you could go.

"Yes it is, and no, not there. Way too expensive for a grunt like me. I live on the spindle, but not on the fashionable lev-els, low down, just above the service levels and the power core. It's the only way to get a bit more space for your money. Garrick owns the quarters and he gives us a good deal. Sev-eral of the single guys live there. Syke's place is two levels above me, bigger, though, and he's got a window."

"A window! That wouldn't suit everyone."

"It would suit me. Great view of the stars from down there, because you're below the main rings."

The tub-cab came to a halt after several twists and turns and Wes jumped out, offering Kitty his hand. She took it to be polite.

"Regular elevators, I'm afraid. Sometimes have to wait a

minute or two for one, but there are two decompression doors between here and home, so no antigrav shafts. There's a bank of comm booths over there if you need to send your message before we go down."

"I do, thanks. Could I have the answer routed through you?"

"Of course." He fistbumped her to transfer his personal data address.

In the comm booth she smoothed the front of her dress and ran her fingers through her hair, then pressed record.

"Hi, Mom. How are you? I wanted to let you know not to worry. I'm on assignment and it might be a while before I can come and see you. You'll probably be back home, fit and well before I get Earthside again, but I want you to know that I'm thinking about you, and that I love you. Here's a code for your reply. Let me know how you're getting on." She blew a kiss at the camera and waved. "Love you lots."

As the record symbol winked out she wiped the corners of her eyes.

"Done?" Wes asked.

"Yeah. How long will it take?"

"Hard to tell. Communications have been up and down for the last week or so. Word is that one of the megacorps has targeted us, but our guys keep rerouting the data packets to get around the blockages. Could be as quick as three days each way, or a lot slower."

"Well, you let me know as soon as you get an answer?"

"Of course. Your mom, eh? I heard your recording. You forgot to punch the privacy baffle."

Had she? A fine spy she'd make.

"My mom's got Ren-Parry Syndrome. She's having treatment, but I worry. You know?"

"Yes, I know. Don't worry. I'll let you know as soon as I have an answer." He guided her toward a bank of elevators.

Doors opened and Kitty followed Wes into the compartment. It had seats on three sides and hanging straps in the center for standing passengers. Wes and Kitty shared a strap, their hands entwined. The elevator shot downward at a speed that made Kitty's stomach lurch, but it decelerated smoothly before each stop. Finally Wes said, "This is ours," and she followed him out onto a gray landing, dimly lit.

"No expense spared, huh?"

Wes grinned. "No expense at all, but at least it's not attractive to the local kids. There are much more interesting places to hang out."

Wes went to the third door down and passed his handpad over the doorplate. "Home sweet home."

The room was square with a sofa and a screen. One corner had a countertop with a hotspot on it for cooking and there was a table folded flat to the wall, the kind that usually had a couple of chairs tucked away behind it. A door, half-open, led into a bedroom. Kitty could see the foot of a bed, another door into a san-unit and concealed closets. Everything was neat.

"Are you always this tidy, or were you planning on company?" she asked.

"I was hoping, but it's easier to stay tidy if you clean up as you go."

Kitty thought of her own cast-off clothing on the floor of her cabin, dropped as she'd rushed to find something to wear. One day she'd get the hang of clearing up as she went.

"Give me a few moments to get rid of the uniform." Wes tapped his chest. "Feel free to call up something on the screen. I have a subscription service."

He disappeared into the bedroom and she heard the shower start up. Subscription service be damned. She needed a little distraction in her life right now. She pushed open the bedroom door, unclipped the shoulders on the sheath dress and let it fall to the ground along with her underwear. Quickly she slipped beneath the silky bed cover and pulled it up to her chin.

The sound of the shower was replaced by the whoosh of the dryer. When the door opened Wes was completely naked.

His eyes widened when he saw her in the bed.

She took in the smooth brown skin, the muscles of his chest, the breadth of his shoulders, the flatness of his belly, and the definite un-flatness of what lay below as it began to respond to his thoughts.

She let the cover drop.

✦ ✦ ✦

Ben tried not to let his frustration show. Everyone was doing their best, but tracking the gate records for the missing ark was proving more difficult than expected. Mother Ramona had a team of hackers on it, but the most recent potential lead had proved fruitless. It shouldn't be this difficult unless someone had deliberately obscured the ark's transit.

It was a relief from the tension of waiting to make the run to Olyanda in the *Solar Wind* with Cara. He left Gupta in charge of security in Blue Seven, but brought along Ronan and Yan Gwenn, who mentioned Dido Kennedy twice in conversation, which was effusive for the normally quiet engineer. Either Kennedy, or her jump drive, must have made quite an impression.

Ben had thought long and hard before adding Kitty Keely to the crew. She'd passed Ronan's psych evaluation, so there was no real reason not to, though he suspected Cara didn't altogether trust her. Keely had previously been on the same side as the mercenaries, so might be a help in persuading them that the Free Company was on the level.

Also he wanted to give her another chance to try handling *Solar Wind* in foldspace. With Gen raising babies they'd need another pilot-Navigator who could handle a jumpship. Kitty was inexperienced, but there was a first time for everything. The principle was the same as gate navigation except you had to find the exit point without a beacon. Theoretically all Navigators should be able to do it, but in practice only a tiny percentage could. If Kitty proved to be one of those, that would be a bonus.

Few pilot-Navigators ever got the opportunity to fly the Folds freestyle. Jumpships were rare and gave twice the opportunity for disaster because without a prescribed gate point for entry and exit it was like entering the mythical Forest of Despair without a path to follow. You couldn't even leave a trail of breadcrumbs, since the last thing you wanted to do was to try and retrace your steps. You had to focus on your destination while avoiding all the monsters.

Unfortunately, foldspace seemed to throw even more monsters at you when flying freestyle. One day, if he had time, he'd like to make a study of the things that inhabited the Folds. Imaginary was the official stance, but he didn't think they all were. His imagination wasn't that good.

Ben's theories were crystallizing even more since that

torpedo had cut through the *Solar Wind* last time out. The swirling creatures of the void were way too complex to have come from his own imagination. The detail manifesting from the shadows wasn't even something he wanted to think about. Sometimes they were small and otter-like, but last time a single creature had manifested as a long, snake-like dragon, perfect in every detail from the color of its eyes to the prehensile claws on the end of its beard. He'd asked Cara, but she hadn't seen it. Gen, however, had muttered something about a big snaky thing, so she undoubtedly saw something similar.

What if the creatures were real? What if nothing was real in foldspace, but at the same time, everything was?

Ben let Kitty take *Solar Wind* through the gate into the Folds without using the jump drive. She managed it without a flutter using the ship's nav systems in conjunction with her own psi-tech capabilities.

◆ ◆ ◆

Ronan, sitting at systems, begins the count. The quicker they get out of foldspace, the better. Ben sees the seconds begin to rack up on the forward screen.

"All right, Kitty?" he asks.

She's following gate procedure correctly, but that's not what he needs her to do. She has to learn to connect through the jump drive to the currents of foldspace. Ben remembers his own first time, working in tandem with Eve Moyo, out on the Rim. Eve acted as den mother to all the new Monitor operatives straight out of basic training. She'd thrown him in the deep end to sink or swim. He'd swum, found the line, and after that had become standby pilot for one of the two jumpships their division needed for fast-response work.

Will sink or swim work for Kitty?

He reaches forward and switches off the connection to the next jump gate, her safety net. She has a brief moment of panic, but he says, "Link with me. I won't let you get lost."

He feels her presence in his head. No amount of theory can prepare for this kind of experience. The creatures come again. There seem to be more of them this time and they're manifesting more strongly. They are furred and sleek, like eel-shaped otters. They swirl through the air like silk and appear, ghost-like, through the skin of the flight deck. They curl around and back on themselves, nosing into instrument panels, sliding past Cara and Ronan, who don't seem to see them, though Ronan is talking to someone or something that Ben can't see and Cara has her eyes closed and is sitting very still, hands squeezed into fists, her knuckles white.

One of the otter-things passes right through Kitty, but she doesn't flinch. Can't she see it?

"Okay, Kitty. Find the line," Ben says.

"What line? Where?"

He feels her on the edge of panic. Her hands freeze on the control panels. She hesitates. The seconds tick past. This isn't going to work. Why can't she see when the line to Olyanda shines so clear to him?

"Two minutes-thirty," Ronan calls.

Ben glances at the timer on the forward screen.

"Kitty!" he says, sharply, but she doesn't respond. Her eyes have that thousand-meter stare.

He takes over from her, fixes his will on where he wants to be, finds the line and nudges the *Solar Wind* toward her destination, the space around Olyanda—not somewhere that he wants to gatecrash without permission.

◆ ◆ ◆

With a pop that wasn't audible, but felt as if it should have been, the *Solar Wind* emerged into realspace two hours from the hot zone.

"Elapsed time: one hour forty-one minutes," Ronan called. "Logged."

Ben swallowed rising nausea and shook his head to clear it. Working out the time differential seemed to help clear his head. A ratio of one to thirty-eight this time. Much lower than last time, maybe because they'd entered foldspace via a gate.

There was always a dangerous moment of disorientation coming out of the Folds. Bursting into a newly militarized zone without identifying yourself wasn't advisable. Oleg Staple, formerly in charge of Crossways' hornets, the defensive fleet that was one of the station's deterrents, had set up a blockade to protect Olyanda from the sky while Leah Nolan, formerly head of Garrick's guard before Syke, commanded troops on the ground and managed the mining engineers.

Once he'd established they were in no immediate danger from friendly fire and he'd heard Cara broadcast their ID, Ben turned to Kitty. "Did you follow my line?" he asked.

She looked at him blankly. "How do you mean?"

"You felt the way I pulled us back out into realspace, right?"

She shook her head. "I couldn't see where you were going until you got there."

"We'll try it again on the way home."

"What if I never get it?" Her voice rose in pitch. "I'm not a Psi-1 Navigator like you."

"Gen's a Psi-3. She got it first time out. Did you see the void creatures?"

"I saw—I don't know—something."

"What did they look like to you?"

"Wisps of smoke. Blood in water."

"No details? No faces?"

She shook her head. "Just shapes, appearing and disappearing. One of them looked like a teacher who used to bully me. Good thing they're not real."

"What if they are?"

She looked at him sideways. "They're not."

"Maybe we're the ghosts in foldspace and they're real. Or maybe, since, theoretically, when we enter foldspace we're passing through every point in space and time simultaneously, we're actually ceasing to exist in any of them for a moment. Maybe reality is only what we can hold onto in our mind."

"So if we decided the monsters were real they could attack us?" She shuddered. "Maybe that's why the first thing they teach us in flight school is that they're not. I'm going to stick with that if you don't mind."

If that was as good as he was going to get, maybe Kitty was right, she wouldn't ever get it. Not all pilot-Navigators did, despite what they told you was possible in flight school. Pity. It would have been very useful to have someone else who could pilot *Solar Wind*, especially with Gen's pregnancy.

"Permission granted to pass through the blockade," Cara said. "Oleg Staple says good luck with the mercs. They've surrendered their weapons to Nolan and taken over what remains of the landing complex as their territory, but they're not showing any signs of wanting to cooperate with the ground troops."

"You know these guys, Kitty," Ben said. "What's your take?"

"They're a tight unit. Good soldiers. Very professional. Did their job well, but liked to keep to themselves when they weren't working. I can see them not wanting to get sucked into a bigger force and losing their group identity."

"I'm not taking *Solar Wind* down there," Ben said. "If something goes wrong with these negotiations I'm not risking the mercs getting their hands on her. Yan can keep her in orbit and I'll take Kitty down in the Dixie to negotiate."

"You're not going without me," Cara said.

"Nor me," Ronan said.

"Be reasonable," Ben said. "The Dixie's only a two-man flyer."

"With cargo space and a couple of bucket seats for emergencies," Cara added. "We're only shuttling down from orbit."

"You need a couple of Empaths," Ronan said, "if you want to know whether Tengue's word is good."

"Did you guys argue the toss as much when the Trust paid your wages and I had Commander on my pocket flap?"

Cara grinned at him.

✦ ✦ ✦

The wider view of Olyanda as they dropped down through the atmosphere was of a planet with significant ice extending from the poles to cover maybe two thirds of the surface. The equatorial band was blue-green with ocean and fragmented landmasses. It had been a land of so much promise to the agrarian settlers who had hoped to make a home here, before the discovery of platinum dashed their hopes. Finding significant platinum deposits was like winning the lottery and then discovering your ticket was coated with poison. Unless you had the backing of one of the big megacorporations—in which case they'd take over administration, for your own good, of course—you might as well kiss your ass good-bye. Keeping platinum required significant firepower and a steady nerve.

From ten kilometers up Ben could already see the gray

scars of strip mining on the alluvial lowlands and a crater in the highlands where platinum nodes had been exposed. He was too high to see it from here, but one processing plant was already under construction and a second would follow shortly.

Not for the first time, Ben wondered about the ethics of resource stripping and the effect it had on the natural environment of a virgin world, but the need for platinum overrode all other considerations. The hungry jump gate system would crash without it. The voices of conservationists had been silenced by the might of the megacorporations.

Ben dropped the Dixie Flyer down to the field where the first shuttle ships had landed. Rows of low tunnel-shaped buildings, known as risers for their speed of construction, clustered around the original colony landing vehicle, a single-use, saucer-shaped craft used as the psi-techs' admin base. Wherever he looked there was blast damage, but the LV had survived and some of the risers still looked weathertight. It had been his home, however temporarily. He'd worked with good friends, shared a bed with Cara, been part of its triumphs and disasters.

Beyond the temporary town the fat silver river flowed on undisturbed, its banks lined with broccoli trees. Suzi had had a fancy Latin name for them, but they looked too much like giant broccoli ever to have their real name applied except on reports.

Everything had seemed so hopeful only a few months ago. Ten thousand Ecolibrians, back-to-basics settlers, building homes and breaking new ground. It should all have been idyllic, but there had been trouble even before the platinum had been discovered. Lorient had been a nightmare from the first, a classic psi-phobe. And they wouldn't be free of him until the colony was resettled somewhere safe, and the thirty thousand missing settlers either found or finally laid to rest.

When Ari van Blaiden had arrived, intending to rip out a fortune in platinum and settle an old score with Cara at the same time, it had brought things to a head. Finally Lorient had focused on a bigger threat than the psi-techs and had accepted Ben's plan to sell Olyanda to the biggest crimelord on Crossways as the only way to get his people out alive.

Ben settled the Dixie a couple of hundred meters short of the flitter bays on an apron of fired earth. Close up, the whole of Landing looked like a war zone. If any of the flitters had survived the final fight, the Crossways ground forces hadn't left them for the mercs.

Ben let power bleed away and popped the door. "We'll wait here and see if we get a welcoming committee."

"It looks deserted." Ronan peered at the scanner, set to magnify. "Just a few wrecks. You're sure the mercs are here?"

"Sure as I can be," Cara said. "Tengue said come in person. He didn't say he wanted to play hide-and-seek."

"Leah Nolan's crew disarmed them," Ben said. "Supposedly. They're on parole. If they don't cause trouble maybe— just maybe—they'll get a lift off planet. Let's hope they're sticking to the deal."

"Captain Tengue was always totally professional," Kitty said. "He kept the mercs in line."

"Had they worked for van Blaiden before?" Ben asked.

Kitty shook her head. "I don't think so. There was a fair amount of negotiation before they took the contract, more than there might have been if they already knew each other."

"Unfortunate to get employed by the losing side. I guess it's an occupational hazard." Ben checked the derri in his thigh pocket and returned it to its place, satisfied.

It took about half an hour before the scanner revealed heat signatures and Ben spotted the first movement among the wrecked flitters. "I make it five—no, six—altogether."

"They'll be armed," Cara said. "These guys are resourceful. They're probably working out how they can get control of the Dixie right now."

"Agreed," Ben said.

"So what are you going to do about it?" she asked.

"I'm going to go and stand outside in full view."

"Let me," Kitty said. "They'll probably recognize me. It doesn't mean to say they won't take a shot, but it's less likely."

"We'll both go," Ben said. "Cara, Ronan, you've got our backs."

Cara primed the bolt gun. Ronan picked up the long-range tranq rifle.

"Got you covered both ways," she said.

✦ ✦ ✦

Ben stepped out of the Dixie onto the fired earth, Kitty a couple of paces behind him, both close enough to make a dash back inside if they needed to. Cara crouched in the doorway, her finger lightly on the bolt gun trigger, barrel pointed down toward the ground. Ronan stood close behind.

Ben watched the approaching figures through narrowed eyes. "Do you know them, Kitty?" he asked, soft-voiced.

"Not all by name. The guy out in front is pretty level-headed. Uh-oh, the one behind him is bit of a hothead. The rest aren't troublemakers, though. The big black guy is Gwala. Wins all the hand-to-hand competitions. The last one is Morton Tengue."

"I'm here to talk," Ben shouted when the shadows stopped moving on the edge of the flitter wreckage.

"What about the two in the flyer?" Tengue shouted back.

"Insurance. What about your five guys skulking in the shadows?"

"Insurance."

"Meet halfway. No weapons." Ben took the derri out of his thigh pocket and placed it on the stubby wing of the flyer.

"There's two of you. I bring one more."

"Fair."

Ben turned to Cara crouched inside. "Close the hatch." He saw from her face that she didn't like it, but she backed into the flyer with Ronan and the hatch slid shut.

I'm listening in, she said.

I hope so.

"Are you all right with this?" Ben said quietly to Kitty.

"It's too late now if I'm not, isn't it?"

"Probably."

They walked forward, as did Tengue and the big black merc Kitty had identified as Emmanuel Gwala.

Ben wasn't short, but Gwala was taller by a handspan and Tengue heavier by ten kilos, all of it muscle.

"What's your combat rating, Kitty?"

"I scored very well in pilot training."

Oh, right. He was on his own if it came to a fight. Worse than on his own if he had to protect Kitty, too. Cara didn't need protecting. She was fast and decisive. Maybe bringing Kitty had been the wrong move.

"Benjamin," Tengue said as they halted ten strides away from each other.

"Captain Tengue." There was a suspicious bulge in Tengue's thigh pocket. Bigger than the derri Ben had abandoned and much bigger than the parrimer blade tucked into his sleeve. "I don't believe we were formally introduced. You know Kitty Keely, I think."

"Yes." Tengue nodded to Kitty. "Ensign Keely." It was almost, but not quite, a question.

"Just plain Kitty, now, Cap. I quit Alphacorp. Didn't like their style."

"Van Blaiden's style."

"That's right. I especially didn't like that."

Gwala stood a pace behind Tengue, face impassive, but something in the line of his shoulders altered at the mention of van Blaiden.

Tengue's mouth turned down at the corners. "I lost good men on account of you and yours, Benjamin."

Ben shook his head. "You lost good men on account of van Blaiden. You signed up for the losing team. No shame in that, but no malice either. I seem to recall you tried to execute me."

"Nothing personal."

"No offense taken."

"What about her?" Tengue pointed past Kitty to the flyer. He couldn't see beyond the darkened screen, now, so he must have been watching them for some time.

Cara was a comfortable presence in the back of Ben's mind and would be watching their every move. "Cara doesn't take offense either. Her beef was with van Blaiden. That's over and done with."

Was it? Would it ever be over and done with or would they be living with the aftermath forever?

"That's generous of her."

"It was her idea to come. We're looking to hire."

"Who is?"

"The Free Company. That's the psi-techs from the Oly-anda team."

"You work for the Trust."

"Did. We're on our own now. Got a little security problem you might be able to help us with. Want to hear more?"

"I'm listening."

"Seems we upset someone when we took this planet off the market."

Tengue put up both hands, palms out. "We're not going up against the Trust or Alphacorp or any other corporation you can name because we'd lose."

"Okay, stay here then. Olyanda's relatively mild in the winter. It only drops to forty below. But if you change your mind . . . We're not asking you to go up against the megacorps on their own turf, only to stand between us and whatever they throw at us on Crossways. Maybe that won't be anything. Garrick's stepping up security station-wide, but there may be sleeper agents. Job's yours if you want it. Trial basis only, of course, and we'll throw in the ride off this rock for free."

"We don't come cheap."

"Didn't expect you would."

"Three hundred per man per week plus accommodations and meals."

"Can accommodate you all together in Blue Seven."

"Got three men banged up bad after the firefight. Olyanda base medic treated them. Wanted to hospitalize them, but we look after our own. Not leaving them behind—and they get full pay, too."

"Of course. Got a medic here now if you want him to take a look."

Tengue nodded. "Be right grateful."

They thrashed out details of who paid for arms and armor, replacements, and necessary repairs while Ronan and Cara combined their Empathy to check for any signs of double-dealing. There were none.

He drives a hard bargain, Cara said. *But we both agree. It's one he's prepared to stick to.*

"And we stay an independent unit," Tengue said. "Chain of command runs from you to me and from me to them."

"Done." Ben held out his hand.

The agreement was quickly registered with Oleg Staple and Leah Nolan, one in orbit with the fleet and the other on the ground with the miners. Tengue insisted on a down payment.

Ben authorized it.

Tengue hadn't finished. "And there's the madwoman. She's not rightly our responsibility, but she can't look after herself. Doesn't eat unless you put food in her mouth. Pisses herself if you forget to put her on the potty regular."

Ben felt sick as he shook on the deal. He had a feeling he knew who Tengue was talking about. Why hadn't he considered the possibility that Cara's abuser had survived? He felt Cara stir uneasily, but he had to ask. "Madwoman?" *Please don't let it be her.*

"Mrs. McLellan," Tengue said.

Ben slammed down his mental shield as Cara's mind began to scream.

Chapter Eight

THE BENJAMIN MANEUVER

I THOUGHT SHE WAS DEAD AND GONE.
  I thought she was dead.
  Why can't she be dead?
  I need her to be dead.
  I have to kill her.
  Donida McLellan, chief mind-bender at Alphacorp's neural reconditioning unit and Ari van Blaiden's pet sadist, was alive, but not for much longer. Cara reached out toward her, mind-to-mind. She'd done it once. It would be so easy to snuff out her former tormentor. All she had to do was lock on and squeeze and squeeze and ...
  So easy.
  Her mind touched McLellan's and she recoiled.
  She's in a room, strapped to a chair. McLellan's mind is boring into hers. Deeper and deeper. In her imagination she can hear a voice saying: You think you're bad, girl? This is how it's done. Learn it well.
  She'd learned it, well enough to kill their assailant in the warehouse, but even in this state, McLellan was the river she could not swim, the mountain she could not climb.
  Madwoman, Tengue had called her. She'd always been mad in her own way, but evil genius rather than babbling idiot. Ari had employed her because of her fearsome psi

abilities, her psychopathic tendencies and utter lack of inhibitions when it came to twisting someone's mind. Cara had suffered her inhumane treatment and had not even been able to remember it until it was almost too late.

Now she remembered.

"You don't have to see her," Ben said.

"Yes, I do." Cara sat on the wing-step of the Dixie and watched Tengue and Gwala as they walked back to the mercs. "Tell him, Ronan."

The young medic hoisted his emergency kit onto his shoulder and frowned. "Cara, I have to go and check on the injured. We should talk about this later."

"No, we shouldn't. I want to see her now." She looked at Ben and then at Ronan. Kitty was wisely hanging back, though she'd actually been a witness to McLellan's final attempt to break Cara's mind. "What? You don't think I'll try and kill her, do you?" She tried to laugh but it came out all wrong. Ronan and Ben were both staring at her. That was exactly what they thought.

"I won't."

If she couldn't do it one way, would she do it another?

"I probably won't." She raised both hands, palms out. "All right. Not today, but sooner or later I will look her in the eye. I need to know she's got no hold over me now."

Ben nodded. "When you're sure you're ready."

✦ ✦ ✦

Ben snapped to attention as Yan Gwenn's general alert from orbit cut through all their thoughts like a klaxon.

Detail? Ben asked Yan.

We've got company. A Trust cruiser just showed up on the edge of our scanning range.

How close? Ben asked.

Close enough and coming in fast. They've deployed fighters.

"Shit!" *Yan, bring the* Solar Wind *down and prepare for a quick pickup.*

There's a second cruiser and—oh bloody hell—a battlewagon, Yan said. *They really mean business.*

We don't need to get caught up in this, Ben said. *Staple and his boys are more than capable. Ronan and Kitty, get*

Tengue and his mercs ready to evacuate. I'm not sure how mobile their injured are.

"I need you to focus," he said to Cara. "Are you with me?"

He could feel her pulling the threads of her mind together, dragging her attention away from McLellan, shoving the trauma deep down where it couldn't hurt her. She nodded and opened up a general channel for him. He felt the connection wobble and then it steadied. Good.

He flashed her a brief smile and her chin trembled as she tried to return it.

"Can we get them all on board *Solar Wind*?" Kitty asked.

"Do we have a choice?" Ben said. "Cara—"

"Already on it." Cara, all business in an emergency, had patched communications through to Tengue and had linked with the Telepath on board Oleg Staple's command ship. "Staple's fighters are on standby," she said. "And there are surface-to-air missiles ready for launch."

As if to echo that statement a bright flare from the east announced a single missile fired from somewhere in the lee of the northern mountain range. A second contrail followed it, and a third.

"Reinforcements on their way from Crossways," Cara said.

"By the time they get here it will be over," Ben said.

Yan Gwenn kept up a running commentary. *ETA twenty minutes. Trust fighters deployed. Two fighters have punched through Staple's outer cordon. Prepare for incoming. They'll be on my tail.*

"Wait with the Dixie." Ben didn't want Cara confronting the shell of what used to be Donida McLellan, not yet. "Guide Yan down. When *Solar Wind* lands, get the Dixie into her cargo hold and prepare for a quick takeoff."

He ran to the hangar where Morton Tengue's mercs were gathering, fully kitted out for combat and carrying their packs on their backs and weapons—the ones they were supposed to have handed over—in their hands. Three antigrav gurneys were neatly lined up. Ronan knelt over one of them. Ben wondered if Donida McLellan was one of the patients, but then he saw Kitty leading a tall, thin woman with dark hair and a vacant expression.

"Is that her?" he asked Kitty.

"It is. Doesn't look like much now, does she?"

"Looks can be deceptive. Are you okay with her?"

"She's pliant enough."

"Keep her away from Cara for the time being."

He checked. There was no flicker of understanding from McLellan at the mention of Cara's name.

"Understood."

He hoped Kitty did understand. He'd felt Cara's intense satisfaction when she'd found a way to *turn off* the Telepath during the warehouse attack. *I can kill you with my mind* was nothing more than an old psi-tech joke precisely because it couldn't happen, but somehow Cara had found a way to make it happen and suddenly the phrase had lost all its humor.

Solar Wind came in low over the horizon, antigravs already engaged. Yan dropped her neatly into the open space just beyond the Dixie and let down the ramp.

Cara rolled the Dixie into the hold on antigravs. Tengue's mercs jog-trotted across the open ground, neat and orderly. Ronan took one gurney, Gwala the second, and Ben picked up the controller for the third, noting it was occupied by a pale young woman, upper body swathed in burn dressings. She was conscious and watching him.

"I hope you know how to drive this thing," she said.

"I can pilot a starship. How hard can it be?"

"I hope those aren't your famous last words. I hear we might be in for a rough ride."

"Don't worry. Getting off this rock will be a piece of cake."

As he said it the landing vehicle, which had been the center of operations during their time on Olyanda, exploded in a fireball.

Incoming, Cara said.

Yeah, thanks, got that. Ben pushed the gurney and ran for the *Solar Wind*, a hundred-meter sprint. Something whomped into the ground beside him: debris from the LV. He sprang sideways, and the gurney wobbled alarmingly.

"I thought you said you could drive this thing?"

"Everyone's a critic." Ben scooped up the young woman, abandoned the gurney and ran like hell.

Three fighters screamed out of the sky and fanned out. Two flew low and straight, heading for where Nolan's troops were based. One strafed the ground behind them. Ben clutched the girl to him and concentrated on the *Solar Wind*, legs pumping, breath rasping. His shoulder muscles pulled beneath the burn scar.

"Run, damn you!" she screamed. As if he needed telling.

He clattered up into *Solar Wind*'s belly as the hangar they'd just left took a direct hit. The shockwave from the explosion shoved Ben forward and he barely avoided squashing the woman as he went down.

"Owww! I want a fucking refund!" The edge of panic had subsided from the young woman's voice.

"Fowler, is that you acting up again?" Tengue picked up the complaining young woman while Gwala dragged Ben up and off the ramp as it began to close.

"Sick bay's this way." Ben led Tengue and Gwala up into the guts of his ship, Tengue carrying Fowler. "Don't worry, Fowler, Doc Wolfe has got some state-of-the-art gadgets up there. Tested them myself."

"I should take your word for it? You can't even drive a gurney."

"No, but I can fly us out of here."

As Tengue delivered Fowler into Ronan's care Ben ran for the flight deck. Gwala stayed with him all the way.

"Do you mind?" the big man asked. "I was supposed to work tactical for van Blaiden before some bastard stole his ship."

"Come and welcome."

◆ ◆ ◆

Cara knew why Ben had asked her to stay with the Dixie, but it galled her. Still, she did the job she'd been asked to do even though her hands shook on the controls. As the *Solar Wind* landed and dropped her cargo hatch she rolled the little flyer in there and locked it down, making a quick exit to the flight deck as the first of Tengue's mercs trotted up the ramp. Ben had a point. It wasn't the right time to confront Donida McLellan. Just knowing she was on board was bad enough.

Cara felt sick.

She took three deep breaths, ran up to the flight deck, slid into the comms chair, and patched into Oleg Staple's channel.

There was a full-blown battle going on above them, two

Trust cruisers, a battlewagon, and their associated fighters versus a Crossways fleet of one cruiser with an array of fighters and six smaller ships. She guessed Crossways wasn't yet up to full strength.

Fighters had mobilized from the planet's surface. The Trust had the advantage of numbers for now, but there were surface-to-air missiles prepped which could tip the balance.

Unfortunately, the missiles weren't picky. *Solar Wind*, being registered to an independent port rather than Crossways, sported a ship code that could get them killed by their own side as well as the Trust.

We can give you eight minutes to clear before we release the next missiles, Staple said. *Eight minutes and counting.*

Cara set her clock.

Six minutes, Ben, she told him as he entered the flight deck followed by the big African Kitty had identified as Gwala.

Yan relinquished the pilot's chair to Ben and took the copilot's space. Kitty moved to systems and Gwala took tactical.

"Strap in." Ben connected with the ship and lifted *Solar Wind* on her antigravs while the drive cycled. "Ready?"

Ready. Four minutes twenty, Cara told him.

Solar Wind shot skyward just as a Trust fighter screamed toward them. It snagged in their wake and, too low to make a recovery at that speed, plunged into the ruins of the settlement.

Solar Wind yawed. Ben fought to hold her steady.

Incoming. Cara pinpointed a second fighter ahead of them and flashed the exact location.

"Pulse-cannon, clear the way," Ben ordered, straightening out their flight path.

The ship reverberated as the pulse-cannon discharged, but the shot went wide. The fighter was still heading straight for them and a second fighter was on their screen now.

"Gwala," Ben said, sharply.

"Got the range now." Gwala fired again. The ship shuddered and the first fighter disappeared. Gwala reconfigured and took out the second fighter as well.

"Nice shooting," Ben said.

"It's my ass on the line as well." Gwala stepped back. "Sorry about the first one. Got the feel of it, now."

"Two minutes forty to ground missile release," Cara said. More blips appeared on her screen. "Trust cruiser dead ahead. Low orbit. Fifteen fighters, ten of them Trust, five belonging to Crossways. The Trust's got the upper hand."

"Damn!" Ben made a course adjustment toward the cruiser.

"What?" Cara said. That thing had ten times their firepower.

"That's our platinum down there," Ben said through gritted teeth. "We lose Olyanda to the Trust and it's going to take forever to pay off all those loans. I've got an idea to help even the odds. Prepare to jump to foldspace."

"We're still in Olyanda's upper atmosphere." Kitty's voice rose to a squeak.

"How long to the missiles, Cara?" Ben asked.

"One minute fifty."

Cara broadcast a shipwide alert. *Prepare for foldspace. It's going to be a rocky transition. Strap in or hold on tight.*

Ben cranked up the jump drive.

"One minute ten."

"Nearly there," Ben said.

The cruiser loomed closer.

"Ah, gotcha." Ben fixed his eyes on the forward screen. "Gwala, stand by, punch us a passage through the gnats. Yan, what's the range on that cruiser?"

"Seventy klicks."

"I want to get close enough to kiss her."

Oh, shit. Cara realized what Ben was trying to do. They'd sucked the missile into foldspace, now Ben was going to try and take out a cruiser by doing the same. It would even up the numbers for the Crossways fleet and give them a chance of holding out until the reinforcements arrived, but it might wreck *Solar Wind* in the process.

Ben—

He looked perfectly calm, perfectly focused. He flicked a glance in her direction and gave her a tight half-nod. Nothing else betrayed his emotions.

She cleared her throat to try and steady her voice. "Thirty-five seconds."

"Thirty klicks," Yan said.

Oleg Staple's broadcast cut in. *Solar Wind I've got missiles launching on your tail in thirty, twenty-five, twenty . . .*

Thanks, Staple, trying to do you a favor as we leave, Ben said. *Stand by.*

"Ten klicks," Yan said.

"Ten seconds to missile launch," Cara said. *Five. Three. Two. Missiles away.*

"Close enough."

Ben slammed open the jump drive and they seemed to collapse sideways, sucked through a space that was too small.

◆   ◆   ◆

"Mayday. Mayday. Mayday. Trust cruiser *Simonides*, Captain James Duran requesting assistance."

A ship's distress beacon flashes a message on the forward screen at the same time as the audio message overrides normal comms.

Ben has successfully dragged the cruiser through into the Folds with them. Drawing them away from the battle is Ben's primary objective. He doesn't want to kill the crew, but without a gate beacon to latch onto they'll never be able to find a way out of the Folds. How many on board?

Friends or enemies, you never leave anyone to die in space if there is an option.

"Captain Duran, stand by." Cara opens up the comm link both ways, almost surprised that it operates so well in foldspace. There's hardly any lag at all, half a second maybe.

She looks toward Ben.

He shrugs, nods and touches the vox control on his collar. "*Simonides*, Captain Duran, this is Ben Benjamin of the *Solar Wind*."

"Benjamin. What happened?"

"You got caught in our jump drive wake, Duran. Sorry about that."

"Like hell you are."

"Well, you were trying to kill us."

"You've got me there."

"Have you got a Psi-1 Navigator on board?" Ben asks.

"Negative. Psi-3. Do you?"

"Affirmative." Ben smiles. "Stand by and we'll try and hook you up to a gate beacon."

There's a pause. "Thanks, Benjamin."

Ben switches off his vox and looks up. "How long since we entered foldspace?"

"Subjective time four minutes," Kitty answers.

"Yan, take the helm while I search for a nav beacon. Just hold her steady."

"You do know where we are, right, Boss?" Yan asks.

"Sure, we're between here and there. It's where we'll end up that we need to know."

Ben reaches out with his senses. He can feel the tides of foldspace. Things are moving out there, sliding between the eddies, but there's no jump gate beacon within reach. The Folds are never the same twice and any vessel entering by a jump gate usually has a choice of two or three different exit points. They've not only come in via the *Solar Wind*'s jump drive, but they've entered from within Olyanda's upper atmosphere, something not technically possible, or at least not desirable unless you have a death wish.

When he opens his eyes, Ben realizes everyone is staring at him, but it's nothing to do with the swarm of void creatures that have gathered around his head. He doubts that they're visible to anyone else.

He shivers. "How long now, Cara?"

"Five minutes thirty."

He nods. The longer they stay in the Folds the less chance they have of coming out the other side. He can get *Solar Wind* out right now, but only by leaving Duran and the *Simonides* behind. Ships have been lost in the Folds before. It's an occupational hazard of flying the vast deeps but ... not on his watch, not if he can help it.

He taps his vox and opens up the comms channel to the *Simonides* again. "Duran."

"Benjamin, where are you? Our instruments are showing ... things swimming about out there as well as in here. I think it's only illusion but ... Hell, what was that?"

The conversation turns chaotic as something happens on the *Simonides'* flight deck to interrupt Duran's calm.

"There is something out there, Benjamin. Can't you feel it?"

"There's always something out there. The trick is not to let it see that you've noticed. Don't draw its attention."

Whether it's real or not, a Navigator learns to ignore it lest it take too keen an interest in the intruding ship.

"Have you found us a gate beacon?" Duran asks.

"No. There isn't one."

"You can't just leave us . . ."

"I don't intend to," Ben says. "Maintain your course. I'm going to swing you out on our coattails like I brought you in."

"You must be mad. You can't maneuver that closely in here. You'll kill us all. We should abandon ship and try and shuttle our crew across to you."

"Without a Psi-1 Navigator? You'd be lost as soon as you launched. You'd rather we left you?"

"No. Please, no."

"Keep steady then."

Ben takes over the ship from Yan. To be honest, he's not sure he can do it, but he has to try. He can't imagine a worse way to die, cut off from all hope of assistance until the ship's life support fails. It could take weeks or months or even years, but no one would ever come to the rescue and eventually everything would break down and people would die like his parents had died.

"What's happening up there?" Captain Tengue asks. "It's like the seventh layer of hell down here. There are . . . things. Are we getting out of the Folds any time soon?"

"Soon enough," Ben says, shaking his head at Gwala. "Stand by."

"You know what you're doing, right?" Cara asks.

"I hope so," he says.

✦ ✦ ✦

Cara's nails cut into the palms of her hands. Either this move will always be remembered as the Benjamin Maneuver or both ships will be scattered to atoms in the next minute and a half.

"What's happening up there?" Tengue asks again from the hold, his voice harsh.

"You really don't want to know, Cap," Gwala answers, his eyes showing too much white.

"Benjamin!" Tengue tries to get Ben's attention.

"Not now!" Cara cuts in. "Give him some space." She severs Tengue's audio connection to the flight deck.

Ben pulls up the holographic nav screen, not entirely reliable in the Folds, but a rough indication of how close the two ships are. Cara's screen mirrors it.

"How close do you need to be?" she asks.

"Maybe three klicks, but to be safe, less than one. If I don't get him on the first go there won't be a second chance. Watch that blip on the screen. Call time and distance as you see it."

"Six minutes forty-five. Fifty-two klicks and closing."

Ben makes a slight adjustment to their course.

"Seven minutes, ten. Thirty-eight klicks and closing."

"Seven minutes thirty. Fifteen klicks and holding."

"We're much closer than fifteen klicks by the feel of it," Ben says.

"What?"

"We're too damn close. The instruments are wrong."

"Pull out, Boss," Kitty squeaks.

"Hold your nerve. We need to be kissing close." Ben grins, but the mirth doesn't reach his eyes despite his flash of white teeth. "Fucking close, in fact."

"Remember the missile." He makes another slight adjustment. "Here we go!"

The prow of the *Solar Wind* nudges the *Simonides* amidships, but instead of the shudder of hull on hull the *Solar Wind* cleaves cleanly through the other ship like a hot knife through butter. For a frozen moment the *Simonides'* bridge appears on the *Solar Wind*'s flight deck like a hologram. The two ships slide through and past each other as if neither is solid, each a ghost to the other. Ben and Duran come face-to-face and Duran's expression is a mask of horror, but he pulls himself together and salutes. Ben nods an acknowledgment. Then they are past and the *Solar Wind* is coming out the other side as Ben fires up the jump drive and roars out into real space.

◆ ◆ ◆

"So that's the Benjamin Maneuver," Cara said, fighting off a wave of dizziness.

"Huh?" Ben looked gray.

"I'll tell you later. It's better than the other scenario I had in mind."

She opened up communications and winced at the onslaught of protests from the mercs and questions from Ronan in the med bay.

"Time?" Ben asked.

"Seven minutes in the Folds and . . ." She checked and

checked again, hardly believing. "Ten hours twenty-four minutes elapsed time in realspace."

"A ratio of one to something close on eighty-nine. Highest yet," he said. "Log it."

How did he work it out so fast?

"Where's Kitty?" Cara counted heads.

"You are one crazy son-of-a-bitch, Benjamin," Gwala said.

"Let's see if I'm crazy enough. Cara, did we bring her out?"

"Captain Duran?" Cara broadcast.

"Safe in realspace. Did we dream that?"

"If you did, so did we," Ben said. "I've had a theory about foldspace for a while, never got to test it quite so intimately before."

"Ben, where's Kitty?" Cara asked. *Kitty?*

Here! Kitty Keely replied.

Where?

On the Simonides. *I got scooped up when the two ships merged and here I am.*

Are you all right? Ben asked.

Apart from hardly believing what happened, yes, I think I am.

That's the other part of my theory you've proved, Kitty. Reality in the Folds is what we believe it to be.

◆ ◆ ◆

Kitty staggered and fell straight into the lap of the person in the command chair of the *Simonides*. She'd barely opened one eye and squinted at his name badge, Captain Duran, when she was seized from behind by someone much bigger and stronger than she was. She briefly considered struggling, but then added up what had just happened. She was on board the *Simonides*. How the hell had that happened? All she'd done was to think, for a moment, that the *Simonides* looked so real.

She relaxed into her captor without struggling. For the moment, play dumb. See how this worked out.

"What the hell . . ." Duran spat out. "Mulligan, hold her." He turned to the Nav Station. "Casey, status."

"We're in realspace, Captain. Benjamin did it." The Navigator, female, fortyish, turned and grinned at him. "He did it."

"Position?"

"Not sure. Give me . . . Oh, bastard. Sorry, Captain. Half-way to the Rim. Closest system gate is fifteen days away. Romanov Hub."

Kitty saw Duran's jaw clench.

"Captain Duran?" Cara broadcast from *Solar Wind*.

Kitty listened to the exchange between Benjamin and Duran. She'd thought Benjamin a bit of a nut with his theories about foldspace, but now she wasn't so sure.

Kitty? Cara sent that thought just for her.

Finally they'd missed her!

And now Benjamin was banging on about reality in the Folds. After what just happened, she barely knew what was real and what wasn't.

She'd think about Benjamin's theory later. In the meantime she needed to get back to *Solar Wind*.

Captain Duran was still blinking in disbelief. She gave her name and her Alphacorp ID twice before he took note of it. "Ensign Keely, I should engage *Solar Wind*, but the circumstances are somewhat unusual."

"Don't go head-to-head with Benjamin, sir, you'd lose. *Solar Wind* has modifications."

Not strictly true. She didn't actually know who'd win in a straight shoot-out, but she needed Benjamin in order to stay on the inside of what was happening on Olyanda. The platinum was more important than Benjamin and his psi-techs. Besides, she had to admit that they weren't actually guilty of most of the crimes they'd been charged with. If the psi-techs were guilty of anything it was making the most out of a rough deal.

"I know Benjamin," she said. "He won't come out shooting unless you do. He could have left you in the Folds if he'd wanted you dead. Besides, could you even begin to write this up?"

He looked thoughtful.

"How about you just send me back and we don't complicate matters?"

◆ ◆ ◆

The mechanical comm rattled into life.

"Well, now this is awkward," Captain Duran said. "We appear to have one of your crew. I don't know how, and I don't want to know."

"On screen," Ben said, and the image of *Simonides'* bridge flickered and stabilized. Kitty stood just behind the captain with a tall corpsman obviously on guard.

Ben touched his vox. "What are your intentions, Duran?"

"I intend to get back to base as quickly as possible without recording an incident which will count against me next time I have a psych evaluation. As far as my log goes *Solar Wind* dragged us out of foldspace just like she dragged us in."

"And Miss Keely?"

"Ensign Keely is an Alphacorp employee."

"She is in our care. Check your records. There's no warrant out for her."

"So I note, or she'd be in the brig already and we wouldn't be having this conversation."

"Kitty, are you all right?" Ben asked.

"Yes, Boss." Her voice sounded a little shaky. Not surprising under the circumstances.

"Do you want to stay with Captain Duran? He can get you back to Alphacorp safely. Right, Duran?"

"Uh, no," Kitty said quickly. "I want to come home."

"Understood. You heard her, Duran. Let's keep it simple. You tried to kill us, we stopped you, and you're still alive to tell the tale."

"Fifteen days from the nearest hub."

Ben's mouth twitched at the corners. "Fifteen days out of the rest of your life, and the lives of your crew. What do you say to a truce?"

"You always had a rep for being fair."

"I'm surprised I have any kind of a rep."

"Word gets around. The Hera-3 thing . . . Didn't figure you for a terrorist and a pirate, though, until we got the warrants."

"It's a twisted world out there, Duran. Look who issued the warrants. Follow the money."

"Anyhow. I want you to know that I'm not unappreciative."

"Thanks—I think," Ben said, "but forgive us if we try and stay far enough away that we never need to put your gratitude to the test."

Duran laughed. "You can have Miss Keely back, but take care, Benjamin. If we ever meet again, come out fighting."

"You can count on it."

Kitty transferred on the *Simonides'* launch. They left Captain Duran and his crew in realspace. By the time they found their way back the situation on Olyanda would be resolved one way or another.

Ben fired up the jump drive and popped the *Solar Wind* through foldspace without incident, four hours from Crossways.

"Gwala," Ben said. "Nice shooting back there. If you want to change outfits I've got a place for you on the flight crew."

"I thought Tengue was a crazy sonofabitch, Benjamin, but right now he looks like my mother. Happy to take your coin and to fly with you again, though." He gave the closed fist sign. "Respect!"

"And to you."

Chapter Nine

JUSSARO

*S*OLAR WIND DOCKED IN PORT 22 AGAIN. CARA hung back while sixty mercenaries staggered out of the hold with varying comments about the rough ride and the legitimacy of Ben Benjamin's birth. Ben booked a clean-up crew to hose down the space and left Gwala to tell Tengue why the ride had been, even by foldspace standards, more traumatic than usual.

Cara waited, torn between charging down to confront McLellan and hiding away in the cabin she shared with Ben. Finally she dithered for long enough that Ronan arranged for McLellan to be taken away to a secure facility.

You can come out now, Ronan told her. *Deal with McLellan another day.*

Grateful for the matter to be out of her hands, she followed Ben down to the dockside where he was making arrangements with Morton Tengue for his mercs to report to Blue Seven later in the day. Their wounded had already been shipped off to Dockside Medical, Fowler complaining every step of the way, but Cara noticed she paused to squeeze Ben's hand as the antigrav gurney carried her past. She also noticed the look on Tengue's face as he relinquished her to the med-techs.

Yan said he needed to get a thorough overhaul for the

Solar Wind after Ben's little trick, and if they were going to resort to the jump drive every time out he needed to re-stock the platinum rods. So it was Ben, Cara, Ronan, and Kitty who shared a tub back to Blue Seven where Cara was looking forward to no more than a hot meal and a few hours' solid sleep.

"How the hell are we going to get any sleep in all this?" she said as they walked through the open doors into the vast warehouse. Her words were swallowed up by noise and a melee of mech-techs with a variety of worker bots drilling, cutting, riveting, sealing. The transformation was underway. Everything was happening at once. And the din . . . Cara switched on her noise cancellers, but that meant she couldn't hear Ben when he spoke, so she linked telepathically.

I said, how are we going to get any sleep? I've a good mind to go back to the Solar Wind.*

We'll manage, even if we have to sleep with our buddy-suit helmets up and the noise cancellers on.

She pulled a face.

On closer examination the chaos began to sort itself out into separate projects. In one section Archie Tatum was su-pervising the installation of medonite walls to create one- and two-room apartments while a team of his Psi-Mech engineers constructed an internal skin as an extra layer of security. Several staircases and a couple of antigrav tubes had already been installed, but at the moment they led to nowhere, as the mezzanine floor was nothing more than a series of major support struts bordering a double-height atrium that would prevent the whole place from being claustrophobic.

Let's see what Wenna's got organized, Ben suggested.

They headed for the cluster of low boxlike structures that formed the basic administration block. Inside it was just a space divided up by a series of portable screens where people could carve out a small kingdom for themselves for as long as they needed it. Cara could tell from the way Wenna was talking to Gen and Max that the noise levels were benign, so she clicked off the noise cancelation on her buddysuit and her ears popped back into the real world.

"Boss?" Wenna's greeting was also a question.

"We've got the mercs. Gupta can start working with them this afternoon. Where is he?"

"Either babysitting or imprisoning Cara's visitor. We can't decide which."

"Visitor? What visitor?" Cara had been about to drop into a spare chair, but she stood up again. "I'm not expecting anyone. Hell, I don't have anyone who'd want to visit me." She swallowed hard. "It's not my mother, is it?" If her mother ever got a whiff of the platinum profits Cara had no doubt that she'd be on the doorstep as soon as she could detach herself from her lover of the month.

"No, not your mother, though that sounds like a story worth hearing just from the way you said it. This is a squat fellow with an eyebrow." She zigzagged her finger across her forehead. "Just one eyebrow. Says he knows you from Mirrimar-14."

"Jussaro?"

"That's the one."

Cara laughed. "Where is he?"

Wenna pointed to the far end of the room where there were screens surrounding a space isolated with sound baffles.

"Cara!" Ben's sharp tone pulled her up. "Make sure it is Jussaro before you barge in there with your guard down."

She nodded but noted he still followed her, though he stood back to let her enter the enclosure on her own.

It was unmistakably Jussaro, monobrow, purple-black skin, nictitating eyelids and all. Though heavily muscled, the top of his head barely reached Cara's nose, which made him tall for one of the natives of the two inhabited planets of the Hollands System, where gravity was twenty-five percent stronger than Earth-normal. The genetic adaptations protected him from the ravages of the harsh Hollands sun. Most of the Hollanders didn't travel far, but Jussaro wasn't most people.

"Jussaro!" Heedless of Gupta's two guards, she stepped forward and hugged him, planting a quick kiss on the top of his bald head. "What are you doing here?"

And then she thought about it. What was he doing here? He'd been a Psi-1 Telepath before undergoing two sessions of Neural Readjustment and finally having his implant decommissioned for the crime of encouraging psi-techs to go rogue and abandon the megacorps that paid to have them implanted and trained.

"Long story. Glad I found the right place at last."

She folded her arms and stepped back. "About that. How did you find us?"

◆ ◆ ◆

Jussaro leaned back in his chair. "Got any caff, Carlinni? I always talk better when I'm caffeinated."

Cara looked around. Gupta had set it up as a typical interview room with nothing but a table and a couple of chairs.

"I think we can manage some caff."

"If you don't need me, I'll send some in," Gupta said.

Would you ask Ronan to bring it? I'd like him to hear this, too, Cara asked him on a very tight band so that Jussaro didn't hear.

Gupta gave an almost imperceptible nod.

Cara sat in one of the chairs, Ben lounged against one wall, saying nothing. Jussaro eyed him up warily and turned back to Cara. "It's a long story."

"We've got time."

"Okay." Jussaro took a deep breath. "After you got away from Mirrimar-14 the line manager at Devantec called us all in—on our own time I might add—and started asking questions. There was a man with him who never said anything, just leaned against the wall and listened." He looked at Ben again, but Ben never moved.

"They were real interested in me because of how close you and I worked and because of my history, but they couldn't prove any kind of connection and I was obviously not helping Telepaths go rogue anymore since I lost my implant. They figured out that I could still receive, because I still had some natural talent, but beyond that I couldn't throw a thought past the end of my nose.

"It was sweet when you contacted me, by the way. First time I'd felt normal in two years. I knew it was all you and not me, but it felt good."

"I didn't put you in any danger?"

"No more than I was in already. They found a security recording of you in the access corridor to my accommodation sector on the night you hid out at my place. It was enough for them to come knocking on my door. Once they were in . . . well . . . you left a blonde hair on my chair, Carlinni."

"Sorry. I really am sorry for dragging you into this."

The door opened and Ronan brought in a tray with four mugs of caff. He placed it on the table and gave Jussaro a curious look.

"Will you stay?" Cara asked.

Ronan took a mug for himself and handed one to Ben, settling next to him against the wall.

Jussaro eyed Ronan, but said nothing about the extra observer. He took a sip of his caff, sighed and settled back in his chair.

"So what happened after they found my hair?" Cara took her own cup of caff.

"Turns out that the man in the interview room was van Blaiden's goon."

Cara nodded. "Thought he might be. Was his name Craike?"

"That's the one. I got a first-class ticket to Sentier-4."

Knowing Craike's propensity for violence, it hadn't been quite as straightforward as that.

"I'm so sorry."

Jussaro shook his head. "No need. There's not much they can do to you if you've already lost your implant. Well, yeah, they can lock you up and throw away the key, but that's about it. I saw Donida McLellan once and before she could start anything I voluntarily told her everything that happened the night you came to visit and about you contacting me. By that time it was old news anyway."

"McLellan's here."

"What?"

"Not quite her old self. Long story." Cara swallowed the rising queasiness in the back of her throat. "Go on. Is that it?"

"Apart from a lot of staring at the walls. McLellan left me alone and I never saw Craike again."

"So how did you get out?"

"That's the interesting bit. I lost track of time." He held up his hand. "This is a new handpad; they ripped off my old one. Months later—maybe more than months—I was transferred. I didn't know where I was being taken or why. I thought they might lose me on a prison planet or just shove me out of the air lock. Turns out it was to the Trust."

"How did that happen?"

"I really have no idea. Anyhow, I saw a very nice lady called Dr. Zuma who said I was a suitable subject for reimplantation."

"Reimplantation? Why would they do that?"

"So that Crowder could let me escape, or appear to, and I could find you and spy on you for him, of course."

Cara heard Ben mutter a soft curse, but he didn't interrupt.

"Did you agree?" she asked Jussaro.

"Wouldn't you?"

She shrugged.

"You know van Blaiden is dead?" Ben spoke up for the first time.

"So I've been told," Jussaro said. "And Craike, too, I understand. Couldn't have happened to a more deserving pair. Sadly I report to a Telepath called Leyburn and he's not dead."

"You're admitting to being a Trust spy?" Ben said.

"I'm admitting to not only being a spy, but continuing to be a spy. Unless I report once a week . . . ." He drew his finger across his throat. "My implant is fitted with a kill switch."

"And you're telling us all this because . . . ?" Ben wasn't lounging against the wall now. He was on his feet and looking as though he was about to come at Jussaro hard and fast.

Ronan hadn't moved.

Cara waved her hand at Ben and turned to Jussaro. "I get it. A spy is only dangerous if you don't know he's there."

Jussaro raised one eyebrow, not an inconsiderable feat with brows like his. "And you're not stupid, you're going to have me repeat all this in front of the best Empath you've got to determine if I'm lying." He looked at Ronan, who nodded.

"Damn right," Ben said.

"But, wait . . . you said kill switch?" Cara leaned forward in her chair.

"Yeah, that's the kicker." He grimaced. "Given that all my old contacts are either dead or have gone to ground, there's no place I'd rather be than here. . . . In any other circumstances than these, that is. The implant in my brain will kill me, maybe not now, but one day. Crowder says it's tamper-proof. Try to disengage or adjust it and it will blow, with messy results, a meltdown cascading through my neural pathways like a stroke. Crowder can trigger it at any time, from any distance, deliberately or by omission. If I don't contact Crowder's Telepath at least once a week I'm toast."

He shrugged. "I might keep Crowder happy in the short-term, but in the long-term it's an unsustainable arrangement. Sure, I can warn Crowder if you're sending any kind of attack against him, but what happens when I've served my purpose? Will Crowder keep me around? Unlikely. I know too much. Besides, Crowder doesn't look like a well man. Too much stress, not enough exercise, not enough sleep. What happens if he dies of natural causes? He's at least a quarter century older than me and doesn't look like the sort of man who'll make it to a well-deserved retirement."

"You think Crowder won't have thought this through?" Ben said.

"Oh, I'm sure he will have, but as far as he's concerned I have two choices. I can either trust you, as I am doing, or hide what I am and try to stay alive. And Crowder's not big on trust himself. In my position what would he do? Either way, if I don't send back information he can just write me off as a failed experiment. I don't like playing the spy, but I'm not sorry to have my implant back and I'm not sorry to be here. Give me time. I'll find some way to screw Crowder over if it kills me." He exhaled sharply. "It might, of course."

Jussaro sipped the last of his cooling caff. "I want shelter here. I don't want to be a part of your Free Company, but I want to work with you. My agenda has never changed."

"Sanctuary for Telepaths," Cara breathed.

"What better place than Crossways?" Jussaro smiled. "I don't want you to bankroll me—well, I do, but not without me working for it. How many psi-techs have you got in the Free Company? No, don't answer that, I don't want to know. Psi-techs are created by the corporations and unless they go rogue like you've done, they're owned by the corporations until the day they die. I not only want to release psi-techs from the control of the megacorps, but I want to have the facility to implant and train independent psi-techs. Think about it. You find me someone who's willing to do the actual implantations, provide me with a place to work and I'll train a new generation of psi-techs for you. It gives your

Free Company long-term stability. What do you say to that?"

◆ ◆ ◆

"Is he telling the truth?" Ben asked as he, Cara, and Ronan walked further into the building site that was Blue Seven.

That was the question, wasn't it?

Cara pondered. Her instincts were to trust Jussaro. She hadn't known him for long on Mirrimar-14, they'd worked together for just a few months, but she'd grown to like him. Dammit, he felt trustworthy, but she'd been wrong before.

They slowed as a team of willing hands led by Archie Tatum manhandled a heavy spar across their path using antigrav limpets. A woman in a protective face mask leaned over a pair of drill bots inserting power couplings into a new section of wall before it was lifted into place.

"As far as I could tell." Cara frowned, wincing at the squeak of metal on medonite. "Ronan?"

"He's telling the truth as far as he knows it. I'm sure."

They came out into a relatively quiet open space that would be for their warehousing and storage.

"That's better," Ben said. "I can hear myself think again."

Cara nodded. "I noticed a bit of a wobble between the long wait in a lonely cell and the offer of a new implant in return for spying on us. I don't think he told us everything, but it may just be that he's skipping the bit where they kicked the shit out of him."

"I'll check him for physical injuries," Ronan said.

"What about the kill switch?" Ben asked.

Ronan frowned. "That's outside my experience, but there's a specialist on-station, a man called Jamieson."

The idea of a kill switch in anyone's implant gave Cara a sick, crawling feeling between her shoulder blades.

"I'll leave that up to you," Ben said. "What about training rogue psi-techs?"

Cara was more sure about that. "It was what he got busted for. Three times. He went through two bouts of Neural Readjustment and then they switched off his implant because he wouldn't stop helping psi-techs to get away from the megacorps. I think it's what drives him. It may be the only thing that drives him."

"Agreed," Ronan said. "I'd trust him."

Ben nodded. "Then let's back him, but keep a close watch. We'll be losing some of our crew once Gen gets them fixed up with new idents. Maybe a source of new recruits isn't a bad idea."

"Max," Cara said. "We can send Max to him for training."

"Is that fair?"

"On Max?"

Ben laughed. "On Jussaro. Max marches to his own tune."

"He's also a pretty good judge of character."

Ben nodded. "Yes, he is. We'll play it your way. It may be that we can use Jussaro to pass back the information we want Crowder to have."

✦ ✦ ✦

"But I've got to go!" Ricky Benjamin couldn't believe what he was hearing. His dad had never wanted him to get an implant and join the psi-techs. Missing this appointment would ensure it never happened. Dad would win and Ricky would have to spend the rest of his life babysitting cattle on the farm, like Kai.

He only just stopped himself from stamping his foot. At eleven he was far too old for those kinds of tantrums, whatever he felt like.

He took a deep breath and turned to Nan. "I'm right, aren't I? This will spoil my chances of getting into the advanced program."

Nan raised one eyebrow and shrugged. "Possibly, but you can still get an implant if you test positive at fourteen."

She took down the old ceramic teapot from the shelf, spooned in leaves and filled it with scalding hot water from the spigot. When Nan got out the teapot it announced a serious family discussion. Dad shrugged off his work jacket, hung it on the back of the door and padded over to the kitchen table in his socks, his outdoor boots, fresh from the farmyard, having been left in the mud room.

Ricky didn't have to be told to get out three mugs and a jug of milk, but he wasn't going to give up so easily. "At fourteen it will just be the regional testing center and you know how that always works out. I'll never get into the space program."

"They take notice of real talent. Always." Nan poured the tea. "Sit, Merrick."

Oh-oh, he was always in trouble when Nan started to use his full name. She always called Uncle Ben *Reska* as well, even though no one else ever did.

Ricky tried again. "But passing this test could get me an early scholarship to the academy in Arkhad City. I could even get my implant next year."

"If you have any talent for it," Dad interrupted. "Kai didn't."

Kai had refused the fast track program at eleven, tested positive at fourteen and again at sixteen, but had turned down the offer of an implant. Twice. Dad didn't know that. Ricky was sworn to secrecy, though he suspected Nan might know. There wasn't much that escaped Nan's notice. Kai had eventually chosen to go to agricultural school. He actually wanted to stay on the farm. Well, that was up to him, but Ricky wanted the stars. He wanted to be like Uncle Ben.

Nan cleared her throat and drew his dad's attention. "Ricky's got potential, Rion. You won't be able to hold him back forever."

"See!" Ricky felt vindicated.

It didn't last. That was the trouble with arguing against adults. They only had to say: *Because I say so*, and you'd lost.

Nan turned to him. "It's not just because your dad doesn't want to lose you." She sipped her tea. "You know we heard from your Uncle Reska?"

"Sure. The reports of the plague on Olyanda were hokum. Uncle Ben's all right."

Nan nodded. "But he's in trouble with the Trust, specifically with Mr. Crowder. He told us to watch our backs and lay low. We're half a planet away from Crowder here, but Arkhad City is right in Crowder's territory."

"But Kai's there already." Ricky frowned. The university was on the outskirts of Arkhad City. "And we're not in trouble with the Trust, are we?"

"No, we're not, but Reska is worried that Crowder might try and use the family as leverage. Besides, Kai's on Tobar studying the new arcology. He's in no danger until he gets back. No one can get to him there." Tobar was the smaller of Chenon's moons.

"You think Mr. Crowder will try and hurt us?" Ricky asked. "Can he do that?"

"Not legally."

"Well, then."

Nan frowned. "Uncle Reska doesn't trust Mr. Crowder to limit himself to what can be done legally."

Ricky drank his tea. He knew when to stop arguing. Sometimes, however good your reasons, you just couldn't change someone's mind when they'd made it up in advance. He wasn't quite sure what Nan and Dad expected Mr. Crowder to do, but he was pretty sure that being eleven years old exempted him from whatever it was. Besides, it wasn't even as if Nan or Dad had to take him to Arkhad. There was a party going from the region. One of his teachers was the supervisor. All he had to do was present himself at the dock in Corrigar four days from now. He could get a lift with the Pastorio family. Their twins, Luna and Sala, had both been called for appointments just like him. It was a regular school day. If he left the house at the same time as usual he could be there and tested and safely on his way back before Dad and Nan even missed him.

Who was going to notice him if he was in a party of thirteen other kids? Every one of them had psi potential. They all had close relatives who were psi-techs: parents, grandparents, uncles, or siblings. The talent ran in families. The megacorporations, the planetary government, and the Monitors all kept an eye on likely kids. They needed psi-techs as engineers, communications operatives, exozoologists, pilots, navigators, medics. Whatever his specialization turned out to be, he could apply for space-based work. He wanted to be a pilot, maybe rising through the ranks in the Monitors, or setting up colonies like Uncle Ben, or even captaining a survey vessel out in the uncharted territories, seeking out habitable worlds. If Uncle Ben was in trouble with the Trust he could apply to any one of the other megacorps. Arquavisa, Sterritt, Rodontee, and Eastin-Heigle all had offices on Chenon.

Whatever Dad said, Ricky wasn't going to miss out on the opportunity of a lifetime.

But he wasn't going to be totally stupid about it. He'd call Kai and tell him what he planned. He was keeping Kai's secret. Kai was obliged to keep his.

Later that night Ricky settled down in front of his screen. Dad was asleep in the chair upstairs in the living room, tired out from a day in the open air, as usual. Nan was in her office writing a message to her friend Lucy, who was back on Earth and who didn't have an implant, so they still exchanged old-fashioned honest-to-goodness mail.

The screen scanned him. "Hello, Ricky," it said in a female voice. "What can I help you with this evening? I have the programs you asked for."

"Which ones?"

"Megacorporation ships and logos."

"Later."

"I have a new documentary on the platinum conundrum."

"No." Ricky knew all about the desperate need for platinum. Platinum was everywhere in the known galaxy, but it was usually only found in small quantities. A platinum prospector who found a large lode could get very rich very quickly. Perhaps if he didn't set up colonies like Uncle Ben he could be a platinum prospector, but it was unlikely he'd ever get off-planet unless he made it to this appointment at the test center.

"Call to Kai Benjamin," he told the screen.

"Kai is off-planet."

"I know. He's on Tobar."

"Station time on Tobar is three a.m."

Ricky bit his lip. "Call him anyway."

It took a while for Kai to answer. When his face flashed onto the screen the angle was skewed, his eyes were red-rimmed, and his voice thick and drowsy.

"Hey little brother, what's up?"

"I got called to Arkhad City for the fast track test."

"Great news, but did you need to ping me in the middle of the night?" He turned and spoke over his shoulder. "No, it's okay, go back to sleep."

"Is someone there with you?"

"No one you need worry about. Hang on a minute." The picture spun as Kai sat up. Lights flared as he entered a room with a long table in the middle flanked by fixed benches. There were doors every couple of meters, lots of sleeping cabins, probably, but no one else was up and about.

"Okay, we can talk now," Kai said. "What's up? You

didn't call me to tell me about the test. Is Uncle Ben all right?"

"As far as I know. It is about the appointment, though. Dad and Nan don't want me to go." He was going to say it wasn't fair, but was suddenly aware of how babyish that would sound.

"Oh, I get it. You think you're missing out."

"Well, yes. They think it could be dangerous."

"They might have a point."

Ricky shook his head. "You know how important the testing is."

"I guess, but Uncle Ben's pretty savvy. I get back to Arkhad at the end of the month and Dad asked me to come home, but it's finals. I have a couple of places where I can keep out of sight, though, just turn up to sit the papers and then disappear again."

"You're taking all this seriously?"

"So should you, little brother." Kai always managed to make things sound reasonable.

"Maybe." Ricky scrubbed a hand through his tousled hair. "Thing is, Kai, I'm going. I can't miss this chance. There's an official supervised trip. All I have to do is turn up. My name's already on the list. I can get a lift to the hub at Corrigar with the Pastorios."

"Don't be dumb—"

"I can't miss out on this, but I figured that someone should know where I am."

"So you thought it was okay to get me into trouble with Nan and Dad?"

"They can hardly blame you. There's not much you can do to stop me."

"I can call Dad."

"I keep your secrets. You keep mine."

Kai frowned.

"Besides," Ricky continued, "I'm pretty sure Dad's actually pleased I'll miss out on the test and the fast track program. He's never wanted me to try for the psi-techs. You know what he's like about space."

"He's always been like that, ever since his parents ... well, you know."

Dad had been nine when his parents' ship had been lost in the Folds.

"Nan's on your side, Ricky. Don't forget what her job was before she gave it up to look after Dad and Uncle Ben."

"Yeah, a negotiator for the Five Power Alliance, I know. She made us sit down and drink tea."

Kai shook his head. "That's pretty serious negotiation tactics. You don't suppose she knows I turned down an implant, do you?"

"She's psi, an Empath. She always seems to know what's going on. She hasn't said anything, though."

"Good. Look, Ricky, if you're intent on going to Arkhad, just don't do anything to draw attention, right?"

"I'm only going to sit the test. I don't think we'll be in Arkhad for more than a couple of hours. By the time they know what I did I'll be safely on my way home." Ricky smiled.

"How long do you figure they'll ground you for?" Kai asked.

"I don't know." Ricky bit his lower lip. "It'll be worth it, though."

"Yeah, I suppose." Kai looked over his shoulder again. "Coming," he said.

"You do have someone with you," Ricky said.

"Only my bunk-mate. We don't get our own bedrooms, you know. This isn't a hotel. It's pretty cramped up here."

"Was that a girl's voice I heard?"

"Look, Ricky, it's great talking to you, but I have an early class and I need some sleep. Let's talk again soon, just you and me, huh?"

"Yeah, that'd be great."

"Okay, then, take care of yourself and don't get into trouble. I'll call after your test, just to make sure you've arrived home safely. Okay?"

"Yes, thanks. You're a pal. Bye."

"Bye."

Kai's face disappeared and Ricky felt better about what he was going to do.

Chapter Ten

FAMILY TROUBLE

*N*OT NOW, REMUS, PLEASE!*

Kitty jerked awake, wondering where she was, saw the plain interior of Wes' bedroom in the dim light from the holographic clock and tried to relax.

Beside her Wes stirred and muttered something unintelligible before subsiding into sleep again.

Report!

Better get it over with.

There's a Telepath called Jussaro turned up. Emil Jussaro, a Hollander. He's got some kind of connection with Cara Carlinni from before Olyanda. I don't know the details.

Emil Jussaro. Noted. What else?

Benjamin has employed the mercenaries van Blaiden took to Olyanda to run security for the Free Company on Crossways. The Trust sent a flotilla to try and retake Olyanda. They failed. Benjamin tangled with one of the Trust's cruisers, the Simonides, *dragged it into foldspace and out again. Dumped ship and crew fifteen days away from the nearest gate without casualties. Neat bit of flying.*

You admire him.

He's a good pilot.

Anything else?

Isn't that enough?

It will have to be.

My mom, Remus. What about my mom?

I don't have that information.

Well, dammit, can you find out?

I'll ask for next time. Stay sharp, Keely.

He disengaged from her mind. She hadn't mentioned her unorthodox trip from the *Solar Wind* to the *Simonides*. It never happened, she told herself.

She rolled over and checked the time. Still a full hour before either of them needed to get up.

Wes' arm snaked around her waist and he pulled her back against his warm body. She could feel something hard against her butt cheek. She smiled and pushed herself against him. He spread his fingers against her belly and stroked downward. His hot breath tickled her neck and she felt his lips tracing a warm line across the back of her shoulder. A little jiggle and his other arm was beneath her, wrapped around caressing her breasts. He had big hands, warm hands, gentle hands. Oh gods! Talented hands. His fingers found their way between her legs, already sensitive from their lovemaking the night before.

Her breath hissed between her teeth and she arched. He pulled her back gently until his cock slipped between her thighs and found its home.

"Wes, I—"

"Shhh."

He moved inside her slowly and languorously from behind. His fingers worked lightly, gently, until she ached for more. She reached between her legs, sliding her own hand across his until she touched that part of him that wasn't inside her, hot and swollen, and brought forth a shuddering gasp. He pulled her hips firmly toward his own and began to thrust.

Afterward they snuggled together until the alarm reminded them that they had someplace else to be. Still, they found time to shower together, and despite Wes' compulsive tidiness, the tangle Kitty had left her underwear in the night before almost set them off again.

Finally, dressed in buddysuits, his in Garrick's colors, hers workaday black, they stepped out into the hallway, still warm and fuzzy from sex, straight into Wes' teammate

Ellen Heator, who lived across the hallway and was, herself, heading to duty at Port 22. She said good morning and gave Wes a knowing smile and a wink. Wes blew her a cheeky kiss, grinned and took Kitty's hand as they waited for the elevator. Two levels up Syke joined them, nodded to Wes and Ellen, said a polite good morning to Kitty, but kept his expression completely neutral. Stiff-ass. Kitty tried not to laugh at his formality.

The elevator disgorged them into early morning crowds at the cab station and Syke took the last place in an eight-seater going to the port hub while Ellen shuffled further up the platform to see if she could grab a space. It was hot and noisy. How on earth could anyone tell where some of the tubs were heading? They all looked the same to her.

A warning rippled through the crowd.

"Pickpocket," Wes said. "Stay sharp."

Exactly what Remus had told her.

"How can anyone tell what's happening in a crowd like this?" she asked.

"You'll see."

The crowd parted and Ellen Heator stood over a prone body, a hypo stick fully extended. She grinned at them. "Tell the captain I'll be late."

"What happens next?" Kitty asked.

"It depends if he's been caught before. If it's his first time he'll probably get off with a warning and a fine since no one was hurt. If he's part of a gang, the gang will get a warning and a fine, too. Second time he's caught the fine will be hefty. Third time all his possessions will be impounded and he'll be removed from the station. If anyone's been injured he may be removed without benefit of ship."

"I see. Isn't there a prison on the station?"

"Only a temporary cooler for suspects awaiting questioning, or trial if it's not an open-and-shut case."

"There's a courtroom?"

"Not really, but there's a judge, a class one Empath."

"That's a hell of a responsibility."

"For the really big stuff, terminal stuff, there's a panel of three, but the council has the last say. I suspect Garrick can sway the council on most issues if he wants to, though."

"Is that good?"

"Crossways has been a safer place to live since Garrick

took over from Chaliss. Garrick's solid. Chaliss was—how can I put it?—whimsical."

"You like Garrick?"

"What I know of him, yes. And he pays my wages, of course. I think Garrick's good for Crossways."

✦ ✦ ✦

Ricky wiped his nose on his sleeve. The floor was hard under his skinny buttocks and the wall unyielding against his back. He could sit on the chair, of course, but it was fastened to the floor and the camera eyes stared across the middle of the room. A spigot and basin on the far wall with a pull-out san-unit completed the facilities. Tucked into the corner, half-shielded by the narrow bed, he finally gave in to the tears.

Crying wasn't what his Uncle Ben would have done, he suspected, but in view of his stupidity he reckoned he was allowed some childish behavior. Nan had warned him, Dad had warned him, even Kai had warned him, and he'd still walked straight into a trap. He hadn't even had any kind of test. He'd entered the testing room of his own free will and there was a tough-looking woman in a buddysuit who had simply slapped a blast pack to his neck. He'd felt a cold sting and the next thing he knew he'd woken in a groundcar, blinded by a hood.

He'd counted the journey time by heartbeats and listened carefully to external sounds, more as a way to keep his mind off what was happening than with any idea that he might be able to put any information to use, but he got lucky when he heard the unmistakable sound of the wheezy BX98 airtruck engines, the workhorse used by the Trust. He figured he was somewhere on the Trust's massive Colony Operations site just outside Arkhad City itself. All his studies of the Trust had paid dividends in a way he could never have imagined.

His prison was either very high up or very low down according to the length of time they'd spent in an elevator. An elevator, not an antigrav shaft, Ricky noted. The ride was so slow and smooth that he'd have had difficulty telling up from down if it hadn't been for the very slight grav-pull as they stopped.

Down.

He was almost sure.

The hood had made him dizzy and he'd gasped for fresh air. Logging the turns and the number of paces from the elevator as they marched helped him to keep it together. The sounds of booted feet on the hard floor sometimes echoed as if they were passing through a hall, and sometimes the space sounded narrow and confined. No one spoke, but he was fairly sure the scary woman was still there. He'd noticed she had a habit of clearing her throat softly, and every so often he heard the sound.

When they'd finally unlocked a door and shoved him through it, she'd removed the hood. Yes, it was the same woman, tall and broad-shouldered, dressed in a buddysuit with a Trust flash on the shoulder.

At least he'd told Kai he was going on the trip to Arkhad. Kai would call home this evening. Nan and Dad would be worried when he wasn't on the school shuttle. Kai would confirm what they'd probably already guessed.

But even if they knew where he was, how could they get him out? If this was Mr. Crowder's doing—and the scary woman had not given anything away except by her uniform—he had all the resources of the Trust behind him.

Would they use Ricky as bait for a trap for Uncle Ben, or was there, even now, some negotiation going on? *Give yourself up, Ben Benjamin, or the boy gets it.* Was that even possible? Was Crowder so ruthless?

Ricky began to tremble.

✦ ✦ ✦

"Louisa Benjamin is in the main lobby, sir." Crowder's secretary, Stefan French, commed him on audio only.

"Louisa Benjamin?" He'd been expecting the brother, Rion.

"Yes, sir."

Crowder crossed quickly to his desk and accessed Ben Benjamin's file, pulling it up on the holo-screen. Had Benjamin's ex-wife turned up? No, the ex-wife was Serena, not Louisa. Crowder had never heard Ben talk about a Louisa Benjamin.

He looked up the brother's wife, but they didn't have her name on file.

He did a search for Louisa.

Of course! Benjamin's grandmother. Ben had always referred to her as Nan, obviously a title, not a name.

"Have we got a visual on her?" he asked.

"Patching it through, sir."

A separate holo-image popped up beside his screen. A tall, rangy woman paced the waiting area in the lobby, her long leather coat flapping around her calves. She paused briefly at one end of the room with hands on the windowsill, then turned and paced back, energy evident in the set of her shoulders and her determined stride.

Unexpectedly, Louisa Benjamin was of European descent, though bronzed by the sun and weathered by the wind. Surely not Benjamin's grandmother. It wasn't her skin tone that surprised him most, however, it was her age, or lack of it. This woman's hair was steel, not snow, and she didn't look much more than fifty—maybe sixty. She could have been through intensive rejuv, of course, but there weren't many farmers on Chenon who could afford that kind of treatment.

She raised her head and glared at the cam as if she knew he was watching. Bronze skin, steel hair, and iron eyes. Was there anything about this woman that didn't remind him of metal? Farming was a tough life and looked to have honed a tough woman. This wouldn't be an easy meeting.

"I'll see her in the visitors' lounge, Stefan. Make her a caff, be pleasant, but don't comment on the boy's disappearance or the Olyanda mission. As far as she knows the whole colony died of plague. Call Pav Danniri."

Pav Danniri was the twin of Thom Danniri, one of Crowder's recently deceased bodyguards, killed by Benjamin. If it meant a chance to get revenge Pav would not question Crowder's orders or spend time checking the rule book. She'd already secured the boy.

"I'll keep Mrs. Benjamin waiting for . . ." He glanced at his handpad. "Ten minutes should be long enough. Then give me another ten and come and remind me about a scheduled conference call. When you show her out make sure she uses shaft 4B."

"Yes, sir."

Ten minutes later Crowder fixed a sad smile of condolence on his face and prepared himself to be solicitous.

When the lounge door whooshed open he could see immediately that condolences were not called for. Any ideas of dealing sympathetically with Ben's grieving Nan went out of his head at the look on Stefan's face. On the spectrum of uncomfortable to terrified, it was as close to terrified as it could be without any weapon being pointed in his direction. He was pressed back into his chair with Nan on her feet towering over him.

Crowder didn't catch any of the conversation because at the sound of the door opening she whirled around, coattails swirling. "Gabrius Crowder, I trust you've not come to give me any more of this condolence crap. Where's my great-grandson?"

Stefan took the opportunity to bolt for the door.

"Mrs. Benjamin—"

"It's *Miss*. I never married Reska's grandfather."

"Miss Benjamin—"

"Don't patronize me. I can hear it in your voice and I can smell bullshit from ten klicks away. I haven't flown halfway around Chenon to be fobbed off with platitudes. My great-grandson, Merrick Benjamin, was in a party of youngsters from Russolta called for fast track testing at the Academy two days ago. He hasn't been seen since. His supervisor was told he'd been singled out for further tests."

"You need to make enquiries at the Academy, then. I'm afraid I have no knowledge of any young people asked to remain."

She gave him a look that said she'd done all that and more. "There were no further tests, Mr. Crowder. Merrick went in for his appointment and never came out again. What's going on?"

Crowder raised both hands in a nothing-to-do-with-me gesture.

"I have, of course, informed both the local police and the Monitors that Merrick is missing."

"The natural thing to do." Good thing Crowder had contacts in the local force.

"I know there's something going on."

"Has Ben been in touch?" Crowder asked.

"What do you think?"

"Miss Benjamin, I've heard so much about you from Ben, may I call you Nan?"

"No, you may not. And while we're at it, why is there a warrant out for Reska on three counts of murder, terrorism, armed insurrection, hijacking, grand theft, and kidnapping? What's he supposed to have done?"

"I'm so deeply disappointed, Miss Benjamin, but a fortune in platinum can turn the best of men."

"Go on." The woman's complete lack of reaction was unsettling. Crowder resisted the temptation to tug at his collar.

"Commander Benjamin was in charge of setting up a colony on the frontier planet of Olyanda for a bunch of back-to-basics Ecolibrians."

"That much I know."

"They found platinum, large deposits. Your grandson sold the platinum rights and forced the settlers off the planet. In the process he stole a state-of-the-art jumpship and murdered Ari van Blaiden."

"Van Blaiden runs the Special Operations Department for Alphacorp, if I've kept up with appointments correctly." She raised one eyebrow. "An Alphacorp official on a closed planet being settled by the Trust. Hmm. Go on. Three counts of murder, the warrant said."

How the hell had she got hold of the warrant? It was classified, need-to-know only. Perhaps one of Ben's ex-colleagues in the Monitors had broken security for old time's sake.

"Two were here, in this very building, in a terrorist attack. My own associates. I believe I may have been the intended target, but I'd left earlier." He found himself rubbing the dressing on his ear and shoved his hand in his pocket. "There's one more thing, an ark ship containing thirty thousand settlers in cryo has been hijacked. Thirty thousand very vulnerable settlers who would have been a huge complication to Benjamin's plans had they been allowed to land on Olyanda."

Ben's grandmother sniffed, but said nothing. Got her on the run, Crowder thought. See how she likes the idea of her darling boy gone rogue.

"I'm so sorry to have to be the one to tell you all of this, Miss Benjamin. Obviously the Trust is doing all it can, and the Monitors have been informed, but there's a press blackout, for security reasons, you understand."

"Oh, yes, I understand perfectly." Her nose twitched and she rubbed it with the back of her index finger.

"I'm sorry I couldn't arrange for you to hear the news in a more gentle manner," Crowder said. "I realize this must be an enormous shock for you."

"Shock? Not exactly. I know what my grandson is capable of, and I know what motivates him."

"Greed is a terrible thing."

"Indeed, it is. I think you should know, Mr. Crowder, that I have contacts who will be very interested in Merrick's safety, powerful contacts." She narrowed her eyes and gave him an iron stare.

"Is that a threat, Miss Benjamin?"

"I wouldn't be so crass, Mr. Crowder. It's just a statement of fact. Whatever beef you have with my grandson, the rest of the family will be kept out of it. I would appreciate your assistance to find Merrick, and would anticipate that since you have the resources, you'll be able to do that soon and deliver him safely to me. I'll be at Reska's apartment. You know where that is."

Crowder's neck prickled. Did she have contacts or was she bluffing?

She gave him a long, steady look before turning and stalking out.

He breathed out. He hadn't even needed Stefan's intervention to cut the interview short. So why did he feel as though he was the one who'd been dismissed?

He commed Stefan. "Is Pav Danniri in place?"

"Yes, sir."

"Good. Steer the Benjamin woman in the right direction. When Danniri has her safely confined I want to know more about Miss Benjamin—a lot more."

✦ ✦ ✦

Ricky checked his handpad, wafer-thin and grafted onto the back of his left hand. He'd been really proud to have it fitted on his tenth birthday, a proper grown-up model, but it was no help now. Still no comms signal. He suspected the room was shielded, otherwise they'd have ripped off his handpad, and that hurt. He'd done it accidentally once and it had bled like the very devil.

On the fourth day of captivity, just as he was getting used to a twice-daily food delivery by a silent guard, and had played Upstix and Braintease on his handpad way too many times, Ricky heard feet in the corridor outside. The door's lock mechanism whirred. The scary woman came in first and motioned for Ricky to stand over in the far corner, then an antigrav chair floated in, operated by a thickset man. In the chair, ashen and very still, was Nan.

Ricky started forward and the scary woman caught him around the shoulders.

"Nan! What have you done with her?" He'd heard his own voice rise childishly. He fought to lower it and sound less desperate, less petulant. If there was one thing Nan had taught him it was that childish demands usually failed to get him what he wanted.

"The old woman's been in the med bay."

"What's wrong with her?"

Silence.

"Please."

"Her life is not in danger."

"What's wrong with her?"

"Her leg is broken. We underestimated her physical capacity."

"But—"

Even from across the room Ricky could see that Nan's right leg was encased in a protective fracture sleeve with the telltale indicating that she'd already had two sessions of bone regeneration. Her damaged leg stuck out stiff, supported by an extension of the float chair. She didn't really focus on anything in the room, just stared straight ahead with a blank expression that was so unlike her that Ricky, who had been scared enough before, felt the bottom fall out of his world. Nan was the rock that anchored their family when Dad's moods swung between sour and mellow.

He'd never seen Nan helpless before.

The thickset guard lifted her from the chair and deposited her on the freestanding bed, then unlocked and pulled down a narrow bunk from the wall, which took up almost half of the remaining floor space. "This is yours, now, kid."

Ricky ignored the furniture. "What have you done to her?" He tried to keep his voice strong and level but it wobbled right when he didn't want it to.

"Fixed her leg," the scary woman said.

"What's going to happen to us?"

"Same thing that usually happens to criminals."

"We're not criminals!"

"Helping Ben Benjamin commit murder. That's a criminal offense."

"It's not . . . We didn't . . ." *Shut up, Ricky, before you say something stupid. Deny everything.* "Uncle Ben's not a murderer."

He saw the look in the woman's eye and shut up.

When they'd gone, Ricky turned to his great-grandmother. "Nan?"

She continued to stare at the ceiling.

"Nan?" He touched her shoulder lightly.

No reaction.

"Nan?" He shook her with a little more determination.

Nothing.

Again. Nothing. More shaking.

"You wake up, now. I need you."

He heard himself shouting and realized he was gripping her shoulder too hard and shaking her. What was he doing? He stepped back, balled his fists, and took a deep breath.

"Okay, Nan. It's okay." This time he patted her shoulder gently. "I'll think of something. I'll get us out of here. Don't worry."

He looked around the room. What resources did he have? What would Uncle Ben do?

❖　❖　❖

Stefan hadn't been able to find a thing on Louisa Benjamin. Crowder almost fired the young man on the spot, but assistants with discretion weren't easy to find. Sure that he could do better himself, and that Stefan would be abjectly apologetic when he did, Crowder accessed the link and found . . . nothing.

Nothing more than her basic identity, that is: name and address, the will left by Ben's parents, deeds to the farm, and her date of birth, which surprised him because she didn't look anywhere near her age, but almost nothing else of any value. In these days of information overload to have a record that was so devoid of detail and nuance was almost unheard of.

Maybe she did have connections.

He'd assumed she was bluffing, but what if she wasn't?

Oh, hell, there were two alternatives. She'd either paid a

lot of money or had a lot of influence to have her identity scraped from public view, or she'd never been anywhere, done anything, or met anybody important in her whole life. She was a farmer living off the grid.

Which was the most likely?

He began to smile.

He wasn't in the habit of waging war on old ladies, but Louisa Benjamin was fair game. Ben had never offered much detail, but it was pretty obvious that he loved his Nan. Why sit around waiting for Ben to pay him an unauthorized visit? Why not take the initiative? His grandmother and nephew would be the perfect bait for a trap.

Crowder heard voices in the outer office.

"Come in, Danniri," he called, still finding it rather odd to be using the name of his onetime bodyguard who had died trying to take down Benjamin.

Crowder tried not to stare at Pav Danniri. She looked so much like her dead brother that it was uncanny. He had wondered whether using her to capture and guard Louisa Benjamin was a good move, since she harbored such a grudge against Benjamin himself, but she'd been completely cool and professional with both the boy and the grandmother.

Crowder waved her in. "You've done well."

Pav scowled. "The old woman's broken leg was unfortunate, but it's responding to treatment."

"Hardly a major disaster given that her only role in this affair is as bait in a trap."

"Were you aware that she has a psi implant?"

"No." Had he misjudged Louisa Benjamin after all? "What's her specialty?"

"I don't know. I put her on reisercaine as soon as I realized, so between that and the pain meds she won't have been able to get a message out even if she's the strongest Psi-1 Telepath ever. I checked her handpad. Not much on it that I could find."

"What about the boy?"

"He's just a kid."

"Any psi abilities?"

"Too young."

Crowder smiled. Everything was under control.

✦ ✦ ✦

The first time he tried to escape, Ricky barely got twenty strides down the corridor before the thickset guard, Minnow, caught up with him and hauled him back. But escaping hadn't been the point. Getting to the bend in the corridor had been his objective, to see what was around it: an emergency staircase, leading both up and down; a grav shaft that may or may not be switched on. A comms device on the right-hand wall.

And now he also knew Minnow wasn't as slow as he looked.

With that information Ricky went happily back to the cell where Nan dozed the hours away, sometimes almost lucid and other times freshly doped and quiet.

The second escape attempt fared little better, but he got to see that the corridor in the opposite direction looked less promising. Long and featureless, it dead-ended in solid looking double doors. It wasn't Minnow he slipped past this time, but a wiry older chap whose name he didn't know. For this attempt he received a couple of hard slaps on the side of his head that left him reeling. He was lucky that it wasn't any worse than that. He hoped that meant they didn't take him seriously. With Nan still doped it was up to Ricky to get out and get help.

The scary woman, Danniri, had said they were in trouble with the law, but they hadn't allowed him to call Dad. He had some vague notion from old reality vids that anyone detained for any kind of suspected crime was allowed one call, whether a lawyer or a family member, but Danniri wasn't a Monitor or even part of Chenon's planetary police, she was Trust. Ricky wasn't sure whether the Trust had to play by the same rules.

Chapter Eleven

SETTLING

RION BENJAMIN PACED ACROSS THE KITCHEN, turned and paced back again. He glared at the pan, still half-full of an egg and paruna grain mixture he'd cooked, but couldn't face eating.

Two days.

He stepped out onto the balcony of their energy-efficient pit house. The dome of the inner atrium was open to the sky and gentle rain splashed down onto the tomato plants growing two floors below. He couldn't think in here, even with the fresh air filtering down from above.

He grabbed his work-worn jacket and took the steps up, two at a time, emerging into the barnyard where the brisk breeze funneled between the byre and the barn, spattering his face with raindrops. The sweet smell of the farmyard always steadied him.

Something was very wrong.

Nan had vanished just like Ricky. She'd left him strict instructions not to follow her to Arkhad whatever happened, but to send the message she'd stored on her machine. It was to her friend Lucy on Earth, a person with some influence, Nan said, but Rion knew no more than that. He'd done it, though.

Rion had called Kai, still on Tobar, Chenon's smallest moon.

"No, Dad, I've not had any contact with Ricky since the day he told me what he was planning. You need to get a message to Uncle Ben."

"Even presuming I can get hold of him, what can he do? If Crowder is using Nan and Ricky as bait he wants Ben to trade himself for their safety, and Ben is damn fool enough to do it. And there's no guarantee that Crowder would release your Nan and Ricky even if that happened."

"Uncle Ben could probably rescue them."

"Oh, sure. We don't even know where they are."

"Uncle Ben's got the resources. Psi-techs. Telepaths, Finders. Didn't he once rescue Crowder from pirates when he was in the Monitors?"

Rion resented Ben rather more than he should. He was still the exciting brother, and still young. Their age gap, a mere three years officially, had increased significantly with all the cryo Ben had done. What was the gap, now? Eighteen, no, nineteen years. Rion had gray hairs, a family, and the responsibility of running the farm. What responsibility did Ben have, roaming across the galaxy, here, there, and all over?

And this was all about one of Ben's scrapes. Nan had gone haring off to find Ricky. That should have been Rion's job, but Nan had been a negotiator. Her Empathy could tell her whether she was being fed a line of bullshit or not. It made more sense for her to go, but he felt impotent, stuck here at home, letting his grandmother attempt what he could not.

"This is the only time I wished I had an implant," Rion said. "If we could contact Ben or Cara direct . . ."

"I know, Dad. Didn't they give you any idea where they were?"

"No."

"Didn't Nan get copies of Uncle Ben's arrest warrant? Is there a clue in there?"

"She did. It's worth a try. Well done, Kai. Good thinking."

He had a whole heap of reading to do.

Four hours later he looked up from Nan's screen, bleary-eyed. He had a clue. Ben had apparently sold Olyanda's mining rights to Crossways, some kind of criminal organization. He looked up possibilities and found records of a space station that went rogue a century ago, supposedly the home of several criminal gangs. That sounded about right. How did a person go about getting a message to anyone on Crossways? When in doubt, ask.

Rion had never been fond of social networks. He kept in touch with other local farmers on farm-net, but that was all he had time for. Once more he called Kai.

"Have you ever heard of a space station called Crossways?"

"Rumors. Some folks say it's real, others say it's one of those tales that grows in the telling."

"Well, according to the warrant, one of the things Ben's accused of is selling the rights to mine platinum on Olyanda to criminals on Crossways. If Ben's not there, someone should know how to get a message to him. I don't know where to start, though."

"The university's net usually has good access to information. Let me ask a couple of contacts."

Rion felt relief wash through him. "I can leave it up to you?"

"I'll let you know how it goes."

As Rion reached to power Nan's screen down he noticed a message waiting from Lucy. He opened it. It simply said: *Investigating from this end. Stand by. Please keep me updated. There is already some concern about Trust activity.*

He responded: *Thank you. Trying to get a message to Ben Benjamin to apprise him of the situation. I believe he can be contacted via Crossways. Can you help?*

It would be at least a couple of days before he could hope for a response, but he'd done all he could do for now.

◆ ◆ ◆

Ben stared at the schematics for Blue Seven. The warehouse space had been neatly divided into accommodation, storage, work, and recreational space. Archie had managed to link directly to the external docking cradle on Crossways' upper deck and Max had arranged for secure connections to the banking hub. Marta had sourced kitchen equipment from a dubious restaurant that had gone out of business, and Ada Levenson, the formidable cook that none of them dared to cross, had declared it usable and set about cleaning and sterilizing it to provide food for the hungry workers, none of them so appreciative as Morton Tengue's mercs, now rebranded as Blue Seven Security.

All of Tengue's injured were out of danger now, though Fowler, the young woman Ben had carried through the air-borne attack, would need reconstructive surgery. Ronan planned to move her to his new med bay in Blue Seven so he could keep an eye on her personally.

Techs finished installing the matrix, and with the addition of the datacrystals Wenna had preserved from Oly-anda, the new offices, though still a little raw around the edges, became fully operational.

"I like it!" Max said as he polished an imaginary scuff off the surface of his new desk with his sleeve. "My own office right next to Wenna's. Do I get an assistant?"

"Do you need one?" Ben asked.

"I'm going to be in charge of company accounts. I shouldn't be the only one who knows where all our money is."

"Good point. Pick your own team, but have Ronan do a psych eval."

"He hasn't done one on me."

"Another good point. Does he need to?"

"No, I trained as a tax accountant. I'm always going to fail a psych eval." Max grinned.

✦   ✦   ✦

Ben may have been feeling more comfortable in Blue Seven, but Norton Garrick wasn't happy. And when the *de facto* head of Crossways wasn't happy, headaches cascaded down the chain of command like birdshit from a tree branch. Though he wasn't in the Crossways chain of command, the problem had landed at Ben's feet.

The good citizens of Crossways were protesting the temporary closure of their stadium while the Olyanda refugees were in residence.

Protesting loudly.

"You see my problem?" Garrick leaned over the balcony, which jutted out from an upper reception room of the Mansion House.

"I've got problems of my own," Ben said, glancing down at the throng of protesters. It said a lot for Garrick's style of governance that the gathering was not being dispersed with extreme prejudice.

"It should be the grapple quarterfinals next week and at the moment the game's on hold until we get those damned settlers out of there."

"You promised—"

"I know, that I would resettle them, but that man—"

Ben knew he was talking about Victor Lorient by the way Garrick's mouth tightened when he spoke.

"That man has turned down four perfectly suitable planets, so far. I'm running out of time. What more does he want?"

"He wants to be absolutely sure that there are no hidden platinum deposits, and he wants a planet that is completely independent of any of the megacorps."

"We've done a thorough survey of all of them. They'll support human life. They don't have any native sentient beasties above the level of a cockroach. There's no more platinum than there was on Earth—not on any of them. As for independence, that's up to him to turn away anyone who comes knocking, but we can hack the central systems of all the megacorps to show whichever planet they choose as uninhabitable."

"Have you explained all this to him?"

"I have, and I've offered him all the help he needs to set up."

"Well, then, what else can he possibly want?"

"He wants you."

"Huh?"

"He wants the set-up team he had on Olyanda."

"He hated us. He thought we were deliberately trying to make life difficult for him and never accepted genuine offers of help if he could do something the hard way. This is the man who thinks psi-techs can take over his mind and use him like a puppet."

"I know all that, but he says better the devil he knows. Will you at least talk to him?"

"I'll talk to him." Ben could feel himself being manipulated. "But if he wants me to find his missing settlers, I can't

go back to babysitting duties." He frowned. "Though ...
maybe there is a way."

✦ ✦ ✦

Cara sat with Ben, quietly sinking into the luxury of the
sofa, which adjusted beneath her for maximum comfort.
Conducting business in the Mansion House was all padding.
First drinks, then dinner, and only after good food and fine
wine had induced an air of relaxation and cordiality did
Garrick start to negotiate what surely must have been his
most pressing business.

"Here are the choices, Director Lorient." Norton Garrick dropped four slim folders onto the low table by Lorient's chair. "Robinet, Jamundi, Darwen, and Lexolan. Four
planets all guaranteed as close to platinum-free as can be.
Two of them are virgin, so they come with all the attendant
risks you were prepared to face on Olyanda. One is already
thinly populated, but there are unsettled continents and the
current incumbents would be happy to share. There are, of
course, no sentient or developing life-forms to endanger,
though the planets are by no means empty of life. Darwen
has some rather interesting flying herbivores and Lexolan
is nine-tenths ocean. Robinet's gravity is heavier than
Earth's, but not beyond human tolerances."

Garrick paused to top up Lorient's glass.

"In fact," he continued, "the folks on Lexolan would be
eager to welcome you as your goals match theirs in most
respects. They're New Amish and your back-to-basics phi-
losophy fits neatly with theirs."

Cara had drunk sparingly. Excess alcohol inhibited a psi-
tech's implant. Mother Ramona had taken Rena Lorient,
Jack Mario, and Saedi Sugrue to show them the garden so
that Garrick could have Victor's undivided attention. Cara
had all her powers of Empathy turned toward Victor, ready
to nudge him toward any of the possibilities he seemed interested in. They had to have a decision soon or Garrick
was going to have a meltdown, and his sports fans were
going to openly rebel.

Garrick cleared his throat. "Jamundi is interesting as
well. It was one of the early terraformed planets. Already
atmosphere and gravity compatible, it was successfully
seeded with Earth flora and fauna some two hundred years

ago. There was a brief attempt at colonization a hundred years ago, but the colony failed due to bad management and internal strife. It was one of the Shorre Company projects and its demise went unremarked while the Ramsay-Shorre Alliance was being negotiated."

Cara and Ben had studied all the possible planets. Any one of the four would make a good settlement site, but Jamundi's seeding would give them a head start. As soon as Victor chose they could swing into action and start moving the settlers to their permanent new home.

"What guarantees do we have?" Lorient asked.

"About what?" Garrick asked.

"That Alphacorp and the Trust will leave us alone this time."

"They won't know where you are," Ben said. "Mr. Garrick has specialists who'll wipe all records of your location from the star maps. If you pick one of the uninhabited planets your new home will show on all systems as a barren rock. If you go for the inhabited one, you'll simply be hidden by the people who are already there."

"Someone might find us."

"They might, but space is big. The chances of an accidental flyby are less than a speck of dust getting close enough to notice a single pea in a grapple arena."

Laughter trilled outside as the door to the Mansion House's reception room opened and Mother Ramona, resplendent in turquoise silk, led in her guests. Their conversation died away and Jack and Saedi uncoupled their entwined fingers as Victor turned toward them.

Jack and Saedi. Saedi and Jack. Theirs had been a good working relationship that had grown into something more without anyone suspecting, but a young psi-tech had died on Olyanda for the simple crime of loving a settler girl, and now Jack, Victor's chief administrator, and Saedi, the Psi-1 Telepath assigned to settler communications, had ceased to hide their affection. Victor might not like it, but here on Crossways he couldn't do anything about it. Jack, who had seemed to lack a backbone for much of their time on Olyanda, had now begun to grow one. It helped that Rena Lorient had championed their relationship, though Cara wondered whether that was because she approved or because she knew that her husband didn't. She suspected the latter.

"Have you decided?" Rena barely glanced at her husband as she walked over to the balcony window and gazed out with her back to him.

"One of them has a settlement already and the other two—well—I'm not sure they're safe. We should look further."

Cara bit back a comment. Ben huffed out a *here-we-go-again* kind of breath while Garrick and Mother Ramona exchanged a sidelong glance.

Victor looked up from one to the other. "You're mind-talking about me again, aren't you?"

"Actually," Cara said, "we're not. Mr. Garrick doesn't have an implant and it would be rude of us to exclude him, but you hardly need telepathy to guess what we're all thinking. Crossways station has extended enormous goodwill, but it's time to go now."

Rena turned and acknowledged Cara over her husband's head.

"Yes. It's time to go." She walked over and selected one file from the four on the table in front of Victor. "Jamundi. We'll take Jamundi. If Victor can't make up his mind, Mr. Garrick, I'll do it for him."

She looked across to Jack and Jack nodded back.

"But—" Victor leaned forward in his chair.

"These good people need us out of their hair. We've taken advantage of them for long enough. And our own people are ready to go. They're miserable and confused. They've been yanked out of the life they expected and dumped in a refugee camp with only what they could carry. They don't even really know why, but they'll listen to you and do what you ask. They've always listened to you. Now it's your turn to listen to them. Give them a new home. It's what they want."

"I . . ." Victor Lorient was, for once, at a loss for words. He sank back in the chair and massaged his forehead with his fingertips.

Jack stepped forward. "Commander Benjamin will provide a set-up team for us again."

"Not such a large team as last time," Ben said, "But they can stay for as long as you need them."

"Thank you," Rena said. "And this time we'll welcome them as part of our community for as long as they want, or need, to stay. We may have lost our planet, but the psi-techs turned their backs on their old lives, too. They protected us at the expense of their homes and jobs and families. If any of them need a home with us they can have it and they can bring their families, too."

Jack reached out and took Saedi's hand again. "And you should know, Director, that Saedi and I are together. That means she'll be staying on Jamundi permanently. If you have a problem with that, please say so now and I'll start looking for another job."

"But the whole point of leaving Earth was to found a new world on true Ecolibrian principles, leaving behind—" He paused and Cara thought for a second that he was going to say *abominations*, but he reined himself in. "Engineered and implanted humans."

"We'll get there, Director," Jack said. "It will take a generation longer than we expected, but since we'll have no facilities for testing youngsters for latent psi abilities or performing implant surgery, any psi-techs staying with us will be the last generation of their kind on our planet. Their children will grow up implant-free. *Our* children will grow up implant-free." He squeezed Saedi's hand and she blushed, but wisely said nothing.

Victor nodded. "I don't want to lose you, Jack. You're too good an administrator." He glanced at Saedi, but barely made eye contact. "Welcome to the fold, Miss Sugrue."

Cara realized she'd been holding her breath. Mother Ramona clapped her hands delightedly. "That's all settled, then. Good! Who wants another drink? I think it's time for a toast to Jamundi."

❖   ❖   ❖

"I thought we'd go to the farm today," Wes said as Kitty met him on the concourse outside Port 22.

"The farm?"

"I told you, I volunteer. I can't let a simple thing like glorious sex get in the way of teaching kids how to milk a cow."

"That's where you get all your practice!" She giggled and evaded his reaching arms, just beating him to a tub-cab as it pulled in. "Farm first, sex afterward."

"Now there's an offer I can't refuse." He laughed.

The journey took longer than Kitty expected because they had to change cabs at the major hub points. Crossways' transport system was a chaotic web of interconnecting tubes. They traveled hubward, but rather than going all the way to the spindle they changed at the main ring and transferred to a pod that took them halfway around the circumference of the station, past manufacturing units, warehouses, dockyards, upmarket shopping malls, less salubrious street markets, and residential pockets blossoming like villages with cafes and stores. Once they passed through a brightly lit strip.

"Casinos?" she asked Wes.

"Yeah, they belong to Lord Roxburgh."

"Lord Roxburgh?"

"Self-styled. Fancies himself. He's rolling in credits, though. Casinos, brothels, entertainment establishments."

"You mean strip joints."

"That's the least of it. Strippers of all ages and genders are just the floor show between the serious business of fights. Legal fights and probably illegal ones as well. Roxburgh is the only serious rival Garrick has. He's on the council. Some say the only reason Garrick is in power is because Roxburgh doesn't want to put the effort into governance."

"Sounds like a charmer."

"Steer well clear."

The tub-cab trundled on until they came to the next hub. From there, a moving walkway took them rimward once more.

"This is a really cranky section of the station," Wes said. "It's half of what used to be an O'Neill cylinder, part of an old station decommissioned when artificial gravity first became viable and O'Neill cylinders were rendered obsolete. It was brought here, repurposed and incorporated, and now has half a dozen levels of farmland, market gardens, and hydroponics, powered by indirect solar and also lit by mirror arrays."

"Did it come in sections?"

"They say it was fitted with one of the first jump drives and brought through the Folds by some maniac who didn't know it couldn't be done. It's a good story." He grinned. "I don't know if it's true. I like to think it might be."

Kitty frowned.

"What's up?"

"Jump drives aren't as easy as they tell you in flight school. I can take any ship you like, even an ark, through a jump gate, but I can't get the hang of *Solar Wind*. It's like I have a puzzle, but I can't make it fit together because there's a missing piece."

"In the *Solar Wind*?"

"No, in my head, or in my implant. Ben does it effortlessly. Even Gen Marling can do it and she's only a Psi-3 Navigator. Whatever she does, I should be able to do, but I can't."

"I thought jumpships were as rare as hen's teeth anyway."

"Yes, they are, but I know Ben was hoping I'd be able to fly *Solar Wind*. I think it's the only reason he kept me around after Olyanda. That and the fact that he's kind. Do you know how rare that is?" She reached for his hand and squeezed it. "You're kind, Wes Orton."

"No, I'm not. I'm a mean man who wants to keep you all for myself." He tugged on her hand, and as she turned toward him he kissed her.

She pressed against him and let herself get lost in the warmth of his lips until she felt dizzy. She put out her hand and her knuckles brushed the stationary side of the walkway.

"Steady." He laughed and caught her as she staggered.

"I like it when you're there to catch me."

"I'll always be there for you if you want me to be."

Did he mean that? How was she supposed to answer? Part of her wanted to say she did, but she wasn't free to do that. Instead of an answer, she kissed him again.

The walkway spit them out into a lobby with three layers of insect mesh curtains that they treated like an air lock, making sure each layer was secure behind them before moving on to the next.

"They have bugs in here," Wes said. "Valuable ones, and they don't want to lose them. They're all part of the ecosystem."

Once through the mesh they came out into a vast curving crescent of greenery, brightly lit.

"What is it?" Kitty asked.

"Hi-yield wheat."

"It goes on forever."

"Looks like it, doesn't it? We need to go up a level to the farm." Wes indicated an open elevator big enough to lift a hefty piece of machinery.

On the next level the scenery was different. The farm-yard was, as Wes had described it, a collection of animal sheds, a cattle byre, a horse barn, pig pens, and paddocks with goats and sheep. Chickens fluttered underfoot. A couple of dogs bounded up to them, but by the lack of barks and the way they greeted him they obviously knew Wes. He bent and scratched one behind the ears and the other on its back just above its tail.

"This is Moss. She's a bit head-shy, but scratch her just there and you'll be her friend for life. Domino, on the other hand, likes his ears rubbed gently."

"Hey, Wes!" A young woman with practical cloth trousers and shirt, her hair shoved under a battered cap and stout boots on her feet, came out of the horse barn. Under the cap her face was pretty, if you didn't count the smudge down one cheek.

"Hey, Lana, this is Kitty."

Introductions followed. Lana Grissom managed the farm and also administered the leases on the market gardens that began beyond the farm's own orchards and stretched around the crescent on this level. She had three full-time staff members and a large team of volunteers, all of whom she knew by name and capabilities.

"I wanted to give Kitty a taste of the great outdoors, Crossways style. Can we take a couple of the horses out?"

"Sure. Do you ride, Kitty?"

"I . . . not for a long time."

Lana turned to Wes. "Take Robin for Kitty, and Cordelia could do with some exercise if you don't mind."

"Thanks."

"We've got a bunch of kids from Yellow in later."

"We'll be back in time to help."

In the horse barn Kitty watched Wes tack up a quiet roan pony and a restless bay mare with a glossy coat. His movements were economical and the mare steadied under his gentle hands. *I know what that feels like*, she thought.

"Do you need a hand?" Wes led out Robin and handed the reins to Kitty.

"I can manage."

She scrambled aboard with more determination than grace as Wes brought out Cordelia and swung into the saddle. Their ride was surreal: through an orchard, along a track between market garden plots, and back by an open water course that drained the land and recycled the water into gentle rain that fell each night. How could such a thing be taking place on an artificial world hanging in space? But it was. No wonder Wes loved the farm so much. Logic said there was no room for such a thing on a space station, but Crossways was more than a station, it was a world in miniature.

They arrived back in the barnyard in time to deal with a party of awestruck kids from Yellow sector. Kitty helped by keeping an eye on them and making sure no one was left behind, but, peering over their heads, learned as much as they did. Wes answered every question, no matter how trivial. He'd make a good father, Kitty thought, and then found herself shocked that she'd arrived at that conclusion and was profoundly grateful that Wes didn't have an implant. She'd have been mortally embarrassed if he'd caught that thought.

On the way back to Wes' apartment they stopped at a booth for street food, spicy vat-meat kebabs in a lentil flour wrap with extra sauce, and a crisp apple big enough to share and with a price tag that made sharing the best option.

"There's a message," Wes said as he pushed open the door. He groaned. "I hope the captain hasn't swapped me on to the early shift tomorrow." He passed his handpad over the reader and a message popped up on the screen. A man's face appeared, frozen partway through a word. He wore medical whites.

"Is it for me?" Kitty pushed past him as Wes activated the message.

"Ms. Keely, I regret to tell you that your mother is no longer with us."

Kitty's heart began to pound and she reached for Wes' hand.

"I'm afraid I don't have a forwarding address. I believe she's been relocated to somewhere with a more benign climate than Shield City, but I thought you should know that her treatment was entirely successful. We discharged her on the 18th November. She left us a well woman. That's all I can tell you, I'm afraid."

"Oh." Kitty sat down suddenly and began to laugh, while wiping tears from her cheeks.

"That's wonderful," she said to the image on the screen as if he could hear her. *Thank you, Alphacorp.*

Chapter Twelve

WHITE KNIGHT

BEN HAD ALREADY PUT IN THREE EIGHTEEN-hour days to organize transfer of the settlers from Crossways to Jamundi before he got the message that Serafin was allowed visitors, though only on condition that their stay was short. He dropped everything, hopped into one of the multihued tubs that had taken to waiting for fares outside Blue Seven, and headed for Dockside Medical with only one guard for company. He dreaded what he might find, but was much relieved when Serafin greeted him with a husky, "About time. You look like shit!"

"You're a fine one to talk."

"I'm allowed to look like shit. They tell me I died twice and they had to take out half my left lung."

"Okay, I revise that. You look pretty good for a corpse."

"Thank you."

Ben sat down where Serafin could see him without twisting his head too far. "How are you feeling?"

"Fine. Better than fine. But it's all down to the drugs. I'm guessing that underneath it all I feel like I died twice, but my brain isn't getting the message. Did you get the bastards?"

"All accounted for. When it turned out that the prisoners

didn't know anything, they had unfortunate accidents in an air lock."

"You spaced them?"

"Not me. I can't fault Garrick's efficiency, but I hope none of ours ever gets on his bad side. He said he had a point to make."

"Can't say I'm sorry."

"Me neither, but on the whole I tend to favor the fair trial method of dealing with criminals, even ones who've tried to murder me and mine. Summary executions and accidents when everyone is looking the wrong way don't sit right with me—even though I've occasionally taken the expedient way out." He didn't elaborate. Better change the subject. "What's the prognosis? How long will you be in here?"

"Long enough. Lungs are all to hell. Looks like I'll need new ones once I'm fit enough for the transplant. They're growing them for me now. Truth to tell, I'm thinking it's time to retire. Suzi's been telling me so for long enough. We might just settle down and find a quiet corner on some remote colony; build a house, grow cabbages."

A gaping hole opened up in front of Ben. The old man was always talking about retiring, but he'd kept putting it off. Just one more job, he'd said. Just one more. And now it looked like this might really be it.

"What am I going to do without you?"

"Work the bollocks of Archie Tatum instead." Serafin's laugh turned into a cough that brought a nurse to the doorway. "It's okay." He waved the young man away. "I'm all right, no need to fuss."

"Seriously, Serafin, the Olyanda mission ate section heads for breakfast. Now you, and Suzi, too. What am I doing wrong?"

"Nothing, except perhaps not rolling with the punches. You take too much on yourself. You can't take responsibility for everything that goes wrong. We all knew the risks when we signed up. It's time you stopped carrying the dead around with you."

"That's what Cara says."

"Then listen to her, man. Besides, you don't want us old folk slowing you down, especially not now that you need to keep one jump ahead of the Trust and Alphacorp. It's time to let the youngsters shine."

"I could do with your experience behind me right now. We're living on credit until Olyanda produces the first platinum. We're taking a chance on hiring the mercenaries van Blaiden used against us on Olyanda. We're no closer to finding the missing settlers. Crowder's hidden himself behind a double security screen operated by the Trust and the Monitors, in particular by a slippery bastard called Sergei Alexandrov who's been brought in precisely because he has a grudge against me."

"Is that all?"

"Isn't it enough?" Ben sat back in his chair. "Ah, you're right. I suppose it's not all bad news. There's a woman here called Dido Kennedy who thinks she can manufacture jump drives that can be retrofitted to any spacecraft. Yan Gwenn's working with her and he says she might be on to something. Don't tell anyone but I think Yan's sweet on her." He smiled. "Lorient has finally agreed to a new planet, Jamundi, in the Penda System. Yeah, it's going to be a hassle getting the settlers there, but it's sweet. Better real estate than Olyanda and no platinum to speak of. It's got a jump gate hub only eight days away for supply. I'm sending a smaller set-up team, though, because we need to split resources to find the missing settler ark. In fact I could sure do with Suzi to lead the agriculture team. If you're thinking about retiring, how do you fancy growing cabbages on Jamundi?"

Serafin's chuckle turned into another cough. "I'll think about it."

✦ ✦ ✦

Crowder had hated space travel ever since the Londrissi hijack. He always insisted on a sedative for the journey through the Folds, but he still felt as though his body had been turned inside out. His palms were damp, his mouth dry. He'd woken with the nagging worry that unremembered dreams had snagged in the dark corners of his consciousness and were waiting for an unguarded moment to manifest.

It was possible to attend board meetings via a high-speed holo-link—the signal routed through three jump gates and the time lag was barely five seconds—but as the newly proposed member of the board he really needed to make the effort to be there in person. Despite the Olyanda fuck-up, he'd earned enough kudos from getting control of Hera-3's platinum to warrant the invitation.

He'd landed at King Shaka Spaceport, in KwaZulu Natal, north of the tourist city of Durban. He'd left Stefan with a watching brief to let him know of any developments on the Benjamin front, and since he'd just seen the most recent colony mission launch, he had a few days' grace before he needed to think about the next one. His deputy could handle the pre-mission planning for the time being.

He needed to devote himself utterly to the business of board politics for the next few days. He had plans once his seat was secure—and those plans involved making an impact quickly and building up his own faction.

He transferred to Mangosuthu in a maglev pod. The shining headquarters complex occupied the land where Umlazi Township had once stood, before the demise of the USA and China in the meteor strike, combined with the advantageous distribution of platinum, had left Africa ascendant in Earth's political arena.

Sifiso Kweyama, his designated personal assistant, met him at the door with a schedule as a bot took his luggage to his suite. There was much lobbying to be done if he was going to work his way up and eventually oust John Hunt from the position of CEO. Hunt was a formidable opponent, but though his age had been wiped from the records sometime around his second or third rejuv treatment, he had to be pushing ninety-eight at least. It wasn't his age that Crowder took issue with, but his leftward political leanings. For some time he'd been in the pocket of the European prime minister, Vetta Babajack, and some of the decisions he'd made had been to Babajack's advantage over the Trust's. Rushing the Ecolibrians off Earth before a particularly finely balanced election had been inexplicable unless you knew of Hunt's connection to Babajack.

That had meant rushing the Olyanda planetary survey to speed up the exodus, which resulted in the Trust missing one of the biggest platinum finds ever.

"And look where that got us," Crowder muttered to himself as he rose in the antigrav tube.

"Sorry, sir?" Kweyama said, floating by his side.

"Nothing, just talking to myself. Has Ms. LeBon left any messages for me?"

Tori LeBon would support him, for a consideration of course. She was as good as her word as long as he delivered on his promises. Isaac Whittle was on his side; he owed Crowder a favor, having been tipped off to buy Hera-3 shares at rock bottom prices before the platinum news broke. He'd sold at a massive profit. Yolanda Chang would do whatever Tori told her to, and Adam Hyde always went with the majority. The problem, apart from Hunt himself, would be Beth Vanders, Sophie Wiseman, and Andile Zikhali. Vanders and Hunt had had a child together once upon a time and, though they might not be lovers now, had always retained an affection for each other that ran deep. Wiseman was a wild card, easily swayed by rhetoric and ruled by her heart. Zikhali was ruled by his head, cool and logical, and always looking at the bottom line.

Wiseman and Zikhali were the ones he needed to win over if he was going to eventually move Hunt out of the top job and himself into it.

Kweyama interrupted his thoughts. "Ms. LeBon said she'd see you in the Atrium at sixteen hundred for afternoon tea with Mr. Zikhali."

"Good, thank you."

And so it began.

✦ ✦ ✦

Cara recognized Ully's mental handshake.

What's up, Ully?

Mother Ramona asked me to pass on some news for Commander Benjamin.

He's going over loading manifests for Jamundi with Marta. Do you want me to patch you through?

No, just tell him that she got a report from one of her sources. Gabrius Crowder has been appointed to the Board of the Trust. He was proposed by Tori LeBon. That's all the information she has.

Tori LeBon? The name didn't mean anything to Cara but maybe Ben knew more.

Thanks, Ully.

Cara wandered through from the alcove where she'd

been helping herself to a cup of caff and found Ben in the open workspace that would eventually be divided up into smaller units. Ben sat at one side of a desk and Marta, a damp scarf wrapped around the delicate gill slits on the side of her neck, sat opposite. They had a holo-screen each and they were moving items from column to column, the loading weight totals changing with each move.

Both of them looked up when she entered.

"A snippet of news from Mother Ramona," Cara said. "That woman is well-connected. She must have people in every megacorp head office."

"I believe she does," Ben said. "To our advantage, I hope."

"Well, I don't know how advantageous this is, but I suppose it's best to know. Crowder's got himself a seat on the board."

"The hell he has." Ben's mouth tightened and he shook his head. "He always said he would, and I never doubted him for a minute, but if it means more power and influence for him it's bad news for us."

"He was proposed by Tori LeBon. That's not a name I know."

"She was head of the Trust's Research and Development unit in Pretoria," Marta said. "A bit of a whiz kid by all accounts. Followed her father onto the board when he bowed out due to ill health."

"I met her once, briefly," Ben said. "She came to Chenon to see what went on in Colony Operations. It was soon after Hera-3 and we were still waiting for the final hearing. She asked a lot of intelligent questions. She also spent a lot of time closeted with Crowder. She may be up to her elegant armpits in whatever Crowder is planning."

"Maybe the whole board is," Marta said.

"Could be. I just don't know anymore. I'm not stupid enough to think we can take on the whole Trust. Crowder's still my main target. Besides, if we could shake the Trust apart what would happen to their colonies? Not all of them are self-sustaining. A lot of people could get hurt. A shake-up would be good, but not a breakup."

How could you manage one without the other, Cara wondered.

✦ ✦ ✦

Kitty had angled to join the party heading toward the settlers' new planet, but all the available space had been taken up by the advance team of psi-techs and the core group of settlers, the decision makers. She'd heard the planet's name mentioned several times, but Jamundi wasn't on any of the star charts. When Remus contacted her early in the morning the day after *Solar Wind* had departed, fully laden, she had to admit that she didn't know where the Olyanda settlers were going.

How can you not know? You're a Navigator, Remus said.

That's right, a Navigator, not a psychic. Look, Remus, I'm doing my best, but I don't get included in everything that happens around here.

Ms. Yamada wonders if your best is good enough. You haven't been able to get the platinum production figures for Olyanda. You don't know where the settlers are going. What else are you missing?

There's nothing to miss. The station heads, Garrick and Mother Ramona, are unhappy about the blockade, but shortages haven't begun to bite yet, so there's no general unrest. Serafin West is out of danger and likely to recover slowly. The psi-techs are busy building. Benjamin and Carlinni heard the news that Mr. Crowder had been appointed to the Trust's Board of Directors. There are no figures for platinum production on Olyanda yet because it's still too early. There is no production. It will take at least six months. I can't give you information that doesn't exist yet. There's a woman who thinks she can retrofit spacecraft with jump drives, but the word is that she's a crackpot.

Ms. Yamada asked you for the new IDs for the departing psi-techs.

I'm working on it.

Now that her mom was free of disease, how hard did Kitty have to try to please Ms. Yamada?

Remus, where's my mom? I want to know how she is.

All in good time.

The time's good now. I messaged the clinic. They said the treatment has been successful, but Alphacorp has moved her to somewhere with a better climate than Shield City.

Oh yes, much better.

I want to message her, hear her voice, see for myself how well she is.

When Ms. Yamada has her information. The platinum figures, the whereabouts of the settlers, the new identities of the departing psi-techs. In the meantime take my word for it that your mother is being very well looked after. She has the best of everything. Of course, she hasn't had the bill yet.

Bill?

Her accommodation is very luxurious.

Kitty's heart began to pound. Her mother, formerly a data clerk, had been living on a very small welfare payment since her illness began. Her reserves were gone.

Does she know . . . that you're going to bill her for everything?

Not yet, and she need never know as long as Ms. Yamada feels as though she's getting value for money.

I see.

Yes, I think that you do.

◆ ◆ ◆

Cara stared at the forward screen. Rena Lorient had chosen well. Jamundi hung before them, bathed in light from its yellow sun. Blue-green with intermittent cloud cover, it looked as close to Earth as any planet might be. Its second moon, an irregular rock barely big enough to be worthy of its status, orbited between them and the planet, leaving a small eclipse shadow on cloud and land alike.

Because they had to route through independent gates, the journey time from Crossways for the massive superliners was a month, but Rena, Jack, Saedi, and fifteen settler volunteers were on board the *Solar Wind* as an advance party, together with a small group of psi-techs led by Gupta. Cara had suggested Mel Hoffner as Gupta's second. She was the young medic who had proved so capable at dealing with the settlers back on Crossways. Ben had added four resourceful Psi-Mechs and several crates of bots, a botanist, an exozoologist, a surveyor, and two agronomists to the team, including Suzi Ruka, who had said if she was going to retire and grow cabbages she might as well plant them on Jamundi. Serafin would follow as soon as he was well enough. Suzi had seniority over both Gupta and Hoffner, but she said she didn't want the headache of administration and would much rather just do her job.

It had taken only days to mobilize ten thousand settlers, but considerably longer to arrange for basic agricultural equipment, tools, temporary shelters, seeds, and provisions. Horses, cattle and sheep, chickens, pigs, and goats were more difficult to source with the quarantine still in force.

Marta, based in the organized chaos of Blue Seven, was still hunting down supplies as the superliners departed Crossways. Before they'd reached the first jump gate she had found five independent colonies willing and eager to sell surplus stock at the right price and contracted a commercial fleet to ship them, making sure the animals were well-sedated in the Folds.

Cara received the good news as Ben put the *Solar Wind* into orbit around Jamundi and set the long-range scanners working.

"It's beautiful," Rena Lorient whispered as she gazed at the planet from space.

Jamundi's axial tilt gave it slightly more seasonal variety than Earth, but as it was springtime on the vast southern continent, Ben settled the *Solar Wind* on the edge of a broad river valley that had been the site of the original colony. Fast-growing sycamores had invaded the remains of stone buildings from the long-abandoned earlier settlement, but there were cut stones available to be reused once the Psi-Mechs and their bots had cleared the site.

After mistakes made on Earth—even at the height of the Great Colony Grab, humankind's first and fastest expansion into the galaxy—all the megacorporations and the independent settlers had upheld the Chenon Accord, which stated that no more than thirty percent of the land surface of any planet could be taken for settlement and the remaining seventy percent must be protected as a natural reserve. But Jamundi had originally been semibarren and any native growth had long ago been overtaken by the vigorous imported flora.

Fauna, too. A herd of bovines, descended from Earth stock, spooked by *Solar Wind*'s approach, stampeded across the rolling grassland beyond the thick swath of trees that crowded along the river bank.

As the ramp lowered, Cara took her first breath of plan-etside air and looked out onto a virgin vista: tall trees to one side of the ship and rolling grassland to the other, if indeed it was all grass, since it was intermingled with blue-green growth exhibiting soft fronds. She sighed. It would end up being called grass since that was the nearest equivalent. That was the way it always happened. Humans always brought familiar names into unfamiliar landscapes. It made it feel more like home. In the far distance a range of hills rose to the horizon.

She smiled at Rena Lorient and stepped back. "It's your planet. Want the honor of being first down the ramp?"

"Should I? Is it safe?" Rena asked.

"We're right behind you," Ben said. "Besides, the colony that failed didn't do so because of the planet. They found it mostly benign—at least, no more dangerous than Earth."

"So only earthquakes, volcanoes, super storms, floods, blizzards, and wildlife to worry about?"

"You forgot landslides, quicksand, poisonous plants, and drought."

Rena laughed. "So I did." She walked down the ramp with a light, firm step and jumped the last stride, planting both feet in a puff of dust. "Jamundi, I claim you."

An insect the size of a small sparrow fluttered upward with a startled chitter and several more followed it. They circled once and flew away.

Rena stepped back.

"Not dangerous." Kayla Mundy, their exozoologist, was already tapping something into her handpad. "They're on the survey. Prey on a leaf-eating grub, so probably going to be the farmer's friend."

"Well . . ." Rena gathered herself together. "I guess we'll get used to them." She looked at Ben and Cara, who'd flanked her, and at the rest of the settlers and psi-techs on the ramp. "I'm going to make you all a promise. We made mistakes on Olyanda and I'm sorry for it. We'll probably make mistakes on Jamundi, too, but they won't be the same ones. We were too ready to think of ourselves as different from psi-techs, but we're all people and we should all treat each other with respect."

Jack Mario started to applaud and everyone caught his mood and joined in.

"What about the Director?" one of the settlers asked.

"Leave him to me," Rena said.

"And me." Jack Mario stepped forward, still holding Saedi's hand.

Cara glanced sideways at Ben and saw that he looked satisfied.

Were you expecting this? she asked.

I was hoping.

◆ ◆ ◆

It had been five days on Jamundi, and nothing and no one had tried to kill them yet. Things were getting better. Cara had almost begun to relax. Of course it might all dissolve to shit when Lorient arrived, but so far, so good.

They set up a base camp for the newly arrived settlers, erected perimeter beacons, surveyed the surrounding area and agreed on a plan for the first year with Jack and Rena.

Suzi set about taking soil samples in the river valley and Kayla went with her, examining anything that crawled, ran, wriggled, or flew. The settlers started to erect temporary shelters using an old method of pumped quickset over an inflatable frame. The inflatables provided an interior lining and the quickset slurry added strength and durability and had the advantage of using local materials, mostly dirt, with a powdered catalyst.

Cara thought Ben began to relax a little, too. He hadn't been sleeping well, but he wouldn't open up to her. She figured that was down to a number of things. He seemed to want to keep her around, or said he did, but she'd brought him nothing but trouble, or, at least, compounded the trouble he had already. She'd put him in the position of having to kill van Blaiden. Admittedly it was self-defense, but Ben wasn't a natural born killer. He couldn't just take someone down in cold blood and shrug it off. Maybe it was different if someone was shooting back, but van Blaiden had been unarmed, even if his guards hadn't been.

Apparently she could kill and forget, and though she didn't like herself for it, at least she still slept at night. She knew that some of Ben's nightmares involved van Blaiden. But it was more than that.

Before they met he'd survived a pirate attack on Hera-3 which had killed three-quarters of his team and a few thousand settlers. That he'd rescued fifteen hundred settlers and brought them out against near impossible odds didn't seem to count.

And then, before working for the Trust, he'd been in the Monitors, out on the Rim. Millions of klicks of blackness with too few personnel policing too many far-flung settlements, mining operations, and resupply hubs. He never talked about that, though Marta had known him then and said he did three tours despite the fact that most Monitors burned out after one. He'd once said that the bad guys didn't always wear black hats and she knew he'd had a run-in with at least one of his seniors, as evidenced by the recent altercation with Sergei Alexandrov and the Monitor ship.

Stress could be cumulative. Hell, enough stress could affect even the strongest person, and Ben was strong.

Now he was planning to search for the missing settlers without any personal recovery time and if that meant a run-in with Crowder, then so be it. In fact she suspected he would find a way to confront Crowder to resolve the unfinished business from Hera-3.

She counted the days on Jamundi as a holiday with nothing but straightforward, practical tasks.

And then the message came.

They'd spent a long day marking out blocks for the new town plan and were walking back to the *Solar Wind*, shoulder to shoulder. For a moment she'd considered reaching out for his hand. Though they still fell into bed together, exhausted, they'd not crashed through the sex barrier, and he might take hand holding as a sign.

She was just working out whether she intended it to be a sign or not when she felt the mental handshake that announced Cas Ritson's presence in her head. Cas was the other Psi-1 Telepath in the Free Company, solidly dependable.

Hey, Cas, everything all right?

No more assassins, if that's what you mean.

Serafin?

Recovering as expected.

*Then . . . *

Message for Ben. Kind of an odd one.

Odd in what way? Cara had brought Ben in on the conversation and he frowned at the word, odd.

It came in on an old ident code via S-MAIL on a public channel. Mother Ramona picked it up. Said it took a couple of days for one of her people to wonder if it was significant and pass it on, but then they had a second message from— believe it or not—the president of African Unity on Earth, and it tallied with the first one.

Go on, Ben said.

A message from Rion Benjamin. Your brother Ben?

Ben stopped walking.

Yes.

All it said was: Nan and Ricky are missing. Crowder has them.

Shit!

Ben clamped down on anything else he might have said and withdrew from the triad. Cara watched him intently, feeling mixed fear and anger coming off him in waves as his jaw clenched.

She'd only met Nan once, but she knew how much his formidable grandmother meant to Ben, and his nephew was only—she calculated quickly—eleven years old.

"I should have pulled them out of there. Should have known Crowder would try and use my family."

"You warned them."

"I should have insisted they all move to somewhere safe—though whether Nan could have pried Rion away from the farm is debatable. My brother can be—stubborn." He ran his fingers through his hair, just starting to regrow after being shaved down to stubble. "Damn! I wanted to keep them out of it."

Ben, Cara? Cas was concerned.

It's okay, Cas, we're still here, Cara said. *Was there anything else in that message?*

No. It was sent three days ago, though.

Thanks, Cas, we'll take it from here, Ben said.

Cara wasn't a slow walker, but she had to put in little hops and skips to keep up with Ben. He said nothing, but one look at his face told Cara everything she needed to know.

"First things first," she said, slightly out of breath as she labored to keep up and talk at the same time. "I'll try to contact Nan for you."

"Makes sense. Now?"

She nodded. Ben's brother was a complete deadhead. Cara hadn't met him, but the impression she got from Ben was anything but favorable. They didn't seem to have much common ground, though Ben adored his nephews. Cara had met Ricky once, a bright boy with hints of undeveloped psi potential. He was still too young for an implant.

They stopped on the crest of the hill above the camp. In the distance *Solar Wind* hunched behind newly constructed risers, waiting for the influx of settlers. All around them the air was silent, not an insect call to be heard, which was unusual, since the bird-sized grub-eaters were rarely quiet and there was a type of burrowing beetle that rattled its ninth pair of legs against its carapace for echolocation whenever it surfaced.

Cara checked for crawling things and then sat down on a rock. "Anchor me." She held out a hand, thumb uppermost, and he grasped it firmly. It wasn't at all the same kind of handclasp she'd been contemplating just a few minutes before. This was all business. As the two of them stilled, the insects broke into a cacophony of warbles and clicks.

She called up an image of Nan: elderly, but not weak; forceful, sometimes irascible, sometimes loving, always practical. Cara had liked Nan immensely on their first and only meeting.

She aimed a thought toward Chenon, seeking out just one mind out of hundreds of planet-bound psi-techs. She sensed a flicker of something familiar and thought she'd found Nan. It was the right pattern, but the mind was weak and confused, not at all how she recalled Ben's grandmother. She thought at first that she'd found the old lady sound asleep, but then realized she couldn't wake her.

"What's wrong?" Ben asked as Cara disengaged.

"She's sick, or drugged. Drugged I think. I got no clear focus."

Ben swore. "Try again."

She did, with the same result.

Ben released his grip on her hand and she could hardly bring herself to look at him. "You're going to Chenon."

"Of course I'm going to Chenon."

"It's a trap."

"I know."

"I'm coming with you."

"No."

"You need a Telepath."

"I'll manage."

"And a team."

"I'm not dragging anyone else into this."

"We'll see about that." Cara skipped after him as he strode toward the *Solar Wind*.

Chapter Thirteen

INTO THE BLACK

THERE WAS NO WAY BEN WAS TAKING CARA, or anyone else, into a trap. They'd barely got out of the warehouse in one piece. Serafin might never recover fully. Max and Gen had almost been poisoned. Wenna might have lost an arm, if she hadn't already lost it on Hera-3, on his watch. Back on Olyanda he'd lost three of his team leaders. He had a piss-poor record for keeping those he cared about alive.

Trouble was, he knew any one of them would back his play if he called on them, and he knew that rescuing Nan might need a fully trained team. If he went in unprepared and undermanned he was likely to get himself killed without rescuing Nan and Ricky.

Though with him dead, Crowder had no reason to hold his family to ransom. It was almost a solution in itself.

"Are you even listening to me?" Cara snapped at him from the comms chair on *Solar Wind*'s flight deck.

"What? Yes, I'm listening. I'm just not agreeing."

"You'll get yourself killed and that won't help Nan and Ricky."

Had she been listening in to his thoughts? Probably not, she just knew him well enough by now to guess what he was thinking. He shrugged. "I'm still not taking you. Crowder knows your face. Knows you . . . mean something to me. You'd be his first target. Any of our psi-techs would be a target."

"Then take a team Crowder doesn't know. Take Tengue and Gwala and some of their people. They get paid for the rough stuff."

"I promised I wouldn't send them up against Alphacorp or the Trust."

"Crowder's not the Trust. He's gone rogue. The Trust just doesn't know it yet."

Ben set a course for Crossways, jumping into the Folds at the earliest opportunity and out at the latest to save flight time, popping back into the real world barely fifty clicks out from the station and earning an ear full of abuse from the traffic controller.

"Sorry, it won't happen again," he said into the vox as Cara glared at him.

"See that it doesn't," the controller said. "Me and the boys arranged a little party for the last hotshot who thought he could break the rules. He didn't walk so good after that. Makes us look bad, see, when ships collide. Space is kinda big, and Mr. Garrick figures it doesn't take too many brains to keep two ships apart, so if we get it wrong, we'll be busted to the maintenance bays, or worse. And there are some jobs on this station make the sanitation detail look glamorous."

"I get the picture."

"Good. Port 22 is open and waiting for you."

"Thank you, Control."

The crackle of static that followed sounded like a string of obscenities.

Ben nudged *Solar Wind* into the now-familiar Port 22 and docked, feeling the slight judder as she touched down and the docking clamps engaged.

Ben didn't need to meet Cara's gaze to know she was mad at him. Not that long ago she'd told him she needed some recovery time. Now he was offering it and she was mad at him.

"Can't win," he muttered.

"What?"

"Forget it."

Cara's face took on a momentary blankness, a dead give-away when she concentrated really hard on some difficult mind trick. In this case, he figured she was talking about him. Probably to Gen or Wenna. Damn, he wished he could tap in. He'd been at the back of the lineup when chance gave out Telepathy skills. He might be a Psi-1 Navigator, but he could barely throw a thought from here to the floor without another stronger Telepath to work through. Cara made it super easy for him, so easy he sometimes forgot that the skill was all hers. This time she kept him locked out. Conspiring.

Shit, he was getting as bad as Victor Lorient.

He powered down, completed *Solar Wind*'s final checks and sat staring at the blank forward screen. Cara didn't move.

He sighed. "All right, I give in. You're right, it's not a solo job. But volunteers only."

"Finally!"

"I get there in the end."

She stood up. "I'll go and see if Tengue is bored with babysitting Blue Seven."

"I need some thinking time. I'll catch up with you."

She dropped a light kiss on top of his head. "I like it that you're not afraid to change your mind, Ben Benjamin."

◆ ◆ ◆

"Volunteers only." Cara drew Gen to one side in Blue Seven. "Crowder's out for blood and knows Ben's coming. Even without Jussaro, Crowder knows Ben well enough."

Gen knew about Jussaro since Max had been having daily lessons. "Right now I've got to think about more than myself, so I'm not volunteering." Gen's belly was expanding rapidly, now a very obvious pregnancy. "And don't even think about asking Max."

"It hadn't crossed my mind."

"Liar!"

Cara shrugged. Max was a psi-tech Finder of lost things. Ben was going to need a good Finder if he was going to locate Nan and Ricky. A Psi-Mech would be an advantage, too, and a Telepath to keep everyone connected and working in gestalt.

"Come on, we can go over potential volunteers. I'll buy you a coffee," Gen said. "That new place across the way is doing great business, especially since the alternative is Ada Levenson's bland brew."

"Real coffee?"

"It had better be for the price they charge."

Leaving the bustle of the building site behind, Cara followed Gen outside, past Hilde, one of Tengue's Blue Seven Security guards, and across the footbridge that spanned the transport tub channel. Three taxi tubs lined up in the pull-in, waiting for customers.

"Looks like we've arrived on the Crossways map," Cara said. "The locals are already touting for business."

"Tengue's very thorough," Gen said. "He's vetted the companies and only two are allowed access to the bay."

"I'm liking him already."

Gen led the way into the busy little coffee shop, enterprisingly named Blue Mountain, and slipped into an empty booth. A real waitress followed them over and took their order. As she left, Cara activated the sound isolation baffle. The hum of conversation around them immediately stilled.

"Tengue's good at his job," Gen said. "But running security might be a little tame for him."

"Ben promised Tengue they wouldn't have to go up against the Trust or Alphacorp."

"Crowder stepped outside the limits of the Trust when he tried to kill us all on Olyanda."

"That's what I told Ben, but you know how stubborn he is. Thinks he has to protect the whole universe from harm. Counts every death as a debt he has to repay personally— as if it's his fault."

"Are you saying that it's bad that he values the lives of his team?"

"Of course not. Hell, we're both here, aren't we? But he carries the dead around with him, like links in some personally forged chain, and it's weighing him down."

Their coffee arrived and Gen flashed her credit chip. "And now it's his grandmother and his nephew in trouble, which makes it even more personal."

Cara sipped her coffee, strong and black with a layer of cream on top and tasting every bit as good as it smelled. "You think Tengue will be up for it?"

"You wait here. I'll send him across." Gen clipped a lid onto her coffee. "I'll take mine with me. You enjoy yours." She stood as if to leave and then turned back. "I would come if it wasn't for, you know." She patted her belly.

"I know."

Cara sipped her coffee and waited for Tengue, nodding to the big, bronzed merc as he paused in the doorway and checked out the room. It looked habitual, never stepping into a place until you were sure you'd be likely to walk out again unscathed.

"How do you do it?" Cara asked him as he sat down.

"Do what?"

"Spend so much time in a combat zone without ending up jumpy as all hell with your nerves frayed to pieces."

"How do you know what my nerves are like?"

"Empath."

"Ah."

"So?"

"Lack of imagination. I cultivate it. And I don't let myself get too close to anyone. Nothing personal. I look after my team like a good farmer looks after his prize dairy herd."

"Is that what they are to you, cattle?"

"That's what I tell myself."

"And does it work?"

"Mostly."

That would never work for Ben. People were always people to him, and he had imagination by the bucket-load. Cara moved on to the business at hand. "Word is that you find working security a bit tame."

"Is that what the word is?"

Cara raised her eyebrows.

"No one's taken a potshot at me in ... days." Tengue laughed. "Could be that I'm beginning to feel unloved."

"I can remedy that."

He smirked.

"Not in the love department," she put in hurriedly. "Ben's got a job to do and could use backup."

"And what would this job be?"

"An extraction. Old woman and a boy."

"From?"

"Chenon."

Tengue blew air past his teeth. "I didn't sign on to go up against the Trust."

"Crowder's gone rogue, he just hasn't told the Trust yet. What he's doing, holding Ben's grandmother and nephew, is illegal. He's got a squad of folks answering to him, but if the rest of the Trust found out he'd be answering questions faster than he could speak."

"It's still Trust heartland."

"Yes, it is. That's why Ben needs backup."

Tengue nodded thoughtfully. "Could be I might find you a few volunteers." He grinned.

◆ ◆ ◆

Ben dismissed the skeleton crew aboard *Solar Wind*.

"Do you need me for anything else tonight?" Yan asked, the last to leave. "Dobson's doing the post-flight check. Ship'll be ready in six hours, tops. In the meantime I've got a date with Dido Kennedy."

Ben smiled. "Dido Kennedy or her jump-drive project?"

Yan wiggled his hand. "Maybe a little of both."

"Good for you. I'll stay until Dobson arrives."

"I can be ready to leave for Chenon as soon as you give the word. Your family—"

"It's private business, Yan."

"You're not taking off alone, are you?"

Ben squashed down irritation and answered Yan with a shake of the head. "Volunteers only."

"This is me volunteering. You know there's a bunch of us only too happy to give Crowder a kicking if you just say the word."

"I know, thanks."

Ben raised the ramp and sealed the hatch behind Yan, then made his way to his cabin, yanked off his buddysuit and headed for the shower. He needed thinking time to plan the mission to Chenon.

What was the point in having a state-of-the-art jumpship if you didn't use it to its best advantage? *Solar Wind* couldn't dock at any one of Chenon's spaceports—she was probably on every watchlist in the galaxy—but Ben figured he could bring her out of foldspace in the lee of Tobar, Chenon's second moon, and then, in a snap, jump back through the Folds into the upper atmosphere above the southern continent and land at the farm. If he did it fast enough, a small blip on anyone's screen would vanish almost immediately and would be taken as an unverified anomaly.

Rion would snark, but he'd empty out the big barn to get

Solar Wind under cover. It would be good to see Rion again, if they could avoid bickering.

His team could catch a variety of regular flights to Arkhad city in ones and twos without raising suspicion. If there was one thing Mother Ramona excelled at it was forgery, so false idents weren't a problem, though they took time to set up properly.

Extracting Nan and Ricky was his primary objective, but if he got the opportunity to have a significant, and possibly terminal, conversation with Crowder about lost settlers, he'd take it.

Ben wasn't looking forward to convincing Rion that leaving Chenon was the best option. His brother was pigheaded. You could only do so much to persuade Rion if he didn't want to be persuaded. He'd made an art form of intransigence. The boys would be upset, too, Kai, at any rate, since he was close to the end of a university course. Ricky, not so much. The kid would love to see something of the galaxy, though he wouldn't want to leave his dad behind.

Think about that later. Getting Nan and Ricky away from Crowder safely was the first task.

Out of the shower he flicked on the external monitor in his cabin while he pulled on the bottom half of his buddy-suit and a singlet and sipped a cup of tea from the dispenser. Dobson should be here soon.

Something flickered on the edge of his screen. Not Dobson. Six figures in buddysuits wearing helms and breathers. They moved quickly with no wasted effort, reminding him of the Alphabet Gang who had originally stolen the *Solar Wind* with him, snatching it from Ari van Blaiden's private dock. Mother Ramona had employed them, had trusted them, and they'd done their job well and been paid well for it. Six thieves he'd known briefly as Bravo, Delta, Echo, Papa, Oscar, and Sierra. He counted the moving figures again. Six.

Oh shit! He raced for the *Solar Wind*'s flight deck, tea mug spilling behind him, forgotten.

◆ ◆ ◆

Ben felt the limpets engage, saw the intruders running for the exit, heard the klaxon that announced the bay doors opening and dock depressurization. He'd never make it out in time if he left the *Solar Wind*.

Four limpets.

Enough bang to take out the ship.

And the ship's drive had enough power to blow a hole in Crossways. This wasn't just about killing him, it was about asset denial.

If only he had more telepathic ability, but without Cara close by he was useless. He scrambled up the access tube to the flight deck and opened the comms on a general frequency.

"Emergency. Port 22. Clear the port. Seal all the internal blast doors." He dropped into the pilot's chair. "Get all your security teams to safety."

What's going on, Benjamin? Mother Ramona's Telepath, Ully, linked instantly.

Four limpets. I don't know how long we've got. Protect the station. Could be the Alphabet Gang, he told her.

Sealing the area. Sending a team to Port 22.

There was a pause and Mother Ramona cut in on Ully's link. *Bastards disabled guards and left them inside to chew on vacuum. I'll get their sorry asses for this, Benjamin. Suit up and get out of there.*

"No time," Ben muttered to himself. He had options, but none of them good. "Four options," he said out loud, but two of them were certain death.

Ben. Cara tried to connect and he pushed her away mentally. The drives were online now and he needed all his concentration.

Four: stay where he was, die with the *Solar Wind* and anyone inside the blast radius. Chance of survival: zero.

Ben!

Three: get out into space and as far away from Crossways as he could before the limpets blew. Save the station. Chance of survival: zero.

Ben!

Two: get out into space and set the *Solar Wind* on an automatic heading and try to hit an escape pod before she blew. Chance of survival: minimal.

Ben! Cara's urgent mental cry tore down his defenses. She sounded so close.

Where are you? he asked.

On my way to Port 22.

Get out. Get out of the sector. Behind blast doors. Go! Run!

They're going to repressurize the docking bay.

No.

Ben saw the outer jaws begin to close. He lifted *Solar Wind* on her antigravs, praying that the limpets were on a timer, not docked to his drive ports. He engaged and shot forward.

One: hit foldspace immediately and hope to hell the laws of physics didn't follow him in. Chance of survival? Who the hell knew!

With a rush, the Folds took him.

◆ ◆ ◆

Humans shouldn't be here. The black is unfathomable. Beyond comprehension. How can flesh and blood pass through every point in space and time at once—and live? Foldspace is infinite, as the universe is infinite, yet small enough to vanish inside a single neuron in the human brain.

It's not real, Ben tells himself as a creature swims through the flight deck—one that he fervently hoped he would never see again. Pilot-Navigators, when they're drunk enough, talk about dragons in the depths of foldspace, void dragons. According to the training manuals they are nothing but figments of the imagination, but it's difficult to remember that when faced with one.

The creature is huge, its head as big as a man. It's like a cross between a lizard and a giant sea horse with a beard, prehensile strands with claws on the end that move as if sentient. Part scales, part leathery hide, it does have a color, but he's not sure whether he can describe it in words that relate to the spectrum he knows. Iridescent would be the closest. It has a long, snake-like body coiled into the center of the flight deck, wings furled.

In its own way it's beautiful, but utterly terrifying, not because of any threatening behavior, but purely because it shouldn't exist, but somehow it does. Any creature that lives in this void between realities should, logically, be completely alien, beyond understanding, yet here is a creature from Earth's mythical past. Logic tells him that this cannot be. The only way a void creature could own this shape is if it's stolen the image from humankind, and if that's the case he doesn't want to think how.

Even as he rejects the idea, he wonders what really happens to the ships lost in foldspace with their human cargoes. His insides turn to liquid and he wants to throw up.

The void dragon turns toward him as if it's noticed him for the first time and he quickly looks away, his heart pounding, breath coming in rapid gasps.

Calm down.

Nothing is real in the Folds unless belief makes it so.

The limpets, they are real or they will be when . . .

He tries to stop thinking about them. They are not real. They are not going to blow. They are not!

He closes his eyes and remembers the muffled clang-thud as they attached to the outer hull. He can track their position by those sounds. The hull is real, the sound is real, but the limpets aren't. What limpets? No limpets here. Nothing to see. Move along.

He releases his harness and stands quickly, shooting upward.

No bloody gravity! Great. Just what he needs.

And then because he's forgotten to believe the *Solar Wind* is real for a moment, he drifts up through the deck plating, through the insulation cavity and breaches the outer hull into the vacuum of space.

Unprotected.

Thirty seconds? A minute? Two minutes, maximum.

That's all he's got, if he's lucky.

Ten seconds before the saliva on his tongue starts to boil. Fifteen seconds to unconsciousness. After that nothing matters. No one is out here to snatch him back.

Fifteen seconds. That's all he's got.

His instinct is to hold his breath but he has to breathe out to protect his lungs.

He pushes panic away and scrambles for a handhold, suddenly believing intensely in the reality of the *Solar Wind*. She rewards him by crushing his left wrist in solid plating. He gasps and tries to drag free, but she holds him in her bone-grinding grip.

Why isn't he dead yet?

Is there air? No, of course not, that's ridiculous.

His lungs begin to ache.

Yes, yes. Of course there's air. Air and pressure and warmth. A little pocket of atmosphere around him. Believe it.

He inhales.

There's air.

He sees movement out of the corner of his eye. He turns in slow motion, still caught by the wrist, still in zero gravity.

The void dragon—the bloody enormous void dragon—rushes toward him, scaled and clawed, eyes bright as hot coals. It unhinges its lower jaw, belches flames and roars.

Of course it does, it's a dragon.

His heart stops.

This is not the way he planned to die.

Then . . .

Two things. How can he hear a dragon roar in space? And what are those flames feeding on in a vacuum?

No!

He doesn't believe in fire.

The dragon snaps its jaws shut on nothing and looks puzzled. Such a human look on an alien creature emboldens him. Nothing is as it seems.

Ben believes his left hand is free, so it is, though it still damn well hurts. He pushes off the outer hull of the *Solar Wind* and believes with heart and soul that he will grasp the dragon's neck between the jutting spines.

His fingers touch scales, warm, liquid metal. Alive. Sentient.

There, got it. Now, fly, my friend.

I believe you can fly.

It twists in a leisurely manner, a helical dance. Ben hangs on, weightless, and rolls with it, getting a good view of the underside of the *Solar Wind*. He's going to believe that the hull is solid, but until he's close enough to kiss them, the limpets are no more than pimples, teats on the underbelly of the mother ship.

The void dragon unfolds great ribbed wings that creak like old leather. They beat down with a snap. He doesn't let himself wonder how wings work in space, he just believes that they will. It flies him to the first limpet. He reaches out. As his fingers touch the device he believes in its reality, disengages it, snaps on the safety and hurls it away.

It speeds along its trajectory, diminishing in size and threat.

The dragon waits for him.

He deals with the second limpet, and the third in similar manner.

As the third one speeds away he wonders how far his belief can affect this strange place. He concentrates on the receding limpet until it's a tiny dot in the distance and then he reimagines its existence. The safety is off. Its interrupted countdown resumes. It explodes, a brief, silent flare as the available molecules consume themselves in a vacuum.

This is too easy, the void dragon is too compliant. This should never be working. He starts to wonder what might go wrong.

The backlash of the blast hits him. He's ripped from the void dragon as it fragments into a cloud of shards, each with the velocity of a bullet. All he can think is how beautiful it is as it envelops him.

It's beyond pain.

Meat, bone, blood. He's reduced to his component parts.

And when his body is no more, only his mind is left. He sees a network of neurons and synapses, glittering like a helmet that he's worn all his adult life, but on the inside.

A sinuous shape glides through what's left of him. Void dragon. How can he see it without eyes?

How can he still be conscious? Is this how death works? He's always believed that death is the long dark nothing. . . .

Belief.

He's stopped believing.

He must believe again.

Rebuild himself.

Meat, bone, blood into skeleton, organs, muscle, and skin. He tries to think how a man is made, but his knowledge of anatomy isn't up to the task. Besides, there's more to a man than his component parts. Can he reconstruct every blood vessel, every organ? Dammit, he doesn't even know how the bones in his wrist fit together. Though he knows how much they can hurt when they are smashed.

His left wrist begins to ache where the *Solar Wind* held it in her not-so-tender embrace.

Hurts. ▪

Good. Fasten onto the pain, that sense of a wrist and use it to build on. Wrist, hand, fingers, handpad—as much a part of him as his own flesh and blood. Forearm, elbow, upper arm, shoulder . . .

It takes an eternity.

It's done in a flash.

He's complete again.

A glittering neural net floats beside him for a moment. The void dragon noses it, seems to inhale and it's gone.

No matter.

He does an elegant backflip, glides to the last limpet, releases it from the hull, and hurls it away.

Success.

For a moment he thinks how unlikely this all is. Hard vacuum rushes in on him again. Moisture on his bare arms evaporates. He blinks. Ice on his eyeballs crackles. He has fifteen seconds before he passes out. The plating is solid to the touch. He can't imagine it soft enough to move through. He lets air dribble out of his lungs and tries not to suck on the searing nothingness.

Hatch. Emergency hatch.

Dizziness threatens to overwhelm him. His chest is one fierce ache.

He pulls himself hand over hand, but his left hand is barely functional. He yanks the release mechanism with his right. It springs. He tumbles inside. As darkness closes in he smacks the air lock control.

He comes to in a disordered heap on the air lock floor. Gravity drags him down, chokes him with his own weight. He rolls over sideways, throws up, and passes out again.

The next time he comes around he manages to reach the door release and he commando-crawls into the corridor dragging his left arm. The ship feels solid beneath him.

Keep believing it's solid.

Got to get the ship out of the Folds.

How long has it been?

Too long.

If he can't find his way out again, it's all been for nothing.

Slowly, slowly, he climbs up from the belly of the ship to the flight deck, through the cargo hold and crew quarters, past his own cabin and to the final shaft. No antigrav here, just a steep companionway halfway between a ladder and a stair. He wraps his good arm around the rail and pushes his feet onto the first tread.

He arrives at the top sweating and shaking, but manages to stagger to the pilot's chair and collapse into it. He powers up the jump drive and searches for a way home.

Home to Crossways.

The Folds are black, amorphous, ineffable. He can't see a way through. Is he so deep in that he'll never get out? He checks the time. No, that can't be right.

He sinks a little more deeply into the chair. Out is more important than where right now. But he can't see the way.

He's lost the line.

Lost the line . . .

Chapter Fourteen

LOST

CARA JUMPED UP, SPILLING COFFEE ACROSS the table into Tengue's lap.

"Attack on Port 22," she said unnecessarily. Tengue had received the news at the same time as her.

It would take ten minutes at least to get to Port 22 by tub-cab, but it was the only option. Cara reached out for Ully, Mother Ramona's Telepath.

Update on Port 22?

Ully brought Mother Ramona in on the conversation instantly.

Can you reach your security? Cara asked.

Negative, Mother Ramona said. *Assume they're down. Sending reinforcements.*

How long?

Minutes.

Cara called a general alert as she ran for the tubs. Tengue and Gwala and their squad had beaten her to the first available transport so it took at least another minute, though it felt like hours, for another tub to pull in for passengers. She leaped in, rocking it wildly. Ronan hit the seat next to hers, emergency pack in hand, and Archie landed next to him with a bag of bots slung over his shoulder, trailing little critters coming to his call. He lifted the flap of his bag and scooped up the last few. Surprisingly, it was Kitty who made it to the last seat.

As Cara's tub pulled away blast doors rumbled closed across Blue Seven's access. Wenna was locking down and going into fortress mode. An attack on the port may be a diversion preceding an attack on their HQ.

"Come on. Come on!" Cara muttered as the tub bounced into the main traffic lane. "Is this the best we can do?"

Ronan reached forward, slapped off the auto and shoved both hands into the manual control gloves. They ricocheted off the track wall, sideswiped a laden goods tub and pulled clear of the traffic.

"Faster!" Cara heard sirens in the distance, Crossways security she hoped.

Ben?

Limpets.

On the Solar Wind*?*

At least four.

Hang on. Tengue's team's coming. We'll defuse the bastards.

No time.

Cara could feel part of Ben's attention taken and then she realized what was happening. He was firing up the *Solar Wind*'s drive aiming to get her out of the docking bay before she blew. Before she blew with him inside it.

Ben!

✦   ✦   ✦

"Ben!" Cara pounded her fists ineffectively on the solid docking bay door, leaving a smear of blood from broken knuckles. Through the view panel *Solar Wind* all but leaped between the closing jaws of the docking bay and winked out into foldspace.

Any closer and he'd have hit the Folds inside the docking bay and turned the whole station inside out.

Ben! "Fucking idiot!"

She didn't know whether that last was for Ben or for herself on the wrong side of the window behind reinforced blast doors with no more hope of being heard than a spider-fart. Once he hit the Folds, Ben was lost to any mental contact.

Ben had opted for the hero's way out. He'd saved the

docking bay and possibly the whole sector of the station, but at what cost? The only course now was to repressurize the bay as quickly as possible and get the surviving security guards out of there.

Tengue slapped the control panel to flood the bay with air at maximum speed. He hit the door release. The emergency protocols wouldn't allow it to open until the levels were safe. It seemed like hours, but was probably only a couple of minutes before the door cracked and a rush of wind from the corridor as the pressure equalized gave Cara a push through the opening along with Tengue's mercs and a squad of Garrick's guards. Tengue's mercs immediately began to check for survivors. Garrick's squad checked exits and sealed off the hangar as a crime scene and administered emergency oxygen. Ronan dealt with survivors, moving between them quickly and efficiently. The bay had been fully open to space for less than two minutes. Any guards who had not been sucked out of the open air lock stood a good chance of surviving, especially if they'd managed to activate their breathing tubes. Even so, two of them were dead, one with his skull caved in and the other with a chest wound.

"Wes! Oh, Wes." Kitty dropped to her knees by the side of the one with the chest wound. Cara hadn't immediately recognized him, though seeing Kitty's reaction she remembered the young man. He'd been handsome, but he didn't look so good now. His lips were swollen, his brown skin dull and gray, his eyes open. Kitty closed them gently.

Shaking inside, Cara barely registered Kitty's distress. She didn't have any spare capacity for comfort. All she could do was stare at the empty space where the *Solar Wind* had been. She pushed down the snakes that were turning somersaults in her belly. Think logically.

There had been no explosion before Ben entered foldspace. Once in foldspace the laws of physics changed in ways no one really understood. She remembered the missile punching through *Solar Wind*, in and out like a needle with no explosion or hull breach. The limpets were clamped on, however. What would happen when *Solar Wind* emerged into realspace again?

She swallowed a sob.

A small and deliberate throat clear caused her to stiffen.

How long had she been standing there? She turned to find Gwala at her left elbow.

"He's good," Gwala said. "He may even be the best I've ever flown with. If anyone can come back from that, it's Benjamin."

If was such a tiny word with such a big meaning.

✦ ✦ ✦

Kitty sat by Wes' corpse, shock keeping tears at bay. She might as well have been sitting alone for all that she registered medical staff working on the living, engineers checking the bay doors and interior pressure, maintenance staff going over the docked ships for damage. It was only when an antigrav gurney dropped into the space next to Wes that she realized she'd been muttering, "No," repeatedly.

"You can't—" she began, but they obviously could. "Where are you taking him?"

"Morgue at Dockside Medical, Miss," said one of the orderlies. "Are you next of kin?"

Kitty started to say no, but Ellen Heator came up behind her and put her hands on Kitty's shoulders. "Yes she is—as good as."

Kitty swiveled and looked up. "Isn't there anyone else?"

"Captain Syke would stand in, but Wes has no family."

"They died in an accident," Kitty said, "before he was dumped here as a child."

"That's more than he ever told me, and I worked with him for four years. You go with them, complete the paperwork, say good-bye. It may seem like indecent haste, but we cremate our dead immediately unless there's a forensic reason not to."

Kitty nodded numbly. That was standard on most space stations. She'd seen it happen before, but she'd never considered what it might be like to turn the body of a loved one, so recently vital, to ash. She reached out and touched Wes' face, already cooling, already empty of the spark that made him Wes.

"You know where I live. Come by tomorrow," Ellen said. "Someone will have to clear out his stuff. We'll do it together."

Kitty wanted to scream that he wasn't even cold yet.

The orderlies lifted Wes' body onto the gurney where an open body bag waited. Kitty gulped back a sob as they sealed the bag, but Ellen helped her to her feet with a strong arm under her elbow and nudged her to follow Wes on his last journey.

Keely, report.

In her haze Kitty had not even noticed Remus' implant handshaking with her own. She stiffened and by some miracle kept putting one foot in front of the other, helped by Ellen's guiding hand.

Remus, not now, please.

Report!

There's been a thing. They're dead.

Who? Make sense, Keely.

People. Guards. She wanted to say Wes Orton, but she held the name back. It was too precious to give to Remus. *An attack on Benjamin and the* Solar Wind. *He's gone.*

Who's gone where?

Benjamin. She swallowed. And Wes. *Limpets. Flew the* Solar Wind *off station and into the Folds. I don't see how he could have survived. Casualties on-station.* She didn't even know how many. Wes was all that mattered.

Clarify.

Fuck off, Remus. Leave me alone. They're dead! Have some respect!

She cut him off and blocked him out. He tried twice to reconnect, but with growing anger she refused to acknowledge him. He was stronger than her; he could force a connection, but thankfully he didn't try again. She'd pay for it next time.

She thought about the bill they threatened her mother with and fought down nausea. Wes was dead. What could be worse?

But a little voice at the back of her mind said: *Take care of the living.*

✦ ✦ ✦

All Cara could do was to keep trying to contact Ben. The longer a ship was in foldspace the less chance it had of coming out again.

She was dimly aware of Archie leading her out of the dock to a waiting tub. She was concentrating so hard on finding Ben that she missed her footing. If Archie hadn't caught her she'd have ended up in a heap on the floor.

Wenna grabbed her hand as they led her into Blue Seven. "Keep searching. Cas is on her way."

And I'm here, too. Gen was in her head immediately, adding her Telepathic whammy to Cara's. Then Cas Ritson joined them, adding her considerable Psi-1 strength. One by one, as they realized what was happening, every other Telepath in the place, from strong Psi-2s down to weak Psi-5s, joined them in the search. Even Max, so recently outfitted with an implant, tagged along.

Can I help? Jussaro asked.

Damn right, you can, Cara replied, drawing his consciousness into the whole.

Work stopped. Blue Seven fell silent as every psi-tech with any talent for Telepathy, however slight, formed a gestalt. Cara took the focus and concentrated on Ben outside in, inside out: warm brown skin; ready smile; the planes of his cheeks; the strength in his muscles. And inside: level-headed intelligence; desire to bring out the best in people; loyalty; the burden of dead souls he carried; damned annoying white knight syndrome that sometimes led him by the nose; his talent for Navigation and spatial awareness. All that was Ben and more she put into her search for him.

How long had it been? Minutes? Hours?

Three hours and fifty-six minutes, Ronan said, slipping into the mix. *Sorry I'm late. Work to do.*

Casualties? Cara asked.

Five survivors, two dead and three missing presumed lost into space. There are Finders out now, looking for the bodies.

Damn.

Yeah. Ronan settled down. *Any hint of Ben?*

Not yet.

In foldspace?

Seems likely. We keep trying.

At four hours and twenty-eight minutes one of the Psi-5s collapsed and Ronan pulled out of the gestalt to seek him out where he'd fallen.

Enough, Cara. Ben wouldn't thank you for burning out half his Telepaths, Ronan said.

She was about to protest, but he was right. *Take a break, everyone.*

As they all pulled out she wobbled and would have fallen, but she was wedged into a chair with arms. When had that happened? She didn't even remember getting here. She looked around. Wenna's office, of course. It was the heart of Blue Seven's operations. Sooner or later everyone gravitated there. She was surprised to see it empty of everyone except Wenna, Gen, and Max when just a few moments ago her head had been filled with individual Telepaths, but of course, they didn't need to be together physically to form a gestalt.

She blinked, as if emerging into the light.

"Drink." Gen pushed a cup of water into her hand and she drained it on the spot.

"Ben ..." Cara's voice cracked.

"Four and a half hours."

Cara groaned. "Sixteen. The record is sixteen—that we know of."

"It is, and Ben's good enough to beat it if anyone can, but ..."

Gen didn't need to elaborate.

Cara allowed herself three deep breaths and opened her mind to search for him.

"Wait!" Gen cut in and yanked her attention back. "You'll kill yourself like this."

"Sixteen hours," Cara said. "I can give him sixteen hours before I rest. Give everyone else a break now and then divide them into three shifts to join me, one hour on, two hours off until we find him."

"You're sure we'll find him?"

"I have to be."

At nine hours thirty Jussaro's consciousness joined hers. *Get some rest, Carlinni, I'll take over.*

He brought in several other minds, refreshed by the short break.

I said I'd give him sixteen hours.

Suit yourself.

At sixteen hours and five minutes she felt a slight sting on the side of her neck and lost her grip on the gestalt. "What the hell ..."

"You'll be no good to Ben if you burn out," Ronan said.

"What did you do to me?" She massaged the sting with her fingertips.

"Mild sedative laced with a reisercaine derivative. Don't worry, the effects are temporary. You'll be back to normal in a couple of hours. In the meantime, sleep."

"You bastard. How can I sleep when . . ."

"When he's out there somewhere." Cara came to with the second half of the sentence on her lips. For a moment she didn't realize she'd been out cold, then she realized she was stretched out on an airquilt on the floor of the cubicle that was Ben's temporary office.

"Ronan sends his apologies," Gen said, seated on the floor next to her. "He's only just left. Got a call from the med center. Serafin's taking it pretty badly."

"Taking what pretty badly? Ben? There's news?"

"Nothing. I'm sorry." Gen's mouth was set in that particular way that said she was using all her willpower not to let her chin tremble.

"How long was I out?"

"Three hours."

"So it's been—"

"Nineteen hours and six minutes. No one's ever come back from foldspace after that—"

"Ben will."

"Cara . . ."

"He will. You'll see. You haven't stopped looking, have you?"

"Of course not. Three shifts, one hour on, two hours off until . . ."

"Until we find him."

Gen didn't reply.

Cara slid straight back into the gestalt. *I've got the focus, now,* she told Cas. *Take a break.*

Follow your own orders, Cas said. *One hour on, two off.*

Right, Cara said, knowing perfectly well Cas could tell she was lying.

Ronan won't hesitate to put you under again if you endanger yourself.

He can try.

A memory surfaced. *I killed him with my mind!* Oh shit! She didn't mean that. Please let her not have meant it!

Cara!

She could hear the alarm in Cas' mental voice.

It's all right. Truly. Ronan won't need to do anything. I'll do two hours on and one off.

See that you do.

And she did. Two hours on and one off throughout the night, accompanied by uncomplaining Telepaths.

"Cara. Cara!" Ronan's voice brought her back to reality as she handed the gestalt over to Jussaro.

She clamped her hand over the side of her neck.

"Leave me alone."

He crouched in front of her chair, hands up to show they were empty. "It's been thirty-two hours."

"I know."

"Twice as long as the longest time anyone's ever stayed in foldspace."

"I know."

Ronan dropped his voice to a whisper. "He's my friend, Cara. I love him like a brother, but it's time to stand your Telepaths down. They're exhausted. You're exhausted."

"I know." She didn't realize she was crying until tears splashed from her chin onto her folded hands.

Ronan rocked back on his heels and looked up to meet someone's gaze over Cara's shoulder. His head tilted in a nod of acknowledgment.

"Come with me," Gen said from behind her. "Time to get some proper sleep."

She shook her head, but didn't resist when Gen's grip raised her to her feet.

"You want a shot?" Ronan asked.

She shook her head and let Gen lead her to a room with four bunks in it: the standby room.

"You need to talk?" Gen asked.

She shook her head.

Gen tweaked back the quilt. "Buddysuit."

Obediently Cara shrugged out of the suit, top first, and, stripped down to singlet and shorts, sat on the edge of the bed.

"In."

On Gen's command she rolled into the bed and Gen pulled up the covers.

"You want me to stay?"

Cara shook her head one more time and Gen left, leaving the light to power down.

There was a gaping hole in Cara's insides. How could she sleep?

She closed her eyes and stared at the inside of her eyelids for what seemed like hours. Then she opened her eyes and stared at the inside of the dark room. Same picture.

Ben: her first glimpse of him leaning against Gordano's bar on Mirrimar-14, tall and so sure of himself.

Ben: in his bed that first night. He'd been her ride out to freedom—a convenience fuck—she'd barely considered him. Her head had been too full of Ari van Blaiden. How could she have been so stupid?

Ben: catching her when she fell.

So stupid for so long . . . and then . . .

There had been a time when it had been so right between them, just a very short time before Ari van Blaiden and Donida McLellan's neural conditioning had turned her into something she wasn't. Or perhaps turned her into something she was, but something she didn't want to be.

Ben had saved her. They'd saved each other.

Why had she told him to take it slow?

What was her problem?

It wasn't Ben.

Except now it was. He'd left her—like everyone else she'd ever valued.

Gone.

She couldn't even cry herself to sleep.

◆ ◆ ◆

Ben crawled up out of blackness in stages. At first he was only aware of the world behind his closed eyelids. He was awake, but not awake. Gradually he felt a pain external to his head. His left wrist throbbed in time to his beating heart.

That he had a beating heart surprised him.

He shivered and coughed.

Realspace.

Where was he?

That was a question he hadn't had to ask in many years, not since a fifth-year med student admitted that his was the first implant she'd ever carried out, but not to worry, her supervisor was watching.

"Oh, great," his sixteen-year-old self had responded. "Do I get a refund if it doesn't take?"

Her supervisor had leaned across his field of vision. "Don't worry, Mr. Benjamin, if it doesn't take, you'll be the last to know about it. Glad you signed the consents, now, huh?"

So . . . where was he?

On the floor for starters, his left arm crushed beneath him. He pushed his right hand flat to the deck plating—deck plating, that was a clue—and raised his upper body off the floor just far enough to move his left hand.

Arrgh! Not quite a yelp, more of a groan. Broken. He rolled over and scrambled with his feet until he was sitting up, leaning against something solid, something cool against his right arm.

No buddysuit top, hence no painkillers for the break. Ah damn.

Flight deck. *Solar Wind*. The limpets. The Folds. What was all that about?

(He didn't let himself think of the void dragon.)

Had it been a particularly lucid dream? He forced his eyes open and examined his wrist. Swollen. Bruised. His wrist certainly hadn't been dreaming.

A violent tickle in his lungs brought on a percussive cough. The first cough felt good, scratching the itch. The second still satisfied. The third scraped. The fourth and the fifth stung. The sixth, seventh, eighth rattled his skull, set his eyes watering, scraped his lungs raw. He coughed and coughed again, helpless. His chest spasmed and the coughs kept on coming, wave upon wave. He tried to suck air in and hold it to break the cycle, but he was hacking so hard he could barely snatch air. Coughing so hard that his chest locked.

Then the coughing stopped, but he could neither breathe in nor out.

Relax, he told himself, trying not to panic. Relax.

His vision was tinged with black spots.

Okay, pass out if you must. Let your body take over.

He couldn't take his own advice. He fought his chest again and managed to suck in something, air of sorts. And again. He sat back against the chair, all but finished, taking one shuddering breath at a time.

He lost track of how long he sat there, concentrating on the next breath, and the next, until . . .

Warmth. He needed warmth and he wasn't going to get it here. There was an emergency blanket in the first aid kit if he could only reach it. He was suddenly grateful to the designer who had thought far enough ahead to put the emergency kit in a locker less than arms' reach above the floor. He crawled, one hand, two knees, one hand, two knees . . . The journey, barely four strides for a healthy man, seemed to take years, but he got there and hit the release catch, dragging out the contents of the kit, scattering them on the floor.

Painkiller first. He slapped a blast pack to the side of his neck. Just one shot because he needed to stay awake. Emergency blanket. He tore open the slim packet with his teeth and discarded the wrapper. One-handed, he shook out the folded foil sheet and managed to get it around his shoulders. The heater circuit kicked in and he felt warmth seeping into his upper body. Thankfully he had the bottom half of his buddysuit on.

Sentient trousers. He would have laughed if his chest had not been raw. Wouldn't want to get frostbite down there.

He crawled back to the pilot's station, but the chair seemed like a mountain. He needed to get into it to check the ship's readouts.

Where was he?

Where the hell was he?

His link with the universe was broken.

He was broken.

Hauling himself into the chair was neither easy nor quick, and the analgesics only dulled the edge of the pain in his wrist. He didn't look too closely, aware that his hand was tight as a balloon and he had a bad case of livid purple sausage-fingers.

Upright in the chair he realized the *Solar Wind* was yawing. Luckily he'd emerged from foldspace into the middle of a vast nothing. Well, the odds were always good for that.

First, stabilize the ship.

He reached for the ship's systems with his mind, but it was like clawing his way through fog.

"Activate voice," he told the ship. "Stabilize the trajectory and do a systems check. Why can't I connect?"

"Trajectory stable, Systems functioning within normal parameters. Suggest switching on your implant."

"It's never off . . ."

He tongued the switch on the inside of a back molar, or tried to.

"My tooth."

The ship didn't answer him. How could it? There was no answer for this. The tooth that had been implanted on the same day the med student had successfully completed her first solo procedure was now devoid of any switches. In fact, it felt like a real tooth again. Weird.

"Awaiting instructions," the ship said.

"Bloody wait a bit longer." The vehemence of his words started him coughing again, but this time he managed to control it before it took hold. No implant control. He felt at his forehead. He hadn't been able to see the tiny implant scar for years, but he could still feel it, a knot smaller than a grain of wheat just under his skin. He probed with his fingers. Nothing.

Where had he been? What had happened? He thought he remembered, but were they his real memories? Donida McLellan had thoroughly fucked with Cara's head and her real memories had taken months to surface, and then only slowly and painfully. But it had taken McLellan weeks to work on Cara, he'd only been in the Folds for . . . He checked his handpad, expecting it to tell him that minutes had passed. Thirty-three hours. Nearly a whole fucking day and a half! How long had he spent in the Folds and how much of that time was due to the time differential?

"Time."

The ship flashed the time onto the screen. It matched the time on Ben's handpad.

"Is there anyone else aboard this ship?"

"Negative."

"Has anyone else been aboard this ship since we left Port 22."

"Negative."

"Do you have audio and video recording of the flight deck for the whole time of out flight."

"Positive."

"Step through it. Show twelve frames per minute."

The image fast-forwarded across the screen. Just as Ben

remembered it showed him standing, floating up with the momentum and disappearing from out of the range of the lens, which wasn't positioned to show the ceiling. Some time later gravity returned and he reappeared from the direction of the access ladder.

It didn't help.

"Do you have video of the ship's hull during the time I was out of camera shot?"

"Negative."

"You didn't record?"

"The hull cam is black."

He shouldn't expect anything else. Hull cams were always black in the Folds.

He shivered and pulled the emergency blanket tighter around his shoulders. He didn't know whether he was still affected by the deep cold of space or whether it was fear. He wasn't used to being disconnected from his sense of location. He closed his eyes and reached out with his mind.

Nothing.

"Coordinates."

The forward screen sprang into life with a star chart. Ben stared at it and blew air out past clenched teeth. "Well . . . fuck, and double fuck. That's . . . not good."

"May I recommend—"

"No you may not!" Ben cut the ship off. It was going to recommend a jump through the Folds that would carry them halfway across the galaxy. And without his implant he was helpless to navigate. He'd have to rely on the automatic systems.

And there might be another one of . . . those things.

His gut churned at the thought of the void dragon.

This was ridiculous. He'd never been afraid of flying the Folds before. But on previous occasions he'd always been completely in charge. Now he felt helpless. The chance of getting through foldspace was significantly reduced when flying on automatics.

And now he knew what was out there. Waiting. He'd looked into infinity and it had looked back.

✦ ✦ ✦

"If I may make a suggestion . . ."

Ben jumped awake at the sound of the ship's voice. He

was slumped in the pilot's chair, not even realizing he'd closed his eyes.

He knew what it was going to say.

"Suggest if you must."

"Your vital signs are erratic. If you intend to return to the Folds you should do it now while you still have strength."

"I don't have my implant."

"Suggest switching it on."

"No. I don't *have* my implant." He closed his eyes and drew a deep breath which stabbed him in the chest. "Implant is malfunctioning."

"Understood."

"Is that all you can say?"

"Your implant is malfunctioning. There is no other human aboard this vessel. Therefore if the vessel is to reenter the Folds it must be done on the automatic guidance system."

"How long to travel back to Crossways through real-space?"

"Forty-four thousand years at best speed."

"That's what I figured." He pushed down the roiling snakes in his stomach. He shivered, chilled to the marrow, while sweat beaded on his forehead. Damn, his hands were shaking. The Folds loomed like a bottomless pit in his imagination. Dragons swirled in its depths. The souls of the dead—his dead—swam up in front of his eyes, glared accusingly and sank down again. Ari van Blaiden, knife buried to the hilt in his eye socket, loomed up. *You were the only one who deserved it, bastard!*

He swallowed hard. There was one way out. Not a good way, but maybe better than facing the Folds again.

"Make the calculations."

"Calculations complete." The answer was immediate.

"Are you sure? Have you checked them?"

"Calculations complete."

Bloody hell, the machine managed to sound offended.

He strapped in. "Go on then, do your worst." Hmmm, maybe not the best way to phrase it. "Take us to Crossways in . . ." He glanced at his handpad. "Five minutes from my mark. Mark."

The ship began to count down.

Ben prepped the sedative, dialing the lowest possible

dose. It should put him out for no more than a quarter hour. He cradled it to the side of his neck and started to count. By three he was pleasantly light-headed. By four he was sinking. By five the darkness of unconsciousness was coiling through his brain.

Chapter Fifteen

KEEPING IT TOGETHER

CARA WOKE NOT KNOWING WHAT TIME IT WAS or whether she'd slept for a minute or a day. The room was still dark.

"Lights," Cara said, and the overhead panels began to glow, gradually increasing in intensity.

Someone, Gen probably, had been in while she slept and left fresh underclothes. Of course, all her clothes had been in the cabin on the *Solar Wind*. The cabin she shared with Ben.

Ben.

A hole opened up and threatened to swallow her. She skirted around it.

Pretend it's an ordinary day.

She hit the bathroom and went through her usual morning routine, emerging into Wenna's office ten minutes later, clean if not bright.

"Cara, how are you feeling?" Wenna looked up from her desk. "I know. Stupid question, but it has to be asked."

"I slept. I don't know how. I don't even know for how long." She glanced at her handpad. "Oh two hundred. It seems I slept the day away."

"You did. Ronan said not to disturb—"

"That's okay. Catch me up."

"Mother Ramona says it was the Alphabet Gang, highly skilled operatives. They were the ones Ben worked with to steal *Solar Wind* from van Blaiden in the first place."

"She got them, right? Tell me she got them."

Wenna shook her head. "Garrick closed down all out-bound flights, but we figured they cleared the station within ten minutes of setting those limpets."

"Fuck!"

"Yes, as you say."

Cara didn't even ask if the Telepaths had managed to contact Ben. It would have been the first thing Wenna told her. Hell, they'd have woken her up. So . . . no Ben. What next?

She backtracked. "Ben's Nan. We still need to spring Nan and Ricky. Ben would have wanted that." Oh, gods, she was saying it as if she believed he was gone . . . dead.

"Of course."

"And find Lorient's missing settlers."

Wenna looked uncomfortable. "Some of the crew are talking about shipping out."

"You've got to hold them together, Wenna."

"Me?"

"You were always Ben's second."

"That's what I'm good at, being a second. I'm not . . . I don't have . . . any desire to run the whole show. You need to step up."

"Me? I'm an outsider. I not only came late to the party, but I brought trouble with me."

"Everyone knows how Ben feels . . ." She swallowed hard. "Felt about you."

"Gah! Later. I'll think about it later."

"There may not be a later."

Cara took a deep breath.

Ben would want this.

She gave herself five minutes to prepare, then opened up a broadcast to catch all the Free Company currently on-station. *You all know what's gone down.*

There was a ripple of assent, a sense of loss, condolences, uncertainty.

It's hard—for all of us.

Agreement.

*And I know some of you are thinking about cutting your

losses. There's no shame in that. Take your share of the platinum and have a nice life.

A mixture of relief, denial, confusion, guilt.

We're all hurting, but Ben left us with a job to do and we have already split our strength. Fifty psi-techs had shipped out to Jamundi with the settlers. *Thirty thousand settlers are still missing. Lost. Nobody looking for them except us. And Ben's family, back on Chenon, in danger because of what we did on Olyanda. The Free Company's still here, still working. I'd appreciate volunteers to help finish what we all started.*

I'm in it for the long haul, Wenna said.

Max and I are here. Goes without saying, Gen added.

I'm saying it, Ronan chipped in.

Me, too. Archie Tatum and Yan Gwenn started a flood of responses.

In the end they lost only nine people, and they were ones who'd been borderline about deciding to stay with the Free Company. That left a hundred and fifty-two committed psi-techs, and another fifty on Jamundi.

"Well done," Wenna said.

Cara shook her head, not knowing how to answer.

Wenna took her hand. "You know you're not alone, right?"

Not alone. The door whooshed open and Gen entered, followed by Max carrying a tray of coffees in cups with Blue Mountain logos on them.

"We didn't know how many to bring." Max put the cups down on Wenna's desk. "May have overestimated."

"I'll take one." Ronan was barely a few paces behind.

"If there's a spare . . ." Archie followed him in.

They all took a cup.

"A toast," Ronan said. "To Ben."

"To Ben," they echoed, raising coffee cups.

A dam inside Cara shattered. She gulped and sobbed, trying to get words out. "We should be toasting him with tea."

◆ ◆ ◆

Once she let go, Cara cried so much that her eyes puffed up and her nose blocked, and still she couldn't stop.

"Is . . . this even . . . normal?" she asked Ronan, who had

ushered everyone else out of the office and stood patiently with Cara's head buried in his waist, one hand resting lightly on her back.

"Don't worry about normal," he said. "There's no such thing as normal in a situation like this. Everyone deals with it differently. You might feel lots of emotions all mixed up: shock, grief, anger, regret.... It's still too fresh, you've hardly accepted that he's gone yet. I know I haven't." He let her snuffle some more and then handed her a tissue. "Did you know Kitty had been seeing Wes Orton?"

"Wes?" Cara tried to recall who Wes Orton was.

"One of Garrick's security guards. He was killed when the docking bay depressurized."

"Oh, Ronan, I'm sorry. I'm so busy thinking about myself."

"Garrick sent a team out to recover the bodies sucked out of the air lock. Lewis Bronsen volunteered to go with them. They brought them all home."

Lewis was a phenomenally good Finder. Cara wondered whether his talents worked in foldspace.

"I can't bear the thought of Ben being out there, alone, in the cold and the dark."

"I know. We've all lost a friend."

"I shouldn't hoard all the grief for myself. That's such a Ben thing to do. How long has Wenna known him? She's worked with him on so many missions. Gen, too. They used to be ... close. And Serafin ... I know you went rushing off to the old man yesterday. How is he?"

"Sedated. Mildly sedated, not out cold. I can offer you—"

"No thanks. I'll cope." She sniffed and Ronan passed her another tissue.

"Thanks." She applied the tissue and then cleared her throat. "We were ... still getting to know each other. There never seemed to be enough time to ... just swap stories. You know. Our time on Olyanda lurched from one crisis to the next. What about you? When did you meet Ben?"

"I think it was my first mission for Crowder, Ben's third. We were escorting a bunch of scientists and exozoologists to Connemara, the planet, not the place in Ireland. There was a settlement there already, but these guys wanted to study what looked like archeological remains out in the rain forest, so they needed a nursemaid crew since no one from the settlement was willing to volunteer. Can't say I blame them either. Bug-ridden place with temperatures hotter than hell and enough humidity that it was like breathing soup. There were a fair few poisonous critters, too, some of them actively looking for humans, others just out to poison each other."

"Sounds charming."

Ronan shrugged. "Didn't figure Ben had much of a sense of humor at first. He can be, could be, a bit dry . . ."

"Yes, I know."

"Besides, it was the sort of place that any sense of humor you might have brought with you would have hightailed it back to the nearest settlement—mine certainly left me quickly enough—but Ben managed to keep smiling. Nothing fazed him. About ten days into the trip he found a critter, not one of the poisonous ones, but it was pretty strange: six legs, about the size of a sheepdog; not so cute unless you think bug eyes are sexy. Anyhow, it seemed to take to Ben and pretty soon it became the camp mascot. He called it Trixibelle. Having Trixibelle around kinda lightened the atmosphere a little bit. Helped us all get through."

"What happened to Trixibelle when you left?"

"Ben found a home for her at the settlement—a family with two kids. And then he had pins made for everyone with her face on them."

"He should have had pins made for all the Olyanda survivors with Lorient's mugshot."

"Or maybe Crowder's."

For some reason she found this funny and laughed until her sides hurt and then laughed some more, knowing that if she stopped she'd cry again.

"Is this a party anyone can join?" Mother Ramona stood in the doorway.

Cara waved her inside. "Ronan was just telling me about the first mission he went on with•Ben. When did you first meet him?"

"When he was in the Monitors. He came here chasing someone—someone I was happy for him to remove from circulation as it turned out. Oh, he wasn't in uniform, but I'm a specialist in fake IDs. Spotted his a mile off and sent

one of my ... associates to check him out. My guy got his
ass handed to him on a plate, so instead of sending two guys
I went myself. Had a little talk. We conducted some business."

"On your couch?" Cara asked, knowing Mother Ramona's method of sealing business deals.

"As it turns out, yes." She smiled. "And I ended up giving
him my access code for the next time he passed through
Crossways."

"Thornhill Renaissance."

"That's the one. Next time he came with a boatload of
Burnish refugees, artisan glassmakers, jewelers, and metal-
workers and their families, displaced by a land tussle between Eastin-Heigle and Arquavisa. His orders were to
take them to a subsistence camp on Dounreay—a pretty
inhospitable place by all accounts. He wanted new idents
for them so they could settle on Scarra where there were
opportunities for artisans."

"And you provided them?"

"For a consideration."

"Money?"

"An exchange. I needed someone taken to safety. Scarra
was as good a place as any. I wouldn't have asked Ben if I
hadn't known his word was good."

"His word was always good," Cara said. "And we have to
make it good again. His Nan's in trouble and there's still
Lorient's settler ark to find."

"We may be able to solve the problem of his grandmother. Crowder's got her as hostage, right?"

"We presume."

"So once Ben's declared legally dead, why would
Crowder need to keep her?"

"You think it's that simple?"

"It's worth a try. We've got a lead on the perps, the Alphabet Gang. Garrick thought we should give them time to
report their mission a success before we terminate them
with extreme prejudice. Oh, don't look at me like that.
Don't you want to see them dead?"

Cara nodded.

"The Alphabets have worked for me and Garrick, and I
introduced Ben to them. They turned against me and mine

for money. That's not something we can forgive. We'd never be able to trust them again. There's a code and they stepped beyond it."

"I should—"

Mother Ramona shook her head. "This job's ours. On the house. Garrick and I agreed that having you all on Crossways would be an advantage. Garrick wants to spruce up our reputation as a free-trade port, play down the shady side, attract legitimate business. You don't do that by letting incidents like this happen without sending a clear message. The Alphabet Gang is toast, but we'll give them time to be useful first."

"Crowder sent them."

"We don't know that for sure, but if he did, then he's yours."

Cara nodded. "Mine."

She understood why Ben had been reluctant to kill Crowder in cold blood when they last met. Ben and Crowder had been friends for a long time. Maybe Ben didn't want to believe that Crowder was irredeemable. Cara didn't feel any need to give him the benefit of the doubt. Crowder was a dead man. He just didn't know it yet.

◆ ◆ ◆

Kitty avoided Cara as much as she could. There was only so much grief she could take and Cara's was palpable. In fact Blue Seven was a big old pile of grief. It was Ben this and Ben that. Did any of the psi-techs care about Wes and the other dead guards?

Kitty found her feet taking her to the cab lane and she automatically programmed in the coordinates for Port 22. The hangar was empty except for the little Dixie Flyer and one of Mother Ramona's smuggling ships docked in one of the repair gantries. Yan Gwenn and an odd-looking woman in half a buddysuit had the drive casing off the Dixie. Yan waved and Kitty waved back but didn't go over to start a conversation. She'd come down here to get away from psi-techs.

Syke nodded an acknowledgment, almost a formal bow. He was going through the motions, but even behind his usually impassive expression Kitty recognized emotion. It was tightly constrained, but it was there.

Ellen Heator pulled off her half-helm and scrubbed her hair just like Wes used to do, except Ellen had considerably longer hair. "Kitty, how are you?"

"All right, I guess. Well, no, not all right if I'm honest. You know."

"I do. I'm not sure I can do this anymore. I'm thinking of resigning."

"I heard that, Heator," Syke said. "Come into my office."

"You don't have an office . . . sir," Ellen said.

"I'll have to make one, then." He led her gently into the guard post and thirty seconds later the four guards who'd been in there came out and stood looking at each other.

When Ellen came out again she still wore Garrick's colors on her sleeve.

"Not leaving, then?" Kitty asked her.

Ellen just shook her head. "Syke said if I really wanted to go I could, but give it a few months. He didn't want to lose anyone else from this team. He said I might feel differently if I waited. Said I'd gain perspective. I might, I suppose. But what if I don't want to?" She cleared her throat. "You should come over and help me clear Wes' apartment."

"I was thinking . . ." Kitty said. "Is it up for grabs? I wouldn't mind staying there . . . for a while at least." She jerked her head over her shoulder. "Then we wouldn't need to clear it."

"As far as I know the rent's paid up two months in advance. Are you looking for perspective, too?"

"I don't know what I'm looking for."

✦ ✦ ✦

Ricky watched the big guard, Minnow, slap a blast pack to the side of Nan's neck, then quickly looked back down to the slate he was pretending to read.

Minnow had dropped the slate off after Ricky's last escape attempt with a gruff, "Here, kid, this'll keep ya occupied."

Ricky had plenty on his handpad to keep him occupied. He'd even caught up on all his homework and had worked ahead on a bunch of math problems and done some of the extra reading for his project on pre-meteor Earth history, but Minnow's slate, a basic model with no connectivity, sadly, was a welcome distraction.

"Look, kid, I know it's hard, but settle down and ya won't get hurt and neither will Granny."

Nan was his great-grandmother, but he didn't bother to correct Minnow. It was only a halfhearted attempt at a veiled threat and Ricky paid it no mind. He'd already figured out that they weren't in any immediate danger, but the uncertainty was eating at him. Surely Dad had reported them missing by now.

Ricky had only a vague idea of how the police might go about looking for them. Was kidnapping serious enough to call in the Monitors? They mostly operated on newly established colonies where there wasn't such a good local policing system. Chenon had been the first colony. The founders had left Canaveral Spaceport pre-meteor, so it was a point of pride that Chenon considered itself culturally superior. It had the oldest uninterrupted strand of human history. North America had been smashed back to the Stone Age by the meteor, but the Chenonites had preserved the best of it: a pioneering spirit, democracy, education, and law.

"What ya readin' today?" Minnow asked, shoving the remains of the blast pack into his pocket.

"The Curse of the Chinese Whisper," Ricky said. "It's set on Earth, before the meteor strike, before jump gate travel, even. What's a Chinese Whisper?"

"Something 'at comes from China, I expect," Minnow said. "China was a town once, way back, a big town somewhere near Australia and they had black and white bears. Got flattened by the meteor. I ain't read that Chinese Whisper one yet but my wife finds all this quirky old stuff an' puts it on my slate."

"Nan read me *Don Quixote* once. That's quirky and old. From before people even got off the planet."

"Donkey Hoeteh? Ain't even heard o' that one. I'll tell Ginny to look for it."

"It's weird, but good weird."

He thought Minnow was softening toward them. He'd brought Ricky an extra blanket and the slate, stuffed with a weird selection of books, and had told him the Arrows had beaten the Rockets fifty-nine to forty-three in the grapple quarterfinals. He'd laughed then and said, "Tickets twenty creds each, an' I got to watch it for free. This job's done me a favor."

"How so?" Ricky had asked.

But Minnow had just laughed and tapped his nose with his index finger.

Ricky had puzzled over that and then remembered a couple of nights ago, after Minnow had delivered the evening blast pack and departed, he'd heard the low rumble of some kind of engine. Well, not so much heard it as felt it in his bones. He'd put his hands against the wall and his fingers had tingled, then he'd put his ear hard to the wall and heard a low hum. He'd felt it in his teeth, too.

It was an antigrav drive. He'd felt funny. It was possible they were close to, or maybe even beneath, a grapple arena. It couldn't be the Arrows' home arena because that wasn't allowed in quarterfinals, semis, or finals. They had to be close to the De Barras Stadium, the only independent stadium on the planet. Independent because it was owned by the Trust, not a team. Of course, and the De Barras Stadium was on the edge of the Trust compound.

Yes! Ricky knew where he was now. All he had to do was get out, or get a message out.

The smile that was starting to form died unborn. How was he going to do that?

He so needed to talk to Nan.

✦ ✦ ✦

"Dead?" Crowder received the news with mixed feelings. He put his plate down on the table and stared at the screen on the wall of the penthouse's small kitchen. Dammit, he wanted Benjamin dead, didn't he? Of course he did. He needed him dead, but Ben had been ... *Like a son,* kept coming into Crowder's head. Families had disagreements, chose different sides; it didn't make them not care about each other.

He touched his ear, newly grafted and still very tender. Ben could have killed him, but he hadn't.

"What would you like me to do about the Alphabet Gang?" Stefan French asked.

"Release the rest of the payment."

Stephan nodded. "There's a message from Crossways, from Norton Garrick's office. Someone called Ramona."

"Mother Ramona?"

"That's the one. Says she has a proposition for you."

"I'll come down and take the call."

Briefly Crowder considered removing the damper that isolated his receiving implant, but even though Benjamin was dead, there was still Carlinni to reckon with, and three hundred psi-techs, his former employees, who all had good reason to carry a grudge.

He stood up slowly and stretched the knots out of his back. He put his coffee cup and breakfast plate into the cleaner and headed for his private antigrav shaft in his shirtsleeves, then thought better of it and went to get his jacket from the bedroom closet. He didn't always wear the Trust's uniform, but today he would, whether out of respect for a dead frenemy or to keep up appearances, he wasn't entirely sure. It just felt right.

Stefan nodded to him as he entered the outer office. "The call's on your screen now, sir."

"Thank you, son." Son? When had he started to call his secretary son?

Mother Ramona's hologram hovered a few inches above his desk. Her eyes followed his approach.

"Gabrius Crowder. I don't believe we've had the pleasure of a direct link before."

"Mother Ramona. I've heard a lot about you, and heard from your lawyers, of course."

There was a delay while the call routed through jump gates, then the screen sprang to life again. "I thought this deserved a face-to-face conversation. Ben Benjamin's dead, though you probably know that already if you were paying the Alphabet Gang."

"Dead?" Crowder thought he injected just the right amount of surprise into his expression. "I'm sorry to hear that. We may have had our differences, but he was like a son to me before he went rogue."

Another delay.

"Your idea of family isn't the same as mine. No matter. There's an outstanding situation. Ben's grandmother and his nephew."

"What about them?" Now Crowder tried wide-eyed innocence, thought it might look too obvious, and went back to keeping his expression neutral.

Delay.

"Let's be straight with each other, Mr. Crowder. Ben was

a friend of mine and I would be remiss in my duties as a friend if I didn't address a situation which I see now is eminently resolvable without any further recriminations. You no longer need the old woman and the boy as leverage. Release them. Get them to sign a confidentiality agreement first, if you like, but let them go."

"What if I don't have them?"

Delay.

"With your resources I'm sure you could find them. They might even be grateful for your intervention."

"Quite. I'll consider it. In the meantime, the platinum on Olyanda—"

This time the delay was slightly longer than the transit time accounted for.

"It doesn't work like that. You can't use Ben's family as leverage on me. Sure I'd like to see his last wishes carried out, but I don't have a personal stake in this. You weighed the value of Olyanda's platinum against a whole colony and your own psi-tech team and found the platinum more valuable. Believe me when I say that one old woman and a boy are not worth a single concession on Olyanda. Our security there has beaten off your fleet—"

"Not mine."

Delay.

"Whatever." She waved dismissively. "We've repelled everything you've been able to throw at us and set up a planetary defense grid that you'd be foolish to try to breach."

Crowder shrugged. "You can't blame a person for trying."

Delay.

"So what about the old woman and the boy?"

"I'll see what I can find out. Maybe they've been taken as hostages by criminals for ransom. I'll look into it, as a favor . . . in memory of Benjamin."

Delay.

She nodded. "Thank you."

Crowder let the holo-image fade. "Stefan!" he called.

"Here, sir." The young man was already hovering in the doorway.

Crowder adjusted his voice accordingly. "What's the latest on Louisa Benjamin's condition?"

"Stable. Still under sedation."

"Have Pav Danniri report to me. No need to waste resources, we just need to find a way to release the Benjamins without any kind of media fuss. Maybe make it look like I've staged a rescue. No need for any more bloodshed now."

Chapter Sixteen

FOUND

BEN HAS NEVER FLOWN THE FOLDS LIKE THIS before.

He's supposed to be unconscious. Is this an anesthetic dream or is he somehow aware? He's always been in control. He's always known the way out, a thin thread of silver light in the ultimate darkness that leads him to where he needs to go. Now it's all up to the machine that has control of *Solar Wind*. An intelligent machine, to be sure, but not a sentient one. It's programmed to preserve life, but ultimately it doesn't care if it fails.

He's come this far. He doesn't want, "Oops, sorry," carved on his tombstone.

He searches for the line in his mind.

Gods! It's always been so easy before.

Inside his head is a fog, thick, black, and tarry, but ... there's a pull that favors one direction above all others. If not a line, then at least a faint trail where the fog rolls back to reveal a glimmer.

In his dream he touches the nav plates, one hand is swollen like an overripe plum about to burst, but he can just about move his fingers.

"May I suggest—" the ship says.

"No. We go this way."

"But—"

"This way, damn you. Go offline. Taking manual control."

Ben's wrist throbs. His head begins to pound, but still he follows the pull. He starts to cough again. He tastes blood—iron and salt.

The exit point. There!

Spinning. Out of control. As the ship tumbles into real-space the anesthetic kicks in and the blackness takes him.

✦ ✦ ✦

"Cara!" Max burst into Wenna's office. "Cara! It's Ben. I . . . I'm sure he's out there. *Solar Wind*. I . . . I can sense her, out there."

Gen was close behind him. "Don't get your hopes up. Max is still a beginner, but it's worth checking. Even if it is the *Solar Wind* . . ."

"I know. It may just be wreckage, but . . ." Max said.

Cara reached out to contact Ben. Nothing. Was he dead? Did she really have so little faith?

Wenna was already on the vox to Crossways' traffic control. She looked up, face pale. "They've got an incoming object on the extreme edge of scanner range. Unidentified, not answering hails. It's on a direct trajectory with the station, so if there's no response by the time it reaches the 1000 klick mark they'll launch a missile to deflect it."

Cara was on her feet in an instant. "Get Garrick to call them off. If it's *Solar Wind* we'll do an intercept. Hell, even if it's not *Solar Wind* we'll do an intercept."

Wenna hit the vox and Cara reached out for Yan Gwenn, bringing him up to speed in an instant, mind-to-mind.

The Dixie's ready, Yan said. *She's in Port 22.*

On my way.

Not without me, Ronan said. *There may be someone incapacitated on that boat.*

Ben. Let it be Ben. Oh, please let it be Ben.

We need a second pilot, Yan said.

I'll come, Gen said.

"Just a minute, is this dangerous?" Max grabbed her by the arm.

She shook him off. "Don't treat me like I'm made of

glass just because I'm carrying your child. You said yourself it could be Ben."

"And it could be dangerous." Cara glanced down at Gen's twenty-week bump. "More importantly, it could need an EVA and suits aren't made for two."

Gen growled in frustration and Max swept her up and held her tight. "Do you need me?" he asked over her shoulder.

Cara shook her head. "We've got accurate coordinates and not enough crew space. We can't take more than four and we need someone to fly *Solar Wind* home—if it is *Solar Wind* and if she's in one piece."

Let me, Kitty Keely chimed in.

Yan? Cara checked.

She's good.

Okay, Kitty. You're in.

Cara raced for the entrance and grabbed the nearest tub with Ronan and Kitty close behind. The ten-minute journey to the dock seemed interminable. Cara stared at Kitty, wondering if she exhibited the same puffy red eyes. What was her dead friend's name? Oh, yes.

"Sorry to hear about Wes, Kitty. I understand you and he were—"

Kitty nodded. "Just friends, at least that's all we'd got around to. It might have been more, given time. He was very sweet. Volunteered at a community farm."

"Farm?"

"Surprised me, too. Station kids can go there to pet baby animals. I ... I've volunteered in his place." She shrugged. "Yeah, I know, not like me at all, is it?" She dropped her eyes to her hands, splayed over her knees. "I just felt as though I should ... that he might have liked it."

"Doing the things now that we should have willingly done when they were alive is like plugging a hole after the water's drained."

"Oh, you too?"

Cara nodded. "'Fraid so."

Kitty cleared her throat. "I hope Ben's alive, but ... one way or the other ... I hope it's him out there."

"Thanks."

The tub rattled to a halt and Kitty leaped out and

through the open doors of Port 22 with a brief wave to Mother Ramona's guard—twice as many of them as there had been previously—beating Cara to the dock by half a stride.

Yan was already powering up Ben's Dixie Flyer and filing an emergency flight plan.

Crossways Control, do we have clearance? Cara asked as they settled into the Dixie and clipped the harnesses. Yan and Cara in the pilot and copilot seats, Kitty and Ronan in the bucket seats behind.

Clear to go. All other traffic's on lockdown, Mother Ramona answered through her Telepath, Ully.

Kitty dogged the hatch as Yan primed the drive. The air lock cycled and the outer jaws opened.

I'm here in flight control, Mother Ramona said. *Ask for whatever you need, it's yours.*

Thanks. Mother Ramona couldn't fail to be aware of the wave of gratitude Cara emitted.

That's all right, she said. *If that's Ben in there, bring him home.*

Will do. Or die trying, Cara thought.

Under Yan's competent handling the Dixie rose on antigravs and shot out of the air lock into space.

They had to take turns suiting up because of restricted space in a cabin ideally meant to accommodate only two, but by the time the unidentified ship was in visual range they were all ready.

"Oh, shit!" Yan said from the pilot's seat.

"What's the matter? Is it *Solar Wind*?" Cara had a lump in her throat big enough to choke on.

"Yes, it is."

She didn't know whether to be relieved or terrified. It was *Solar Wind*, but she still couldn't raise Ben. She'd been maintaining a search for his mental presence all this time.

"But she's spinning end over end," Yan said. "Ass over tip, and there's some yaw in there as well. We can match velocity, but to lock on we'll have to match her spin as well."

"Can we do it?" Ronan asked.

"No," Kitty said.

"Yes," Yan said.

"We've got to." Cara gripped the arms of her couch.

Crossways Control, Cara broadcast. *It is the Solar Wind. Repeat it is the Solar Wind. Hold your missiles.*

Copy that, Mother Ramona said. *I'm standing over my guys. You'll have all the time we can give you, but I can't risk a collision with the station.*

Understood.

"What next?" Cara asked Yan.

"She's doing one full rotation every thirty-four seconds, left wing down. If we match velocity and come at her from above we can glom onto the upper hull plating toward the tail with a mag lock and use the Dixie's thrusters to try and slow the spin. Just a few degrees in any direction will deflect her away from a direct hit on Crossways and buy us some time."

Cara relayed that to Crossways Control.

Is that the best you can come up with? Mother Ramona asked.

Cara looked around the cabin, Yan nodded and a second or two later, Kitty agreed. Ronan shrugged. "If Yan says so, it's all right by me."

It's the best we can hope for, Cara told Mother Ramona.

Then I'm going to say a very loud prayer on your behalf.

Thanks. I think.

Cara relinquished her place on the copilot's couch to make way for Kitty, who would be much more useful at the controls. She settled into the bucket seat beside Ronan.

"Do you think—" she began.

"I'm trying not to think," Ronan said. "If I think, I'll pee in this beautifully clean space suit, and I'm not plumbed in."

"Helmets," Yan said. "I'll get her as close to the access hatch as I can, but this isn't an exact science. Strap in if you haven't already. It's going to be a bumpy ride."

Cara pulled on the helm and locked it down tight, suddenly feeling very alone. Her HUD showed the suit was functioning normally and she tried to breathe evenly.

"Check audio," Yan said.

"Check."

"Check."

"Check," they all responded.

"Here we go."

The Dixie was flying straight and level on the same trajectory as the freewheeling *Solar Wind*. In space terms they were kissing close, but that still meant they had a kilometer between them. Yan gradually closed the distance. Nine hundred meters, eight hundred.

Kitty called the numbers, but kept her hands away from the controls. At four hundred meters her fingers twitched.

"Not yet," Yan said.

Three hundred.

Two hundred.

One hundred.

Yan let the Dixie drop back just behind the *Solar Wind*'s tail, watching the tail come up beneath them, flip over the top and then see the belly fall away, followed by the nose, repeating the pattern.

From this angle she looked like a diving dolphin, or maybe a humpback whale.

"On the next rotation, Kitty," Yan said. "Get ready to match thrust. Left wing down."

"Ready." Kitty took the thruster control.

"Hold tight."

As the *Solar Wind*'s nose dipped and the tail started to come up, Kitty hit the aft thrusters and Yan hit the short-burn maneuvering ones. The Dixie dived after the *Solar Wind*, belly to back.

Cara felt rather than heard the scrape of ceramic on metal, and a shielding plate bounced off the forward screen. A judder strong enough to rattle her teeth all but shook her out of her seat, saved only by her harness. Then they were tumbling end over end with *Solar Wind*.

"Kitty, hit forward thrusters." Yan ran his hands over the controls in a complex dance until the speed of their tumble slowed and evened out. "Course correct."

"Done." Kitty's voice sounded strange over the suit comms and Cara realized she was holding in hysterical laughter.

All right, Kitty? Cara asked.

I am now.

"We're a bit further aft than I'd hoped," Yan said. "You've got a bit of a trek to the emergency hatch."

"Not a problem," Cara said, already on her feet. "I've got clamps. I'll string a line to the hatch."

The Dixie's air lock was so small that it would only take one fully suited human at a time, even though two could squeeze in under normal circumstances. Cara secured her line as the air cycled and hefted the magnetic clamps which magically bled weight as she floated free of the Dixie's half gravity. She secured the first clamp to the *Solar Wind*'s hull and clipped the line to it, then the second, and the third until she worked her way toward the emergency hatch. By this time Kitty and Ronan were close behind her. They'd have to go through this hatch one at a time, too, and though she wanted to push in front, it made sense to send the pilot in first and the medic in second.

As it turned out it was Ronan who pushed in front and dropped feet first into the tubular air lock.

Heart thumping, she watched the lock cycle.

Is he there? Is Ben there?

He is.

Kitty relinquished her place to Cara as the air lock cycled again.

Is he . . . ?

Alive. Just barely.

Cara's knees gave way as gravity and emotion hit her all at once and she all but fell out of the air lock and scrambled for the companionway to the flight deck.

She unclipped her helmet and let it fall to the floor. "Ben!"

Ronan had unclipped his own helmet and torn off his gloves. He'd stretched Ben out on the deck plating and strapped an oxygen mask to his face. Cara could see the blue tinge to Ben's lips through it, accentuating the gray pallor that had bleached the health out of his brown skin.

Ben! she tried.

"Save it, Cara, he's totally out of it." Ronan administered a shot and then another. "Get some blankets. I don't want to move him."

Cara could feel Ronan's talent for healing pouring energy into Ben. As she came back from the nearest cabin with an airquilt she heard Ronan saying to Kitty, "Is this thing flyable, and if so how quickly can you get us back to Crossways?"

"Yes, and thirty minutes. Whether we'll be able to dock is another matter altogether. I don't know if there's any external damage."

"Docking clamp four has sustained minor damage," the ship cut in.

"Where were you when he needed you?" Cara asked.

"Offline as ordered."

"Damn and double damn. Just get us home." Cara wasn't sure whether she said it to the ship or to Kitty, but she sank down on the floor beside Ben and Ronan and wondered whether Mother Ramona's prayers might be effective, but decided Ben's best chance lay with Ronan.

She connected with him. *Need some extra whammy?*

I'll take anything I can get right now.

She felt the clunk as the Dixie disengaged and saw that Kitty was taking care of business, flight-wise.

Coming in, she flashed to Mother Ramona.

Have a medical team standing by for immediate transfer to Dockside Medical, Ronan said. *It looks like Ben's been trying to chew on hard vacuum.*

Cara looked at him sharply. *How did that happen?*

Ronan shrugged. *If we get him through this, we can ask him.*

◆ ◆ ◆

Ben wasn't sure how long he'd been away.

There was a point when he felt as though he'd walked into a crowded room and everyone had stopped talking at once, then resumed in hushed tones.

The next time he walked into the room everyone was leaning at an odd angle and he realized that he was horizontal.

He recognized Ronan first and then Cara's face swam into view. She looked puzzled. Perhaps she was trying to contact him mind-to-mind. Good luck with that.

He tried to make his mouth work to tell her about his implant, or lack of it, but neither his tongue nor his throat would obey him.

"Ben." She spoke out loud.

He tried to twitch his lips into a smile. Maybe he managed it. Maybe he didn't, but she smiled at him anyway.

"Relax, we've got you."

Maybe he should do as he was told for once.

◆ ◆ ◆

For the first twenty-four hours in the High Dependency Unit Cara didn't move from the chair outside Ben's door except to stand and look through the clear panel and to pace up and down in short, tight turns to get the blood flowing in her legs again.

"He's strong," Ronan told her. "If anyone can pull through, it's Ben."

But despite his words, Ronan spent a lot of time in there pouring as much healing energy as he could spare in Ben's direction.

What had happened? Ben had been away for five days from her perspective, but how long had it been for him? His hair had been just starting to grow again after the all-over shave to change his appearance before tackling Crowder — she counted back — less than sixty days ago. Now it was back to being long and bound into a tight plait, long enough to dangle down to his shoulder blades. It looked like it did when they first met. How had that happened?

It seemed such a small thing to focus on when he was so sick, but it was a puzzle her mind couldn't leave alone.

First Gen and Max came and sat with her. Then it was Wenna's turn. While Wenna was still there, Serafin arrived in a float chair, guided by a pretty nurse who fussed about him in a way he seemed to like.

Hey, there has to be some compensation for being in this place for so long, he said. *She may be young enough to be my granddaughter, but a man can appreciate a good-looking woman, can't he?*

Wenna and Serafin left together and when Archie Tatum arrived it became obvious that they'd set up a rota to keep her company. Kitty, Yan, even Tengue, who said he was just passing through on his way from visiting Fowler. Fowler sent her best regards to the worst gurney driver in the system.

Some time in the middle of the night it was Jussaro's turn.

"Hey, Carlinni." He sat down next to her.

"Hey, yourself."

"How is he?"

"Still too early to tell, but he's hanging in there."

"You know I'm going to have to report this to Crowder, right?"

"I know. Maybe you could delay a short while. Mother Ramona's been trying to get him to release Nan and Ricky."

"Maybe I could, at least until Ben's out of danger."

"Thanks." She covered Jussaro's hand with her own. "You're a pal."

The next day she was allowed to sit in with Ben as his vital signs had stabilized. He still hadn't spoken. Cara hadn't been able to get a flicker out of him mind-to-mind, and a machine was breathing for him. A temporary necessity, Ronan assured her, but it was scary as hell.

The rota of visiting psi-techs continued. Jussaro came again in the middle of the afternoon. "I still haven't reported, but I'm going to have to do it now."

"I know. Thanks for being straight with me."

"Do you want to ghost in on the link?"

"If you think you can keep me hidden."

Jussaro nodded.

"Let's do it, then."

She connected to Jussaro with the lightest of touches and felt him reach out and find Leyburn, Crowder's Telepath.

Tell Mr. Crowder that my earlier report was a bit hasty, Jussaro said. *Ben Benjamin is not dead after all.*

Mr. Crowder knows that already, Leyburn said. *He wants to know why you didn't tell him right away.*

Cara felt a cold chill between her shoulder blades that had nothing to do with the ambient temperature of the station air. Did that mean Crowder had another informer planted in the Free Company? Or did it mean he had someone on Crossways who'd heard the news and reported back?

Mr. Crowder asks me to remind you that he has options where you are concerned, Leyburn said.

She felt Jussaro's level of anxiety rise.

Tell Mr. Crowder that until this morning Benjamin didn't look likely to pull through, Jussaro said. *He's still very sick, but he's stronger now.*

He says that wasn't your call to make. Next time anything happens he wants to hear about it immediately.

Of course.

See that you remember.

How could I forget?

Cara felt Leyburn disconnect.

"Damn!" Jussaro leaned back against the wall.

"We've got a leak," Cara said.

Jussaro nodded. "Another leak—and it's not me."

◆ ◆ ◆

The following day Cara stood back with Ronan, watching anxiously as a med-tech took out the tubes connecting Ben to the machine that had been breathing for him. After what seemed like an hour, but was probably only a few seconds, Ben's chest began to rise and fall on its own.

"I told you it would be all right," Ronan said, but his voice trembled with relief.

"You could have warned me . . ." Cara said. "You could have said how bad it was."

"Then there would have been two of us sick with apprehension." Ronan slumped into a chair by the bedside, his face as pale as Ben's was bloodless.

"I had a right to know."

"Yes, you did. I . . . I'm sorry. I just couldn't . . ." He scrubbed his eyes with the heel of his hand. "Ben's my friend, too, you know, not just my patient."

"Oh, gods, Ronan. You're exhausted. You've poured so much energy into him, you don't have enough to keep yourself upright. Get some rest."

"I'm all right. I'll just close my eyes here for a moment . . ."

In an instant he was deeply asleep. Cara found a spare blanket in a cupboard and draped it over him, then perched on the remaining chair.

It broke her apart to see Ben semi-reclined on the bed, so still. His left arm was a mottled blue-black bruise, darkening his brown skin alarmingly from fingertips to elbow, or at least what could be seen of his arm beneath the protective sheath that held the wrist flexed slightly inward.

She stared at him, wondering exactly what it was that Ronan did to transfer healing energy. She'd never shown any aptitude for healing, but she'd felt the flow when Ronan had drawn it from her. Maybe she could . . .

Ben's eyes flicked open, slightly unfocused.

She stood up so she was in his field of vision without him having to turn his head.

"Hey," she said, following it with a *Hey.*

He blinked and frowned as if trying to force his eyes to focus.

His lips twitched as if he was trying to speak. It might have been, "Hey," but no more than a breath of a whisper came out, so soft she couldn't quite catch it. He didn't answer the mental *Hey.*

"You're back with us." She stuck to words.

He blinked. Maybe that was a slight nod.

"I'd ask how you feel, but I can see from looking at you."

His mouth tightened. He widened his eyes and glanced upward in a brief look that said he was both affronted by his condition and resigned at the same time. Sometimes it didn't take more than half a second to transmit a world of feeling. She was used to doing it with thoughts, but looks worked as well.

"Are you hearing me?" She asked the question aloud, tapped her forehead, and transmitted it mind-to-mind at the same time. "In here?" It was like trying to talk to a deadhead.

His eyebrows knotted together in a frown and he raised his right hand to his forehead and poked with his fingers. His mouth moved as he worked himself up to say something.

"Gone." He managed at last. "Im . . . plant."

Cara felt as though spiders were crawling up her spine. *Ronan!* The young medic jerked awake in an instant. *We have a problem.*

Chapter Seventeen

CIVILITY

KITTY SLIPPED INTO THE BACK OF THE CHAPEL behind three uniformed guardsmen. They were calling it a Service of Respect for the dead guards, now numbering six in total because one had died later from his injuries. There were a lot of faces she didn't know, mostly in uniform. Gupta was there, too, and Wenna, probably as a token of respect and to represent the Free Company. She knew Cara and Ronan Wolfe were at Dockside Medical where Benjamin was still in critical condition, so she didn't expect them to show up.

Mother Ramona and Norton Garrick had come to pay their respects, though. That was kind of them. She didn't know much about the rest of the dead, but Wes had only been on the second pay grade, one step up from a grunt, not especially important. Even so, the head of Crossways had come.

"Kitty, don't hide at the back." Captain Syke came in and shepherded her to the front to stand beside Ellen Heator, who had declared her to be Wes' next of kin. She felt a fraud. Wes was there, or at least his ashes were, in a polished black medonite cylinder about thirty centimeters tall, standing on a small pedestal in front of a holographic scene of his face superimposed on woodland, the leaves of the trees rustling in a gentle breeze. Wes would have liked that. There were other cylinders as well. The bodies of the guards sucked out of the air lock had been recovered by Finders and brought home.

She'd been very fond of Wes, despite latching onto him originally for a purpose. More than fond, perhaps. She'd not lied to Cara when she'd said they might have been more than friends, given time, though she was always acutely aware that neither her life nor her time were her own. She'd never fully committed herself.

Lately she hadn't felt good about the information that she passed back to Alphacorp on a regular basis, but she consoled herself that the Free Company, as far as she was aware, had no plans that would be detrimental to Alphacorp and none of the information that she'd passed on would really hurt the Free Company. It wasn't as if she was passing information on to the Trust. She'd reported Benjamin's loss and early this morning had reported his miraculous rescue, leaving out her own part in it.

Syke stood up and read out a list of the dead and said a few words about each of them. He said how good Wes was at his job. An elderly woman stood up and said what a good boy he'd been when the port immigration officer had brought him to the orphanage. "He was all elbows and knees." She smiled. "Took him a while to grow into his height."

There was no one there from the farm. Had they even been notified? Wes hadn't said he kept that part of his life separate from his job, but maybe he had.

"Do you want to say something, Kitty?" Syke asked.

"Me?"

"Don't be shy, just say what you feel."

She stepped out to the front. "I didn't know him long, but Wes made me laugh. He was kind and gentle and loved animals and children. He volunteered at the community farm." There was a small susurration of surprise among his fellow guardsmen. "I wondered if you knew about that. It would be the biggest thing you could do for him if you went and visited there, and maybe volunteered sometimes. They'll miss him. I'll miss him."

When she ran out of words she stopped and sat down again, her eyes moist. Wes Orton had been in the wrong

place at the wrong time and the Trust had killed him. He
was collateral damage. That whole segment of the station
could have been collateral damage but for Ben Benjamin's
insane idea to fly a bomb-laden ship into the Folds where it
could do no damage.

Thank you for my life, Ben Benjamin.

She suppressed a flare of anger directed toward the Trust
and the team it had sent. The best she could do for Wes was
to keep Alphacorp strong, otherwise the Trust would be the
uncontested pack leader of all the megacorporations, and
that would be a disaster.

✦ ✦ ✦

Ben felt like a freak.

Ronan, two more doctors he'd already forgotten the
names of, and an implant specialist had all trooped in and
out of his room in Dockside Medical, each offering different opinions about how and why his implant had disappeared. One doctor said it had dissolved, the other held to
a weird alien technology theory. There was also the odd
question of why his hair had reverted to his old style, adding
a year's worth of growth in just a few days. It didn't seem
like a big question in itself, but it raised plenty of others. He
didn't think he'd been in the Folds for long, but his hair said
something had happened.

He remembered being meat and rebuilding himself. Ridiculous.

The implant specialist wasn't interested in sudden and
unexpected hair growth. He just shook his head and said he
needed to call in someone else, a specialist.

"I thought you were a specialist." Ben managed a soft
croak.

"He's special, even among specialists. Not the most
charming of characters, but he knows his stuff."

Which was how Civility Jamieson came to be standing at
the foot of Ben's bed, frowning down from a striking height.
Ben was tall, but if he were standing next to Jamieson he'd
be looking up. The man was cadaverously skinny, pole-like
in stature, with steel gray hair and eyes to match.

He didn't offer an opinion as to how it happened, just
tilted his head to one side as if Ben and his lack of implant
were a particularly interesting puzzle to solve.

"I'd like to see if you can be reimplanted, if, that is, you wish to be." He tilted his head to the other side. "Under the circumstances."

"Circumstances?" Ben asked. His voice was a little stronger today, but his chest still felt raw.

"Well, it's not as if you're a Telepath," Jamieson answered, as if that was the only specialization that mattered. True, Telepaths were the ones who tended to go nuts without their implants. Ben wouldn't go nuts, not screaming-and-banging-your-head-on-the-wall nuts, but he'd been open to the tides of the whole universe since he was sixteen years old. You couldn't lose something like that and remain the same. Being a Navigator was what he was.

Even though . . . He heard his own pulse pounding in his ears. Even though he didn't know whether he'd ever have the guts to go into the Folds again.

Did he have a choice? Maybe he did.

Part of him wanted to walk away from it all. Never have to fly anywhere again. When he thought about what had happened, the deep cold returned to gnaw at his bones.

Had it all been real?

Space-burned lungs and a broken wrist told him it had, but common sense told him it couldn't have been. Void dragons? EVA without a suit? Not possible, not for more than fifteen seconds anyway. Fifteen seconds to loss of consciousness, then death. Yet he'd been outside, not only in space but in *foldspace*, and removed four limpets from the hull of *Solar Wind*. Fact—otherwise he wouldn't be here now.

He dragged his mind back to Civility Jamieson.

Cara had come in on the tail end of Jamieson's last comment. She drew down her brows and pressed her lips together. He didn't need to be telepathic to know she was angry. Some communication must have flashed between her and the specialist's specialist that Ben wasn't privy to. Jamieson suddenly stiffened and then flushed red.

"I'm sorry, Commander Benjamin, I didn't mean to . . ."

Ben waved away the apology with his good hand.

"I can arrange for some tests: scans; a synapse map; a full assessment; aptitudes."

Cara walked around and insinuated herself between Ben and Jamieson. *Bastard*, she mouthed silently where Ben could see her lips and Jamieson couldn't.

"I think Ben needs a few more days to recover before you start taking his head apart, Mr. Jamieson."

"Yes, of course. Whenever you're ready, Commander Benjamin."

"Take your time," Cara whispered as Jamieson departed. She reached for Ben's good hand and squeezed it briefly, their only touch since he'd returned, not that he was counting. She'd been there when he woke and had been back and forth several times in the last few days, but conversation was still difficult. He missed having her in his head almost more than he missed having her in his bed.

Almost.

He was as weak as a kitten in that department, too, right at this moment. He hated to admit it, but, in all respects, he needed time.

He groaned inwardly. Nan to rescue, and a boatload of settlers to find. He didn't have time. He needed to be functional, and quickly, with or without an implant.

"What happened out there?" Cara asked the question he'd been dreading. Tell her the unbelievable truth and sound like a madman, or avoid saying anything?

He shook his head, "I really don't know."

And that was the truth. He didn't know. He knew what his memories told him, but was that what had actually happened?

✦ ✦ ✦

Ben didn't need to be an enhanced Empath to know that Cara was worried and trying not to show it. He'd never been able to rely on his telepathic abilities, so he'd always been sensitive to body language, naturally good at reading people without needing to be in their heads.

She squeezed Ben's hand briefly. The touch, skin on skin, was electrifying and he tried to hold on to her fingers for a few moments before she slipped out of his grasp. She flopped back into the chair, just out of his reach.

Ben stared at the hand she'd just released. That touch still thrummed through him. She really cared, despite all she'd been through and everything that had conspired to come between them. Here he was, feeling sorry for himself after just a few days and she'd been powered down for almost a year while she was on the run from van Blaiden.

"How did you do it?" Ben's voice was still little better than a grating whisper.

"Do what? Rescue you from *Solar Wind*?"

He shook his head. "On the run. You kept your implant powered down. Pretended to be a deadhead. How did you do it . . . and not go nuts?"

"I didn't have any choice. I knew they could track me the instant I used it. I wanted to live. I wanted to live more than I wanted to be a Telepath."

He huffed out a breath and touched his fingers to his forehead. "I don't have time for this shit."

"I know. Things to do, people to rescue. Windmills to tilt at."

"*Don Quixote.* Nan likes old books." He cracked a rueful smile. "Used to tell us the stories. I guess she figured we'd never read them for ourselves."

"I've made a start."

"On *Don Quixote*?"

"On rescuing Nan and Ricky. Mother Ramona tried to negotiate their freedom, but Crowder found out you'd survived before she finished the deal."

Ben started to bristle. Rescuing Nan was his job.

"Oh, don't look at me like that. We thought you were dead. If you had been dead wouldn't you have wanted us to finish off what you started, free your family and find the settlers?"

He felt a shiver run through him. Of course he would, but not at the expense of any more lives.

"I . . ." He shrugged. "I've got a bad reputation for getting people killed."

"You're in no position to be overprotective."

"I guess I'm not." It galled him to admit it.

She searched his face, possibly wondering if he meant it. Finally she must have been satisfied because she nodded and continued, "I've sent Tengue and Gwala to Chenon to nose around. They've taken Fowler."

"Fowler? The mouthy woman with the burns?"

"That's the one. She sent you her best wishes—well—not phrased quite like that."

"I can imagine." Ben smiled. He liked Fowler. She said what she thought, not what people wanted to hear.

"She needs reconstructive surgery," Cara said. "Ronan recommended a burn unit in Arkhad City."

Ben nodded. "Neat."

"Well, it was one way of giving them a good excuse to get in. I wanted them there as fast as possible. So far, so good. Hilde's gone independently. Max has given her the details for that contact of his in central records."

"Lorin?"

"That's the one."

"Hilde will scare her off."

"I don't think so. You'd be surprised at Hilde out of uniform. She cleans up well and looks as though she's got a few thousand credits to spare. Lorin responded to bribery last time, right?"

He nodded. "Though Crowder will be operating off-record, so I don't know what Lorin can find."

"She doesn't have to find anything. Hilde's going to bribe her to introduce an anomaly bug into the system. Mother Ramona has a backdoor analyst who claims she can find where the holes are in accounts and see where things aren't. That's where you're likely to find the things Crowder's hiding." She sat forward. "Once we've got likely areas of search we'll go in via the normal shuttle routes. Just a small team. Me on comms, Lewis Bronsen as Finder, Archie Tatum and his bots. We'll rendezvous with Tengue, Gwala, and Hilde for muscle. A six-man team—"

"No!" Ben pushed his voice and it came out sharper than he'd intended.

Cara jumped visibly. "What do you mean, no?"

"There are too many people to get hurt. I should—"

"Oh, yeah, right. What did we just say about overprotective?" Cara jumped up, paced toward the window, pivoted around and leaned on the foot of the bed, arms stiff. "You should just get out of your sickbed, make an instant recovery and do it all your fucking self. Again. Well, fuck that!"

Ack! Was it what he'd said or the way he'd said it? It wasn't that he didn't trust her, he just didn't want to put her—or anybody—in any danger. A good commander shouldn't send other people out to do what he wasn't prepared to do himself.

She flushed with anger and then swallowed whatever she'd been going to say. The flush faded to normal and then beyond, to pale. She took a couple of deep breaths, in through the nose, out through the mouth, and then straightened up. "Try it if you like, but if you leave me now, don't expect me to be here when you get back."

And then she simply turned and walked out.

Ben felt as though someone had doused him in ice water.

"Cara," he called after her. "Cara!"

But she just kept on walking without looking back.

Oh, shit, he'd done it now. She'd taken it as a slight on her competence. In truth it was a good plan, a lot better than the one he'd had, which was to get Rion to start screaming to the news networks and watch Crowder to see where his key people were concentrating their efforts. His hand hovered over the comm unit, ready to pick up and send a message. What could he say that would make it any better?

At that moment Civility Jamieson arrived with an entourage of young student types and proceeded to ignore Ben completely while he explained the barrage of tests that he was going to conduct and which student would be assisting with which test.

"Now?" Ben asked, surprised by the haste.

"You're a very interesting case, Commander Benjamin. As Miss Carlinni reminded me, quite forcibly, this station owes you a debt of gratitude which medical attention can hardly begin to repay. Now, Nine, here will make notes on everything you can remember, while—"

"Nine? That you?" Ben turned to a moon-faced kid who barely looked old enough to be out of school.

She nodded, shyly.

"Got a name?"

"Vina. Vina Daniels."

"Well, Miss Daniels, your job is easy. Just write down CRAFT."

"Craft?"

"Can't. Remember. A. Fucking. Thing."

"Commander Benjamin," Jamieson said.

"Yes, you're perfectly correct, Doctor. I shouldn't be rude to your students. I guess you never are."

"Oh, I'm rude to them all the time. They're hardened to it. Just don't get in my way while I connect this."

He came at Ben with an electrode and a tube of snot glue.

Half a day later Ben had been hooked up to four different machines, had had a succession of scanners pointed in his direction and had been tested eight ways from Sunday and still Vina Daniels sat waiting patiently with her recording pad.

"All right, Miss, Daniels. What do you want to know?"

"Everything you can remember."

"Hmm, well, okay. I was half-dressed from the shower when a team of bastards I think I recognized tried to blow me and my ship to atoms without much care for station safety. I sprang the ship for the air lock and straight into the Folds before she blew. While in foldspace, I floated through the hull of my ship, had my wrist crushed, breathed vacuum for hours and rode a void dragon to peel off four limpets. Then I ran out of luck, and air, and warmth. I managed to get to safety through an emergency hatch, whereupon I crawled back to the flight deck and let the ship find an exit point back into realspace."

"Commander Benjamin." Civility sounded anything but civil. "If you're not going to cooperate, please don't insult my student's intelligence. She's got marks riding on this assignment."

"You're perfectly correct, Dr. Jamieson. Sorry, Vina. Just put that I exited the station air lock, made the jump to foldspace as soon as it was safe to do so and passed out almost immediately. I must have fallen awkwardly on my wrist. The ship must have depressurized and repressurized while I was out cold. When I came to, I managed to find an exit point and came home."

"Thank you, Commander Benjamin."

"You're welcome, Vina . . ." He turned to the student and whispered, "Believe which explanation you like best."

"What happened to the limpets?" she asked softly.

"That's the question, isn't it?"

"Ahem!" Jamieson cleared his throat like a bad stage actor. "I've collated the test results. I believe we can fit a new implant, an upgraded CC22, but it's not without risk. I'm slightly puzzled as to why the pathways that hosted your first implant are still open, so though it's a little unorthodox, I believe that this implant should be fitted without anesthetic. If anything's going to go wrong I need instant feedback to minimize damage."

"What kind of damage?" Suddenly Ben was glad his croaky voice could be attributed to his lungs.

◆ ◆ ◆

Solar Wind was hoisted up on the repair dock, crawling with techs and bots. Cara was only allowed on board because she agreed to wear a high-vis jacket and protective headgear.

"I need my stuff," she'd explained to Garrick's chief engineer at the top of the ramp. "I live here, at least I do when it's not a crime scene or in the repair shop. Is there a lot of damage?"

"Not as much as there would have been if those limpets had blown."

"Four limpets, right?" she asked.

"You can see where they were clamped on and wrenched off again. Those babies aren't meant to be removed easily."

"Would they have to have been detached manually, from the outside?"

"Oh, yeah." The engineer removed his helmet, scratched underneath it and put it back on again. "Not an easy task in a pressure suit."

"Quite. Might Commander Benjamin have had to remove a glove to detach a limpet?"

"Only if he wanted to lose the hand at best, at worst die horribly in a depressurized suit."

"That's what I thought. Thanks."

She let the cabin door slide closed behind her and breathed a sigh of relief.

Ben's buddysuit top was still draped casually across the bed, its functions hibernating. She picked it up, folded it in half and hugged it to her chest like a long-lost child.

"Cara." The door opening startled her.

"Ronan. I see they've got a good supply of hi-vis vests. Yellow's not your color, though."

She rolled the buddysuit top swiftly and stuffed it into her bag, then started to gather her underwear and sleepsuit.

"You and Ben had a disagreement?" Ronan asked.

"He's a stubborn bastard." She kept packing.

"He's Ben."

"That's what I said." She swallowed before her voice cracked. "I only just got him back and now he wants to dump me and go off on his own to be noble. He's not even on his feet yet, and already he's trying to fling himself between me and trouble. Between anyone and trouble. Stupid white knight. He thinks he's invulnerable and he's not. He's going to get himself killed and . . ." She dropped the bag on the floor and kicked it. "And then I'm going to have to go through this whole dead thing again, only next time it will be real."

She hadn't meant to say it aloud, hadn't even realized she had until Ronan put his arms around her and she found herself leaning into his shoulder, sobbing as though it was the end of the world.

"Silly bloody man," she managed between sniffs and gulps. "I could kill him myself."

"He won't be going anywhere for quite a while. Whatever he thinks, he's not fit yet. Besides, the test results are in. Jamieson's getting ready to fix him up with a new implant."

"Is that good? I mean, will it take?"

"There are problems—anomalies. Jamieson needs to do the implantation with Ben conscious. No anesthetic."

"What? Is that even possible?"

"It's irregular. He needs to be able to abort the operation if it's not going well."

"Define not going well."

"The implant's a seed, it grows through the brain organically."

"Implant 101, Doc." Cara tapped her own forehead.

"The tests showed Ben's neural pathways from the first implant are still open—there's just no implant there. The new implant should grow along the lines of least resistance, the old pathways. If it doesn't, if it tries to forge new pathways . . ." He shrugged. "Jamieson doesn't know what damage it might do."

"He's explained all this to Ben and Ben's willing to go along with it?"

"Yes and yes."

"He doesn't have to do it, especially not for me. Psi-tech or not, he's still Ben."

"I think you should tell him that yourself. Go now. There's not much time."

Chapter Eighteen

CAPTIVITY

RICKY HAD LOST TRACK OF TIME. HE'D BEEN trying to mark off days by the number of meals and number of sleeps, but with nothing much to do all day except read or play yet another pointless round of Braintease on his handpad, he'd been dozing more and more and sleeping through the night less and less.

He'd never read so much in his life before—not all at one time. The choice of books on the slate was an odd one, mostly fiction, and not for kids either. Minnow's wife had chosen them. He wondered what she was like. Her taste in books was certainly strange. There were a lot of books about crime.

He'd always got the impression that the police on Chenon generally didn't have much work to do. The crime rate was low and, except at the ports, which had more crime than all of the rest of Chenon put together, mostly consisted of misdemeanors, some fraud, and the occasional murder, more shocking for its rarity. Everyone had enough for their needs, which cut down on them trying to take whatever someone else had.

Ricky had been learning about crime on Chenon from a series of Adam Perry books on Minnow's slate. Adam Perry was an ex-Monitor turned private security cop, one of the fully licensed ones. Though crime was low, Adam Perry seemed to solve most of it together with his partner Jane Cox, who was smarter than Perry. Perry was a short-range Telepath and a Psi-4 Empath who often jumped to conclusions that were always good guesses. "Trusting his gut," he called it. Cox had been a local police cadet who'd exposed a corrupt superior and had been bought off with a pension, but she hated herself for taking the payoff and tried to be better than the best cop. She worked everything out logically. Between them they were a good team, though sometimes Perry made guesses that were nothing short of magic. Ricky kept going back over earlier chapters to see if there were clues that he'd missed. How did Adam Perry do it? Ricky took to reading bits out loud to Nan, hoping that she could hear him. He was worried that the drugs they'd given her would addle her mind permanently.

They'd kept up the bone regeneration treatment. After six sessions the fracture sleeve had been removed in favor of a smart-stocking. He'd heard an argument between a med-tech and Danniri. The med-tech said the old lady needed to put some weight on the leg now, Danniri had said to keep up the medication and told him to put Nan back on the bed.

Ricky had to find a way of stopping them giving Nan all the stuff that made her dopey. He understood it was so she didn't contact anyone. Nan was only a short-range Telepath, but she still had friends from the old days, from her time working for the Five Power Alliance on Earth, who contacted her regularly. He wondered if any of them were starting to worry. If he managed to get her a reprieve from the drugs could she send a message out?

He thought hard about it and came up with a plan. It wasn't a good plan, and it was going to hurt, but it was the best he could do.

He pushed his folding bunk against the wall and sat down behind Nan's bed with his back to the camera eye. He pulled off his right shoe and sock and put his shoe back on. He figured out where it might rub him if he walked without his sock and then he took off the shoe again and, using the sole, started to rub at his heel.

Oww, he was right, it did hurt, but he kept on rubbing anyway. Then he put his shoe back on and started to pace.

By the time Minnow came to deliver dinner and Nan's nightly meds the nasty blister he'd started had flowered and burst, but he was still pacing the length of the cell smacking the wall and pacing to the other end. Smack and turn. Smack and turn.

"What you doin' now?" Minnow asked as he balanced the tray on the table and gave Nan her usual shot.

"What's it look like I'm doing? I'm exercising. How many days have we been here? I'm going to lose the use of my legs if I don't make them work. Owww!" He sat down on the floor and pulled off his shoe, making sure Minnow could see the blister. "See. I've gone so soft, my feet are blistering."

Minnow bent over to look.

If I were Adam Perry I'd jump right up and hit Minnow under the chin with my head and escape, Ricky thought. But he wasn't Adam Perry and he wasn't going anywhere. He'd tried that already.

"Nasty blister." Minnow tapped his pockets. "Got no skin gel, but I'll bring some tomorrow. In the meantime, if you've got to walk, do it barefoot."

"Okay, thanks," Ricky said meekly, shuffling sideways to get out of Minnow's way and trying not to let the big man see that he'd dropped the empty blast-pack on the floor when he'd checked his pockets.

Mine. Ricky casually placed his hand over the fallen pack. He wasn't sure what he could do with it, but something, surely.

The following morning Ricky was suitably grateful to Minnow for the tiny tube of skin gel. When he figured it was close to time for Nan's evening shot he squeezed out a centimeter and smoothed it on the side of her neck. Chameleon-like, it darkened to her wind-weathered skin tone and looked like any patch of normal skin.

It wasn't Minnow who came that night, it was the small wiry guard whose name Ricky didn't know. Ricky held his breath, but the guard didn't suspect. He slapped the blast pack onto the skin gel patch and left.

Ricky jumped up and wiped the film of the drug off the gel with a corner of wet towel, making it look as though he was wiping the old woman's face.

"Nan," he whispered, close to her ear. "Nan!"

But it took several hours before the residue of the drug leached out of her system.

✦ ✦ ✦

"Ricky." Nan's voice was little more than a whisper in the darkness of the night, but Ricky rolled to his knees immediately and put his head close to hers.

"Nan, hush, there's a camera. I don't know what they can hear."

He jumped up and felt his way to the spigot, turning it to full so that the sound of running water filled the room, then made his way back to the bedside.

"You've been asleep, Nan. You don't even really wake when they put food in your mouth."

She made a kind of guuurrgh noise and then managed, "How long?"

"About eighteen days . . . I think. I may have missed one or two."

"Where?"

"I worked it out. I think we're under the grapple arena, the De Barras Stadium."

"Good boy. You're going to be like your Uncle Reska." Nan didn't question him or ask what his reasoning was. "My leg . . ." she said.

"You broke it when they captured you, I think. They've been treating it. Six bone regeneration sessions and now it just has a smart-stocking on."

"Must be almost healed, then. It aches. Help me up."

"No, they'll realize you're awake. Stay still."

"No strength, anyway," she said.

"Door's locked. We couldn't just walk out even if you could. Walk, I mean. Can you call anyone? You know . . . telepathically."

There was a pause. "Uh, no. Shut down, mentally. Whatever they've given me there's reisercaine in the mix. How come I'm awake now?"

"I faked a blister. One of the guards brought me skin gel. I put it on your neck. Don't have much, though."

She put her hand up to the side of her neck. "Clever boy."

Ricky felt himself smiling. Nan's approval had to be earned.

"And I got outside the door a couple of times."

Carefully he described the corridor: double doors at one end, an emergency stair, and antigrav shaft at the other. "The staircase goes both up and down, so we're not on the lowest level. I'm not sure whether the grav shaft is turned on or not."

"Have they asked any questions, about Reska or ... anything."

"No, nothing. I'm sorry, Nan, this is all my fault. If I hadn't ..."

"Hush, boy. You made it easy for them, but they might have come after us anyway."

"What next?"

"Wait. Watch. Be ready. If they don't want anything from us, we're bait in some kind of trap they've set for Reska. That means he'll be coming."

"You're sure?"

"Oh, yes."

"Can't we get in touch? If I use the skin gel again, how long will it take for the reisercaine to wear off?"

"A day or two, maybe, but my Telepathy range is too short. The people who could help are worlds away."

"Uncle Ben?"

"Reska may try to contact me via Cara. I have to listen. Listen and be ready to respond."

"Should I use the gel every day? I'm not sure how long it will last."

"Every day, night and morning for three days until the reisercaine wears off. I need to see if someone is trying to contact us. Have you got enough for that?"

"I think so. I wish I had an implant."

"You will, eventually."

If we ever get out of here, Ricky thought. But somehow talking about normal things made it seem more possible.

"Will Dad be really upset if I do?"

"Well, he won't like the idea, but he'll get over it."

"Is it just the idea of space?"

"He was a bit younger than you when your grandparents died in the Folds. He never developed a taste for space travel after that."

"Uncle Ben did."

"Reska was three years younger than Rion, always a bit more adventurous."

"I want to be a psi-tech and explore like Uncle Ben."

"It sounds more glamorous than it is, take my word for it. There are wonders out there, but there's an awful lot of nothing between them."

"You used to work in space."

"Not exactly. I used to work on planets, mostly, but that meant traveling between them."

"I always wanted to work for the Trust, but now . . ."

"There's more places than the Trust if you want to be a psi-tech. Your great-grandfather has connections."

"My great-grandfather is still alive?"

"Oh, yes."

"You never talk about him. I just thought . . ."

"That's what I always let people think. Even Rion and Reska have never met him. Listen, Ricky, if anything happens to me you need to contact Malusi Duma and tell him everything you know."

"Malusi Duma, do you mean *that* Malusi Duma, the president of African Unity."

"That Malusi Duma. Yes. Just tell him who sent you."

Ricky and Nan talked on and off through the night until the light level in the room rose to indicate a new day. Nan lay on the bed as still as if she were drugged again. Ricky turned off the spigot and climbed into his narrow bunk, his eyes gritty from lack of sleep.

Minnow appeared with a breakfast tray just as Ricky drifted off.

"Not reading this mornin'?" Minnow asked. "Or exercisin'? You all right?"

"Tired. Water spigot's faulty. Kept me awake."

Minnow put down the tray and turned the spigot on, then off again. "Seems all right."

"It does now. Thanks for checking."

Ricky sat on the edge of his bunk.

Minnow pressed the controls that raised the head end of Nan's bed so she was sitting upright. Ricky had described carefully how this part of the day went and Nan stared resolutely ahead and swallowed the mush Ricky spooned into her mouth while Minnow watched.

When they were done Minnow took a blast pack from his right pocket.

Always the new one from his right pocket, the spent one goes into his left, Ricky noted, fingering the spent one in his own left pocket. There was little difference between a new one and a spent one if you didn't look closely at the telltale.

Also it meant that Minnow had the blast pack in his right hand, so he always applied it to the left side of Nan's neck. Ricky remembered reading in his Adam Perry book that regular habits could get you into trouble. He began to take note of Minnow's regular habits.

✦ ✦ ✦

Crowder finished the holo-vid call to his daughter, Tamsin. It was his monthly ritual. They'd been estranged for half her life, but she'd taken the initiative to get in touch when Nini was born and he'd grasped the opportunity eagerly. He'd never held his granddaughter in the flesh, they were worlds apart physically, but seeing her grow from a baby to a bright toddler had been an intense pleasure. Nothing was allowed to interrupt and he liked a moment or two after each call to reflect on the joys of being a grandfather.

He looked up in mild annoyance, therefore, when he found Stefan hovering in the office doorway.

"Sorry, sir, but you said you wanted to be informed if anyone of the mercenary persuasion showed up on immigration scans."

Crowder's insides lurched.

"Who?"

"Not sure, but definitely mercs. Three of them, two upright and one badly wounded. Seeking medical treatment. We don't have much detail. I took the liberty of arranging for them to be interviewed."

"Send Danniri—no, wait." That was overkill. He scratched his ear. "Are they still at the port?"

"Yes, waiting on an immigration officer in an interview room."

"Patch me through and give me a direct audio link to the interviewer on Priority One Protocol."

"Yes, sir."

Crowder scanned their credentials on screen. He didn't recognize any of their names. They were each listed as *pri-*

vate contractor working out of New Rio. He didn't have long to wait before a holographic display of a bare interview room opened up on his desk. There were three individuals, two of them seated, the other lying on a medevac float.

The interviewer, Masood, entered, wearing a small earpiece. He went through their credentials with each one and rechecked their handpad readings. Everything correlated, including their DNA.

Masood asked all the right questions and got all the right answers from Tengue and Gwala: private contractors here to purchase reconstructive surgery for an injured colleague.

"Check the injured woman," Crowder said directly into Masood's earpiece. "Make sure she's genuine."

Masood gave a slight nod and moved over to the float. "Would you mind showing me your injuries?"

"You want to look at my tits?"

"No, I want to see your injuries."

"That's what I said. Amounts to the same thing. Go ahead, there's nothing there to stir a man up anymore."

"What'd I say?" The merc who seemed to be the leader had a warning note in his voice.

"Oh, yeah, that I'm still a hot chick even with half my chest looking like barbecue. Go ahead, Agent Masood, grab an eyeful while the painkillers are still doing their job. Can't feel a fucking thing."

The woman's chest was a pulp of red. Masood stepped back when he saw it and Crowder's gorge rose, even though he was viewing it on a holo.

"Seen enough of the freak show?" The woman's voice cracked.

The boss merc reached forward and held her hand. "We'll get you fixed up. Surgeons here are the best we can buy." He looked at Masood. "And the sooner we can get you to the burn unit, the sooner they can get started. Are we good to go, Agent Masood?"

"Let them in," Crowder said, and closed the connection.

He turned to Stefan, who was still hovering. "Keep a watch on them. Let me know if they step out of line, but they look genuine to me." He sucked in air through his teeth. "I think it's time I took a little trip out of town."

He'd planned to take a trip anyway while the Grapple Championships moved into the stadium. He couldn't reschedule a national sporting event for his own convenience. He hadn't expected Benjamin would take this long to walk into his trap.

"Where will you be, sir?"

"Where no one will expect to find me. It's time I paid my ex-wife a visit. Let Mr. Leyburn know that I'll be on Norro if he needs to contact me."

✦ ✦ ✦

"Cara!"

She stood in the doorway, looking tough in black. There was no softness in her expression as she glared at him. Ben had hoped she'd come back, had rehearsed what he wanted to say to her half a hundred times, but he wasn't sure he'd see her again before the implantation procedure, and afterward, well, who knew?

"You're an idiot," she said.

"I'm an idiot. Hey, I was going to say that first."

"Just shut up and listen. You don't need to have this implant restored just because you think you need to be a psi-tech to run the Free Company, and you certainly don't need to do it on my account. No one gives a shit whether you're connected or not. We all . . . I love you. Just as you are. Tell Jamieson to go fuck himself."

She stepped into the room and he held out his good hand. She came close and took it. Their fingers connected and suddenly everything was right with his world.

"Thank you."

"You'll call it off, then?"

He shook his head. "I'm not doing it for you. I'm doing it for me. Because I have to. When it happened . . ." He took a deep breath. "And if I tell you what did happen to me out there, you'll tell me I'm a fantasist, but in case this doesn't go well I've recorded it all on my handpad. It may have been a big hallucination, but it felt real.

"Anyhow, after I got rid of the limpets I was pretty beaten up, but I made it back to the flight deck. I was in foldspace and I couldn't see the line to an exit point. There's always a line, a way to go. *The* way to go. It was like swimming through tar. I've never been *lost* like that. It scared me. Really scared me. Maybe I realized I didn't have my implant anymore, maybe I didn't. I'm a bit fuzzy on that.

"Then, instead of a line there was a ... path is too strong a word. It was like following a trail of breadcrumbs where there's one or two crumbs every hundred paces, and you're never sure if this will be the last one."

"Your underlying talent."

"I guess so, but it was so insubstantial."

"It brought you home."

"Not the first time. It took me to some point at the ass-end of the galaxy."

"You had to make a second jump?"

"Blind. Using the ship's automatics. It wasn't enough. I knew it wouldn't be enough."

Her grip on his fingers tightened.

"I've never been scared of foldspace before, but I was scared then. Scared sick."

"But you did it."

"I tried to knock myself out with anesthetic but ... well, let's just say if I hallucinated it was all remarkably consistent with what I thought I'd seen before. But I had to do it, scared or not. It was the only way home ... back to you."

"You're here now. No need to—"

"I can't live my life terrified of the Folds." He squeezed her hand back. "After our parents were lost, Rion said he was never leaving Chenon, never going into the Folds. He never once took an aptitude test. Never wanted an implant, never wanted anything except the farm, especially if it meant he could stay put. Kai tested negative for psi talent. Now Rion's worried that little Ricky will test positive, and he's right to be worried. All the signs are there. I wanted to talk to him about it, but Rion wouldn't ... We had words ..." He shrugged. "Families, you know?"

"I know."

"Nan's trying to sit back, to let Rion and Ricky sort it out between themselves. Rion's not going to be able to keep him on the farm. The kid's going to fly."

Cara had her head on one side, as if trying to make sense of him.

He took a deep breath. "I can't live my life like Rion, afraid of going anywhere, doing anything. My implant's too much a part of what I am now. If I can get it back ..."

"You're willing to risk everything."

He cleared his throat. "Damned if I do, damned if I don't."

Ronan arrived at the door with a float chair. "They're ready for you now, Ben. I'll take you down. Civility Jamieson's supposed to be the best there is, but I'm not going to let him do this without me there."

Ben looked at Cara. Her pale face said everything. "Will you come too?" he asked.

"Try keeping me out."

Chapter Nineteen

CONNECTED

CARA HAD NEVER BEEN PRESENT AT AN IM-
plantation before, only her own, but the anesthetic was
all she remembered. A pleasant, muzzy feeling as she
drifted to sleep and waking slowly to a world that was so
different. It was like being dropped into a rainbow after
being blind her whole life. It was all noise and color and
brightness inside her head. That was the point at which
some new implantees started screaming, but Cara had
taken a deep breath and plunged right into it, reveling in
the experience. After a while she'd learned to tone down
the brightness, tune out the unwanted sounds, focus.

And it had all started like this.

Ben sat in a treatment chair, his head immobilized by a
padded clamp. A complicated-looking piece of equipment
with a robotic arm loomed behind him, but it was still offline while a techie loaded a cartridge into the business end.

It brought back the image of herself in such a chair with
Donida McLellan . . . No, don't go there. What McLellan
had done to her was irrelevant. She'd be useless to Ben if
she was wrapped in her own misery. McLellan was on-
station somewhere, little more than a vegetable. Sooner or
later Cara would go and confront her own nightmares, see

the woman and get it over with. Until then, better to keep the memories sealed away.

"All right?" Ronan asked her as if he knew what she was thinking. Hell, he probably did.

"I'm fine. Holding together at least."

He nodded. "Good. I'll be monitoring Ben throughout. If I need extra whammy—"

"I'll be here."

"Good, thanks."

Me, too. Another mental voice inserted itself into the conversation.

Jussaro? Cara recognized him instantly. *Where are you?*

Corridor waiting area. Close by. I heard what was happening. You can't keep anything secret when your company is psi-tech. I've been through something like this, recently. Oh, not without an anesthetic, and my neural pathways had completely closed up, but I know what it's like to wake up to something you thought you'd never experience again. Let me help.

Cara looked at Ronan and he nodded.

You're in, Jussaro.

Standing by.

A gaggle of student types entered the observation gallery, a slightly raised box enclosed by a clear wall. Their conversations stilled as they came through the door. One of them, a round-faced girl with sawn-off dark hair and almond eyes, moved to the front and waved at Ben. He responded with his good hand.

"Hey, there, Nine. Get a good mark for your assignment?"

She nodded. "I went with the unlikely explanation."

"Good for you."

"If you've finished . . ."

Cara hadn't seen Civility Jamieson come and slide into the surgeon's chair behind a bank of equipment with shaped pads for the operator's hands and a gantry above with a jointed arm carrying a full facemask.

"Sorry, professor." The girl Ben had called Nine sat down with her fellows.

The techie finished installing the cartridge and patted the machine fondly. "All ready at this end."

"Places everyone," Jamieson said. "Commander Benjamin, the bot will give you a shot to immobilize you."

"It won't be necessary. I can keep still."

"It will be necessary, trust me. There's zero tolerance for movement, but we need you to be able to communicate, so you'll have use of your right hand. Doctor Wolfe is going to monitor you and Miss Carlinni will have your hand." He looked at Cara. "Well, what are you waiting for?"

Cara stepped forward.

"Hey there," she said.

"Hey there, yourself."

"I'm Doctor Wolfe's assistant."

"So I understand." The corners of Ben's lips twitched and he squeezed her fingers. "Once for no, twice for yes?"

She nodded. "And squeeze like hell for ohmygodsthathurts."

"Will do. Is there a sign for I love you?"

She brushed her thumb lightly across the outside of his hand. "Maybe."

The bot sidled into position behind Ben's head and its arm snaked over and tapped the side of his neck. Cara felt all the tension go out of his body as the immobilizer kicked in. She squeezed his hand and he squeezed back.

"Stand by." Jamieson pulled the face-piece down from the control gantry and rested his head into it while his fingers found the sensor pads. "Commencing."

Ronan moved to Ben's other side and rested his hand on Ben's arm, just above the wrist case. Cara reached across Ben and took Ronan's free hand with hers to close the loop.

The robotic arm moved up to Ben's forehead and suckered on. She felt Ben's fingers twitch and through Ronan's connection knew that the tiny hollow needle had pierced Ben's skull. She held her breath.

❖ ❖ ❖

It hurt. Everywhere. Not just the needle through Ben's skull, but the implant, stretching its tendrils through his brain, triggered sensations in body parts unconnected with the process, or so he'd thought. His left foot was on fire, but he couldn't do anything about it. Then his hip. The pain flowed like acid across his belly and down to his groin. Oh, gods, he was going to cut off the circulation in Cara's fingers at this rate.

Relax, it's not real. Let it flow through.

Easy to think. Harder to do.

The fire ate his spine and burst through the top of his head.

He heard Jamieson's voice from a vast distance. Something about pathways, but it wasn't directed at him.

"Ben." Cara's hand squeezing his. "Are you still with us?"

He twitched back. Once. Twice.

"Does it hurt?"

He twitched back. Once.

"Liar."

Twice.

"Not lost your sense of humor, then?"

Once. Then: twice.

"Jamieson says the implant's in place and it's spreading along the expected pathways. Can you feel it?"

Twice.

"Ronan says you're doing fine."

He didn't know how to answer that. They hadn't agreed a prearranged signal for bullshit. It was comforting bullshit, though. Had the pain eased slightly? Probably not, but at least Ronan was telling him there was no external damage. His legs weren't actually on fire. The top of his head didn't have a crater in it. The implant was—

Ohgodsohgodsohgods.

A void opened up in his head and foldspace rushed into it. He was outside the *Solar Wind* once more, turning to catch the bony crest of a void dragon, only this time it was rainbow-hued. Slick oily blue-green shimmering with a thousand different colors. It turned its head and breathed on him, a mighty wind roaring in his ears.

Fire. Consuming the void dragon from tail to tip. It burned blacker than emptiness and he began to slip and slide away into the hard reality of foldspace, sucked down and down.

A voice that belonged to neither Cara nor Ronan said something about new pathways and abort. Ronan's voice said, "No, if you do that now you've lost him."

"Keep going. We'll bring him back." That was Cara's voice.

Ben, hold on.

He grasped Cara's hand and she drew him upward. Ronan was there as well, and someone else. Ben struggled to identify the third person, but he had wiry strength. They weren't going to let him go. He clawed upward, searching for the line. He must find . . .

There.

"Ben."

He squeezed Cara's fingers. Once. Twice.

"We've got him," Cara said.

"He's stabilizing." Ronan's voice this time.

Reality came back slowly, one jumping muscle at a time, until a wave of shudders rolled through his body from feet to scalp.

◆　◆　◆

Cara wobbled and would have fallen but someone grabbed her shoulders from behind and steadied her. A purple-black hand reached over and held her own hand over Ben's so she couldn't let go.

Ronan had already disengaged and had slumped backward into a chair against the observation gallery wall.

"Don't let go yet." Jussaro's lips were close to her ear. "He's relying on you."

"Not letting go," she said.

"You can when I tell you."

"Don't want to."

"No, but you will. You're exhausted. I'll take it from here. It's what I'm good at—teaching. It's what I did before they caught me teaching more than they wanted their psi-techs to learn."

Cara felt Jussaro's presence ease between herself and Ben. There was a surge as Ben realized she was backing off.

It's all right. I'll be back.

She needs to rest, Jussaro said. *I'm going to stick around for a while if that's all right?*

Whatever you say.

Cara disengaged her mind and, finally, her hand. Jussaro stepped around her and took her place. One of the students, the one Ben had called Nine, guided her into a chair and shoved a bottle of water into her hand.

"You'll be dehydrated. Drink."

She drank. "Thanks."

Across the room another student was attending to Ronan. Civility Jamieson had departed without a word.

"Where's your boss?" Cara asked.

"He's not strong on bedside manner," Nine said.

"I'm surprised you stick with him."

"He's the best there is. I'd like to be half as good as he is one day and if I can learn from him I'm willing to put up with his rudeness."

"Don't tell me, he really cares about his patients."

"No, I don't think he does, but he cares about his reputation and every patient he loses puts a dent in that. Patients are a game to him, a puzzle to be solved, and he doesn't like to lose. He'll take on cases other specialists won't touch, because he wants the challenge."

"I'm glad Ben was a sufficiently intriguing puzzle."

"He's certainly that," Nine said. "Has he told you what happened to him in foldspace?"

She shook her head. "Not entirely."

"Here, check this out." She held out her right hand and fistbumped Cara to transfer a file. "That's the original recording from when I was taking Commander Benjamin's notes. You might find it interesting. I did."

Two of their security team waited outside Dockside Medical to take her back to Blue Seven with Ronan. Cara didn't have the privacy in the tub to play the file Nine had given her, but Gen had a room ready. It showed signs of still needing work, but there were four solid walls and a door that closed. It was furnished with a bed, a chair, and a table, and it had a window. Currently it looked out onto a building site, but it would eventually look out onto an enclosed courtyard. Maybe there would be plants in tubs, a place to sit, and a blue-sky ceiling.

Until then . . . she activated the privacy screen and the window darkened.

Right, let's see what we've got here.

She sat on the edge of the bed and accessed the file. It was unmistakably Ben's voice, if a little husky. She listened to all of it and felt her mouth going slack in surprise.

That couldn't be right.

She activated it again and listened through as if the recording might change, add something or leave something out.

On the third pass, she decided to take it a section at a time.

Ben's voice said: *I was half-dressed from the shower when a team of bastards I thought I recognized tried to blow me and my ship to atoms without much of a care for station security. I sprang the ship for the air lock and straight into foldspace before she blew.*

That much was absolutely true. She'd picked up the abandoned buddysuit top herself and left it at Dockside Medical for Ben. And she'd seen *Solar Wind* exit Port 22 and wink out into foldspace. If the station had been merely ship-sized it could have been pulled into the Folds like the *Simonides* had been.

All right, so far, so good, but the next bit ... She activated the next section of the recording: *While in foldspace I floated through the hull of my ship, got my wrist crushed, breathed vacuum for hours, and rode a void dragon to peel off four limpets.*

Well ... something or someone had peeled off the limpets, and when Kitty Keely had stepped through onto the *Simonides* in the Folds she'd proved that the term "solid" had little meaning in foldspace, but void dragons? Come on. She'd never seen a void dragon, but still there were navigators' tales. She'd always thought they were made up to perpetuate the myth.

Ben's voice continued: *Then I ran out of luck, and air, and warmth. I managed to get back to safety through an emergency hatch.*

Ben certainly had the broken wrist. Ronan had confirmed that it was more like a crush injury than the sort of break that resulted from a fall.

She didn't know what to think. Ben himself had told her: *If I tell you what did happen to me out there, you'll tell me I'm a fantasist,* but he'd admitted: *It may have been a big hallucination, but it felt real.*

She didn't know what scared her most: the fact that Ben had had a massive hallucination in foldspace, or the fact that maybe he hadn't. If he hadn't, then maybe the stories were true. There were things living in foldspace, things not only alien, but things from another dimension.

✦ ✦ ✦

Ben lay cradled by the contour bed, semi-recumbent, eyes closed, listening to what was in his head, exploring what he could sense around him. His arms and legs felt like jelly but his thoughts were jumping all over the place.

His bed faced hubward. That one thought gave him immense satisfaction. It didn't prove he was a Psi-1 Navigator, but it did prove his skills were not completely lost.

"Feels strange, doesn't it?" a voice said.

"Jussaro?" Ben recognized the voice and ran it through his mental checklist of who he'd expected to find in his hospital room and frowned. He opened his eyes and blinked rapidly before screwing them up against the glare.

"Sheesh, Benjamin, your eyes are like drill holes, all pupil. Lights down," Jussaro said, and the ceiling panels dimmed.

"Thanks." Ben shaded his eyes with one hand. "Cara?"

"Exhausted. Sent her home to sleep it off. There are a couple of nurses close by if you need anything."

"No." Ben shook his head and winced.

"Pain?" Jussaro asked.

"Not exactly. Not now."

"Feels weird?"

Ben grunted agreement. "It's almost the same, yet entirely unlike . . ."

Jussaro grunted. "Me, too, though I was out cold when they did my second implant. I guess yours hurt."

"You could say that." Pain was always difficult to recall. There was a memory of the fact that it hurt, but the feeling had gone. Truly gone. Endorphins, probably. That was the mind's own protective mechanism. If you really remembered pain you'd never risk doing anything dangerous again.

"It didn't go quite according to Jamieson's plan," Jussaro said.

"I guessed there was a bit of a fuss."

"Jamieson wanted to abort, but Ronan said no, and Cara made the decision to continue."

"Should I thank her?"

"You should. She probably saved your life, or at least your mind."

"Second time in—how long?"

"Five days."

"Getting to be a habit," Ben said. "How much does Crowder know about all this?"

"He knows you're alive, but in bad condition. He doesn't know about the implant, because I didn't know when I made my last report. I'm going to try not to let it slip when I make my next report."

"What difference does it make?"

"My implant's got a kill switch. I have to play by Crowder's rules."

"You believe what he says about a kill switch?"

"Let's put it this way, I don't want to put it to the test."

"If mine had had a kill switch I'd be dead by now," Ben said.

"Not necessarily. Have you ever seen what they do to remove an implant?"

"Only seen the results. It doesn't happen often."

"Exactly." Jussaro touched his own forehead. "They can't take it out, they kill it instead. Every implant has a kill code. To kill it they need to input the code from short range. It powers down instantly. Bang, gone. Over the next few months the remains gradually shrivel, but that hardly matters. The real damage has been done."

"How short is short range?"

"Line of sight. Two meters, maybe three. The kill switch isn't meant to be used as a weapon," Jussaro continued, "but it could be, if the right person had the right code."

"I went up against Crowder on Chenon and he certainly didn't have a kill switch then."

"He wasn't expecting you then."

"Fair point." Ben was silent for a moment. "He'll have Cara's code, too."

"I think it's safe to say he'll have the codes for everyone on your team, but it's not like firing a pistol. The code has to be programmed into the machine, and it's not a device you can carry around in your pocket. It's handheld, but not small. It's about half a meter long and twenty centimeters wide and deep. The machines I've seen can maybe do one deletion per minute if the operator can program quickly enough." Jussaro let the information sink in. "You're free of that, Benjamin. New implant, new design. No kill switch. I checked with Professor Jamieson. I can help you make the most of what you've got, but in return I need to know how you managed to get rid of your implant so effectively."

"If I knew I'd tell you."

"You do know. The information's in there somewhere. Work with me and we'll find it."

"Right now?"

"Right now. You need to work it, expand the pathways, make the most of what you've got."

"I feel as though I've been through a mincer and reconstituted with some of the bits in the wrong place."

"That's remarkably astute."

"Bits in the wrong place?"

"In a way. The implant filled up all the old pathways, taking the line of least resistance, but it burrowed into new areas, too. You've almost certainly not lost anything you had before, but you might have gained a grade or two."

"I was already a Psi-1 Navigator."

"But not much of a Telepath, Cara told me. You might find that's changed, or maybe you'll have acquired a talent you didn't used to have. You might be a Finder or a Psi-Mech, a Healer or a little of all of them."

"Is that likely?"

"It's rare. Thing is, there's a window of opportunity, and if you let it slip past, you might never know."

"Window of opportunity?"

"You're buzzing now, right?"

"Buzzing, yes. Energized, perhaps, mentally anyway."

"It won't last. You'll crash soon. Before that happens we've got work to do."

"Work?"

"You'll thank me later."

◆ ◆ ◆

Ben wasn't sure that he was ever going to thank Jussaro, but by the following afternoon he realized that not only was he not as tired as he had been, but he was beginning to make noticeable improvements in his Telepathy. Maybe he wasn't ever going to be more than a Psi-4, but he'd been almost a deadhead before, able to receive but hardly able to throw a thought further than the end of his nose.

Contacting Cara for the first time was a breakthrough.

Ben! She almost overwhelmed him with the strength of her answer, shot through with pure delight.

There's nothing more they can do here, I've been discharged.

I'll come and get you.

I can manage.

No, I'll come and get you. Crowder's had two tries to take you out. Garrick's got enough security at Dockside Medical to start a small war, but we're all vulnerable moving around the station. I'll bring a team. Besides, Ronan says you've got to take it easy.

He sighed. She was right, dammit, but that wasn't going to stop him. *All right.* He tried to sound meek, but he wasn't sure he'd fooled her.

Ben refused a float chair and walked out of the med center with a look of grim determination on his face. Cara was watching him. He fancied she was waiting for him to stumble and admit weakness.

He wasn't going to.

He knew he hadn't fooled her, but they were playing a game. One falter and she'd be on him like a tiger.

The waiting tub was at the far end of the pull-in. At a signal from Cara the guard brought it front and center. It was still almost too far. His thigh muscles trembled and he had to sit down quickly to cover his shakiness.

Cara slid in opposite. Two tubs with three guards in each flanked them in the transit lane.

"Ronan says you're nowhere near fit yet."

"I'm getting there."

She grunted, not an encouraging sound. "I'll go after your Nan."

"No."

"I'm not asking." She hissed out a breath, angry. "This is how it all started in the first place. Why can't you accept help when it's offered?"

"Because I don't want to see anyone else injured on my behalf."

"Especially not me."

"I didn't say that."

"You didn't have to."

What could he say? She was right. Was he being overprotective? Of course he damn well was and he knew it. Not just of Cara, but of everyone. That had always been one of his failings. She'd accused him of having White Knight Syndrome before and she was right. Getting over it wasn't going to be easy. He'd never liked sending somebody to do a job he wasn't prepared to do himself.

He took a deep breath.

"Go. I'll just hold you back."

"Was that so difficult?"

"Hardest thing I've ever had to do in my life."

"No it wasn't." There was a smile hovering behind her eyes. "Besides, you're in no condition to stop me."

"I know. Try not to get anyone killed."

"I'll do my best."

"Including yourself."

"I'll do my best."

"Take Ronan, too."

"Why, so that he can look after me for you?" She scowled.

"No, because of Nan. You haven't been able to get through to her implant. She could be drugged up to the eyeballs on reisercaine. At her age, who knows what that might do? You need a medic and Ronan can handle himself."

"Yes, he can. You're right."

She reached over and squeezed his hand, briefly.

"Hilde reported back. We've got a lead."

"When were you going to tell me this?"

"Depended on whether you were willing to see reason."

"I've seen it, now tell me."

"Max's old flame Lorin planted the bug in the matrix on condition they got her safe passage off Chenon before everything kicked off. She's already made a run for it with a hefty credit balance. I figured you wouldn't begrudge the cash."

Ben shook his head.

"The bug is burrowing deep. Mother Ramona's number crunchers have found a few holes. Does Building 18 mean anything to you?"

"Building 18? Yes. You've been there yourself, or at least walked over its remains. It's an old underground facility that was closed off when the grapple arena was built on top of it."

"There's a building under there?"

"Nine floors of it."

"We think that's where she is."

"It's going to be a tough extraction," Ben said. "Crowder's heartland."

"Yes, but we know the ground."

"If you can cope with a direct infodump, I'll show you a full plan of the place, a Navigator's insight into the twists and turns."

"I'll take that. Thanks."

"I'll meet you on Chenon in four days at the farm."

"Four days?" She gave him a disapproving look.

"Now who's getting overprotective?" he said. "I won't take any risks, but you'll never pry Rion out of the farm and off Chenon without me, and *Solar Wind* will give us a clean getaway. I may not be much use in a scrap, right now, but I can still drive the bus. And I won't be alone."

◆ ◆ ◆

Cara was about to depart when she got a call from Jussaro.
I need to speak to you and Ben.
   Can it wait? I have a shuttle to catch.
   I don't think so.
Cara left Ronan, Bronsen, and Archie rehearsing their personas for their false identities, newly acquired from Mother Ramona, and found Ben and Jussaro in Ben's office, which had been made more comfortable with the addition of an armchair that Ben had taken every advantage of.

"I don't want to worry you unnecessarily," Jussaro said, "but you've got another singer in the choir."

"How do you mean?" Ben asked.

"When I called Crowder to tell him you weren't dead he already knew. I thought he was going to fry me right then and there. He's getting information from someone else."

"It was an open secret that we got Ben back," Cara said. "Can we narrow it down?"

Jussaro shook his head. "I have no idea how Crowder knew, or even how much he knew."

"I don't want to believe it's anyone from the Free Company," Ben said. "These guys have all been through hell together. How could any of them still be in contact with Crowder?"

Cara shrugged. "It could be any one of them if Crowder

used the same tactics on them as Ari used on me. It could be someone who might not even realize he or she is doing it."

"Is there any way to tell, Jussaro?" Ben asked. "You're probably the best Empath we have."

"I'd have to get close, and even then . . ."

"Can it be done on some pretext? A health check on everyone's implant?"

"Possibly."

"Borrow Nine from Jamieson. She can give them a genuine checkup while you look for anything amiss."

"It will take some time."

"Better get started, then."

Jussaro left and Cara turned to Ben. "What do you think?"

"It affects your mission."

"No, it doesn't. Jussaro's going to have to report our departure anyway, otherwise he'll get fried."

"He won't have to tell Crowder the details."

"True, but Crowder knows we'll be coming. He's laid a trap; we have to spring it. Hopefully on our terms, not his."

Ben nodded, but he didn't try to stop her leaving.

Chapter Twenty

GAME ON

KITTY KNEW THAT CARA HAD TAKEN A SMALL party and had left by shuttle. Though she wasn't privy to the details, she figured that they were going to try and extract Benjamin's family from Chenon. If they were moving against Crowder it might be something Alphacorp could use to their advantage.

Where was Remus when she needed him? Today was the day for contact, but he was haphazard about the timing. She wished he'd make a note of the station time. All too often he pushed into her mind when she was sleeping, or trying to. She didn't sleep so well these days.

She had barely an hour before meeting Captain Syke, Ellen Heator, and two of Wes' fellow guards. They were going to scatter Wes' ashes across the green acres of the community farm and afterward she was going to take them to pet baby goats. She'd been back twice since Wes' death and each time she felt just a little closer to him, but no more at peace with his loss.

She'd taken over Wes' apartment, keeping his sparse furniture, but adding her own careless clutter. Ellen had helped her to recycle Wes' clothing, but she kept his bed linen, fancying there was still something of him sleeping next to her when the bed felt too big for one.

Wes' affairs were all in order. What little he had in his account went to the farm at his request, and she offered his personal possessions to his fellow guards: an antique chrono that might have been his father's, or might have been some random thing he'd picked up somewhere; a reading pad loaded with an assortment of nonfiction; an antique hairbrush with a pearlized back and bristles nearly worn away. Whatever significance these few items held was lost now, and would forever be.

Kitty kept his image album for herself. There was a video and some stills of two dark-skinned people with a small boy. She studied their faces, trying to see where Wes' solid good looks came from. Both of them, she decided eventually. There were other stills of people she didn't recognize. She'd have to ask Ellen if she knew who they were and offer copies to anyone who wanted them.

Half an hour came and went and still no Remus. It would be just her luck that he'd intrude as they scattered Wes' ashes. She made her way to the elevator. The journey to the farm was much shorter from Wes' low spindle apartment than it was from Port 22, but it still took fifteen minutes to the last hub where she met the others.

They stepped onto the walkway in a line, standing in companionable silence.

"Are you all right, Kitty?" Ellen whispered as they passed through the insect netting, layer by layer, and entered the farm.

"I'm fine," she said. When someone asked if you were all right, the last thing they really wanted to hear was that you were not.

Captain Syke said the words as they scattered Wes' ashes. They were good words, maybe not inspiring words, but solid, dependable ones, just like Syke himself. She hadn't expected him to be a baby animal kind of person, but he seemed to take delight in the goats and their kids. Well, who didn't love cute babies of all kinds. There was that phrase that stuck in her head: In the midst of life we are in death, but once you took the babies into account maybe it should be: In the midst of death we are in life. There was something so hopeful about babies. Life to come. Mistakes not yet made.

Remus didn't contact her while she was at the farm, for

which Kitty was thankful. Instead she was just settling down with a cup of caff and Wes' entertainment subscription when she felt the familiar mental handshake.

Report!

You're late, she told him.

It's the appointed day.

You're later than I'd like. A small team left by shuttle. I think they're going to try and extract Benjamin's family from Chenon.

Who?

Cara Carlinni, Lewis Bronsen, Ronan Wolfe, and Archie Tatum.

Not Benjamin himself?

He's still recovering.

Anything else?

Isn't that enough? Yes, there's more. We scattered the ashes of my lover today. Caught in the wrong place at the wrong time.

She would have liked to tag along with Cara and company if they were going to stick it to Crowder. Wes Orton had been a good man, but Crowder had not cared about killing good men when he sent in the Alphabet Gang. The best she could do was keep Akiko Yamada and Alphacorp fully apprised of the situation. The Trust was rotten to the core.

Ms. Yamada has authorized a message from your mother. It's in a regular mail packet. Watch out for it. You can send a reply via this office.

Thank you. She was surprised, but tried not to show it too much.

Perspective. It was all about perspective. Maybe Alphacorp was not so bad after all.

✦ ✦ ✦

Ben paced the length of Blue Seven's cavernous interior and tried not to worry about Cara. She was more than capable and he had to get over the idea that he was personally responsible for setting right the wrongs of the universe.

"Hey, Boss, shouldn't you be resting?"

Dammit, if he heard that one more time . . .

He turned to find Wenna close behind him. "Did Ronan prime every single person in this outfit to ask me that?"

She smiled. "Pretty much. He guessed you'd be trying to do too much as soon as he was out of the way."

"I'm just taking a gentle walk around the block."

She hrmphed at him as only Wenna could. "Ronan said to tell you if you were going to get yourself back into shape, be sure to take plenty of fluids and rest between bouts of exercise."

"I will."

"Starting now." She held out a water flask.

"Starting now." He took it and grinned.

"And he said to tell you he's cleared you for pilot duties as long as you have a full crew. No more gallivanting solo through the Folds."

Ben shivered. He wasn't looking forward to that part of the journey. Truth to tell, the thought of going back into foldspace scared him more than a little. It happened to pilots and Navigators sometimes, occasionally on their first flight, occasionally on their hundred and first. You stare into the void often enough and it starts to stare back.

"Are you all right, Boss?"

"Yeah, Wenna, fine, thanks."

"I've known you a long time, and I'd say you're anything but fine."

"Hones—"

"And if you're going to say, *honestly I'm fine*, then I know you're bullshitting me."

He shrugged. "I'm as fine as I can be. I'll make sure I've got a good crew with me. Yan Gwenn for starters."

"Make sure one of them is a psi-tech Navigator."

"I'm not taking Gen."

"I didn't say it had to be Gen, though you could do worse. She won't thank you for coddling her just because she's pregnant, and she's pretty much finished sorting out false idents and travel permits for all the guys who are bailing out." Wenna shrugged. "There's Kitty Keely. She's the highest-rated Navigator you've got after you."

"Yeah, Kitty Keely . . . She didn't do so well last time out."

Would Ben do any better himself, this time? Had the void stared back a little too intently? Had it said: I know you, tiny man?

"Ben!" Jussaro caught up with him, taking two quick steps for every stride of Ben's. "I need to come with you."

"Why?"

Jussaro lowered his voice. "Because there are two scenarios. One, I call Crowder's Telepath as soon as you depart for Chenon and let him know you're coming—or, two, I don't call and the instant Crowder discovers I've deliberately gone against his orders he hits that kill switch. I don't want to betray you, Benjamin, but I don't want to die either."

"Fair point, but how will coming with us help? You'll be getting even closer to the source of your problem."

"I need to get into the Folds and see if I can float this implant out of my head like you did. Don't look at me like that. I know it's a long shot. But just in case, I've got Jamieson on standby to replace it as soon as we get back. He's real interested in whether this can be done to order. You can see the possibilities, can't you?"

"I can, but you're taking a lot on trust. I didn't do it on purpose and I don't know how I did it, or even if it was me that did it. Things got a little strange out there. What if you have to breathe vacuum and stick your head in a dragon's mouth or be shredded to a pulp before it works?"

"I'll take my chances."

Ben nodded. "Come and welcome. It's going to be an interesting ride, but not in a way that would make you want to post it to your S-LOG afterward."

"More than interesting. I just reported to Crowder's Telepath. Don't worry, I managed to leave out all the relevant bits of information, but I gleaned one piece of news. That Telepath's not as tight as he thinks he is. Crowder's no longer in Arkhad City."

"He isn't? Any idea where he is?"

"I got an echo of a thought. He's someplace called Norro. You know where that is?"

"Norro? Oh, yes." Ben grinned. "He thinks he's being clever. Thinks it's the last place I'd look for him."

"Why?"

"It's where his ex-wife lives. She hates him. He knows I know that. He's got to be desperate to put himself anywhere near Agnetha Sigurdsdottir."

✦ ✦ ✦

"Agnetha. So kind of you to extend your hospitality."

Crowder stepped down from the flyer only after Wyndham, Danniri's second, had sent a security detail to check out the house and grounds and declared the area safe.

"Gabe, welcome. So good to see you again," the ex-Mrs. Crowder said in her public voice. As he got close enough to kiss the air beside her cheek she whispered, "You didn't give me much choice." She eyeballed Wyndham. "Bit of a thug, isn't he?"

"A very efficient thug. Come and meet him."

Crowder put his arm around Agnetha's sharp shoulders and though she shook him off she still turned to meet Wyndham with a glassy smile on her face.

"Aggie, this is Drew Wyndham, my captain of security. His men answer only to him, and to me, of course. He'll be in charge while I'm here."

"And how long will that be?" Aggie asked under her breath.

"As long as it needs to be. Do I have to remind you that I own this property?"

"You don't have to, but you always do." She cleared her throat, offered her hand, and in her public voice said, "Drew. Or is it Captain?"

"Wyndham will do, ma'am." He didn't return the shake. "Welcome to my home." There was a slight emphasis on both *my* and *home*.

Crowder had to hand it to Aggie, she was always a mistress of last words and verbal one-upmanship. Perhaps coming here wasn't such a good idea after all, but with the report from his man at Alphacorp that the long-expected rescue bid was imminent, staying in Trust HQ had lost its appeal. The big grapple game had to be a factor. If he were trying to mastermind a rescue he'd do it under cover of the big game. Perhaps they would, too.

There was enough Trust security to stop a small army, but a well-placed bomb would be hard to hide from. He didn't think Benjamin would willingly cause collateral damage, especially with his grandmother and the boy imprisoned on the premises, but it wasn't a risk he was prepared to take.

He'd laid his trap carefully and, he hoped, with subtlety. It was the pitcher-plant method, sucker them right in and then let them have it.

Having Jussaro watching Benjamin was a distinct advantage. It was obvious that hirelings weren't going to be enough to take Benjamin down, at least not on Crossways. He'd been so relieved when he'd thought Benjamin dead, but the man obviously wouldn't stay dead. Time to finish it once and for all, lure him to Chenon and end it using the best men he had. Pav Danniri was itching to settle the score for her brother.

He'd hoped to be there when she took Benjamin down, but a deadly skirmish in narrow corridors wasn't a spectator sport. He'd have to make do with the security footage.

He'd given Danniri Benjamin's kill code. Carlinni's had come from Akiko Yamada. She'd been eager to get it for him as soon as he let slip that Cara had accessed van Blaiden's handpad.

No one knew what information might have been on there. Handpads were generally coded with permanent and living files. The permanent files remained after death or detachment. The living files automatically erased in the event the handpad was forcibly removed or if the power source, the body's own electrical energy, died. There was a very short window of opportunity between death and dissipation of the body's natural power supply.

The thought of what might be on that handpad ate at him. Until Benjamin, Carlinni, and all the psi-techs from the Olyanda mission were taken care of, he couldn't relax. He fingered the small device in his right-hand pocket. The only way he'd been able to get Benjamin's kill code onto a hand-held device was to have it uniquely embedded into a one-time-use implant-killer. The one in his left-hand pocket was Carlinni's. If either of them evaded Danniri and got too close to him, he had the ultimate weapon. All he had to do was to get line of sight.

✦   ✦   ✦

Ricky had a flotilla of butterflies in his tummy. He'd tried to cultivate Minnow's sympathy and to a large extent he thought he'd managed it. The big man was noticeably more friendly and relaxed than any of the other guards. He'd even brought him another tube of skin gel when Ricky had showed him the blister on his foot wasn't healing as well as it should, largely due to Ricky picking off the scab and rubbing it raw again.

The skin gel had done its job. Nan had been conscious for three days, and by the third day her psi ability had returned. Ricky had hoped for a miracle, but when nothing happened he was forced to admit that if anyone had tried to contact Nan they had probably given up by now.

Nan was a marvelous actress, but there was no point in wasting the second tube of skin gel until they had a better chance of getting out. They discussed the possibilities and Nan had admitted that Ricky's plan was probably the best chance they had.

"You're going to have to do it all by yourself," she'd said.

"I know. I'm not scared."

"Aren't you?"

"Maybe. Just a bit."

"It's all right to be scared," Nan had said. "It means you won't take stupid risks. But when it comes time to act, don't let the fear freeze you."

"How do I stop it?"

"You give yourself a moment to let it have its way, then you count to three and tell it to get lost. It doesn't control you."

"And does that work?"

"Always."

Now Ricky was going to try something a lot more dangerous than picking off a scab. He had the used blast pack hidden under the edge of Nan's mattress. If he could swap the used one for the fresh one in Minnow's right pocket he'd have a single dose of anesthetic. Surely if he could catch one of the guards unawares he could use it to knock him out. Maybe not Minnow, he was too big and the drug would take longer to work. Maybe the scrawny man who'd never let his name slip and who rarely answered questions. He was probably half Minnow's weight so the drug would work faster—he hoped.

He scrubbed at his eyes to make them red, as if he'd been crying, took the blast pack from the bed and palmed it. His heart was beating like thunder. What had Nan said? Count to three and shove the fear away. One, two, three.

He was ready when the door lock bleeped. By the time

Minnow came in with the tray of mush for Nan's evening meal he was sitting on the floor, head in hands, looking about as low as he could.

"What's up, Ricky-boy?" Minnow kicked the door shut and put the tray down on the table. "I got you a bar of choc. Figured every kid loves choc."

That was Ricky's opening. He jumped up and hugged Minnow around the waist, lurching into him so that he spun him with his right side away from the eye on the wall. "Minnow, you're my only friend. No one else even talks to me." He let his voice break and managed what he hoped were pretty convincing sobs into Minnow's jacket front.

"Aww, Ricky. This ain't going to last forever. You'll soon be out of here." Minnow hugged him back.

Yes, that was just what Ricky had been waiting for. He dipped his fingers into Minnow's right pocket and substituted the used blast pack for the fully charged one, then pulled away from Minnow's embrace.

"Sorry. Just feeling a bit helpless, you know. With Nan so . . ." He nodded toward the bed. "It's like she's dead."

"Oh, no, boy, she ain't dead."

"What's going to happen to us?"

"Truth, boy, I don't know. Danniri don't tell us much, but her regular squad is hanging around all the time."

"Are they watching us all the time, on that?" Ricky pointed to the camera eye.

Minnow dropped his voice. "Well, we do that, but truth to tell you two are pretty boring, 'specially at night."

"So if I want to take a dump in private I should wait until night and you might not be watching?"

"Pretty much, yeah."

"Thanks. It doesn't get any easier, having the san-unit on camera, you know."

"I guess not. Good thing your granny's not aware of it, right?"

"Yeah, good thing."

Minnow raised the head of the bed to sit Nan up, then watched Ricky spoon the nutri-paste into her mouth. Between them they put her on the potty. She was completely compliant.

Sorry, Nan, Ricky thought, but the alternative was even worse.

Then Minnow slapped the empty blast pack to the side of Nan's neck and dropped it into his left pocket.

After Minnow left, Ricky hid the fully charged blast pack under the mattress and sat on the bed so he shielded Nan's face from the camera eye. She looked up at him and winked. They had plans to make.

✦   ✦   ✦

Cara fought down her nerves as the liner landed at Arkhad Spaceport and spat them all out into the immigration lineup. The only way to get through this was to relax into the part of the new identity. Believe it. Otherwise the Empaths employed to do random checks might pick out a sense of unease and start asking too many questions.

Cara looked at them all. It was amazing what a difference a few simple formine injections and a new haircut made. Bronsen's cap of tight curls had given way to a severe tonsure that made him look bald except for a fringe of close-cropped hair around the back and sides. Archie had exchanged his normal mouse-brown for ginger everything, and Ronan's skin had been darkened to copper, his luxuriant mop bleached blond and his lips thickened.

"Have we all got the details straight?" Cara asked.

Archie said he could handle it, but Bronsen had been nervous until Ronan had given him something to calm him down.

They got through without a hitch, thanks to Mother Ramona's careful work and their thorough immersion in their new characters. Once out of the spaceport they headed straight for the nearest dockside bar, still quiet at this time in a morning, and ordered beer all around, though Ronan wouldn't let Bronsen have more than a sip of his until the sedative wore off.

Cara contacted Hilde. All of the mercs had receiving implants, but only a handful were true psi-techs. Hilde was a Psi-3 Telepath.

I'm good to go whenever you are, Hilde said. *I put Lorin on a shuttle to New Rio. Where she goes from there is her own business, but I advised her to make it somewhere she can get lost and settle down with her bank account for company.*

But when Cara contacted Tengue it was a different story.

We're being watched, he said. *We got through immigration with a few awkward questions. Fowler's in the burn unit. She had her surgery and she's doing well. We can give 'em the slip as soon as we need to, but not until we need to, otherwise they'll get suspicious.*

"So we'll have to do the recce ourselves," Ronan said.

"The sooner the better." Cara drained her beer. "Drink up, let's go."

They checked into a cheap hotel, once quite plush, but now showing signs of age and neglect. Maybe it had once had a name but it didn't now. All it said on the sign outside was "Rooms."

"I've been here before," Archie said. "Not *here* here, but places like it."

"Even smells familiar," Bronsen said.

Cara wrinkled her nose. "Well, it's got a functioning link, plumbing, and beds without fleas. That's a plus in a place like this."

They hit the link.

"There's a grapple match tomorrow evening," Ronan said. "The semifinal. It means there will be more people around than usual and tickets for tourists. It's probably the best opportunity we'll get."

"For a recce or the job?" Archie asked.

"Maybe both," Cara said. "We might not get a second chance."

"I'm going to try Nan one more time." Cara closed her eyes and put the image of Nan upfront, then let her thoughts roam.

Cara! Is that you?

Nan! You're all right?

If you can call going stir-crazy all right. We're in the grapple arena—underneath it, anyway.

We're coming to get you.

Ben?

Driving the getaway bus. He's all right.

I never considered he wouldn't be. What's happened?

It's a long story. How are you?

Broken leg and I've been completely immobile. I'm not going to be fast on my feet.

Understood. Ricky?

*Very resourceful. Managed to drug-proof my neck with

a tube of skin gel. Nan got right down to business. *We're underground, not right down at the bottom level. Ricky managed to get a look outside. We're close to an antigrav shaft, but we don't know whether it's active or not. There's a long corridor with solid double doors to one side of us and on the other a corner with steps, an antigrav shaft, and a comm station on the wall. We get two visits a day from our keepers, but we have a camera eye in the room. Ricky got some information, though. The guards are all on an upper level and though they're supposed to watch us all the time from the control room, they think we're boring and they have a running card game to pass the time.*

Good one. Stand by. There's a grapple game tomorrow evening. That's when we'll come.

◆   ◆   ◆

Hello.

Hello, yourself. Ben sat back in the booth of the Blue Mountain coffee shop and smiled. Though he was drinking tea, the smell reminded him strongly of Cara's preferences. *Where are you?* he asked.

A poxy little flophouse on the edge of the port. 95 City-side, Cara said.

Cityside, huh? Watch your back.

Don't worry.

News?

I've made contact with your Nan.

Ben discovered it was possible to feel elation and sick apprehension at the same time.

How is she? Ricky?

Both fine, though your Nan's got a broken leg that's only half-healed and she's been drugged. Ricky managed to figure a way around that.

Smart kid. Ben smiled and touched the corner of one eye, suddenly moist.

There's a grapple game tomorrow night. That's our opportunity.

They'll probably expect that.

I think they'll be ready for us whenever we go in. At least this way we can figure out some monumental distraction.

Agreed.

Has Jussaro had any luck with finding our leak yet?

Not yet, but he has gleaned some information. It looks like Crowder may be on Norro, keeping a low profile. It's an island in the middle of the Calman Sea where his ex-wife lives. Your news?

Crowder—

Later. Sit-rep first.

Okay. Tengue and Gwala are being watched, so for now they're sitting tight at the burn unit until·we need them. Hilde's in the best hotel in town enjoying five-star service. Are you intending to go after Crowder?

Fowler? Ben asked, ignoring her question. Was he? It was a pity to waste the opportunity.

Doing well. That's a bonus. Not sure we can get her out even if this goes according to plan. She might have to find her own way home after rehab, but her bills are all paid up and she knew that when she agreed to come.

Tengue won't be happy.

Tengue?

He's fair with all his crew, but there are signs if you look for them. Fowler's special to him. Not sure if she knows it or not. We don't leave without Fowler if we can help it.

Talk to me about Crowder, Ben. This thing's getting complicated. Is he bait for a secondary trap? Do you think they're planning to move Nan and Ricky?

Jussaro believes Crowder is just laying low. His ex-wife lives on Norro. There's a lot of enmity. It's the last place anyone might expect him to hide out. It's the last place I would have expected.

So you are planning to go after him?

Hell, yeah.

A waitress came over and asked if Ben wanted a refill. He nodded and sighed as she poured fresh coffee into his cooling tea.

"Oh, I'm so sorry, I'll get you another."

"No, it's all right." He waved her away but she came back a few minutes later with fresh tea and a lemon cake.

"On the house," she said and gave him the kind of smile he might have once found difficult to ignore. She was cute in a not-Cara kind of way.

What's happening? Cara asked.

I think I've just been propositioned with a lemon cake.

She laughed, a warm, tingling sensation in his skull.

How are you? Cara ventured.

Fitter every day. I'll see you tomorrow.

We'll make our move during the match. Hilde's hired a private flyer for a tourist trip. It will take us five hours to get to the farm.

Scrap the farm idea. He came to a decision. *Let's rendezvous on Norro. I'll pick up Rion, make arrangements for Kai to go and visit Fowler at the hospital where we can scoop them both up.*

After you've dealt with some unfinished business?

He laughed. *Oh, yes.*

Chapter Twenty-One

FOLDSPACE

BEN ASSEMBLED HIS TEAM FOR *SOLAR WIND*. The repairs had been completed to Yan's satisfaction and everything was A-okay—with the ship, at least. He was going through the motions as if everything was normal, yet when it came to the crunch, how would he deal with the Folds?

Getting a copilot was going to be the biggest problem. Kitty wasn't up to it. He hadn't asked Gen, but she'd already told Cara she wasn't going to volunteer for the rescue mission. Ben couldn't blame her, but neither Mother Ramona nor Garrick knew of anyone else who could pilot a jumpship. A million people on the station and not one jumpship pilot, or at least no one who admitted to the talent.

"There was one," Mother Ramona said when Ben stopped off at the Mansion House office to ask her to check her freelancer files. "Name of Jules Charnock, if I remember rightly." She flicked through the files on her holo-screen, pulling a few forward, discarding others. "Here she is. She had a solid rep for staying sober and getting the job done with a minimum of fuss. She took a succession of jobs while she was here, including some for me. Did well out of it, bought her own ship, nothing fancy. May have been one of the oldest jumpships still flying."

"Where is she now?"

"That's a good question. She took one trip too many. Started drinking, doing Amfital, losing herself in it for days on end. It didn't take long before she wasn't fit to fly. Sold the ship to pay off debts. Ended up in Red One. I lost track after that. Dido Kennedy might know more, but if Charnock's still around I wouldn't trust her to drive a tub-cab." She frowned at him. "Aren't you up to the job yourself, Benjamin?"

He didn't answer. He didn't know how to answer. He didn't know whether he was up to it or not, but the fact that there was doubt in his mind was almost an answer in itself.

"Oh, like that, is it?" There was sympathy in Mother Ramona's voice. "Don't beat yourself up over it. You're not the first and you won't be the last. You should ask Marling."

"Gen's pregnant."

"It doesn't make her ill or incapable."

"No one really knows whether flying the Folds affects the unborn child."

"That ship left the dock a long time ago. How many fold-space jumps has she made in recent months?"

"Yeah, that's what she said."

"Your Dr. Wolfe has said everything's normal, hasn't he?"

"He has, but this could be dangerous. Besides, she already told Cara she wasn't going to volunteer when Cara was putting her team together."

"Ask again. That was different. This time you only need her to drive the bus. She doesn't need to set foot on Chenon itself. She won't turn you down."

"That's why I can't ask her."

"For a smart man you can sure be a fool, Benjamin. You can't wrap up the people you love and hide them away from danger."

He shrugged. "She's my last resort, and only because not having a backup pilot would seriously jeopardize everyone on board. If I crack . . ." He finished the sentence with an open-handed gesture. *Anything could happen.* "I'll try to find Charnock first, see if she's made any kind of recovery."

Mother Ramona made a dismissive noise.

Yes, she was right. Ben was fully aware that pilots who lost it didn't usually recover.

✦ ✦ ✦

Kitty did as Remus had told her and checked her messages, then checked again hoping for something, anything, from her mother. Two days later her inbox flickered and Kitty rolled out of Wes' bed to tap the icon on the bottom corner of the screen.

From Norma Keely.

It was the only message in the box. Kitty felt herself start to smile even while her eyes were flooding.

Then a second icon began to flash. Captain Syke. She decided to get that one out of the way first so she could enjoy her mother's message—at least she hoped it would be enjoyable—with no pressure. She tapped the icon.

"Kitty, I wanted to make sure you were all right," Syke's image said. "Do you need anything? Have you been crying?"

"Oh." Kitty wiped her eyes with her fingers. "It's nothing. Just some soppy movie I was watching."

"At this time in the morning? You need to get out more."

"Yeah, probably."

"A bunch of us are going to the Ocean coffee shop at close of shift today. You should join us. You know you'd be welcome. You're practically one of us."

"I'll think about it, Captain."

"Arran . . . that's me. No need to be formal. It's not like I'm *your* captain."

"Okay, Arran. I'll remember that."

"So you'll come?"

"I'll think about it." She smiled. It was nice of Syke to check up on her. Ellen Heator had knocked on her door a couple of times on fairly flimsy pretexts. Wes' crewmates were adopting her. She found she liked the concept.

As Syke's image faded, Kitty leaned forward to watch her mom's recorded message. Mom was smiling, eyes bright, and her mousy hair, so lank the last time Kitty had seen her, curled softly around her face, which was now plumped out and healthy.

"Is this thing on? Oh, yes, so it is," Mom's image said to someone in the background. She turned to the camera.

"Hello, Kitty. How are you, my lovely? As you can see I'm much recovered. In fact, I'm completely recovered and having a restful break here—though I'm not actually allowed to say where here is, for some reason. Still, it's enough to say that it's a private resort. Sun, sea, sand, great food. There's not much company, but I've been able to catch up on my reading. Can you believe it, I got through five novels last week? I'm not sure when I'll be going home. I'd hoped to be back in Shield for Midwinter. You know how much I enjoy having everyone over for dinner, even Aunt Bessie, picky as she is. I hope whatever you're doing out there is going well and that you're safe and enjoying yourself. Message me if you can. Take care, my lovely. I hope to see you on your next leave." She blew a kiss to the recorder.

Kitty kissed her fingers and blew toward the screen. "I love you, Mom," she said out loud, even though her mother would never hear it.

Then she frowned. What had her mom been trying to tell her? Aunt Bessie, her father's sister, had died a decade ago.

She recorded a response and sent it by return to the Alphacorp address it had come from. It was full of: I'm fine, and don't worry about me, just enjoy your break. She finished with: "If you get home for Midwinter, give my love to Aunt Bessie."

There, Mom, just letting you know that I got your message. I know that you know that something's going on.

✦ ✦ ✦

Ben didn't tell anyone where he was going or why, but he hopped a tub to Red One, not the worst place on the station, he now realized, just poor. Dido Kennedy hadn't said much about her life there, but Yan had remarked that the folks seemed to be eating better since she'd been paid for the work she was doing. Ben wondered whether all the platinum they supplied actually made it to Kennedy's workshop, but as long as she got the job done he wasn't going to carp. It was pretty obvious that if she was siphoning some of the platinum off, it wasn't for her own benefit.

Though she did look a bit smarter than she had when he'd first met her. The buddysuit top, sleeves ripped out, was still her work garment, but the shirt beneath it wasn't as frayed, and she might even have brushed her hair.

She was bent over her workbench when he entered her den, a headset covering her eyes and a micro-drill in her hand.

"That you, Yan, sweetie? Did you bring the mag-couple I asked for?"

"It isn't, and if I'd known I would have brought you one."

"Oh, Benjamin. Gimme a minute."

Ben stared at the piles of what looked like scrap but were sorted into discrete stacks, so were obviously being tagged for something.

A rustling in the corner attracted his attention and a scrawny child, maybe about seven, emerged backward from a cupboard, eyed him up suspiciously and yelled, "I'm done."

"Okay, Todd." Kennedy didn't look up. "Wash your hands. Sonic and scrub. You know the routine."

The child disappeared through a narrow doorway behind the couch that seemed to be Dido's only comfortable piece of furniture. Ben heard water running.

"Show me." Dido stood up to inspect his hands when he came back out. "Do your nails?"

"Twice with the brush and once with the sonic."

"Good boy." She fished a small credit chip out of the pocket of her grease-stained trousers and gave it to him. "Don't waste it."

The child nodded and scampered away.

"Yours?" Ben asked.

"They're all mine, but not biologically. That one's got a sister to support. He strips down some of the pieces I get. Nothing too toxic. Got a steady hand and a quick mind. Might make an engineer of him when he's a bit older. But you didn't come down here to see my kids. What can I do for you? If you want to know if it's finished yet, the answer's no, but I'm getting a bit closer. Going to need to test it out soon, and for that I'm going to need someone who can fly a jumpship."

"That's what I came to ask you about. I've only got one other pilot who can and I need a backup. Mother Ramona said you might know where I can find Jules Charnock."

"Jules? You don't want to find her."

"She's a jumpship pilot, right?"

"She was. Psi-2 Navigator. Managed to buy out her own

contract from Arquavisa and was sitting pretty for a while. Did good business, but on her last run she burned out."

It was always the last run.

"Did she recover?" Ben was afraid he knew the answer already.

Kennedy shook her head. "You know how it affects some people."

Oh, yes, he knew.

"Have you ever wondered why some people can fly a jumpship and some can't?" Kennedy asked.

"Who hasn't?"

"I heard about the Benjamin Maneuver. You've got fold-space figured out. Nothing's real."

"I don't know that I've figured it out, but I've certainly got a lot more questions, and they're not ones the academy trainers ever answered."

"You've seen 'em, haven't you?"

"Seen what?"

Kennedy stared intently at Ben, her tongue peeping over her bottom lip. "Tell me you've seen 'em. Void dragons."

"I've seen them," Ben said. *Touched one, ridden it through foldspace. Looked into its eyes.* "They tell us whatever we see is an illusion."

She shook her head. "There are illusions in foldspace, ghosts from your own past and the like, but if the void dragons are illusions why does everyone see the same thing?"

"Do we see exactly the same thing? They don't show up on any video recording."

She yanked open a tool chest drawer, causing the stack to wobble alarmingly, and pulled out a sheaf of plasfilms. "Recognize these?"

"Oh, gods, yes." Ben breathed out the words while he looked at sheet after sheet. Some of the drawings were outline sketches, others were detailed and lifelike. They all depicted the same thing: void dragons. He stopped at one of the drawings. It was his dragon, perfect in its detail. It even had the prehensile claws in its beard. And the eyes, even from the plasfilm, seemed to stare into his soul.

"You know the big fella, huh? That's Jules' drawing. Good, wasn't she? I told her she could make a living as an artist, but she could never bring herself to draw anything else but these." Kennedy shrugged. "Last time I saw her she was heading for an air lock. Said it was the only way she could find any peace. For all I know she took a walk into the black. She never came back, anyhow. Sometimes there's nothing you can do for folks who are determined to go."

Her voice choked off and she cleared her throat. "Jules said that nothing in foldspace is real—except these fellas—and at the same time everything's real. You're nowhere and everywhere all at the same time. You'd think that was obvious, but from what I understand they train it out of pilots early on. If my jump engines are going to be any use, you need flyers who know what one of these looks like." She flicked the edge of the plasfilm in Ben's hands. "Ones who are open-minded about what's out there and what can be done with it."

"You aren't psi-tech, are you?" Ben asked.

"Nah. They offered me an implant." Her mouth turned down at the corners. "Said I tested real strong. But I added up the credits and it made no sense. Figured I'd go my own way, and I have. And look where it got me." She laughed. "The credits still don't make sense, but at least I don't have a debt the size of a small planet."

She gestured to the workbench with the single piece of equipment on it. "Going to be in the money soon, though. That there is a hundred percent, bona fide jump engine with retrofit capability, or it will be soon. And if I adjust the power ratio it won't take one any bigger than that to take a battleship through the Folds. With the right pilot and the right ratios you could take this whole damn space station through foldspace. When I've got the engine. You give me someone to fly it." She tapped the plasfilm. "It had better be someone who's seen the big feller."

✦ ✦ ✦

Ben went direct to Port 22 from Kennedy's workshop clutching one of the rolled up drawings but avoiding looking at it. As he walked down the length of the dock, he could see a figure sitting at the top of *Solar Wind*'s ramp.

"Were you planning on going without me?" Gen asked as he stopped halfway up the ramp, his eyes on a level with hers.

"You already said to Cara—"

"That was a different gig. You need a pilot, Cara didn't. Besides, I've probably got more flight time on *Solar Wind* than you, thanks to the shuttle runs from Olyanda." She didn't quite meet his eyes.

"You know, don't you?"

"That foldspace took a bite out of you? Yes. I guessed." There was a world of understanding in her voice. "You're not just talking about your wrist, are you?"

Ben looked down at the smart-case wrapped around his broken wrist. He'd barely thought about the break. Apart from not being able to bend or flex his wrist he had full use of his fingers, and while the case was in place it didn't hurt unless he gave it a real sharp knock.

He shook his head and sat down on the top of the ramp next to her.

"I've got your back." Gen reached over and squeezed his arm. "How bad is it?"

"We'll find out soon."

"But you think it might be bad."

"Let's put it this way, I'm not taking *Solar Wind* into the Folds unless there's someone else on board who can get her out again."

"Have you . . . spoken to anyone about this?"

Ben shook his head.

"You know no one's going to judge you for it, don't you?" Gen said. "Anyone who's ever flown a ship through foldspace knows that it could be them next."

"I know. Let's see if there's anything to it before we start to put my phobias through a meat grinder, shall we?"

She nodded. "How about we go into foldspace via a gate? The effects are always . . ." She frowned. ". . . intensified in a jumpship. If we go in via a gate then find a new line to our exit point maybe we can minimize them. It should reduce the time differential, too."

"It's worth a try. Thanks, Gen . . . for stepping up and for understanding."

"Yeah, well, it could happen to any one of us at any time. What's that you've got?"

He unrolled the plasfilm. "What do you make of this?"

Gen's sharp intake of breath said it all. "That's come straight out of my head. Our hallucinations in foldspace are not supposed to be real. Is that exactly what you see?"

"Scale for scale," Ben said, "even down to the claws on the end of its beard."

"So if it's an illusion, how come those of us who see this guy see the same thing?" Gen leaned over and traced the outline with one finger. "Where did you get this?"

"It was drawn by a woman called Jules Charnock."

"A jumpship pilot?"

Ben nodded. "Dido Kennedy's theory is that only those pilot-Navigators who can see the void dragon stand a chance of being able to pilot a jumpship."

"Have you shown the drawing to Kitty?"

"No. I'm betting she doesn't recognize it, though."

Gen hauled herself to her feet a little awkwardly. "Wouldn't it be interesting if you could identify potential jumpship pilots by whether they recognized the void dragon or not?"

On the flight deck, Ben saw Max sitting in the bucket seat reserved for nonessential crew.

Oh, sorry, I should have said. Gen aimed a private thought at Ben. *Max insists on coming. He says he'll keep out of the way, but he's not getting left behind.*

Ben was saved from making a comment by the arrival of Toni Horta from Blue Seven Security, to operate tactical. She was somewhat shorter than the rest of Tengue's mercs, but supposedly a first-class marksman. No sense of humor, Tengue had said, but an icy calm that could freeze the balls off a baboon. He was certainly right about the humor. Ben would just have to take the baboon's balls on faith.

It was a good team. Frankly, if anyone was going to mess up, it would be Ben. Every time he thought about the Folds his mind seized up in panic. The closer they came to departure, the more he felt immobilized by his own fear.

They had almost completed pre-flight checks when there was a general *knock knock* broadcast ship-wide as Jussaro arrived.

"You're still intent on this?" Ben asked him.

"I am. I don't have much choice."

"Okay. Your decision."

Ben settled Jussaro into the other bucket seat next to Max and strapped him in. It would have been better if he could have been put in an empty cabin, but if he started to float through the walls Ben wanted someone to be able to pull him back. That someone was Max.

"It's all you have to do, Max. Stop him from leaving the flight deck by any means imaginable—or unimaginable."

"That's not comforting."

"I'll let Jussaro explain it to you. It's all a bit . . . unorthodox. Watch him, but don't do what he does, understand?"

"I think so."

"Right, everyone, stations, please. Let's go. Two things you need to watch out for on this run. One is that Jussaro will be trying to think his own implant out of his skull—and no, neither he nor I know whether it can be done. The other thing you need to watch out for is me. This will be my first time since . . . well . . . you know what happened. I stared into the Folds and they stared back. But I want you to know I will not put you all in danger. Gen's got my back and can get you home safely if I turn into a gibbering heap of jelly on the floor."

"Ewww, I hope that's not literal," Max said.

Gen looked daggers at him, but it broke the moment.

Ben laughed. Sure, it was a slightly hollow laugh almost bordering on hysterical, but it was a laugh. "Me, too, Max," he said. "Me, too."

✦ ✦ ✦

"I don't like Wyndham," Aggie said as she watched the man depart to check on his squad. "Does he have to hang around all the time?"

Crowder sighed, trying not to let his irritation show. "I told you. It's his job."

Aggie crossed her elegant legs and her skirt rode up her thighs. He'd loved those legs once. Dancer's legs, shapely but strong. He tried not to remember how they'd felt when they were wrapped around his back. It was a long time ago. He hadn't thought about sex for . . . how long? Not even with Mrs. Hand and her five daughters.

"Jusquin and Danniri were lighter on their feet," Aggie said. "Less intrusive somehow."

They hadn't been light enough on their feet when they'd tried to take out Benjamin. The image of them both lying dead on his office floor burned in his memory. The blood . . .

He forced a smile. "It was only because you were used to them."

"Maybe."

"Danniri's sister is very like him. I'll bring her next time I come to visit."

"Are you going to make a habit of this?"

He thought about her legs again. "I don't know. Am I welcome?"

"You can please yourself. It is, after all, your house, as you keep reminding me."

"Then I might come again."

"Message ahead so I can find somewhere else to be." She stood up and stared out of the window so that her skirt fell to knee level again. Damn.

"What kind of trouble is it this time?" she asked.

"I'm just being cautious. I always take precautions."

"I've known you a long time, Gabe. I may not be one of your psi-techs, but I can tell when you're lying."

Crowder steepled both hands over his nose and breathed out into his sweaty palms, then he scrubbed his fingers over his lips. What to tell her that would keep her quiet, keep her on his side.

"Remember Ari van Blaiden?"

"How could I forget. Your protégé, your rising star. You brought him home to dinner three times. I once wondered whether you were swinging toward men."

"It was purely business. I had you. I was never, have never been, unfaithful to you, you know. Not then, not since."

"Maybe not with another warm-blooded being, but you're married to the Trust. I didn't know I was signing up for a threesome when we met. Even the girls learned very quickly that the Trust always comes first."

Crowder frowned. He couldn't deny it. He hauled himself off the couch and went to stand beside her, placing both hands squarely on the windowsill and leaning heavily on them.

"You were telling me about Ari van Blaiden," she said.

"When he defected to Alphacorp—that was my idea, you know, to get someone on the inside. When he went we kept up a working relationship, but after a few years it became obvious he was out of control." *No lies yet, Aggie,* he thought. "Van Blaiden did something stupid and dragged me into it. People died. A lot of people. Not my fault—I'll swear that on the lives of our daughters."

She glared at him. "Leave our daughters out of this."

He stood and spread his hands in a gesture of surrender. "Some of my own psi-techs died."

"Hera-3. You're talking about Hera-3, aren't you?"

He didn't deny it. "I picked up the pieces as well as I could."

"Very well indeed. The Trust ended up with a platinum planet."

"I can't deny it, but there were a lot of unhappy people and . . ." He glossed over Olyanda completely. "Benjamin has gone rogue." He touched his newly regrown ear. It still itched. "I'm here for a few days, until something is settled. Permanently." He sighed. "I bought this place as an island retreat. We've got a few days to get to know each other again. I could make it up to you, Aggie."

"No you couldn't. You're in the guest room tonight."

He shrugged. It had been worth a try.

❖   ❖   ❖

"Trap? Of course it's a trap. All we have to do is to figure out how to spring it from the outside." Ben's words stuck in Cara's head as she made plans to break into Building 18 under the grapple arena. Ben had given each of them all the information he had on the building in a direct infodump. A Navigator's spatial perspective was slightly alien to Cara, but she was getting used to it.

Ronan and Archie had said little about how the information affected them, but Bronsen had developed a thousand-meter stare for a couple of hours and then come back into himself with a soundless, "Wow!"

"It's a bit like when I'm Finding something," he said. "Now I have a grid overlaid with a mental map. Let's hope I can pinpoint Ben's Nan accurately on both the grid and the map."

Cara had only met Nan and Ricky once, so Ben had given Bronsen his memories of them to make them easier to locate.

Ronan had managed to secure tickets for the grapple

semifinal from a scalper, though it had cost a small fortune. The six tickets were all in different parts of the stadium. Hilde had hired a flyer big enough to take nine of them and was standing by. Tengue and Gwala were waiting patiently in the burn unit until it was time to move.

"Are we ready?" Cara asked.

"Ready," Ronan, Archie and Bronsen answered together.

"Ready to get out of this place." Archie looked at the damp-stained walls of their hotel room and patted the bag of bots slung over his shoulder. "Even the boys aren't used to this standard of accommodation."

They'd all reattached the Trust insignias to their buddy-suits, hardly out of place here in Arkhad City.

Cara contacted Nan one more time. *We're on our way.*

Chapter Twenty-Two

GRAPPLING

CARA REACHED BEN BEFORE *SOLAR WIND* hit the Folds.

Ben, Nan's still okay. I've managed to talk to her again.

How is she?

Looking forward to getting out. We're heading for the grapple arena now. We've got tickets for a game.

Cara let the link drop. Had she sensed some deep-seated worry behind Ben's thoughts? She hoped not, but she had the feeling that something was going on that he wasn't letting her in on.

She linked her arm through Ronan's as they waited in line at the gate to the grapple arena where once, before setting off for Olyanda, they'd played a friendly match of three-on-three with no audience.

Hard to imagine this was our playground, isn't it? Ronan kept the thought tight. *How carefree we all were.*

Speak for yourself. I was on the run from Ari van Blaiden. You were carefree.

I love it, shooting hoops and loops. A freefall game of free-for-all where every way is up and no mayhem is out of bounds short of actual physical damage. I used to play semi-professionally, while I was still at school.

*I know, Suzi told me. You played for Magna Colony and

*you took the Trust's interdepartmental grapple champion-
ship three years in a row.*

*It could have been four, but we lifted off for Olyanda
before the finals. I had to bail.*

*Perhaps you'd like to skip this mission and stay and
watch the match.*

No, it's never as much fun watching as playing.

She gave him a light smack on the arm as the line began
to move and they filtered into the arena and collected magnetic plates for their boots to anchor them to the inner surface of the spherical arena. No seats here, you just snagged
your feet magnetically onto the plating and took up a position in whichever segment your ticket said. Gravity was already off and would remain off until the last member of the
audience had left after the game. If it came on, the entire
crowd of around five thousand would gently fall to the floor,
a real public safety issue, not from the fall, because gravity
would return slowly, but from the potential crush.

They split up and headed for their allocated sectors,
clunking on the floor plates as they walked up the walls and
onto the ceiling, which, of course, was still the floor from
their perspective.

The hollow sphere was punctuated by a series of inward-
protruding bars and platforms and the goals were loops of
medonite, through which teams had to post hoops to score.
Because this was a pro match there were five to each team.

In such close quarters with everyone in a state of height-
ened excitement, Cara had to damp down her Empathy so
as not to be overwhelmed.

Me, too, Ronan said.

Archie and Bronsen, who had been a few meters behind
them in the lineup outside, had found their designated
places, unaffected by the mental hubbub. The interval after
the first set was when they were going to make their move.
In the meantime, though he looked as if he was watching
the match intently, Archie had released his bots, one at a
time, from his bag. They were already scuttling for the arena's control panels and wiring grid. Cara hoped Archie
knew what he was doing. They needed to inflict very specific
damage if they weren't going to kill a few hundred innocent
people.

In the arena two teams were arrayed against each other,

standing on ledges, holding on to handgrips. At the first beep a hoop sailed between them out into the center of the arena and all ten players pushed off to where they expected it to be. It was balletic sport, graceful, as bodies glided into the center of the sphere, bending and weaving in slow motion, trying to keep from being bounced into another trajectory while trying to knock their opponent off-course. In null-G the play wasn't fast, but it was relentless and the cheering and catcalls from the whole crowd ratcheted up the tension.

Cara kept a tight grip on her Empathy and was relieved when the beep announced the end of the first segment. Most of the spectators stayed where they were but Cara made her way back toward the entrance from segment six, just above the equator of the sphere.

Archie? she asked.

Ready, he answered.

Ronan?

Almost down to ground level.

Bronsen.

Over here.

Tengue? Gwala?

Here.

Have any trouble at the med center?

Nothing to worry about. Amateurs. They don't even know we've left yet.

Hilde?

Close by. The pilot's reply was weaker. *Ready when you all are. Just give me the word.*

Cara clamped her feet to the plating by the entrance and spotted Bronsen standing by a stairwell that was taped off with warning tape and sported a notice saying, DO NOT CROSS THIS LINE, in big bold letters. Cara looked up. Segment Eight was directly opposite the stairwell, two hundred meters across the empty interior of the spherical arena.

Now, Archie.

The people down at ground level didn't know anything had happened for a few moments, until the screaming started. Six hundred people in Segment Eight began to fall from the ceiling in slow motion as their magnetic boot grips failed and a whisper of gravity drew them slowly down. The floor space would easily accommodate six hundred without a crush, but there was going to be a lot of flailing around and motion sickness. Not a good combination. The big worry for the management would be that if one segment had failed then the others might follow. They would need every security guard they could draft to get people out of the danger zone as quickly as possible.

The alarms began to sound. That would relay to the emergency services. The whole place would be full of first responders within minutes.

As the first few tumbling people reached the head of the stairwell, Cara, Ronan, Archie, and Bronsen abandoned their mag plates and jumped. Tengue and Gwala were ahead of them.

Bronsen? Cara asked.

Fifth level down, directly below us, Bronsen replied.

Nan, we're coming to get you.

We're not alone, Nan said. *There's a guard. He's armed and he has an earpiece and transmitter. I think you've got a welcoming committee.*

Shit.

They landed on the stairs, the antigrav effects less here now that they were below ground level, though they were still light. This wasn't the ideal place to be if there was a welcoming committee waiting.

Guards erupted from a room on the landing below them. Tengue and Gwala got off four shots in quick succession, all smart-darts loaded with quick-acting anesthetic. Four guards fell, blocking the shots of the two who were still on their feet. Gwala's fists took down the closest one and Tengue got in another shot, which took care of the last one.

"Is that it?" Bronsen asked aloud.

"Doubt it," Tengue answered.

Cara glanced into the room: a series of screens showed various corridors from ground level to the basement, nine floors down. As she'd hoped, the chaos was blocking access to the stairwell. There was a room with a woman lying prone on a bed and a boy. Nan and Ricky. Sitting on a chair in the middle of the room was a hulking figure of a man with a bolt rifle across his knees, grim-faced, staring at the door.

What's your situation, Nan? I can see from the screen it doesn't look good.

The man's called Minnow. He's been kind to Ricky, but he's never come with more than a sidearm before. He's not a natural born killer, but I'm an Empath. I can tell he's scared, and a man who's scared will do stupid things.

Is he still talking on the wire?

He's listening. There are people out there.

I can't see anything on the screen. All the corridors are empty.

It's a trap.

Yes, but where?

She turned to Tengue.

"One man with a bolt rifle in the room with Nan and Ricky. Somewhere there's a trap set for us, but where is it?"

"Keep going?"

"We don't have a choice."

"Proceed with caution then." He jerked his head and Gwala advanced down the stairs. The rest of them followed.

◆   ◆   ◆

Ricky sat on the edge of Nan's bed keeping up a conversation with Minnow that was more like a monologue, as the normally talkative guard barely answered. Most of it was for Nan's benefit, as she lay unmoving but wide awake.

"What's happening, Minnow? Why are you just sitting there? What kind of gun is that? Is it a bolt rifle? What's that thing in your ear? Is it a receiver? Have you got a transmitter? Why are you wearing a buddysuit today? Is there something special going on? Are we getting out of here? You wouldn't hurt us, would you?"

He felt Nan's foot twitch. Was that good or bad? He sure wished he had an implant right now.

"Shut up, kid, and read your book. Stay still and quiet and nobody needs to get hurt."

"Who are you listening to on that earpiece? Isn't it the big game today? Aren't you missing it? Have you got a commentary in your earpiece? You have!"

"No commentary. More than my life's worth. Shut up, kid."

"Aww come on, Minnow, be a pal."

"I ain't your pal. Not today."

"I need to pee, Minnow. I need to pee real bad."

"Hold it, kid."

"I can't. Just a quick pee, Minnow, please. Then I'll sit back down here and you'll not hear another word out of me. Promise."

"Make it quick."

Ricky held the blast pack of anesthetic in his sweaty palm. If there was a time to use it, that time had come. If he could. He jumped down from the bed and padded over to the san-unit on bare feet, pulled the pan out of the wall and hoped he could manage to pee, even if it was only a little bit. Minnow kept his eyes fixed on the door, his back straight, listening to something over the earpiece. Ricky waved his hand over the sensor that would retract and clean the bowl, then while the swirl of cleaning fluid and the hum of the pump covered up any sound his bare feet might make he crossed the couple of meters to the back of Minnow's chair, and with all the strength that he had, slapped the blast pack to the side of Minnow's neck just beneath his ear.

"Wha . . ." Minnow elbowed Ricky hard in the chest, flinging him backward. Ricky tried to draw a breath and failed. Minnow was on his feet now. The barrel of the bolt rifle came up in an arc, drawn to him like a magnet to iron. The blast pack was having no effect. It was probably calibrated for someone Nan's size and Minnow was a lot taller, a lot heavier. And he was angry. Ricky could see it in his eyes, hurt and betrayal. He'd tried to be a decent human being and Ricky had turned on him.

"Minnow!" Nan sat up and rapped out Minnow's name.

Ricky saw the surprise in his eyes and his head snapped around, the gun's nose following it a fraction later.

"No!" Ricky forced himself to his feet and jumped at Minnow's back. The pair of them hit the floor and the rifle clattered against the ceramic. Ricky rolled over, groaning, but Minnow didn't move. The blast pack had finally done its job.

"Well done, Ricky." Nan looked up at the eye on the wall. "If they saw that they'll be down here in no time. If they weren't watching we may win a few minutes. Help me drag him out of the cam view."

She stood up, or tried to, but her healing leg let her down and she fell across the bed. "Shoot! How long have I been lying in that bed?"

"Too long." Ricky helped her on to her feet and then

steadied her when she sat down. When had Nan got so light? "I'm not sure. It's hard when every day's the same."

"You've done marvelously."

Ricky felt himself swell with pride.

"But it's not over yet. Cara's coming, but it's likely there's a trap waiting to be sprung."

"Just Cara? Where's Uncle Ben?"

"Coming, and no, not just Cara, she's got a team with her."

"Will this help?" Ricky teased the receiver out of Minnow's ear and handed it to Nan.

She looked at it distastefully, wiped it on the blanket, then pushed it into her own ear. "Hand me the gun. Now, can you move Minnow by yourself?"

Ricky pulled the gun out from beneath Minnow's chest and passed it to Nan, who checked the safety and placed it on the bed. He pulled at Minnow's arm, but barely moved the man. He was heavy. Pushing had no better success. Minnow had slumped half on his face with one arm beneath him. Ricky grabbed hold of his shoulder and tugged until Minnow flopped onto his back, slightly closer to the bed. Then using the same technique, he rolled him over again, this time onto his face. He was alongside the bed now. Ricky pushed. Minnow moved a couple of centimeters at best. Nan slithered to her knees and started to push as well. Five centimeters, ten, twenty. Gradually they got him tucked away.

"That's better." Nan's tan was suspiciously pink and she could barely catch her breath to speak. She laughed, a kind of gurgle. "And now I don't think I can get up again. Give me a hand, Ricky."

She wasn't such a dead weight as Minnow. Ricky managed to get her on her feet and she rolled herself back onto the bed.

"Now what?" Ricky asked.

"Now we wait for Cara."

✦ ✦ ✦

Archie sent a handful of bots scuttling down into the pit of the stairwell. "Floor below is clear," he said.

Cara switched to silent mode. *Check for booby traps: ordnance, gas vents, anything unusual.*

Nothing, he said after a short interval.

On the fourth level they paused for the bots to check the next floor down, Nan's floor, even more thoroughly, but the corridor remained stubbornly empty.

This isn't right. There's no way we could get so lucky, Cara said. *Is the antigrav shaft working? Are they going to come at us that way? Rappel down?*

Antigrav tube isn't working, but I can reset it, Archie said. *They switch it off during matches.*

Power it up. At least it will slow them down if they try to come that way.

Cara nodded to Tengue and Gwala and fell into step behind them down the last flight of stairs to Nan's level. From the landing there was a corridor with a comm station in it and beyond the comm station a bend. This was how Ricky had described it.

The grav shaft was just behind the stairwell, a faint hum announced that it was operational. Beyond the grav shaft the corridor dead-ended. She compared it with Ben's schematics that he'd infodumped into her head. There used to be doors there, but they'd blocked off the corridor.

Bronsen put his hand on the left-hand wall. *Nan and Ricky are behind this. The door must be around the next corner.*

Cara nodded. *Thanks. You've done your bit. Go back up a level. Guard the antigrav and the stairs. Don't do anything heroic, just yell if anyone comes close.*

Understood.

Cara let her senses roam out to see if she could feel any human presence. Ronan joined with her. Just Nan and Ricky.

Nan, we're outside. How's your guard doing? Cara brought Nan into the gestalt so that everyone got the answer.

Sleeping like a baby. My great-grandson is a very smart kid.

Tell me the details later. We're on your floor, by the side wall. There's still no sign of a trap. Sending a bot to hack your door lock. Don't come out until we're sure it's clear.

Got that. Staying put. I don't have much choice, my legs aren't up to much right now.

Don't worry, we've got that covered, Ronan said. *Got an antigrav harness for you.*

Oh great, I get towed along like a balloon on a string.

Ronan chuckled. *That's about it. Are you complaining?*

I wouldn't dare.

They moved to the corner. Tengue used a scope to confirm what the bots had told Archie. *Empty. Door on the left, five meters. Corridor dead-ends.*

What? Had they blocked off the corridor since Ricky had seen it on his abortive escape attempt? Ben's schematic said it was a set of doors, too.

Oh shit. Each end of the corridor. Archie, send your bots down, don't just look. Check for a holographic screen. There should be doors there.

The blank end wall of the corridor behind them disappeared. A dozen buddysuited figures boiled out of the space. A barrage of bolts hit the ceiling beyond them—deliberately fired high.

"Stand down. Raise your hands in the air," a female voice shouted.

They jumped back to the bend in the corridor. At the other end the blank wall had disappeared and another dozen figures stood, six abreast across the corridor, bolt rifles aimed.

Tengue and Gwala moved in opposite directions. They each hurled a flashbang while at the same time banging a shield-stick on the floor. A shield rippled across the corridor, one on each side of Cara's group. Stride by stride they moved around the corner and to the open door of Nan and Ricky's cell. A barrage of bolts pounded into the shields simultaneously, but they held firm.

"Very useful gadgets," Cara said. "How long will they hold?"

"About long enough to get into here." Tengue and Gwala held the barrier while they all piled into the cell and then doubled up what was left of the shield while they slammed the door.

"Know how to make an entrance, don't you?" Nan said.

"Hi, Nan. Hi, Ricky," Cara said. "Seem to have made a mess of this. How are you?"

"Well, we were all right. Not sure now," Nan said as Ricky threw himself at Cara, almost bowling her over.

"Where's Uncle Ben?"

"He's meeting us later." She jerked her head sideways. "This is Ronan. He's our medic."

"Hi, Miss Benjamin."

Nan checked him over for a few moments. "You can call me Nan."

He grinned at her then produced an antigrav harness from inside a slim pack. "I brought a spare pair of legs. May I fit them?"

"Cara, is Uncle Ben all right? I mean, why didn't he come himself?" Ricky was at her elbow, face all concern.

"He's coming, Ricky. In the sleekest spaceship you can imagine, a raider with a jump drive."

"Oh, boy."

We just have to get out of here first, she thought.

Bronsen, activity on the floor above us?

Nothing yet.

Right. "Archie, what can your bots do to break through the ceiling? Can it be done?"

"Some of the boys are still outside, I'm sending them up to the floor above. Oof!" He clutched his head. "Sorry, they just totaled them. Just these guys then." He sent five small spider bots up the wall and across, each drilling into a different section of the ceiling and disappearing through into the void.

Something whomped into the door from the outside.

"Archie, can you hurry?"

"Three charges, here, here, and here should do it." Archie pointed and brought down three bots.

Cara took a single charge from her belt and handed it over, Archie added one of his own, and Gwala a third.

"I suggest making a makeshift shelter out of the bed and mattress. There's going to be a lot of debris."

Another whomp shook the door.

"Everyone behind the bed," Cara said. "Whoa, he's a big boy." As they moved the bed Minnow's recumbent body was exposed. He snored loudly once and fell silent again.

"Three of us could shelter under him," Gwala said.

"That's Minnow," Ricky said. "He was kind to me. Don't leave him out there to get hurt."

"Look, kid—" Gwala began.

"Pull him into the corner," Cara said. "Get down, use the

bed frame and the mattress. Right, Archie, best we can do. Blow it!"

She'd barely said the words when three sharp cracks and a tearing groan dropped a section of ceiling on the far side of the room, filling the air with dust and the acrid reek of explosives.

Tengue was on his feet first, coughing, followed closely by Gwala. There was another whump against the door and a sprinkling of rubble cascaded down from the raw hole above them.

"Quick. I can hear movement." Bronsen peered down from above.

"Tengue," Cara said.

"On it." Tengue cupped his hands, Gwala stepped into them and got a boost upward. He caught the reinforcing beam that projected from the hole and swung up easily. Archie did the same for Tengue, boosting him up to Gwala's waiting grasp. They didn't wait, but ran to secure the stairwell. The building shook as they dropped a charge down it to slow down the opposition.

"Ronan, Nan, get up there now," Cara said. "Drop a line."

Ronan flicked a switch on the side of Nan's antigrav casing and pushed off, rocketing upward to be caught by Bronsen. Archie boosted Ricky up next.

Another whump on the door. The next one would batter it down.

"You next," Archie said, cupping his hands for Cara's foot and shoving as she sprang. Bronsen caught her hand and pulled.

Ronan lay down and dropped a thin line for Archie, whose head appeared through the hole as another whump blew the door inward. He swung his legs up and rolled clear of the hole as a bolt gun discharged into the space he'd just cleared.

"Grav shaft, quick," Ronan said.

"Got an idea," Cara said. "Tengue, can you blow the stairs?"

"One charge left." Tengue pulled it from his belt.

A head appeared above the hole in the floor. Cara put a smart-dart into the man's cheek and he fell back.

Nan thumbed the safety off the bolt rifle, set it on spray

burn and heated up the floor around the hole until it was glowing red and the reinforcing bar was twisting in the heat. "Stay back, you bastards," she yelled. "First one through goes home without a head." She glanced sideways at Cara. "What? I was trained in negotiation. Sometimes things got a little rough."

They ran for the grav shaft.

"Push off hard," Ronan said. "Like you would if you were playing grapple. Follow me." He bent his knees and pushed, soaring upward with Nan in tow. Cara took hold of Ricky's hand and followed him. Bronsen came next, closely followed by Archie. Gwala and Tengue came last, and Cara heard the crump of explosives as the stairwell collapsed below them.

"Archie, can you take care of the grav shaft once we're into the arena?" Cara asked.

"Got one bot left."

Hilde, are you there?

Affirmative.

Hover over the roof of the stadium. There's a vent.

They shot upward into the stadium where spectators were still being evacuated. The null-G was back up to full strength. Cara caught the lip of a platform and pulled Ricky onto it. "You ever played grapple before?"

"No." His voice trembled. "But I've watched it plenty on the vid."

"Well, now's your chance. See that bar up there?"

"Right up there?"

"Yes, that one. Push off from here, grab it with both hands, then get your feet on to it and aim for where Ronan is up there on the loop with your Nan. I'll be close behind. You can't fall. Don't think of it as up and down."

"What if they cut the power?"

"Gravity will come back slowly, just like it does in a grav shaft."

"Yeah, but there are no ladders to grab."

"Just jump for it, before the guys with guns get past that blockage on the stairwell."

Ricky jumped. Cara jumped after him. Bronsen and Archie had each taken different routes and were traversing across to the loop. Tengue and Gwala had halted by the head of the grav shaft to throw a flashbang down now that it was deactivated. There was a lot of healthy screaming as the crowd jostled to escape what had become a fiasco.

Tengue had torn the marker tape from the head of the stairwell and was busy directing fleeing spectators down the staircase Crowder's militia would be coming up. Cara suppressed a smile. Good man.

Ricky had reached the bar, but hadn't taken off again yet. "Like this." Cara swung her feet up and launched herself toward the goal. She grabbed on to the loop and looked back. Ricky was still on the bar. She beckoned him toward her.

"Hold Nan," Ronan said and launched himself over to where Ricky clutched the bar, frozen. Everyone else had made it safely and Gwala was working on the roof vent catch three meters above their heads. One of Archie's bots would be perfect, but they'd used them all up.

Cara could see Ronan talking calmly to Ricky, but the boy had a thousand-meter stare. Suddenly he doubled over and puked, globules spraying out. Ronan just rubbed his back, took his hand and launched through the vomit, delivering Ricky to the loop.

"Don't worry about it. Most of us puke in free fall the first time," he said as they landed. "Don't make me tell you about my first time in a grapple arena. They made me clean it up myself. Didn't tell me until afterward there were bots to do it."

"Got it," Gwala said as the hatch cover sailed away.

"Hilde's in place," Tengue said.

The sound of a flyer's drive droned above the roof canopy.

"Okay, everyone," Ronan said. "The antigrav field extends beyond the external skin of the sphere. Outside, grab onto anything you can to anchor yourself. The field weakens about three meters out and it is possible to slip out of it altogether. It's a long way down." He took Ricky's hand firmly and powered off the loop toward the roof hatch and through it. "Come up one at a time and I'll guide you through."

Bronsen shot up first and would have gone straight through at some speed, but Ronan caught him by the arm and pulled him sideways, out of sight.

"Not so fast. Next," Ronan called down.

Archie went next, then Cara with Nan. She handed Nan through, then pulled herself over the lip and found everyone sitting, delicately balanced on the roof plate of the giant geodesic dome. Looking down made her head spin and she quickly looked up to where the flyer was hovering a couple of hundred meters away. Gwala and Tengue completed the crew.

A roof plate to her right shattered and a bolt streaked upward, visible against the darkening sky.

Tengue waved Hilde in and she hovered above the roof, the downdraft almost dislodging Cara from her precarious hold.

"This is the difficult bit," Ronan said as the craft's open hatch loomed about four meters away from their position.

He let go with both hands and bent his knees to jump, but Gwala beat him to it, the African's powerful legs and long reach giving him the extra impetus to grab on to the hatch with what looked like his fingertips. He hung there for a few heart-stopping moments, then hauled himself inside and lowered a line. Ronan and Ricky first, Cara and Nan second. As Cara passed into normal gravity her limbs felt like lead. She teetered on the edge of the hatch, trying to push Nan upward. Gwala leaned down and grabbed Nan's hands, then Cara's, and she tumbled into the flyer, gasping.

Another bolt shattered the roof plate where Cara had been sitting moments before. Nan rolled forward and covered the hatch with her bolt rifle still set on spray burn. Once the last man, Tengue, was safely on board, she sprayed the roof struts to heat them up.

"Whoo-hoo!" She sat back on the floor of the flyer, clutching on to a cargo net. "That was a wild ride, children. I thank you all very much."

Chapter Twenty-Three

CHENON

*N*AN AND RICKY ARE SAFE.* CARA'S MES-sage rattled through Ben's brain.

Everyone all right? he asked.

Yes. No casualties, except Archie's bots, but they died in a good cause.

A trap?

Yes. We had to get creative in zero gravity. Nan's still laughing, though I think it's relief. Did you know your Nan was a dab hand with a bolt rifle?

Nothing Nan does ever surprises me. Much relief all around. See you soon.

Soon.

Ben eased *Solar Wind* out of the dock. It was a clean exit, completely different from lurching out with four limpets ready to blow. The Folds had been his salvation then. Keep that in mind.

"Jump drive powered up and online," Kitty said.

He almost snapped at her. He knew the bloody jump drive was online. He could feel it coursing through his body. "Thanks, Kitty," he said, trying to keep his voice even.

Jussaro looked at him sharply. *Can I help?*

No one can help. This is my fight.

You don't have to do it alone.

He's not alone, Gen said.

Okay, I get that, Jussaro said. *Let me swing along for the ride. A bit of mental ballast.*

Just don't get in my way. Ben looked across and scowled.

I won't.

Ready, Gen? Ben asked.

Ready.

The jump gate in front of them grew from a pinprick on the screen to a maw big enough to swallow a ship three times their size. Ben positioned *Solar Wind* ready for the leap into foldspace, the hairs on the back of his neck standing to attention—or maybe it just felt like that. They got the signal from the gate Telepath.

Ben continued to stare at the void.

"Go," Gen said quietly.

He gave a short, sharp nod, but still hesitated.

Go! she said again, but this time directly into his head.

He swallowed convulsively and took a deep breath. He'd been scared of water as a small child. This felt like the first time he'd stood on the bank, afraid to jump even though Dad was there in the pool to catch him. In the end the anticipation had been worse than the fear of jumping. He'd jumped so far and so fast that he'd barely touched the water and had landed on Dad's chest, knocking him over backward and submerging them both. Dad had quickly fished him out, but not before that moment of infinite mortality when the water had closed over his head.

Now Dad was somewhere in the Folds, no longer there to catch him.

Ben swallowed convulsively, took a deep breath, and nudged *Solar Wind* through the gate.

And that's when it all fell apart.

◆ ◆ ◆

The flight deck is suddenly swirling with creatures of all shapes and sizes. They nudge and buffet him, their hot breath drying his eyeballs. Then they scatter, fleeing through solid bulkheads. In their place, one huge void dragon coils around him. It must be twenty meters long, snout to tail, and is etched black on black. The claws on its prehensile beard curl toward him and tickle his cheek while its dragon breath cools his flesh. He crosses his forearms in front of his face and its attention is taken by the protective casing around his wrist. It nudges it; once, twice, three times. It's not just a creature. Its eye is infinity—his past and his future. His present is somewhere else entirely, but he doesn't know where.

Ben, I need the line, Gen says from a very long way away. *Ben, are you with me? I need the line.*

He can't answer her.

She reaches across and smacks the void dragon's snout. So she can see this one as well as he can. Kennedy was right. He's not going completely crazy. He stares into its lambent eye and is lost.

Fuck it, Benjamin. Gen's voice comes from far away. *I didn't think you'd really flake out on me. Taking control.*

He hears her, but the dragon has him transfixed.

✦ ✦ ✦

They emerged into realspace with a gentle pop. No more dragon. Ben felt sweat cooling on his face. His heart rate must be off the scale. He forced himself to breathe. Without a word he unstrapped his harness, stood up, and walked away from the pilot's chair. Gen slid into it.

"Go and sit next to Gen," he said to Max, his voice shaking.

He couldn't look Max in the eye. He flopped down into Max's still-warm seat, next to Jussaro. Damn, he hadn't given a thought to whether Jussaro had managed to get rid of his implant.

It's real, Jussaro said directly to Ben and Ben only. *I saw what you saw, a wyrm or a dragon or an alien. I don't know what it was, but it was real and it was trying to make contact. It knows you. It's not your mind playing tricks.*

Gen saw it, but it didn't scare her.

It wasn't as big to Gen, not as threatening. The rest aren't looking. They don't believe. You're not imagining things. You have to find a way to deal with this thing because it won't leave you alone until you acknowledge it.

Ben got his breathing under control. *How the hell do I do that?*

I can't help you there. All I can say is that you're not going nuts.

Thanks, Jussaro. Believe it or not, that is a help. But you've still got your implant.

Yeah, your void dragon sidetracked me and I expected to have more time, but we're doing another jump, aren't we? A short one?

A shorter distance covered doesn't always mean a shorter jump.

"Get ready everyone," Gen said, meaning, *Get ready, Ben.* "Jumping to foldspace in three, two, one."

❖ ❖ ❖

Ben feels the jump drive kick in and immediately the void dragon is back. It coils itself around him again, making a mockery of the cabin dimensions. Half its body is through the bulkhead. One coil pierces Max's chest, but he doesn't react. He obviously can't see or feel anything. Its tail snakes across the flight deck and out through the far bulkhead. Ben is heavy with fear. Paralyzed.

Even though his mind tells him the void dragon can't possibly be real, his gut tells him that it is. He's ridden it, out there, in the vast deeps of the Folds, the nothing place between realities.

He tries to imagine it gone, but it remains. Belief is not that easy to deny. The void dragon is real in this reality, and it wants something from him.

• Its head snakes around. He feels the whisper of breeze, ice cold on his mouth and nose. He holds his breath, afraid to breathe the air that the dragon has breathed out. The claws on the strands of the dragon's beard twist and reach out to touch his forehead. He feels a pinprick on the tiny scar left by the implantation needle.

No. No. No.

His insides turn to liquid. Between one blink and the next he understands how he parted from his last implant. It wasn't lost. It wasn't an accident.

You took it! He tries to communicate that thought.

The void dragon echoes it back to him with a hint of assent. Or maybe it's intent. It doesn't seem to have words, but it has ideas.

Well, you're not having this one. He puts a thought into his mind that's a mixture of no and stop.

The void dragon responds with, *?*

Ben wonders how to communicate the fact that his implant is supposed to be there, that he wants it to be there, that removing it will be a bad thing. Does the void dragon even have a concept of good and bad, of right and wrong?

Across the cabin he sees Jussaro bent double in his seat, held in place by a lap strap. There's a look of fierce concentration on his face.

Oh, gods! He's misled Jussaro. The thought sits like a stone in his gut. It wasn't the effect of belief or the fluidity of foldspace that separated him from his first implant, it was the void dragon itself.

Ben reaches out, trembling, and tugs at the strands of the void dragon's beard.

Over there. He puts Jussaro at the front of his mind, turns the great saurian head and points. *Take that implant.* (And leave me alone.)

He hears a gasp as the beast turns its attention on Jussaro, which is less of a movement and more of a rotation of its coils until its head is in the right place.

"What's it doing?" Jussaro's voice trembles.

"It's doing what you're trying to do."

"I can't . . . I don't . . ."

Jussaro gives a wordless cry. A glittering net of delicate tendrils floats beside him. He cranes his neck and looks at it, reaches for it with his fingers. Some of the strands begin to unravel.

The void dragon breathes in and the implant is gone.

Jussaro collapses over his own knees, sobbing quietly. For a few moments, Ben's own misery is deluged by Jussaro's.

✦ ✦ ✦

"Ben, get your ass back in this chair," Gen yelled. "We're in Chenon's atmosphere and likely flaring across Corrigar's tracking screens like an incoming meteor."

Ben blinked images of the dragon away and pushed down the terrors as if shaking off a nightmare. "Someone see to Jussaro. He might need a sedative."

Kitty jumped up from systems, but Max beat her to it and flopped back into the bucket seat Ben had just vacated.

Gen slid over to copilot, and Ben once more had the *Solar Wind* under his control. This was okay. Flying in realspace was what he needed right now.

All right? Gen asked.

Yeah, I'll manage.

She looked at him sideways.

Don't worry, I can handle it from here.

He brought *Solar Wind* screaming through the upper atmosphere, swept around and let her speed bleed away. "Kitty, what have we got on the screen?"

"Airliner." She snapped out the coordinates and heading.

"That will do." Ben matched speed and shadowed the liner across the southern continent to confuse any tracking signals, peeling off for Russolta just before Corrigar and skimming low over ancient woodland until the Benjamin family farm was on the horizon.

The landing pad was a little small for the *Solar Wind*, but he dropped her in neatly on antigravs, her fully flexed wings overhanging the pink grass equally on both sides.

"What the hell is this?" Rion was waiting for him at the bottom of the ramp, Tam and Lol sitting by his side, their tails thumping the ground, but too well trained to leap and greet Ben without permission.

It was always a shock to see Rion, only three years older according to their birth certificates, but because of Ben's long periods of cryo on missions, effectively much older, steel gray at his temples already. His skin, actually lighter than Ben's when they were children, had weathered to a deeper shade of brown. Rion's mouth habitually turned down at the corners. The crinkles around his eyes were from squinting into wind, rain, and sun, not from laughter.

"I love you, too, brother. This is a spaceship. My spaceship. I stole her."

"So the accusations are true. You've gone rogue."

Ben raised one eyebrow. "We can talk about it while you're packing."

"I'm not going anywhere."

"We can talk about that while you're packing, too."

"Nan and Ricky—"

"Safe. Pack for them as well. Do you need some help?" Ben started to walk toward the house.

"Dammit, Ben, what's going on?"

"I wondered when you'd ask that. Short version: Crowder tried to shaft ten thousand people on Chenon in order to get his hands on a planet-load of platinum, and he tried to kill three hundred psi-techs to stop the news from getting out. We weren't too keen on the idea. Conflict ensued and now we're on the wrong side of the law because the law is on the wrong side. Clear so far?"

Rion's mouth was still open.

"And in addition there's a missing boatload of settlers which we need to find. And you might be Crowder's next target, so get packing."

"I can't leave the farm. A thousand head of beef cattle, horses in the barn, the chickens, the dogs, the dairy herd."

"You won't be any use to them dead. Call Bunty Jaeger. Get her boys to farm-sit for you until further notice."

"Dead?"

"Cara had to bust Nan and Ricky out of Crowder's holding cell. There's no way Crowder's going to forgive and forget. Call Kai. I need him at the hospital in Arkhad City visiting a burn patient called Fowler. Tell him to keep his head down."

"I . . . I already told him that when Nan and Ricky went missing. They're really safe?"

"I promise you."

Rion's shoulders sagged.

They walked together to the house in the deepening gloom. Ben usually came here between missions. It was his safe haven. Even though he only used it once every couple of years his room was still his, with all the reminders of his childhood, his art portfolio and several sets of half-used, dried-up paints, a wooden spaceship that had once belonged to his father, and hard copy images of his parents, the same as the ones he carried in holographic form on his handpad.

The house was pure Chenon frontier, a circular pit house, like a four-story bagel set into bedrock with an open central atrium. Kitchen and living space were on the upper level, with a horizontal row of slit windows to the outside up close to the ceiling where someone standing on a stepladder could peep out beneath the eaves and see out at ground level. Bedrooms and storerooms occupied the lower three levels. They grew tomatoes, peppers, grapes, and soft fruit in the atrium. It collected heat in winter and cooled the house down in summer.

The only part of the house substantially above ground level was the entrance and the thatched roof sloping from center to edge of the outer ring. When Ben was a boy the central atrium had been roofed over with a plasglass dome, but that was long gone and now it was open to the weather. A shallow sunken pool collected rainwater.

He'd brought Cara here once, to visit Nan, back when he thought his main problem was going to be the upcoming mission to Olyanda with a bunch of fundy settlers. Rion had been away, which probably added to the pleasant memories he had of Nan and Cara laughing together over the kitchen table. Rion had always been curmudgeonly about Ben's girlfriends, and he'd never liked Serena, Ben's college sweetheart and later his wife. Their relationship hadn't been strong enough to survive Ben's few years in the Monitors, so perhaps Rion had had some insight that Ben lacked. He wondered what Rion would make of Cara, or, indeed, what Cara would make of Rion.

He came up from his room with the wooden spaceship.

Rion eyed it. "You're not intending to come back, then."

"I hope it doesn't come to that."

"Taking the spaceship . . . it seems so final." Rion turned away and gazed through the curved glass down at the forest of grapes and tomatoes. "I can't leave here, Ben. I'm too much of a fixture, too old to change. Not cut out for space travel. Take Nan and the boys somewhere safe. I'll wait it out here."

"No, if you do I'll only have to come back and rescue you from Crowder."

"You needn't bother."

"Rion, you're my brother. Why wouldn't I bother?"

Rion just shrugged.

"Make the calls, pack your things and Ricky's. I'll throw some of Nan's clothes into a bag. Hurry."

Ben headed for the stairs, then realized Rion hadn't moved. He stopped, hand on the banister. "Come on, man. You know it makes sense."

"Not going anywhere."

Ben sighed. He was going to have to do this the hard way. He crossed the living room into the kitchen area and reached into the cupboard for two mugs.

"Nan thinks tea solves the problems of the universe,"

Rion said, following him to the door and leaning on the frame. "You can't change my mind with tea."

"I'm not trying to. Sit and drink it anyway. How long is it since we've sat down together?"

Rion shrugged. "A year? Two?"

"Try three. Three for you, anyway. Two for me, subjectively."

Ben held the pot under the spigot. Nan always insisted on proper tea, brewed in a prewarmed pot.

"Cryo has torn this family apart," Rion said.

It wasn't just Ben's cryo trips he was talking about.

"Our parents are long gone," Ben said. He let the water heat up the ceramic and tipped it down the drain. He shoveled three heaped teaspoons of leaves in, set the spigot temperature to boiling and half-filled the pot.

"You never cared like I did."

"Don't fool yourself. I was younger. Maybe I bounced back faster. I haven't forgotten. Every time I fly the Folds I wonder if their ship is still out there, a hulk full of dried-out husks."

"*Cassandra*. Their ship was called the *Cassandra*."

"I know." Ben looked at the wooden spaceship he'd set on the kitchen counter. It had never had a name, but he'd named it in secret, his childhood self imagining his parents inside it. Sleeping into eternity. Safe and untroubled.

"Tea for two." He placed the pot on the table and put two mugs next to it. "Sit, Rion."

"Have you got time for this? Shouldn't you be going?"

Ben found milk in the cooler, poured a splash into his own mug and offered the jug to Rion. Then he sat down and waited.

"Sit, Rion. I've got time. It may be the last time if you're so stubborn you're going to risk your life here just because you're afraid of the Folds."

"That's not why—"

"Bunty Jaeger's boys are more than capable of looking after the farm. It'll still be here. You can come back when we resolve this."

"You think there's a resolution?" Rion walked over to the table and poured a few drops of milk into the second mug and held it out for Ben to pour tea into. He sat, cupped his hands around the mug and breathed in the steam.

"I hope so. I have information that will discredit Crowder completely, I'd have gone public with it sooner, but I wanted to make sure the settlers were safe first. Then I heard Crowder had Nan. Once all my family is safe—and that includes you—Crowder is toast. Then you can have your life back."

"The Folds..." Rion took a sip of his tea. "I don't think I can."

"I'll not pretend foldspace isn't dangerous, but statistically—"

"Are our parents only a statistic to you now?"

Ben wanted to say, *I was almost a statistic,* but Rion didn't need to hear that. "We've got a medic on board. You can have a sedative if you wish. A lot of first-timers do. There's no shame in it." He took a deep breath. *I might even be joining you,* he thought.

"There's got to be an alternative..." Rion's speech slurred. He frowned at his mug and looked up at Ben. "You didn't..."

"I'm afraid I did."

Ben took the scalding mug out of Rion's hands as he collapsed slowly forward onto the table. *Okay, you can come and get him now,* he said. *I had to use the goodnight drops.*

On our way, Boss, Yan replied. *One antigrav gurney and two packers coming up.*

◆ ◆ ◆

All set? Cara reached for Ben across Chenon. His newly achieved Psi-4 rating wasn't strong enough for him to contact her from halfway around the planet.

Rendezvous at Norro in thirty minutes, Ben said. *I had to knock Rion out to get him on board, and we've got Jussaro curled up in a cabin mewling to himself, but apart from that we're okay.*

He flashed the whole Jussaro story to her in an instant. There was something else he wasn't telling her, but Cara didn't pry.

Is there a plan? Cara asked.

Yeah, improvise.

"That's Norro ahead," Hilde said over her shoulder. "Should I put down on the beach?"

"Overfly it a couple of times so we can take a look," Cara said. *We're ahead of you,* she told Ben. *Just checking it out. There's a village on the south side, plenty of lights, fishing boats in the harbor, and a couple of larger craft anchored off the bay.*

Tourist yachts most likely. Good beaches at the west end, sheer cliffs north and east. Commercial landing pad center-island and a private one at Northcliffe, that's where the ex-Mrs. Crowder lives when she's not attending functions. I never met her. Crowder used to keep all his family well away from his work, but I do know their split was not amicable. There was a lot of very unpleasant fallout.

There's a Trust flyer on the landing pad at Northcliffe.

Size?

Not a huge one, maybe capacity for ten or twelve. It's guarded. Two heat signatures. More in the house. Twelve or fifteen people.

Have they spotted you?

We flew over at about a hundred meters. Yes, they spotted us, but we're in a rental flyer. Hopefully we look like tourists.

Land on the commercial pad. Pay the landing tax. Take a walk with Bronsen, see if he can confirm whether it's Crowder there. Don't act suspicious.

Suspicious? Us? Wouldn't dream of it. What about you?

Water landing.

◆ ◆ ◆

Ben brought *Solar Wind* across the last fifty klicks of the Calman Sea submerged. Rion slept like a baby in Ben's own cabin and Jussaro, having refused a sedative, was curled up further down the corridor, alone with his misery.

Cara had confirmed that Bronsen had Found Crowder located somewhere within the complex at the north end of the island. Now that they were so close Ben was able to contact her directly rather than having to wait for her to contact him—still a joy to him. He'd even been able to have a conversation with Nan, recovering spiritually from her confinement, if her anger was anything to go by, but still weak-muscled after a month of sedation. Ricky, Nan said, was bouncing off the walls of the light flyer, confined to an even smaller space than their cell, and sharing it with Ten-gue and Gwala, keeping out of sight so as not to arouse suspicion. Tengue and Gwala, having been in this kind of situation before, took their confinement philosophically, and sat back, talking quietly, playing games on their handpad or reading. Neither of them connected into the planetary network, of course, since they needed to stay invisible.

Ben had a package for the planetary network: the vid of his confrontation with Crowder, and Crowder's admission of guilt for the attacks on Hera-3 and Olyanda.

Olyanda had backfired on the Trust spectacularly.

Once Ben had extracted the whereabouts of the missing settlers from Crowder he'd happily throw him, and the Trust, and possibly Alphacorp as well, to the wolves, and let the combined might of the press and the law deal with them all. He'd even be willing to return to answer for Ari van Blaiden's death if he had to. He hadn't told Cara that part yet. He knew what her reaction would be. As for the Free Company, they'd manage without him.

❖ ❖ ❖

"Everyone clear about what's going to happen?" Cara asked out loud for Ricky's benefit. They were crammed into the cargo space behind the flyer's seats, down and safe in the area of the airport reserved for private flyers.

"Clear." Tengue, Gwala, Hilde, Archie, Bronsen, and Ronan all responded quickly and concisely.

"As long as I get a chance at Crowder once you've got him," Nan said. She still clutched the bolt rifle that she'd taken from Minnow.

"You planning on using that?" Tengue nodded toward the weapon. "Because if you are, would you give us all fair warning, please?"

Nan sighed. "I don't need a bolt gun to blister Crowder's ears off."

"I bet you don't, lady," Gwala said.

"Nan, why can't I go, too?" Ricky put his hand on Nan's sleeve. "I knocked Minnow out."

"You did," Cara said. "You did absolutely the best thing you could have done. You kept your head and you used your brains. What you did was very smart. Without you I doubt we could have gotten in and out without someone getting hurt. Ben will be so proud of you. Do you know what the best thing you did was?"

"Figuring out how to use the skin gel as a barrier on Nan's neck?"

"That was clever, but it wasn't the best thing."

"Switching the used blast pack for a fully charged one?"

She shook her head. "Same again, clever but not the best thing."

"Knocking Minnow out?"

"Uh, no. That was courageous, though."

"What then?"

"When we blew the ceiling you insisted we protect Minnow as well. He was your enemy, but you treated him with respect and human kindness. That was the best thing. It shows that you know how to fight when you need to, but you don't let people get hurt if you can help it. You're more like your Uncle Ben than you know."

"Really?"

"Really."

"But you've got to understand that if you come with us it will be dangerous and you're not fully grown yet. So someone would have to look after you instead of looking after themselves, and that's when people get hurt under fire. And you know that you don't let people get hurt if you can possibly help it. Understand?"

He nodded. "Yeah, got it. Stay with Nan and Ronan on the perimeter."

"Yeah, buddy. I'm missing all the fun, too," Ronan said. "Not that I'm complaining."

Nan looked sideways at Cara and winked. *Are you sure you were never a negotiator?*

Sure.

Cara, you all ready? Ben made contact.

Abandoning the flyer now, she said. *We'll be up-island in an hour. Rendezvous as planned.* "All right," Cara turned to the rest of them. "Me, Hilde, Archie, and Bronsen first, making a loud noise through the main gate. The rest of you, quietly and quickly as we take all the port master's attention. Ricky, stick with Gwala until you get to the perimeter. All right with the antigrav legs, Nan?"

"Oh, I'll just bump along behind Ronan like a half-deflated balloon. Don't worry." She slapped Ronan's upper arm. "We'll be fine."

"Who's got my buddysuit?" Hilde asked.

"It's in my pack," Gwala replied. "Don't worry, you won't have to scale any walls in your high heels."

Cara slipped on Hilde's brightest, most outrageous coat, a swinging swirl of lemon and crimson. It covered her from chin to midcalf. "I feel a bit ostentatious in this."

"You look wonderful, dahling!" Hilde put on the voice to go with the high heels, white sheath dress, and gauzy wrap that fairly sparkled in the daytime lights.

Archie and Bronsen wore the same green flight suits that they'd worn to come through immigration, lightweight coverings to disguise the buddysuit beneath.

"Let's go give them a show," Cara said.

"Walk this way." Hilde sashayed out in front of them, hips swaying, heels clacking on the floor.

"If I could walk that way . . ." Archie left the old joke hanging as they followed her out into the morning darkness.

Chapter Twenty-Four

GETAWAY

BEN STUDIED THE CLIFFS. THEY COULD BE climbed, though his lungs weren't completely healed yet, and with his wrist still in the case he'd make heavy weather of it. Better to make an entrance and cause a distraction, let Cara's crew slide in over the perimeter wall. He wasn't going to put Gen in danger, though she wouldn't thank him for coddling her. Max was about as much use as a sugar teapot and Kitty had already admitted to being no use in a scrap, but he could use them behind a screen with smart-dart rifles to protect the entrance and draw fire. He only had Yan and Toni Horta, the taciturn merc, and he needed Horta on tactical. Just him and Yan as a landing party, then.

But he did have a very neat spaceship.

Everyone in place? he asked from the ladder in the upper hatch.

He got a chorus of affirmatives.

Here we go. He gave Gen a mental nod.

She raised *Solar Wind* from the ocean like a leviathan, perfectly level. Nose to the cliff face, she rose up and loomed over the cliff edge. A shudder through the body of the ship announced Horta letting loose with the pulse-cannon.

Yes! Horta's triumphant affirmative was the nearest

Ben had ever heard her come to joy. *Crowder's flyer, destroyed.*

A second shudder, smaller this time, signaled that she'd blown out part of the perimeter wall.

Gen planted *Solar Wind* firmly on the landing pad and the main hatch lowered. Max and Kitty, armed with smart-dart rifles, were lying flat in the hatch behind one of the portable body shields, the muzzles of their rifles poking through. It didn't matter how accurate they were, the object of the exercise was to draw as many of Crowder's people from the house as possible. If any of them looked close to boarding *Solar Wind*, Horta would lay down lethal fire, but until then, smart-darts would be enough. One dart would knock a man out. Two would probably not be lethal unless there was some underlying medical condition. Three would be fatal. Each dart was movement- and heat-seeking, so even if Kitty and Max were the worst shots in the world, the darts should find their marks in mobile, warm bodies. With luck, they should be able to knock out two or three in the first rush. After that it might be a standoff.

Ben heard pings as bolts ricocheted from *Solar Wind*'s skin, but they were no more than gnat bites on her armor. He opened the upper hatch and slithered over to the far side, followed by Yan. By grabbing the handholds designed for use in space, they slithered down the hull, along the wing, now fully extended for atmospheric flight, and dropped down close to the cliff edge under cover of darkness.

We're in, Cara said from the opposite side of the compound.

Ben and Yan circumnavigated the firefight going on at *Solar Wind*'s hatch. There were four bodies on the ground.

Good shooting, guys, Ben said.

It's Kitty, not me, Max responded. *Even with the heat-seeker things I've not hit one. Kitty's a whiz.*

Keep it up. Pin down as many as you can. I'm counting at least another four still throwing bolts in your direction. If your shields show low power get back inside and dog the hatch. Don't take any chances.

Do I look like the kind of man to take chances? Max said. *I'm an accountant, remember?*

Ben and Yan ran for the wall at the corner of the compound. Ben boosted Yan to the top and Yan dropped a line, holding it firm from the other side while Ben climbed.

Yeowch, it hurt his wrist. He'd been overconfident about it. His lungs, too. His breath rasped in his chest. At the bottom of the wall he stopped, panting.

You all right? Yan sounded concerned.

I will be when we get Crowder.

The house and gardens were ablaze with light. Figures moved inside. Someone screamed. Definitely not Cara or Hilde. Mrs. Crowder, then. Two figures ran across the manicured pink lawn from the direction of *Solar Wind*. Ben hit one of them with a smart-dart, Yan felled the other.

Cara? he asked.

All secured in here. We've got Crowder.

Any other guards?

Not in the house.

By my count, there might be one more watching Solar Wind.*

I'll check. Yan doubled back.

Ben let himself in through the garden doors.

✦ ✦ ✦

Crowder raised his hands.

How the hell had they figured out he was here?

Why hadn't he had a warning from Jussaro? The man was dead as soon as Crowder got his fingers on that kill switch.

He didn't recognize all of them, but he knew he was in trouble when Carlinni followed the thick-necked soldier type into the room. If his heart had been capable of beating any faster than it already was, it would have hammered its way out of his chest as soon as she arrived. Benjamin. Where was Benjamin?

Danniri had been blindsided at the stadium and Drew Wyndham had been worse than useless here, the first out at the sound of the alarm and not seen since. Crowder had managed a call to Danniri, but it would be four hours before she got here with reinforcements. About three hours and fifty-nine minutes too late. He'd told her to send a squad to the Benjamin farm and to the university where Kai Benjamin was studying, but he doubted they'd find anything. Benjamin wasn't stupid enough to leave any of his family exposed.

"Is this him?" A statuesque blonde female jerked the business end of a smart-dart rifle in his direction. Benjamin may not be here, but this had all his hallmarks, a soft operation. He recognized the weapon for what it was, nonlethal, and started to breathe again. This was one of the weapons he'd taken precautions against. You could never be too careful. Building an immunity to the anesthetic had not been particularly pleasant, but suddenly it all seemed worth it.

"Meet Gabrius Crowder," Carlinni said. "Would-be mass murderer."

"Unsuccessful, if I may remind you," Crowder said, pleased that his voice hadn't broken. "I didn't actually kill anyone."

"Don't tempt me to use this, Crowder. Not before Ben gets here. We've got two assassination attempts to add to your butcher's bill. One of them almost killed Serafin the day we arrived on Crossways and the second one, the Alphabet Gang, killed six station guards trying to take out Ben."

"That wasn't me, honest. I tried once, sure. You can't blame me for that, but—what did you call them, the Alphabet Gang?—they're not mine. Never heard of them. Sounds like Alphacorp to me. Alphacorp. Alphabet. Know what I mean?"

"You're lying."

"What? You think Alphacorp was completely innocent of all van Blaiden's wrongdoings? Didn't you know about Akiko Yamada? Of course not, why would you? Ari fucked his way to the top."

Stall for time. Benjamin was on his way, good. If he was going down he was damn sure he was going to take Benjamin and Carlinni with him. The implant killers were still in his pocket. Right pocket for Benjamin, left for Carlinni. Pity those were the only two, but if he had to guess who else might be on the team that came after him he might have guessed Vijay Gupta, Gen Marling, and Wenna Phipps, possibly Ronan Wolfe. He'd never have picked Archie Tatum and Lewis Bronsen, and who the hell were the soldiers? Mercenaries. It was written in every line of their body language. Crossways hirelings, perhaps. Oh—his brain caught up with him—the mercs who'd brought in the injured woman. Damn, he'd been suspicious, but he thought they were contained at the burn unit.

"Check the other rooms," Carlinni said.

The big black soldier and the woman left without a word. Within minutes there was a loud scream followed by a faint thud.

"You found my ex-wife," Crowder said. "She never could stand me."

"A woman of taste," Carlinni said.

He shrugged. "Can I put my hands down?"

"No. Keep them up there until they fall off."

"Just one woman," the tall female said as they came back in. "She's sleeping off a smart-dart."

Carlinni nodded. "Secure the house. Ben's here."

As she spoke, Benjamin stepped over the threshold of the garden door. "Hello, Crowder. What a very fine day it is."

Crowder's guts churned. This might be a soft operation, but Benjamin's expression was anything but soft.

"I see you've got a new ear. I don't like the color. It's still a bit too fresh and it doesn't quite match the other one."

Crowder started to lower his hand to touch his ear, but the muzzle of Carlinni's rifle reminded him to keep it up.

"How did you know I was here?"

"Jussaro. Information goes both ways sometimes. Your Telepath was careless."

I'll have him brain-wiped, Crowder thought. Fucking useless asshole.

"You've heard from the stadium, of course?" Ben asked.

"Yes, well played."

"It wasn't me." Ben jerked his head sideways to Carlinni. "These guys orchestrated it. What possessed you to go after my family, Crowder? Surely you knew I'd come for them?"

Crowder shrugged, trying to appear more in control than he felt. "What are you going to do with me?"

"Extract information for starters. The whereabouts of thirty thousand settlers."

"I don't know."

"Arcturus, you said. That was a lie."

"I still don't know." He truly didn't. Oh, gods, he wished he did. "I can't tell you what I don't know. And why should I tell you? You'll kill me anyway. Even with that popgun." He jerked his head toward the rifle in Carlinni's hands. "One dart won't kill me for sure, three will. Two might. I'm not as fit as I used to be. Two could do it for me, you know. Not feeling so good right now, in fact."

"Nan wanted a word with him," Carlinni said to Benjamin. "She's blue blazing mad and she picked up a bolt rifle in the stadium and won't let go of it."

Crowder remembered the look on the terrifying old woman's face. Benjamin might not murder him in cold blood, but he'd locked up Louisa Benjamin for a month. "Ari van Blaiden," Crowder said. "Van Blaiden was supposed to find them a planet and dump them."

"You're stalling," Carlinni said. "Just a few minutes ago you claimed that you hadn't actually killed anyone yet. Thirty thousand settlers, Crowder. Do you really want them on your conscience? Where did you send them? Don't give us that Ari van Blaiden crap. You knew him. Handing them over to Ari would be a death sentence." She turned to Benjamin. "Let me clean him out, Ben. Strip it out of his mind." She pressed the muzzle of the rifle into Crowder's belly. Reached up and tore one of the psi-dampers from the collar of his jacket. "Been relying on these, Crowder, to keep you safe from nightmares like me. I can kill you with my mind."

"That's an old joke. You don't get me with that one."

She reached up and ripped off the second damper.

"Cara, no!"

The genuine alarm in Benjamin's voice sparked icy fear in Crowder's gut. The double damper had kept his implant inviolate since the discovery of platinum on Olyanda. It had been inconvenient, but he wasn't a full psi-tech. Losing the facility to receive messages hadn't crippled him. He'd seen psi-techs with their implants decommissioned. It wasn't pretty. He'd had it described to him as like being hit on the head with a spiked club—from the inside.

Carlinni was inside his head, now, drilling down through layers of consciousness. He felt stripped naked; his thoughts started to unravel. He couldn't see, couldn't breathe.

Through a fog, he heard her say: "He's telling the truth, damn him."

He dropped his arms, fell to his knees and folded over, desperately concentrating on moving his hands, managing to get them into his pockets. He didn't need to be an ace marksman to make these work.

Everything was happening in slow motion. As Crowder reached into his pockets and began to clasp the implant killers, Benjamin wrapped his arms around Carlinni. Maybe he was telling her to stop, but Crowder's ears were filled with a cacophony of bells and buzzers, whoops and whistles. Memories surfaced and sank as if she was rifling through them, keeping some, discarding others.

He brought the implant killers out and pointed them, his thumb on the triggers. Carlinni's mind contact snapped off. She flopped like a rag doll in Benjamin's arms. But Benjamin didn't fall. The implant killer had no impact whatsoever. He thumbed it again. Still no effect, but Carlinni was down and Benjamin was on his knees, lowering her to the floor, cradling her head, shouting something.

Tatum and Bronsen both sprang forward. Crowder felt one dart puncture his thigh and a second one pierce his shoulder through his shirt. He'd built up immunity, but he wasn't invulnerable. Two certainly wouldn't kill him. He wasn't so sure about three.

Benjamin picked up Carlinni's fallen dart rifle with one hand and fired it directly into the middle of Crowder's chest.

He felt the jab. His last thought was that he didn't even have time to be afraid.

✦　✦　✦

"Cara, hold on. Hold on!" Ben cradled her head. "Fucking kill switch! Hold on. You've survived without an implant before. We'll get you back to Crossways—get you a new implant."

She moaned in his arms and tried to claw at her face.

"Archie, get the devices."

"Crowder?"

"Leave him, he'll be dead in minutes. Got to get Cara back to Crossways, to Civility Jamieson."

Ronan, everyone on board Solar Wind, *now.* He flashed what had happened.

He would normally have been able to carry Cara, no problem, but he was so out of condition that Bronsen scooped her up instead and they ran back to *Solar Wind*, through the gap that Toni Horta had blown in the wall.

Ronan was close behind with Nan and Ricky.

All accounted for? he broadcast.

Except for Fowler and your nephew, Tengue said.

Fuck! Fuck! Fuck! In his panic to get Cara back to Crossways, he'd forgotten the hospital pickup. He couldn't leave Kai, and Tengue wouldn't want to leave Fowler.

"Gen, get us back to Arkhad City."

"Right away, Boss."

"Reska!" Nan's voice cut across the chaos.

"Nan, find a cabin and strap in; it's going to be a bumpy ride. Ricky, stay with Nan."

"Cara?" Nan asked.

"Not good."

Ben turned to find Bronsen and Ronan had already taken her to sick bay. He wanted to go straight after her, but everyone was shouting at once. He took a deep breath.

"Essential crew only on the flight deck. Everyone else, find a cabin. Archie, show Nan and Ricky where my cabin is. If Rion comes to from the goodnight drops, better that he sees them first. Nan, Rion's going to be as mad as blazes with me. Tell him he can have a piece of me later, but to stay clear of the flight deck and sick bay."

"Has he got a right to be mad at you?"

"He certainly has. Tell him Bunty's boys are farm-sitting and the dogs are in a crate in the hold for the duration of the flight. They're fine. That might help."

Archie led Nan and Ricky up a level, chatting normally to Ricky, trying to defuse the tension.

Ben turned. "Tengue, Gwala, are you in touch with Fowler?"

"Hilde is. She's the better Telepath."

"Hilde, is Kai with Fowler?"

"Yes."

"Tell her to tell Kai to get a float chair and take her down to the west side of the hospital building. They're to wait where they can see the autopark. That's where we're putting down."

"What about the hoverpods in there?"

"What about them?"

Hilde grinned.

"As soon as the ramp goes down, you three are responsible for getting Kai and Fowler on board safely. Any questions?"

They all shook their heads.

"Max, you're making the place look untidy. Get strapped in."

"Only essential crew to the flight deck?"

"Hell, what a time to start listening to what I say. Get yourself up there with Gen."

Max flashed him a grin and turned just as the drives began to power up with an urgent hum.

Ben turned the other way and headed for sick bay.

"Ronan, how's she doing?" He'd expected Cara to be flat out, but instead she was sitting up in a chair, wrapped in a blanket.

"I'm still here," she said, and reached out a hand.

He took it.

"Has Ronan given you anything for the pain?"

She shook her head and winced. "He can't."

"Why not?"

"Because she has to be fully conscious when you hit the Folds so that she can get the dead implant out of her head." Jussaro's voice came from behind.

Ben turned. If a man with purple skin could look pale, Jussaro was pale. Bloodless might be a more accurate description. "I heard the fuss, asked a nice old lady in antigrav leggings what had happened." Jussaro stepped forward unsteadily. "The moment an implant is killed it begins to shrivel. It doesn't take long for the pathways to shrivel with it. Sometimes that makes it impossible to replace. I was lucky the first time. But if the implant can be removed, it leaves the pathways open. Reimplantation should be simple."

"So you want me to what? Think this ruined thing out of my head?" Cara said.

"Well, you might need some help," Jussaro said. "From a void dragon."

Ben squeezed her hand. "You had your implant switched off when I met you, trying to hide from Alphacorp. Once, when I asked you how you'd coped, you said it was because you wanted to live more than you wanted to be a Telepath. How about now?" He kissed her fingers. "I want you to live. I need you to live."

"Go drive the bus. Get me home."

He squeezed her fingers one more time and left.

✦ ✦ ✦

The comm gave a small whoop and then crackled into life. "Arkhad City ATC to unknown craft, identify. You are in controlled airspace. Repeat, you are in controlled airspace in the lanes reserved for emergency services."

Ben slid into the pilot's seat and left Gen to monitor comms. "Stall them," he said.

"Let me." Max leaned low over her shoulder, kissed her ear, and reached for the vox. "Hey, hi, Mr. ACT . . . er . . . Mrs. ATC lady. You in charge up there?"

"Identify yourself."

"Hi . . . err . . . yes . . . This is the good ship . . . err . . . Lollipop."

"Lollipop?" Ben said quietly.

Max turned and grinned, his eyes alight. "You don't watch old movies? Got to do something when the girlfriend dumps you and even the cat goes out on the town."

Ben shook his head.

"When this is all over I need to educate you, my friend. Beer and old movies." Max turned back to the comm.

"Lollipop, state your ident code and your destination."

"Ident code? Heading for the hospital. This is an emergency. Got a pregnant lady on board. Keep everything out of our way."

"Ident code, please, Lollipop."

"Ident code . . . ident code . . . I had one of those somewhere. Is it in this pocket? No. In this one? Uh-huh—"

"Lollipop, you are in controlled airspace. Ascend to one thousand meters."

"Now how am I supposed to get my lady to the hospital from one thousand meters?"

"Lollipop, who's in charge there? Do you have an emergency medical situation?"

"Sure do."

Ben blocked Max's performance out of his mind as they approached the hospital. *Tengue?*

In position.

Like an overeager horse, Ben reined in *Solar Wind* above the hospital. The auto park below them was a sea of small hoverpods jostling for space on automatics. It was the largest space without people, and as a bonus was close to the west side of the building. He didn't even let down the stabilizers, just crunched down onto the roofs of close to a hundred shiny pods, opened the hatch and dropped the ramp.

On the forward screen he saw Tengue, Gwala, and Hilde run forward. Tengue scooped Fowler from the float chair. Hilde grabbed Kai's hand and urged him to run while Gwala covered them all with a smart-dart rifle. Though there were people huddling in the lee of the building, no one tried to stop them.

"Hey, Boss, you might want to see this . . ." Gen flicked a local news broadcast onto the screen.

There was *Solar Wind* nestling on top of what had become a scrapyard, filmed from above. One of the hospital's security cams, he thought.

"In breaking news, an unidentified craft has landed outside the Centenary Wing of Arkhad City Hospital, crushing private vehicles. Emergency services are rushing to the scene. Bystanders are urged not to get involved. It's not known yet whether there are any casualties."

"They're on board. Ramp retracted. Hatch secured," Kitty said from Systems.

"You want me to fly the bus, Boss?" Gen asked.

The quickest way to get Cara back to Civility Jamieson was to flash into foldspace from low orbit and emerge less than fifty klicks from Crossways itself. Gen would balk at that. He should do it himself. He could do it. Couldn't he?

One mistake and none of them would make it. Better to arrive safe and slow than not at all.

"Do it, Gen." He took his trembling hands off the control pad.

"Warn them we're coming. Tell them to clear a path. Have Jamieson standing by to do two implants."

Gen boosted *Solar Wind*'s antigravs just as ground vehicles were screaming into the hospital precinct. They shot steeply upward on extended wings. One thousand meters, two thousand meters, three thousand.

The comm sounded again. "*Solar Wind*, this is the Monitor ship MS *Lomax*. You are impounded by law. Please stand down and prepare to be boarded."

Four thousand meters. They were still well below the altitude of commercial liners. *Lomax* must be above them.

"Get her position, Kitty," Ben said.

"Right there." Kitty put *Lomax* on screen.

She was, indeed, between them and escape.

Ben left Gen to take the pilot's seat and activated his vox. "Alexandrov, is that you again?"

"Benjamin, stand down."

"Like hell I will." He muted his vox and turned to Gen. "Now Gen, into foldspace."

"We're still in Chenon's atmosphere."

"Do it."

Alexandrov didn't waste time on a warning. *Lomax* released a missile. Gen gave a strangled squeak and plunged *Solar Wind* into blackness.

✦ ✦ ✦

The void dragon comes at him, just the big one this time. Ben's fairly sure it's the same one. It's come looking for him. Why him? Why can't it leave him alone?

It wants to talk. How can it? They don't even share a language.

No. Not me. Cara. Find Cara, please. He wraps his arms around his head. It seems to be telling him that he can't avoid a conversation sooner or later. He's on the riverbank again, his dad's in the water. The chasm of darkness swirling at his feet. Jump, his dad says.

Talk, the void dragon says.

"No," he replies and steps back.

His dad floats effortlessly away into midstream. The void dragon dips its head in acknowledgment and vanishes, leaving the flight deck empty of hallucinations. But there's an echo of *soon*.

Chapter Twenty-Five

RENEWAL

THE SICK BAY SHUDDERS AND THOUGH THE lights don't dim, darkness swirls in, tangible. They are in the Folds. Cara hardly feels the jump; she's far too preoccupied with what's in her head, or rather what's not in her head.

It's just like it was before, she tells herself. *I survived nearly a year with my implant turned off. I can do it again.*

But she'd needed an array of tranqs to help her through it and she'd always known that with one flick of her tongue against a back tooth she could power it up again.

She pulls the blanket around herself, shivering, though it isn't cold.

"Breathe," Ronan says. "You've got to get rid of that thing. Jamieson can replace it when we get back to Crossways."

"You don't know that for sure, Ronan. Stop bullshitting me."

"Look at me, Carlinni." Jussaro cups her cheek and turns her face toward him. "You have one chance. Imagine . . . no, not just imagine . . . You have to know that your implant is not you. It's a thing apart. You have to believe it. Really believe it."

"That's all it takes?"

"Uh, not really, but it's a start."

"You got rid of yours."

He nodded. "With some help."

"You look like shit, Jussaro."

"Welcome to the club."

Something swirls into sick bay, a formless shadow. It bumps Jussaro, nose to forehead.

"Here," she hears him tell it. "Another one for you."

He pulls her upright. She shrinks back.

"It's all right Carlinni. It wants your implant. I'm not sure why."

"Talk." There's an audible rumble that she can feel all the way down to her toes. Is the thing speaking?

"Learn."

"Holy shit!" Jussaro chokes on his own words.

Ronan is looking around in amazement. He hears something, but obviously can't see the source.

"Mind," the thing growls.

Is this Ben's void dragon?

"It's learning from the implants." Jussaro's voice is filled with wonder. "Give it yours. Imagine you want it gone."

She can't. She knows she can't. Getting rid of her implant is the last thing she wants to do. She wants to reactivate it, restore it, retain it. She tongues her tooth, but nothing happens.

"It's mine. It's me."

"Not anymore," Ronan says. "It's dead. Diseased and dead. Let it go before it kills you."

She wraps her arms around herself and tries to act small.

Ronan kneels at her feet and pulls her hands into his. "Trust me, Cara."

Ronan helped her when she was mind-blocked on Olyanda, when she knew there was something in her head that she'd been prevented from sharing by McLellan. He helped her to break the conditioning. She trusts him more than anyone except Ben. She sees his expression. He's scared for her.

"Trust me. Let it go."

Diseased. If she thinks of it as diseased, she might want to get rid of it.

"Yes, you can do it," Ronan says, his voice urgent. He transfers both her hands into one of his and with his thumb rubs her forehead where the slight bump of her implant scar still hides beneath her skin.

"It's not you anymore," he says gently, squeezing her fingers.

She nods and squeezes back.

"All right. I'm ready."

"Stay very still, Carlinni," Jussaro says.

Something ripples through her head with butterfly softness.

She relaxes. Then sharp pain stabs through her skull.

Ronan catches her as she falls forward. "It's over," he whispers. "It's out. Gone. Sucked away into nothingness."

"It's his now," Jussaro says. "The void dragon has it."

She bursts into tears.

✦ ✦ ✦

"Shit, Benjamin, you really know how to make an entrance. Don't make a habit of this." Mother Ramona was waiting for them on the dockside by the time the air pressure had returned to normal.

Cara and Jussaro were both in float chairs, one from the *Solar Wind*'s med bay and the other requisitioned from Fowler, who would follow at a more sedate pace.

"I love you, too," Ben said, not stopping as he pushed Cara's chair toward the entrance. "Got the clearance we asked for?"

"The tub lanes are all clear," Mother Ramona said. "You'll have a straight run. Now can we get this station running normally again?"

"Thanks. I'm sorry." He left her behind.

"No, you're not."

"You're right. Not sorry, but I am grateful." He turned his head to shout back. "Please introduce yourself to my family. My grandmother's looking forward to meeting you. My brother may not be quite so civilized. Go easy on him."

"Not so civilized. That's one way of putting it." Ronan, pushing Jussaro's float chair, kept pace with Ben to the entrance and they loaded both patients, still in their chairs, into the waiting tub. Syke and three guards shot ahead of them and a second tub of guards followed behind.

"Do we still need a guard?" Ronan asked. "Now that Crowder's dead."

Crowder dead. Ben hadn't let himself think about the third dart he'd pumped into Crowder. The tub careened around a corner and he reached over to steady Cara. No time for Crowder right now. "Are you still with me?"

"Still with . . ." she said. "Not getting any easier."

"I guess it's not." He clasped her hand, small and frail, like a bag of bird bones, with no answering squeeze.

"Professor Jamieson's in the implant suite." Nine met them at the front door.

"He knows he's got two patients, right?" Ben asked.

"He knows. He says he'll take Jussaro first because he's already done the preliminary tests. While he's doing that I'll run Cara through the tests, so she's ready."

Ben didn't ask what happened if the tests proved Cara wasn't suitable for reimplanting. She sat very quietly in her chair, eyes closed, but he was sure she was listening.

"Don't worry." Nine put her hand on Cara's shoulder. "Professor Jamieson is the best."

Cara nodded, but didn't reply.

"Professor Jamieson also said to ask whether you got either of the implants out whole."

"Both of them," Ben said. "But we didn't get to keep them. Would you believe me if I told you a void dragon sniffed them up like they were some drug?"

"I might, but Jamieson . . . not so much."

"Make something up then, but don't tell him until after he's done the implantations. We might have a recording of the whole thing, but don't tell him that until afterward either."

Nine flashed a grin at him. "I see you're beginning to understand what makes the professor tick."

"I've met men like him before. Single-minded to a fault, but frankly, I don't care what makes him tick as long as he can do the job."

◆ ◆ ◆

"Do you understand me? I'm going to clamp your head so that you can't move."

Cara heard Jamieson's brisk voice as if from a long way away, but she could see shadows cross her closed eyelids as figures moved between her and the light.

"I said do you understand?" His voice was up close now. She could smell him. Dry, clean, antiseptic.

"Yes."

"You sat in on Benjamin's procedure, so you know how this works. I don't need to immobilize you completely. I've tweaked the head restraint since then. This isn't an experiment."

"How's Jussaro?" she managed.

"Fine, recovering quietly. He screamed like a girl, but it all went according to plan."

"Am I supposed to say girls don't scream and then try to prove it?"

"Scream all you want, just don't move. And for the record no one goes through this, awake, without screaming."

Ben squeezed her hand and that was the first time she realized he was still there. She squeezed back. "Once for no, twice for yes?" she asked.

"You've got it. I'll be here."

"I know you will."

"Ronan's here, too."

"Hey, let's have a party."

"Ready for the head restraint?" Jamieson asked.

"Yes. No. Ben . . ."

"Here."

"Kiss me."

"For goodness sake we haven't time . . ." Jamieson protested.

"Out of the way, Professor. There's time for this," Ben said.

She felt Ben's lips on hers, warm, tender, full of promise. There was no need to say the words, but she did anyway. "I love you."

He kissed her again and breathed the words back to her.

"All right, Professor," she said. "I'm ready now."

The head restraint was a tight fit. She had a moment of claustrophobic panic, but Ben grasped her hand. The restraint shaped itself to her skull, covering crown, eyes, cheeks, and lower jaw, while leaving a cool open space in the center of her forehead and a triangular opening over her nostrils and mouth. She heard the robotic arm begin to move above her head and felt a slight pressure as it made contact. Then there was a blinding pain as the needle bored through her skull.

Surprisingly that part was over quickly and she felt the needle withdraw. The implant must be in place already.

"All right so far?" Ben asked.

She squeezed twice for yes, and then it began.

A million baby snakes frolicked through her brain, wriggling, tickling, fondling, jostling, and just plain thrusting through. Pain and pleasure followed in waves like good sex for all the wrong reasons or bad sex for all the right ones. She was losing her virginity all over again at the same time that her head was being sawed in two. She clutched Ben's hand and held on tight as her body spasmed from top to toe.

It could have been a minute, it could have been a lifetime.

Cara. Cara! Are you back with us? Are you back?

Yes. Oh, gods, yes. Yes!

She began to laugh.

◆   ◆   ◆

"I'm fine, Nine. Don't fuss," Cara said.

"Professor Jamieson wanted a full set of bloodwork six hours after implantation."

"I've had so many sharps stuck in me I feel like a pincushion."

"Sorry."

"I'm not sick. In fact I feel better than I've felt for years."

"Euphoria. When it drains you'll crash. Jussaro's already sleeping like a baby."

"Well, I don't intend to stay in here another hour, let alone another night. Time I was gone."

And you called me a bad patient!

Cara whirled around to find Ben in the doorway. "See, Nine, my transport awaits. My Knight in Shining Armor has come to whisk me off to his castle and make mad, passionate love to me."

"Don't bother to wrap her, I'll take her just as she is!" Ben said. "That's the best offer I've had since . . ."

"Since Olyanda." Cara ducked around Nine and grabbed Ben's outstretched hand.

"On the other hand, wrap her." Ben grabbed Cara's hand and twirled her around, laughing. "Singlet and shorts are very fetching, but maybe a wee bit underdressed for Crossways."

"You're no fun, Benjamin."

"I am. Really, truly, a lot of fun."

She pulled on her buddysuit trousers and then flung herself straight at Ben, plastering herself to his front so hard that their suit bottoms rubbed together like rhinoceros hide and her breasts were squashed against his chest armor. She pulled his head down to meet hers and liplocked so fiercely that she felt his utter surprise and then delight as he gave back in good measure.

"Unhhh," Ben surfaced. "I've got this, Nine, if you've got all the bloodwork you need."

There was a gap where Nine had been.

"Are we alone?" Cara asked.

"Oh, yes, just us and a ton of nurses and doctors, not to mention patients just the other side of that glass. Here, put this on."

She shrugged into the buddysuit top but didn't stop to anchor it to the trousers or to fasten it, but wore it like a loose jacket. "Back to the *Solar Wind*, right?"

"With you in this mood? No way. There's a hotel around the corner."

The hotel was literally around the corner from Dockside Medical. Cara let Ben sign in with a wave of his handpad and clung to his side like a limpet. It was a lot like being drunk, something Cara experienced only rarely because alcohol messed up her Telepathy in the worst way. They rode up the antigrav tube together and Ben grabbed the rail and exited at the correct floor. By that time she didn't know whether she was on her head or her heels. Normal weight returned as they hit the hallway ceramic and the second door down on the right opened at the wave of Ben's handpad.

All she focused on was the bed, huge and soft with fluffy pillows and an airquilt that rippled with their entrance.

"Oh, yes, perfect." She flung herself on top of the quilt and bounced.

"Come on, let's get your clothes off." Ben held her jacket while she shrugged out of it.

"Yours, too." She yanked at the touch-and-close fastening around his suit neck. "Ooh, Ben Benjamin, you don't know how much I've missed you." She ran her hands across his chest, over his singlet, and around the side of his well-muscled ribs. "How long has it been?"

"Too long." His voice was husky.

She tugged at the fastenings on her own trousers and his. It was complete and utter magic how two people could shed clothes so quickly and completely when the need was so urgent.

"Oh, yeah. It's long, but it's not too long." She slid her hand between them and heard him gasp. "I can take that."

He groaned as she pulled him onto the bed and he cradled her with his right arm while his left stroked her breasts and down her ribs to her belly. She writhed against him.

"Thing about euphoria . . ." he said.

"Hmmm?"

"Is that it's great while it lasts . . ."

"Oh, yeah."

"But when you crash . . ."

"Not gonna . . ."

"You crash . . ."

❖   ❖   ❖

". . . completely."

Ben felt all the tension melt out of Cara as she flopped against him, utterly relaxed, half-asleep already. He reached for the airquilt and pulled it over both of them, willing his hard-on to subside. He'd known she wouldn't go the distance, but his body had betrayed him anyway.

"Hmmm." She made a comfortable sound and curled against him.

He stroked her flank gently as if she were some favorite pet.

"I'll give you just four hours to stop doing that," she murmured.

He kissed the top of her head, her cropped hair little more than fluff. "Go to sleep. You're safe."

"My white knight."

"You've saved me more times . . ."

"Who's counting?"

"No one. I love you."

"I love you, too." Her voice trailed off as sleep overcame her.

He'd not planned to sleep as well, but he did.

"What time is it?" Cara's voice was thick and low.

"I don't know. Lights."

The lights came up in a soft glow.

"Enough!" Cara screwed up her eyes to look at her handpad. "It's four in the morning, station time. What's that Chenon-time?"

He could probably work it out, though Arkhad time was two hours adrift from Norro time.

"Does it matter?"

"No." She wriggled around to face him and stroked his naked chest with one hand. "I believe I might be embarrassed if I could remember much. Did we . . . ?"

"No."

"Ah, pity."

"Pity?"

"Yes, well, it would have eased us past that awkward moment when we both remembered that this is our first time since I slept with Ari van Blaiden. Willingly if I remember rightly, though I'm not sure I do. It was all a little confusing."

"Shut up."

"What?"

"About Ari van Blaiden."

"Yes, Boss."

He drew her to him and cupped her cheek and neck, feeling her pulse jump under his touch, kissed her on the mouth, chin, throat, shoulder, breast.

She hissed as he found the hardness of her nipple with his tongue and caressed the length of his leg with the sole of one foot. She pulled him between her thighs and worked a minor miracle with her fingers.

Rational thought left him.

◆ ◆ ◆

Cara had never felt more comfortable than here in this strange room in Ben Benjamin's arms.

"Are we good?" he'd whispered after their second bout of lovemaking.

"Better than good, we're fucking fantastic." She'd laughed out loud. "Though I may not be able to walk straight in the morning."

They'd dozed together until nearly eight and then she'd slipped out of bed for a pee and a shower. He joined her as she stepped into the steaming jets of water and they soaped each other all over. He kissed her as he soaped her breasts and down her belly and slipped his hand between her legs. One thing led to another and they made love again, pressed against the massage wall of the shower unit, the vibrations at her back chiming with the waves washing through her.

✦ ✦ ✦

Ben could have stayed in the hotel room for the rest of the day, possibly for the rest of his life, but sex made him hungry.

"Eat here or—"

"Blue Mountain," Cara said as they dressed. "I need good coffee."

After breakfast, during which they put away a large stack of pancakes between them, Ben took Cara's hand and they walked into Blue Seven, past the new facade and into the central atrium.

"Good morning." Jussaro passed them heading in the opposite direction. "I gather everything went well and now I presume you've slept off your euphoria, had coffee, and are ready to greet the day."

"Something like that." Cara tried not to smile and failed.

"Good, then the three of us should get together sometime soon with Civility Jamieson."

"Not more bloodwork," Cara said.

"Not at all. We need to talk about the future. Do you realize what a remarkable breakthrough this is for psionics?" He tapped his head. "Some people I used to work with will be very interested, but I won't talk to them until we've agreed a strategy."

"Strategy?" Ben said as Jussaro exited Blue Seven whistling happily. "That's something I don't really have. I seem to lurch from one near-disaster to another, getting no closer to finding these missing settlers while life catches up with me. We've got enough criminal warrants to send us all to the toughest prison planet for three lifetimes; mounting debts until Olyanda starts to produce; a potential fortune in platinum, but only if we can hold on to it; the Free Company; finding Lorient's settlers; and now I have the problem of what to do with my displaced family."

He didn't say, *and I've lost my nerve and can't fly the Folds anymore.* Cara had been in no state to notice that it was Gen who'd brought them home safely.

"Your displaced family probably has to decide for itself."

He shrugged. "Yes, but Rion won't want what Ricky wants, Kai will have his own ideas, Nan will try to find a compromise, and when that doesn't happen she'll lay down the law. Have you ever heard one of Nan's this-is-how-it's-going-to-be speeches?"

Cara shook her head.

"Trust me, you don't want to." He'd been much younger the last time he'd heard one of those.

"So we need to make plans . . ."

"We do. We need to be ahead of the game, not half a step behind. The Trust—"

"Not just the Trust, Alphacorp as well," Cara said. "Crowder claimed he didn't send the Alphabet gang. I didn't entirely believe him, but while I was inside his head I found that Akiko Yamada and Ari were lovers."

"We need to check with Mother Ramona to see what they've extracted from Ari's files." Ben frowned. "Crowder's gone, but the Trust won't let up, and now Alphacorp is out to get us as well. Cut off one head and another two grow in its place. I'm not stupid enough to think we can take down two of the biggest megacorporations that have ever existed, but we can seriously inconvenience them and maybe teach them to leave us alone. Let's go see Mother Ramona now. There's something I have to show you."

◆ ◆ ◆

"Dad, you're just not being fair!" Ricky jumped to his feet and balled his fists, aware that his voice had squeaked. At home he would have run to his room and slammed the door, or gone out into the yard and saddled up for a long ride, but here in the *Solar Wind*'s mess, there was nowhere to run to except to Uncle Ben's quarters, and that wasn't fair either.

"Sit down, Ricky. Sit down, Rion. Kai, pour the tea. Let's start over." Nan had abandoned the antigrav leggings and was pacing the room, round and round the long refectory table, somewhat slowly for her, and with frequent rest stops. She lowered herself onto a chair at one end and leaned on her elbows, breathing heavily.

"Are you all right, Nan?" Kai asked.

"I will be," she said. "Thanks to Ben and his friends. We

all will be." She turned to Rion. "Admit it. Your brother just saved your intransigent ass. Sure, he didn't do it politely. Was there any way he could have talked you into leaving the farm voluntarily?"

Dad sat down. "Probably not."

Nan pushed a mug of tea toward him and took one herself. "You slept through foldspace. He did you a favor."

"I dreamed . . . Things."

"What did you see, Dad?" Ricky asked. "I saw otters swimming through the air like it was water. One of them kept whirling around my head. It was awesome."

"You weren't scared?" Nan asked.

"Uh, no. They were playing." Ricky sat at the head of the table. "Can we go and look around Crossways? We're in space, but I haven't seen anything yet, just the inside of the *Solar Wind*. I didn't even get to see what she really looked like on the outside."

"Shut up and settle down, Squirt," Kai said without animosity. "Time you started thinking about other people for a change. This isn't a tourist trip, it's serious business. Life-changing serious business, for all of us."

"Oh . . ." Yeah, okay, Ricky got it. It wasn't just about him and Nan. Dad had been dragged off the farm that he'd given his life to, and Kai . . . He looked at his brother's usually smiling face and saw strain lines around his mouth. Kai had spent three years at university and been dragged away just days before his final exams. And the farm—that was as much Kai's as Dad's.

He sat down and pressed his lips together.

"Time enough to see everything later, Ricky," Nan said. "Everyone's busy right now. Let's try not to give them any more headaches."

"I wonder how Cara is," Kai said.

"She's fine." Uncle Ben spoke from the doorway. "Or will be as soon as she gets used to her new implant. How are you all?"

Dad stood up, took a couple of paces forward and glared at Uncle Ben. Ricky had never appreciated how alike they were, Dad older, of course, and a bit heavier, but they had the same profile as they stood almost nose-to-nose.

"If you're going to take a swing at me, get it over with," Uncle Ben said.

Ricky held his breath.

There was a long pause, during which neither of them said anything, but then Dad hugged Uncle Ben in that back-slappy way of men who find hugging unnatural. Suddenly everyone was talking at once and Kai was pouring an extra mug of tea for Uncle Ben and it looked like everything was going to be all right.

Chapter Twenty-Six

STRIKE AND COUNTERSTRIKE

"WHY DIDN'T YOU SHOW ME THIS BEFORE?" Cara sat stiff-backed on the edge of her chair while Ben leaned back against Garrick's office wall. She hadn't known this existed. This was their proof that Crowder had tried to wipe out the Olyanda settlement. It seemed like a lifetime ago, but it was barely two months. Ben had left her on Olyanda while he flew back to Chenon to confront Crowder. She knew what had happened, but seeing it was different.

"I left a copy with Mother Ramona when I returned to Olyanda," Ben said. "She knew how to use it if ... things didn't work out well. I'm not proud of it. I killed two men."

"Did you watch it?" Cara turned to Mother Ramona, sitting on the couch next to Garrick, her long legs crossed elegantly.

"I confess that I did," she replied. "I wanted Benjamin to use it against Crowder straightaway, but he thought it might do more harm than good while there was potential danger to psi-tech families. With hindsight, he was probably right."

"Okay, enough. Let's watch it and get it over with," Ben said.

The screen flickered into life and Ben's face appeared. His hair was newly shaved to stubble. "This is Reska Benja-

min. I swear that this is a true record. I was lately an employee of the Trust assigned a mission to transport a group
of Ecolibrian settlers to the planet Olyanda. On arrival, a
detailed survey of the planet revealed considerable platinum reserves which the settlers did not wish to exploit—
their right under contract. Unknown to the settlers or my
technical team, Gabrius Crowder, Director of Operations
for the Colony Division of the Trust, erroneously declared
the colony infected by a plague and issued a quarantine
order, falsely declaring settlers and crew alike dead, or as
good as.

"Here follows a true recording of my confrontation with
Crowder."

Then it flipped into a recording of a room, an office,
brightly lit with a Trust motif in the decoration. The angle
was odd, foreshortened as if taken from high on a wall, but
Cara recognized Ben in the shadow of the doorway.
Crowder sat at his desk talking to someone on audio.

Ben stepped into the office and the door closed behind
him.

"How did you get here?" Crowder asked. The sound was
tinny, but the words were clear enough.

"Not important. Do you want to ask me why I got here?"
Ben waited for an answer but didn't get one. Cara hadn't
seen Ben get angry very often, but when he did his voice
went quiet. He was angry now.

"I want to know what you've got planned for Olyanda,"
Ben said. "I know half of it already. Now you can tell me the
other half. Let's start with why you didn't trash the platinum
data."

Cara followed the argument while Crowder tried to
make excuses.

She gasped as two men came into the room and shot at
Ben. If this had been a training video Cara would have
given Ben maybe only seven out of ten for style, but ten for
effectiveness. Part of her watched it dispassionately while
the other half was anxious. Ben was here with her, now.
He'd survived it, she told herself. Then why was her heart
pounding?

It was almost too fast to follow. Ben snapped a throwing
disk from his belt buckle and with a flick of his wrist sent
one man reeling back, blood everywhere, Spurting. Spray-

ing. She was watching a man die. Her scalp crawled and it was only when she gulped air that she realized she'd forgotten to breathe.

The other man landed a good kick in Ben's ribs. Ben went down almost on top of the dead man, grabbed the gun, twisted, and fired. The second man fell.

"Two down, one to go," Crowder said. "Would it be me next, Ben?"

Cara's eyes had been on Ben and she hadn't noticed Crowder pull a gun of his own. It looked like a toy at the side of the hefty guns the two men had carried, but she knew it wasn't. Ben watched it like it was a snake as he climbed slowly to his feet, hands open, palms toward Crowder.

"Not until I'd wrung every bit of information out of you that I could." Ben's voice was low and even. "Go on, then, Crowder. From this range you shouldn't have any problems, though the blood might stain your shirt. What's one more life on top of all the rest?"

Crowder's hand never wavered. His eyes remained steady, but he didn't fire.

"It's not quite the same as killing people on another world, is it? Give an order. Make a payment. That's easy, but this . . . this is messy." Ben flicked an eye to the bodies on the floor. "It's messy and very personal. Is it worth it?"

Still Crowder didn't fire. Eventually he said, "I never intended any harm to you or your team, either on Hera-3 or Olyanda, but . . ."

"But platinum trumps all other considerations." Ben exhaled sharply and shook his head. "I trusted you, Crowder. I trusted you with my life . . . and theirs. What next? Airborne attack? Neural blast bombs to turn us all to zombies, then send in a mop-up division?"

Crowder didn't blink. "You're too late already. Probably . . ."

Ben twisted sideways and leaped over the desk, grabbing the gun and pinning Crowder to the floor.

"Biological strike? What have you released, bacteria, a virus, neurotoxins?" Ben put the gun against Crowder's neck.

Crowder didn't need any persuading to talk. In fact, he was positively gabbling, his eyes wide. "A superbug. A weapon from more than one viral source."

Ben pulled Crowder up from the floor, then shoved him down hard on the float chair, which wobbled dangerously until he jammed it against the wall.

"There's nothing you can do." Crowder began to laugh, but it was more like nerves than humor. "A killer. Human specific. Airborne. Virulent as all hell. It's fierce, but it's fragile. Lifespan of six months, but that's enough to do its job. Within a year the planet will be safe again."

Ben dragged Crowder to his feet. "What about the second ark? What have you done with it?"

"It's safe. Safe. I'm not a monster." Crowder started to wheedle. "You're not stupid, Ben. Forget all this. It's already too late to do anything for the poor sods on Olyanda, but there's still time to save yourself. I'm sorry it worked out like this. You were my best man, you know. Your only flaw is your integrity. You're too honest."

"There was a time when I would have died for you, but not anymore. You might still be useful, so . . ." Ben put the gun close to the side of Crowder's head and pulled the trigger. Crowder shrieked and fell back clutching his ear, blood pouring between his fingers. Ben leaned over him and said something too quiet for the recording to catch, then ran out of the office. Crowder rolled onto his knees, tried to get up, slumped to the floor and lay still.

The recorder kept going for another three minutes. The stillness and silence horrific after the violence. Cara felt sick. She looked up at Ben. His face was a stony mask.

"Clearly self-defense," Mother Ramona said. "That slams right through those two counts of murder on the Monitor warrant. Send a copy to them, too."

"I maimed Crowder for nothing more than revenge," Ben said. "That was petty."

"I'd have killed him." Cara didn't mention that if it hadn't been for Crowder's implant killer, she would have turned his mind inside out right there on Norro. It seemed a little redundant once Ben had told her about firing the third dart.

"I think it's time to go public with it," Ben said. "With Crowder dead, we should be able to get the warrants against all of the psi-techs rescinded."

"Except for you," Cara said.

"Except for me," he agreed.

Garrick scratched his embryonic beard. Its gray stripes made him look older, but it suited him. "Let's be canny about this," he said. "We've decoded a lot of the information from van Blaiden's handpad. Akiko Yamada was his lover. That's filled in one of the blanks. He's used a code name for her and for Crowder. We can begin to tie it all up together. The Trust and Alphacorp are both in this up to their necks and when we release the information I want them both to take a hit at the same time. Anything that weakens them helps Crossways and protects the platinum on Olyanda."

"My guys are information specialists," Mother Ramona said. "Let's send copies of this vid and some of van Blaiden's files to the GBC on Earth and CBC on Chenon. I can release it across the space logs on forty different channels simultaneously. You should set up a Mouth account for the Free Company."

"It's nothing but idle chatter," Ben said.

"Idle chatter that influences millions across the known galaxy. The megacorps can't control it, even though it's their own Telepaths who sustain it, or at least the transmission from world to world. Cara, is that something you can do?"

"I have been known to participate." She nodded. "I can do that."

"Maybe someone out there knows about the missing thirty thousand," Ben said. "Post a reward."

❖ ❖ ❖

Cara set up a Mouth account, "*&freec-crossways,*" and then sat back and monitored reactions. The initial comment went out via a network of Telepaths and was then transmitted in written or audio form, sometimes both, depending on the sophistication of the various planetary networks. It took longer for the responses to come back because they could only be transmitted by data packet via the jump gates. Half a second to get there, anything from half a day to get back.

She picked up the packet from Chenon and scrolled through. Her own message was at the top and then the replies came thick and fast, some sensible, some just hot air, but the trend was toward outrage. Good.

❖ ❖ ❖

MOUTH
Tells it straight
+++
&freec-crossways: Have you seen this vid? Top Trust official tries to wipe out Olyanda colony for platinum reserves. Thirty thousand settlers still missing. &freec-crossways wants to know where they are. Alphacorp involved. Reward for info.
+++
&sevenbaby: Is this for real?
+++
&cors: It happens. Look up Hera-3.
+++
&brontoman: Mighty suspicious. Benjamin involved in Hera-3 and Olyanda.
+++
&cors: wake up &brontoman That's Benjamin nearly getting his ass kicked by 2 thugs on the vid. Fat guy is Head of Colony Ops for Trust. Much higher up the foodchain.
+++
&brunt: Looks like he ate the food chain.
+++
&brontoman: to &brunt So the guy's got a little weight on him. So what?
+++
&sevenbaby: What's the Trust say?
+++
&trust: Investigations being made into Olyanda accusations. All fabrication.
+++
&alphacorp: No links with Trust. Ari van Blaiden killed in an accident. All else is false
+++
&cors: that's what they say.
+++
&sevenbaby: Is that vid a forgery?
+++
&pranadeep: Vid encoding clean. Not a forgery
+++
&sevenbaby: Looked up Hera-3. Serious shit. Thousands of civilians missing or dead. 1500 survivors brought out by Benjamin.

+++

&brontoman: He's a fucking hero.

+++

&yerad: I lost a sister on Hera-3. Trust should answer.

+++

&brontoman: Yeah, Trust should answer.

+++

&pranadeep: Selling my shares.

+++

&sevenbaby: If I had shares I'd be selling them too.

+++

*&pranadeep: Arquavisa looks like a better bet for invest-
ment, or maybe Eastin-Heigle.*

+++

*&cors: Sterritt Corporation has a better rep for ethical op-
erations.*

+++

&sevenbaby: Yeah, that's what they say. Do U believe it?

+++

Cara scrolled down the comments on Mouth from her
desk in Wenna's office, then checked the ones from Earth,
Kemp's World, the Hollands System, and Aqua Neriffe. It
was all more of the same, but one thing was sure. The vid
had gone viral.

She wandered through into Max's office next door. "You
know about the markets. Is there any way to tell if this
adverse publicity is hitting the Trust and Alphacorp finan-
cially?"

"I'll check." He flicked through several options on his
holo-screen. "Well, would you look at that." He looked up.

"Good news?"

"Alphacorp's down a little. The Trust is down significantly."

"That's good, right?"

"It looks promising."

❖ ❖ ❖

Kitty sat in a booth in the Ocean coffee shop. The coffee
wasn't as good here as the Blue Mountain, but it was the
venue preferred by the station guards, and since Wes' fu-
neral she felt closer to them than to the Free Company's
psi-techs. It was midmorning and Syke wouldn't be here for

another hour. She'd heard Benjamin had released a vid and some files into the S-LOGosphere, but she hadn't had the opportunity to sit down and study it yet. Obviously Alphacorp had seen it by now, so there was nothing to report to Remus than wasn't already known.

She activated the privacy baffle on the booth and watched the vid all the way through on her handpad, then read the transcription. Her scalp prickled when she saw Crowder actually admit to trying to wipe out a whole colony.

She read on. Ari van Blaiden's files linked him to Crowder and the attack on Hera-3.

Then she saw something in van Blaiden's files that made her blood feel as though it was congealing in her veins. She left her coffee cup still almost full and bolted outside to hail a passing tub. She could be back at Blue Seven in five minutes. She waved at the man on reception and he unlocked the door through the barbican and let her in.

"Where's Cara?" she asked Wenna when Cara's desk was empty.

"Getting a new apartment habitable for Ben's family."

"Where?"

"Upper deck, 2B, but you might . . ."

That was all Kitty heard because she was already halfway across the atrium with the door softly closing behind her before Wenna finished.

"Cara. Cara!"

The apartment door stood partly open and Kitty rapped loudly and went straight in. Cara was on her knees in front of a large pot filled with growing medium and surrounded by smaller pots containing various plants, some green and some pink.

"Oh, hi, Kitty. Do you know anything about flowers? Ben's family will be moving in here and I thought they might appreciate a planter. It's hardly a replacement for a farm, but it's a bit less clinical if there's something growing. Only I've forgotten everything I ever knew about gardens."

"I think you pretty much just stick them in and water them. Make sure you disturb the roots as little as possible."

"I don't know if the pink-leaved plants and the green-leaved ones are compatible."

"There's only one way to find out." Kitty knelt on the opposite side of the planter. "Tallest one in the middle?"

"Back corner, I think. Yes, there. You hold it, I'll firm up around it. Thanks."

"Cara, I watched the vid and read the reports. How did you get those files from Ari? Surely not after his death? Wouldn't they have self-erased?"

"They would. They did. All Ari's private files self-erased."

"So ..."

Cara sat back on her heels and looked at Kitty through the foliage. "Did he make you think you were the only person in the world for him?" she asked. "Was he witty and smart and devastatingly great in bed? No, don't answer that. Ari slept his way to the top in Alphacorp, did you know that? He used sex to get his own way. You, me, Craike—"

"And Akiko Yamada?" Kitty's voice shook.

"That's how Ari got a seat on the board and promoted to head of Special Operations so quickly. Oh dear, Kitty, did you think you were the love of his life?"

"What? No. I just didn't know about Ms. Yamada."

"She wasn't just his lover, she was his business partner. Crowder confirmed it."

"Crowder must have been lying."

"About many things, but not about that. Crowder certainly had a mole in Alphacorp."

"You're wrong. You've got to be wrong!" Kitty jumped to her feet and ran out into the atrium.

If Cara was right, it meant that information Kitty'd fed to Alphacorp had fed straight through to the Trust and had probably contributed to the attack on the *Solar Wind*.

It was her fault that Wes had died.

◆ ◆ ◆

Even the trip to Blue Seven in one of the crazily painted little tub-cabs had been exciting. Ricky had craned his neck to see everything as the cab whirled them through canyons, into tubes and along wide-open roadways where other cabs, manned and automatic, jostled for position. It was as good as a fairground ride. All the time, Dad had stared resolutely at his own feet.

Gwala and another of Captain Tengue's men—or maybe it was a woman, hard to tell under the buddysuit and helm—rode with them. Gwala's helm was in his lap, but his hand wasn't far from a sidearm that Ricky guessed was not a smart-dart gun. Despite his obvious on-duty attitude Gwala pointed out one or two things as they passed: a side tunnel that led to a street market, but not the sort of street market a boy should go to on his own; a residential area which was respectable enough to have a school; a warehouse district. Ricky had asked about the hum of machinery as they passed through one area. Waste recycling, he was told. Human waste. Ricky had curled his nose, but he knew that a space station couldn't afford to ignore resources, including bodily byproducts.

With one last whoosh their tub popped up from its tube into the open and pulled in next to the tub that carried Nan and Kai and two more of Blue Seven Security's finest. He recognized Hilde even though she wore her helm, but the other one was completely anonymous. He wondered what Nan and Kai had been talking about. Kai was bummed about leaving university, and his friends. He understood why, but he was still bummed.

Well, that put him one step ahead of Dad, who was still insisting none of this drama had been necessary.

Uncle Ben met them at the pull-in, hugged Nan and shook Dad and Kai's hands before patting Ricky on the shoulder. "Well, this is it," he said. "Blue Seven. It will be great when it's finished."

"It looks finished to me," Ricky said.

"This is just the entrance, there's a whole lot of work happening behind the facade."

The triangular entrance had two glass-fronted offices, one on each side, which funneled down to a set of doors, firmly closed. Their guards nodded politely and went into the left-hand office. Ricky tapped the glass. It looked like glass, but didn't feel like it or sound like it.

"Metal." Uncle Ben saw him. "Blastproof. This way." He led them through the right-hand office, nodding to the man behind the counter and the woman working on a holo-screen on the back wall. "This is manned 24/7. Don't let the bright young things fool you, they may look like receptionists, but they're all combat trained and at least Psi-4 level

Telepaths. And across the way the other office is manned by Morton Tengue's guards."

Uncle Ben passed his handpad across the code block and the door in the back of the reception office opened into a tunnel twenty meters long. Ricky looked up. There were ports in the ceiling and security cams to cover the place from all angles, plus vents at floor and shoulder height.

"It's like a prison," Dad muttered quietly.

Not quietly enough. "This is a barbican," Uncle Ben said. "There have been two serious attempts on us since we arrived here. The perimeter precautions are not overdone, believe me. There are multiple independent surveillance systems in here and two separate gas release systems. Nothing lethal, but very effective. And the ports are for weapons. It's like the killing-ground entrance to medieval castles that had murder holes in the ceilings and a portcullis at either end."

"You have portcullises?" Ricky asked.

"Kind of, but they're blast doors."

"Cool," Ricky said.

"What's to stop people cutting through the walls or the floors?" Nan asked.

"Reinforced internal skins with sensors. And no service vents, ducts, or plumbing wider than twenty centimeters. This place could even sustain its own atmosphere in case of extreme emergency, for a while, anyway."

The outer door closed behind them before the inner door opened. Inside Blue Seven the scene was completely different. The grays of the barbican gave way to a bright open space with a central atrium open to an azure blue roofspace that looked an awful lot like sky even though Ricky knew it couldn't be. Under the atrium at one side was a set of doors.

"Offices that side," Uncle Ben said. "Mine, Max's, Marta Mansoro—she looks after stores and supply. Wenna's is the main one. She's in charge here."

"I thought you were," Ricky said.

"Well, sort of, but the only way this works is if you let people do what they're best at. Wenna's a great administrator and she keeps things running smoothly. Max is good with figures, so he has that end office there, and he looks after all our finances, which at the moment are in minus numbers."

"I thought you were rich."

"It's not quite as simple as that."

"Nan told us about the platinum."

"It may be a year or even longer before we start to see much of a return from the platinum on Olyanda. There are surveys and construction before the ore is even mined. The extraction process can take another six months. Platinum isn't found on its own; it's usually mixed with other platinum group metals, gold and palladium. It takes around four and a half tons of ore to produce a single gram of platinum. Once you've got the pure platinum it has to be baked in a reaction chamber to make the jump gate rods."

"So you're not rich."

Uncle Ben laughed. "Not so much. Not yet, anyway."

Dad looked around. "So where did all this come from?"

"Mother Ramona and Norton Garrick arranged a line of credit against future expectations."

"So you're up to your ears in debt," Rion said.

"Yes, brother, if you want to put it that way, we are. We're psi-techs. We're used to debt. It's how the megacorps hold us close."

Nan was nodding. "I was lucky enough to be released from my contract, thanks to your grandfather."

"Now that's a story I'd like to hear," Uncle Ben said.

"And it's a story I should tell, at last. There are things you all need to know, but let's settle in first." She winked at Ricky and put her finger to her lips in a brief shushing gesture.

Malusi Duma. Ricky pinched his mouth together. That was something that he knew that neither Kai, Dad, nor Uncle Ben did.

Uncle Ben led them further into Blue Seven. The atrium ran through the middle like a two-story canyon with a balcony running the length of the upper deck, both sides with lots of doors and windows.

"Are these apartments, Uncle Ben?"

"That's right. They're not all finished yet, but this is where we'll all be living."

"Rabbit hutches," Dad said, but Uncle Ben ignored him and led them up an open stair to the upper balcony.

Two black and white farm dogs met them at the door, tails wagging, turning ecstatic circles.

"Tam, Lol." Rion dropped down on one knee and let the dogs try to bowl him over in their happiness.

"You'll all be staying here, for a while at least," Ben said. "I know it doesn't look like much, but ask Marta Mansoro for anything you want—within reason, Ricky, please—and she'll try and get it for you."

"Is there any chance I could get a message through to . . . someone on Chenon?" Kai asked. "I left in a bit of a hurry and she . . . well, she deserves an apology and a good-bye, at least."

"Someone special?" Uncle Ben asked.

"Just a good friend. She would have been heading back to Drogan's World after exams, anyway."

"Has she got an implant?"

Kai shook his head. "Does that make it difficult?"

"Audio and video messaging has been sporadic since the Trust started trying to jam our data packets at the gates. You know how that works, right? Messages sent to the local gate, squirted through in compressed bursts while the gates are open and forwarded from the receiving gate into the local network. As soon as the Trust hacks into our feeds we counter it, of course, but that means the network is unreliable. Generally we've asked people to save it for the really important stuff. The tel-net is still up and running, though. That's short messages transmitted mind-to-mind over interstellar distances and then committed to whatever global network is open locally. The Trust can't stop that, even though some of their own Telepaths are unofficially involved. Cara would normally—"

"Oh, I wouldn't want to ask her right now."

Uncle Ben smiled. "She'll be good as new in a few days. Better, maybe. In the meantime Cas Ritson can get a message through the Telepath network. Keep it short."

"Open sky." Dad looked around him with disapproval and peered into the long apartment, a bare living space in the middle with doors at either side and a window at the far end.

Ricky peered out. "What's outside?"

"It'll be a garden eventually, but right now it's just a building site," Uncle Ben said. "I told you it's not finished yet."

"I'm finished." Dad leaned on the far windowsill and

Ricky thought he was staring out at the people working below, but he rested his forehead against the glass. "I can't stay here. I can't."

Nan walked up behind him and put her hand on his shoulder, soothing him like he was a child. "It's only for a short while, Rion. Reska will find us somewhere else to stay, a planet with open skies and good grassland." She turned to Uncle Ben, a pleading look in her eyes. "Won't you, Reska?"

"Uh . . . I'll try."

Nan motioned him out with a sideways jerk of her head. Ricky looked at Kai and Kai looked back at Ricky. With such a large age gap they'd never been really close, but they each recognized a look that said: *I've never seen Dad like this before.*

Ricky's world began to crumble. His dad, who always knew what to do and how to do it, was having some kind of meltdown. He turned to Uncle Ben, but in the face of his brother's discomfort, he'd fled.

Chapter Twenty-Seven

DEFECTION

GABRIUS CROWDER WOKE UP.

That was a surprise.

He was in a hospital bed, drips in his arm, and Aggie was sitting by his side. Another surprise.

"How are you, Gabe?"

"Unless this is a very strange heaven, or hell, I seem to be alive." His voice cracked. He cleared it, then swallowed. "Rough throat."

"You were on a ventilator. They took the tubes out about two hours ago. You nearly died."

"Three darts."

"Doctor Mayweather says you have the constitution of an ox. He's never seen anyone survive three darts before. Lucky for you that you've put so much weight on."

He didn't tell her that he'd spent some time building up an immunity to a variety of toxins. There was still no guarantee, depending on the dosage.

"How long?"

"You've been out for five days."

"And you've been here all this time? How touching."

"If I had, it would be."

"I'm disappointed."

"I'm sure you're not. A young man called Stefan has

been calling on the hour every hour. Do you intimidate your staff so much that they daren't sleep?"

"I like to think so."

"Pav Danniri has sent you her resignation. She says it didn't happen like you said. It was a fair fight. Her brother was careless and he paid the price."

Crowder's scalp crawled. Had Danniri been talking to Benjamin?

"And Victoria LeBon called once to say the Board has met and unanimously decided to ask for your resignation once it was obvious you weren't going to save them the embarrassment by dying."

"They what?"

"There's a vid of you confessing to trying to kill some settlers on a platinum planet. It's gone viral on every major planet in the inner systems and beyond."

Crowder groaned.

"Did you?"

"What?"

"Try to kill ten thousand people."

"You don't understand what was at stake."

"I think I do."

"Platinum, Aggie."

"People, Gabe."

"The Trust—"

"I don't care. I stayed here until you woke up for one reason and one reason only. I wanted to tell you face-to-face that you are not to have any further contact with our daughters or our grandchildren, and if you ever come near my home again I have a smart-dart pistol and I'm prepared to use it. Four darts should do the trick. Maybe five to be sure. Oh, yes, and my lawyer is sending you the bill for my house repairs, with an added amount to cover compensation for my mental trauma, which includes you signing over the deeds of the property to me and an amount which, if properly invested, will keep me and mine comfortable for the rest of our lives." She stood and loomed over him. "If you want to fight me through the courts, I'm happy to do just that. Your credibility is about as low as it can go right now and you seem to be out of a job. Do we understand each other?"

"I think we do."

"Good."

She flounced out of the room, leaving only a waft of Longest Day, her favorite perfume. He watched her go, her perfect behind swaying. *I should have died,* he thought. *It would have been simpler if I had—and cheaper.*

✦ ✦ ✦

"I've never seen Rion like this before," Ben said. "Oh, sure, he's got his quirks, but I think he's losing it."

Ben and Cara were in their new apartment, one floor below and one apartment over from the one Ben's family shared. They could hear Rion's voice from here, though they couldn't make out the words. Finally a clump of pink leaves landed outside their front window, scattering growing medium and peppering the glass.

They heard Nan's voice and then Rion's high-pitched reply. "It's no substitute!"

"That's it," Ben said. "Enough's enough. Someone's going to get hurt."

He headed up the balcony steps, Cara close behind.

Kai was on his knees trying to rescue the remains of a planter, and Ricky was as far away from his dad as he could get, his eyes wide. Nan stood in the middle of the floor, her face impassive, but Rion leaned against the doorframe, breathing heavily.

"Rion," Ben began.

"Get me out of here, Ben. I can't stand it. Take me home." His red-rimmed eyes overflowed.

"Sit down. I'll think of something," Ben said. "Ricky, why don't you make us all some tea."

"That's usually my line," Nan said.

"I'm learning," Ben said. "How are you this morning, Nan?"

"I ditched the cane yesterday. My leg's a lot better. Your Doctor Wolfe is a fine young man. He called in to see us last night with his partner, Jon. Just a social call, he said, but managed to check on us all while he was here. Gave Rion some pills, but he's too stubborn to take them. I've seen this kind of reaction before in space virgins."

Ricky carried six mugs of tea to the table on a tray, and Ben sat down, looking at Rion to follow. Nan sat, Cara sat and then Kai and Ricky followed suit. The social pressure

worked, Rion flopped into the last empty chair and reached
for a mug.

"Fine," he said. "Sit. Drink tea. Things will all work out.
Yeah, right."

"Take a pill, Rion," Ben said. "If Ronan gave them to
you he must think you need them. He's an Empath as well
as a doctor and he knows his job."

"What are they? I won't be knocked out again." He put
the pill pot down on the table.

Cara reached across to take a look. "Tranqs. Macadom.
I've taken them myself. They won't slow you down, just buf-
fer your anxiety a little. Make it more manageable."

"I don't have an anxiety problem."

"Yes, you do," Nan said. "Take a pill."

"Space doesn't suit everyone," Ben said. "It's big, but the
habitats we build in it are small. Sometimes too small."

"I can't see the sky."

"I know. I have an idea. A planet you can wait out your
time on."

Cara looked up from her tea and mouthed, "Jamundi?"

He nodded at her and she nodded back, completely in
agreement.

He's a damn good farmer, Ben said to her privately.
*Suzi Ruka doesn't have such a big team as she did on Oly-
anda, so maybe the settlers would appreciate some sound
advice, especially from someone who isn't a psi-tech.*

What about your Nan?

We give her the choice. Give them all the choice.

"A planet?" Rion asked. "What kind of planet?"

"A new settlement. A virgin planet. Jamundi. The settlers
from Olyanda are going to need a lot of help, experienced
help."

"What's it like?" Kai asked.

"Basically very Earth-like," Cara said.

"We've never been to Earth," Ricky said.

Ben compared it to Chenon. "Much shorter days than
you're used to. Temperate zones with a good climate for
agriculture. Seasonal shifts. Green vegetation. Gravity
slightly less than Chenon. Three main continents. Some serious mountain ranges, but plenty of lowlands, too, very
promising farming country. Rivers and oceans. Polar ice-
caps. The occasional desert, some massive forests of tree-

like growths that will look a little strange at first, but you'll soon get used to them. There are few native nasties to worry about. Some volcanic and seismic activity but mostly confined to where our settlers aren't."

"And these settlers?" Rion asked. "Ecolibrians, yes?"

"Set out with the intention of getting back to basics," Ben said. "They want a colony free of genetic engineering, and that includes psi-techs. They've begun to compromise after their experiences on Olyanda. They're beginning to see the advantage of not shutting themselves off from help should they require it."

Cara leaned forward. "Victor Lorient, the colony director, pretty much lost his grip back on Olyanda. He's got a few hard-line colonists, but the rest of them just want to get on with their lives. Given a choice I'm pretty sure that some of them will vote for retaining more tech. They've found out how hard it can be going back to fire and the wheel."

"So how much tech can they afford?" Nan asked.

"When I did the deal with Crossways I cut them in for five percent of the profits from Olyanda's platinum," Ben said. "It's not producing yet, but once it is they can afford whatever they need." He turned to Rion. "It's a good planet. They're good people. Right now it's the best I can offer. A safe place with ground beneath your feet and sky above you."

Rion nodded. "Let's do it."

He took one of the small white pills, popped it into his mouth, and washed it down with a gulp of tea.

✦ ✦ ✦

"What about me?" Ricky heard his voice squeak and everyone turned to look at him at once.

"I'm sure there will be other youngsters your age," Dad said, completely missing the point.

"The Ecolibrians don't do implants. What happens when I'm old enough to be tested? If I'm on Jamundi I'm not going to get an implant, am I? I'm going to be stuck there and never learn to pilot a starship or fly the Folds."

"That's a long way off." Dad frowned. "You might not even be suitable for an implant. Kai wasn't."

Ricky saw the look on Kai's face.

"Yes, he was. He turned it down to make you happy."

You could have cut the silence with a knife. Ricky turned pleading eyes to Kai, knowing he'd said the unsayable. Kai stared resolutely into his tea mug.

"Nan, you know I have psi potential," Ricky tried. "I might even get onto a fast track program."

"And put yourself into the hands of some ruthless megacorp?" Dad said. "No way!"

Nan shrugged and gave Rion a long, appraising look. "The boy has talent, Rion. He's going to test positive and if you try and hold him back you'll lose him."

"I ... I didn't ..." Dad turned to Kai. "Did you really turn down an implant, son?"

"I really did. I just figured that if I had an implant I'd have to go where I was sent, do what I was told. It's okay if you want to be a small cog in a big machine—" He looked up. "Sorry, Uncle Ben, I don't mean that like it sounds ..."

"No problem, Kai."

Kai nodded. "I didn't want the debt. I just wanted to learn to be the best farmer I could and then stay on the farm and be who I wanted to be. My choice. No need to feel guilty, Dad. You didn't make the decision for me."

"But I don't want to be a farmer," Ricky said. "Yeah, all that about cogs and machines and doing what you're told and owing lots of money doesn't sound so good unless you're doing the thing you most love doing in the whole world. In the whole darn galaxy."

Nan cleared her throat. "Well, you can't stay here, Ricky, so we'd better reach a compromise."

"Why can't I stay here?"

"Your schooling for a start."

"There are schools on Crossways."

Uncle Ben nodded. "Schools and a university, too, though the degree is not always accepted on the inner system planets."

"See. I could stay here."

"I want you safe, Ricky," Dad said, "with me."

"But ..." Ricky felt a swell of righteous indignation. It was his life.

"Your Dad's right, Ricky," Uncle Ben said. "We have a job to do and there are people after us who won't stop to ask if you're an innocent bystander. You don't want to have to watch your back every minute of every day and be taken to school by an armed guard. You've already experienced the Trust's hospitality." He spread his hands on the table, big capable hands. Ricky had never noticed before how alike Uncle Ben's and his dad's hands were. "Jamundi isn't going to be completely isolated. We'll come by and visit whenever we can and I promise you that we'll arrange for your preliminary testing at fourteen, and if you are suitable you can have your implant fitted here, so as not to be tied to a megacorp."

"And learn from Mr. Jussaro, yes?"

Uncle Ben smiled. "Possibly. It's still three years in the future. A lot can happen in three years."

"Yes, a lot can happen," Dad said, in that kind of way that made Ricky think he'd be getting a lot of lessons in farming between now and his fourteenth birthday.

"No pressuring the lad, Rion," Nan said. "It's his life. He'll be what he'll be."

Dad sighed and nodded. "Agreed."

✦ ✦ ✦

"What do you know about Cotille?" Garrick asked Ben on a visit to Blue Seven. They'd settled in Ben's office over caff, which Garrick drank with good grace.

"Not much," Ben said. "It was set up by the Trust just as Hera-3 was kicking off. It's a planet with some small potential for platinum, but not enough to draw unwanted attention. It's heavy in iron and coal, so several manufacturing firms took out industrial contracts and sent out engineering specialists. Sofia Lake was the officer in charge of a two-year setup program. She's a very competent administrator, so I doubt there were any problems with the initial mission. Sofia's team would have left behind a Trust officer in charge of a small admin staff, but I'm not sure who that would have been. It should be on the Trust's open records."

Garrick checked his handpad. "It was Lake herself who stayed behind. She's enquired about terms for a potential trading agreement. They're interested in discussing a move to declare independence."

"Interesting. I worked with Sofia a couple of times, just after I joined the Trust. She was my boss on my very first colony setup. She always said she might retire into colony admin eventually. Looks like she's finally done it. She has a family who used to go with her on missions, so I expect they've all settled together."

"What did you think of her?"

"Psi-3 Telepath and a skilled pilot. Very reliable, even-handed, a good person to learn the ropes from. Was always particularly good at bringing on new talent in her team. Several of her younger officers have since gone on to command positions."

"Loyal to the Trust?"

"Yes, but not slavishly. She'll always stand up for what she thinks is right."

"Ah, good."

"Does that fit with what you wanted to know?"

Garrick nodded. "One of the reasons she's quoted for wanting to talk to us about leaving the Trust is that she's seen the vid of your confrontation with Crowder and says that she knows you well enough to believe your account. She wants to talk to you."

"To me?"

"Might it be a trap?"

"If you're sure the message was from Sofia Lake herself and not someone else on her behalf, I would be inclined to give her the benefit of the doubt."

"Good, because on your behalf I turned down the invitation for you to visit Cotille, but I invited Lake here."

"And?"

"She accepted. She'll be here tomorrow morning."

"I'm planning to take Rion and the family to Jamundi and then to get on with hunting down the lost colonists."

"I know. Please bear with me and meet with Ms. Lake first."

◆ ◆ ◆

Ben waited on the concourse outside the public dock for Sofia Lake's ship to cycle through the air lock and her delegation to emerge. The port operated on a low-pressure, thin-air system designed to cut down on incidents. For anyone newly arrived it was like experiencing high altitude without the slow ascent to acclimatize. Try and cause a ruckus and you'd most likely fall over and pass out. The port officials wore a bio-grafted breathing tube in various imaginative ways. Some snaked along their jawline, up and around the side of their mouth to their nostrils, others had the tubes grafted horizontally from above their ear with slim oxygen packs worn as hats.

Ben watched from the glazed arrivals gallery as Sofia led three individuals to the immigration gate. With Garrick's personal invitation, the small party was quickly admitted, though, Ben noticed, they still had to pass through a scanner that would pick up most kinds of weaponry, including minute traces of explosives. All four were clean.

Ben scooted down a short flight of steps and arrived at the main gate in time to meet them at the outer air lock where Syke and Nan were already waiting. He'd enticed Nan away from her packing duties. Her Empathy was much more reliable than either Ronan's or Cara's when it came to reading emotions and intent from both psi and non-psi.

"Benjamin." Sofia held out both hands and Ben took them. "It's good to see you again."

She'd aged well, her hair iron gray, now, instead of black, but she was still trim and carried her height well. Her skin was barely lined.

"Good to see you, too." Ben only just stopped himself from calling her Boss. "You retired into colony admin like you always said you would."

"I did. Got a bit tired of all that cryo."

"How is your family?"

"Well. Janie is with me on Cotille, but the kids are off doing their own thing. Bran got his implant and is at university on Earth—Edinburgh—studying exobiology and contracted to the FPA. Juno tested negative for psi, but did rather well in engineering. She's an independent contractor on the rim, married to a very nice couple from Walder-5. I'm a grandma four times over. I'll show you the baby pictures later."

"Sofia, this is my grandmother, Louisa Benjamin."

"The Louisa Benjamin who negotiated the peace on Scarra?"

"That's some time ago." Nan smiled.

"But still quoted in the textbooks."

"I believe so." Nan inclined her head.

"And this is Captain Syke," Ben said, making a final introduction. "Norton Garrick and Mother Ramona's Chief of Security. Forgive us for being overcautious. We've had some close calls over the last few weeks."

"No apology required. These are my colleagues from

Cotille, Elder Zakhar, Elder Gully, and Andrew Hoffman."
Everyone shook hands with everyone else except for Syke,
who settled for a bow of acknowledgment and stepped
back with his crew. "Elders Zakhar and Gully have been
recently elected as Speakers on Foreign Affairs," Sofia continued. "Andy is my legal guru."

Ben led the way to the tub system where one of Syke's
men had a flotilla of cabs waiting to take everyone to Garrick's Mansion House. Nan sat with the two elders and Syke
while Ben settled himself in with Sofia, Andy, and one of
Syke's guards. Two tubs of guards, one in front and one behind, escorted them.

"You're looking well, Sofia," Ben said. "Does colony life
suit you?"

"Surprisingly, it does. You should try it. You look like
hell, Benjamin. What have you been doing to yourself?"

"Had a small argument with the Folds."

"Sorry to hear that." Tactfully she didn't inquire any further. *Tell me what happened to put you on the wrong side
of the Trust.*

You heard about Hera-3?

*Who didn't? Hell of a bad break. Platinum pirates and
most of your colonists slaughtered. You were damn lucky to
get out alive.*

*We got fifteen hundred settlers out, but I lost all but forty-
seven of my crew. Wenna Phipps—remember her?—lost an
arm. Most of the rest weren't so lucky.*

Bloody pirates!

*It's worse than that. Follow the money. Who ended up
with the platinum from Hera-3?*

*The Trust, but you don't mean ... *

*I suspected an inside job, someone leaking information.
I didn't expect to find Crowder and Ari van Blaiden in it together.*

Van Blaiden defected to Alphacorp years ago.

Yes, but who was his mentor in the Trust?

Oh, gods, Crowder.

Exactly.

*And this Olyanda thing? I've seen the vid. Crowder and
van Blaiden.*

*Platinum again, only this time Crowder decided to wipe
out the whole colony with a plague. We stopped him.*

He left Cara's part out of it altogether, figuring she would prefer not to have the details shared.

Van Blaiden?

We stopped him, too.

And landed on the wrong side of the law, Lake said.

Pretty much.

Tell me about Garrick.

Clever, manipulative, ambitious, ruthless. Ben shrugged. *Everything you might expect from someone who's scrambled to the top of the heap on Crossways, but he's got vision and a long-term plan that could see this place legitimized.*

An empire builder.

In a way, yes, but not for personal gain. I don't think it's even for personal power, though don't get me wrong, he's not a pushover. He's on top and he intends to stay that way. He's a born politician, but as I understand it, raised on a prison planet for the first sixteen years of his life, not exactly the sort of environment where you can take up politics. He landed on Crossways after a few adventures around the galaxy and spent twenty years working his way to the top.

Can we trust him?

You can trust him to do what he says he'll do.

That's your considered opinion?

It is. He didn't let me down. My team and the colonists would be dead if it wasn't for Garrick and Mother Ramona.

Fair enough.

You've got problems on Cotille? Ben asked.

First couple of years were fine. We're self-sufficient in food production now, but we export high-cost, low-volume goods such as quality cocoa beans and luxury chocolate, but more importantly, catechin and epicatechin for the pharma industry. The Trust is now only offering half the market value while trebling the cost of transport. The Elders have seen the way the Trust's stock has nosedived since your vid hit the S-LOGS and it's given them the push they needed to look for a better deal.

The tubs pulled up at the central hub where the visitors could instantly appreciate the colossal waste of space of the area, open through seven levels to an artificial azure sky. Hub Park, replete with specimen trees and lush tropical plants, filled the whole of the center. Opposite, flanked by more modest but still impressive residences, stood Gar-

rick's Mansion House. This time they took the external stair
to the grand entrance where Garrick and Mother Ramona
formed a welcoming committee.

"Ms. Lake, Mr. Hoffman." Garrick stepped forward and
shook hands warmly as Ben made the introductions.
Mother Ramona had dressed more conservatively than she
normally did and drew Elders Gully and Zakhar along with
her to the impressive state reception room with its elegant
proportions and tasteful furniture. A butler and two smartly
dressed waiters offered trays of drinks and canapés. Ben
caught the eye of one of them and recognized her as one of
Syke's guards, then spotted the bulge beneath the bow of
her apron that denoted a weapon. Garrick was taking no
chances.

Ben glanced at Nan. She smiled and nodded. *Genuine,*
she said. *They are who they appear to be and they're looking for a better deal than they're getting with the Trust.*

He felt a wash of relief. He could leave the details of the
negotiation to Garrick. He'd played his part.

Four hours later he excused himself, the main points
having been agreed upon. From now on Cotille's trading
agreement with Crossways included several mutual obliga-
tion clauses including a minimum market price for various
staple foodstuffs and protection from everything from ha-
rassment to a full-scale attack.

✦ ✦ ✦

Cotille's defection from the Trust brought new complica-
tions. The jump gate system, though nominally governed by
interstellar treaty, was largely controlled by the megacorporations. The usage tolls, though supposedly standardized,
often had a high premium for any ship not affiliated with
the gate operator, though some megacorps had reciprocal
agreements. Without exception they all charged independents through the nose.

Dido Kennedy's jump drive, if she could get it operational and iron the kinks out of it, was going to revolution-
ize travel and make it possible for the independents to
operate a wider trading network.

"It's the independents who are going to make a difference," Ben said as he and Nan watched Ricky, Kai, Ronan,

Cara, Max, and Hilde having a knockabout session in the smaller of Crossways' two grapple arenas.

"You need to send out ambassadors," Nan said. "Draw in the independents and the undecided."

"Not me," Ben said. "Garrick and Mother Ramona."

It was the first real training session in null-G for Ricky, Kai and Max. Ronan, Cara, and Hilde were good teachers. Anyone who mucked around in space for long enough would encounter null-G sooner or later, and it was always better to know how to handle yourself when your world turned upside down. Learning how to negotiate obstacles and get yourself from one end of a spacecraft to the other without throwing up was a skill in itself. Unsurprisingly, Rion had turned down the offer.

Nan smiled as Ricky managed to somersault across the width of the arena from one of the projecting bars to the glass window of the referee's box they'd settled in. He flattened his hands against the window, blew a raspberry on the glass, turned in midair and pushed off again to shoulder-charge Ronan, who had just grabbed a medonite hoop with the idea of showing Ricky how to shoot it through the loop for a goal.

"The boy's a natural," Nan said. "What're the odds on his testing well for Navigation when he gets his implant?"

"Wouldn't surprise me," Ben said.

"They rely on you," Nan said.

"Huh?" Ben had lost the thread of the conversation while watching Cara gracefully glide like a slow-motion diver, snagging the hoop before Ricky could get his hands on it and passing it to Max, who promptly lost it to a tackle by Hilde.

"Garrick and Mother Ramona. Keep up, Reska!"

"Garrick's got close to a million people on Crossways. Plenty to rely on. He doesn't need me."

"You think alike."

"Are you trying to find an outlet for my talents?" He shook his head. "You know I lost it—in the Folds. A pilot-Navigator who can't fly the Folds isn't much good. Better retire him into administration before he kills someone."

"That's not what I said."

"You didn't need to. I say it to myself all the time. Here

I am trying to reassure Rion and I can't hack foldspace myself."

"Give it time."

"Yeah, right. Time. That'll help. It seems the longer I leave it the harder it gets to go back. I've got a date with a void dragon, but I'm terrified to keep it."

"You know you'll have to sooner or later."

"I know." He stared out at the grapple arena without actually looking at the figures. "What were you saying about ambassadors?"

Nan accepted the change of subject. "That if it's the independents who are going to make a difference to Crossways, you—Garrick, that is—should be sending out ambassadors to win them over."

"We'd need someone with a real gift for negotiation to head up a team." Ben looked at her sideways. "Are you thinking about coming out of retirement?"

"I might be." She watched Ricky do a lazy corkscrew around Kai and this time catch the hoop. "I might even take the boy with me if Rion's willing."

"I'll talk to Garrick and Mother Ramona if you talk to Rion and Ricky."

"Deal." She nodded. "And then you need to talk to a void dragon."

"Let's get Rion and Kai settled on Jamundi first."

It was another excuse and they both knew it.

Chapter Twenty-Eight

FAMILY SECRETS

BEN TOOK RION, RICKY, AND KAI TO THE FARM. Kai had been studying arcologies on Chenon's moon as part of his university course and he wanted to see how Crossways handled intensive food production. Rion had taken some persuading, as he expressed an opinion that a farm without open sky above it wasn't real. Ricky was happy to tag along because he wanted to see more of the station.

Of course they had to be accompanied by a phalanx of guards, in this case, Gwala, Hilde, and half a dozen of Tengue's finest.

To keep Ricky happy Ben decided to take the long way. From Blue Seven they circled around the outer rim of the station anticlockwise, through the huge market, where it was possible to buy almost anything if the price was right, and past the public docks. Ben kept up a running commentary. From the docks they moved into an upper-class shopping area that was indistinguishable from the kind of mall that could be found in any sophisticated capital city anywhere in the colonized worlds. Toward the far end stores became smaller and shabbier and beyond them was an open souq leading onto the accommodation levels organized into gated communities occupied by clans, factions, and possibly the wealthier gangs.

Farther along still there were laboratories, engineering works, and factories which then opened up onto three huge shipbuilding and refitting yards. They'd left the privileged areas far behind by the time they came upon the ship-breakers, where the poorest gleaned a living from stripping down hulks for their component parts and reusable materials. Ben suspected not all the derelicts in there had been officially decommissioned, but some were the proceeds of piracy. He knew Garrick turned a blind eye, but had hopes of legitimizing some of Crossways' more dubious businesses.

Rather than continue around the station's rim, they cut in toward the central spindle and dropped a couple of levels to Hub Park before taking the radial direct to the farm.

Once at the farm, Ricky attached himself to Gwala and Hilde. Ben suspected that he figured that guard-talk would be more interesting than anything his dad and Kai were going to be discussing, and also that he didn't want to give his father the chance to change his mind about the possibility of traveling with Nan on her ambassadorial mission.

Rion wasn't keen on Ricky gallivanting off with Nan, but when he learned that they would be traveling in a state-of-the-art jumpship, actually Garrick's private yacht, fully armed and with a crew used to protecting their VIP passengers, he softened toward the idea a little. Nan had reminded him that Ricky would eventually go his own way and that trying to overprotect him now was a good way of losing him later. But it was Kai's quiet good sense that prevailed in the end, and Rion admitted that trying to settle Ricky on a planet full of farmers was the best way to make sure he never wanted to farm.

Though Rion was his usual skeptical self as they looked around the station's farm, Kai was in his element, checking the figures on wheat production and weighing the ethics against the practicalities of intensive pork rearing. He was entranced by the community farm, too, and admitted that it was worth sacrificing a few acres of production for the project.

It had been a pleasant half day away from the demands of the Free Company and the pressures of what lay ahead, until Cara interrupted. Ben felt her implant handshaking with his own.

Mother Ramona has just sent a message, she said. *Crowder survived your three darts.*

And that was a good day spoiled.

◆ ◆ ◆

"Any idea why Nan wants to talk to us all together?" Ben asked Rion as he settled the dogs in a corner of *Solar Wind*'s mess.

"None at all. She has a clean bill of health, hasn't she?"

"According to Ronan she's fitter than anyone her age has a right to be."

"Talking about me?" Nan came in with Kai and Ricky.

"Just speculating on the family meeting," Ben said. "I programmed the server for tea. It seemed appropriate."

"Tea is always appropriate. I made most of my best negotiations over a cup of tea."

"You're negotiating?"

"Not quite," Nan said. "Before we all go our separate ways I wanted to give you a family history lesson. There may not be time later and it could be important." She smiled at Ricky and he winked back. "You've all heard of Malusi Duma?"

"President of African Unity on Earth," Kai said.

"That's the one. He's your great-grandfather." She turned to Ben and Rion. "Your grandfather."

Grandfather. Ben heard the word but for a moment the importance eluded him.

She cleared her throat. "Don't all speak at once," she said into the silence.

"Sorry, Nan, still trying to take it in," Ben said. "I mean, I knew we had a grandfather, out there, somewhere. I think I just assumed he was . . ."

"Dead?" She smiled. "No, Malusi is very much alive, though he's had rejuv treatment and at least one new heart that I know of. I met him at university, Cambridge, way back. I was studying history and psychology and Malusi was studying politics. Always politics. I already had an implant and was signed up to the Five Power Alliance. Malusi didn't have an implant, and still doesn't. We stayed together through university and afterward, when I joined the Diplomatic Corps, he went back home to Pretoria and became a career politician."

She smiled. "We had an off-and-on relationship after that, though more off than on. I was apprenticed to Gerda Swanson and learning my job. Some of our negotiations took us away for long periods, and I lost three years in cryo.

"We met up again when I was twenty-four and he was twenty-seven. I'd booked leave. I was ready to settle down and tie the knot. I wanted children, specifically his children. Oh, that man was something. Don't look at me like that, Kai. I was young enough to have a sex life once. Get over it."

Ben was glad she'd aimed that at Kai and not him, though his thoughts hadn't been far from there.

"Anyhow, that's when he told me that he was settling down, too, but not with me." She sighed. "It seemed like a pity to waste the leave I'd booked, so we said good-bye properly and promised to stay friends forever, which we've done. Robert was born nine months later. Malusi doted on him and Malusi's wife proved to be very amenable to having an extra member of the family. They eventually had five children of their own.

"Anyhow, we couldn't travel together in cryo until Robert was six, so I did a PhD at Cambridge while I was out of commission, then the FPA called. A skirmish out on the rim that needed mediating and Gerda was busy elsewhere, so I left Robert with his father for a couple of years and went back to work. As soon as Robert was six I scooped him up again and we spent the next fourteen years jumping around the galaxy. Of course, we only aged five years in that time with all the cryo. By the time Robert was eleven he decided for himself that he wanted to go back to his father and not rack up so much cryo time, but by then Malusi was a rising star in Pan-African politics. That was the year he was elected to the vice presidency and seconded to the FPA. He'd been widowed and had remarried, but his new wife wasn't so amenable to having Robert around. It didn't seem prudent to call attention to Malusi's bastard child. There had already been several assassination attempts and it was safer to keep Robert hidden.

"Well, you know the rest. Robert decided on a boarding school, we picked Kingston College on Chenon. He graduated, married, took up farming and he never left the planet again until . . ."

"Until he left for the last time," Rion said.

Nan nodded. "And I came to look after you two. It was Malusi who got the FPA to cancel my contract. I could never have afforded to buy myself out. We keep in touch."

"Your best friend, Lucy," Rion said. "All these years . . . written messages."

"Lucy, yes, Malusi's code name."

"And you haven't seen him in person since?" Ricky asked.

She shook her head. "Not in person. Anyhow, I thought you should know. Trapped in that cell for a month, I suddenly realized that I might not see you again and that there were things I hadn't told you. Your grandfather might have remained anonymous, but he's always taken a keen interest in your various adventures, even though it's been at a distance."

"I'd like to meet him one day," Kai said.

Nan smiled. "I'm sure that can be arranged."

✦ ✦ ✦

Rion accepted the offered sedative gratefully. As *Solar Wind* slipped out of dock he felt the drug making him drowsy and settled back in his bunk. It was okay for Ben, who was used to all this gallivanting through space, but Rion found it terrifying. All he could think of was his parents, gone forever into some black hell.

He may have dreamed, but whatever was floating around his brain dissipated as he woke to the sound of Kai scrabbling for his boots. Kai had also decided to sleep away the journey, though probably more to show solidarity than out of fear. There were times when Rion felt profoundly grateful for Kai, but the last few days had proved that his boy had become a young man. Maybe it was time to take stock while the farm was so far away. Kai had to make his own choices, not shape his future to placate an increasingly old-fashioned and cranky father.

Ricky and Nan were nowhere to be seen. Not surprising. Ricky was all talk about the forthcoming trip to Blacklock with Nan. They'd probably gone hunting for monsters in the Folds, looked them straight in the eye and laughed.

The door whooshed open and Ricky bounced in, excitable as a puppy.

"You're going to love it here, Dad."

It was only then that Rion realized they must have landed on Jamundi already. He hadn't even been aware that the faint hum of the drive was now silent.

"Come on." Ricky thrust Rion's boots at him. "There are ten thousand settlers arriving tomorrow, but right now there are probably fewer than a hundred people on this whole world, and most of them are psi-techs preparing the ground. Literally. They're cutting great paths into the jungle and clearing ground for a town. There's this enormous plow, and a road-laying machine that fuses silica with—oh, I don't know—something—to make a road surface. It's kinda glass, but not brittle or slippery. And houses called risers 'cause they go up so fast, and—"

"Slow down, son."

"Sorry, Dad. Nan's talking to Mrs. Lorient—she's in charge—about off-world trading when the settlement gets established."

Rion stomped his feet into his boots and nodded to Kai. "I expect we'll only be here for a few months until things on Chenon settle down."

"If you say so," Kai said.

"You're not convinced?"

"I wonder whether there will be anything to go back to. Will the authorities have impounded the farm?"

"Why should they do that? We're not guilty of anything." But even as he said it, Rion had doubts.

"Neither is Uncle Ben. It doesn't seem to have stopped them from turning him into a wanted criminal."

Kai had a point. Rion had never been away from the farm for so long. He'd put blood, sweat, and tears into it. He'd been born there and expected to die there. He'd suffered poor harvests, cattle pestilence, and the occasional bad decision, but he'd also had bumper crops and won awards at the regional shows for the quality of his herd. He'd married there. His children had been born there. His wife had died there.

From the *Solar Wind*'s ramp all he could see was green. On one side the green-gold of wild grassland, and on the other growth halfway between a dense forest and a jungle, though without the tropical heat. There was something about green vegetation. Even though he'd grown up on a pink planet whose only patches of green were crops introduced from Earth, there was something in the human psyche that felt at home in green surroundings. A broad river sliced through the growth. Above them the sky hung heavy with ragged clouds. Darker clouds crowded low over the upstream horizon, but not knowing the land he couldn't tell whether they were rolling in or out. Well, he'd soon find out.

Forward of the ship, as Ricky had said, there was a quickly raised town ready to shelter ten thousand new settlers before they set off to conquer whatever was out there. Beyond the buildings, clearings had been torn into the virgin earth and stacks of lumber were lined up ready for use. Two heavyweight plows trundled along, eating green and shitting out strait brown furrows.

Brother Ben, looking seriously austere in his all-purpose buddysuit, was talking to a man and two women on the edge of town. One of the women spotted him and said something. Ben looked up and waved him over. She was in settler garb, casual soft trousers and tunic, made for comfort not for fashion. It made him feel at home already.

"Rion, come and meet Mrs. Lorient and Jack Mario. They're in charge," Ben said. "And this is Suzi Ruka, the Free Company's agronomist."

Agronomist. Just a fancy name for a farmer who didn't like to get dirty, but Rion noticed the soil under Suzi Ruka's fingernails. Maybe she wasn't so bad after all.

"Paruna grain." Suzi anticipated his first question. "Fastest-yielding crop for this type of ground."

"Makes sense," he said. "What are you going to diversify with? I've always favored spelt over bio-engineered wheat."

"Spelt, oats, corn, linseed, barley, beans. Vegetables, of course: potatoes, parsnips, carrots, brassicas of all kinds."

"I've always been fond of peppers and tomatoes."

"We've got acres of grow-tunnels . . ."

And they were off, comparing cultivation methods and seed varieties. The conversation drifted to stock raising and Suzi mentioned Charolais cattle. He countered with Blonde d'Aquitaine and Belgian Blue and the composite breed he raised on Chenon, the Russolta Brindle, which she admitted was a very fine breed for beef production and asked his opinion on the Magenta lineage, which he almost knew by heart.

It was only when he caught Ben's meaningful expression

that he realized he'd been totally ignoring Mrs. Lorient. Luckily she laughed when he apologized.

"It's a good thing we've got four hundred acres marked out for you, Mr. Benjamin," she said.

"Please, call me Rion. Four hundred acres?" He glanced at Kai, who grinned back. Well, that would do very nicely to be going on with.

"We're not exactly short of land here. If you need more . . ."

"Thank you."

"And cattle. Good breeding stock, though I can't promise you Russolta Brindles."

Rion felt himself smiling. "We'll take what we can get, won't we, Kai?"

"We need good farmers," she continued. "I hope you'll stay. You and Kai and Ricky."

"I'm going with Nan," Ricky piped up.

Rion didn't mean to frown.

"For a while, anyway."

Rion sighed. "My youngest is determined to be a psi-tech and be like his Uncle Ben."

Rena Lorient smiled. "He couldn't have picked a better role model."

Ben looked sheepish. Damned idiot never could take a compliment.

Cara was supervising the unloading of crates from *Solar Wind*'s hold with the help of some psi-techs he didn't recognize. Seeing him glance around, she waved and pointed to a livestock carrier. Tam and Lol! Tam barked once through the door's grid.

"Excuse me, Mrs. Lorient—my dogs."

"I like a man who knows how to treat his animals. Go ahead. I'll see you after you've said hello to your dogs and good-bye to your family."

Rion hurried over and let the two dogs out of the carrier to frolic around him. He gave then a few minutes to run and sniff and mark their territory before he called them to heel.

He heard Nan's laughter before he saw her. She was with a couple of psi-techs who had apparently been showing her around the embryonic settlement. The dogs broke away from him and streaked toward her. She stooped and gave them both scritches along their curly-coated backs.

"They're going to miss you," Rion said. "I'll miss you."

"Nonsense. You and Kai will have everything organized before I get back, and you'll enjoy not having me under your feet. I'll keep in touch via Jack's wife, Saedi. If you have any messages for me, send them via her."

"Will do."

With promises to visit and to keep in touch, Ben headed back to his precious ship.

Nan hugged Rion and Kai, not once, but twice. "We'll be back soon," she said, "and I have a full set of schoolwork for Ricky, so he won't miss out while he's traveling."

"Aww, Nan ..." Ricky started to protest, but she gave him one of her this-is-how-it-will-be looks and he shut up remarkably quickly.

Ricky's good-bye to Kai was a brotherly punch on the arm, neither sure whether they wanted to lose their dignity by hugging, but Rion pulled Ricky into a gruff embrace. "You'll never be too old to hug, son. Behave yourself and don't get into trouble."

"I won't." Ricky straightened up and started to turn, then shot back, clamped his arms around Rion's chest and squeezed. "I love you, Dad."

"Course you do." The lump in Rion's throat kept his response necessarily brief. "Now go on and don't keep Uncle Ben waiting."

The clouds rolled closer as they said their good-byes, and it started to rain as *Solar Wind* rose on her antigravs, which was just as well since Rion's face was already wet.

◆   ◆   ◆

Ricky wanted to make the journey to Crossways on the flight deck, but Uncle Ben said no very firmly and he didn't feel he could argue. It wasn't too late for them to turn around and take him back to Jamundi. *Best behavior* became his mantra. *Best behavior. Best behavior.*

They arrived back on Crossways to find that Mr. Garrick had made his own private yacht, the *Glory Road*, available for Nan and Ricky's ambassadorial trip. Next to *Solar Wind* it was the coolest ship ever. Yacht made it sound small, but it was much bigger than a runabout and sleekly elegant, decked out in green livery with a red flash, just like Mr. Garrick's guards. In fact all the crew had the same smart uniform. Surely it didn't take thirty people to fly a ship of this size.

"My own personal flight crew," Mr. Garrick explained. "Smart as whips, the lot of them, and dangerous when backed into a corner." He walked down the lineup on the dockside with Nan and Ricky. "This is Captain Nelka Dorinska, a fine pilot and a Psi-3 Navigator extricated from the clutches of Arquavisa when she took out two senior officers in a bar fight. She hasn't touched a drop of yahto ever since, have you, Captain?"

"Not a drop, sir, not of yahto, anyway." Dorinska saluted smartly. "Please to have you on board, Miss Benjamin, and you, too, Master Ricky."

Master Ricky. Did being the ambassador's great-grandson give him a title now?

They followed Mother Ramona up the ramp and through the open air lock. "The best way to attract friends is to look like you don't need them," she said as she showed Nan the elegant reception cabin. Cabin was hardly the word for it. Salon was the word he thought he heard Mother Ramona use. It was all so . . . so . . . fancy. Ricky ran his fingers across the plush sofa, noting that it was firmly clamped into place in case of loss of gravity.

The master cabin opened off one side of the salon. It had a huge soft bed, a couple of easy chairs and a desk, once again, all clamped down. It was sumptuously cushioned and only a little less fancy than the salon.

"There's a cabin for Ricky next door," Mother Ramona said. "And you'll have a personal staff of four, including Chander Dalal from the Free Company, a Psi-2 Telepath and also an excellent cook. He'll be your contact person."

"Namaste." Chander gave them a palms-together greeting, which Nan returned elegantly and Ricky more awkwardly, but was rewarded with a quick smile and a nod of approval. Good, he didn't fluff it too badly.

"There are two other Telepaths in the crew," Mother Ramona said. "And everyone has a receiving implant."

"Wow," Ricky said, looking around the cabin. "Is all this for real?"

"Real enough," Nan said. "But none of it prevents you from doing your schoolwork. Deal?"

"Deal. If I do extra can I go on the flight deck?"

He saw Nan glance at Captain Dorinska and she gave a brief nod. He felt himself start to grin.

✦ ✦ ✦

Crowder's recovery was slow, but while his body trapped him in a hospital bed, he began to plan. Aggie, true to her word, didn't come back, and though he tried to send messages to his daughters they were returned unwatched. Stefan French visited with paperwork that confirmed Aggie's diagnosis. He was, indeed, off the Board and out of a job, or at least on extended personal leave. In his weakened state this hardly seemed to matter, but as he recovered he began to seethe.

He'd only done what any one of them wished they had the guts to do.

Lawrence Archer was holding Crowder's post as head of Colony Operations temporarily. He was efficient, but had no vision. Crowder had Stefan, who had not been told to cut off his former boss from the information stream, comm the hospital three times a day. He wanted to know everything that Archer did and all the news as it happened.

Cotille Colony's declaration of independence incensed Crowder. Sofia Lake had served the Trust well for thirty years and now she'd turned traitor. He got Stefan to check the records. Damn! He'd forgotten she'd worked with Benjamin.

He watched the vid that Aggie had warned him about. That particular cat was well and truly out of the bag now, but since the Monitors weren't standing guard outside his door he presumed that the Trust had enough influence to ensure he wouldn't be called to account. Someone would be answering awkward questions, but for the moment it wasn't him. He decided that extended leave, for personal reasons, suited him just fine as long as he could keep up his contacts and influence. He'd bide his time until it all blew over.

He called Tori LeBon only to be fobbed off and left worrying for a day. When she eventually called him back it was with accusations.

"You were careless," Tori said of the vid. "You left the Board no choice. We reluctantly accepted your resignation."

"I didn't tender my resignation," he growled.

She merely looked at him, expressionless.

"John Hunt?"

"Was the first to say you should go, but not the only one."

Crowder shrugged, outwardly calm, but inwardly raging. He'd get the bastards.

"What's done is done." He sighed theatrically. "There will always be leaks. Speaking of which, you know I have an insider in Alphacorp?" Several insiders, actually, but he wasn't going to reveal that.

"You'd better put me in contact."

"I don't think so. You know I have every respect for you, Victoria, but there are some things that remain sacred. I will however, while I remain on extended personal leave, work on the Trust's behalf, and my own of course."

"Of course."

"You'll get the benefit of my considerable network of contacts and my business advice. I want back in."

"Of course you do."

"Not right now, naturally, but when the time is right."

"It's a pity your contacts didn't warn you about the vid, or Benjamin's destination." The long silence and the sour look on her face told him exactly what she thought of the fiasco on Norro.

"Is Benjamin back on Crossways?"

"As far as we know."

"We need to do something about that."

"We've tried. Alphacorp has tried. Their security is tight and getting tighter."

"Doesn't Alphacorp have a claim on Crossways?"

"Theoretically." She frowned. "It's not enforceable."

"Might it be enforceable if they had help? Den of thieves. Should be cleared out for the good of everyone traveling the space lanes. Yadda, yadda . . . Scare tactics. Didn't Arquavisa lose two ships last month?"

"Probably in foldspace."

"Maybe to pirates? Wouldn't it be the duty of all the megacorporations to help eradicate piracy? It's time to take action against Crossways."

"You want us to take down an armed station of over a million people?"

"Not alone. It might take some careful planning, but it's time Alphacorp and the Trust recognized that they had a significant overlap of objectives. If we can bring in Arqua-

visa and Ramsay-Shorre so much the better. The others will
follow suit. We'll need the Monitors, of course. This has to
be a legally sanctioned intervention. Joint fleet and all that.
A million crooks inhabiting a haven for pirates. The galaxy
would be better off if Crossways disappeared completely."

She smiled. "And an attack on Crossways would force
them to pull back the fleet they have protecting Olyanda,
which we do have a legitimate claim on."

"Now you're thinking, Victoria."

"So we use the attack on Crossways as a feint and grab
Olyanda's platinum reserves?"

"Grab *our* platinum reserves," he said. "There may be a
cost in ships, but the gain would be incalculable." He raised
one eyebrow.

Tori LeBon smiled back.

Chapter Twenty-Nine

SECRETARY

"WE GO AFTER ARI'S SECRETARY." BEN SAT back in his new chair behind his new desk in his new office. The armchair was gone and it now looked less like a sickroom. "Secretaries always know more than the boss gives them credit for. That's why I don't have one. Besides, Wenna does all the hard work around here. She needs a flotilla of secretaries."

Cara recalled Ari's secretaries. He'd had two in the time she'd known him. Pete Gaffney had been efficient but impersonal. She'd never really got to know him and didn't even know where he'd gone when he'd moved on. Etta Langham had been much friendlier. They'd exchanged pleasantries a few times when Cara had been in the office between assignments. Etta had to have known about the relationship between her and Ari, but she was supremely incurious, at least to all outward appearances, a good attribute for someone running Ari's office.

Kitty had been in Ari's office more recently than Cara. Perhaps it was time to ask her to step up. She said as much to Ben and he agreed.

Cara's message brought Kitty to Ben's door in less than ten minutes. "You wanted me?"

Ben waved her in and Cara stood and indicated that

Kitty should sit. Looking a little nervous, Kitty did so. "If it's about the trips to the farm . . ."

Ben shook his head. "It's not about the farm. It's about Alphacorp. We need your help."

Something changed in Kitty's demeanor. Suddenly she was more guarded. She'd had a tough time with Ari, though . . . Hell, Cara shouldn't make excuses for her. Whatever tough time Kitty had had was nothing to what Cara herself had gone through. She'd cut the younger woman some slack because of their shared Ari experience and because of Wes. His loss had certainly hit Kitty hard, but they needed her now and there was no time to dance around her feelings.

It would have made sense for them both to sit down and compare notes, but Cara hadn't offered the details of her relationship with Ari to anyone and she didn't intend to start. She was comfortable with Ben now, and remembering Ari would only mess her up again. That was one of the reasons she'd been putting off confronting Donida McLellan. It was all part of the same tangled package.

She concentrated her Empathy on Kitty. Ronan had done a psych evaluation and cleared her, but Jussaro and Nine hadn't pinned down the leak yet. Cara had made a careless mistake when she'd dismissed her feelings about the false Mirakova before the attack in the warehouse. She needed to trust her instincts, not rationalize away her worries.

While Ben explained that they needed to get hold of Ari van Blaiden's secretary, Cara concentrated on Kitty.

"It's not Etta Langham now," Kitty said. "Etta left months ago. Ari's current secretary is Barb Rehling."

"Damn!" Cara said. "I remember her from the admin office. A bit of a martinet. Not Ari's type at all, but then Ari was always careful to keep his relationships with his secretaries strictly business."

"Barb by name, barbed by nature," Kitty said. "I think she liked me, though. She did try and warn me off Ari at first. I thought she was jealous, but then I figured that she was trying to be kind in her own way."

"Do you think you could arrange a meeting with her?" Ben said. "Outside of work, of course."

"We're actually going to Earth?"

"Unless you think you can get at Rehling any other way," Cara said. "Does she have an implant?"

"A receiving implant, but she's generally wearing a damper."

"So it would be better to talk to her face-to-face," Ben said. "If we can get you to York, do you think you can do that?"

"Maybe. It depends on what information they have about me. It's not like I'm officially off payroll, I probably just show up on the files as missing. Officially, I'm on detached duty seconded to Ari. Now that he's dead I don't know where that leaves me. I guess they have to give me time to find my way back before they suspend me." She flashed a rueful grin. "I wonder if they're still paying wages into my bank."

"We're going to have to go by a roundabout route to disguise our origins, and we'll need false IDs again," Ben said. "Let's see if Mother Ramona will oblige."

"Who's going?" Cara asked. "Do we need muscle?"

Ben shook his head. "You, me, and Kitty. Let's keep it small."

Cara let her attention drift back to Kitty, but whatever she'd caught before was well under control now.

◆   ◆   ◆

Three false identities, some cosmetic facial changes (temporary), and four hub hops later, Cara, Ben, and Kitty landed at Lakenheath, England's major spaceport, and caught the shuttle train to York, dressed as tourists for an English winter.

"Expect rain," Kitty had said, and Cara concurred. "Except in the old city, of course."

The old city of York was protected by a massive bubble dome, itself an ancient monument, a four-hundred-year-old structure protecting a museumized city stuck forever as it was in 2120 with its Roman remains, its medieval churches, including the magnificent but fragile Minster, buildings from the 1300s, the Georgian era, some Victoriana, and two beautifully preserved twenty-first century shopping streets between the River Ouse and the market. Such was the attraction that the still-functioning city employed thousands in the tourist industry, everything from street cleaners and gardeners to shop workers, catering, and hotel staff. The whole place was owned by the Old City of York, itself a small corporation. It advertised an authentic historical experience, which brought in tourists not only from around the world, but from all over the galaxy.

Cara's short hair was now sleek raven black and her skin color olive with almond eyes that made her look more Asian than Gen. Kitty had turned into a flaming redhead, with unruly hair framing pale skin and freckles. Ben's color had been deepened to a rich ebony from his normal mid-brown and his hair had been curled into a wild springy mass. There was yet another layer of names and backstory to memorize. Cara hoped she'd fixed it in her mind, but it would be so easy to slip into one of the previously learned personas. Luckily they slipped through immigration with no trouble, especially when they showed their reservations for one of the most expensive hotels in the country.

Mother Ramona, operating behind several layers of identity screening, had booked them two coveted rooms in the Royal York Hotel, restored to its Victorian glory, apart from the sanitary facilities and the connections to the globalweb. They changed from the shuttle to the local monorail at York's Hunslet interchange, with both Cara and Kitty keeping their heads down as an extra precaution. Anyone who knew them well might see through the cosmetic changes.

York and Old York were separated by barely twenty klicks in distance but five hundred years in time. York had been built over the ruins of what was once Leeds and had become one of Federal Europe's foremost cities. It was not only a banking and communications hub, but also a cultural marvel. It was the administrative center for Alphacorp's Special Operations and Colony Operations, separate from the main HQ in the Saharan Rainforest. It had its own shuttleport at Yeadon to the north of the city, linking it to the main intergalactic spaceport on the Moon.

Cara had once thought of the city as home. She'd lived in a small sub apartment sunk deep into the rock strata. Ari had owned an apartment in a center city high-rise as well as a garden house discreetly nestled into a gentle hillside between the old city and the new.

She wondered what had happened to Ari's homes. He had no relatives that she knew of who might inherit, but it was likely his estate would be tied up in litigation forever with the files that they'd released into the wild. Alphacorp's investigators might be all over his office, which was an added complication when it came to seeking out his secretary.

She said as much to Ben and Kitty while green fields flashed past their pod window.

"Let Kitty make the first contact," Ben said. "We'll worry about the rest if and when we have to."

"Do you entirely trust Kitty?" Cara asked when Kitty had made her way down the pod to the washroom.

"I have wondered about her," he admitted. "But her psych evaluation was clean despite her time with Ari."

"Cleaner than mine, I expect."

He reached for her hand. "Just for the record, I've always trusted you."

"I know. That's sometimes been a mistake. It might still be. Just because I think I've beaten Neural Readjustment doesn't mean I have. Donida McLellan was good at her job. There might still be things planted in my subconscious that I don't know about."

"If there are, I'm trusting that you'll let us help you deal with them."

She subsided into quiet contemplation of the scenery as Kitty returned. The shuttle to Old York terminated outside the dome and they had a choice of entering the city by steam train, open-topped omnibus, horse-drawn carriage, or on foot.

"It's not far to the hotel," Cara said. "Let's walk. I've been sitting on shuttles for far too long. Come on." She tugged Ben's hand. "I'll give you the guided tour."

And she did. They diverted to walk through the ruins of St. Mary's Abbey and its gardens, complete with mature specimen trees and the Roman remains of the Multiangular Tower, then, though it was out of their way, walked up to Bootham Bar, one of Old York's medieval gates, and from there to the magnificent Minster with its cool towering interior, fantastical stone carvings, and stained glass.

"I wish we had time to be real tourists," Kitty said as they cut down Stonegate and worked their way toward Lendal Bridge. "I should have taken the time to come here when I was transferred to York."

Cara looked at her sideways. There weren't many people who would ignore the opportunity to visit Old York if they lived and worked in such close proximity. Ari had been fascinated by it, even though the whole place had been turned into a giant museum. He'd brought her here on many of their early dates. Hadn't Kitty had the same treatment?

Their hotel was sumptuous, plushly decorated in keeping with its Victorian origins and offering every modern convenience neatly hidden behind a historical facade. The check-in was smooth and efficient. Yes, their reservation was in order, two rooms with garden views, all paid for.

Once in their room, at the head of an elegant sweep of staircase, Cara flopped down on the bed, so soft that she bounced, and stared at the ornate plasterwork ceiling.

"How come Kitty's never been here before?" she asked.

"At this price? Are you kidding?" Ben flicked on the entertainment center built into the wall. It was full of restored movies and TV shows from the twentieth and twenty-first centuries, some of them historical even when they were made.

"No, I don't mean the hotel, I mean Old York. If she'd been dragged into Ari's orbit she would have been here. He'd have taken her to the Café Concerto near the Minster and for a cruise along the river and possibly even to the Theatre Royal, or to Evensong at the Minster to hear the choral singing. There's something not adding up about her. Don't trust her, Ben. I didn't warn you about Mirakova when I had suspicions. I didn't mention what I thought about Crowder. I might be wrong about Kitty, but . . ."

Ben sat next to her, took her hand and kissed her fingers. "I hear you. We'll trust her only as far as we must to get at Ari's secretary. So far and no further until she's proved herself."

"Thank you."

Then anything else she might have said was forgotten as Ben stretched out beside her and she pulled him close.

✦ ✦ ✦

Kitty closed the hotel room door. Had she seemed so totally clueless about Old York? She should have taken time to do the tourist thing when she'd first been transferred to Ari's department, but she was too busy getting herself noticed.

Yes, he'd shown an interest in her, but it took more than being blonde and pretty to attract him. She'd had to work at it while letting him think that he was making the running. She'd only been included on the Olyanda trip at the last minute because she'd said she could fly a jumpship through the Folds. A slight exaggeration—she'd completed the theoretical training, but only on sims. Having tried to shadow Ben through the Folds she now knew that she'd have been completely overwhelmed. Ben's theft of the *Solar Wind* had done her a huge favor even before she knew of his existence.

She idly flicked through the entertainment channels on the screen, but her mind wasn't really on them. She had a dilemma. Alphacorp would love to get their hands on Ben and Cara. Kitty only had to send in a report and there would be a black ops team here to take them out within the hour. Did she want that?

Did it matter what she wanted? Akiko Yamada still had her mother secreted away at some resort, mounting up bills that she'd never be able to pay off. Unless Kitty continued to do as she was told her mother would be declared insolvent and shipped off to a labor compound for the rest of her days.

But Akiko Yamada had been Ari van Blaiden's lover. She had a share in all the nastiness he'd been involved in. A sleeping partner in all senses. Kitty shuddered. Had Yamada been involved in the disappearance of thirty thousand innocent settlers, too?

Remus was probably here on Earth. She was close enough to contact him herself rather than waiting for him to contact her. She'd managed to shut him out the last time he barged in on her thoughts, but he'd call again. If Kitty reported Cara and Ben to Alphacorp not only would it be the end for them, but it would end all hope of the missing settlers being found.

Whose side was she on?

Weighed against her mother's future were thirty thousand settlers. If there was even a chance of finding them she had to play her part and give Ben and Cara time. After that—well—she'd see.

First things first, contact van Blaiden's secretary.

She'd tried mind-to-mind and, as before, there was not a

glimmer of a reply, but Barb Rehling usually wore a damper, so that was no surprise.

Van Blaiden's office would no doubt be in upheaval. Maybe Barb was trying to hold everything together. Kitty attached a disruptor to the public comm link and deactivated the video so that no one could put a trace on the call or see her. Getting through to a secretary on a local line was usually pretty easy, but she hadn't figured in whatever internal chaos was going on.

"Mr. van Blaiden's office is closed," the receptionist at the other end informed her.

"Closed? What about Mr. van Blaiden's secretary?"

"Mr. van Blaiden's secretary passed away very recently after a short illness. I can put you through to the Internal Affairs team. Who's that calling, please?"

"It doesn't matter. Thanks for your time." Kitty cut off communications. Internal Affairs and Barb Rehling dead wasn't a good combination. The woman had looked well enough the last time Kitty had seen her. She wondered if the short illness was an allergy to a blade between the ribs.

What had happened to Ari's previous secretary? Etta Langham surely hadn't contracted the same short illness. Kitty needed to access Alphacorp's central files. She had clearance, but she couldn't do it without leaving an imprint. Would Ms. Yamada find out?

Oh, hell! Do it anyway.

✦ ✦ ✦

The lobby of the Royal York was dim enough for privacy, with chairs arranged, four at a time, around low tables on which rested reprints of newspapers from the nineteen hundreds to approximately 2030, when the last paper copies were printed.

Cara picked up one at random. It was from 1979, detailing the remains of a tenth-century Viking settlement discovered while digging the foundations for a shopping center. Tenth century, and still preserved fifteen hundred years later.

"Fascinating," she muttered to herself.

"What is?" Ben asked from behind his own newspaper.

"The layers of history preserved in this city. If I hadn't tested positive for psi I would have liked to study archaeol-

ogy. Did you know there are rock groupings on Aqua Neriffe that might indicate pre-colonial remains. Intelligent
aliens."

"Might."

She sighed. "Well, we have to start somewhere. Surely
humans aren't the only species in the galaxy."

"Ah, that's the big question, but it's not only if, it's when.
Maybe other species have already evolved to intelligence
and destroyed themselves again. We damn near did it with
catastrophic climate change in the twenty-first century and
the great meteor almost wiped us out a couple of hundred
years ago, at least on Earth. Who knows how many civiliza-
tions have risen and died. Maybe the next intelligent species is at this very moment dragging itself out of some
primeval methane swamp halfway across the galaxy and by
the time it's asking, 'Are we alone?' we'll be long gone."

"Maybe. Ah, here's Kitty."

Though there were only a few residents in the lobby and
no one seemed to be taking any interest in them, they immediately switched to silent communication.

Any luck? Ben asked.

Cara could see from Kitty's expression that the answer
was no.

There's already an investigation underway into Ari,
Kitty said. *Barb Rehling is dead.*

Cara was getting an odd feeling from Kitty. She glanced
up. *There's more.*

Kitty nodded and licked her lips. *I still have access to
records. I checked on Etta Langham.*

And?

She's been transferred to Sentier-4.

As an inmate or staff? Ben asked.

That's the big question, isn't it? Kitty kept her eyes
averted from Cara's gaze. *What do you think?*

A cold chill ran down Cara's back. The name Sentier-4
invoked dread. The neural readjustment facility was the
place of last resort for any errant Alphacorp psi-tech. Until
lately Donida McLellan had ruled supreme there. Cara had
escaped, thinking herself lucky to get out with her mind
intact, only to have the memories of what McLellan had
done to her surface later.

She pushed away the memory of McLellan's eyes, mad eyes, boring into her brain.

Breathe. Ben was holding her hand.

She breathed. *Sorry, was I that obvious?*

Only to me. You don't have to come.

You're actually going to Sentier-4? Cara asked.

Is there a choice?

She shook her head. *No, but . . . you'll never get in . . . unless.* Oh, shit! Part of her brain put together a plan while the other part was screaming.

We've got McLellan, she forced herself to say.

We have indeed, Ben said. *But you don't have to be involved in this.*

Yes, I do.

✦ ✦ ✦

Cara's guts lurched every time she thought about Sentier-4, but Etta Langham was there and she was the last potential link they had to the missing settlers.

Such a tenuous link, she told herself. *But the only one we've got,* the logical part of her mind answered.

"I need to talk to Jussaro," Cara said as they grabbed their bags and headed for the checkout desk. "He has a lot more experience than I do. He'll know what's possible, and he's been imprisoned in Sentier-4 himself."

"Can we trust Jussaro?" Ben asked.

"Now that he's free of Crowder, I think we can trust him implicitly. Ronan agrees."

"I'll take your word on it."

Cara waited until they'd cleared the city and the three of them were seated in the pod on the way back to the transport hub at Hunslet before she reached for Jussaro, mind-to-mind.

Sentier-4! You think you can do it? Jussaro's interest was plain. Not only interest, but excitement. *I'm coming with you.*

What? No, that's not why I called you.

Don't deny me this, Carlinni. That place is a resource beyond imagination.

It's dangerous, she said. *Possibly the most dangerous place in the universe for people like me and you. McLellan's *out of action, but we don't know who else they've got in there. Maybe someone as bad as McLellan. Maybe someone worse.*

And what about the prisoners?

We're only concerned with Etta Langham right now. We don't have the resources ...

We'll make the resources. If there are broken psi-techs in there we need to get them out. Mend them.

Cara glanced at Ben, who shook his head. *It's going to be dangerous enough, Jussaro,* she said. *There's no way we can guarantee getting anyone else out.* She could taste his disappointment. *All I need to know from you is whether it's possible to get inside McLellan's head. Make her appear to be her old self, if only for long enough to get us into the place and give us access to Etta.*

You want to take over what's left of her mind? Animate her?

Is it possible?

It's not impossible. I could do it—I think.

But could I do it? Cara asked.

You've got too much history with McLellan. He didn't say: you might kill her, but he meant it.

"I don't like it," Ben said when he realized what Cara's idea entailed.

"Me neither, but can you think of a better way?"

"Not without Tengue's mercs mounting a full-scale raid."

"Well then ..." Cara tried to ignore her belly doing backflips and schooled her face into a semblance of calm. "I'll contact Ronan, shall I?"

Ben scowled, but he didn't say no. She was surprised, however, when Ronan was dead set against it.

You can't, Ronan said when Cara contacted him.

Can't? Cara asked. She could sense that she'd caught him at the wrong time and off guard. *Sorry, Ronan. Is there a better time to contact you? We need to discuss this rationally.*

It doesn't matter how rational you want me to be, there's a line I can't cross. Donida McLellan is technically my patient. Whatever she's done in the past, she's currently completely helpless and harmless. You want to get inside her head, wear her like a skin, use her as a meat puppet. How would you like it if she'd done that to you when you were helpless?

She might have, for all I know.

That's beside the point.

Ronan, you know what she did to me.

I do, and that's precisely why you shouldn't try this with her. It's not only McLellan, Cara. You're my patient, too. Neither of you is going to come out of this well.

"Let me speak to him," Ben said.

Cara backed out of the conversation and left Ben and Ronan to it.

What if it wasn't Cara? Ben asked. *Jussaro could do it.*

My initial objection still stands. The ethics are—

Gray at best. I understand, but Sentier-4 is like a fortress and there's an innocent woman in there. Etta Langham was van Blaiden's secretary. She's not in Sentier-4 for the good of her health, probably just the opposite. And we have thirty thousand settlers to find.

So the end justifies the means?

I understand your concerns, but in this case I think it does.

Cara knew that the settlers had clinched it.

✦ ✦ ✦

Kitty felt awash with guilt. She could have found out about Barb Rehling and Etta Langham from the safety of her room on Crossways, but she'd never have been able to explain away her access to Alphacorp's central files. At least the trip to York had covered up where the information came from. Dammit, she could possibly flash her Alphacorp ID and walk into Sentier-4 any time she liked, but if she did that she'd definitely be switching sides, and there would be no going back from that. What would happen to her mother then?

Much as she hoped Ben and Cara could find the settlers and deliver them safely to Jamundi, she couldn't bring herself to sacrifice her mother's security to make life easy for them.

There was a chance they could pull this off without blowing her cover, so she had to let them take it. She could turn a blind eye for a few days, but she couldn't be a part of the operation. One camera in the wrong place and there would be tough questions to answer.

She'd answered honestly when Ben had asked what she

knew about Sentier-4. She'd never been there and said as much.

"You don't want anything to do with this, do you?" Ben asked her as their shuttle sped south from Hunslet toward Lakenheath.

"Is it that obvious?"

"I don't blame you. When we meet up with *Solar Wind* at the Dromgoole Hub, you head back to Crossways by the same route we came. No sense in putting you in danger, too."

"I hope you find Etta."

"Thanks."

And she did, but not enough to put her mother on the line to help them achieve it.

Chapter Thirty

SENTIER-4

BEN FIGURED IT WAS THE WORST PLAN ANY-one had ever come up with, but without bringing a private army in to do a full-scale raid, it was the only option they had.

By the time they caught the commercial flight from Lakenheath to Dromgoole Hub, and he and Cara watched Kitty head for the next flight, the *Solar Wind* had docked in the adjacent terminal, this time disguised as a private yacht belonging to a pan-African billionaire with interests all over the galaxy.

Ben had been tempted to ask Mother Ramona to supply an ident code for Malusi Duma. Now that he knew who his grandfather was he itched to meet the man, but it was a bad time to piss off a long-lost family member. One day, he promised himself. One day he would look up his grandfather.

They made their way to the private dock. *Solar Wind*'s ramp dropped for long enough to take them on board and then rose behind them again. Within minutes they were disengaging from the dockside and nudging out into space under Gen's steady hand.

"Hold on to your hats," Gen warned, and then eased into foldspace and almost immediately out again before Ben had had time to more than clutch the arm of the copilot's seat he was strapped into.

"Where are we?" Cara asked.

"Nowhere, or as good as," Gen said.

Ben nodded. "Fourteen light-years from the nearest inhabited system. As good a place to hang out as any."

"Permission to enter the flight deck, Captain?" Max hovered in the entrance tube.

"Yes." Gen and Ben spoke together, looked at each other and shrugged.

"Is this where we're supposed to say: Let's get this show on the road?" Max asked. "Because I am so not feeling optimistic about this."

"Why did you come, then?" Cara asked.

"Until you find yourself a new pilot with clearance to fly this ship in and out of the Folds, you're calling on my sweetie and our unborn child to carry you into ever-riskier endeavors. She's not going without me. And besides, you might need a Finder. Jussaro says I'm training up nicely." He flopped down into the spare bucket seat. "Ronan's in sick bay with Mrs. McLellan. He's still not happy with all this, but he says you can go down whenever Cara's ready."

Ben glanced at Cara. Was it his imagination or was she paler than usual?

Ronan wasn't happy with the plan.

Cara wasn't happy with the plan.

He wasn't happy with the plan.

Oh, yes, this was going to be great.

❖ ❖ ❖

Cara's insides churned.

Ben asked again. "Are you sure about this?" It must have been the tenth time. In truth, she wasn't, but it had to be done sooner or later. As they approached sick bay the corridor seemed to get longer, or she was slowing down, and then, with a rush they were in front of the door. Ben waved his hand across the panel and the door whooshed open.

Cara paused on the threshold.

Donida McLellan sat in a float chair, Ronan half in front of her as if protecting her. Maybe he was.

She's back on Olyanda. Harsh sunlight slants down onto

*the temporary town they've all taken to calling Landing.
Ari's mercs are standing around watchfully, all armed. Her
memory doesn't acknowledge the fact that those same mercs
have since become friends. Ari and Donida McLellan are a
safe distance away, but McLellan is hovering on the edge of
Cara's mind. Cara knows what she's supposed to do. It's
Ari's special treat for her, make her kill her lover and one of
her best friends. Her body's moving while her mind is
screaming. No!*

*Ben and Ronan have been forced to their knees in the
open space in front of the saucer-shaped landing vehicle and
she's standing behind them with a knife. It's a good knife, a
killing knife. She can see Ben's blistered flesh beneath the
burn across his buddysuit shoulder. Ronan must have done
a good job because Ben's awake, upright, and holding in his
pain.*

*"How are you?" Ben asks her as though they've met
during a walk in the park on a spring morning.*

*"I'm fine, now," she murmurs, not daring to risk mind-to-
mind contact. Donida McLellan is too close. "How are you?"*

*"I've been better." Despite everything, his voice carries an
implicit smile that's just for her. "But I'll hold together for a
while longer."*

*She raises the knife, holding it lightly in her right hand.
"I'm supposed to use this."*

"I know. Do it quickly if you're going to."

**Finish him!* Donida McLellan is in her mind again.
Cara feels her grip on the knife tighten, and she takes a pace
forward involuntarily.*

*She glances back to Ari and McLellan. McLellan has one
hand out. Ari's supporting her.*

So McLellan isn't invincible after all.

*A light switches on in Cara's head. McLellan has taught
her some hard lessons, but she's always been a good student.*

*She turns back to Ben. He looks at her over his shoulder.
She feels energy flow, feels Ronan in the mix. She seizes Mc-
Lellan's last thought and turns it back toward her. McLellan
drops to her knees, scrabbling at Ari's arm. He steps back,
shaking her off like a street beggar, his face a mask of surprise and revulsion. She doesn't even look human anymore.*

Cara took a deep breath. "Don't worry, Ronan, I'm not

going to kill her, though there are times when I've dreamed of it."

"I'm sure you have. You understand why it's a bad idea?"

"Killing someone?"

"Killing her. Specifically, you killing her."

"Because she'd be dead and we wouldn't be able to use her?"

"Apart from the obvious."

"Because it would hurt her more than it would hurt me?" She kept her voice flippant, but something cold had lodged itself in her throat.

"Try that the other way around."

She swallowed. "I've killed with my mind. I'm already a monster, but I'm a monster that's not going to let anyone hurt me again."

It was the first time she'd said it out loud. She heard Ben draw breath behind her.

"That was an accident," Ronan said quietly. "You only intended—"

"To knock him out, I know."

"Cara," Ben said softly. "You probably saved everyone. It gave me the chance to get a weapon, evened up the odds a bit. Don't beat yourself up over it. It's not who you are."

"It's what I can do."

"It's not all you can do." Ben moved up close.

She nodded—an acknowledgment of sorts—and turned toward McLellan, her heart skipping a beat as she noticed something close to recognition in McLellan's eyes. It was gone as soon as she spotted it, but it made her gut flip over one more time.

"You're sure she's completely out of it, Ronan?" she asked.,

"If there's anything of McLellan left in there it's buried so deep I can't find it."

"Okay." She held on to Ben for support and reached for McLellan's mind.

The next thing she knew she was on the floor and Ben was on his knees next to her, his voice full of concern. "Cara. Cara!"

"Mm . . . All right. All ri . . . What just happened?"

"You tell me."

She squinted up at him, then at Ronan, who was just

fixing McLellan's safety restraints on the float chair so he could leave her for a moment. She couldn't have been out long.

Ronan knelt too, and together he and Ben eased Cara upright. Her knees felt like jelly, and she was grateful to be able to sit on the end of Ronan's exam table. She held out her hands. They were shaking.

"Let's go over it," Ronan said. "You tried to make a connection—and then what?"

"I thought she was fighting me."

Ronan shook his head. "I don't see how she could be. Maybe it's your own hangups. She screwed you over pretty well, got inside your head, messed with your memories. There's residual McLellan in your own head. Perhaps—"

"Yes, that must be it. Give me a minute and I'll try again."

"Take as long as you want."

Was it just Cara's imagination that told her McLellan sniggered?

She took several deep breaths and centered herself. "All right. Take two."

She thought of Donida McLellan as she had first seen her on Sentier-4 when Cara had been completely at her mercy. She walked ramrod stiff, never smiled, cocked her head slightly to the right when listening intently, had a voice that was hard and crisp—imperious. She expected to be obeyed.

And her mind . . . Cara was usually trying to avoid close contact with her mind, but McLellan had been too strong for her. Cara, on reisercaine, couldn't resist.

Well, she wasn't on reisercaine now.

She reached for McLellan's mind again.

Ben caught her as she teetered sideways. "That's enough, Cara. It was an idea worth trying but it's not working."

"No, I can do it."

The bitch was fighting her. Whether it was McLellan herself, or the echo of McLellan in her own mind, there was only one way to do this.

She didn't give herself the opportunity to wimp out. She reached again, this time pushed past any resistance and she was in.

The world slipped sideways, suddenly she was looking at

herself, propped up between Ben and Ronan, eyes glazed. "Is that me?" Her voice sounded sharp to her own ears. "I look like hell."

She tried to stand, but the safety straps on her float chair kept her seated.

"Cara!" Ben was caught between her body and her consciousness, not knowing which one to take more notice of. She wanted to giggle, but McLellan would never giggle. She sat up straight. Held her head just so. "I can do this," she said. "Let's go."

✦   ✦   ✦

Ben shook with relief when Gen brought *Solar Wind* in to land on the pad carved out of compacted ice. The creature in foldspace had come too close for comfort, ever more curious and demanding of his attention. *Soon,* he'd promised it. *We'll talk soon.* But he was lying. Did it know?

He'd barely even noticed Gen giving their ship ID—forged again—to Sentier-4's traffic control, and informing them that Mrs. McLellan was coming home.

He took a few deep breaths—*Pull yourself together, Benjamin!*—and nodded an acknowledgment to Gen. "Once we're in the tunnel, pull up the ramp and don't open it again for anyone except us."

"I know the routine."

"Good."

"Boss—"

Ben turned.

"Don't let anything happen to Max. I'm not ready to be a widow yet."

He wanted to reassure her that it wasn't going to be dangerous, but the platitudes dried in his throat. "I'll do my very best."

"You always do."

The first thing he saw at the top of the ramp was Mrs. McLellan, upright, walking and talking, but it was Cara who looked out at him through her eyes. Cara's body, dressed in nothing but a soft-suit, was slumped in the float chair, eyes glazed, drool glistening on the corner of her mouth. Ronan tightened the safety straps and wrapped a foil blanket around her. It was twenty below out there, a serene summer day on Sentier-4.

"She can't manage to operate both bodies at once," Ronan said. "If you want McLellan walking and talking this is the best we can do."

Ben nodded. Cara in a float chair. Oh, yes, this was going to be great.

Sentier-4 was little more than a rock, just on the far edge of the habitable zone of its star. The atmosphere, while not actively poisonous, was thin and unsustaining and all the surface water was frozen at the poles. The desolate South Pole was where Alphacorp had chosen to build its Neural Readjustment facility, a cube of Brutalist architecture on the surface with many levels carved into the rock beneath. Life on Sentier-4, such as it was, was confined to a few single-celled microorganisms and the inmates of the cube.

"How are you doing, Cara?" Ronan asked.

"All right for now." Cara answered through McLellan's mouth. "Not sure how long I can keep it up. Let's get in and out as quickly as we can."

"I'm not intending to hang about." Ben pulled on his helmet and snapped on the heads-up display. "Ready?"

"Ready." Ronan followed suit.

"Wait a min—oh, got it," Max said. "Whoa, this is neat."

Ben tapped the back of Max's helmet sharply. "Don't step out of line. Gen will roast me if anything happens to you."

"As if—"

Ben tapped again.

"Yes, Boss."

"Good man."

Breath puffing out in clouds from below the unsealed helms, they exited the *Solar Wind* and crossed a few hundred meters of ice to a lonely entrance built of gray block and sprinkled with diamond-bright crystals, the closest this planet got to precipitation.

McLellan, dressed in the buddysuit she'd been wearing on the day Cara had downed her on Olyanda, walked smartly, hands gripping the handles of the float chair, cheeks glowing pink with the unaccustomed cold.

"Mrs. McLellan, it's really you!" A man waited for them in the shelter of the entrance. Ben wasn't sure whether he was happy to see her or not.

"Of course it's me." Cara/McLellan pushed the chair

past him. "Get out of the way, man. It's cold enough to freeze the balls off a baboon."

"Yes, ma'am." He saluted smartly and stepped sideways.

The float chair, and McLellan's feet, coped with the stairs and Cara/McLellan didn't turn around until they were all on level ground again in a gray-walled access tunnel where a car and driver waited with a trailer attached behind.

"I'll take the prisoner, ma'am, if you want to sit up front with Cameron." The man reached for the float chair handles, but Cara/McLellan snatched the chair back, causing it to wobble alarmingly.

"I'll decide where I sit. Ms. Carlinni is my special guest and I will see to her personally. You sit up front. I'm sure Cameron won't mind, will you, Cameron?"

"Uh, no, ma'am."

Ben and Ronan maneuvered the float chair and McLellan into the trailer, while Max slid into the car. The tunnel lights flashed past overhead as they rolled steadily forward. Ben had already estimated the distance at about two klicks, but at their steady speed the journey took a little over six minutes. They could almost run it as fast if they had to make a hasty retreat—though maybe not with a float chair, McLellan, and a secretary who may well be doped up to the eyeballs. And not in this thin atmosphere, though those of them in buddysuits had five minutes of emergency oxygen.

The car slowed down and Ben noticed the telltales of the security system: camera eyes, gas grids, panels behind which would be ordnance. He'd installed similar in the barbican entrance of Blue Seven. The tunnel was a killing ground.

The entrance to the facility was through an air lock, and they all took grateful breaths of recycled air as the inner door opened. There was a welcoming committee, though they didn't look so welcoming.

"Mrs. McLellan, good of you to join us." The man in the middle spoke up. "I'm Robinson Gorse, your replacement."

❖ ❖ ❖

Cara was almost at the end of her strength. Holding on to what was left of Donida McLellan's brain was like trying to steer a very large codfish by its tail, not that she'd ever tried that. She was dimly aware of her own body shivering in the cold, gasping in the thin atmosphere, trundling along on the trailer. Then she gagged on the sudden rush of warmth and air as her float chair was propelled into the reception hall.

She held Mrs. McLellan's body stiffly upright and even made her nose curl into a sneer at her replacement. Was she supposed to know Robinson Gorse? Hide behind formality. Hope for the best.

She'd been nervous of being face-to-face with McLellan again, now she was looking out from that face, wearing it like a glove—a meat puppet—that's what Ronan had said. So strange.

Even while she was trying to work out what to say next she remembered being dragged along a corridor very like this one on her way to an isolation cell. She felt a surge of satisfaction from McLellan. No, it wasn't real, it was just a shadow of her personality hanging around in Cara's own head.

"Gorse, this is nonsense. I have work to do." Cara tried to get McLellan to push the float chair past Gorse, completely ignoring the six people flanking him with weapons. They weren't going anywhere. "I see we need to talk."

"We certainly do. You were reported missing, presumed killed in action, along with Ari van Blaiden."

"A slight exaggeration—about me, anyway. Mr. van Blaiden, sadly, is no more, and neither is Mr. Craike, though I suspect few will weep for him. In the meantime I've been undercover."

"Undercover?" Gorse sounded skeptical.

"You are aware, of course, that the Trust has . . . issues . . . with some of its former employees and"—she slapped the chair handle—"this one of ours."

"I'd heard."

"I was sent to bring them into the Alphacorp fold under an amnesty. They have valuable information about the Trust's activities on Olyanda."

"That's been all over the S-LOGs," he said.

"Not all of it. Nowhere near all of it. Let me introduce you to Commander Reska Benjamin."

Cara managed to turn McLellan's body to wave flamboyantly. Ben removed his helm. She sensed his surprise, but blessedly he wasn't actively trying to kill her for her betrayal. She caught his glance and then turned and tried to hold Ronan's gaze through the helm. She didn't know how sharp Gorse's guards were. They could all be Psi-1 Telepaths. She tried to put her feelings up front. Ronan was an Empath. Come on, man, get it.

Exhausted. Not going to last much longer.

"And who are the other two?" Gorse asked.

"Ah, if I told you that I'd have to shoot you, or they would," Cara/McLellan said. "Need-to-know only. I hope you understand."

Ronan saluted by tapping one finger on his helm. Max just stood there but thankfully said nothing. In that outfit even Max looked intimidating, so his stillness worked for him, not against him. Outwardly his posture said: I don't need to acknowledge you. Inwardly he was probably shaking like a jelly.

"Sorry to take you by surprise, gentlemen," Ben cut in smoothly. "Mrs. McLellan is a very persuasive advocate for Alphacorp's hospitality. I'm here under an offer of a truce, and with information as to the whereabouts of a large haul of platinum. I need to speak with Etta Langham, van Blaiden's former secretary."

McLellan's right knee buckled suddenly and Cara had her grab the float chair to steady herself. Ronan stepped in to stabilize it and put his hand on her shoulder. She felt a surge of energy, which she drew on gratefully.

There wasn't time to say anything else. Gorse was leading off down the corridor and everyone had fallen into step. What had Ben been saying? Something about information from Ari's former secretary. Yes, get Etta Langham into an interview room and her job was over. Ben, Ronan, and Max could take it from there.

She manipulated McLellan's body into a shambling walk, but McLellan tripped over her own feet.

Ronan grabbed McLellan by the elbow. "Are you all right, Mrs. McLellan?" he asked, then turned to Gorse. "She's done everything Alphacorp has asked, but she's not been well, Mr. Gorse. If there's an interview room on hand where we could ask Miss Langham a few questions, that would be a big help."

"This is all very irregular."

"But necessary," Cara said out of McLellan's mouth. "Platinum makes allies where it must."

Gorse nodded and snapped out a few orders, dispatching two of the guards. They followed him to a gray door in a gray corridor, which he unlocked with his palm print. The four remaining guards split up, two stayed outside the door and two followed them in. Inside there was a table and a row of chairs along the wall. Cara lowered McLellan's body into the nearest one, trying to keep her posture upright. Once McLellan was sitting, the talking was easier.

So far, so good.

Do you really think you can get away with this? McLellan said straight into Cara's mind. *You've brought me back home. Now suffer the consequences.*

❖ ❖ ❖

Cara gasped and opened her eyes. She was back in her own body and strapped into the float chair. *Ben!*

She saw Ben's expression change as he realized that McLellan was in her own body.

That was the point at which it might all have fallen apart, but Cara surged back into McLellan's mind, finding her very much at home. Had she been there all along, waiting her chance, or was it reconnecting with Cara that had brought about such a rapid return?

Stay down! Cara brought pressure to bear, trying not to overdo it. She wanted McLellan's compliance, she didn't want her to drop down dead, at least not before Gorse had produced Etta Langham.

She felt McLellan's surprise as she retreated before Cara's onslaught. Her body shuddered all over and drew the attention of both guards.

She held out a hand, palm outward. "No need for concern."

Cara concentrated on keeping McLellan still and trying to look as though she was completely in charge of the situation. It took longer than expected to retrieve Etta Langham from her cell, though, and Cara felt every second of it as she squashed McLellan's personality down.

The two who delivered Etta were orderlies, not guards, both female, physically strong, one tall and black, the other rounder, shorter, and brown. Tough, the pair of them, but not armed, at least not with conventional weapons, though they probably both had anesthetic blast packs on hand.

Cara suspected they'd tried to clean Etta up, but they hadn't done a very good job. Her gray hair was matted into clumps and there was a trace of something on her chin, food or vomit. She was wearing the kind of trilene prison one-piece that Cara remembered so well. It still had creases where it had been folded in the packet, so they'd probably just put it on her.

She didn't look capable of putting it on herself.

Cara felt a thump of disappointment in her belly. Had they come all this way and taken all these risks for nothing? Was this another dead end? Etta had been such a cheerful, lively woman with a ready smile. She'd been motherly and round, but the weight had dropped off her and the flesh around her jowls had loosened and sagged.

Cara glanced at Ben and could see he was thinking the same thing. Etta's thousand-meter stare wasn't a good sign. The smaller orderly pulled a chair from the row and sat Etta next to the table. Etta stared at her hands resting limply on her knees. The back of Cara's neck crawled. Is this what she'd been like when she was in here?

"What have you done to her?" Cara asked through Mc-Lellan's mouth.

"What have we done?" Gorse asked and looked to the orderlies.

"She's just as you left her, Mrs. McLellan," the taller one said. "We continued the medication as ordered. Mr. Gorse—"

"There hasn't been time for a full review, yet. I've only been here four days," Gorse said, walking over to a screen on the wall and pulling up a file. "Ah, I see. One of your little projects, Mrs. McLellan. There have been a few irregularities."

"No irregularities, only necessities." Cara tried to snap out the words, but she felt McLellan resisting her and she hesitated.

Cara's body, in the float chair, was breathing heavily. She was going to crash any minute. Cara perched McLellan on a chair and thrust herself deeper into the woman's mind.

Did things look different? Same gray-walled room, same

chairs. Gorse, two guards, two orderlies, Max and Ronan anonymously helmeted. Ben standing close enough to Gorse to take him out if necessary.

She even recognized one of the orderlies—no, wait a minute, she, Cara, didn't.

But Mrs. McLellan did.

Oh, fuck!

Chapter Thirty-One

THE LEAD

DID YOU THINK YOU COULD GET RID OF ME so easily?

Cara separated her consciousness from her former tormentor and sat bolt upright in her float chair.

Donida McLellan stood under her own steam and turned to Cara. *It's way past time for you and I to have a little conversation, head-to-head.*

Had they played right into McLellan's hands after all?

Cara's heart tried to pound its way out of her chest and her mind spun. All the abuse that she thought she'd begun to leave behind flooded back, spiky as an ice pick to the brain.

This place.

This woman.

She'd never be able to leave it all behind.

"Cara!" Ben's voice snapped like a gunshot. It jerked her to her senses.

Then several things happened at once.

Cara slapped the fast-release and dived sideways out of the float chair, drawing the attention of the two guards.

Etta Langham shot forward, grabbed a sidearm from the nearest guard's holster while his back was turned, leveled it at McLellan and screamed, "You bitch!"

There was a loud crack. Blood sprayed. McLellan flew backward into the wall, sending her chair flying. She collapsed in an undignified heap, headshot.

Etta tried to turn the gun on herself, but Max flung his arms around her and barreled her to the floor.

Ben smacked his elbow into Gorse's temple, putting him out with one blow, then he swung toward the nearest guard who was only just releasing his sidearm from his holster and tackled him to the ground.

Ronan ran to McLellan at the same time as the taller of the two orderlies.

Max, slow off the mark, got with the program. Without releasing Etta he swung his foot into the remaining guard, knocking him off balance. Max grabbed the gun Etta had used, but wisely did nothing with it except snap on the safety. In such a confined space he'd be more likely to hit someone on his own side if he tried to use it.

Without even stopping to consider, Cara grabbed the consciousness of the guard Max had tripped and squeezed, trying oh-so-carefully not to apply too much pressure.

The smaller orderly reached for Etta with a blastpack in her hand and smacked it onto the side of her neck.

Cara moved then and grabbed the orderly by one hand, twisting it behind her back. She reached into the woman's pocket, found another blast pack and knocked her out, letting her down gently as her knees buckled.

Ronan and the tall orderly worked on McLellan, oblivious to all the mayhem happening around them. By the time they sat back on their heels everything was over.

"She's dead," Ronan said. There was anger bubbling under the tone of his voice.

"It was her," Cara said, voice shaking. "Really her. At the end. She was still in there, biding her time. Waiting for a chance."

Ben cursed. "Are you all right?" He didn't take his eyes off Gorse and the guard who was still conscious, but he had them both on the wrong end of a gun.

"Yes." Cara was surprised to find that she was. McLellan had been the monster in her closet for so long and now it was finished.

Max rolled over, stood up, and dusted off his pants. "Now what?" he asked.

The tall orderly shuffled back from McLellan's corpse, both hands in the air. "I'll just stay over here, out of the way, shall I?"

"Now we go," Ben said. "But not the way we got in." *Gen, are you ready? Punch us a new door.*

Sure, Boss. Where are you?

Below ground level.

Stand by.

"What's above the main entrance on the ground level?" Ben asked.

"Canteen," the orderly said.

Knock first, Gen, Ben said.

I will.

There was a whoomp as something punched against the exterior wall somewhere above their heads.

"Blast packs." Ronan held his hand out and the orderly put three packs into it from her own pocket. "Sorry about this. Thanks for your help."

He slapped a pack to the side of her neck and she went limp and flopped over. Then one for the conscious guard and one for Gorse, who was moaning and shaking his head. Everyone who needed to be was out cold.

"Can you walk?" Ben asked Cara.

"Do I have a choice?"

Together they lifted the unconscious Etta into the float chair and strapped her in.

Another whoomp from upstairs. Yelling, screaming, and the clatter of running feet announced their new doorway. It would be leaking good air into the thin atmosphere, which would give them an edge. Ben pulled up his breathing tube and pointedly slapped Max's arm.

"Breather."

"Oh, right." Max engaged the breathing tube on his own suit.

Cara wrenched the one from McLellan's suit, but it was smashed and bloody. She hurled it away in disgust. Etta didn't have one either. Never mind, the atmosphere wouldn't kill them, not between here and *Solar Wind*.

Ben opened the door cautiously. Dust and debris showed him the direction of the stairs. They ran for it, pushing the float chair along into the chaos of people running for safety. They pushed against the tide. Nobody even questioned them as they clambered across rubble into the canteen where steam from dinner formed a fog as two air fronts met in a mini weather system. Hot and steamy. Icy and dry.

Solar Wind, her atmosphere wings extended to full, rolled closer on her antigravs, ramp lowering as they scrambled through the breach in the wall and ran across the ice. Within six strides Cara was gasping for air.

Someone in the building woke up and a hail of hard-case bullets followed them.

Solar Wind fired a warning shot from her pulse-cannon and crumbled a crater out of the upper wall without actually punching through. The gunfire stopped. Ronan and Max each grabbed one of Cara's arms and practically lifted her flailing feet off the floor. Ben shoved the float chair and ran, half-turning to cover their getaway with pistol fire barely aimed.

Go! Ben snapped as the ramp rose under their feet. Cara staggered and grabbed onto a handhold as *Solar Wind* levitated and shot forward.

She coughed. "Does that count as a win?"

"Maybe." Ben headed for the flight deck. "Unless your name is McLellan. Let's not celebrate too soon until we see what Ronan can do with Etta Langham."

✦ ✦ ✦

Ronan refused point-blank to let them see Etta.

"She's traumatized," he said on the second day, having installed her in the newly furnished medical center deep in the heart of Blue Seven. "Both by what happened to her and by what she did. On top of that she's suffering the aftereffects of a particularly nasty cocktail of psychotropic drugs designed to destabilize her memory. She doesn't know what's real and what's not. She can barely remember who she is."

Ben was grateful Ronan hadn't said I-told-you-so about McLellan. No one could have predicted Etta's reaction, but even so, they had taken a vulnerable woman into a dangerous situation. That they had rescued Etta, whose trauma was all from McLellan in the first place, was just another twist in the ethics of the situation, as was the fact that McLellan had not been as damaged as they had all believed.

He wasn't sorry that McLellan was dead.

He didn't think Cara was sorry either, though she hadn't said anything beyond, "I'm all right, now," since they'd arrived back from Sentier-4.

"Etta's memory," Ben asked. "Will it return?"

Ronan shook his head.

"Is that a no?"

"I don't know."

"Are you sure she is what she appears to be?" Cara asked. "I mean, after McLellan . . . Etta's been in Sentier-4 long enough for . . ." She waved expressively. "Changes to be made."

"I'm as sure as I can be that Etta's no ticking time bomb," Ronan said. "I can't blame you for asking, but Ari sent her there to make sure she wasn't going to pass on any of his information."

"I'm surprised they didn't just have her killed," Ben said. "Though sooner or later someone would notice the high mortality rate among Ari's secretaries."

Ronan nodded. "Better to have her harmlessly released back into the world with a pension. If McLellan hadn't been caught up in Ari's demise, they might have finished the job before we found her. She'd be a little old lady in a fluffy jumper with a neat little apartment, a couple of cats, and only a very vague memory of her former boss."

Ben had to be satisfied with that. He left Etta entirely to Ronan's care, tending instead to the everyday demands of running the Free Company, sharing Nan's daily reports with Mother Ramona and Garrick, and keeping count of the number of incidents reported involving unrest between the megacorps and their colonies.

Dissatisfaction was contagious. Cotille had been the first, but in the last week alone fifteen colonies had declared independence. Three of them had sent delegations to Crossways and a further six had formed an alliance of their own. It didn't take much to drive a wedge between those exploited and those exploiting.

On the morning of the eighth day after leaving Sentier-4, Ronan announced, *You can see Etta now, but don't expect miracles.*

Just me? Ben asked.

And Cara. Etta might remember her.

Etta was fully dressed in a violet shirt that brought out the paleness of her blue eyes. Her dove-gray hair had been trimmed and washed and her cheeks had begun to fill out, though her expression still looked haunted. She sat in an armchair between her rumpled bed and a screen showing a landscape of rippling barley framed by trees rustling in a light breeze.

She looked up as they came in and smiled at Ronan.

"Here are the visitors I promised you, Etta. Remember, we talked about it."

"I know you." Etta looked up.

"I'm Cara."

"Not you. You." She looked at Ben. "I've seen you before."

"Have you?"

"He said you cost him."

"Cost who?"

"You brought them home."

"Is it Hera-3 she's talking about?" Ben asked Ronan.

"Could be, couldn't it?"

"I don't think she was Ari's secretary at the time of Hera-3," Cara said. "That was Pete Gaffney."

"Gaffney," Etta said. "What happened to him? I should have known better. Secretaries. Such a fast turnover. I know you, too." She looked at Cara. "He's bad for you. Don't get involved. It won't end well. Pretty things. They come and go."

"He's dead." Cara reached forward and held Etta's hand. "Ari's dead. He can't hurt me any more. He can't hurt you any more."

"He was so sweet. He brought me flowers. It always starts with flowers. He sent you flowers. I made sure they got there on time. Always use the best florist. Did you give her flowers?" She looked at Ben.

"No, he's never given me flowers." Cara dropped her voice and leaned in conspiratorially. "I don't think he knows about flowers."

Etta giggled.

Ben opened his eyes wide. "Should I have given her flowers?"

"It's traditional," Etta said.

"I'll remember that for future reference."

"You see that you do, young man."

"Etta, do you remember when you were working for Ari, for Mr. van Blaiden?" Cara asked.

"I should have known, shouldn't I?"

"He wasn't a very nice man."

"He bought me flowers."

"Did he take calls from Gabrius Crowder? Do you remember the name? Crowder."

"The elephant man. I remember the elephant man. Very sad story. Very old book. True, though. People didn't understand."

"What?" Ben asked.

"A man called Joseph Merrick, back in the 1900s," Ronan said. "He had a deformity that resulted in elephantine growths all over his body."

"No, she's talking about Crowder," Cara said. "When I first saw him he reminded me of an elephant: the size of him and his ill-fitting skin with a grayish cast to it. He looked like a pachyderm."

"You saw it, too," Etta said. She leaned over and patted Cara's hand. "He wasn't a very nice man either."

"Did Mr. Crowder ask Mr. van Blaiden to find a home for some settlers?"

Etta's eyes clouded over. "I used to live in a very nice apartment. There was a park opposite. It had a statue of the Black Prince. From before. Very old."

"Settlers, Etta," Ben said. "Do you remember the settlers? Where did they go to? What did Mr. van Blaiden do with them?"

Etta just shook her head, wrapped her arms around herself and began to rock back and forth.

"I think that's enough for today," Ronan said. "You can come again tomorrow, but I don't know how much good it will do. Half the things she says appear to be nonsense, but they mean something to her."

As they turned to go, Etta stopped rocking. "An ark ship shouldn't be piloted by a freelancer, not alone. He told me not to worry. He was sending someone to get Jake Lowenbrun, the best in the business. Best at what, that's what I want to know."

"Jake Lowenbrun? Is that who piloted the ark with the settlers, Etta?"

But Etta had gone back to rocking.

◆ ◆ ◆

Chenon's predominantly pink native foliage blended effort-lessly with green Earth imports. It was false spring and the long day was just beginning. Earthy aromas with a faint tang of spices rose from the dewy grass. Crowder paused to stare at an agglamentia, but though his gaze rested on its perfect bell-like flower, his mind was far away. Coming back to himself, he bent and plucked the tender stem, pink sap staining his fingers. He'd never had the time to appreciate his garden before. Not that this was his garden, but it was a garden in a very nice suburb of the city, surrounding one of the Trust's safe houses. The guard posts were subtly dis-guised, but Tori LeBon had authorized a small army to keep him safe round the clock. He had full connectivity to his network, a personal Telepath on the premises, and Stefan flitting back and forth each day.

Things were going to plan. Tori had engaged two of the younger Board members to put forward Crowder's plan as their own, and John Hunt himself had come down in favor with his deciding vote when the Board had been divided. He would have never done that on principle if he'd known whose plan it was.

If the plan worked, then Crowder would reveal himself as its instigator and Hunt would be left with egg on his face. If it failed, then Hunt would still suffer.

Perfect.

Taking down Crossways would be a massive undertaking requiring a huge fleet and careful negotiation with the FPA and the other megacorporations. Earth didn't keep a stand-ing fleet of any great size. The FPA relied on levies from the colonies and the spacefaring corporations, each providing according to their resources. Crowder had hoped for actual support from the FPA in terms of ships, but when ap-proached, both Vetta Babajack, Europe's First Minister, and Malusi Duma, the pan-African president, vetoed any mili-tary support. Now the best they could hope for was an agreement not to interfere. Disappointing, but Crowder was confident they could still achieve their objective as long as the FPA wasn't in active opposition.

Meanwhile John Hunt was busy in the United States of Canada, deep in talks with the Monitor Council at their

Calgary headquarters. Composed of the eight sector com-
missioners and Sebastian Rodriguez, the Chief Commis-
sioner, the Council was responsible for the fair allocation of
policing resources across the galaxy. No single organization
could hope to cover the vast distances involved, so the
Monitors, thinly spread, also worked closely with the
megacorps' private police forces and planetary legal systems.

Ben had been on duty out on the Rim when he'd been in
the Monitors. Crowder knew all the details. In the early
days, before Hera-3, before Olyanda, they'd been close.
He'd begun to think Ben might be someone he could trust
with some of those delicate matters that cropped up from
time to time that were not strictly legal, but Crowder soon
came to realize that Ben's rule-bending had its limits. Ben
hammered the rules into his own shape to force the letter
of the law to conform to the spirit. No one sensible ever
expected the law to be fair, but Ben had risked his career
more than once to try and make it so.

If Ben had disappointed Crowder with his unsuitability
for somewhat shady jobs, he'd unwittingly made Crowder
aware of his ex-boss, Sergei Alexandrov, who would take
any shady job offered as long as it paid enough.

Crowder smiled. Sergei had proved very adaptable.

✦ ✦ ✦

The last time Remus had called, Kitty had told him she was
sick and had been in bed for three days. Lying mind-to-
mind was one of the most difficult things any Telepath could
do. The only way around it was to tell the truth, just not the
whole truth. She was genuinely sick, thanks to taking an
emetic. She'd given Remus a genuine wave of nausea, not
without a ripple of satisfaction for all the times he'd barged
into her mind without so much as a by-your-leave. Imperious bastard! Take that!

If she could give Benjamin a chance to find the missing
settlers she would. Unfortunately Akiko Yamada had other
ideas.

So, today, Kitty was sitting in the Ocean coffee shop with
Arran Syke, whom she'd become rather fond of despite his
social stiffness and somewhat stern appearance. He wasn't
easy to talk to like Wes had been, but she'd gradually come

to appreciate his dry sense of humor. He reminded her of Wes. They'd started meeting at lunchtime whenever his duty allowed it, at first in a group, but now just the two of them.

Kitty had begun to admit to herself that she was comfortable on Crossways, that she'd miss it when Alphacorp called her home. She'd even begun to wonder whether she wanted to go home. If it hadn't been for her mother . . .

She'd never been in this position before, but she knew that deep cover invariably meant a false life with false friends. One that would eventually have to be abandoned.

She'd almost coaxed a laugh out of Syke when a stabbing intrusion caused her to falter and drop her half-empty coffee cup back onto the table with a clatter.

It took a few moments for her to realize that Syke was asking her if she was all right.

Not now, you'll blow my cover, she managed to say to Remus, who had broken into her thoughts like a hammer blow.

"Yes, I'm fine. I just caught the end of a transmission that wasn't meant for me. It surprised me, that's all."

You're well now? Remus asked.

Better, but nothing to report.

A station of a million people and nothing to report?

"Sometimes I think I'm missing out not having an implant," Arran said. "Other times I realize that they're more trouble than they're worth."

She forced a weak smile and aimed a thought at Remus. *Back off. I'm having coffee with the head of Garrick's guard. Call me in two hours.* She slammed down her shield.

Syke tapped the earpiece that all Garrick's guards wore. "This works well enough for me on-station, and who do I know from away?"

"Well, there's me," she said. "I'm not always on-station and it would be nice to keep in touch."

"Yes, it would." He actually smiled. Was that a first?

Two hours later, Kitty locked herself in the tiny room she'd been allocated in Blue Seven. She'd only slept in it a couple of times. Mostly she went back to Wes' spindle apartment—she still thought of it as Wes'—where she felt she could be herself. This room was barely bigger than an onboard cabin on a utilitarian transport, but it did have a bed, a chair, a table, and a narrow window onto what would become a garden when it was finished. She'd wheedled a garden view not because she liked flowers, although she did, but because directly across the garden was the Benjamins' window, somewhat bigger than hers and with a garden door.

Your two hours are up. Remus again. *Ms. Yamada wants to know why she didn't receive advance warning of the raid on Sentier-4.*

I can't tell you what I don't know. That wasn't a lie, not exactly.

They took Etta Langham. What do they want her for?

Benjamin thinks she might know what happened to the missing ark.

And does she?

She's a mess. They won't get any sensible information from her. Sentier-4 broke her completely.

Better not to take any risks. Your orders are to end her.

Kill Langham?

Do you have a problem with that?

I'm not an assassin.

You're whatever Alphacorp needs you to be.

Kitty sat down on the edge of her bed and stared out at the mess that would become the garden. She'd like to be a gardener.

Kill Etta Langham.

Or maybe she'd like to go to work full time on the community farm.

Kill Etta Langham.

Or she could see if they needed help at the Ocean coffee shop.

Anything except be an Alphacorp operative with a kill order.

Etta Langham today. Cara and Ben tomorrow.

✦ ✦ ✦

Cara was worried about Ben. His personal battle with fold-space was weighing him down. He needed to face up to it or admit that he was never going to fly a ship through the Folds again. Until he found his own solution he was putting that part of his life on hold, but it was eating at him.

"We need to see Mother Ramona if we want to find Lowenbrun," Ben said. "High-grade freelance pilot-

Navigators are pretty rare, and it would take a Psi-3 at least to fly a ship the size of an ark through foldspace."

"Or into foldspace and lose it forever," Cara said quietly.

"We'll deal with that possibility when we get there. If we get there." His mouth was set in a grim line.

They collected muscle from Gwala, who was on duty in the guard post.

"Hilde, is that you?" Cara asked the bucket-helmed guard.

"How'd you know?" Hilde's voice held amusement.

"Because try as you might, you don't walk like a man, and that's not an insult." Cara laughed. "Do you mind doing a routine run to the hub?"

"I'm up for it if it gives me an hour away from this big lug . . ." She jerked her head at Gwala. "He only wants to talk about the grapple league and who's going to win the series. As if I care."

"Only because your team got knocked out in the first round," Gwala said without rancor.

She checked her sidearm, tapped her helm in a half salute that was more a friendly *up yours* than a *yes, sir*, and called up one of the private tubs in the new siding.

Traffic was light. They reached the Mansion House and Hilde settled into the tub to wait for them. Mother Ramona was in Garrick's office. Garrick wasn't in evidence, but there were now extra desks, a receptionist, and a staff of ten. Cara supposed that he needed to increase his staff as Crossways' interests expanded to take more planets into the Protectorate.

"Garrick's inspecting the troops," Mother Ramona said, inviting them into her own inner sanctum.

"Troops?" Cara asked.

"We have eleven colonies to protect now, plus Olyanda. We need something to protect them with—ships, pilots, hardware. The station is well armed and we have our hornets and drones, but not enough of them to send them out to patrol settlements. We need skiffs, cruisers, battlewagons."

"And you need them with fast-response, jumpship capability," Ben said. Cara could hear the wariness in his voice.

"Yes, we do," Mother Ramona said. "Being able to get ships from one place to another in the blink of an eye cuts down on the size of fleet required and eliminates our reli-

ance on potentially antagonistic jump gates owned by the
megacorps. How's the research and development coming
along?"

"Dido Kennedy has adapted a jump drive, but it's
platinum-hungry. Yan Gwenn says she's ready to retrofit it
for field testing soon. She says she can put any size of ship
into foldspace with the right pilot and enough platinum."

"So we need a test pilot."

"I'm not the right person—"

"Then find me someone who is."

Cara watched Ben's expression. She was a Telepath and
an Empath, but even so there were times when Ben's shielding was so good she didn't have a clue what he was thinking
or feeling.

He nodded. "I believe I have a way to find potential
jumpship pilots. In the meantime I need a favor—some research. You have a lot of contacts. I need to know where a
freelancer called Jake Lowenbrun hangs out between jobs.
He's got to be a Psi-3 Navigator or above and not too particular about who he works for."

"You've got a lead on the settlers' ark?" Mother Ramona turned to her screen. "I'll check it out."

A short while later she looked up. "Interesting."

"What's interesting?" Cara asked.

"Vraxos seems to be the most likely place."

"Vraxos?"

"Jake Lowenbrun calls it home when he's not working.
Montego is the main spaceport. There are a couple of bars
where freelancers hang out along Sunshine Strip. You'll
need to watch your back."

"We always do, these days," Ben said.

"There's a man called Solpek who acts as an unofficial
agent for freelance flight crews. Word is that he can be
bought for the right price, allocates crew for jobs according
to sexual favors or how much they're willing to tip him over
and above his fifteen percent, and he gets tough with anyone, crew or hirer, who tries to cut him out of a deal."

"Pleasant individual, then," Cara said.

"Not very, but if you want a cover you can do some re-
cruiting for Crossways while you're there. See if he's got any
jumpship pilots available."

"When do we go?" Cara asked as they rejoined Hilde in the tub-cab.

"As soon as we can," Ben said. "Within the hour if Gen can get herself ready."

"You can't keep using Gen to pilot for you. She's twenty-five weeks pregnant."

"I know."

"When are you—"

"I don't know." The muscle in his jaw twitched. "When I'm ready."

She nodded, tight-lipped. His talk with a void dragon was way overdue and the longer he left it, the worse it would be.

✦ ✦ ✦

Report!

Remus again. His intrusions were getting painful. Luckily, this time Kitty was on her own, kneeling over a new raised bed filled with compost, smoothing it and firming it down with her hands, getting honest dirt under her fingernails.

Etta Langham.

She's under close watch, Kitty said.

You have orders.

She's weak. The situation might resolve itself.

See that it does.

Kitty opened the seed packet. Poppies, fast growing. They'd continue flowering for months and self-seed, providing a riot of color from the palest moon-yellow through oranges to fire-red. The seeds were mixed, from simple, single-headed cornfield poppies of Earth to the heavy-headed double varieties cultivated in the glasshouses of Kemp's World, which were every shade from white to deep damson.

Etta Langham had been kind to her. If the woman had any chance of recovery after what had been done to her on Sentier-4, she should be allowed it. Besides, Ben and Cara had taken off this morning in *Solar Wind* with Gen. They hadn't told her where they were going, but they'd taken Hilde and Gwala, and that meant business. It seemed likely that they'd still be hanging around if they were waiting for Etta to produce some useful information.

So either Etta had told them something, in which case killing her was pointless, or they'd decided she wasn't going to, in which case killing her was equally pointless.

And it was just plain wrong.

But orders were orders.

She tried to weigh Etta's life against her mother's future security.

Chapter Thirty-Two

VRAXOS

BEN RELAYED BASIC INFORMATION ACROSS *Solar Wind*'s screens. Vraxos was a mining planet in the Straw Bear System affiliated with Dominion, a subsidiary of the Arquavisa Corporation. Copper, iron, and tin were its main exports, in addition to a small but significant amount of platinum—significant enough that the spaceport had a high-security freight section.

Montego and its hinterlands suffered from a hot and humid climate except when the monsoon hit, and then it was slightly cooler but miserably wet. According to the data the worst health hazard was a particularly nasty fungal infection, though one of the main causes of death, statistically, was accidental. Mining was still a dangerous business.

Gen settled *Solar Wind*, carrying false ID as *Cruel Sister*, into a berth on the edge of the spaceport on the south side of Montego.

"Stay with her, Gen," Ben said.

"Oh, don't worry, I'm not intending to go anywhere." Gen patted her belly. "Bump and I are happy with the quiet life for a change."

"Ronan said I wasn't to let her out of my sight," Jon Moon said from systems.

"Funny, he said the same to me about you," Gen said.

They left a crew of five to guard the ship. Ben, Cara, Hilde, and Gwala, dressed for business in anonymous flight suits, paused at the top of the ramp. Humidity hit them like a hammer, a soggy, wet, warm hammer.

"It's like breathing soup," Cara said.

"Cabbage soup," Hilde said. "What's that smell?"

The smell, a cross between rotting vegetables and a laundry, lingered all the way through the main terminal, but at least the air conditioning inside the building took care of the humidity. They exited through a wide, low-ceilinged foyer dominated by a bronze sculpture representing, according to its plaque, *Everyminer*, a muscular, androgynous figure wearing a hard hat and sleeveless vest top perched on the back of a vast trepanner with a series of spiral drill bits sporting cog-like teeth. Vraxos was either very proud of its mining industry or it was trying to prove something to new arrivals.

They took a shuttle pod into the town. First stop: Sunshine Strip, a long street, lit even in the daytime. A heavy cloud layer held in the humidity and filtered out the light. It probably didn't get any better than this.

"Hey, Manny, remember that summer we did on Vortigern?" Hilde asked.

Not many people, even in Tengue's tight-knit bunch, got to call Emmanuel Gwala "Manny." These two must have worked together for a long time.

"I remember the leech-alikes. What were those things called?"

She pulled a face. "Quillias. Nasty things. Was it hotter than this?"

"Hotter than hell, not sure it was hotter than this, though. Sure wish we hadn't decided on coveralls instead of buddy-suits."

They sauntered down the strip, checking the bars whose names Mother Ramona had given them. Trojan Solpek worked out of a bar called Rangoon. Midstrip was the best address they had, so despite the heat, they trudged past a few run-down stores selling everything from clothing to antifungal powder, past restaurants that made the pot stall outside Dido Kennedy's place look like high cuisine, and from bar to bar, some advertising liquor—get drunk for under five credits, dead drunk for under ten—some selling sex as well.

"Ladies, we got the best boys in town," one pimp called from the open doorway of the Mother's Ruin. "Money back if you're not completely satisfied, at least twice." She laughed. "And something for the gentlemen, too. Got a herm who specializes in couples."

"Maybe another time," Ben called out. "Looking for Solpek."

"Flyers." The smile left her face, but she didn't quite spit on the ground. "Other side of the street. Keep walking, 'bout ten minutes."

"Thank you, lovely lady." Gwala gave her a low sweeping bow. "Maybe we'll return when we're in funds."

"Go on with you." She half-smiled. "And watch out for Solpek's cat. Evil beast."

They found Rangoon as directed, an unprepossessing frontage leading to a dingy interior populated by a few knots of people at tables, men and women of all ages, sizes, colors, some drinking, some eating. One table of four was deep into a board game of some kind. The miasma of cabbage and laundry was overlaid in here with beer and something spicy.

"Cinnamon." Cara inhaled. "That's more like it." She elbowed her way to the bar between two lone drinkers who looked to have planted themselves permanently. "Four cinnabeers," she said, tossing a credit chip onto the counter.

"Coming up." The bar man took her chip. "You want change or are you starting a tab?"

"Start a tab. Why not? Looking for Solpek."

"Should have known you was flight crew when you ordered cinnabeer."

"Yeah. Dead giveaway." Cara passed full glasses back to the others. Cinnabeer had a fiery kick without being alcoholic or intoxicating. "Solpek?"

"'Tween you and me, ain't no one been hiring for the last month. Solpek's over there, in the corner."

"Might be able to change his luck," Ben said.

"You hiring?" The drinker on Cara's right, an androgynous individual, suddenly took notice.

"Could be. Depends."

"You know the rules," the bar man said, waving at Solpek. "Do it right."

"Yeah, I know, only I don't pay the little shit more than his fifteen percent, so I never get the best jobs."

"Well, that should tell you something, Esterhazy." They hadn't even seen Solpek move, but suddenly there he was, his hand descending on the out-of-work flyer's shoulder.

"Yeah, it tells me I never should have broken my contract with Eastin-Heigle."

"Navigator as well as pilot?" Ben asked.

Esterhazy straightened up and nodded.

"Recognize this?" Ben held out his handpad and Dido Kennedy's drawing sprang into being as a hologram.

Esterhazy's eyes widened. "Jesus! It's even got the beard talons. How'd you get that?"

Ben smiled. "I think you might have just secured yourself a job, through Mr. Solpek of course."

"Yeah, of course."

"Why do you think Eastin-Heigle let Esterhazy go so easy?" Solpek scowled, and Esterhazy seemed to shrink back under the man's disapproval. Then Solpek said, "Come into my office. I've got better."

"I'll be the judge of that," Ben said. "I'm looking for very special qualities."

Solpek's office turned out to be the back room of the bar, sparsely furnished with a single table, a few chairs, and a cat. A very big cat, its back as tall as the table, a riotous mix of tiger stripes on its flanks, leopard spots on its face and neck, and everywhere else filled in with brindle. Its ears were tufted like a lynx, and when it saw them it showed sharp fangs in a silent snarl.

"Don't mind Liana. She doesn't bite unless I tell her to."

"Right." Gwala moved away to the other side of the room, as if the caged window gave him an emergency exit.

"Oh, she's gorgeous." Hilde knelt in front of the cat and bowed her head, carefully avoiding eye contact. The cat responded by sniffing delicately at Hilde's hair and then bumping heads. Hilde raised her head to look at the cat and scratched behind the tufted ears. Liana began to purr loudly.

"How'd you do that?" Solpek said. "It took me weeks to get to that stage."

"She's a Gollerian. Grew up with them." Hilde sat on one of the available chairs and Liana immediately tried to climb into her lap, but settled for draping her front half across Hilde's knees while Hilde stroked the creature's short, sleek fur.

"So . . ." Solpek sat back on one side of the desk and gestured to the remaining chairs. "Are you buying or selling."

"Buying very selectively," Ben said. "Pilot-Navigators, but I want to interview each one of them personally. Temporary short-term contracts to start off with. Could be long-term if they shape up."

"How many do you need?"

"How many have you got?"

"In port now?"

"Right now."

"Maybe thirty. Thirty-five tops when word gets around there's a buyer in town. And a pair who work together, she's a Nav, he's a pilot, but they work in tandem."

"How do you get so many nonaligned psi-techs gathered in one place?" Cara asked.

"Well, aren't you the curious one?" Solpek's snarl matched his cat's, but the Gollerian was currently far too interested in Hilde to bother with anyone else, including Solpek.

"It's a fair question," Ben said. "If we hire any of your people, we need to know they don't have some angry megacorp on their tail. Fair enough?"

Solpek nodded. "Mining transportation company based here went bust. Spectacularly. Sold off the ships, left the pilots behind. Now they freelance. Once you get a rep for supplying good flyers, no questions asked, other freelancers gravitate in. They all have a slightly different story, but it all points to slipping through the corporate net for one reason or another."

"So none of them are likely to be traced by their implants?" Cara asked.

"On my honor."

Cara's glance told Ben that she didn't think Solpek's honor was worth much, but Mother Ramona's people could check the backstory of any of the pilots they hired when they got them back to Crossways. They already planned to check Esterhazy's status with Eastin-Heigle.

"Got a list of who's available?"

"Might have. How much are you paying?"

"A thousand a month, all found."

"Signing bonus?"

Ben sighed as if to indicate this was stretching his budget, but knew this was what furnished the signees with enough to pay Solpek's commission. It was customary to pay him fifteen percent of the first two months' wages in advance.

"Three hundred, tops."

"How about—"

"A thousand a month and a three hundred signing bonus. Don't carp. I'll take all thirty-five if they fit the bill." He knew very few of them would. "Show me the list."

❖ ❖ ❖

Is Lowenbrun on the list? Cara asked.

Don't see him, Ben said. *Maybe he's not here. Maybe he's still en route to somewhere with the ark and the settlers are safe.*

Or maybe Ari had him killed. One less loose end.

One more dead end if he did. Ben sounded glum.

They were running out of options.

One by one Solpek's potential recruits came into the office, presented their credentials, answered Ben's questions and looked at the image of the void dragon. Of the first ten, no one recognized it and all were turned down with the offer of a beer on the tab for the trouble of applying. Then two women, Chilaili and Tama Magena, obviously sisters, recognized the image and were quickly signed up. The androgynous Esterhazy was next, and then a string of rejections.

The couple Solpek had mentioned, Alia and Grigor Kazan, were in their thirties. Alia was tall, black, and handsome. Grigor was short with a pale complexion that spoke of someone who'd spent a lot of his life in space.

"He's the pilot, I'm the Navigator," Alia said.

"Combat experience?" Ben asked.

"Some," Grigor said. "On the wrong side in the Burnish Rebellion."

"You fought for the Burnish?"

He shook his head. "No, I fought against them. We won, but it was the wrong side."

Ben nodded. "I was out on the Rim myself at that time. Monitors."

"You were in the middle of it, stuck between two sides. Bad deal."

"Yes." Ben didn't elaborate, but Cara remembered Mother Ramona's story of Ben and the Burnish refugees.

"Yeah, I've seen him." Alia gazed at the image that Ben showed her. "Hard to miss."

"Not for everyone."

"That's true. Grigor never sees him. I've seen him maybe twice."

"Job's yours if you want it."

"We have to bring our children."

Ben shook his head. "Too dangerous."

"Not on flights, but we have to have a home base."

"We can provide that."

"Where do we sign?"

While Ben interviewed the last half dozen candidates, Cara excused herself and went out into the bar. The three Ben had taken on sat together in a corner. The Kazans joined them. Cara wandered over and ordered another round of cinnabeers.

"So what's the job entail?" Esterhazy asked.

"You didn't want to know that before you took the contract?"

"A job's a job."

"Anything to get off this rock," one of the Magena sisters said.

"Jumpships, fast response."

Esterhazy whistled. "Never flown a jumpship before. Don't you need Psi-1 Navigators for that? I'm only a Psi-4."

"Your Psi grade isn't as important as the way you work in foldspace. You all recognized the image."

"What's that got to do with it?"

"It means there's a good chance we can train you to fly a jumpship."

"And what if we don't make the grade," Esterhazy asked.

"Crossways still has regular ships. You won't be out of work." She took a long pull of her cinnabeer, then put the glass down carefully on the table. "Heard there was a freelancer here called Lowenbrun. Jake Lowenbrun. Anyone know him?"

Esterhazy's head jerked up in surprise. The Magenas looked down at the table and said nothing. She knew she'd asked the wrong question.

"Gotta find a washroom." Alia Kazan stood up.

Cara recognized a signal when she saw it.

"Where are they?"

"Out this way, I'll show you."

Cara followed Alia through a door, down a corridor and into a washroom that had all the charm of a back alley.

"Lowenbrun," Alia said. "You don't want him. He's unreliable. Came back from his last job broken. Must have had a bad deal, a hard look into the Folds, maybe. Been hiding his head ever since. I wouldn't have known, but Vel, my youngest, saw him buying a crate of booze, the hard stuff. I guess he's gone off on one. Might come out of it, might not. You know what it's like for Navigators."

Cara did. Ben knew even better.

"Where can I find him?"

"Has a place on Lemont, out of town on Top Mine Highway, but you'll more than likely find him at Sally's. Cheapest joint in town and Sally's been soft on him for years. Always good for a pity fuck."

"Sally or Jake?"

"Either. Both."

"Thanks."

Alia looked around as if checking they were alone. "You're not the only one looking."

"For Lowenbrun?"

"Don't know what his last job was, don't want to know, but some hard-assed Monitor came sniffing around a couple of days ago."

"Monitor? Did he have a name?"

"Didn't stick around for a tea party. Tall chap, iron gray hair. Cold eyes. He's gone, now. Leastways I haven't seen him around, but he handed out a contact. Offered a reward. We cut him dead, but there are a few of Solpek's favored flyers who haven't gotten any work out of this. They may think again about trying to collect."

"Thanks, Alia." Cara turned to go.

"Not going after Jake, are you? I told you that so you'd leave him alone. We need this job. Ain't gonna get it if you're in jail."

"It won't come to that. Get everyone to the spaceport. Meet us in departures, on the concourse by the big statue."

"Departures. Right."

✦ ✦ ✦

You need to finish up business fast, Cara told Ben. *A Monitor's been here asking questions, looking for a freelance Navigator called Lowenbrun. He's offered a reward. Don't trust Solpek.*

No further than I can throw him.

Send Hilde out. I've got a lead.

Wait for me.

Might not be time. Doesn't sound like he'll be in much of a state to resist. We'll be at a joint called Sally's.

She met Hilde in the bar and jerked her head toward the door. "Going to get some air. Want a walk?"

"Sure."

As they left, Alia was gathering the flyers. There were two kids on the doorstep, one a boy of about eight and one a girl of maybe thirteen.

"You Alia's kids?" she asked them.

They nodded.

"Good, grab your stuff. Your folks have a job."

"We've always got our stuff." The little one patted a bag at his side.

"Good boy."

Cara looked up at the sky. Dirty gray clouds, rumpled like an unmade bed, rolled in from the north; beyond them, the dark underbelly of thunderheads, but here on Sunshine Strip it was still too hot to breathe.

The first cool blast, icy in comparison, hit them before they'd got halfway to Sally's. It was a relief after the heat and humidity, but by the third blast they were shivering.

"Think I'm going to regret trying to blend in," Hilde said. "Should have worn buddysuits. At least they're water-proof."

They picked up the pace, and as the first medallion-sized raindrops fell they sprinted for Sally's, obvious by the voluptuous girl on the sign flickering on and off haphazardly above the door.

"We're not taking on, ladies," an unexpectedly cultured voice said from the shadows. "And we don't keep boy whores on the premises. Try the Red Snake by the Belly-buster Diner."

"We're not looking for action," Cara said. "Looking for information. Jake Lowenbrun."

"Who? Never heard of him."

"Yeah, right, then why did I just hear footsteps running across the floor above?"

Hilde darted for the back door. Cara pushed Sally to one side and took the stairs two at a time. A man stumbled across the landing toward a narrow back stair, bottle in one hand, scrabbling at an empty leg holster with the other.

He didn't stand a chance against Hilde, who came up from below and took him with a shoulder to the gut. He went down like a sack of potatoes. The bottle flew out of his hand and smashed against the wall.

He groaned, whether from the pain in his gut or the loss of the bottle Cara couldn't tell. She bent over him, grimacing at the acrid stench of vomit and secondhand alcohol.

"Get away from him."

A sharp voice behind her made Cara pull back. She stood and turned. A young woman, hardly more than a girl, scantily dressed in a few wisps of silk, held Jake's missing pistol in a two-handed grip. Her hands were shaking so much it would be touch and go whether she hit Cara, Jake, Hilde, the ceiling, or herself on a ricochet.

"Back off or I'll shoot."

It was a projectile weapon, small caliber, potentially lethal. Cara's buddysuit would have protected her from anything except a lucky shot to face or hands, but this flight suit was no barrier at all to bullets.

Behind her, hidden from the girl's view, she heard Hilde's sidearm snick out of its holster. Hilde would shoot to kill if she had to.

Cara raised both hands so the girl could see she hadn't drawn a weapon. "No need for anyone to get hurt."

"Yeah? Tell that to Jake. C'mon, honey, this way." She encouraged Jake to his feet, but Hilde had whomped the breath out of him and though he tried to get to his knees he collapsed onto the floor again.

"Just need to ask your boyfriend a few questions," Cara said.

"He's my cousin, but ... family ... ya know?"

"You pulled clean-up duty, then?"

"He's not himself. Leave him alone."

"Maybe we can help." Cara pitched her voice into reasonable mode. "We're not from the Monitors."

"How do I know who you are?"

"Put the gun down, let's talk."

"Uh-uh." The girl shook her head.

Duck sideways, I'll take her as soon as you're clear, Hilde said.

She's only a kid.

A kid with a gun.

"You don't want to do this," Cara said to the girl.

"Oh yeah, I really do. You people have screwed him up enough already."

"Not us, we just want to talk to him." Cara tried to sound sincere, burying the thought that if Lowenbrun was responsible for firing thirty thousand settlers into a sun, or losing them in the Folds, it would be a short conversation and it would be unlikely to end well.

A shadow moved behind the girl.

Get ready, Cara told Hilde. *Going to drop to the right.*

Gotcha.

But the shadow wrapped itself around the girl. Sally turned her toward the wall. The gun cracked out and a chunk of wood flew out of the doorframe.

Ears still ringing, Cara darted forward and grabbed the gun from the girl's hands.

"Thanks," she said to Sally.

"I didn't do it for you. I know what a safety clicking off sounds like. Dree might have taken you if she'd been lucky, but your goon would have taken her out in a heartbeat."

"Yes, I would've," Hilde said, thumbing the safety back into place and reholstering her sidearm. "Glad I didn't have to, though."

Jake groaned again and Hilde hauled him into a sitting position by the scruff of his stained shirt.

"He in trouble?" Sally asked. "Monitors, and now you looking for him. Doesn't look good."

"How much do you know about his last job?"

"Nothing, 'cept he came back drunk and got drunker."

"You?" Cara asked the girl, who was now hugging her arms around herself and shivering.

"Said it was paying enough to set us both up, but wouldn't say what it was. Something about an insurance job.

That guy who came looking for him, though . . . Looked different in a Monitor uniform with a half-helm on, but I've got a thing for voices. Could swear it was the same guy who hired Jake in the first place, otherwise how would he have known to look here?"

"What are we going to do with him?" Hilde nudged Jake with her foot.

"Take him with us," Cara said, shooting a thought to Ben to tell him they'd need an escort with strong arms and weak noses.

"No, you can't!" Dree started forward, but Sally held her back.

"Is he mixed up in anything bad?" Sally asked.

"Could be. Less you know the better."

"He's not bad," Dree said.

"Then he's got nothing to worry about," Hilde said.

"And if he is?" Sally asked.

"What's he told you?"

She shrugged. "Nothing, like I said, but I've known Jake since he turned up here with Dree still young enough to need her nose wiping. I've never seen him this troubled, or this drunk. I'd have staked my life on him being a decent man. Maybe not law-abiding, but decent."

Neither Cara nor Hilde spoke.

"I see." Sally drew a deep breath.

Cara heard Gwala's voice downstairs. The big merc shouldered past Sally and hauled Lowenbrun to his feet.

"Where are you taking him? Can I come?" Dree asked.

"That would be mighty nice." Gwala flashed her a broad grin that took in her clothing and what was showing through it.

Cara cleared her throat meaningfully and Hilde managed a light slap around the back of Gwala's head.

"You'll be safer here," Cara said to the girl.

Sally cocked her head sideways, her voice resigned. "Whatever happens, don't leave us guessing."

Cara nodded once. "We won't."

◆ ◆ ◆

"Let's get him to the spaceport and away from here," Ben said, striding down the street through sheeting rain, which had already penetrated the shoulders of his flight suit. "The pilots are there already."

"How many did you get?" Cara asked.

"Just the four, counting the Kazan family as one. I'm going to need Gen to train them to handle a jump drive."

"No."

Lowenbrun, who'd shown little resistance up to then, tried to pull out of Gwala and Hilde's grasp. Gwala pulled his arms back and snapped a pair of ferraflex restraints around his wrists.

"Not going back!" Lowenbrun muttered. "Can't make me." He shook his head, spraying water from his hair.

Ben felt a pang of sympathy. He didn't want to go back into the Folds either. He clenched his jaw. Gen would handle the transit this time. All he had to do was to hang on for the few minutes it took to get through. Though a few minutes could seem like forever.

Lowenbrun found his feet along with his voice. Though he was a shambling mess he kept himself upright. "He made me. Bastard made me. Didn't want to. Bastard told me it was freight. Insurance job he said. But I know an ark ship when I see one. I know."

Ben's stomach roiled.

"What did you do?"

"Bastard told me it was freight."

"What did you do?"

"Insurance claim."

They were going around in circles. Ben needed Lowenbrun sober. Better get him aboard *Solar Wind* as quickly as possible.

As they boarded the shuttle for the spaceport Gwala took off the shackles so as not to attract undue attention. "Try and run and I'll take both your legs off at the knees," he said. "Understand?"

Lowenbrun nodded.

The public terminal handled barely a dozen passenger flights a day, mostly mining crews and their families coming and going. Though it wasn't large, it was bright and comfortable with a blast of cool, dry air meeting them in the entrance. Ben shivered and wiped rain from his face with the back of a hand.

The Magena sisters and Esterhazy stood by the statue of Everyminer with just a single bag each. The Kazan family was missing. He spotted them over by the restrooms, mum, dad, a teenage daughter, and a boy somewhere under ten, plus four big bags and a couple of transit crates. He waved for them to come over, but they didn't move.

Alia jerked her head to her left just once and that was all the warning they had. A phalanx of Monitors with automatic weapons and armored buddysuits complete with half-helms emerged from opposite sides of the concourse and arrayed themselves between the Navigators and the exit.

"Stand down, Benjamin, you're bound by law. Place all your weapons on the floor."

"Sergei, even with a mask on I'd recognize you anywhere."

The girl, Lowenbrun's cousin, thought she recognized the Monitor's voice, Cara said. *He was the one who hired Lowenbrun in the first place. There's something very odd going on. Your old friend is in it up to his neck.*

Why doesn't that surprise me?

"Weapons," Alexandrov said again.

"All right, Sergei, I get it. Weapons on the floor." Playing for time, Ben took his sidearm out of its holster slowly and carefully with finger and thumb and dropped it on the floor with a clatter, feeling the comfortable lump of the tiny derri still sitting in his thigh pocket.

"Parrimer blade, Benjamin. I've never known you not to carry one."

"And you know me so well, Sergei, almost as well as I know you. What's this about? You're here after Lowenbrun, aren't you? We're just a bonus you never expected. What have you been up to? What do you know about thirty thousand missing settlers?"

Ben noticed one of the helmeted Monitors glance toward Alexandrov.

"Is that you, Jess? Did Sergei take some personal time a couple of months back? He did, didn't he? Would that have been about the time an ark loaded with thirty thousand settlers in cryo went missing? Am I ringing any bells here? Come on, Jess, wake up. Why is he so keen to get Lowenbrun? Is there even a warrant out for him? He's cleaning up after himself."

Alexandrov raised his weapon, his finger tightening on the trigger. Ben flung himself sideways and grabbed his dropped gun.

Lowenbrun screeched, "You bastard," and ran at Alexandrov full tilt, arms outstretched.

Alexandrov's gun barked. Lowenbrun fell. Ben brought his own weapon up, fired and hit Alexandrov square under the jaw. The man's head snapped back, a ruin of blood and bone.

Everyone dived for cover as a volley of shots rang out.

Chapter Thirty-Three

VOID DRAGONS

AFTER THE FIRST FLURRY OF SHOTS, SCREAMS of bystanders and deafening cracks as energy bolts slammed into walls, there was a pause. Ben's ears rang. He blinked, realized he wasn't hurt and reached for Cara, who'd taken refuge behind Everyminer. All Ben had between him and the Monitors was a row of flimsy seats and someone's flight bag.

All right? he asked.

Yes. You?

So far.

She linked him to Gwala, Hilde, and the newly appointed pilots. Everyone had found shelter.

"Ben, hold your fire. Give yourself up. We've got you outnumbered." Jessop's voice cut through the shocked silence.

"Don't be too sure about that, Monitor man." Alia Kazan's voice carried across the concourse.

Over by the washrooms the Kazans had hunkered down behind their transit crates and three muzzles pointed over the top, directly at the Monitors.

"Jess, you don't want us," Ben shouted. "Think of the paperwork. I warned you about Alexandrov before. He had something to do with the disappearance of the ark, and I aim to find out what."

Lowenbrun groaned and rolled over. He was approximately halfway between Ben and Jessop, spattered in blood. How badly was he hurt? Ben needed whatever information he had. Lowenbrun was their last lead.

"Check your warrants," Ben called. "I'll bet you won't find one for Lowenbrun. You've been dragged here on false pretenses because Alexandrov wanted to shut him up."

"Check it." Jessop spoke to the man on his right. "Come talk to me, Ben. Just you and me."

Ben raised his head above the seat he was crouching behind.

Ben! Cara's alarm was sharp.

It's okay, Jessop's straight. I worked with him on the Rim. He's no Alexandrov.

Is that what I should carve on your tombstone?

But as Ben stood, so did Jessop. For a tense moment neither moved, but no one fired. Jess pulled off his half-helm and walked forward. They'd been the same age when they worked together, but grizzled hair and the lines on his face said he hadn't done any cryo. They met in the middle, by Lowenbrun.

"Good to see you again, Jess."

"I could have wished for better circumstances."

They shook hands.

Jessop glanced at Alexandrov. He didn't need a medic to certify death.

"Mind if I check Lowenbrun?" Ben asked and knelt by the fallen man.

"Go ahead. Did you have to kill my boss?"

"You tell me. You're my witness for the defense."

"Hell, Ben. You've put me in an awkward position. No one liked Alexandrov, but he was one of ours."

"He was bent. Taking bribes on the Rim years ago and working on the side for van Blaiden if what Lowenbrun said made sense."

Ben turned Lowenbrun over, relieved to see that the blood appeared to be Alexandrov's.

Jessop knelt too. "Pshaw! He stinks. You can have him. You're right. I checked. There's no warrant."

"Lowenbrun, where does it hurt?" Ben asked.

"My knee. I twisted it as I fell."

"You were lucky you did fall. Bloody idiot."

"Is he dead?"

"Alexandrov? Yes."

Lowenbrun screwed his eyes up and started to shake, weeping silently.

"What's going on, Ben?" Jessop sat back on his heels. "Make it quick." He glanced back at his men. "I can't keep them standing around all day."

"Short version? When we found platinum on Olyanda, Crowder tried to wipe out the colonists so the planet would revert to the Trust."

"Yeah, I saw the vid."

"Crowder and Ari van Blaiden were hand in glove. Not just Olyanda, Hera-3 before that."

"Alphacorp's saying van Blaiden acted on his own. Nothing to do with them. The Trust is saying the vid is a well-staged fake."

"Yeah, right."

Lowenbrun rolled over and sat up.

Ben steadied him. "Crowder got van Blaiden to get rid of the highly inconvenient second ark that was in transit to Olyanda, and unless I'm very much mistaken, van Blaiden subcontracted the job out to Alexandrov, and Alexandrov hired Lowenbrun for his Navigation skills." He took out the image of the void dragon. "Recognize this, Lowenbrun?"

"Shit! That's one of them."

"Give the man a gold star, he passed the test."

Jessop stared at the image, uncomprehending. "What's that got to do with—"

"Lowenbrun can pilot a jumpship. That right, Lowenbrun?"

"Yeah, but I'm not going to—ever again."

"Tell us what happened."

"That bastard hired me to pilot a ship through the Folds. I was supposed to lose the cargo. Insurance claim he said. Offered a small fortune. Seemed like a good deal. The pilots were supposed to be in on it, too.

"I didn't figure Alexandrov for a real Monitor, but he looked like a good fake. I thought he'd pass any inspection.

He did, of course. Nothing like disguising yourself as something you are. We boarded the ark at Dromgoole Hub under the pretense of a spot inspection. They took his flyer on board, no problem. I stayed hidden in the flyer while the ark transited into the Folds, then Alexandrov called me up to the flight deck.

"It was obvious right from the start the other pilots weren't in on it. Even more obvious when Alexandrov killed them. By that time I knew damn well what the cargo was. Cryo pods. People. I don't know how many."

"Thirty thousand," Ben said.

Lowenbrun closed his eyes. "Just kill me now."

"What happened?"

"We abandoned them. In the Folds." His voice broke. "I tried . . . No, I didn't try hard enough. I should have let Alexandrov shoot me right there. He wasn't a Navigator. I was the only one who could get us out. He'd have died in foldspace with the ship. He deserved that at least." Lowenbrun shook his head. "He forced me to fly him home, out of the Folds. I could have killed both of us. I should have, but I didn't. I didn't want to die. I slipped away at Rio Hub and hitched a ride on a freighter."

"And then you went back to where he found you? Smart move," Ben said.

"I was going to get Dree and run for the rim, but I lost it. Thirty thousand, you say?"

"Thirty thousand."

"I can't—" He smeared snot and tears across his face with the heel of his hand. "It's not just numbers, is it?"

"No, it's not."

"You want me to take him in?" Jess asked. "There may not be a warrant yet, but I can fix that."

Ben shook his head, a sick feeling in his gut. He didn't want to think about it, but it was the last chance the settlers had. "No. We're going back into the Folds to look for the ark."

"They're gone, Ben," Jess said. "No one has ever found a missing vessel in foldspace."

"No one ever had a void dragon before."

"Huh?"

"Long story. There are things in foldspace, Jess. Things

that are not supposed to be real, but they are. Those cryo pods are good for years. I'm not giving up on the settlers without one last try. I'll take Lowenbrun and a Finder."

"No. Nonononono." Lowenbrun began to shake his head.

"You don't have a choice." Ben gripped his shoulder. "Neither of us has a choice. Let's call it a chance for redemption."

"Get going, Ben," Jess said. "I can give you thirty minutes head start."

"What about them?" Ben nodded toward Jess' crew.

"They hated Alexandrov, but that doesn't mean they love you. I'll talk them around. But if you're not out of here in thirty minutes . . ."

"That's all we need. Thanks, Jess."

"Good luck."

✦ ✦ ✦

"Clean him up and find him some clothes." Ben shoved Lowenbrun up *Solar Wind*'s ramp behind the new pilots and handed him to Hilde and Gwala at the top. "I don't want to see him again until he's completely sober. I don't care how you do it, just don't kill him in the process."

"Leave him to us." Hilde pushed the unfortunate pilot toward sick bay. "You need any more information? I can work wonders with a stiff-bristled brush."

"Don't scare the man. The stiff-bristled brush was my fallback plan."

He heard Cara stifle a laugh behind him. "I take it that Jake Lowenbrun is not what you were expecting to find."

"I don't know what I was expecting. Certainly not a shootout with Alexandrov."

"Are you all right?"

"I'm not going to waste tears on Alexandrov, but . . ." He shrugged. "Killing someone . . . anyone . . . even a bastard like Alexandrov . . . does things to your insides."

"I know." She put one hand to his face and he leaned into it for a moment.

"Okay." He kissed her palm and took a deep breath as *Solar Wind* rose on her antigravs.

"Get into the mess," he told the pilots. "Strap in. We'll be entering foldspace from the upper atmosphere."

Gen, have you got this?
Got it, Boss. Crossways bound.

"Cara, stick with Gen and Jon Moon on the flight deck. As soon as we hit foldspace we're going to get a visit from a void dragon."

"You're so sure? Why?"

"Because there are seven people here who can see them, including Lowenbrun and Gen. The big guy won't miss an opportunity like this. It's curious. And I've got an overdue appointment. I've put it off for too long already."

"Are you going to face the dragon or face your own fears?"

"Both."

She frowned and nodded.

"Aren't you going to try and talk me out of it?"

She shook her head. "If I thought that was what you wanted, I would, but you don't. You don't have a death wish, have you?"

"No! Gods, no. This may sound weird because I know we're under stress about so many things, but I've got a lot to be thankful for right now: my family, the Free Company . . . and you."

"I'm hurt. Only third on your list?"

For a moment he thought she meant it until her mouth twitched, then she turned deadly serious. "Getting your mojo back is one thing, but you're not really intending to go hunting the missing ark in the Folds, are you?"

"I am."

"Last time . . ."

"That's why I need to make my peace with the void dragon. If I'm going to be any use as a Navigator and pilot I'm going to have to confront it, or at least confront my reaction to it."

She stared at him, her face not giving away her thoughts. "You don't have to do it alone. I'm staying with you. If I connect to you I may be able to anchor you in some kind of reality. I'm not losing you again."

His jaw started to move to say no, and then her words sank in. He held her hand and leaned forward to kiss her lightly on the cheek. "Thank you. I can't let this thing get between me and doing what needs doing. What use is a Navigator who's too scared to fly the Folds?"

"You're not just a Navigator, you know."

She was going to give him the self-worth lecture. He'd had it before, from Nan, from Jussaro, and much as he appreciated her efforts, now was not the time.

"I know, but being a Navigator is an important part of who I am and I don't intend to let it slip away."

She gave him a sharp nod.

"We need to keep the heat off Gen. Let's invite the void dragon to join us all in the mess."

✦ ✦ ✦

Cara looked at the five Navigators strapped to the benches against the walls of the mess—Ben, Alia Kazan with Grigor next to her, the Magena sisters, and Esterhazy, who'd identified as gender neutral and had requested the pronoun "it."

The Magenas—Chilaili and Tama—were somewhere between forty and fifty, both Amerind and close enough in looks to be identical twins, though Chilaili cut her hair very short and Tama wore hers in a long braid. The Kazans were polar opposites. Grigor was short, skinny, Caucasian, and probably not as old as his balding head made him look. Alia was statuesque and black, in her mid-thirties with wiry hair pulled back into a tight knot.

Cara gave each one a mental handshake.

The door clicked open and the Kazan kids peered in, the girl almost as pale as her dad and the boy deep brown. Alia waved them over and they strapped in between their parents.

Ben frowned, but Alia shrugged. "Nothing they haven't seen before."

"Your kids have seen void dragons?" Cara asked. "They haven't even tested for implants yet."

"It doesn't seem to matter about the implant," Alia said. "Either you see them or you don't. Must run in the family. Reckon they both have Navigator potential if they find someone to sponsor their implant."

"The Free Company will see to it," Ben said. "We need jumpship pilots."

"Obliged to you." Grigor nodded. "Hear that, kids?"

Get ready, Gen broadcast.

✦ ✦ ✦

The transition to foldspace takes Cara by surprise. As soon as Gen says the words, they are plunged into a darkness so absolute that she thinks she's gone blind. She feels as though she's floating, but when she checks her harness, she's still strapped in.

"Ben?"

He doesn't answer, so she reaches out with her mind.

Ben?

Can you see them? he asks.

See what?

Otters. No, not quite otters, but long and otter-like. They undulate as if they're in water.

I can only see blackness. Show me.

And then she sees through his eyes. It's still black but it's as if black is a natural medium for vision. She sees the shapes, long and sinuous, playfully swimming through the cabin air, turning somersaults for the joy of it, twirling around each other in mad helical spins and then separating to explore something with their snouts. One bumps into her chest, backs off as if surprised, seems to sniff at her, then takes another run and passes through. She can't feel it.

Oooh, that's weird. They're like children, exploring new things.

She links to all the pilots. They can all see the squirming, rolling otter-kind.

Childlike, yes, Alia says as one bumps noses with her son. *But this one isn't.*

A creature enters the mess through the aft bulkhead. Cara can't see it when she opens her own eyes, but when she sees it through Ben's it's quite clear, black on black but with an iridescence that suggests every color of the rainbow and possibly some that she's never seen before.

She sees the image from Kennedy's plasfilm drawing: sea horse head, wings folded against its sinuous body. It's beautiful, but she suddenly understands Ben's terror. It's too familiar where familiarity should play no part in its makeup. It's a being from another dimension, it shouldn't bear any resemblance to anything earth-like, yet it does. Its form can only come from human imagination, which means that somewhere, somewhen, the creature has meshed minds with humanity.

It's the fact that it shouldn't look like something we rec-

ognize that disturbs me most, Ben said. *I keep thinking about all those souls lost in the Folds and wonder if the last thing they saw was this.*

It swirls around the mess, taking in the Navigators. Cara almost thinks it's smiling, but only humans treat the baring of teeth as a gesture of friendliness. Is it even possible to interpret the facial expression of such an alien creature as an indicator of its emotional state?

Ben holds out a hand, palm up, fingers open. Cara can sense that he's trembling inside, but his hand is steady. The dragon lowers its snout. The prehensile beard snakes out to touch. Ben twitches as the claws connect, but doesn't jerk back.

What are you? Ben asks, not in words, but in a thought, literally translated simply as *?*

The dragon replies, again, not in words, but with a concept Ben understands simply as, *I am,* and asks the same *?* of him.

I am, Ben replies, and then he reaches for Cara's hand and says, *We are.* He tries to say Ben and Cara by putting the essence of who they are to the front of his mind, but the creature doesn't have language. It doesn't offer a name. *I am* is the closest they're going to get.

Then . . .

Know you, it says.

Words.

Learn you. Learn your mind thing. It turns to her. *And yours.*

Cara remembers something taking her implant. What had Jussaro said?

It's learned from our implants, Ben, ours and Jussaro's. It's trying to communicate.

Communicate. The void dragon echoes. *What is?* The creature looks around at the interior of the flight deck.

Ship, Ben says and pictures safety, air, and warmth.

Many.

Many ships? Yes. Ben pictures ships passing in and out of the Folds. *Must leave. Stay means die,* Ben says.

The creature doesn't understand. It asks *?*

Cease to be, Ben says, offering the image of a person winking out to nothing.

The creature still doesn't understand. Death is a concept it has never dealt with. How old is this thing?

Cease. The creature projects an image of a ship. Not the *Solar Wind*, this is smaller, a nipper class transport perhaps, or something older. It flashes into being as if it has come through a jump gate and then flashes out again.

Through, Ben says. *In and out again. From outside.* *?*

Elsewhere. Beyond.

The creature has no concept of a place other than its own environment. It transmits curiosity.

Ben tries to picture life on a planet. Cara recognizes it as the farm on Chenon: Nan, Rion, cattle. He adds Ricky.

The creature doesn't get land, daylight, or cattle, but it recognizes Ricky. *Young.*

Yes.

The otter-children crowd in, sharing the void dragon's sensory experience. They recognize Ricky, too.

Ricky said he'd seen otters, Cara says.

The void dragon turns to her. She forces her eyes open against the blackness and this time she sees it for herself. Its snout bumps against her face gently. Very gently for something so big. One of the talons on the end of the prehensile beard snakes up to her cheekbone. She feels a slight prick and a trickle of warm blood runs down her face like a tear. The dragon takes her blood, maybe it sniffles it up, maybe it licks it, she isn't sure.

Know you. In the recognition there's an implication that it not only knows her now, but will know her again in future. Cara wonders whether she's putting her own interpretation on something so alien she doesn't have a concept for it.

Know you, too, she responds. *Now and always,* and tries to project goodwill.

Ben pictures a variety of ships winking out. Then he projects an image of a ship, an ark ship, hanging in the middle of nowhere.

Lost, Ben says.

The void dragon doesn't understand.

Find? Ben projects hope.

Still no understanding.

"I suppose that would have been too easy," Ben says. "Worth a try, I guess."

There's an audible crash. The mess door flies open. Jake Lowenbrun, naked and wet from the shower, collides with a table, rebounds and stumbles into the lap of Chilaili Magena, or is it Tama? She grabs him by the arm and drags him down to the bench. There's no spare safety harness there, but her sister leans over and they clasp hands across him to keep him pinned down. He reaches out for the void dragon and it swirls around toward him.

Hilde appears in the open doorway. "Sorry. Too much soap, not enough grip." She obviously doesn't see any of the creatures. She walks through the middle of the void dragon and grabs Lowenbrun by the shoulders to haul him back. Her voice is half a second behind her mouth movement.

The void dragon winks out of existence.

The otter children swirl around the mess one more time and then dive out through the forward bulkhead.

Cabin pressure changes with a pop and they emerge into realspace.

✦ ✦ ✦

Ben took a deep breath. His wrist ached, but he thought it was more a memory of pain rather than a flare-up. He wanted to laugh and cry, both at the same time. He didn't know whether he felt relief or disappointment that the confrontation had been so strange. He'd felt that they were on the verge of communication, but that complete understanding had eluded them. He believed the void dragon had been curious. That was the first step.

Pity Lowenbrun broke the moment.

What was he going to do about the man?

Hilde had dragged him back to sick bay and Ben and Cara had followed. Now Lowenbrun sat on a chair, dressed in nothing but a light cotton coverall, his hair still damp and tousled, nursing a bowl in case his insides got the better of him again.

"He smells better than he did," Cara said. "But I bet he has the mother of all hangovers."

Lowenbrun looked up at her without actually raising his head and swallowed hard.

Yes, Ben knew the signs. Lowenbrun's whole posture said: *If I move I'll be sick.* "Has he had—"

"Everything we can give him and still be conscious," Hilde said. "But he's close to sober."

"Lowenbrun . . . Jake . . ." Ben said.

Lowenbrun grunted.

"By rights I should shove you out of the nearest air lock."

"Do it, then." It wasn't bravado.

"That would be too easy."

Another grunt.

"Thirty thousand innocent settlers."

This time a groan rather than a grunt. "I'm a dead man. I've been a dead man since I took that bastard's job."

"Do you want to die?"

He shook his head, clutched the bowl until his knuckles whitened, then swallowed hard again. "Dree and me. All the family that's left. Need to take care of her."

"It looked like she was taking care of you," Cara said.

"Maybe, yeah. Wasn't always that way. D'you know . . . if you mix yahto with whisky the dreams go away."

"I bet they don't really," Ben said. "It's just that you can't remember them afterward."

"Maybe. You got any yahto?"

"No."

"Whisky?"

"No."

"P'raps that's just as well."

"Tell me about the ark, Jake. You went into the Folds at the Dromgoole Hub. And then what?"

"I realized as soon as we got on board that it was an ark, not a cargo ship. At first Alexandrov said there was a change of plan; we were taking the ark to a safe planet. I think I believed him. I wanted to believe him. We went in and out of the Folds again. That's not where we left it. Four more jumps using different Monitor codes to disguise the ship ident."

"So what was your last entry gate?"

"Dromgoole to Pinch Point. Pinch Point to Stamford Haven. Stamford Haven to Terracotta. Terracotta to nowhere."

"So if we go in via the Terracotta gate—"

"You're not seriously going to do this?" Lowenbrun raised his head and stared Ben in the face, bloodshot eye to eye.

"Not alone." Ben glanced at Cara. "I've learned that lesson. You're coming with me."

"And me, too," Cara said.

"And a Finder. I've got an idea about that. Someone ideally suited, if he's willing."

❖ ❖ ❖

Ben waited until they were back on Crossways, in the office at Blue Seven, before approaching Gen and Max together. It was as much her decision as Max's. If she didn't want Ben to put the father of her baby at risk, then he wouldn't, whether Max volunteered or not. Lewis Bronsen was a good Finder, much more experienced than Max, but Max had one advantage: he actually knew a couple of the frozen settlers.

The product of a dozen foster homes, Max had once spent six months with Dora and Alvin Kirchner. An unhappy six months, it had to be said, but any kind of personal connection gave a Finder double the chance of success.

"Jussaro says you're ready," Ben told Max. "He says that if you'd gone through regular training at the Trust academy you'd easily have a Psi-2 grade."

"He's not going." Gen levered herself up from the chair she'd been sitting in. "Don't flatter him."

"I'm not trying to flatter him, just telling him he's capable of doing this if anyone is."

"If anyone is. See, that says it all." She paced and turned. "This is a mad scheme, Ben. Supposing you find the ark, and just supposing that thirty thousand body pods are still functioning after months in the Folds, how the hell do you propose to drag the ark back into realspace? It's twenty times the mass of the *Simonides*. You can't pull the old Benjamin Maneuver again." She swept both hands together to indicate one ship being dragged along by the other.

Ben shook his head. "If we can't drag it out there's still the jump gate option. Another pilot can bring *Solar Wind*, and Max, back safely. I'll see to the ark."

"So you want both of us to come."

"I didn't say that."

"You need another pilot. How many hours of flight time has anyone else got on *Solar Wind*?"

"The Vraxos pilots—"

"Are still untrained."

"Jake Lowenbrun isn't."

Gen exhaled sharply. "You'd trust *Solar Wind* to that little shit? Even if he could stay sober enough to fly her out of the Folds you'd never see her again."

"Maybe we'll take someone to strong-arm Lowenbrun," Ben said. "One of Tengue's. A pilot. Hilde if she's up for it."

"Do I get a say in this?" Max leaned back in his chair.

"Yes," Ben said.

"No. Shut up!" Gen said.

Max shrugged.

Gen glared at him. "When has what I said ever made a difference? What do you think?"

He leaned forward. "I think I'd like to see the Kirchners stuck in foldspace for a very long time, but if they're the key to finding the ark, we've got to give it a try."

"We?" Gen said. "Me and you?"

"We. Me and Ben and Lowenbrun."

"And Cara," Ben added. "And Hilde if she's willing."

"Right! That settles it." Gen pursed her lips. "If you're all going I'm coming too."

Max shook his head. "You should stay where it's safe. Tell her, Ben."

"You're going to leave me behind because I'm pregnant!" She put one hand on her round belly.

Ben shook his head. "You should stay here, Gen, not because you need to be coddled, but because you're the only other pilot with jump-drive experience. Someone needs to train the Vraxos pilots. We can't risk both of us disappearing into the Folds and not coming back."

"So you admit it's dangerous?"

"It's the Folds. It's always dangerous. This time we're trying to do something that's never been done before. Even if we find nothing, we'll be spending more time there than we should."

"And if you find something?"

"Max, Cara, and Lowenbrun get to come back by the fastest route."

"While you try to do a transfer between ships in fold-space." She scowled. "And bring back a crippled ark."

"And thirty thousand settlers."

"Who might be dead already."

"Who might not."

She nodded and turned to Max. "If you get yourself killed I'll tell our daughter that she was the product of a wild night with some deckhands from Altair-4."

"We're having a daughter?"

"It was supposed to be a surprise."

Chapter Thirty-Four

SEARCH

KITTY WAITED UNTIL *SOLAR WIND* HAD LEFT the dock so that Ben and Cara were safely out of the way. She let herself into the outer office of Ronan's medical suite to find Ronan, Jussaro, and Nine having coffee. Nine and Jussaro had been systematically checking everyone's implants. She'd seen them around, heard people talking, but so far no one had suggested she line up for testing, a situation she was entirely happy with. She hadn't realized they were working in Blue Seven's med center until now.

She smiled to herself. It was fate.

"Kitty, nice to see you," Ronan said. "Is this a visit for professional services?"

He'd offered her counseling when he'd done her psych evaluation way back, when she'd asked Ben to give her shelter. She'd refused, and since then she'd had no need to call on him for anything.

She didn't know about Nine, but Jussaro was a top-grade Empath, even better than Ronan.

Definitely fate.

"I came to see if I could help with Etta. I used to know her, back on Earth. I wondered if you wanted me to sit with her a while, see if an old face might cheer her up."

"You want to visit?"

Kitty caught the way Ronan glanced toward Jussaro before he replied.

"I guess you can. She might recognize you, she might not."

Ronan stood up to lead her down a short corridor to the last room on the left. The room was bright and airy, with a false window showing a garden scene and a bowl of scented roses on the table in front of Etta's chair. Etta's legs were wrapped in a snuggle blanket. She had a book on her lap, but the screen had reverted to the cover image, an elfin child in a cornfield.

"Hello, Etta, you've got a visitor," Ronan said.

Etta looked up, her expression far away, then she blinked and recognition lit up her face. "Mr. van Blaiden's girl, how are you, my dear?"

"I'm fine, Etta, thank you. I came to see how you were."

Kitty leaned over to take Etta's outstretched hand, murder uppermost in her troubled mind.

"I'm . . ." Etta screwed up her eyes. "Why are you here? You're with them."

"Alphacorp? Not anymore."

"Are you sure about that?" Ronan said.

Kitty stiffened and turned. Jussaro, Ronan, and Nine stood behind her, shoulder to shoulder.

"We've been looking for the leak for some time now," Jussaro said. "Turns out we were looking in the wrong place. Your reports to Alphacorp are being leaked to Crowder, did you know that?"

"I don't know what you're talking about."

"Don't you?" Jussaro said. "You're good, Kitty Keely, if that's your real name. You fooled Ronan here with your original psych evaluation—"

"Something I'm going to find very hard to live down." Ronan frowned. "But murder is a hard thing to hide."

"I'm not . . . I wasn't . . ." Kitty felt panic rising. Wasn't this what she'd hoped for? Even so, denying it was automatic. "Why would I?"

"Why indeed?" Jussaro shook his head. "Unless you'd been ordered to."

Kitty breathed out and relaxed. The decision was out of her hands. Etta was safe—from her, at least.

✦ ✦ ✦

Ben hadn't given Lowenbrun any choice about staying sober. He'd left him on *Solar Wind* with Gwala and Hilde for
company. On the third day he figured that Lowenbrun had
dried out enough to fly. Ronan had declared him medically
fit if not psychologically sound, but that would have to do.

"You're serious about this, Benjamin?" Lowenbrun met
him at the top of the ramp, face pale.

"Deadly."

"That's not a good word."

"As I see it you've got two choices," Ben said. "Come
with us to find the ark or I'll just give you up to Garrick's
justice. The last criminals he dealt with on our behalf had a
serious accident in an air lock. This way you have a chance
to redeem yourself."

"Is that really a choice?"

"Not at all." Cara came up the ramp behind him, followed by Max. "There's no way you're getting off that easy.
You're in this for the long haul."

Hilde hit the ramp control.

"You guys don't both need to come," Ben said.

"You might need someone on tactical," Gwala said.

"And I can cope with a few days of endless grapple
league talk if I have to." Hilde grinned at Gwala.

It took three days to trace the ark's last journey: Dromgoole to Pinch Point, Pinch Point to Stamford Haven, Stamford Haven to Terracotta. Traveling via the jump gates, they
encountered no void dragons. The otter-like younglings, if
that's what they were, swirled through *Solar Wind* on the
middle leg of the journey, but that was all.

Between Pinch Point and Stamford Haven, Gen told
them that Ronan, Jussaro, and Nine had found the source
of their information leak. *Kitty!* Ben swiveled around in
his chair to see Cara's reaction.

*I said something didn't add up about her account of
York,* Cara said.

I bought her story, Ben said.

*It was probably substantially true. I saw the way Ari
treated her. But she must have been watching him, and when
the opportunity arose, switched to watching us.*

Reporting to Alphacorp, Gen said. *So Crowder's mole got all her information.*

Ben tasted the bitterness of betrayal all over again. *What have you done with her?* he asked Gen.

In the cells. Tengue is watching over her and a field damper is cutting out any telepathic communication. What else do you want us to do?

That's fine for now until we get back. Have Jussaro talk to her. See if he can get more information.

Will do.

From Stamford Haven they flew to Terracotta. Then it was Terracotta to nowhere.

The jump gate hung in space, the larger crew and control module and the smaller gate impeller framing an ellipse of pure blackness.

Cara called Gen as they prepared to enter the Folds via the gate, just as the ark had done. They exchanged progress reports. Ben was pleased to hear that Gen's Navigator students were doing well in the small runabout Dido Kennedy had retrofitted with a jump drive.

While Cara acted as the conduit for Gen and Max to have a few moments to speak to each other through her link, Ben turned his attention to Lowenbrun.

"Try and remember exactly how it went after you transited via the gate. How far in did you abandon the ark?"

"Not far, but you know as well as I do that you can't measure distance traveled in the Folds by speed and time taken."

"I know, but it's a starting point." Ben relinquished the control of the *Solar Wind*. "Try to duplicate everything you can remember of that journey."

Lowenbrun licked his lips and his hands trembled as he placed them on the control pads. Not a good sign. Ben sat in the copilot's seat ready to snatch back control in an instant if Lowenbrun went to pieces.

And who will do the same for you? he asked himself. Don't think like that. He wasn't going to go to pieces. He'd reconciled with the void dragon and hopefully the void dragon had made its peace with him.

"Terracotta Gate has cleared us to jump," Cara said.

"Okay, take us in, Jake." Ben tried to sound calm, as if

jumping into the Folds without any clear intention of jumping out again was an everyday occurrence.

◆ ◆ ◆

The air pressure changes as they pass through the ellipse of black. The overhead lights dip as if something has interrupted the power.

The lights flicker and regain their normal brightness.

Gwala locks down tactical and sits back.

"Thirty seconds," Hilde says from the systems station.

"Forward screen on," Ben says.

"I'm sorry to tell you, it is on." Cara stares at the black screen.

"Okay. Max?"

"Find Dora and Alvin Kirchner. Right." Max closes his eyes. "Considering that most of the time I spent in their household I was trying to hide from them, this is going to be a bit weird. Did I ever tell you about them?"

"Some," Ben says. "Foster parents when you were thirteen, yes?"

"Fourteen. Strict as all get-out. They had four of us to look after and I guess none of us made it easy for them. They tried to make us a family, but Madoc had just lost his parents and cried all the time. Eirich had been in care since he was four and had bounced back from more foster homes than I had. He was a bully and Madoc was fair game. Gonzo was—"

"Gonzo?" Cara says.

"One minute," Hilde says.

"He had a real name but no one ever used it. Gonzo had had a tough time at home. I guess he was about ten or eleven. He used to climb as high as he could on the bedroom furniture in the middle of the night and pee on his bed. Pee on our beds, with us in them if he could. It was—"

"Does all this talk help?" Ben asks, quelling rising impatience.

"Yeah, it does, actually. Helps me to remember the days, focus on the Kirchners. They were aiming for the impossible. Thought they could make us into brothers, respectful of them and just as devoted to the Ecolibrian cause as they were."

"And I guess you were sweetness and light?" Cara says.

"Hell, no. I was determined to get out of there as quickly as I could. There was this girl back at the orphanage, a year older than me and ten years wiser. I wanted to get sent back, so I was an obnoxious little squirt. Yeah, I know. Can you believe it?"

Gwala laughs.

"Two minutes," Hilde says.

"The Kirchners thought they were being strict but fair, but that's not how I saw it. Fair went out of the window when Gonzo set fire to his bed one night."

"This is as close as I can get," Lowenbrun says. "Sorry to interrupt your life story, pal."

Max shakes his head. "No worries. I'm not getting a flicker. Are we even sure that it's possible to Find in fold-space?"

"It's never been tried before, as far as I know," Ben says. "But Navigators and Telepaths can all function in the Folds."

"Though I can't contact anyone outside the Folds," Cara says.

"Three minutes," Hilde says.

"Lowenbrun, what did you do when you left the ark?" Ben asks.

"Alexandrov . . . shot the pilot and the copilot. He had me at pistol point. He set the ark controls to neutral and powered down her drive, then we made our way back to the hold and into the Monitor flyer. That took maybe five minutes. We exited the ark's air lock and I brought us out of the Folds as quickly as I could via the first gate I could find."

"How long between entering and exiting the Folds?"

"I'm not sure. An hour maybe."

"And how long had elapsed when you returned to real-space?"

"If I'm honest, I didn't log it. I thought Alexandrov was going to shoot me next. Get rid of the evidence. It might have been days."

"Okay, we'll keep trying."

By the time Hilde calls thirty minutes they are ready to give up. The longer you spend in foldspace, the less likely you are to escape it successfully.

"No one said it was going to be easy," Ben says. "We'll take a break and try again."

He lets Lowenbrun find the line out of the Folds, shadowing him carefully in case of errors, but Lowenbrun is careful and steady. In other circumstances, with another pilot, Ben would have been impressed, but Lowenbrun still has a long way to go to raise himself above zero in Ben's estimation.

✦ ✦ ✦

Where have you been? Gen was practically screaming when Cara brought them all into the link.

Searching the Folds, Ben said.

For fifty-six hours? I thought you were lost.

Thirty-seven minutes and forty seconds, Hilde said.

Ben worked it out, a ratio of one to a hundred and ten. "I've never been in the Folds for nearly forty minutes before." Except maybe when he'd had that first head-to-head with the void dragon, and he hadn't been counting then.

Is everyone all right? Gen asked.

Take it easy, Max chipped in. *It was hardly any time at all for us. I'm sorry you were worried. We were fine.*

Not even a void dragon, Ben said. *Which, in retrospect, is odd. We'll take a break, then try again.*

Call as you set off and as soon as you get back out. Now, can I talk to Max alone?

Sure. Ben pulled out of the conversation and felt Hilde do the same.

Ben waited until Max and Gen had finished and Cara had closed the link. "Sleep first," he said, "then we try again."

✦ ✦ ✦

They tried again and again, each time with the same disappointing result and each time losing between one and four days in foldspace, depending on elapsed subjective time, but Ben wouldn't give up.

"We haven't seen the otter-things or the void dragon since we began," Ben said after the eighth try in what was four days to them, but twenty-four days in elapsed time. "Given the frequency of its appearance previously, how unlikely is that?"

"Perhaps it's simply lost interest," Cara said.

"Maybe, or maybe it didn't like being asked to help."

"You asked it to help?" Lowenbrun said. "How did you do that?"

"Asked might be too strong a word," Ben said. "It's so alien that there's no real common ground, but it does have a little common language, mind-to-mind. It's curious about us. I wish I understood why."

"If it's so alien, how come it looks like one of our mythical nightmares?"

"Maybe it does, maybe it doesn't," Cara said. "Is that how it manifests because it picked up some deep-seated human fear during an early encounter?"

Ben shrugged. "We don't even know whether the big one is the same being every time we see it, or whether it's an avatar of some strange interdimensional intelligence. Whatever it is, we need to attract its attention. It showed me an image of a ship entering and leaving the Folds. If it can recognize ships passing through, surely it can identify ones that enter and never leave again."

"And how do you propose we attract its attention?" Cara asked. "Wave at it through the window?"

"Almost. Next time we go in I'm going to take a walk outside in the Folds."

"And what, precisely, would you like us to inscribe on your memorial stone?"

He saw the look on her face. "All suited up, of course."

In truth he didn't know whether the suit would make a difference. As if to remind him what happened last time, his wrist began to ache as it had done intermittently since he'd ditched the case and begun exercising it.

"If you're going outside, I'm coming with you," Cara said.

He swallowed the kneejerk refusal and bit down hard on his back teeth. Her decision. She was as capable as he was.

She nodded as if she'd known what his first reaction would be and was pleased he'd overridden it.

✦ ✦ ✦

Cara suited up in *Solar Wind*'s locker room, carefully checking all the seals, connecting her buddysuit into the EVA suit's circuitry and running through all the standard procedures. She felt heavy and stiff in normal gravity.

It doesn't matter how many times I do this, it still gives me the shivers, she said privately as Hilde double-checked everything from the outside and gave her a thumbs-up.

Don't tell him that. Hilde jerked her head in Ben's direction. *I've seen that look in his eyes. Save me from overprotective people who want to save me.* She grinned.

Gwala? Cara let her eyes rest on the big merc who was checking Ben's suit.

No. Gwala would let me storm the gates of hell, though I guess he'd be right behind me if I asked him. Manny and I go way back. It's my mom.

Somehow Cara had never considered that Hilde might still have a mother around to fuss over her. She was glad the suit helmet covered up her surprise.

Mom was a captain in the Militaire before she met my dad, but somehow she figured she'd be able to turn me into a society miss. Didn't work.

Good practice for when you need to dress up. Cara remembered how natural Hilde had looked in expensive, well-cut clothes.

I clean up well. Hilde laughed and drew Gwala's attention.

"You talking about me?"

"Don't flatter yourself."

Ready? Ben asked.

Ready, Cara confirmed.

Prepare for transit, Jake said from the flight deck.

Good luck, Max added.

Cara and Ben grabbed handholds while Hilde and Gwala clipped their own harnesses to safety loops on the wall.

✦ ✦ ✦

Solar Wind transits into the Folds.

Cara sees Hilde pull at her earlobe as if the cabin pressure has changed, but insulated by the suit she feels nothing.

Gwala opens the internal air lock hatch and Hilde clips a line onto each one of them, then she secures a second shorter line between them. *Don't stay out too late, kids.*

The air lock closes behind them and begins to cycle.

✦ ✦ ✦

When the air lock opens, Cara feels her jaw drop. Black and starless, the Folds assault her optic nerves with every color at once, like the iridescence on a crow's feather. It's not exactly like seeing, not at first. Gradually her brain gets used to it. There's an aurora hanging above them, below them, and all around them, but instead of curtains of light, it's curtains of darkness.

It's . . . beautiful. Breathtaking, she tells Ben.

What can you see?

Colors, all of them black. An aurora, black again.

You can't see the void dragon?

No, can you?

Link closer. See what I see.

Cara gasps and jerks backward into the protection of her helmet. The void dragon, or a void dragon, is up close, its eye on a level with Ben's faceplate. It looks at her. Recognition. It doesn't use words, but its meaning is clear.

I know you, too, she responds.

That seems to please it.

Ben puts the thought of the ark uppermost in his mind as a picture and a question. Cara reinforces it. *Lost,* Ben says. *Find.*

The void dragon produces an image of Ben's family farm on Chenon and for a brief instant ceases to be a dragon and becomes a giant cow.

"I guess that tells us a lot about what these guys look like, or rather what they don't look like," Ben says over the suit comm. "They're appearing as something they think we might recognize. Or it is. I'm still not sure if we're dealing with one or many."

No, they haven't gone home, Ben says. *They're still here, somewhere.* He pictures the ark, pot-bellied, hanging against the black of foldspace, unmoving.

This time the void creature pictures it back at him.

Agreement.

There's a shift and suddenly Solar Wind vanishes to black nothingness. Below them, hanging in foldspace, is a different ship.

Cara!

Yes. I'm okay. Cara feels the tug on the line that still couples her to Ben. *Solar Wind?*

Gone.

Gone where?

You tell me.

Is that the ark?

Same bulbous belly shape but . . . might be a trick of perspective . . . I think it's smaller.

Cara reaches out to the Solar Wind's crew. *Can you hear me?*

Gods and little fishes! Where the hell are you guys? Lowenbrun answers first. *You fucking disappeared!*

Good question, but we've found a ship, or rather our guide has. He's skipped town, though, so we're on our own. Max, can you get a fix on us?

I don't think . . . Yes, I can. It's a bit wobbly but it's there.

Share it with Lowenbrun, see if he can follow your lead.

I . . . Owww! Ease off, Jake. That's my head.

Sorry, bro. Yeah, okay, got it. Not sure how long this will take. Are you going to board the ship?

Are we? Cara asks Ben.

Well, we don't seem to have anywhere else to go right now.

True.

Ben uses the jet pack on his suit and tows Cara, as there's no sense in wasting propellant. As they approach the ship it becomes obvious that this is not their ark, but rather a cargo vessel. The shape is similar, but it's tiny in comparison.

There might be someone alive on board, Cara says.

Or it might have been here a hundred years or more.

Ben reaches for the emergency activation on the upper access hatch set just behind the forward crew compartment. It's likely that the cargo hold will be depressurized, since there's no reason for the flight crew to access it in transit.

The seal pops and the hatch cover opens outward. The air lock is only big enough for one at a time, so Ben goes first and reopens the hatch for Cara with the shipboard controls once the air lock has cycled.

Emergency lighting partly illuminates the narrow corridor.

"Breathable air?" Cara asks.

"No. Still partial pressure, but it's mostly nitrogen. There's not enough oxygen and it's cold as the grave. How long has she been here, I wonder?"

Cara fingers a plate by an empty flight suit nook. "The last time they had a flight suit inspection was seven years ago."

"Ah." Disappointment is evident in Ben's voice. "I wonder what went wrong?"

"Maybe we could ask our dragon friend if he shows up before our oxygen runs out."

"You know, it could just be that if we believe there's oxygen, there will be."

"It didn't work for them." Cara opens the door to the flight deck to reveal three figures, two on the floor, and the third, in the pilot's seat, encased in a space suit for a coffin, two discarded oxygen tanks at his feet, serenely upright. A glance at the faceplate of his helmet instantly reveals that he is very, very dead. Cara shudders and tries not to look too closely at the unsuited bodies.

"Frozen," Ben says. "By the state of them they asphyxiated before they froze. Still a slight blue tinge to the flesh and blood-black fingers."

"Do you always assess corpses?"

"Sorry, old Monitor habits fade slowly. You couldn't always call a coroner and you learned to recognize signs of cyanosis. About half the bodies I had to deal with suffocated in the black. Accidents, mostly."

Three crew, all dead, Cara relays to *Solar Wind*. *Looks like they sat here until they ran out of air. One of them suited up and used the oxygen tanks to give himself a few more hours. That must be the very definition of an optimist. The other two are corpsicles. Maybe been here six or seven years.*

"It's the *Bellatkin*." Ben accesses the ship's systems, which come online at a touch. "No shipboard malfunction." He leans over. "They were transiting the Folds on instruments. I guess they lost the line."

Cara passes on the information.

Harsh, Lowenbrun says.

I've found the record, Hilde says. *A Ramsay-Shorre ship carrying vac-packed coffee from Blue Mountain. Crew of three.*

All accounted for, Ben says. *We should try to bring her out of the Folds.*

Salvage? Lowenbrun asks.

I was thinking more along the lines of getting word to these guys' families.

That, too, but the ship is salvage, right? And the cargo?

Technically.

With the suit on Cara can't see Ben's facial expression, but his back is stiff. His parents were lost in the Folds on a cruise ship. They might have ended up like the *Bellatkin*'s crew. What is Ben thinking? She doesn't intrude to find out. He's all business as he checks out the ship's systems.

"Drive's fine, it's just life support that's been powered down. Maybe the last thing Suit Guy did. I wonder how long it took them to run out of food and air?"

Cargo ships don't have room for intensively planted bio-zones that provide both food and air. Apart from the hold, the ship is little more than a flight deck with a crew compartment, sleeping cubicles, sanitary facilities, and storage, including a cupboard which reveals the ship's doc-in-a-box, a diagnostic center still fully stocked with the kind of meds most likely to be needed by flight crews. Behind the box are three body bags.

"The medical profession usually buries its mistakes. That seems to apply to old doc-in-a-box, too," Ben says through the helmet comm.

They bag the two exposed bodies and lay all three of them carefully on the bunks.

"I wonder if we've got them in the right bunks," Cara says.

"I don't suppose they'll mind if we haven't."

Cara checks her cuff readout. Three hours of suit air left.

Solar Wind, can you estimate your arrival time? she asks.

We're every place and no place at the same time, right? Lowenbrun said.

That's about it, Ben replies.

Then we should be there already.

Believe it.

Oh, I am. I'm believing it like crazy, but there you aren't.

So as not to waste precious oxygen they sit quietly, shallow-breathing. Cara glances at her readout. Two hours of air left.

Ben looks up from the control console. "I can see the line out of here to the Crossways gate," he says. "And the drive is functioning. Let's take the *Bellatkin* home. Connect to Lowenbrun."

Cara does.

Can you see the line to the Crossways gate? Ben asks.

Yes.

Meet us at the other side and we'll transfer back to Solar Wind *in realspace and take the* Bellatkin *in tow.*

You want us to leave you in the Folds?

You can't find us, and we're running out of air, You need to get Solar Wind *out. Who knows how much time has passed out there?*

How much time? Max chipped in. *Don't tell me I might be a father already?*

Ben doesn't answer.

Seriously, how much time?

Let's just get out while we're still breathing and worry about that later, Ben says.

Cara straps in to make the transit through the Crossways gate. "How close can Lowenbrun get on the other side?" Cara asks.

Ben shrugs and checks his cuff readout. "Maybe not close enough."

Chapter Thirty-Five

AIR

CROSSWAYS' GATE SPAT OUT THE *BELLATKIN* into realspace.

Jake? Max? Hilde? Gwala? Cara had felt them all drop out of the gestalt as they crossed the gate horizon and now she'd lost them completely. It was as if *Solar Wind* didn't exist.

"I think they're still in the Folds," she said on suit comms.

Ben swore softly. She didn't catch it all, but she heard Lowenbrun's name in there.

"Crossways Control to unknown vessel. Identify."

"The ship's comm is still working," Cara said, patching it into their suit vox. "Crossways Control, this is salvaged ship *Bellatkin*. Cara Carlinni and Ben Benjamin on board. We're suited up with less than two hours of air left. Appreciate two air tanks or we're going to be docking on fumes."

They were still two hours out from Crossways.

"Well, well. I hope you're going to say pretty please. Tell Benjamin we'll trade him air tanks in exchange for the promise not to emerge from the Folds close enough to set off all our proximity alarms."

"Quit teasing, Crossways Control, I promise," Ben said. "Get your ass into gear."

"Already on it, Benjamin. The Free Company has been alerted. There's a pilot scrambling right now."

Ben? Cara? We're on our way. Ronan's mental voice cut in. *Yan and I are in the Dixie, full tanks prepped. Estimate intercept in one hour forty-two minutes. How much air have you got?*

Cara glanced at Ben and then at her own readout. *One hour thirty-eight minutes.*

How much in reserve?

That is the reserve. Step on it.

Conserve what you can.

Yeah.

You got all that? she asked Ben. At least they didn't have to use up extra oxygen to speak.

I got it.

You're the better pilot. You need to be fit to dock with the Dixie. Let me fly the bus until then while you go into shutdown mode.

It almost scared her that he didn't protest, but with the mental equivalent of a caress he almost immediately dropped into a meditative state that would hopefully use up less oxygen from already depleted supplies.

Cara minimized all necessary movements and concentrated only on keeping the *Bellatkin* on course. She tried not to think about running out of air, as that would only cause her to overbreathe and panic. She set the ship's alarm system to sound as soon as the Dixie came within ten klicks and settled back, watching her helm display count down to zero oxygen.

How long had she got after that?

Minutes.

How many minutes? Enough?

She hoped so.

With two minutes of oxygen left on her readout she nudged Ben and contacted Ronan. *Estimated time to rendezvous?*

Five minutes, Ronan said.

Ben?

I've got four minutes left, how about you?

Two.

You can make it. Go into shutdown mode. Leave the rest to me. I love you.

I love you, too.

She knew he'd share his last breath with her if she asked him to, but it didn't make sense. She closed her eyes and concentrated on taking the shallowest of breaths. Her head began to ache and she wanted to fall asleep. What would happen if she let herself drift into the arms of Morpheus? It wasn't such a bad way to die . . .

Her mother is standing over her. "Why did you let him do it?" *she asks.*

"Let who do what?"

"Your father. You knew he wasn't safe on that dam. Did he fall or jump?"

"They said it was an acci . . ."

Her grandfather is holding her close. "Breathe, child, it wasn't your fault."

"But Mom said—"

"She doesn't blame you, Cara. In part she blames herself. He never got over the split."

Prof Rimbaud looks up from his desk. "I expected better, Miss Carlinni. This paper is inadequate. Perhaps if you concentrated more on your studies and less on young men, you might achieve the grades you're capable of."

She opens the envelope, knowing that if her grades aren't A or A+ across the board, she won't get the assignment that her heart is set on. "Yes!" *Air punch! She's on the spearhead team.*

Rydal is smiling down at her with a mug of coffee in his hand. Damn, that man makes good coffee. It's not the only thing he's good at.

"Don't!" *She sees the doc seal the disposal bag over Rydal's face and tries to rise, but a crushing pain in her knee turns her word into a gasp. The doc comes over.* "Rest, now, Carlinni. We've got this." *He peels her fingers back, pushes Rydal's handpad into them. There's no time or space to carry a corpse home. She hears the whomf and the sizzle as the bag's incendiaries reduce her lover to ash.*

Ari scowls at her. "Craike handles severances," *he says, and she suddenly has an image of heads parted from bodies.*

Ben's standing at the foot of the bed, his eyes smiling. "Are you getting up or do I have to come in there and get you?" *She stretches out under the light airquilt.* "Guess."

"Cara! Cara!"

Who was that? She didn't want to wake up.

Her suit helmet was gone and there was a mask over her mouth and nose. Air! Never had anything tasted so sweet. She drew a deep breath and another. Ben's face came into focus, brown skin and concerned eyes over a clear mask. Then a space-suited Ronan, helmet still in place.

All right? Ben asked.

I will be. Doc Ronan to the rescue, again.

Wait until you get my bill. Ronan grinned behind the faceplate.

✦ ✦ ✦

Cara enjoyed the fuss for a while, the instructions to take it easy while Ronan did half-hourly and then hourly checks. Ben was, as usual, a bad patient, shrugging off the attention and pacing the central office, cursing Jake Lowenbrun five ways from Wednesday until the *Solar Wind* popped out of the Crossways gate twelve hours later with Lowenbrun calling for the *Bellatkin* like a cow calling for her calf.

Home safe, already, Cara told him. *Where have you been?*

We were right behind you.

We came through twelve hours ago.

Shit! I'm sorry. You're obviously all right, though. Benjamin?

Both fine.

He docked *Solar Wind* like the pro that he was and stayed there until Ben relented and gave him permission to come to Blue Seven.

It had been four days for the *Solar Wind*, but closer to five weeks' elapsed time on Crossways, so Ben called a break. Gen and Max gained three days together. Gen's belly had expanded visibly, and after only three days she was reluctant to lose Max again, but relinquished him back to his duty with instructions not to take so long next time.

Wenna had everything under control in Blue Seven. There had been news from Nan that another two independent colonies were willing to ally with Crossways.

Ben was anxious to get back to the search. Cara was fully recovered and willing. Hilde and Gwala volunteered again, and Lowenbrun said if it was all the same to them could they please get back into the Folds or space him right now because he was not built for total sobriety.

"You really think we can do this, don't you?" Cara asked Ben as they boarded *Solar Wind* once again.

"I really do. I think there's one small thing we need to change in what we're doing."

"What's that?"

"Take Max out to meet the void dragon."

"Max? Outside?"

"Outside where?" Max caught up with them at the top of the ramp.

"Don't worry, we'll help you with it."

"With what?"

Ben jerked his head toward the locker room. "Your space suit."

"After what just happened to you two?"

✦ ✦ ✦

"You're sure about this?" Max asked for the fourteenth time as Hilde checked his suit.

"Sure as I can be." Ben would have told him not to worry, but he couldn't lie. It was dangerous, especially with someone inexperienced inside a suit for the first time. Max had barely learned how to use his buddysuit, let alone a full space suit. "We go outside, wait for the void dragon to show and ask again, but this time bring you into the mix with your line to the Kirchners."

"And if this doesn't work?"

"Then I'm out of ideas. We admit defeat, go home, and get on with the rest of our lives."

"And I'm off the hook?"

"Pretty much."

Hilde clipped on the line that bound Max to Cara.

Foldspace coming up, Lowenbrun broadcast from the flight deck.

"Hang on to something, Max," Cara said, "And take care not to tangle the line."

Max's reply was lost in the transition.

✦ ✦ ✦

This time the lights don't just dip, they flicker out altogether and it takes Lowenbrun a couple of minutes to restore illumination. Hilde sets the air lock controls using her cuff-light while they wait.

"All right, children," she says. "Take care out there."

The air lock is big enough for two, but not three, so Ben goes through first, latches his line to the ship and waits, alone in the blackness, for Cara and Max to emerge together. He clips his line to theirs.

"Ahh," Max says over the suit comm. "This is . . . unbe-fuckinglievable."

"Breathe, Max," Cara says. "Slow. Steady."

"Yeah, breathe. Right."

There's a swirling sensation. The big void dragon winks into existence, changes into a cow, back into a dragon and then into the *Bellatkin*, though this *Bellatkin* has an eye. Is that a wink?

"The big guy's here," Ben says. He feels Cara link to him and pull Max into the mix.

"Is that the ark?" Max asks.

"It's the void dragon."

"But it looks like—"

I know what it looks like. Concentrate. Put the ark and the Kirchners uppermost in your mind.

"Ark. Kirchners. Right," Max mutters.

Ben picks up a fleeting impression of a middle-aged couple, unremarkable in their looks, but determined to do the right thing by their foster boys. It seems that Max understands them, in retrospect.

Ben touches the surface of the void dragon, smooth under his glove. The spaceship turns back into a dragon and Max loses it. "Holy shit!" He hits the suit's boosters and shoots away to the end of his tether, his momentum snatching Cara and Ben away from the void dragon.

"That thing . . ."

Max is spinning on the tether, tangling himself, drawing Cara into a knot. They collide and it sets her spinning, too. She curses and wraps her arms around Max, at least as far as her suit and his biopack will let her. Ben's tether is longer. He's dragged, but he avoids the spin and rights himself with a couple of short maneuvering bursts of propellant.

"Steady." Cara puts her faceplate next to Max's. "Steady!"

He's overbreathing dangerously. The inside of his faceplate is fogging.

Ben judges their rotation, counters it and steadies them.

"Breathe, Max. Slowly," he says. Cara reinforces it with a

thought and gradually Max gets himself under control. It takes a while longer to straighten things out and untangle the tethers.

The void dragon rolls lazily and follows them. Ben senses amusement and curiosity combined. He wonders whether to apologize, but figures that's a concept the void dragon might not get.

"Kirchners, Max. Kirchners."

"Kirchners, right."

Ben feels Cara pull them all together again mentally as she tugs the line and brings them together physically.

Find? Ben asks the void dragon. *Please.* It never hurts to be polite. He pictures the ark, but lets Max's image of the Kirchners superimpose on it. *This one.*

There's a glimmer of understanding that translates into a repeat of, *This one.* Is the void dragon managing a little more language each time they meet? It's learning. Why would it do that? Curiosity? Kindness? Some ulterior motive of its own? Or maybe just because it can.

Ben looks up. Hanging pot-bellied above him, black in the darkness, is a huge shape.

"Is that . . ." Max begins.

"I hope so."

This? the void dragon asks.

"Kirchners," Max says. "I never thought I'd be glad to be near them again, but they're here, somewhere."

"Alive?" Cara asks.

"I think so . . . I mean . . . would it feel any different if . . ."

"Don't worry about it," Ben says, still hardly daring to believe. "We need to get on board."

"Where's *Solar Wind*?" Max asks.

Ben leaves the question hanging. *One step at a time,* he thinks.

Jake? Cara reaches out mentally.

Still here.

Stand by.

As if we could do anything else.

Ben propels himself to the ark's side, dragging Cara and Max with him. The ark's skin is space-pitted. She's not a new craft, but she's sound. The cargo bay air lock doors are open, presumably from Lowenbrun's departure. He doesn't

mean to include the void dragon in that thought, but it takes
the tether and passes clean through the skin of the ark dragging them all through with it as though the ship isn't solid.
They're in foldspace. Of course the ship isn't solid. Neither
are they.

They've entered the cavernous hold with rack upon rack
upon rack of body pods. Three hundred racks, thirty thousand souls.

The void dragon rises through them in a lazy spiral, then
returns to Ben and asks, *?*

Settlers, Ben says. *People. Farmers. Makers. Mothers.*
He tries the concept for size, not sure whether the void
dragon will understand. He tries to put it into images, but
that's far from the void dragon's plane of experience. Even
so, it conjures an image of the Benjamin family farm,
plucked out of the remnants of Ben's first implant, no doubt.
Then it comes up with an image of a city, lit by a garish
white sun, peopled by stocky purple-skinned individuals,
looking a lot like Jussaro. After that there's a city with elegant white-walled buildings roofed with multicolored, glittering mosaics of tiny power collectors. Each building is
surrounded by lush greenery and sculpted open space.
Ben's never been there but he recognizes it from images.
New Tamanrasset, where Cara went to school.

Others, the void dragon says. It's a concept rather than
a word.

Now it's Ben's turn not to understand.

Many others. Lost in the Folds? he asks, wondering
whether this could be the first rescue mission of many,
whether he could find his own parents' lost ship, but that
was so long ago. It may still be out there, somewhere, but
what good would it do to bring it home? Let it lie in the
Folds, a mass grave.

Others, the void dragon repeats, and Ben gets the impression that *others* doesn't mean more humans. He gets a
fleeting impression of something alien, possibly even more
alien than the void dragon itself. Then the void dragon is
gone and the three of them are left alone in the ark's vast
hold. The image of something alien lingers until he shakes
it out of his head and turns his mind to the task at hand.

His suit reading tells him there's breathable air in here
and the temperature is a steady five degrees centigrade.

Ben releases his helmet seal and draws it off. Cara is already flashing their news back to *Solar Wind*, saying, *Life support is functioning. Stand by until we see if the ship's fully operational.*

They make their way forward from the hold to the crew compartment where the captain, med-techs, comms-tech, cargo master, shuttle pilots, deckhands, and captain are all in cryo, waiting for a wake-up call that might never come. Cara checks the pods. *All working. Everyone's alive. The captain and the med-techs are in auto-revive capsules.*

What did you do with the bodies of the pilots, Jake? Ben asks.

In the ready room.

They go forward to the flight deck. Cara finds the pilots. Apart from two bodies on the floor, the ready room looks like someone just popped out for a moment. There's a half-finished chess game on the console. Piloting any vessel through the vast emptiness of space is ten percent frantic activity, ten percent checking systems, and eighty percent waiting for the automatics to tell you something is happening.

You might have put them in body bags, she says to Lowenbrun, curling up her nose.

The air scrubbers haven't completely taken care of the sickly sweet smell of corruption, but without them it would be a lot worse.

Sorry. Alexandrov wasn't observing the courtesies.

Max looks through the ready room door and turns away, shaking, more than from his first spacewalk.

While Ben checks the ship's systems, Cara finds a pair of body bags in sick bay and gets on with shrouding the pilots herself. She doesn't ask for Max's help but he bends to help her anyway. His face is ashen.

Ben remembers having to deal with his first corpse, a floater out on the rim. It's a long time ago, but still fresh in his memory. No matter how many times you deal with death you never really get desensitized. Well, he never has, anyway. They all count, whether it's a friend, a stranger, or your own kill.

Ben checks the control panel. Relief washes over him and he has to swallow hard to keep his eyes from misting. It's been a long search and there have been times he feared they'd never succeed. Now he knows it's been worth the effort. "All set here. Settler cryo pods are viable."

But finding the ark was only the first hurdle. Now they have to get it out of the Folds and then across the galaxy to Jamundi without being tracked. The ark is too big for the Crossways gate, but Ben doesn't want to take her via one of the regular system gates since her ID will bring the Monitors down on them and probably the Trust and Alphacorp as well. Can Jake Lowenbrun repeat the trick that Cara's been calling the *Benjamin Maneuver* since he pulled the Monitor ship out of the Folds?

"Max, can you Find *Solar Wind*?" he asks.

"Uh." Max straightens up from the body bags and goes still for a few seconds. "I can feel the pull. Yes."

"Good. Cara, can you link us all in to one gestalt?"

She's good at this. No, that's not giving her enough credit. The way she handles mind links is more than technically perfect, it's instinctive. She's absorbed whatever difference her new implant has made and her mental touch is firm but gentle. He sends a whispered kiss in her direction and she echoes it back to him.

You were right all along, she says privately.

He's not one for saying I told you so, but he flashes her a smile.

She brings Max in first. Yes, Ben can see Max's line between the ark and *Solar Wind*. Now all he has to do is get the two vessels close enough to swing the ark out of the Folds on *Solar Wind*'s coattails.

Next Cara brings in Lowenbrun. Ben feels the man's anxiety. By now he's come to the conclusion that Lowenbrun is not any kind of villain. He was caught up in the wrong scheme at the wrong time, a victim rather than a perpetrator. His only real crime was not standing up to Alexandrov as soon as he figured out what was going on, though whether he could have made a difference is impossible to tell. Alexandrov was a mean bastard even when constrained by Monitor regulations. He wouldn't have hesitated to beat Lowenbrun bloody or, more likely, threaten his cousin to get cooperation.

We're going to swing the ark out with Solar Wind,* Ben says.

He feels Lowenbrun's alarm. *What? I've never—*

I have, Ben says. *We have to get close. Hold on, I'm coming to you.*

Cara brings Hilde into the mix. She's enormously strong and confident, a credit to Tengue's leadership. And lastly there's Gwala, who barely registers on the Telepathy scale despite his receiving implant, but that's an advantage now. Gwala never sees any of the denizens of foldspace and isn't even plagued by his own ghosts. He's going to be the linchpin that holds everything together on the *Solar Wind*.

Okay, everyone, we need to get close. Ben brings the ark around in a wide sweeping turn, following Max's line.

Cara slips into the copilot's seat and checks the readout while keeping the link steady. "I've got another vessel on screen," she says. "It's telling me four hundred klicks one second and forty the next, Take your pick."

Ben checks Max's line to *Solar Wind* and nudges the ark over by tiny increments.

Whoa, you're right on top of us! Lowenbrun says. *And the big fella just flew right through the flight deck. Through Gwala, but he never even felt it.*

I don't believe in void dragons, Gwala says. *Makes life simpler. Don't even tell me if it comes back again.*

I thought I saw something, Hilde says. *I'd have liked to see it.*

Not me. I'm not interested in your nightmares, or Lowenbrun's, or anybody's. I'll stick to the ones that come when I'm asleep.

Okay, Jake, are you ready? Ben asks.

How do I—

We need to bring the ark out of foldspace close to Jamundi and then establish an orbit. Can you find the line? Ben searches for it himself and finds it before Lowenbrun, probably because he's already familiar with the planet. He feeds the information to Lowenbrun.

Got it, Lowenbrun says. *Now what?*

Now we match each other move for move and when you shift into realspace, so do we.

And if you don't? We were twelve hours behind you at the Crossways gate.

This isn't a gate. We'll come through together. Trust me.

I'm all trust.

Ben doesn't know whether *believing* is really what makes

this work, but it's the best he can do. He and Lowenbrun share one vision of the line. Like dancers they echo each other's steps, nudging forward, gaining what counts for velocity in foldspace.

Ready, Lowenbrun says.

Ben nudges the ark a little closer to Solar Wind. *Go for it.*

Now!

+ + +

There was a shimmer in the air and the ark groaned around them as if subjected to plate-buckling pressure from the outside. Was that even possible?

"Did we do it?" Max asked. "Oh, gods, I'm going to be sick." He unbuckled and bolted from the flight deck.

Cara had bent forward and was squeezing the bridge of her nose between thumb and forefinger.

"We did." Ben swallowed bile and inhaled deeply. Truth to tell he didn't feel any better than any of them looked, but he fought it and checked their position. *Well done, Jake.* He allowed himself a self-satisfied grin. *Everyone all right?*

Well, Gwala's made out of iron, but Hilde looks three shades paler than her normal Scandi-fair.

How about you?

Better than I have a right to be under the circumstances.

Good. We should be able to establish an orbit around Jamundi in approximately two hours.

Yeah, about that? What happens to me, now? Am I off the hook?

Do you want to be?

I don't want to get spaced, if that's what you mean.

It's your word against a dead man's. I doubt Alexandrov left any sworn statements. Are you willing to have a full psych evaluation?

Anything.

I'm going to need you to stay on board the ark while the settlers are offloaded and resuscitated. There are thirty thousand of them, so that's going to take some time. The ark needs a pilot just to maintain orbit. It'll be a routine job, but it's yours if you want it.

I can do routine.

Good. Maybe when you've done routine we can talk about a real job.

Flying for Crossways?

Flying for the Free Company.

Ben looked at Cara's surprised face. "What? We need jumpship pilots."

"You hardly know him."

"I like him. He strikes me as a decent man who got a set of bad breaks. Isn't that where we all are right now?"

"I suppose."

"You're an Empath. What do you think?"

"I like him too, but I've been wrong before. Spectacularly wrong. Do me a favor and get your Nan to check him out. I can connect them."

He nodded.

"Cool." Lowenbrun sounded happy about the prospect of a new permanent job. *What about Dree?*

I guess we can find your cousin a job.

Cara cleared her throat loudly and he smoothly followed up with, *Depending on what other skills she's got.*

Chapter Thirty-Six

REUNITED

CARA HAD THE PLEASURE OF LETTING everyone know that they'd brought the ark home, and pleasure it was. Gen instantly forgave them for the nine days they'd been out of contact. Max was relieved that it was *only* nine days and Gen hadn't given birth without him being there.

Marta went into a frenzy of sourcing cryo revival units and med-techs to operate them. Then she started muttering about the logistics of supply. The settlement would need extra staples to last them until the first harvest, more agricultural machinery, tools, and livestock. The embryonic trading network that Garrick was setting up was going to be working overtime, especially considering that until Olyanda's platinum was in full production everyone was working on teetering piles of bills and three degrees of credit.

Saedi Sugrue received the news for the Jamundi settlement. If the settlers had lost Max when he transferred to the psi-techs to be with Gen, they'd gained Saedi, who was now thoroughly absorbed into the settler society. She was overjoyed and signed off almost immediately so that she could pass the news along. When she came back to Cara with thanks, congratulations, and questions Cara tried to calm the excitement down. *Tell them not to start roasting the ox *yet. We'll get cryo revival units there as quickly as we can, but it's going to be a slow job reviving thirty thousand, supplying and equipping them with everything they need.**

They debated whether to revive the ark's crew and came to the conclusion that it was better to keep them in cryo and revive them later on a neutral station. Then, if they wished to return to their old lives with the Trust they could do so without having knowledge that would compromise Crossways or Jamundi.

They docked the ark with *Solar Wind* and traded places with Jake. Ben had Max put Jake on payroll as the newest member of the Free Company.

They made a brief visit to Jamundi. Psi-techs and settlers, working together, had already carved a holding out of the dense growth on the bank above the lazy river. While Gupta supervised building, Mel Hoffner took the news of thirty thousand incoming cryo pods in her stride and had already begun to make a list of the resources she'd need to devote to the revival project and how long it would take. She fist-bumped Ben to transfer the lists from her handpad to his and after a brief report was called away to solve some minor problem that someone else could easily have dealt with.

Was I like that on Olyanda? Ben asked.

Cara laughed softly. **All the time. You need to talk to Mel and tell her that other people are capable of solving problems, too, otherwise she'll wear herself out.**

After the obligatory tour of the settlement to see newly cleared fields and timber stacked ready for building, they admired the sprinkling of self-sufficient houses, some built, some still only frames, and then Ben and Cara borrowed a groundcar and headed out to the new Benjamin farm. Cara was worried that Rion and Ben would start bickering again, but Rion greeted them both warmly and immediately took them on a tour of the farm, still devoid of animals except for the two dogs, a nanny goat in kid, a few feral chickens, and a sty sheltering a fat sow with heavy teats for eight squealing piglets.

"Come and look at the barn." He took Cara by the elbow. "Course, there's not much to see yet except the foundations, but I'll show you the plans when we go inside."

The inside he was referring to was still the temporary medonite structure that Cara had sourced for the family prior to leaving Crossways, a series of small geodesic domes comprising a central living pod and three bedrooms, one for Nan, one for Rion, and one for Ricky and Kai to share.

How like Rion to build the shelter for the animals before his own house, Ben said. *My brother never changes.*

You'd be upset if he did.

Maybe.

Kai ran to meet them across the yard, a thin auburn-haired girl trailing uncertainly in his wake.

"Have you seen the barn?"

"What there is of it," Cara laughed. "But I'm sure it's going to be wonderful."

"Dad's been wrapped up in the design for an efficient building for intensive stock rearing. He had these ideas back on Chenon, but tearing down the old barns and starting again would have been too expensive. He still has occasional mood swings, but I think starting again has been good for him."

"How about you?"

"Oh, all right. Pretty good actually." He held out his hand. "This is Thea. With Nan away an extra pair of hands is really useful, and Thea was contracted to a carpenter and his family but didn't get on with them."

"I signed up to work with wood," Thea said, "but they wanted a household drudge, so I told them they were in fundamental breach of contract and walked out. I'm good with a hammer and nails." She grinned. "Much stronger than I look. I don't know much about cattle, but I'll learn, and until then there's a lot of building to do." She smiled and her thin face lit up. "Kai's cooked for us all, but I'm very happy to boil water for tea."

Cara smiled to herself. Thea might look quiet, but there was a layer of steel under the fair skin—another Nan in the making. "It's a very Benjamin thing to do," Cara said. "Tea would be lovely."

While Ben and Rion were deep in conversation and Thea was making tea, Cara leaned over to Kai. "You like this settler girl."

"Well, yeah." Kai grinned back at her.

"And she likes you?"

"Oh, yeah."

"And your dad?"

"He's okay with it. He doesn't have much of a choice, really."

"Like that, is it?"

Kai winked.

✦ ✦ ✦

Visits over, duty done, they headed straight back to Crossways to reunite Max and Gen and to catch up with whatever they'd missed.

They got an unexpected salute from the guards on the entrance to Blue Seven, which Gwala and Hilde grinned at and Ben returned automatically. Gwala and Hilde tried to leave them at the gate but Tengue turned them around and pushed them into the barbican after Cara, Ben, and Max. As they emerged from the tunnel into Blue Seven, the place was crowded with psi-techs who all began to applaud.

"This is for you as well," Tengue said, slapping Gwala and Hilde on the back. "You brought those people out of the Folds. Be proud."

Cara felt a rush of elation. Tengue and his mercs had become integral to the Free Company, not just as employees, but as partners.

Gen rushed forward and flung her arms around Max, pulling him as close as she could to her belly. "Well done."

Max actually blushed and looked overwhelmed by the attention, and then they were all in the middle of a back-slapping congratulations fest which lasted until Ben grabbed Cara's wrist and pulled her into Wenna's office.

Wenna was waiting for them with a smile on her face. "That's a first. I guess you just made history, not one fold-space recovery, but two."

Cara had almost forgotten the *Bellatkin* and her cargo of coffee. It seemed insignificant alongside the ark and thirty thousand settlers.

"How's Marta coming along with the cryo units for Jamundi?" Ben asked.

"I have fifty new ones due for delivery from Drogan's World within the next two days." Marta slipped into the office behind them. "Cotille has offered thirty-five that they've had warehoused since their own planetfall and I've asked Miss Benjamin to inquire of her contacts. Some of the newer colonies may have spares if they haven't recycled them for raw materials."

"How's Nan doing?"

"She's been checking in regularly," Wenna said. "Mostly with Mother Ramona and Garrick. Says to tell you Ricky is loving the trip, even though she's making him do school-work every day."

"He's a smart kid," Ben said. "More sussed than I was at his age."

Wenna continued. "She's signed up four more independent planets to a trade agreement with Crossways. All of them are desperate for platinum at standard price so Garrick has agreed to supply them as soon as Olyanda starts to produce. Evidently the megacorps have been charging premium prices to nonaligned worlds."

"Imagine that," Cara said.

"Yes, who'd have thought it!" Wenna smirked. "Garrick's agreed that Crossways will stick strictly to standard prices, no more, no less. Three more colonies your Nan has spoken to have reneged on agreements with the Trust and formed their own alliance and are now open to free trade. She says to call her when you get back, by the way."

"I will," Ben said. "What about the jump drives and Gen's pilot training program?"

Gen and Max had quietly absconded. Cara didn't need to guess why. Good for them. They should snatch every moment together while they could.

"Dido's jump drives are working well with smaller ships, but she's trying to develop a compact jump drive that will take larger vessels through foldspace. Gen's working her pilots hard, but they've all achieved basic competence, and the Magena sisters are on their way to becoming outstanding. Crossways has acquired a further fifteen pilots, and two of them recognized the void dragon."

"Good," Ben said.

"Is it good enough?" Wenna frowned. "It looks like we might need them soon."

"What's up?" Ben asked.

It was as if icy fingers stroked Cara's spine at Wenna's words. She shivered.

"Crowder's cooking up something for us," Wenna said.

"Mother Ramona's spies are picking up unusual ship movements."

"She's sure it's Crowder?" Cara asked. "I thought he was under suspension."

"For someone under suspension he seems to have a lot of lines of communication open to the top offices in both the Trust and Alphacorp."

"They're going after Olyanda before we get too well-established," Ben said. "It's what I would do."

"You, my love, would offer a clean fight," Cara said. "I think Crowder's coming after Crossways as well."

◆ ◆ ◆

When the door to their apartment closed behind them and they were alone, Cara put her arms around Ben.

He hugged her close, resting his head on her shoulder.

"Crowder," she said.

He groaned. "How much does it take for a man to stay dead?"

"Well, you made a good comeback yourself."

"I suppose I did, but I thought we'd seen the last of Crowder. I thought he'd lost all his credibility with the release of the vid."

"Did you feel guilty when you thought you'd killed him?"

"No guilt. He hurt you. I didn't even think about it."

"You used to be friends. It's always hard when friendship turns sour."

"Crowder didn't get more than he deserved. Next time I'll make it four darts."

"There won't be a next time. He's going to stay as far away from you as he possibly can."

"I think you're right. He's coming after Crossways. He'll throw everything he can at us again and again until this is over. He'll do it through a third party this time."

"You're sure?"

"Oh yes. I need to talk to Garrick."

"It's almost midnight."

"So it is. Tomorrow then."

"So . . . tonight . . ." She kissed his ear.

"You have plans?" He raised his head.

"Unless the station's about to explode around us there's not much we can do until morning."

"Oh yes there is."

Their lips connected.

✦ ✦ ✦

Ben awoke warm and safe with Cara snuggled against him in the nest that their passion had carved out of the quilt. Her regular breathing indicated she was still deeply asleep. Since he didn't want to disturb her he lay still, his arm around her waist, his hand on the silky smoothness of her ribcage, contemplating their future together.

He remembered her, edgy and nervous on Mirrimar-14 when they'd first met. He'd loved her from the very beginning, but it had taken her much longer to develop trust. He got that. He'd have trust issues as well if van Blaiden and McLellan had mindfucked him as thoroughly as they had her. He was amazed and grateful that she seemed to have overcome all that, at least well enough to function, though he knew from the way she mumbled in her dreams that it was still with her and might never leave.

She'd come to trust him, though, and now his past was catching up with them both. It was hardly fair, but when had fair ever been part of the equation?

What did he want? He'd fulfilled his promise to the Ecolibrians, brought home their missing settlers and left them in a safe space. Whatever happened to him, Gupta and Mel Hoffner would make sure the settlement survived, even if they had to be isolated from the rest of humanity. If that's what it took, then that's what it took.

He had a duty to the Free Company, to Wenna and Marta, to Ronan and Jon, to Gen and Max and their unborn child, to the indefatigable Archie Tatum and steadfast Yan Gwenn. Names crowded in. He owed them all.

Was Crowder coming for them as well?

Cara stirred in his arms. "Time is it?"

"Early."

"Too early for coffee?"

"Much too early."

He leaned over and kissed her on the cheek. She turned into him and stretched against him belly to belly. He stiffened against her. She stroked his flank.

"I love you, Ben Benjamin."

"I've loved you since the very first moment we met."

"Prove it." She slipped her hand between their bodies and he gasped. A delicious heat growing in his groin chased away all thoughts of Crowder and the Free Company.

✦ ✦ ✦

It was the smell of coffee that roused Ben for the second time that morning. Cara was out of bed, wrapped in a robe, her short hair wet from the shower.

"The coffee from the *Bellatkin* is good. Marta sold most of it on the open market but kept some for us." She laughed. "I can see the look on your face. Don't worry, there's caff for you. The good stuff is all mine."

"Good. We couldn't have retrieved a tea clipper, I don't suppose. It had to be coffee." He swung his legs over the side of the bed and stretched. "Marta didn't sell the ship, did she?"

"No. It's been overhauled and retrofitted with one of Dido Kennedy's jump drives."

"The pilots?"

"Families have been notified, ashes returned as requested."

He nodded. "I suppose there are loose ends to clear up. The missing ark has been top of the agenda for so long I feel a bit bereft now we've found it. Everything seems to be going our way for a change."

"Apart from Crowder."

"Yes, Crowder."

"And Kitty."

He shrugged. "Her too. Disappointing."

"And protecting Olyanda so that no one else moves in on our only source of income."

"Crowder, Kitty, and Olyanda, right. And I was thinking what a beautiful morning it was."

Cara laughed and tossed a pair of pants in his direction. "You never lose sight of the big picture."

"Except sometimes, just for a few moments, you can make me forget it all."

She kissed the top of his head and danced out of reach of his hands before they quite closed on her waist. "I'll see you in the office."

✦ ✦ ✦

Ben arrived in the central office barely ten minutes behind Cara, still carrying his carton of caff, but now buddysuited and feeling ready to face whatever the day had to throw at him.

Wenna, Gen, Max, Ronan, Jussaro, and Marta were all waiting for him.

"Who called a meeting?" he asked.

"We need to know what to do with Kitty," Ronan said.

"And there's some financial stuff you need to look at," Max said.

"Pilot training schedules," Gen added.

"And Nan says you still haven't called her," Wenna reminded him.

"I get it. I've been off lollygagging, now it's time for work. Okay, let's all sit down. Who's first?"

They pushed together three tables to make one large one and pulled up chairs.

"Max, finance. Tell us the worst."

"I've gone over all the figures for the last month. We're still forty days from the first platinum rods rolling out of the new plant on Olyanda, but the primary loan arranged by Mother Ramona is accruing interest at a frightening rate. I put the word out and this morning I got a better offer from Fawcett and Post, so I propose we borrow from them to pay off the first loan."

"The sale of the coffee cargo from the *Bellatkin* offset some of our running expenses," Marta said. "But I can't source supplies on credit for much longer."

"Garrick has deferred rental on Blue Seven," Max continued, "but we can't pay wages. No one's grousing yet, but they will. Tengue has agreed to defer wages for a fifteen percent increase when the platinum credits come in. I need hardly tell you that if something happens to platinum production on Olyanda we'll be mired in debt so deep we'll not even be able to afford shovels to dig ourselves out."

"What interest rate have Fawcett and Post offered?" Cara asked.

"Six and a half percent instead of eight, and the term is extended for an additional forty days."

"I say go with that," Ben said. "What about the rest of you? Any further comments or suggestions?"

There was a general shaking of heads. "It gives us a breathing space," Wenna said. "I agree."

Max nodded. "Right. I'll see to it. There is always the possibility of selling the *Bellatkin*."

"We need to increase our own fleet," Ben said. "It would cost us more to buy a jump-drive cargo ship than we'd get for the *Bellatkin*."

"That leads straight to pilot training," Gen said. She dropped a plasfilm onto the table. "We've got two jumpships, both small ones. Kennedy's working on a drive that will power a ship with greater mass, but she's not there yet. Anyhow, training has been pretty intense. I'm worried about Esterhazy. It's not consistent. The Magena twins are outstandingly good and I'm not sure how the Kazans do it—they must have one hell of a bond—but they're rock solid. I'd keep them for the Free Company if I had a choice rather than passing them on to Crossways. I think you need to check each one of them out. Some—not Esterhazy—will be capable of the Benjamin Maneuver if you want to teach them."

"It's a risky trick. Is that a wise move?"

"The Magenas are interested and so are the Kazans. Esterhazy wanted to try it but I think it's being overambitious. Valois and Singh, the two new pilots recruited by Mother Ramona, could probably manage it, though."

"Hey, just a minute," Max said. "If you're training pilots like that, does it mean you can pull more ships out of the Folds? Not only would it be a public service, but the salvage would ease our debts considerably."

"Don't you think if it were that easy that someone would have thought of it by now?" Cara asked.

Max shrugged. "Just saying."

"I'll think about it," Ben said. "Next."

"Kitty Keely," Ronan said. "She's still under guard in a cell with a psi damper, but she's not coping well with being cut off, even with tranqs."

"Been there," Cara said. "Has anyone been visiting?"

"Me," Jussaro said. "Etta."

"Etta?"

"She's coming along quite well." Ronan butted in. "Says

she doesn't believe for a moment that Kitty was going to kill her."

"And Syke," Jussaro finished. "Seems they struck up a friendship after Wes Orton's death. He says he's kicking himself for not figuring out she was a spy, but even so, he's kept coming back. We figure she used visits to Orton to get access to a public comm booth, at first, but there's no doubt in my mind that she really did care for him. The attack shook her faith in the megacorps a little—enough to keep quiet about you going after Etta on Sentier-4. I needn't tell you what would have happened if she'd given you up."

"We must be thankful for some things."

"That's why I don't think she would have gone through with killing Etta even though she'd had orders to. I think she made what she was doing so obvious that she knew we'd stop her."

"We need to speak to her. Will this afternoon be good for you?"

"Yes, fine," Ronan said.

"And Nan," Wenna reminded him as the meeting broke up.

"Nan. Yes. Anything else?"

"Nothing I can't handle," Wenna said.

Cara hooked her arm through Ben's as the office cleared and Wenna went back to her desk. "You want to talk to Nan now?"

"Yes, if you're up for it."

Cara connected him smoothly.

Reska, did you find the ark?

Yes, Nan, we did.

And your void dragon?

Yes. Amazing creature. If you ever come across any pilots who claim to have seen one, point them in our direction.

He quickly poured out everything that had happened. *How's Ricky doing? Ready to send him back to school yet? Rion's missing him. Oh, and Kai's got a girlfriend.*

Kai? Good for him. I don't think Ricky's cut out for life on Jamundi. The boy's got ambition, maybe more than is good for him. He does miss his dad and Kai, but he's not going to be a farmer. Reminds me of you when you were his age.

You encouraged me.

Nana gave the mental equivalent of a chuckle. *Maybe I did.*

How's your mission?

Interesting. Chander Dalal has taught me a whole lot about Indian cookery and taught Ricky how to play poker for chores tokens.

I've seen Chander playing poker. I assume Ricky will be doing chores until his ninety-seventh birthday.

He's not losing quite as badly as you might expect, especially when he can talk Captain Dorinska into playing.

Where are you heading for now?

Romanov.

If you see my ex-wife—

I'll give her your best regards.

That's what I was going to say.

Chapter Thirty-Seven

DECISIONS AND DEVELOPMENTS

CARA AND BEN NODDED TO THE GUARD OUT-side Kitty's cell door. She'd been in a converted store-room at first, but a swift rearrangement of walls behind the barbican had created a cell space which could only be accessed via Tengue's security post.

"How is she this morning?" Cara asked the guard.

"She gives no trouble."

"Any visitors?" Ben asked.

"Not today." There was a pause while he accessed information on his handpad. "Yesterday, Doctor Wolfe in the morning and Captain Syke in the afternoon. Captain Syke comes most days. Sometimes Guard Heator or Mr. Jussaro, and twice Ms. Langham."

He opened the door. Inside, the cell—a room with a bed, a chair, a table, a bookslate, and space to pace—was almost homey.

Cara had survived for almost a year with her implant powered down while she'd been on the run from Ari. Before that she'd been in a bare cell, shot through with drugs to suppress her telepathy. It had been a tough time. Kitty had it easier. She hadn't been totally isolated, even though she'd been locked up for almost two months. Her cell had a damping field to prevent telepathic communications from outside. It wasn't as bad as being drugged with reisercaine, but she had to be feeling the strain.

Surprisingly, every available surface in Kitty's cell was covered with pots of earth showing shoots and young plants. Ben picked up a pot and ran one finger gently up a leaf.

"Getting my fingers dirty helps." Kitty looked up from the table where she had a heap of dirt on a plastic film and a couple of empty pots. "I planted poppies in the raised bed outside your window the day they put me in here. I expect they're growing tall by now."

"Yes." Cara hadn't even looked. "How are you?"

"Better now that he can't get at me anymore." She dusted off her hands and wiped them on a cloth. "I suppose you want me to apologize."

"Not really." Ben shook his head. "I guess you were only doing your job. Is Kitty Keely even your real name?"

"Almost. Catherine Keely, but I've answered to Kitty since I was at the Academy."

"How long have you been an Alphacorp spy?"

She shook her head. "You make it sound like a vocation. Maybe I'd have made a better job of it if it was. I was just in the right place at the right time."

"To watch Ari van Blaiden," Cara said. "They didn't trust him—or maybe Yamada didn't trust him."

"Ms. Yamada. My orders came directly from her office. No, she didn't trust him. Would you?"

Cara shook her head. She had, for a while at least, trusted Ari and it had almost killed her.

"So why did you latch on to us?" Ben asked.

"I needed to make myself useful. My mother needed treatment—expensive treatment. I figured if Ms. Yamada wanted to pull me off the case I could always get out, but if I missed the opportunity that presented itself on Olyanda I'd never get another one."

"Did you stop to consider what might happen after you got back to Alphacorp? You'd have arrived home with dangerous knowledge. Did you think they'd let you keep it? You'd have been sent straight off to Sentier-4 for a mind-wipe, or worse."

Kitty's eyes widened. She hadn't considered that. Cara herself might not have considered it either, before raw experience had taught her that the megacorporations were as dangerous, dark, and twisty as the people who helmed them. Was there anyone who rose to the top by being decent and fair? Probably not. The road upward was built on top of good people.

"Did you pass messages on to the Trust?" Ben asked.

"No. Only to Alphacorp, I swear."

Ben frowned. "Did you know about Crowder's mole in Alphacorp?"

"What? No!"

"Crowder's been getting the information almost as quickly as Yamada."

"The information I sent ..."

"Helped to kill Wes Orton."

Kitty shook her head, but Cara figured that had hit home.

"You liked Wes."

Kitty nodded.

"More than liked him."

Kitty nodded again. "We didn't have long together, but he made me feel good. He was kind. A good man." She flicked a glance at Ben and back to Cara. "You know how that feels after ..."

It was Cara's turn to nod.

"And you like Arran Syke," Ben said.

"He's been a good friend since ... Don't blame him for—"

"We're not blaming Captain Syke for anything," Ben said.

"What happens now?" Kitty asked.

"I don't know," Ben said. "We're not interested in retribution. We're interested in a solution to the problem. A permanent solution."

"Please ... don't leave me here like this. I'm done with Alphacorp."

"That's easy to say and harder to prove," Ben said. "As soon as you get out of here they can get at you again."

"I could wear a damper," Kitty offered.

"For the rest of your life?" Cara said. "They're a temporary solution at best; good for deadheads with a receiving implant who don't feel being cut off from the flow like we do. Besides, even with a damper you'd still be a target for a Finder unless you have your implant removed."

Kitty's eyes widened. "You wouldn't . . ."

"Of course not," Cara said. "Would we?" She turned to Ben.

He shook his head, an I-don't-know gesture rather than of-course-not. "What are the alternatives? Garrick would simply throw her out of an air lock. He's offered to do that already. Problem solved. If we let her go she has information in her head that could endanger not only the Free Company, but the whole station."

"I don't want to go back to Alphacorp. I know I said that before, but I really mean it now . . . except . . . I might not have a choice. My mother . . . they have her in their care. They've threatened to bill her for all the treatment—a bill she'll never be able to pay. They've got a hold over me if they need it."

"Only if they have a direct line of communication to you," Ben said. "A threat is useless unless you know they've made it, and they generally have better things to do than terrorize little old ladies."

"You can say that after the Trust used your grandmother?"

Ben shrugged. "Look how that turned out for them."

"Long-term cryo," Cara said. "We can freeze her and send her to the future with a tag on her toe: open one hundred years from now."

"But my mother . . ."

Ben shrugged. "If the choice is frozen, insane from having your implant shut down, or dead, what would she choose for you? What would you choose for yourself?"

They left Kitty in her cell with her seedlings.

"What do you think?" Ben asked Cara.

"She's still cut up about Wes Orton and she does value Syke as a friend, but whether she's really done with Alphacorp remains to be seen. Her mother's a problem. If Alphacorp has a hold, Yamada may not be done with her. Long-term cryo may be the only option."

❖ ❖ ❖

Ben took a tub to Red One with Yan. He needed to see the jump drives for himself and to talk to Dido.

"She's not as wacky as she looks," Yan said. "I mean, yes, she's a bit unconventional, but so would you be if you'd had her upbringing."

Ben couldn't imagine Dido Kennedy as a child.

"She was born on Earth, you know."

"Really?" That did surprise Ben. She looked as if she'd been bumming around the space lanes all her life.

"Parents were solid entrepreneurs, ran a tour company offering holidays on the Moonbase resorts. She was bored out of her skull. Always liked tinkering with engines, but her parents wouldn't send her to school. Wanted her in the family business. She took to dressing down, refusing to be the young businesswoman. When she was sixteen she took one of their tours to the Moon. At the spaceport she talked her way onto a bucket-of-bolts freighter and learned ships from the deck plates up."

"Tough schooling."

"She learned well. I tell you, if I was up against it there isn't anyone I'd rather have holding my ship together than Dido."

Ben tried not to smile. He'd never seen Yan this enamored of anyone before. He'd found his soulmate. It didn't matter that she was at least ten years his senior, had slightly bug eyes, three chins, and dressed like a refugee, she was beautiful to him. To be honest, if she could retrofit ships with jump drives, that made her more than beautiful, it made her brilliant.

In Red One, Dido greeted Yan with a brief but telling smile. Feelings ran both ways, Ben realized, pleased for Yan.

"Hey, Benjamin, come to see where your money's going?" Dido called, looking up over an amalgamation of wires on her workbench.

"I can see where it's going. Those kids out there aren't anywhere near as skinny."

"No apologies. You've got so much and they've got so little."

"Point taken."

"Come and look at this."

Ben looked. The mess of cables and coils was only marginally less confused than a bowl of spaghetti. "I'd probably be impressed if I knew what it was."

"You want bells and whistles? Flashing lights? I can give you those but they won't make any appreciable difference to how well it works."

"So what is it and what does it do?"

"I've miniaturized the hypervoluraic delimiter and stacked the solupene compensators to counterbalance the foraldic nodules on the simsalvic crystals that drive the—" She cracked up laughing as his eyes glazed over. "It's no good, I can't keep it up. That's a load of tosh. I made it up. You wouldn't know what I've done, anyway. Yan can barely follow it and he's smart. Not saying you're not smart, Benjamin, but you're not engineering smart. So to answer your question: it's a jump drive, powerful enough to take an ark into foldspace. Hell, it might even be powerful enough to take the whole of Crossways into foldspace."

"And out again?" he asked.

"With the right pilot."

✦ ✦ ✦

Ben checked all the Vraxos pilots by taking them through the Folds individually in *Solar Wind*. Alia and Grigor Kazan, working instinctively together, passed with flying colors. The pilots Gen had trained were intended for Crossways' own fleet, but Ben liked the Kazans and appreciated their quick thinking on Vraxos in the spaceport.

"I'd like you to try coattailing," he said. "And if that works out, the *Bellatkin* needs a permanent crew."

"You mean the Benjamin Maneuver?" Alia asked.

"I'd really like to get away from that name."

"I'm afraid you're stuck with it, sir," Grigor said.

"No need to *sir* me, Grigor."

"Okay, Boss." He grinned.

Ben had them zip in and out of the Folds a number of times and then, using a hulk marked for scrap, he had them sashay up close and draw it into the Folds.

✦ ✦ ✦

"Whoa, cool!" Grigor says as they pop into foldspace, the hulk in their shadow.

"Now comes the hard part," Ben says. "You have to bring it out again, and in the Folds all your instruments will be lying to you. You need to get close."

Grigor nudges toward the hulk. "Readout says ten klicks."

"Don't believe it."

"Should I use the screens?"

"Won't do you any good."

"We can always stick our head out and take a look," Alia says.

"Uh, if you say so." Grigor nods.

Alia says, "I'll do it."

Ben doesn't say she can just float up through the outer skin of the *Solar Wind* as if it isn't there and breathe in the void. If her belief falters for a second it will kill her as it almost killed him.

He sits back to see how the couple will handle it between them.

Alia suits up and clips herself on a line in the upper air lock. When the lock has cycled she emerges halfway.

It's close, she says. *Maybe only one klick, though distance is hard to judge. Starboard maneuvering thrusters only in half-second bursts.*

Copy, Grigor says, and nudges one more time. *Again?*

No that'll do it. Port thrusters, half second on my mark. Mark.

Grigor blips the port thrusters and cuts the *Solar Wind*'s glide. They still overshoot and touch the side of the hulk. Instead of ship-on-ship collision, the hulk slices through the cabin like a ghost.

Oh, shit! Alia ducks back into the air lock in alarm and slams the hatch. She reaches the flight deck just as the hulk slides out of view.

"I suggest now would be a good time to swing out of foldspace," Ben says calmly. "You aren't going to get any closer than this."

"Right." Alia flings herself into the nav chair. "I've got the line back to Crossways. Let's do it."

"Whatever you say." Grigor hits the jump drive.

✦ ✦ ✦

They popped out of foldspace fifty klicks from Crossways, the hulk in one piece barely two klicks away.

"Pretty good for a first attempt. Just don't exit the Folds until you're sure the two vessels aren't joined. Could be messy."

"So, we've got the job on the *Bellatkin*?" Alia asked.

"You've got the job."

When Ben finished checking the rest of the Vraxos pilots

he cleared them all for jump-drive flight except for Ester-hazy, who hesitated for too long when trying to find the line out of the Folds.

"I can do it. I can do it," the older pilot kept saying, and second time around, it did, but Ben was doubtful and put it on the reserve list.

"Don't worry, you've still got a job. There are ships without jump drives and you're fine on gate jumps," Ben said. "There are plenty of pilots with higher Nav ratings than you who can't see the line either."

✦ ✦ ✦

Ben dropped into a chair opposite Norton Garrick in the basement office beneath the Mansion House. "I'm keeping the Kazans for the *Bellatkin*, but I've got two jumpship pilots for you," he said. "Chilaili and Tama Magena are good enough to start training others. Gen has two more pilots almost ready, Valois and Singh, but this will be the last lot she can deal with before the baby."

"Understood." Garrick laced his fingers across his chest and swung back in his seat. "Thank you."

"Have you got enough jumpships?"

"Nine new ones, so far. I just need pilots to fly them. We've offered Kennedy a workshop facility on level four, but she won't leave Red One. Says all her friends are there, and besides, she's working on something special. I think she's still trying to crack the platinum recovery algorithm." Garrick shrugged. "Good luck with that."

"But her jump-drive retrofit is sound?"

"It checks out in every way."

"Is Olyanda protected?" Ben asked.

Garrick nodded. "It's safe enough for now. There's a planetary defense grid in operation, but a massive fleet attack would be a problem."

"Let me know if you need any help. We have a vested interest in Olyanda. In fact, as Max pointed out, without it we're pretty much bankrupt."

Garrick cleared his throat. "I won't pretend that we're not—shall we say—overextended as well."

"I thought ... Oh never mind."

"What? Have vast personal fortunes? Well, I'm not saying we don't, and combining mine with Mona's—plus what we appropriated from my predecessor in, well, let's just call it a hostile takeover—gave us a pretty good start, but Crossways has always been run on cooperation between . . . business enterprises."

"You mean crimelords."

"If you want to be so indelicate about it, yes. I have to keep them all happy. Happy or dead. Legitimizing Crossways may not be without its casualties, but there's no future in crime. Not when the megacorps get away with murder and we're persecuted for the occasional bout of free trade—"

"Piracy."

Garrick chuckled. "There are some who might call it that, but I swear, Benjamin, if this trading network holds up, we'll be squeaky clean in the future."

"You can't vouch for all your citizens, Garrick, but you're already cleaner than the megacorps. One step at a time."

"Indeed."

"So what do you need? What can we help with?"

"At the moment we have our fleet split between Crossways and Olyanda. A jump gate closer to Olyanda that cuts down on traveling time would give us a chance of moving our non-jumpships between here and there. Until we retrofit more ships with jump drives and train the pilots to use them, our situation is precarious."

Ben laughed. "A jump gate. That's a tall order. Don't hold your breath." He thought for a moment. "Kennedy says her new modifications are powerful enough to handle the biggest ships. If I send Yan Gwenn to Jamundi to retrofit the ark, once the unloading has finished Lowenbrun can bring her home. She's big enough to fit fifty of your hornets into her hold, which is a good way of getting them between here and Olyanda in a hurry."

"You trust Lowenbrun?"

"I think I do."

Garrick grinned. "Go for it."

❖ ❖ ❖

"Everything all right with Garrick?" Cara asked. "How's his bid for galactic domination?"

They stood in the lineup for lunch along with twenty other psi-techs, shuffling forward, trays at the ready.

"Brave given the circumstances, or foolhardy, I'm not

sure which." Ben switched to private conversation. *He's on a financial knife-edge just like we are.*

I didn't realize.

No one does, and he wants to keep it that way. If his creditors find out they'll close in for the kill.

Of course. My thoughts are sealed. I hope Olyanda doesn't turn out to be a poisoned chalice.

The risks are huge, but so are the rewards.

They reached the front of the lineup. Ben checked the board: razorfin on a bed of paruna grain or vat meat lasagna. "What do you fancy?" Ben asked.

"Uh, razorfin, I think."

"Hmm, I think you're right." He placed a plate of fish on Cara's tray and helped himself to another one, smiling at the server who was refilling the hot cabinet. She smiled back and pointed to the dessert counter. "Last two," she said. "Strawberries from the farm."

"Nice." Ben scooped them up and added them to the trays. "Thanks."

"You're welcome."

They took their food to a table close to where five of Tengue's people were busy tucking in to the lasagna.

"So what can we do?" Cara leaned in and kept her voice low. "After all, we need Garrick to stay in business."

"I asked the same question." *He wants a jump gate.*

Garrick wants a jump gate? Cara asked, her fish temporarily forgotten.

Closer to Olyanda—and one not under control of the megacorps. It makes sense. The one they're using at the moment is too far out to be really useful, though it's big enough to take freighter traffic. I told him not to hold his breath.

Ambitious.

*That's Garrick. You've got to admire the man. In the meantime I've offered to retrofit the ark with a jump drive. She'll hold fifty hornets. It's not as good as a jump gate, but as an interim measure . . . *

Ben applied himself to the fish and the grains. The sauce was buttery with a hint of lemon. Nice.

Cara finished hers and reached for the bowl of fresh strawberries. She ran a thumbnail around the top of one plump berry and pulled the calyx away, then stopped with the fruit halfway to her mouth.

What would happen if you flew Solar Wind *close enough to a jump gate to drag it into the Folds?* Cara asked. *Would there be some enormous feedback loop? Would foldspace end up tied in knots?*

I suppose it depends whether the gate was active at the time. Why do you ask?

I just wondered why, with all the assembled criminal minds on Crossways, no one had ever thought of stealing jump gates.

Ben stared at her and blinked.

◆ ◆ ◆

Ben's feelings were on the smug side of self-satisfied as he watched Alia and Grigor Kazan and their two children, Donna and Vel, examining *Bellatkin* inside and out. The newly recoated and refurbished cargo ship stood in Port 22, gleaming. Her refit included one of Dido Kennedy's jump drives, a device not much bigger than a coffin and secured in the ship's drive housing.

"She's sweet," Alia said. "Boxy, but sweet."

The ship was about as wide as the *Solar Wind* but twice the length. Much of her bulk was cargo hold, two separate cubes contained inside a single skin with rounded corners suspended from a spine that extended into a long high "tail" that gave her an insectoid profile, somewhat like a dragon-fly. She had an extendable high upper wing for atmospheric maneuvering, though Ben suspected her aerodynamic qualities were somewhat bovine.

"Is she ours?" Vel asked.

"We're her crew. She doesn't belong to us," Grigor explained. "But we get to call her home."

"All of us? You're not leaving us in school here?" Donna asked.

Grigor looked to Ben.

"That depends on the run," Ben said. "There might be some trips that are . . . less appropriate."

"You mean smuggling," Donna said.

Ben held out his hand, palm down and waggled it. "Free trade. It's up to your parents, but your apartment in Blue Seven is still yours, so you have a choice."

"But we can come on the shakedown run, right?" Vel said, his eyes dark and wide.

His sister nudged him. "Stop putting on the doe eyes, Vel, or you'll get yourself grounded for being impossibly cute."

Ben laughed. "Yes, you can both come if your parents want you to, as long as you sit quiet and do as you're told."

"We know the routine," Donna said, older than her brother by about five years and wiser by five decades.

"Yes, okay. We'll only be out there for three or four hours," Alia said. "We just need to check out the way she handles and the new jump-drive retrofit."

Ben settled into the spare bucket seat on the flight deck and the children strapped themselves into the crew seats while Alia took the nav chair and Grigor the pilot's couch, resting both hands on the control panels.

"Easy. Easy." Grigor spoke softly to himself as he negotiated Port 22's air lock and out into space.

The comm crackled into life. "Crossways Control to *Bellatkin*, you are cleared to proceed and reminded that jumps to foldspace within a hundred klicks of Crossways are strictly forbidden."

"*Bellatkin* to Crossways Control. Wouldn't dream of it."

"Good to hear, *Bellatkin*, but I believe you have Ben Benjamin on board."

"Fair point, Crossways," Ben said. "But I've only done it in an emergency. Besides, I'm in the passenger seat, today."

The comm crackled and Vel laughed until his sister gave him another sharp dig in the ribs.

Ben sighed. "She's all yours, folks. Let's see what she can do."

At exactly the hundred-klick mark, Alia and Grigor linked telepathically and the *Bellatkin* dipped into the Folds and out again, still close enough to see Crossways as a dot in the distance. Grigor experimented with the maneuvering thrusters and tried various seat positions, then flying both with and without internal gravity.

"One more jump," Alia said. "I want to do another quick bodkin jump, in and out, this time to ten thousand clicks distant from the station."

Once more they connected mind-to-mind and the *Bellatkin* transitioned smoothly into foldspace and out again.

"Sweet," Alia said. "Oh, shit!"

On the forward screen, upside down to their orientation,

a whole battle fleet hung in space. Two huge Monitor battlewagons flanked ships from Alphacorp, Eastin-Heigle, Arquavisa, Ramsay-Shorre, and Rodontee. The Sterritt Corporation was the only one of the megacorps without representation. Behind them a gate that should not exist flashed as it spat out a cruiser decked out with an Alphacorp insignia.

"I think the phrase you're looking for is 'Let's get out of here!'" Ben said as he began to count ships.

The Kazans linked again. As the three leading ships fired missiles, they shivered into foldspace sideways.

"Was that a whole fleet?" Vel asked.

"Shh, not while they're concentrating," Donna said. She reached over and took hold of Vel's hand, the only sign of tension being her white knuckles as she squeezed his fingers.

"Blow the rules, take us right up to the front door," Ben said.

"Your ship, your rules," Alia said, and popped them into realspace barely ten klicks from Crossways.

"Crossways Control to *Bellatkin*. I told you—"

"Crossways Control, there's an Alphacorp fleet ten thousand clicks from here and heading this way," Ben said. "Emergency enough?"

Chapter Thirty-Eight

INCOMING

SCRAMBLE SOLAR WIND, BEN SAID AS HE ran down the *Bellatkin* ramp. *We need to destroy that gate before any more of the bastards get through.*

Cara brought Mother Ramona into the link.

I'm here with Garrick, Mother Ramona said. *What have you got for us?*

A combined fleet, backed up by two Monitor battle-wagons, Ben said. *Thirty ships that I saw, but more still coming through.*

How the hell did they—

They built a gate, ten thousand klicks out. They've been planning this for months.

How long have we got? Time to bring in reinforcements from Olyanda?

Hours at most now that they know we've seen them. The jumpships are the only ones that could make it in time, and they're all here anyway. First things first. Their gate needs to be destroyed and ours taken offline.

We can take ours offline from here.

Do it.

And theirs?

Can you lend me three hornets?

Of course.

Ben turned to the Kazans. "I want you to take one hornet in each of your cargo holds, get them as close to that gate as you can, drop them and hop straight back into the Folds. Wait until you see the gate go down, then return for a pickup. Take as few risks as possible."

Alia and Grigor hugged their children and pushed them away. "Go straight back to Blue Seven and stay there unless you get specific safety instructions," Alia said.

"What about you?" Vel asked.

"We'll be busy."

"What can you do? You can't fight a fleet in a cargo carrier!" Donna's voice squeaked.

"They won't have to if they're quick," Ben said. "Do as your parents tell you. Can you do that?"

"Yes." Donna took hold of her brother's hand and ran against the tide of incoming crew who were dashing for Mother Ramona's and Garrick's ships while Syke's guards locked down the port and donned rebreathers and atmo suits.

"Your children are a credit to you," Ben told the Kazans as Donna and Vel disappeared through the inner gates to the concourse.

They nodded. "If we don't come back . . ."

Ben didn't give reassurances he couldn't back up. "The Free Company will look after them as long as there is a Free Company."

"Thank you."

Ben briefed the three hornet pilots, all well-drilled as part of Crossways' defense fleet, then the hornets were loaded, two into the *Bellatkin*'s holds, and one into the *Solar Wind*'s. They launched and, within fifty klicks of Crossways, winked out into foldspace.

Solar Wind's stripped-down crew consisted of Ben, Cara, Yan Gwenn on systems, and Gwala on tactical. Ben looked around the flight deck. "Let's make this quick or we don't stand a chance."

"Quick as you like," Cara said.

"Quicker the better." Yan nodded his agreement.

Gwala just nodded.

They popped out of foldspace above the gate and Yan immediately dropped the hornet from their hold. *Bellatkin* materialized and dropped two hornets, then, while the nearest Alphacorp ships were maneuvering into a firing position, sideslipped back into the Folds to await a recall.

Cara immediately connected the hornet pilots to Ben and to each other in a broad gestalt. The hornets, wickedly fast and with the ability to sting, immediately engaged the larger of the two gate modules, the crew and control section. Their objective was to take out the pulse-cannon and missile launchers, then to lay down covering fire for *Solar Wind* to make a run at the gate impeller.

Ben began his run from above before the nearest ships had registered *Solar Wind*'s presence. A flash showed one missile launched, but Hornet One intercepted it with a sure shot. Hornet Two buzzed gate control and landed a pulse on the upper surface where there was a clear gun turret. It exploded in a cloud of debris.

A thump, felt rather than heard, meant that *Solar Wind* had been caught in the debris field. An alarm sounded.

"Small hull breach in aft section four," Cara said. "Section sealed."

Hornet Two wasn't so lucky. It was caught by shrapnel from its own blast and veered off tumbling end over end. Cara lost contact with the gunner and the pilot let loose a long string of colorful invective while she fought to stabilize the little craft. Hornet Three swung around and took several potshots at the lower turret.

An Arquavisa supply ship, a long series of pods attached to a spinal gantry, began to emerge from the gate.

Aware of the hornets through Cara's link, Ben spiraled toward the gate impeller. Gwala lined up a missile then followed it up with a burst of pulses. The impeller shuddered and split apart. There was no spectacular explosion, since the unit carried no atmosphere, but the gate ellipse winked out. The supply ship hadn't cleared the disk and the aft section simply vanished, leaving the forward flight deck and two and a half pods barreling forward under their own momentum, spilling crates behind like a trail of gifts from a piñata. Hornet One turned and peppered the intact pods.

Leave it, Hornet One, Cara ordered. *Don't miss the bus.*

Alerted by the destruction of the gate, the *Bellatkin* popped back into realspace and scooped up Hornet Three. Hornet One didn't break away in time. One of the Monitor battlewagons had turned to present a battery of pulse-cannon. The hornet exploded, its cabin oxygen providing the briefest of flares.

Cara cut contact as quickly as she could, but Ben saw out of his peripheral vision that she was shaking her head to clear it. She didn't drop contact with the others, though.

Bellatkin, take the one you've got and run, Ben ordered. *We'll get Two.*

The second hornet had been knocked for a loop and was outside of the melee forming around the dead gate. Ben turned *Solar Wind* and dived after it with Gwala laying down covering fire behind.

Hornet Two, can you stabilize? Ben asked.

Trying my best, but I've lost a maneuvering thruster starboard.

Stand by.

Ben swept *Solar Wind* kissing close and popped into foldspace, dragging Hornet Two in alongside. Then he settled the *Solar Wind* over the damaged hornet so that it passed through the outer skin. When it was firmly inside the cargo hold, he flipped out of foldspace again, emerging close in to Crossways.

"Crossways has a medical team standing by for Hornet Two," Cara said as they swept into Port 22, running hot.

Bellatkin? Ben asked through Cara's active link.

Right behind you, Alia said. *Thought we'd better not upset Crossways Control again.*

Well? Mother Ramona asked through her Telepath, Ully.

Mission accomplished, Cara said. *The rest is up to you.*

❖ ❖ ❖

Get yourselves up here to the control room.

Mother Ramona's command hit Cara as she and Ben emerged from *Solar Wind*. The maintenance crew began to crawl all over the ship to repair the hull breach as the emergency team from Dockside Medical moved in to extract the pilot and gunner from the damaged hornet in the hold. The pilot was still cursing fluently, which was a sure sign she was okay, but Cara thought the gunner was probably lost. The *gunner's a goner* kept playing in her head and she felt mean, but knew it was just the letdown from the adrenaline that had been coursing through her system.

"Have you got nerves of steel?" she asked Ben.

He held out both hands and she noticed a slight tremor. "I'm okay while it's all happening, but afterward it always gets me."

"Mother Ramona wants us up in Crossways Control."

"You mean I have to look those Control guys in the eye?"

She laughed. "I'm afraid so."

They took a tub to the hub and then Garrick's private elevator up to where Crossways Control bulged outward into space at the top of the spindle.

"Ah, the famous Ben Benjamin." One of the controllers looked up and grinned at him. "You just won me fifty creds. I bet you'd emerge within thirty klicks of us and you did. Twenty-nine point four nine, to be precise. Briggs here figured fifty and Robbie was way out. He figured you'd actually stick to the rules this time."

"Sorry, guys. Injured pilot. *Bellatkin* came in on the hundred mark." Ben tried to look innocent and failed. "Okay, you got me, sorry."

"Hey, you did all right," Briggs said. "The hornet you brought back—pilot's married to my wife's cousin. Thanks for bringing her home."

"Benjamin, in here if you will?" Mother Ramona waved them into a side room that contained a holographic three-dimensional plan of Crossways hanging in midair above one end of a long table and a second hologram on a different scale, showing the station and its environs.

"Well done, Ben." Garrick looked up from where he was leaning over the table. "We owe you."

"I'm afraid I lost three of your hornet crew."

"Two. The gunner's injured, but he'll pull through. The other two are casualties of war. And I think we can safely call this a war, don't you?"

"I'm sure Alphacorp will call it policing, but, yes, it's war. Have you put out warnings to the independents?"

"It's gone out all over the S-LOGosphere and the tel-net and we've warned Jamundi and your grandmother to keep a communications blackout. They're safely out of it."

Cara glanced sideways, but Ben didn't show any emotion. He was all business again and his hands had lost the tremor.

"What's the defensive capability of the station?"

"Pulse-cannon, missiles and a laser array, four corvettes, five frigates, and eight cruisers. All of the frigates and two of the cruisers have been retrofitted with jump drives, but they haven't been on a shakedown run yet and we only have four jumpship pilots. The Magena sisters are each assigned to a cruiser, Valois and Sing each to a frigate, and I've even assigned Esterhazy to a corvette. There's only you and Gen left. There are a hundred and fifty hornets, but they're as likely to get taken out by friendly fire in this kind of exchange. I really wish I'd sent them all to Olyanda, that's where they'd be the most useful. I've got five hundred remotely piloted drones available, operated by a mixture of regular drone pilots and Psi-Mechs. I've had to call up every reservist and we still don't have anything to outgun a battlewagon. There are various private citizens who have put their firepower at our disposal, but it won't be enough."

"Maybe they only want us."

Cara's spine seemed to freeze at Ben's words.

"No," Garrick said. "They've been looking for an excuse to take us down for years and now they've got it."

"But why here? Why now?" Cara asked. "Wouldn't it make more sense to go after Olyanda?"

"Alphacorp has a tenuous legal claim on Crossways. It doesn't have a claim on Olyanda."

"No, but the Trust does," Ben said. "And I didn't see any Trust vessels among the fleet."

They all looked at each other.

"He's right," Cara said. Alphacorp, Arquavisa, Ramsay-Shorre, Eastin-Heigle and even Rodontee, but no Trust.

"Oh, fuck!" Mother Ramona voiced what they were all thinking.

Cara immediately forged a link to Oleg Staple. *Have you got trouble there?* she asked, opening the link to everyone.

Negative.

Who's guarding the gate?

McPherson onboard Sovereign.*

The nearest jump gate was on the edge of the system,

days away at best sublight speed. It was one of the reasons Garrick had wanted a new gate closer to the planet.

Check.

I have. She's still transmitting . . . oh hell, it's the old code. It should have changed at noon.

Prepare for incoming.

Right.

It could be everything the Trust can throw at you.

Understood.

"Now what?" Mother Ramona asked.

"Now we wait," Garrick said. "And we prepare."

Ben turned to Cara. "Contact Yan and Lowenbrun. See if the ark's ready for the Folds."

Jump drive's just coming online now, Yan said. *Haven't tested it yet.*

How's the unloading? Cara asked.

Two more containers of cryo pods, Jake said.

How quickly can you offload them?

The medical staff on the ground have asked us to keep them up here for a while.

Forget that. We need the ark back here—top speed.

Okay. We can load them into shuttles in four hours if we have to.

Do it. Your shakedown run for the new drive will be straight back here. What about the ark's former crew?

Their cryo pods are still on the ark.

Cara relayed the information to Ben and then got back to Jake. *Ben says to send the crew cryo pods dirtside and keep them on ice. We'll sort them out later.*

If there is a later, she thought.

✦ ✦ ✦

The waiting was the worst. Ben sat in the corner of their war room while everyone else buzzed around him.

"You look too calm, are you even awake?" Cara had drunk so many cups of coffee that she was buzzing with caffeine and had gone to pee four times in three hours.

"I'm awake."

"Want caff?"

He shook his head. "It won't help."

Three hours into their wait, Oleg Staple confirmed there

was a Trust fleet heading for Olyanda. *We're ready for them,* he said. *But any reinforcements you can send would be very welcome.*

An hour later the ark appeared out of foldspace a short fifty klicks from Crossways with a whoop from Jake. *Did we make it in time for the fun?*

In time to get the hell out of here with fifty hornets in your hold, Ben said. *Stand by to load. Take them to Olyanda. Get back for another pickup if you can, but the ark's no warship, so avoid direct confrontation.*

Understood.

And, Jake . . .

Yeah?

Thanks.

Garrick deployed all the available ships with firepower, ordered all blast doors on Crossways closed and the viewports shuttered. The drone operators, some of them operating a single drone, others, Psi-Mechs, meshed into a flotilla, settled into their padded chairs in the room directly below the war room and sent a hundred of the drones to the far side of the station, leaving them prepped and ready. Another hundred were stationed twenty klicks above the spindle, with the third hundred thirty klicks below. All nonessential personnel were directed to the inner core of the station and weapons operators to the pulse-cannon and missile launchers. The remaining two hundred drones were ready to spring from their launchers at a moment's notice. The paid crews had once laughed at the spare-time soldiers, but now they were working side by side with no complaints, or at least none that reached the control room.

Garrick's guards, Tengue's mercs, and private forces belonging to the various crimelords manned the docking bays in case of incursion, for now safely behind solid airlocks.

"Enemy fleet standing off at five hundred klicks." Briggs' voice came over the comm from traffic control next door.

"Incoming comms." Ully, a small white-haired woman who looked older than Nan, had the comms station.

"Crossways, this is the Monitor Ship *Oxford*: stand down and prepare to be boarded."

Garrick leaned into the comm. "Not gonna happen. You have no authority here."

"We have warrants for five hundred individuals believed

to have taken refuge on Crossways and a court order for the reclamation of Alphacorp property, to whit, the station itself."

"Five hundred individuals? Now you're getting ambitious."

"Transmitting the list now."

Ben glanced at it. As expected, his name and Cara's were close to the top, but Norton Garrick and Ramona Delgath were on there as well, together with a number of names he didn't recognize who were obviously notables in Crossways' underworld.

"It's a who's who of the Crossways great and the good," Mother Ramona said. "Well, maybe the not-so-good, if truth be told." She smacked the table with the flat of her hand and the holograms swayed. "This is just an excuse. They'll come at us hard whatever we do."

"Monitor Ship *Oxford*," Ben said. "You are exceeding your authority. This station is home to almost a million people, most of whom are not on your list. Any attack endangering civilians in the pursuit of criminals is regarded as using unnecessary force. Monitor regulation 19, section 1." He turned. "Cara, broadcast that for me, please. It may slow them down."

"Alphacorp has obtained a judgment against Crossways in the Interstellar Supreme Court," MS *Oxford* transmitted.

"Crossways is a hunk of metal and ceramic, not a person. There are people on Crossways. I repeat: Regulation 19, section 1. Officers in breach of this regulation are subject to suspension and investigation."

Cara transmitted the same thing again, and added, *This is already uploaded to the S-LOG, just in case you thought you could shut us up before anyone found out.*

"Stand by and prepare to be boarded." This time it was another voice on the comm, not the Monitor ship.

"Unknown vessel, identify yourself," Briggs answered.

"Alphacorp One, vessel 2C049, *Sea Eagle*. You're outgunned, Crossways."

"Heavy cruiser, armed with pulse-cannon and missiles. Potentially carries five hundred ground troops, and she's just one of at least forty vessels." Mother Ramona brought up the specs on screen.

"Shit!" Garrick held out his hand to silence Ben. "Go to hell, *Sea Eagle*, and take Alphacorp with you."

The combined fleet came in fast and hard. The first missile hit the station just five seconds later.

"Level four, green sector, exterior skin breach," Mother Ramona said. "Automatic sealant repair."

"Laser array target incoming missiles," Garrick said. "Pulse-cannon, fire at will as your sights come to bear. Unless the Monitor ships fire on us, don't target them. There may still be some sense in all this. Make every shot count. Drone group one, get around behind the Alphacorp vessels. Hit them where it hurts."

"Understood."

Ben jerked upright at the sound of Serafin's voice. *Serafin. I thought you were still in Dockside Medical.*

I want to make sure Dockside Medical is still here this time tomorrow. Besides, all I have to do is sit here and fly a few drones. It's hardly going to tax my breathing. Archie's with me, and a few more Free Company volunteers.

The lasers set up a sweeping barrage that took out a proportion of incoming missiles, but some got through and the Crossways' hologram started to show damage.

"Deploy drone groups four and five," Garrick said, and two hundred drones launched from the upper ring.

A corvette, two frigates, and two cruisers, all Crossways' jumpships, appeared in realspace behind the enemy fleet. The cruisers dropped thirty hornets between them, took out a destroyer class ship in a pincer movement and disappeared back into the Folds without receiving any damage. The corvette dithered and slipped sideways into foldspace. The two frigates launched a series of missiles at Alphacorp cruisers and winked out of realspace before they hit, but the missiles took out one ship and damaged three others.

"Yes!" Garrick punched the air.

Ben kept his eyes on the screens. Five ships down out of forty was still a hell of a lot of ships left to fight off.

The hornets began to target the drives of the larger ships. They didn't have enough firepower to take down a cruiser or even a frigate individually unless they got lucky, but they could cripple a ship with a hit to the drive. They had less than five minutes to wreak havoc before three Alphacorp cruisers deployed a flotilla of drones, outnumbering them three to one.

CROSSWAYS 511

All Ben could do was stand by and watch as one by one the hornets were snuffed out. He felt sick. He checked with Port 22, but *Solar Wind*'s repairs were still ongoing.

The Monitor battlewagons, at least for now, were standing back and observing, not taking an active part in the offensive. Hopefully he'd set the crews questioning their officers' commands.

The five Crossways jumpships appeared out of nowhere again, targeted a cruiser, destroyed it and vanished, but not before picking up five surviving hornets. The next time, they all popped into being at different points, delivered significant damage and disappeared. One of their targets was left floating dead, another broke up in slow motion. A third was spinning end over end.

It couldn't last. The next time the ships emerged from foldspace the corvette, Esterhazy's ship, collided with an Alphacorp cruiser that was on its immediate flight path. The resulting destruction was instant and complete. Both ships reduced to space junk in the blink of an eye. The debris took out one of the smaller Alphacorp ships while the four remaining Crossways ships melted back into the Folds.

"I should be out there with them," Ben said.

"In what? The Dixie Flyer?" Cara asked.

With a shimmer, the ark materialized in the middle of the dogfight, very obviously not a fighting ship.

"Hey, whoa!" Lowenbrun broadcast. "I've got thirty thousand innocent settlers in cryo on board. White flag! White flag! Hold your fucking fire!"

The Alphacorp ship on a direct course for the ark broke and rolled away.

"Ark ship, this is Monitor Ship *Oxford*. Identify yourself."

Jake swung the ark between the station and the array of attacking vessels and the great hold doors swung open, station-side. "Ark J, series 982, *Harvest*," Jake said. "Ring any bells?"

"Monitor Ship *Supreme*, here, *Harvest*, please report your status, are your settlers safe?"

"Next fifty hornets, go, go, go!" Garrick said.

The hornets deployed and, while Jake was stalling, slipped into the ark's hold in tight formation.

"Oh, yes, MS *Supreme*, safe, no thanks to Ari van Blaiden and a rogue Monitor called Sergei Alexandrov who tried to abandon them in foldspace."

"Stand by for boarding, *Harvest*. Let's escort you out of the hot zone."

"No, that's not the way it's going to work," Jake said. "The settlers are safe where no one can reach them. Thanks for the breathing space, MS *Supreme*."

By the time the fleet cruisers had woken up to what was happening, Jake was seconds away from closing up the hold on the last hornet. He slid into the Folds from a standing start and the first missile volley hit the space where he wasn't.

"Yes!" Ben breathed again, forgiving Jake Lowenbrun all his former crimes.

A few small successes followed, but the fleet had the edge through sheer weight of numbers. Even with all the drones deployed the station was taking a beating. Enough missiles slipped through their defense to knock chunks out of sections of station. Losses mounted. The hologram hovering above the table in the war room showed all the damage, glowing red. The crescent of the farm took three hits in quick succession, lost integrity and broke away, scattering a trail of ice crystals in its wake from the irrigation systems.

"Losing structural integrity in Gold One," an anonymous voice announced over the comm. "Evacuate Gold Two through Four. Emergency evacuation procedure. All civilians to your evac stations." The public address system repeated the instruction three times and then a klaxon took over. Mother Ramona muted it. The station hologram shuddered and Gold One and Two, the tube-like extension that held the observatory, disappeared under fiery red.

"Let me through. Let me through!" Shouting from next door penetrated their war room. "Bastards. Let me fuckin' through. Benjamin, it's me, Dido. Let me fuckin . . ."

As Ben got to the door, Dido Kennedy kicked the legs out from under the guard who'd been blocking her way.

"Thank all the little angels you're not out there." Kennedy reached and took Ben's hand. "I got it. I did it. I told you it could be done."

"What?"

"It just needs the right Navigator, or maybe Navigators, and we just need them to stop pounding us for a few minutes."

"What does? Take a deep breath. You're not making sense."

"Yeah, I'm making the best sense you'll ever hear. I fitted this whole damn station with a jump drive. Come and see. Red One is gonna be jumpin' tonight."

Chapter Thirty-Nine

JUMP

THE MORE BEN THOUGHT ABOUT IT, THE more he thought it could work. "It's theoretically possible," he told Garrick, yanking Dido back to make her wait for him. "Kennedy's jump drive worked on the ark."

"That whole damn farm section was brought here through the Folds," Dido said. "Granted it didn't arrive in one piece, but it can be done. You've just got to believe me."

"Belief?" Garrick choked on his own voice.

"Tell him, Benjamin," Dido said.

Ben shrugged. "That's as near as I can put it into words. Nothing's real in the Folds. Mass has meaning out here, but it ceases to have meaning in there. We'll need to pull all our ships—the ones without jump drives—back to the station before we can jump or we'll leave them behind to be picked off." He turned to Dido. "You said we needed to get them to stop pounding us."

She pulled a face. "Yeah. I can't guarantee what'll happen if we try to jump with incoming missiles. We'll suck 'em into the Folds with us. They could pass through, but the station's so big that they could still be lodged deep inside when we emerge and then—kaboom—from the inside out. Could blow us apart."

"So we have to get them to stop firing. How the hell can we do that?" Garrick asked. "Ask them nicely?"

"We'll surrender," Mother Ramona said. "But only on our terms. Cease-fire first."

"They'll want a sign of good faith," Ben said. "Tell them they can have me."

"No. No. No!" Dido was almost jumping up and down. "You're driving the bus, Benjamin. I need you down in Red One. Now. Come on!"

"Hold on," Ben said. "We need to sort this or Crossways isn't going anywhere."

"They can have me," Garrick said. "Have you still got the Keely woman in lockup?"

"Yes."

He tapped the hologram control panel and cut and pasted images of damage across the station until it looked about to disintegrate. "There, does that look credible, or does it need a bit more?" He tapped again and the damage began to look even more dangerous. "Keely's got a direct line to Akiko Yamada, right?"

"Yes, but Yamada's not likely to be with the fleet."

"That doesn't matter. Yamada will have a link to her admiral. Keely's a Telepath but not an Empath, right?"

"Yes."

"So she won't be able to read me if I sell her a pack of lies?"

"Not unless you're a really bad liar," Ben said.

"I'm not. It's all a matter of belief, like you said. You really have to believe your own lies."

"Remind me never to play poker with you."

◆ ◆ ◆

Kitty had felt the thumps and knew what they meant. She wondered whether, if she'd not been isolated in this damping field, Remus would have warned her to get out before the attack began, or whether she was an acceptable loss on this kind of operation. What would happen to her mother if she was killed while on assignment? She'd been thinking a lot about what Cara had said about the consequences of knowing too much. She had little doubt that it was an Alphacorp fleet attacking. As much as the Trust wanted Ben and Cara, they had no legitimate excuse to attack Crossways. Alphacorp did.

How long could the station take this kind of battering? It was big. No ship was going to take it out with a single missile, but enough battering and something vital would be affected. As she reached that conclusion the lights in her cell flickered. If only the damping field would blow.

The door hummed and whooshed open.

She shot back to the far side of the cell. They may have decided she was more trouble than she was worth.

"Cara. No armed guard?"

Cara shook her head, face pale. "Not this time. Garrick's got a job for you. I hope you've still got your hotline to god."

"Huh?"

"Akiko Yamada."

"Yes. I hope so, anyway. Her Telepath usually contacts me." Dare she let herself hope there might be a way out?

"Station can't take any more," Cara said. "Garrick will tell you himself. Are you going to be trouble or will you come quietly?"

"No trouble."

"Good. Wear this."

A damping pin. "Is that really necessary?"

Cara shrugged. "Do you want to get out of this cell or not?"

Kitty stuck the pin in her collar and followed Cara to the waiting tub.

"Where are all Tengue's people?" she asked.

"Manning the barricades at the ports."

"Everyone all right?"

"You mean Syke? So far."

Kitty felt a rush of relief. Maybe she was clinging on to Syke because he'd been Wes' friend, but for whatever reason she'd grown fond of him. *As a friend,* she reminded herself.

The tub ride seemed to take forever as they had to keep stopping for blast doors to be opened and closed behind them again. Cara wasn't very communicative. She supposed that was fair. At the hub, crowds had gathered, filling all the street spaces and spreading out into the park. Cara led her past two guards at the Mansion House door, the small entrance on the ground floor, not the elegant front door. So she didn't rate the VIP entrance.

"Garrick's not here. We have to go upstairs." Cara led the way to a small personal elevator, not an antigrav shaft, but a moving box, claustrophobic but fast and smooth. They came out into a flight control room. Norton Garrick waited in the doorway that led into an inner room.

Mother Ramona glared at her and then turned to Garrick. "I'll leave you now. Good luck." She stepped in close and kissed him. Garrick kissed her back, hard, desperation showing in every line of his body.

When he stepped back from her he looked over to Kitty. "Come in, Miss Keely. We have business to discuss."

There was a hologram of the station. Kitty gulped involuntarily when she saw the damage. Garrick gestured to it.

"To put it quite bluntly, Miss Keely, we give in, but there are conditions. I want a guarantee of safety for station personnel who are not on the Monitor arrest list. You can take off the damper now. I want you to relay a message to your Ms. Yamada."

An hour ago Kitty had been worried about being spaced, but now, here she was, effectively taking Crossways' surrender. Would that help to save her from the consequences of knowing too much if Alphacorp got their hands on her again? Would it save her mother from a labor camp?

"I'm not a long-range Telepath, Mr. Garrick. I'll need comms assistance."

"Ully will connect you." He indicated a white-haired woman standing quietly by the comms array. She looked fragile, like a dandelion clock, as if a couple of puffs would blow her away, but when Kitty shut off the damping pin, Ully's mental contact felt no older than Kitty herself. She slipstreamed behind the old woman's talent and found Remus.

I'm here on Crossways with Mr. Garrick. He wishes to negotiate a surrender.

There was a slight pause. *You have been absent from our thoughts for some time.*

Unforeseen circumstances. Can we discuss it later? Crossways is being pounded to a pulp. They've had enough.

There was a pause.

Ms. Yamada, asks whether, in your opinion, this is a genuine offer.

Kitty eyed the hologram. *The station has taken a lot of

damage. I don't think they have a choice, but there are conditions, safety of station personnel, etc.

There was another pause while Remus relayed Kitty's message.

Ms. Yamada says that Mr. Garrick can discuss details with her fleet commander.

I think that will be acceptable.

She asked Garrick and he gave assent.

I want Garrick here in person, Admiral Lloyd said when Kitty had been given clearance to facilitate direct negotiation. *The only way we're going to talk is face-to-face.*

"Face-to-face," she said to Garrick. "I'm sorry."

He took a deep breath, lips pressed together, then nodded. "If that's the only way. Tell him to call off his dogs. I'm not going out there while missiles are flying. I want a cease-fire while I make the transit."

Kitty relayed the message and then came back with, "He agrees to a cease-fire, but he won't stop firing until you launch. You are to come alone in a small craft. And I'm to confirm that it's you that's in it and to pilot it myself."

Damn! She was going back to Alphacorp whether she wanted to or not.

"Right," Garrick said. "Just you and me in a hornet."

"Not a hornet, sir. An unarmed flyer."

"A small shuttle." He paused, then nodded. "There's really no choice, is there? I agree. I'm bringing my ships back in now as a sign of good faith."

"Shall we go down to your dock?" Kitty stood back and waited for Garrick to lead the way.

◆　◆　◆

Ben stood in Dido's workshop in front of a simple drive plate cobbled together from obsolete parts. Cables as thick as his wrist snaked out from under the console and disappeared down a vent in the floor.

"Well?" Dido asked.

"It's either genius or the worst idea anyone ever had in the history of the universe," Ben said.

Will it work? Mother Ramona was up in the control room while Garrick made his way down to Port 22 with Kitty Keely.

One way or another it will finish this thing, Ben said. *If *it doesn't work we'll all be scattered atoms across the whole sector.* *

"Mother Ramona wants to know if it will work," Cara told Dido.

"It'll work as long as the Navigator is strong enough." Dido narrowed her eyes. "Are you, Benjamin? Strong enough?"

"I stand more of a chance with every available jump-drive Navigator in gestalt."

"Can you do that?"

He nodded to Cara and she nodded back. "I can't, but Cara can. Unfortunately there are only three of us."

"Three's better than one," Cara said. "I'll hold everyone together. Ben can take the focus."

Ben would have liked the indefatigable Magena sisters as backup, but they were still in the Folds, as were Valois and Singh. Gen arrived, hugely round of belly, followed closely by the Kazans.

"Gen—" Ben began.

"What, you think I can't hack it just because I'm pregnant?"

"Be honest." Max followed her in.

"Yeah, all right, I might be in labor, but it's really early. Contractions every thirty minutes and hardly pains yet, just tightening."

"I've sent for Ronan, but he's dealing with casualties," Max said.

Ben's mind did that kind of backflip that he figured men's minds often did when dealing with childbirth.

"You'll be fine." Alia put one arm around Gen. "With my first it took twelve hours from this stage until I was cursing the midwife, Grigor, seven gods, and everyone else I'd ever met in my whole life."

Ben eyed Gen doubtfully, but this jump was likely to be over in the next few minutes, so no use worrying about what might happen twelve hours from now.

"Okay, let's do this thing," he said. "Kennedy, get the station thruster controls transferred to the remote rig."

He placed both hands on the panel and Gen and Alia each placed their own hands over his, Gen on his right, Alia on his left.

"Where are you going to take us?" Dido asked.

"Olyanda."

Cara looked at him sharply. *Straight out of one battle into another?*

He nodded. *All our resources together, where we can use them to best effect. I've got an idea for divide and conquer, but first we have to get through the Folds.*

❖ ❖ ❖

Cara took the focus and then brought Gen and Alia Kazan into gestalt with Ben. She hardly knew Alia at all; Gen was an old friend. They'd shared a lot on Olyanda. If Cara had had a sister, they couldn't have been closer.

All right? Cara asked.

So far, Gen said.

The gestalt began to meld into a single unit and Cara flicked her awareness to Port 22, to where Hilde, Tengue, and Gwala were stationed with some of Syke's men.

All quiet here, Hilde said. *Tell Ben they've finished working on* Solar Wind. *She's sound again. Ah, what's this? Garrick and Kitty Keely? Is that right?*

Yes. Be cooperative. They'll want a two-man flyer. As soon as they're out of the air lock I want to know.

"Garrick and Kitty have arrived at Port 22," she told Ben.

Dido Kennedy was almost dancing. "Get ready to hit it, Benjamin."

"As soon as Garrick and Keely are flying and the missiles stop."

"They've cleared the air lock," Hilde said.

"Now," Cara relayed.

Ben hit the station's maneuvering thrusters and then the jump-drive control.

❖ ❖ ❖

Gen and Alia feed all their energy into Ben, each one of them individual, yet part of the collective. The air in Red One ripples and Dido Kennedy's workshop is suddenly filled with the otter-kind swirling around the humans. Cara sees them through the gestalt, but Max, standing behind Gen, and Dido, kneeling beside where the tubes disappear into the guts of the station, obviously don't.

"Did we draw in Garrick's shuttle?" Ben asks.

"Can't tell," Cara says.

She feels Ben searching for a line strong enough to take them out of the Folds and land them close to Olyanda.

"How long?" Ben asks, his voice catching in his throat.

"Twelve minutes," Max says.

Cara feels Ben suppress worry.

Confidence. Believe they'll find the line and they will.

"Ah." Gen doubles over her belly and drops out of the gestalt.

Max catches her and half-carries her over to Dido's couch.

Just Ben and Alia now.

"It's okay. I'm okay, just a sharper contraction," Gen says. "That's normal, isn't it? They're still twenty minutes ap—" She gasps. "Oh, shit!"

"Cara, can you get Ronan?" Max shouts even though they're close enough to whisper. "I think it's now."

Ronan? Gen's in labor.

Can you bring her up to Blue Seven? I'm operating on a spleen full of shrapnel.

We'll try.

"He wants you to get her back to Blue Seven," she tells Max.

"Oh!" Gen gasps and begins to whimper.

"There isn't time." Max's eyes are wide in panic.

Gen bats something away that Cara can't see. She looks through the gestalt. The otter-kind, dense as eels in a barrel, fuss around Gen, curious, excited.

"Enough, get them out of he—"

Her words end in a groan as another contraction follows sharply on the last.

The otter-kind suddenly flee as a void dragon swirls into the workshop. It twists around Ben and Alia then pushes its huge head between Gen and Max. This time Cara sees it herself, not through the gestalt.

"Know you," she says to it.

Know you, it responds, then looks at Gen again. *?* it asks.

"Young." Cara pictures Ricky and then pictures him smaller and younger and finally in his mother's belly. She reverses the process.

"Who are you talking to?" Max asks. "Is Ronan coming down?"

"It's a void dragon," Gen says between contractions. "It wants to know what's going on." She reaches out and puts her hand on its snout. Its prehensile beard-claws wrap around her hand and hold on while she has another monster contraction.

"I want to push," Gen says.

"Wait, no, hold on. That can't be right." Max glances at his handpad. "Hell, this says six hours. We can't have been in the Folds for six hours, can we?"

Cara looks over to Ben. He and Alia Kazan clutch each other's hands now, deep in concentration.

"I don't know," Cara says, "But if she wants to push, better get these trousers off her."

Between them they settle Gen on the couch, strip off the bottom half of her clothing and drape Dido's cheap throw over her.

The void dragon hovers, fascinated by the whole process.

? it says again.

Cara tries to imagine birth for it. It seems to be laughing.

Yeah, I know. It's just the way humans are made. You should see how the baby gets in there in the first place.

The void dragon laughs again as if saying how small human minds are.

You can't just float this thing out. It doesn't work like that.

Cara has never been present at a birth before, but females of every species have been having babies since before midwives were invented. How hard can it be?

Gen groans again and begins to curse.

Hard enough.

"It's all right, Gen, I've got this." Max pushes his sleeves up, sounding a lot calmer than Cara feels. "You're doing well."

"Do you know what you're doing?" Cara whispers.

"Yeah, I'm getting ready to catch a baby and hoping nature takes its course. You got any better ideas?"

"Uh, not really."

"Okay, then. Let's do this thing."

◆　◆　◆

Ben's aware of Gen dropping out of the gestalt and knows why, but he can't spare a thought for her. Cara will deal with it, she always does. Alia Kazan turns to follow Gen, but Ben pulls her back. *I need you here. Find the line.*

They search for the line to Olyanda, finding and discarding those that aren't strong enough to pull a whole station into being.

The void dragon swirls into view and sweeps itself around them like a life preserver. *Find,* it seems to say. Its presence strengthens them and they search again.

Ben hears a cry, but ignores it. *Cara will deal. Cara will deal.*

With no sound at all Alia sinks to her knees and topples over. Dido drags her away and Grigor springs up to take his wife, completely oblivious to the void dragon he's just stepped through.

Just Ben now.

He holds the focus and searches for the line.

A baby cries.

Don't get distracted.

Then Cara's standing behind him, pouring her energy into him.

She wraps her hands around his waist from behind and hugs herself to him, two bodies, one mind. He staggers. She pulls him upright and puts her hands over the top of his.

Find the line.

His vision fogs.

He staggers again and this time she can't save him. They fall together, but Cara doesn't let go.

"Benjamin!" He hears Dido's voice from a long way away.

There's another Navigator in the mix. Gen!

"Are you sure about this?" Max asks.

"Just set me down and hold me steady."

Ben feels someone else on the deck plating beside himself and Cara. Gen, giddy with euphoria. Max is next to her, clutching a small bundle.

"Oh, hell, one in, all in." Dido Kennedy's bulk drops down into the huddle and though she's not a Navigator, she's a human being and she's offering all the support she can offer.

The void dragon knots itself around them all. Is it laughing? It seems to have picked up Gen's euphoria. Another life brought into being. That can't be something a void dragon experiences every day.

Ben feels a surge of energy.

Find the line.

Find. The. Fucking. Line!

There.

Strong and sure, the line that leads to Olyanda draws him on. He grabs it and begins to draw himself toward it.

With a shiver the void dragon disappears.

✦ ✦ ✦

Realspace again.

A shuddering thud announced that they surfaced in the middle of a battle.

Shit!

Ben disentangled himself from the dogpile of humans.

"How is this better, Benjamin?" Dido yelled. "You were supposed to be getting us out of danger."

Benjamin, what's happening? Mother Ramona asked via Ully's link.

Welcome to Olyanda. Just making a few adjustments. With respect, launch everything you've got at the Trust. You should have them well outnumbered now.

He'd intended to put the station into high orbit around Olyanda, but they were too damn close, yawing like crazy in a decaying orbit that would take them into the planet's atmosphere. Well, at least they were here.

He scrabbled for the control and fired the thrusters, easing them into higher orbit and higher still. *Crossways Control, can you stabilize us?* he asked.

We're on it, Benjamin. You leave the shitty job for us, huh?

Don't grumble, Briggs. You can do it.

"Won't the Alphacorp fleet simply follow us?" Cara asked.

"Not without a gate." He stood unsteadily and took in the whole workshop: Alia Kazan, still stretched out, unconscious, Grigor by her side; Dido just rising to her feet; Cara, Gen, Max, and a baby still all in a huddle.

A baby!

"I thought . . . ah . . . I seem to have missed something," he said, taking in the relieved smiles.

"Me too," Ronan dashed in, med kit in hand. "Sorry about the wait."

"Max delivered her," Gen said. "With some help from a void dragon. Meet Olivia May Marling."

"Constant," said Max. "Olivia May Marling-Constant."

Gen gave him a look.

"Well, perhaps there's time to decide that later," he said. "She seems well and happy and that's what counts."

"Better see to Alia, Doc," Ben said. "It looks like Gen can wait a while."

He turned to leave. "Where are you going?" Cara asked.

"I have one more job to do."

"Need me to come?"

"I would appreciate it. Can you get Gwala and Wenna to meet us at *Solar Wind*?"

"Are we going out there into battle?"

"Not quite. Just shutting a door . . . and stealing a jump gate."

Chapter Forty

DIVIDE AND CONQUER

"YOU'RE SURE ABOUT THIS?" CARA ASKED AS the *Solar Wind*'s hatch closed behind them and sealed with a reassuring hiss.

"It was your idea," Ben said. "Why hasn't anyone ever thought of stealing a jump gate?"

"Yes, but I didn't exactly mean you should try it."

"We're going to steal a jump gate?" Wenna asked, sliding into the systems station.

"Our own—well—Crossways' own."

"Good plan," Gwala said, settling in to tactical.

"Leaving the joint fleet without a way home suits me perfectly," Cara said. "Oh, I know they'll get home sooner or later, but it will be a hell of a long way around. The megacorps will either have to build a new gate—"

"Which we can watch for and destroy," Ben said.

"Or they'll have to resupply their space-locked ships with jumpships. It's going to tie them in knots." She smiled. "This is nuts, Ben. I think you should see Ronan for a psych eval."

"Probably, but—your idea, remember?"

"I think I should see Ronan for a psych eval." She grinned and settled into the comms station.

"Crossways Control," Ben said. "*Solar Wind* ready to launch."

"*Solar Wind*, I don't suppose there's any point in asking you to wait until you're a hundred klicks befo—"

"Absolutely not. This will be a short hop into the Folds."

"Good luck, *Solar Wind*."

"Thanks, Crossways Control."

Ben eased *Solar Wind* out of the air lock. The sudden arrival of the station had diverted some of the Trust vessels away from engaging Oleg Staple's fleet but the sudden launch of Crossways' fighting ships, plus the remaining drones, had set them on their heels. The four jumpships had materialized as well and Staple had the Trust on the run.

A Trust cruiser began to circle around to put them in its sights. It lined up.

"*Solar Wind*? Benjamin, is that you?"

"Captain Duran of the *Simonides*, I believe," Cara said. "I recognize your call sign. Ben's here. Want to talk?"

Ben hit the comm link. "You said to come out fighting if we ever met again, Captain, but I think the tide has turned in this particular battle. Let's not fire in anger."

"What just happened?"

"We got a party invitation and decided to accept. Olyanda is doubly protected now. Crossways has it and we're keeping it. You're outgunned, Duran."

"I believe we are. I've just had an order to stand down and withdraw."

"Wise decision."

It would be all over by the time they got back.

"They don't need our help," Ben said, "but I wish I knew whether Garrick's ship had come right the way through the Folds with us. Any news?"

Cara got straight through to Ully.

"Nothing yet," she told Ben. "They're all watching for him, but if his shuttle was dumped in the middle of a battle . . ."

Ben nodded. "I know, it could have gone in a puff of smoke before anyone knew it was there."

Less than thirty klicks from Crossways, Ben hit the jump drive.

✦ ✦ ✦

"Scoot!" Ben brushes something away. "Can anyone else see them?"

"Void dragon?" Cara asks.

"No, the little ones."

She shakes her head. "I saw the big one, though. In Red One."

"We might make a Navigator of you yet."

"Do you want weapons running hot as we break into realspace?" Gwala asks.

"Cold, let's play dumb and see if we can gain a little time."

"Phasing ship ID," Cara says.

Ben takes the line that leads to Crossways' previous location and pops out into realspace barely two klicks beyond the dark gate.

✦ ✦ ✦

Wenna brought up the full display on the forward screen. They'd dropped right in the middle of a swarm of ships converging on the gate: Alphacorp, Eastin-Heigle, Arquavisa, Ramsay-Shorre, and Rodontee, with the two big Monitor battlewagons bringing up the rear. Only the Sterritt Corporation was noticeable by its absence, and the Trust, of course, whose ships had all been concentrated on the Olyanda attack.

"They've seen us," Cara said. "They're all running hot, weapons primed for launch."

"Unknown vessel, this is Alphacorp One. Please identify," the comms unit spat out.

"Sorry . . . err . . . Hi," Cara said via the vox. "This is pleasure cruiser *Oklahoma*. Sorry we seem to have crashed your party accidentally. Changing course now."

Ben swept *Solar Wind* up and over in a wide one-eighty loop.

"*Oklahoma,* your ship ID is phasing. Repeat, your ship ID is phasing. Please transmit registration and port of origin."

"Oh, sorry, is it? I'm a bit new to all this." She thought she'd try a Max on them. "The regular comms operator is in the head with the squits. They only said to sit here until he got back. Captain Skinner, how do I stop the ship ID from phasing and . . . Sorry, Alphacorp One, let me get this sorted."

"*Oklahoma*, you're heading directly for an offline gate. Come about and stand by for further instructions."

"Hang on, let me tell the pilot."

"*Oklahoma*, this is your last warning."

"What? No! We're complying, Alphacorp One."

Cara saw two telltale puffs from the forward ports of the closest Alphacorp ship.

"Missiles launched," she said.

Gwala answered with pulse-cannon and blew both missiles. Five more puffs.

"They're too late," Ben said. "Here we go."

Ben pointed *Solar Wind* directly between the gate impeller and the control housing, where the blacker-than-black ellipse, the gate to foldspace, normally hung, blotting out the stars.

As he passed between the two he hit the jump drive. The flight deck air rippled and they were through, leaving the missiles behind but pulling in both sections of the gate.

"You got them," Cara said.

"Okay, let's keep them. Straight in, straight out again. I've got the line to Olyanda."

Another pop and they were hanging in realspace behind Olyanda's largest moon.

Cara contacted Oleg Staple to reassure him that it wasn't an incursion, then she called Ully to pass on the message that Garrick's wish had been fulfilled, Olyanda had a new gate just as soon as a team of engineers could reconfigure it. Cara smiled as she told Ully the combined fleet had been stranded on the far side of nowhere.

Still no Garrick? Cara asked.

No.

"We should retrace our steps through the Folds," Ben said.

Cara nodded. *Crossways Control, we're going to try cruising the Folds.*

Thank you, Mother Ramona answered through Ully. *You've done wonders already. All I ask is one more minor miracle.*

We'll do our best.

✦   ✦   ✦

Ben settles *Solar Wind* in the black depths of foldspace, cuts the drive and listens. He closes his eyes. Foldspace isn't really black, neither is it empty. It glistens like moonlight on oily water. He can sense the lines that have the potential to lead to anywhere, but those aren't what he's looking for.

Tracks disturb the ripples, faint whispers in the fabric of space-time, maybe where some ship has once passed, maybe a void dragon or the otter-kind.

"Can we help?" Cara asks.

"I don't think so. Keep a watch on the instruments, check the time and let me know if there's anything unusual."

One lone otter-kind appears and settles on the flight deck ceiling, curling around itself like a cat. Another drifts lazily through and out again.

Ben tries to call up the big void dragon by concentrating, but nothing answers. He's never seen more than one at a time, has always wondered if there is only one.

There's something out there, disturbing the ripples like a crosscurrent. What has been smooth becomes choppy.

"There's something on instruments," Cara says.

Ben keeps his eyes closed for a few seconds longer, trying to feel the shape of it, but it's just darkness out there in the iridescent black. He opens his eyes.

"What is it?" Gwala asks.

"It's like nothing I've ever seen," Wenna answers.

The void dragon swirls into the flight deck and asks, *?*

"I was going to ask you that," Ben says, and responds with his own *?*

Ben gets the impression of, *Other,* without any actual words. The void dragon seems almost worried. It changes its shape and becomes foldspace darkness with a bright dot in the center.

"What is that?" Cara asks.

"A ship." Ben recognizes it. "A small two-man shuttle."

"Garrick and Kitty?"

"Could be. We'll check."

As Ben fires up the maneuvering thrusters the otter-kind tumble in, become agitated and shoot out of the flight deck. The void dragon swirls around twice and then disappears.

"Whatever it is, the big fellow doesn't like it," Ben says.

"I'll try the vox," Cara says.

"*Solar Wind* to shuttle. Come in please. *Solar Wind* to—"

"Cara? Ben?" Kitty answers. "Oh, gods, come and get us. This thing—"

"We can see it. What is it?"

"Stay back, Ben," Garrick says. "If it touches you, you'll be stuck here like us."

"I don't intend to let it touch us, but we've got to get you out."

"Oh, yes, please," Kitty says. "It's eating the shuttle."

"Explain."

"Hush, Kitty," Garrick says. "When it first latched on to us it was just the very tail end of the craft that was mired, but very slowly it's drawing us in. Half the shuttle is—I don't know—dissolved into this darkness."

"Can you still move around freely?"

"Yes, within the half of the cabin that's still clear. Neither of us has tried to touch the shadow-thing, though. It gives off a fearful sense of—I don't know—*otherness.*"

"That's what the void dragon said."

"Huh?"

"Never mind. Have you tried imagining that it's not real, that it doesn't exist?"

"No."

"Nothing's real in foldspace. You're not real, your shuttlecraft isn't real. Everything's fluid, changeable. The shadow is not real."

"While you've been talking it's crept toward us by another ten centimeters. Does that sound like it's not real?"

"Okay, we're coming to get you."

Ben nudges the *Solar Wind* ever closer to the shadow and as he does so the feeling of dread grows.

"I'm not liking this," Gwala says.

"I thought it was just me." Wenna tries to keep her voice light, but it cracks.

"Cara?" Ben asks.

"All of that and more."

As *Solar Wind* nudges closer, the shadow billows like a cloud.

"That's as close as we can get," Wenna says. "The shuttle's embedded too deeply."

"We can see you," Garrick says. "You're close, but not close enough."

"Do you trust me?" Ben asks.

"Yes."

"Then all you have to do is step through the front screen of the shuttle and cross foldspace like you were taking a stroll in the park. You can step straight through *Solar Wind*'s skin."

"Oh, yes, that's likely!"

"Everyone doubts."

"Shall we suit up?" Cara asks.

"Not necessary. They'll never be able to trust us if we don't trust ourselves. As soon as we break the integrity of their shuttle they'll choke on vacuum because that's what they believe will happen."

"So we just step out of the air lock?"

"More or less, yes, but we don't need the air lock. We just go out through the *Solar Wind*'s skin, pass through it like the missile did, like the void dragons do."

"And what happens if you don't come back?" Wenna says.

Ben shrugs. "Believe that we will."

"It's all right, Wenna. Ben's done this before." Cara grabs Ben's hand. "Let's do it."

They push off together, rise to the ceiling and through it into the wonder of foldspace, momentum carrying them forward toward the shuttle.

The look on their faces . . . Cara says as they float toward the small craft, still hand-in-hand.

Priceless, Ben says. The skin of the shuttle gives way beneath them and they land gently in the small space.

"Oh, gods!" Kitty collapses into the pilot's couch. "You can't . . . You didn't."

"Can and did," Ben says. "It's the only way out. Or are you going to sit here and wait for that to catch up with you?"

The aft section of the shuttle, including the hatch, is wreathed in what looks like dense black smoke.

"I'm with you," Garrick says.

"I . . . can't," Kitty says. "Couldn't you have brought pressure suits?"

"There wasn't time." Ben eyes the tangible darkness. It's almost touching the back of the couch Kitty has sunk into. "It's up to you, Kitty. It's save-yourself time."

"Save myself for what, an air lock accident?" She looked

at Garrick. "A hundred-year sleep to wake, when and where? My mother abandoned. Alphacorp—"

"You have to help yourself," Ben says. "Come on. There's still time."

"Why would you care after what I've done?"

"Why not?"

The darkness roils toward them.

Ben links hands with Cara again. Cara grabs Garrick and Ben holds out his free hand for Kitty.

She hesitates.

"Come on, Kitty."

He reaches out for her, but the darkness beats him to it. A tendril swirls around her waist, draws her into its embrace.

Her eyes widen.

"Go!" she mouths. Without a sound, she is gone.

"Quickly," Ben says as the darkness boils toward them. They push off through the shuttle skin and dive for the *Solar Wind*, landing in a heap on the flight deck floor.

"What the hell was that thing?" Garrick asks.

"Nothing I've ever seen before," Ben says. "The void dragon calls it *other*. Let's hope we never see anything like it again."

Without waiting to be told, Wenna fires the thrusters and *Solar Wind* slides away just as the shadow swallows the nose of the shuttle and balloons outward toward them.

"I am not going to do that again. Ever," Cara says, dusting herself off as if some essence of shadow is clinging to her buddysuit.

Garrick rolls onto his knees. "I'm just grateful to be here instead of there."

Ben changes places with Wenna. "Now you know how easy it is to slip outside accidentally, you'd better strap in for the journey home."

"Kitty . . ." Cara says.

He shrugs. "She made her choice. Sometimes all you can do is hold out a hand. It's up to them whether they take it. Let's go home."

✦ ✦ ✦

Just for old times' sake, Ben hit realspace only twenty klicks from Crossways.

"Welcome back, *Solar Wind.*"

"Thank you, Crossways Control. Who won the bet this time?"

"Briggs."

"Well, don't bet next time. I'll be sticking to the rules in the future."

"Copy that, *Solar Wind.*"

"Did you get him?" Mother Ramona cut in.

"He's here, safe and sound," Cara said, waving Garrick to the comm.

"Thank the stars!" Mother Ramona was laughing and crying at the same time.

"Hey, Mona, have I got a story for you." Garrick's voice trembled, but he put on a brave face.

Ben brought *Solar Wind* into Port 22 and dropped her gently onto the landing pad. "Thank you, everyone. Let's hope the next journey isn't so unusual."

Gwala laughed. "With you, Benjamin? It's always unusual. You are one crazy son of a bitch, but you're a lucky one, and that counts for a lot."

"I might just stick to admin for a while," Wenna said.

I'm with you wherever you go. Cara reached out a hand.

Ben took her hand and kissed her fingertips. *Thank you. You're forgiven.*

For what?

Your awful coffee habit.

She slapped his upper arm and he grinned at her, as happy as he'd ever been. She was here, she was staying.

Mother Ramona ran the whole length of Port 22 in high heels to fling herself into Garrick's arms.

It's funny, Cara said. *I thought theirs was a marriage of convenience, a joining together of two criminal organizations for mutual profit and maybe a little sex on the side, but they really do love each other.*

They really do.

Captain Syke stood alone, halfway along the hangar, neither with the gate guard nor seemingly wanting to approach.

"Better break the bad news to Syke," Ben said.

"I think he knows," Cara said as Syke turned away. "Kitty certainly got under his skin. I keep wondering if there was anything more we could have done. Now I know she was an Alphacorp plant I think back to all the times she's been around when something was going down. How much information did she pass on? Yet when it came to getting the ark back she held off and let us retrieve Etta from Sentier-4."

"I think she let herself be caught rather than kill Etta."

"I think so, too," Cara said. "She knew Ronan and Jussaro were Empaths. They were bound to sense her intent. She was certainly conflicted."

"I'm sorry we couldn't save her."

"But this time you're not blaming yourself."

"Not this time."

Mother Ramona and Garrick caught up with them and they were swept up in news and plans.

With the extra ships from Crossways, Oleg Staple had soundly defeated the Trust fleet and sent the survivors running back for the far gate. The S-LOGs were already full of the news that Alphacorp had attacked Crossways. Some of the spin was Alphacorp's and phrased in terms of: *Criminal Gangs Evade Capture.* Others were pushing the independent point of view: *Alphacorp Act of Aggression on Indie Station.*

Nan had been in touch, as had Jamundi, and both had been reassured that not only was Crossways still in business, but that their position was stronger now that they were in orbit around Olyanda.

"I'm not saying we're home free yet," Garrick said. "But we've made a start. We've challenged the old order and made way for the new."

Cara twisted her fingers with Ben's. *To the new order, then.*

And whatever it brings next.

❖ ❖ ❖

Crowder turned his back on the garden, relaxed into his float chair and watched reports of the Trust fleet limping home. At least the survivors were coming home, which was more than could be said for Alphacorp's ships. Akiko Yamada must be spitting feathers over the trap Benjamin had sprung. It would take months, if not years, to get their fleet home again, depending on the resources Alphacorp was willing to commit.

They'd tried the Benjamin Maneuver, dragging a ship through foldspace in the wake of a jump-drive vessel, but something had gone wrong and both ships had been lost, which made them reluctant to try again. They had choices, none of them good. They could build another gate, but Benjamin would be waiting for that and would surely destroy it. Or they could send in jump-drive lifeboats to lift off the crews and abandon the ships themselves, an expensive last resort, but better to lose the ships and retrieve the crews than commit them to the long, long sublight journey to the next nearest gate.

With the situation as it was—colonies defecting, platinum supplies dwindling—there would be cutbacks. Alphacorp was losing its grip. That was not an entirely unappealing situation from the Trust's point of view, as long as they didn't follow down the same route.

The Trust had taken a beating in the skies above Olyanda, but for once he wasn't the whipping boy. In fact Tori LeBon had sent a message to say that the major shareholders were extremely upset and there had been several calls for the chairman's resignation. Crowder smiled to himself. He'd engineered a win-win situation. If the trust had regained Olyanda he'd have revealed himself as the architect of the plan. The failure, however, was all falling on Hunt's head. The chairman's loss could only be his gain. Everything he'd warned them about had happened. He'd soon be back in favor. Tori LeBon had practically promised it. His way was clear.

Time to regroup and rethink. This wasn't over yet. Benjamin had made it personal with that third dart.

Crowder eased his back into a better position. His right thigh had a numb patch that ached abominably. How could something be numb and painful at the same time? Permanent nerve damage, his physician said, and since he was lucky to be alive he shouldn't grumble.

Stefan appeared at his elbow with his pills and a tumbler of water. He popped a painkiller.

"What do you think, Stefan?" He nodded to the holographic readout.

"I think you'll use the opportunity to the Trust's best advantage, sir."

"Right answer, boy. Right answer."

S. Andrew Swann
The Apotheosis Trilogy

It's been nearly two hundred years since the collapse of the Confederacy, the last government to claim humanity's colonies. So when signals come in revealing lost human colonies that could shift the power balance, the race is on between the Caliphate ships and a small team of scientists and mercenaries. But what awaits them all is a threat far beyond the scope of any human government.

PROPHETS
978-0-7564-0541-0

HERETICS
978-0-7564-0613-4

MESSIAH
978-0-7564-0657-8

To Order Call: 1-800-788-6262
www.dawbooks.com

DAW 161